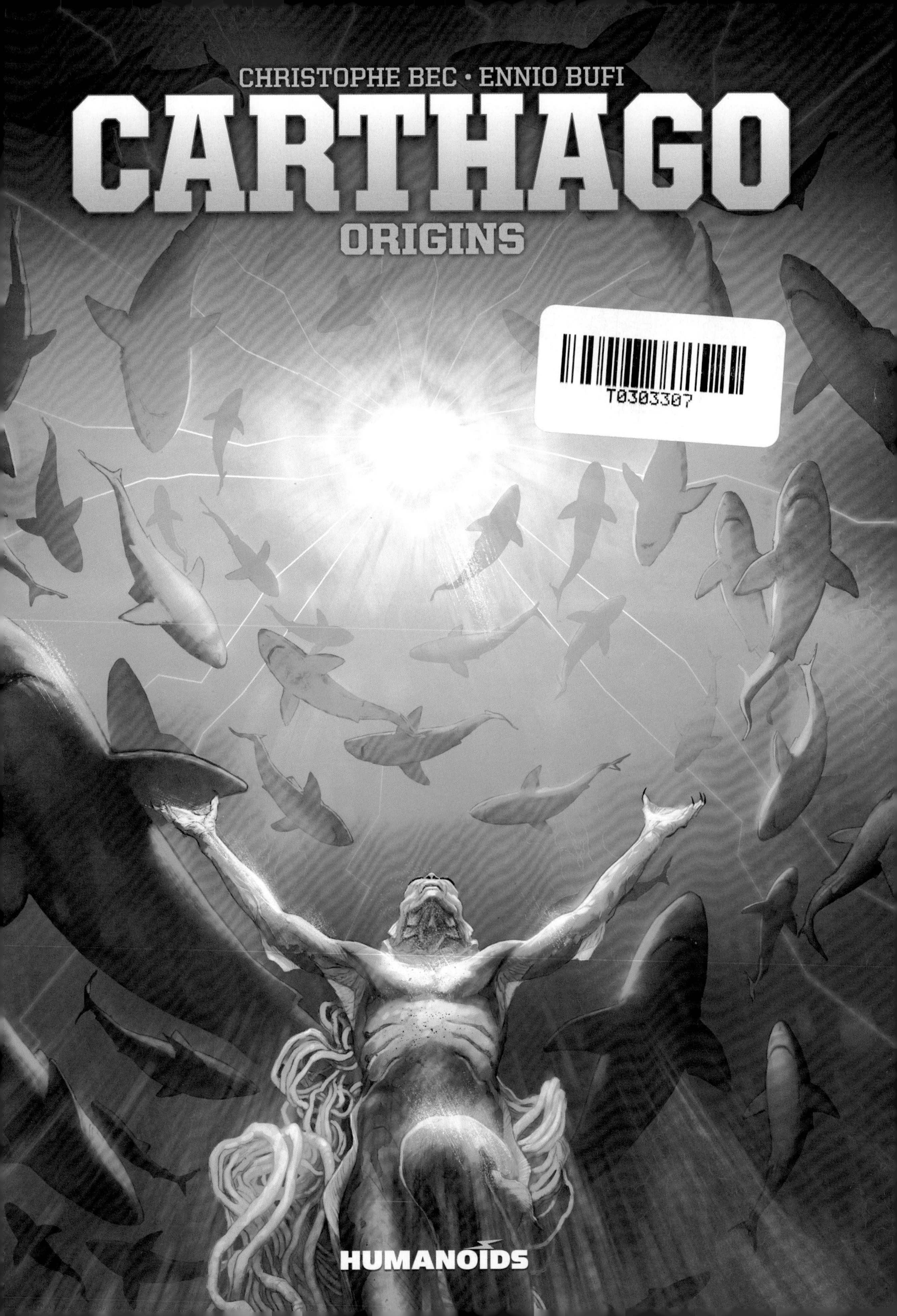
CHRISTOPHE BEC • ENNIO BUFI
CARTHAGO
ORIGINS
HUMANOIDS

CHRISTOPHE BEC
Writer

ENNIO BUFFI
Artist

BERTRAND DENOULET
(pages 5 to 58)

ANDREA MELONI
(pages 3 and 61 to 282)

PHILIPPE SCOFFONI
(page 59)
Colorists

MONTANA KANE
Translator

FABRICE SAPOLSKY
& AMANDA LUCIDO
US Edition Editors

ALISA TRAGER
Assistant Editor

BRUNO LECIGNE
Original Edition Editor

JERRY FRISSEN
Senior Art Director

FABRICE GIGER
Publisher

Rights and Licensing - licensing@humanoids.com
Press and Social Media - pr@humanoids.com

Series created by Christophe Bec and Éric Henninot.

CARTHAGO, BOOK 2: ORIGINS. This title is a publication of Humanoids, Inc. 8033 Sunset Blvd. #628, Los Angeles, CA 90046.

Library of Congress Control Number: 2019918241

Book 6:
HEIRESS OF THE CARPATHIANS

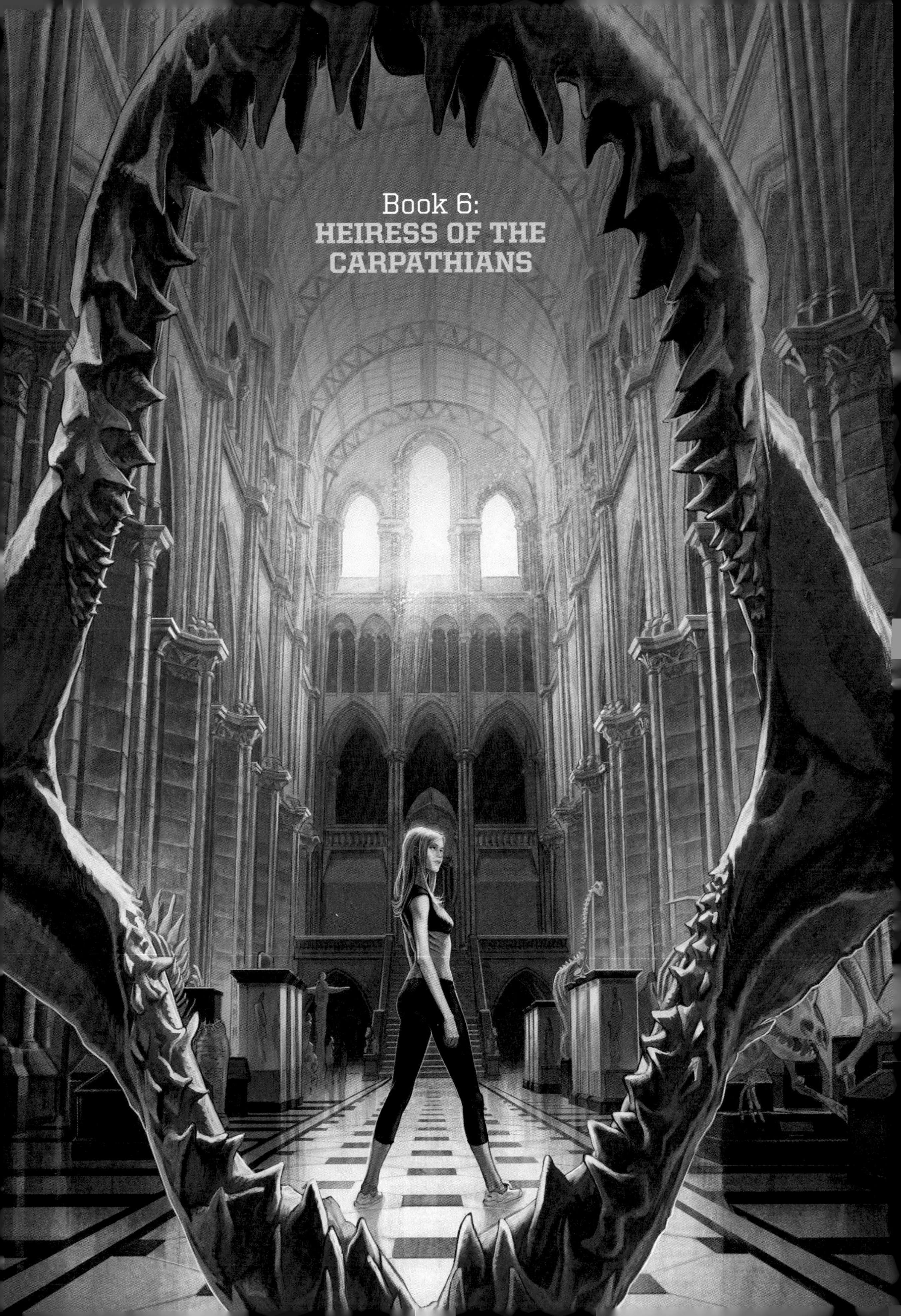

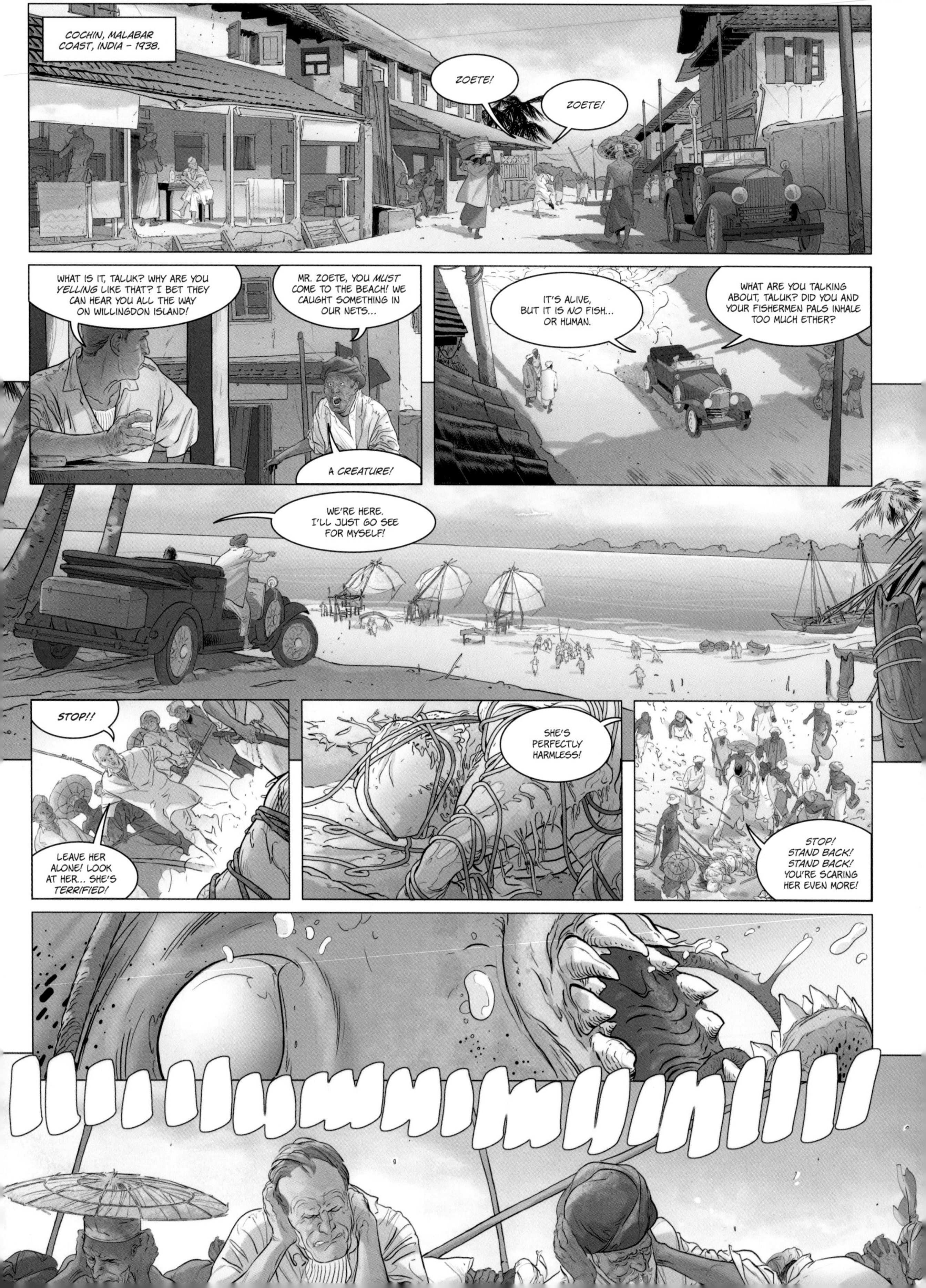
COCHIN, MALABAR COAST, INDIA – 1938.
ZOETE!
ZOETE!
WHAT IS IT, TALUK? WHY ARE YOU YELLING LIKE THAT? I BET THEY CAN HEAR YOU ALL THE WAY ON WILLINGDON ISLAND!
MR. ZOETE, YOU MUST COME TO THE BEACH! WE CAUGHT SOMETHING IN OUR NETS…
A CREATURE!
IT'S ALIVE, BUT IT IS NO FISH… OR HUMAN.
WHAT ARE YOU TALKING ABOUT, TALUK? DID YOU AND YOUR FISHERMEN PALS INHALE TOO MUCH ETHER?
WE'RE HERE. I'LL JUST GO SEE FOR MYSELF!
STOP!!
LEAVE HER ALONE! LOOK AT HER… SHE'S TERRIFIED!
SHE'S PERFECTLY HARMLESS!
STOP! STAND BACK! STAND BACK! YOU'RE SCARING HER EVEN MORE!
IIIIIIIUUMMHHIMMMHHIIIIII

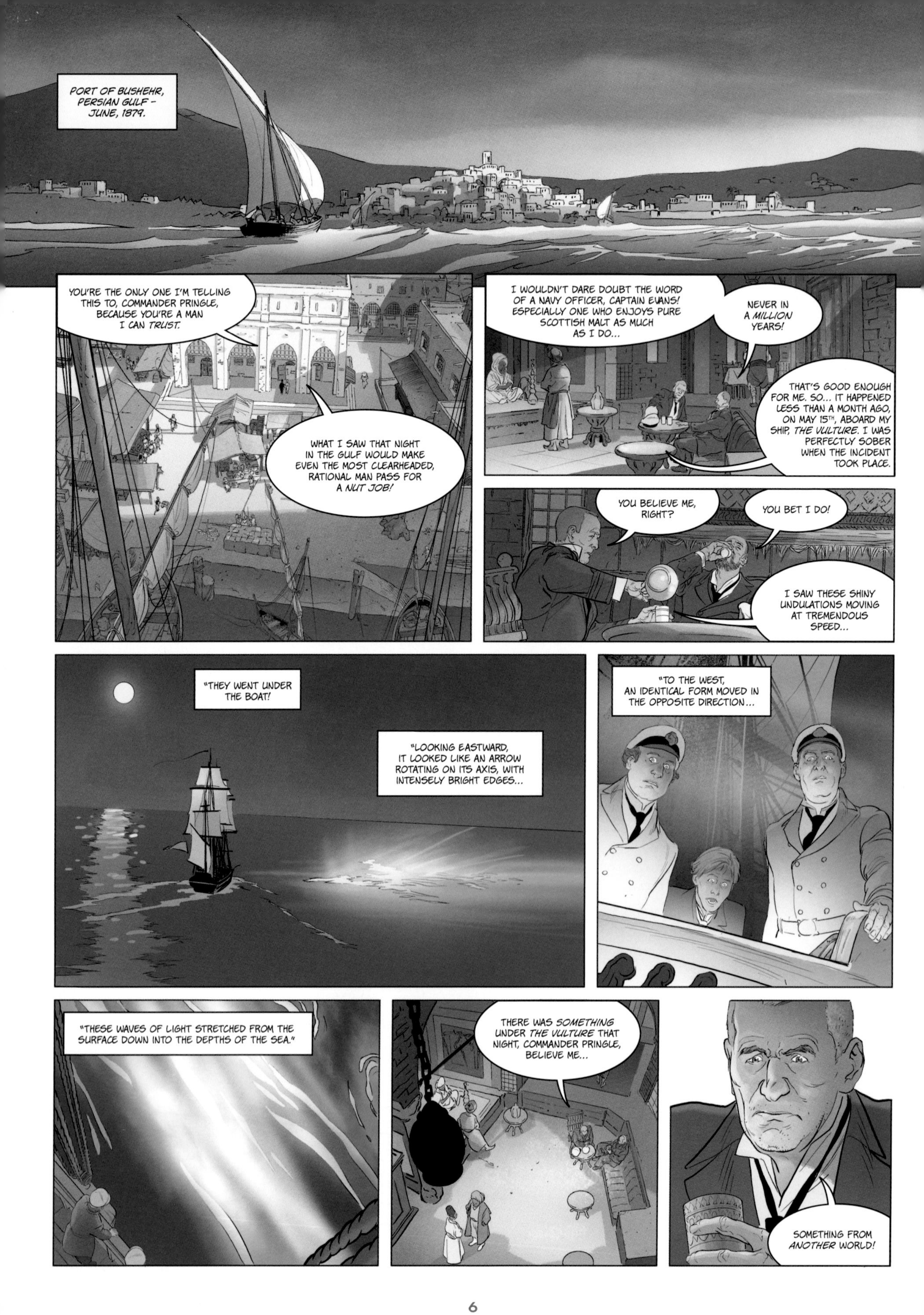
PORT OF BUSHEHR, PERSIAN GULF – JUNE, 1879.
YOU'RE THE ONLY ONE I'M TELLING THIS TO, COMMANDER PRINGLE, BECAUSE YOU'RE A MAN I CAN *TRUST*.
WHAT I SAW THAT NIGHT IN THE GULF WOULD MAKE EVEN THE MOST CLEARHEADED, RATIONAL MAN PASS FOR A *NUT JOB!*
I WOULDN'T DARE DOUBT THE WORD OF A NAVY OFFICER, CAPTAIN EVANS! ESPECIALLY ONE WHO ENJOYS PURE SCOTTISH MALT AS MUCH AS I DO...
NEVER IN A *MILLION* YEARS!
THAT'S GOOD ENOUGH FOR ME. SO... IT HAPPENED LESS THAN A MONTH AGO, ON MAY 15TH, ABOARD MY SHIP, *THE VULTURE*. I WAS PERFECTLY SOBER WHEN THE INCIDENT TOOK PLACE.
YOU BELIEVE ME, RIGHT?
YOU BET I DO!
I SAW THESE SHINY UNDULATIONS MOVING AT TREMENDOUS SPEED...
"THEY WENT UNDER THE BOAT!
"LOOKING EASTWARD, IT LOOKED LIKE AN ARROW ROTATING ON ITS AXIS, WITH INTENSELY BRIGHT EDGES...
"TO THE WEST, AN IDENTICAL FORM MOVED IN THE OPPOSITE DIRECTION...
"THESE WAVES OF LIGHT STRETCHED FROM THE SURFACE DOWN INTO THE DEPTHS OF THE SEA."
THERE WAS *SOMETHING* UNDER *THE VULTURE* THAT NIGHT, COMMANDER PRINGLE, BELIEVE ME...
SOMETHING FROM *ANOTHER WORLD!*

WHILE THE EL NIÑO OF 1998 WAS THE NIÑO OF THE CENTURY, THE ONE WE ARE EXPERIENCING NOW, IN 2021, IS BEATING ALL RECORDS.

MÉGA *EL NIÑO* 9

EL NIÑO'S INFLUENCE AFFECTS THE ENTIRE PLANET.

HEAVY RAINS AND FLOODS HAVE DEVASTATED THE ENTIRE EASTERN BOARD OF THE SOUTH PACIFIC.

OCEANIA IS DEALING WITH DEADLY DROUGHTS AND ENORMOUS WILDFIRES.

THE SEA LEVEL EAST OF THE PACIFIC HAS RISEN...

LUCKILY, THE WATER IS RISING GRADUALLY. NO TSUNAMIS.

IT'S LIKE THE WHOLE ATMOSPHERE HAS GONE *HAYWIRE*... AND IT'S MAKING A HUGE MESS EVERYWHERE!

THIS ALL COMES FROM THE OCEANS.

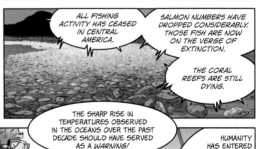

ALL FISHING ACTIVITY HAS CEASED IN CENTRAL AMERICA.

SALMON NUMBERS HAVE DROPPED CONSIDERABLY. THOSE FISH ARE NOW ON THE VERGE OF EXTINCTION.

THE CORAL REEFS ARE STILL DYING.

THE SHARP RISE IN TEMPERATURES OBSERVED IN THE OCEANS OVER THE PAST DECADE SHOULD HAVE SERVED AS A WARNING!

HUMANITY HAS ENTERED A TERRIBLE CYCLE, WHICH WE'VE TRIGGERED OURSELVES! NATURE ALWAYS RESPONDS WITH STUNNING VIOLENCE.

THE NUMBER OF HURRICANES IN THE CENTRAL PACIFIC HAS GONE UP RADICALLY, HITTING THE WESTERN COAST OF AUSTRALIA AS WELL.

RECENT STUDIES BY PALEOCLIMATOLOGISTS USING SEDIMENT AND MARKINGS ON TREES SHOW THAT THERE HAVE BEEN SIMILAR MAJOR CLIMATE IMBALANCES IN THE DISTANT PAST.

THE GREAT PREDATORS ARE COMING BACK UP TO THE SURFACE ON A MORE REGULAR BASIS.

THAT WASN'T A GREAT WHITE... IT WAS MUCH BIGGER THAN THAT!

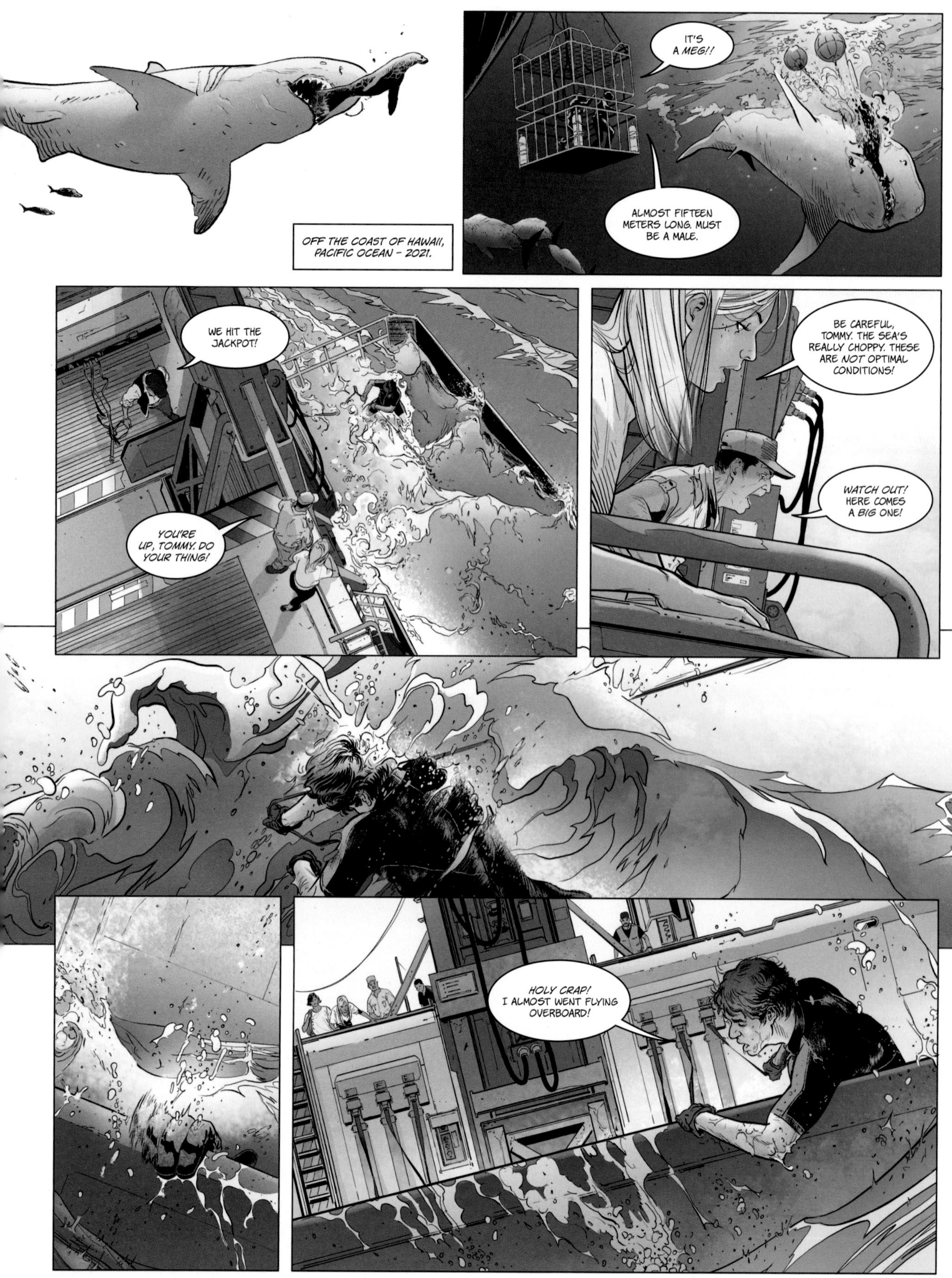
OFF THE COAST OF HAWAII, PACIFIC OCEAN - 2021.
IT'S A MEG!!
ALMOST FIFTEEN METERS LONG. MUST BE A MALE.
WE HIT THE JACKPOT!
YOU'RE UP, TOMMY. DO YOUR THING!
BE CAREFUL, TOMMY. THE SEA'S REALLY CHOPPY. THESE ARE NOT OPTIMAL CONDITIONS!
WATCH OUT! HERE COMES A BIG ONE!
HOLY CRAP! I ALMOST WENT FLYING OVERBOARD!

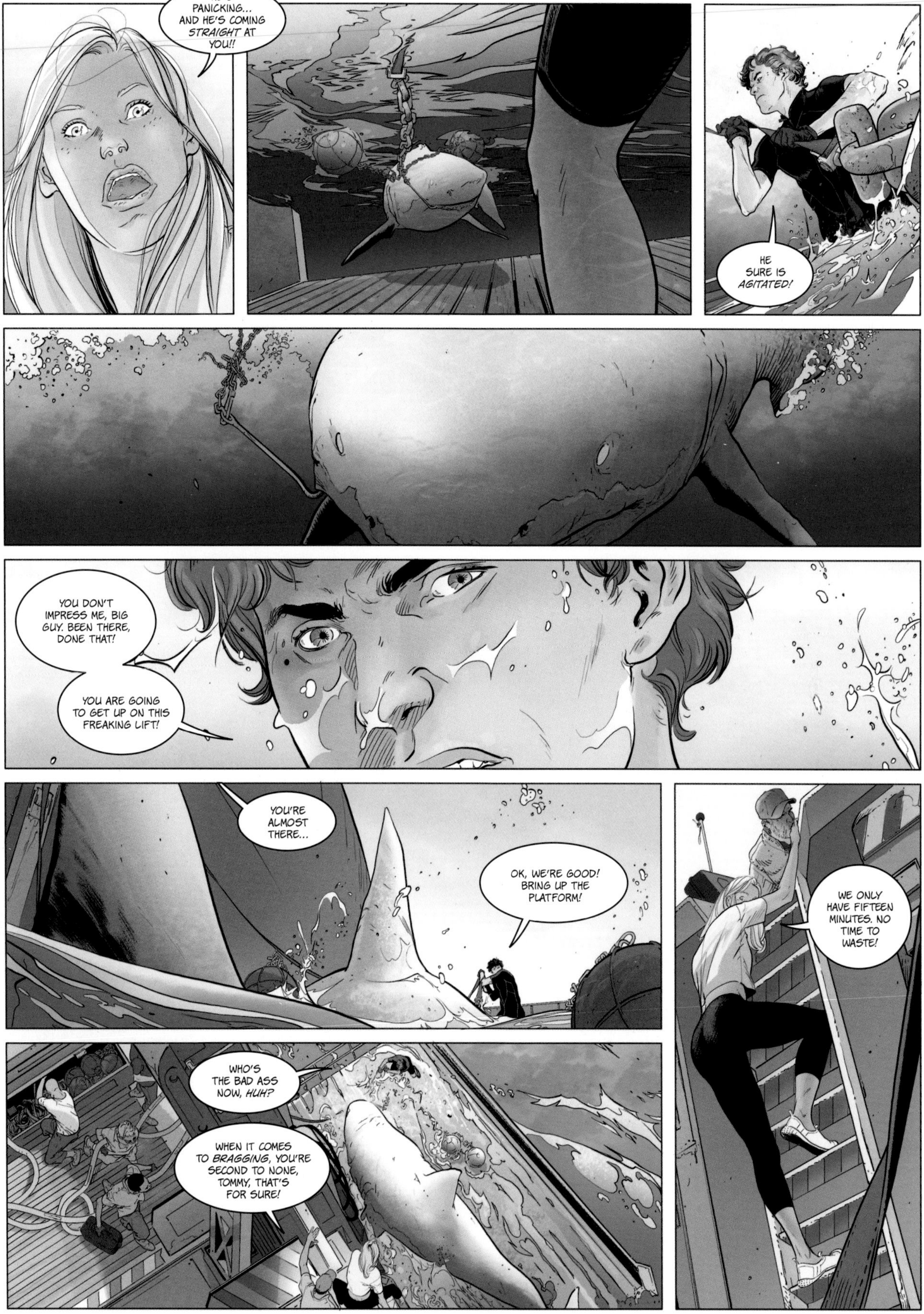

HE'S PANICKING... AND HE'S COMING STRAIGHT AT YOU!!
HE SURE IS AGITATED!
YOU DON'T IMPRESS ME, BIG GUY. BEEN THERE, DONE THAT!
YOU ARE GOING TO GET UP ON THIS FREAKING LIFT!
YOU'RE ALMOST THERE...
OK, WE'RE GOOD! BRING UP THE PLATFORM!
WE ONLY HAVE FIFTEEN MINUTES. NO TIME TO WASTE!
WHO'S THE BAD ASS NOW, HUH?
WHEN IT COMES TO BRAGGING, YOU'RE SECOND TO NONE, TOMMY, THAT'S FOR SURE!

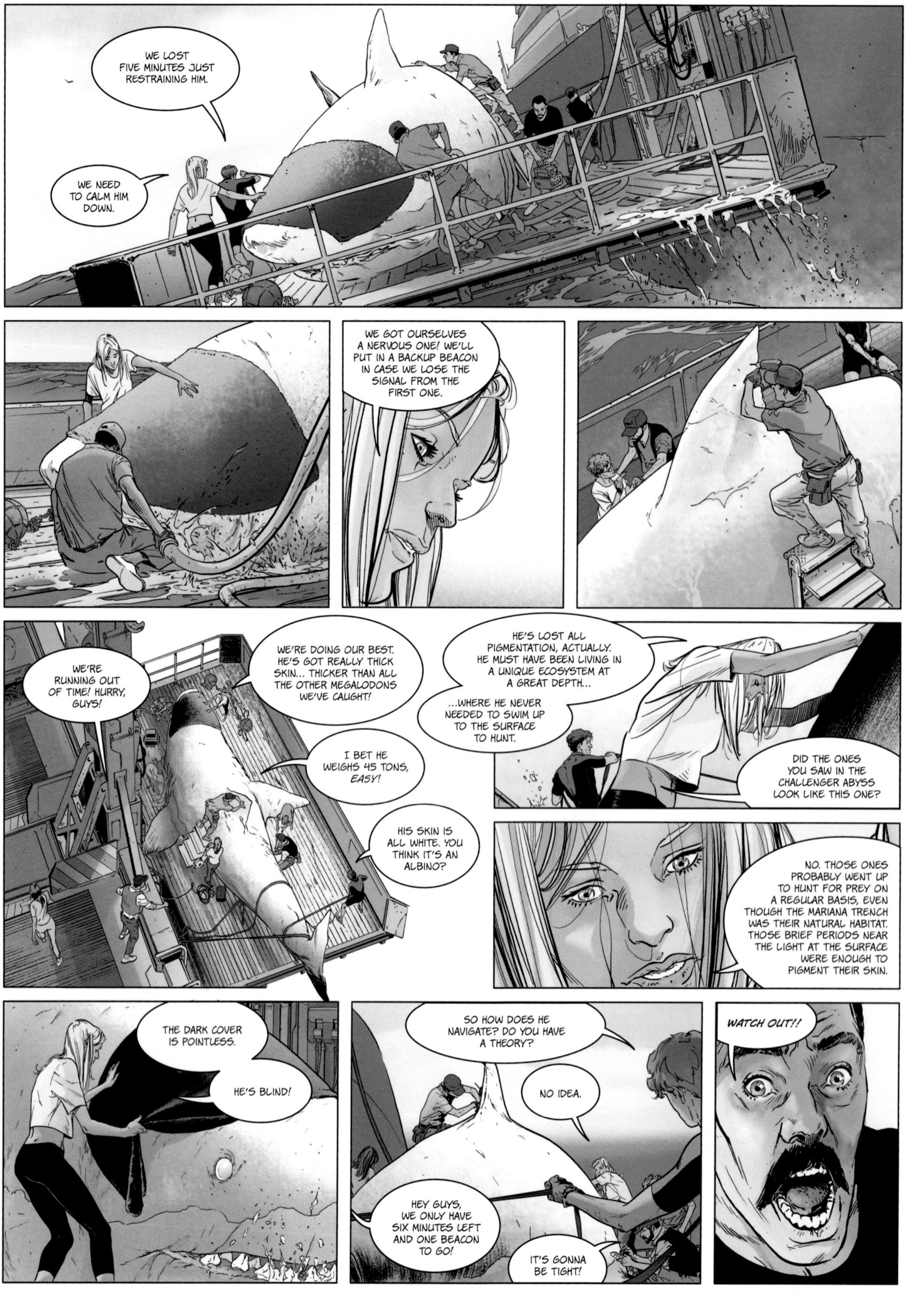
WE LOST FIVE MINUTES JUST RESTRAINING HIM.
WE NEED TO CALM HIM DOWN.
WE GOT OURSELVES A NERVOUS ONE! WE'LL PUT IN A BACKUP BEACON IN CASE WE LOSE THE SIGNAL FROM THE FIRST ONE.
WE'RE RUNNING OUT OF TIME! HURRY, GUYS!
WE'RE DOING OUR BEST. HE'S GOT REALLY THICK SKIN... THICKER THAN ALL THE OTHER MEGALODONS WE'VE CAUGHT!
I BET HE WEIGHS 45 TONS, *EASY!*
HIS SKIN IS ALL WHITE. YOU THINK IT'S AN ALBINO?
HE'S LOST ALL PIGMENTATION, ACTUALLY. HE MUST HAVE BEEN LIVING IN A UNIQUE ECOSYSTEM AT A GREAT DEPTH...
...WHERE HE NEVER NEEDED TO SWIM UP TO THE SURFACE TO HUNT.
DID THE ONES YOU SAW IN THE CHALLENGER ABYSS LOOK LIKE THIS ONE?
NO. THOSE ONES PROBABLY WENT UP TO HUNT FOR PREY ON A REGULAR BASIS, EVEN THOUGH THE MARIANA TRENCH WAS THEIR NATURAL HABITAT. THOSE BRIEF PERIODS NEAR THE LIGHT AT THE SURFACE WERE ENOUGH TO PIGMENT THEIR SKIN.
THE DARK COVER IS POINTLESS.
HE'S BLIND!
SO HOW DOES HE NAVIGATE? DO YOU HAVE A THEORY?
NO IDEA.
HEY GUYS, WE ONLY HAVE SIX MINUTES LEFT AND ONE BEACON TO GO!
IT'S GONNA BE TIGHT!
WATCH OUT!!

DAMMIT!

YOU OKAY?

EVEN THOSE RESTRAINTS CAN'T HOLD HIM DOWN!

WE REALLY NEED TO HURRY. LET'S PUT HIM ON HIS BACK WITH THE WINCH AND COLLECT THE LAST SAMPLES STRAIGHT FROM HIS MOUTH.

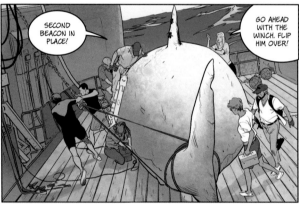

SECOND BEACON IN PLACE!

GO AHEAD WITH THE WINCH. FLIP HIM OVER!

AAAAAAA!!

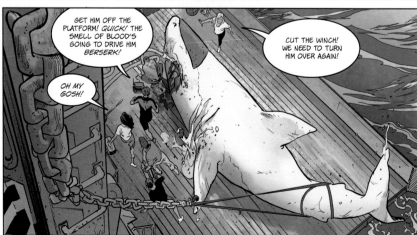

GET HIM OFF THE PLATFORM! QUICK! THE SMELL OF BLOOD'S GOING TO DRIVE HIM BERSERK!

OH MY GOSH!

CUT THE WINCH! WE NEED TO TURN HIM OVER AGAIN!

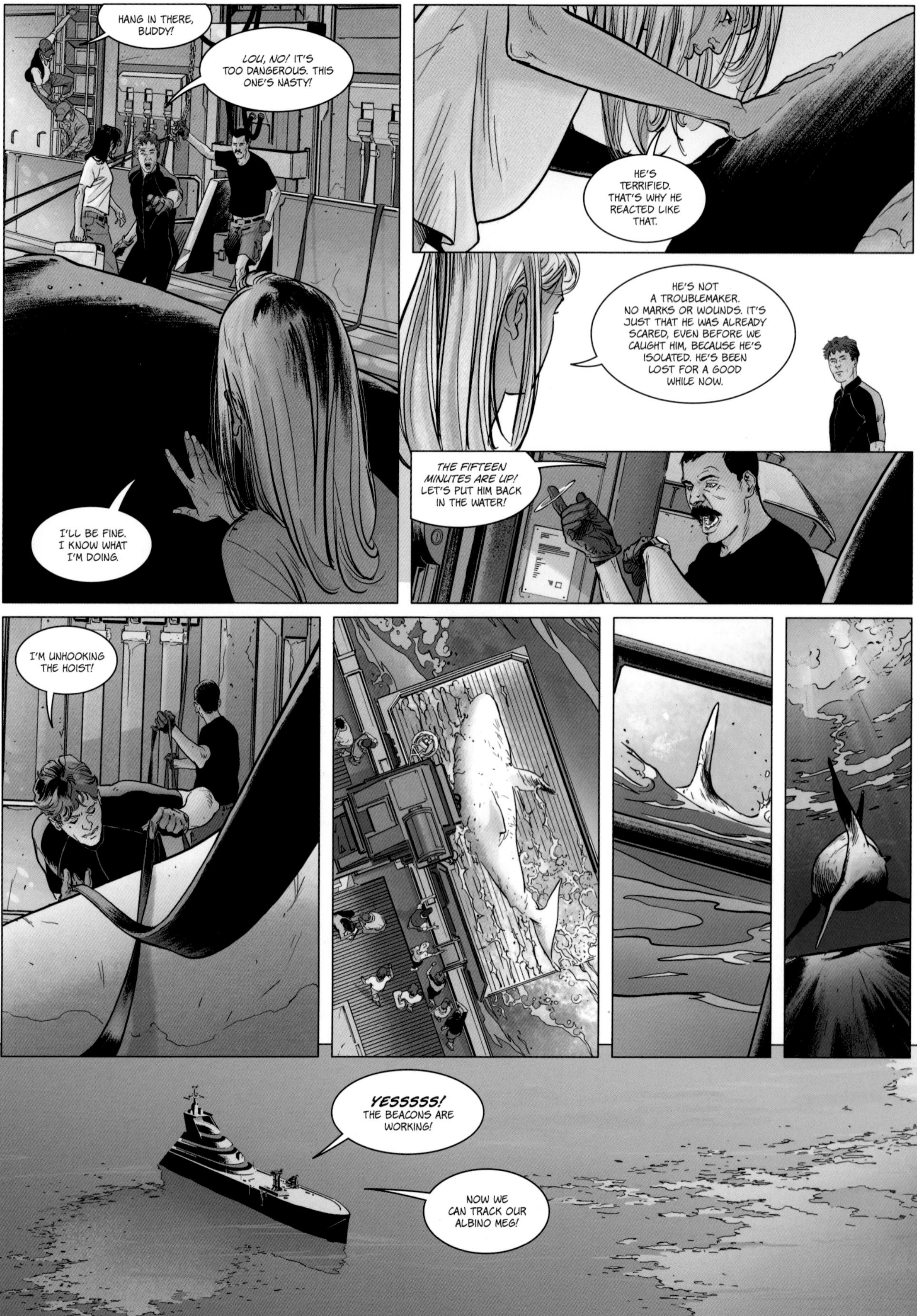
HANG IN THERE, BUDDY!
LOU, NO! IT'S TOO DANGEROUS. THIS ONE'S NASTY!
I'LL BE FINE. I KNOW WHAT I'M DOING.
HE'S TERRIFIED. THAT'S WHY HE REACTED LIKE THAT.
HE'S NOT A TROUBLEMAKER. NO MARKS OR WOUNDS. IT'S JUST THAT HE WAS ALREADY SCARED, EVEN BEFORE WE CAUGHT HIM, BECAUSE HE'S ISOLATED. HE'S BEEN LOST FOR A GOOD WHILE NOW.
THE FIFTEEN MINUTES ARE UP! LET'S PUT HIM BACK IN THE WATER!
I'M UNHOOKING THE HOIST!
YESSSSS! THE BEACONS ARE WORKING!
NOW WE CAN TRACK OUR ALBINO MEG!

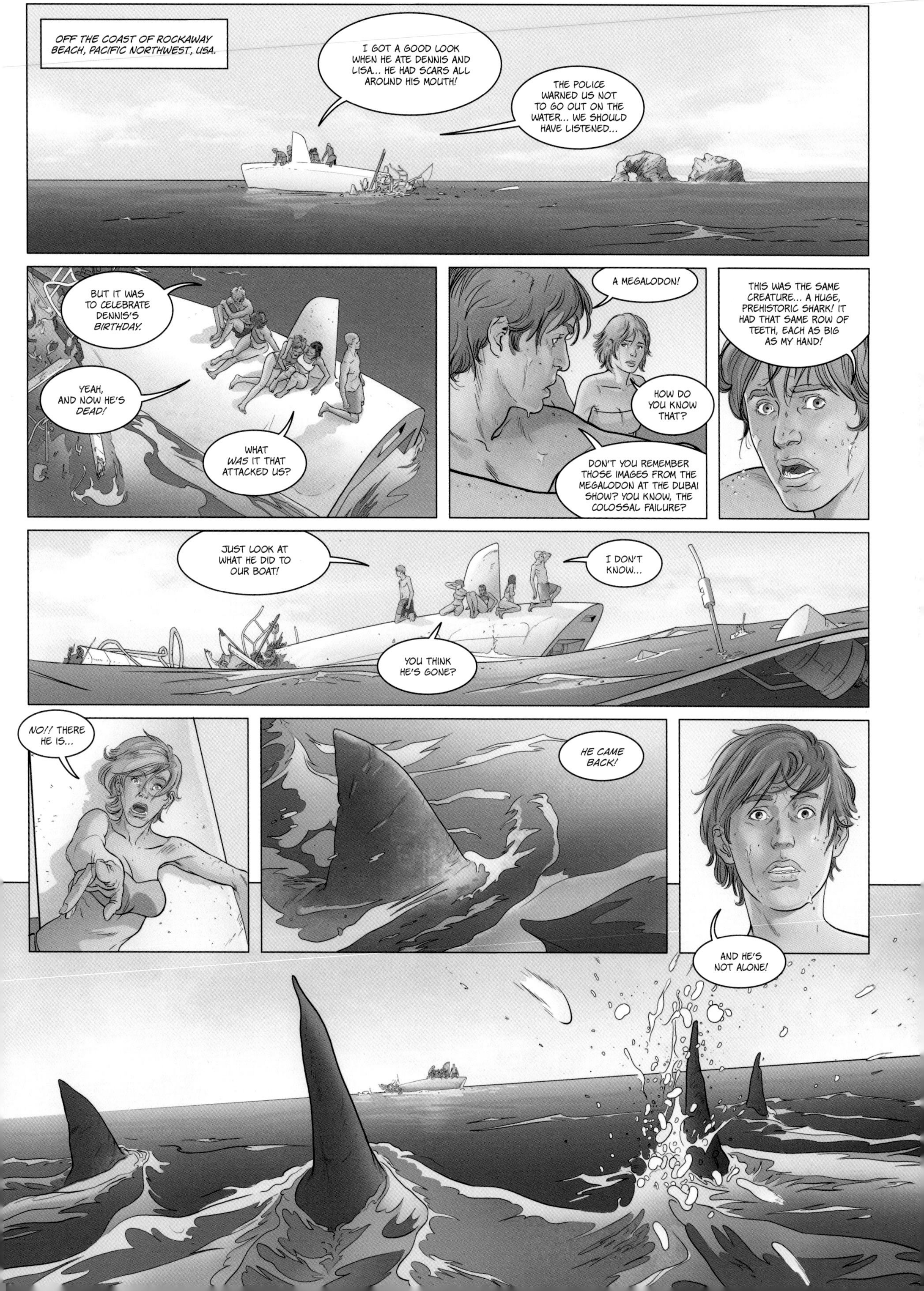
OFF THE COAST OF ROCKAWAY BEACH, PACIFIC NORTHWEST, USA.
I GOT A GOOD LOOK WHEN HE ATE DENNIS AND LISA... HE HAD SCARS ALL AROUND HIS MOUTH!
THE POLICE WARNED US NOT TO GO OUT ON THE WATER... WE SHOULD HAVE LISTENED...
BUT IT WAS TO CELEBRATE DENNIS'S BIRTHDAY.
YEAH, AND NOW HE'S DEAD!
WHAT WAS IT THAT ATTACKED US?
A MEGALODON!
HOW DO YOU KNOW THAT?
DON'T YOU REMEMBER THOSE IMAGES FROM THE MEGALODON AT THE DUBAI SHOW? YOU KNOW, THE COLOSSAL FAILURE?
THIS WAS THE SAME CREATURE... A HUGE, PREHISTORIC SHARK! IT HAD THAT SAME ROW OF TEETH, EACH AS BIG AS MY HAND!
JUST LOOK AT WHAT HE DID TO OUR BOAT!
YOU THINK HE'S GONE?
I DON'T KNOW...
NO!! THERE HE IS...
HE CAME BACK!
AND HE'S NOT ALONE!

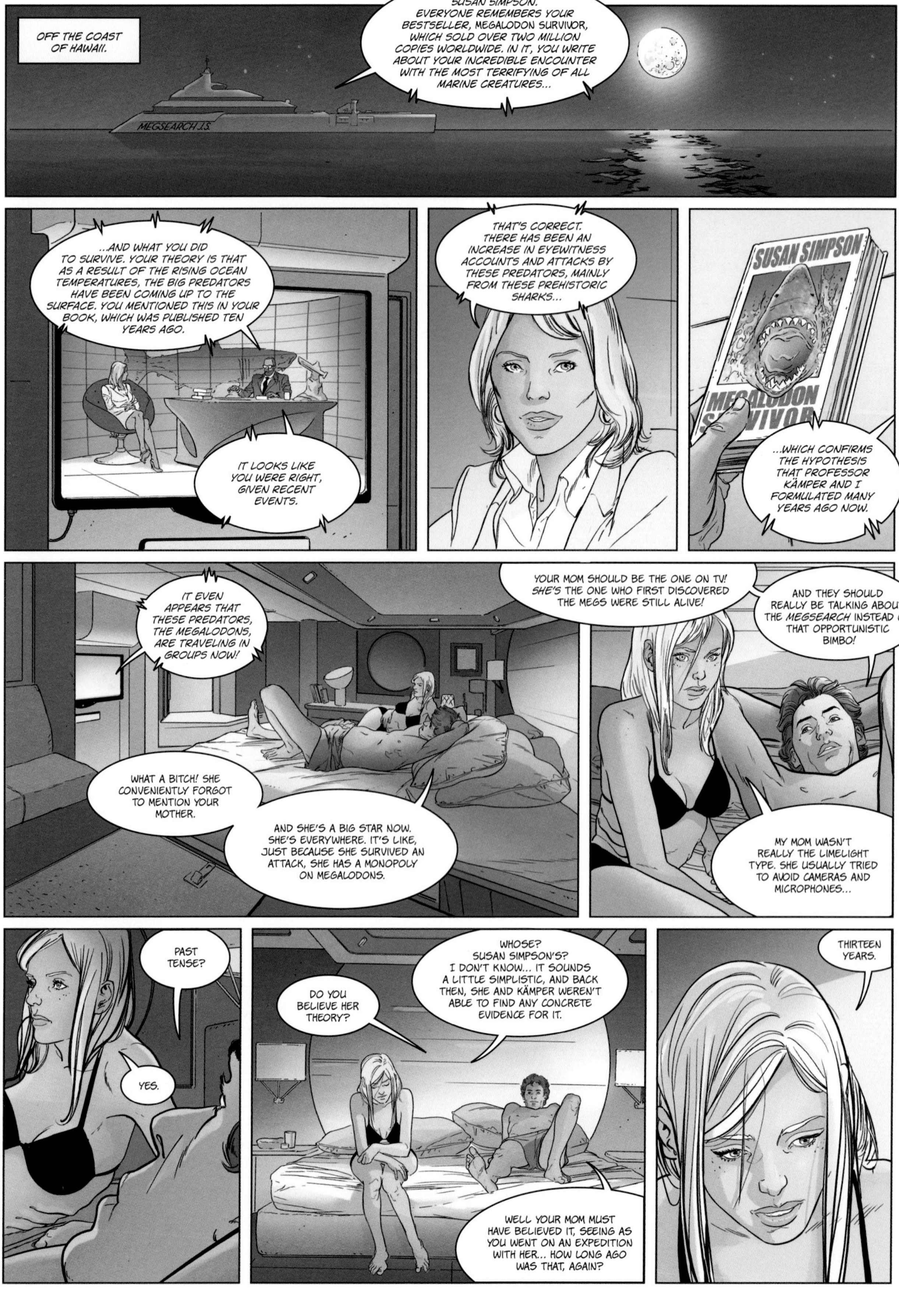
OFF THE COAST OF HAWAII.
SUSAN SIMPSON. EVERYONE REMEMBERS YOUR BESTSELLER, MEGALODON SURVIVOR, WHICH SOLD OVER TWO MILLION COPIES WORLDWIDE. IN IT, YOU WRITE ABOUT YOUR INCREDIBLE ENCOUNTER WITH THE MOST TERRIFYING OF ALL MARINE CREATURES...
MEGSEARCH I.S.
...AND WHAT YOU DID TO SURVIVE. YOUR THEORY IS THAT AS A RESULT OF THE RISING OCEAN TEMPERATURES, THE BIG PREDATORS HAVE BEEN COMING UP TO THE SURFACE. YOU MENTIONED THIS IN YOUR BOOK, WHICH WAS PUBLISHED TEN YEARS AGO.
IT LOOKS LIKE YOU WERE RIGHT, GIVEN RECENT EVENTS.
THAT'S CORRECT. THERE HAS BEEN AN INCREASE IN EYEWITNESS ACCOUNTS AND ATTACKS BY THESE PREDATORS, MAINLY FROM THESE PREHISTORIC SHARKS...
SUSAN SIMPSON
MEGALODON
...WHICH CONFIRMS THE HYPOTHESIS THAT PROFESSOR KÄMPER AND I FORMULATED MANY YEARS AGO NOW.
IT EVEN APPEARS THAT THESE PREDATORS, THE MEGALODONS, ARE TRAVELING IN GROUPS NOW!
WHAT A BITCH! SHE CONVENIENTLY FORGOT TO MENTION YOUR MOTHER.
AND SHE'S A BIG STAR NOW. SHE'S EVERYWHERE. IT'S LIKE, JUST BECAUSE SHE SURVIVED AN ATTACK, SHE HAS A MONOPOLY ON MEGALODONS.
YOUR MOM SHOULD BE THE ONE ON TV! SHE'S THE ONE WHO FIRST DISCOVERED THE MEGS WERE STILL ALIVE!
AND THEY SHOULD REALLY BE TALKING ABOUT THE MEGSEARCH INSTEAD OF THAT OPPORTUNISTIC BIMBO!
MY MOM WASN'T REALLY THE LIMELIGHT TYPE. SHE USUALLY TRIED TO AVOID CAMERAS AND MICROPHONES...
PAST TENSE?
YES.
DO YOU BELIEVE HER THEORY?
WHOSE? SUSAN SIMPSON'S? I DON'T KNOW... IT SOUNDS A LITTLE SIMPLISTIC, AND BACK THEN, SHE AND KÄMPER WEREN'T ABLE TO FIND ANY CONCRETE EVIDENCE FOR IT.
WELL YOUR MOM MUST HAVE BELIEVED IT, SEEING AS YOU WENT ON AN EXPEDITION WITH HER... HOW LONG AGO WAS THAT, AGAIN?
THIRTEEN YEARS.

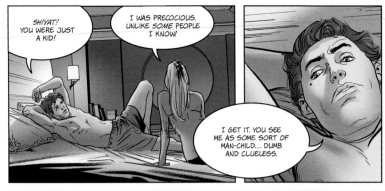

SHIYAT! YOU WERE JUST A KID!

I WAS PRECOCIOUS. UNLIKE SOME PEOPLE I KNOW!

I GET IT. YOU SEE ME AS SOME SORT OF MAN-CHILD... DUMB AND CLUELESS.

TO DO WHAT YOU DID ON THE PLATFORM, YOU HAVE TO BE CLUELESS, YES!

OH YEAH? WHAT ABOUT YOU, LOU? TO GO AND TOUCH THE MEG'S MOUTH WHEN HE WAS THRASHING ABOUT... YOU COULD'VE HAD YOUR ARM RIPPED OFF, JUST LIKE POOR BUDDY.

TOTALLY DIFFERENT. I TOLD YOU, I WAS IN CONTROL OF THE SITUATION.

RIGHT... BY THE WAY, YOU TRIED TO EXPLAIN IT ONCE, BUT I STILL DON'T GET WHY YOUR MOM AND SUSAN HAD A FALLING OUT.

MY MOM AND HER FREAKING PRINCIPLES...

WHY DID SHE QUIT HER JOB?

WHEN MY GRANDMA DIED FIVE YEARS AGO, MY MOM LOOKED AFTER HER DAD. SHE HAD TO GIVE UP HER RESEARCH.

WASN'T THERE AN ALTERNATIVE?

PROBABLY, BUT IT WAS A WAY TO ESCAPE.

FROM WHAT?

HER DESTINY. OWNING HER DISCOVERY AND ALL HER ACCOMPLISHMENTS.

ARE YOU EVER GOING TO TELL ME WHAT HAPPENED BETWEEN YOU TWO ALL THOSE YEARS AGO?

NO.

OKAY, I GET IT.

IT'S NONE OF YOUR BUSINESS, TOMMY.

YOU WON'T BE JOINING OUR LITTLE MELVILLE FAMILY ANYTIME SOON.

A FEW DAYS LATER.

ANY NEWS ON BUDDY?

SO NO NEED FOR A STOPOVER?

YES. THE SURGERY WENT WELL.

NO. THE DOCTOR SAID IT WON'T BE NECESSARY SINCE THERE WEREN'T ANY COMPLICATIONS.

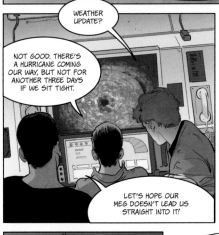

WEATHER UPDATE?

NOT GOOD. THERE'S A HURRICANE COMING OUR WAY, BUT NOT FOR ANOTHER THREE DAYS IF WE SIT TIGHT.

LET'S HOPE OUR MEG DOESN'T LEAD US STRAIGHT INTO IT!

SO FAR, HE'S JUST GOING AROUND IN CIRCLES.

HOW ABOUT THAT BUDDY, HUH? NOW HE CAN BRAG ABOUT GETTING HIS ARM CHOMPED ON BY THE GREAT WHITE'S ANCESTOR... NOTHING TO SNEEZE AT!

NOT NECESSARILY, PHILIP. THE QUESTION IS STILL UP FOR DEBATE.

WHAT DO YOU MEAN?

THE GREAT WHITE MIGHT NOT BE THE DESCENDANT OF THE MEGALODON, AS MARINE BIOLOGISTS CLAIM.

THEY COULD HAVE A COMMON ANCESTOR, WHICH IS WHAT MY MOTHER, KIM MELVILLE, THOUGHT.

YEAH, WELL, ALL'S I KNOW IS THAT WHEN THOSE BEASTS SHOW UP ON DECK, THEY STINK TO HIGH HEAVEN!

SHE AND OTHER PALEONTOLOGISTS THOUGHT THAT THE TWO SPECIES CAME FROM THE GIANT MACKEREL SHARK THAT LIVED IN THE EOCENE EPOCH.

GREAT, THANKS FOR THE NATURAL HISTORY LESSON. SO HE GOT EATEN BY A DESCENDANT OF THE GIANT MACKEREL SHARK. THAT'S STILL PRETTY COOL!

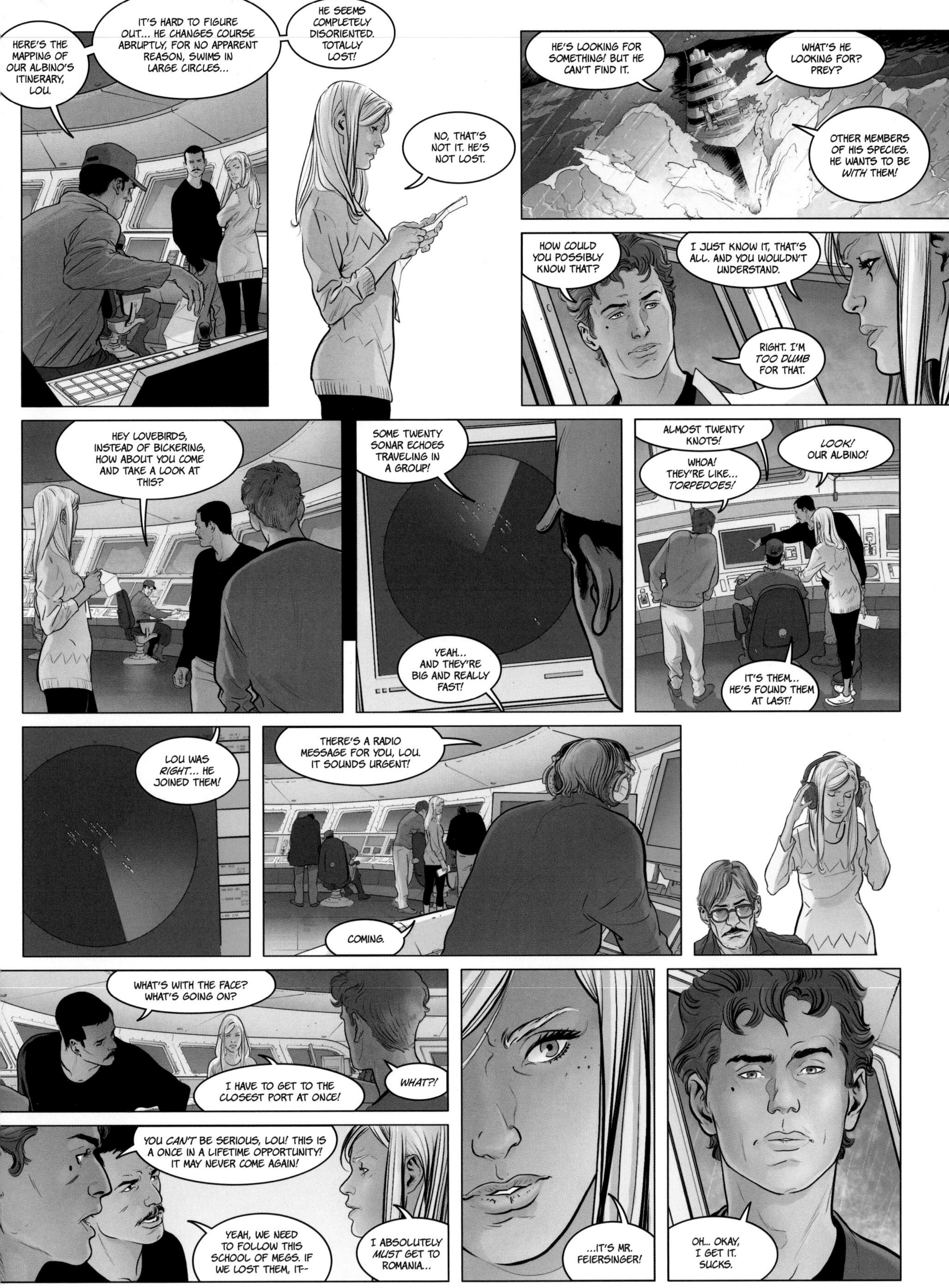
HERE'S THE MAPPING OF OUR ALBINO'S ITINERARY, LOU.
IT'S HARD TO FIGURE OUT... HE CHANGES COURSE ABRUPTLY, FOR NO APPARENT REASON, SWIMS IN LARGE CIRCLES...
HE SEEMS COMPLETELY DISORIENTED. TOTALLY LOST!
NO, THAT'S NOT IT. HE'S NOT LOST.
HE'S LOOKING FOR SOMETHING! BUT HE CAN'T FIND IT.
WHAT'S HE LOOKING FOR? PREY?
OTHER MEMBERS OF HIS SPECIES. HE WANTS TO BE WITH THEM!
HOW COULD YOU POSSIBLY KNOW THAT?
I JUST KNOW IT, THAT'S ALL. AND YOU WOULDN'T UNDERSTAND.
RIGHT. I'M TOO DUMB FOR THAT.
HEY LOVEBIRDS, INSTEAD OF BICKERING, HOW ABOUT YOU COME AND TAKE A LOOK AT THIS?
SOME TWENTY SONAR ECHOES TRAVELING IN A GROUP!
YEAH... AND THEY'RE BIG AND REALLY FAST!
ALMOST TWENTY KNOTS!
WHOA! THEY'RE LIKE... TORPEDOES!
LOOK! OUR ALBINO!
IT'S THEM... HE'S FOUND THEM AT LAST!
LOU WAS RIGHT... HE JOINED THEM!
THERE'S A RADIO MESSAGE FOR YOU, LOU. IT SOUNDS URGENT!
COMING.
WHAT'S WITH THE FACE? WHAT'S GOING ON?
I HAVE TO GET TO THE CLOSEST PORT AT ONCE!
WHAT?!
YOU CAN'T BE SERIOUS, LOU! THIS IS A ONCE IN A LIFETIME OPPORTUNITY! IT MAY NEVER COME AGAIN!
YEAH, WE NEED TO FOLLOW THIS SCHOOL OF MEGS. IF WE LOST THEM, IT-
I ABSOLUTELY MUST GET TO ROMANIA...
...IT'S MR. FEIERSINGER!
OH... OKAY, I GET IT. SUCKS.

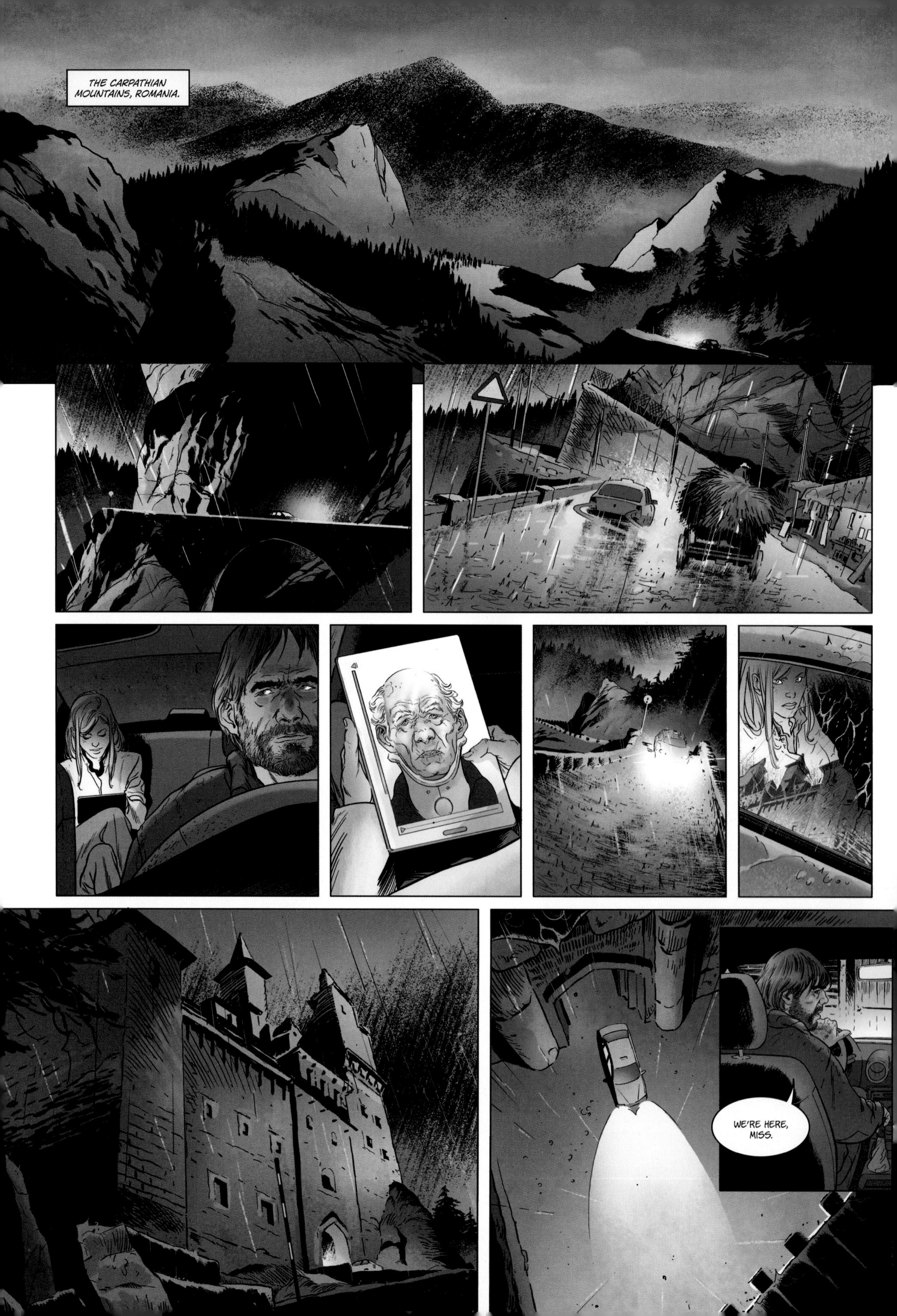
THE CARPATHIAN MOUNTAINS, ROMANIA.
WE'RE HERE, MISS.

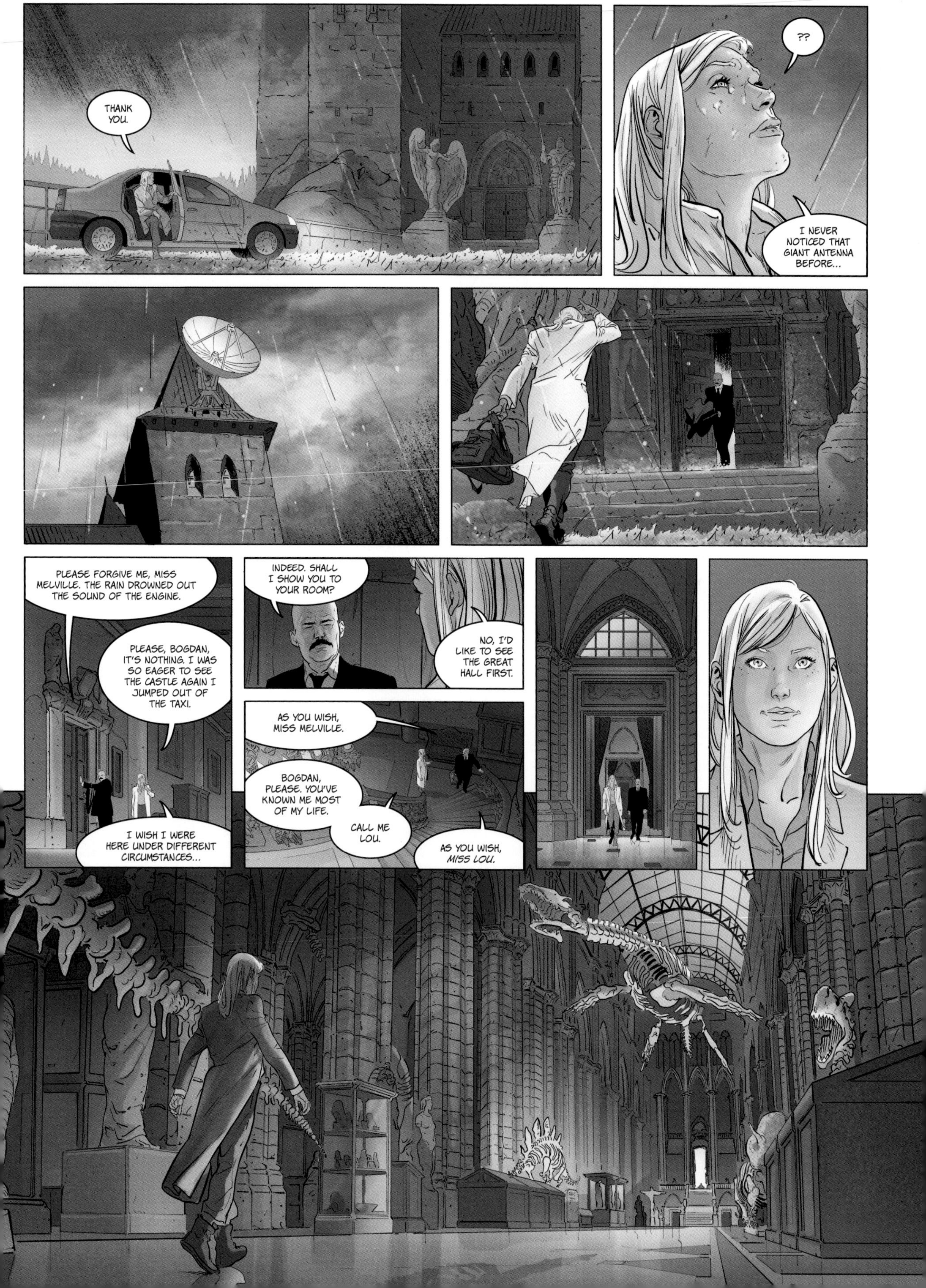
THANK YOU.
??
I NEVER NOTICED THAT GIANT ANTENNA BEFORE...
PLEASE FORGIVE ME, MISS MELVILLE. THE RAIN DROWNED OUT THE SOUND OF THE ENGINE.
PLEASE, BOGDAN, IT'S NOTHING. I WAS SO EAGER TO SEE THE CASTLE AGAIN I JUMPED OUT OF THE TAXI.
I WISH I WERE HERE UNDER DIFFERENT CIRCUMSTANCES...
INDEED. SHALL I SHOW YOU TO YOUR ROOM?
NO, I'D LIKE TO SEE THE GREAT HALL FIRST.
AS YOU WISH, MISS MELVILLE.
BOGDAN, PLEASE. YOU'VE KNOWN ME MOST OF MY LIFE.
CALL ME LOU.
AS YOU WISH, *MISS LOU.*

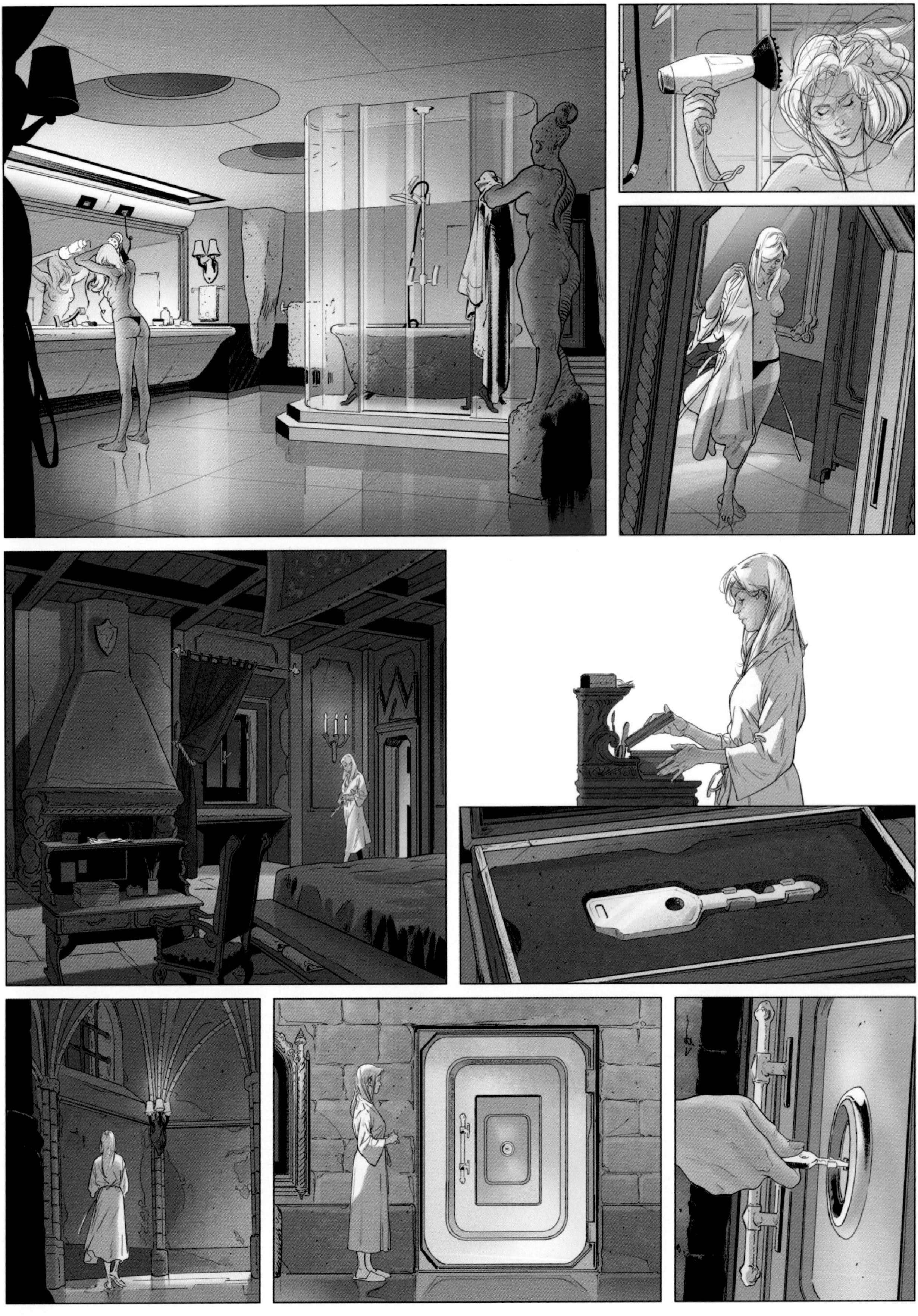

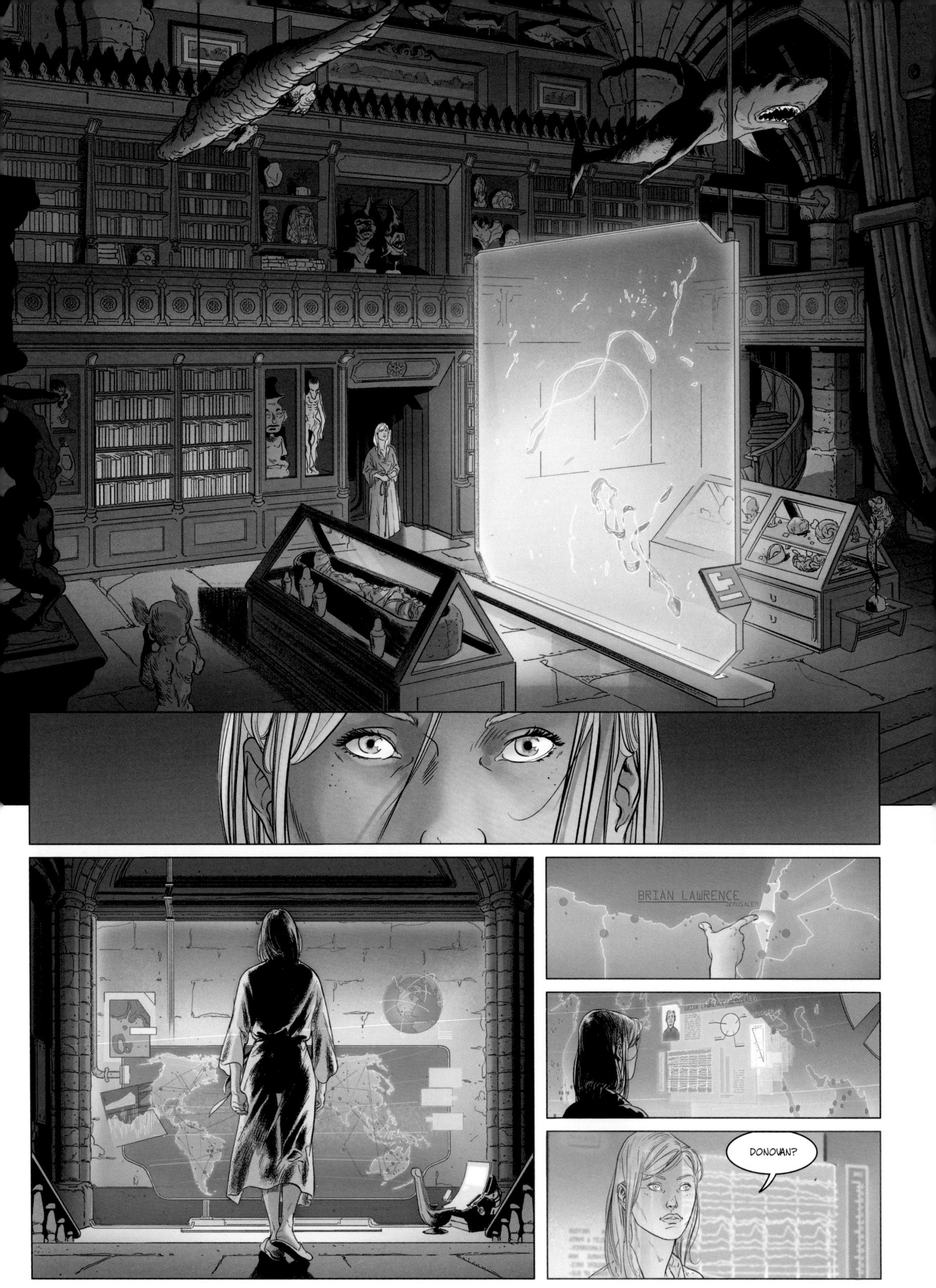
BRIAN LAWRENCE
DONOVAN?

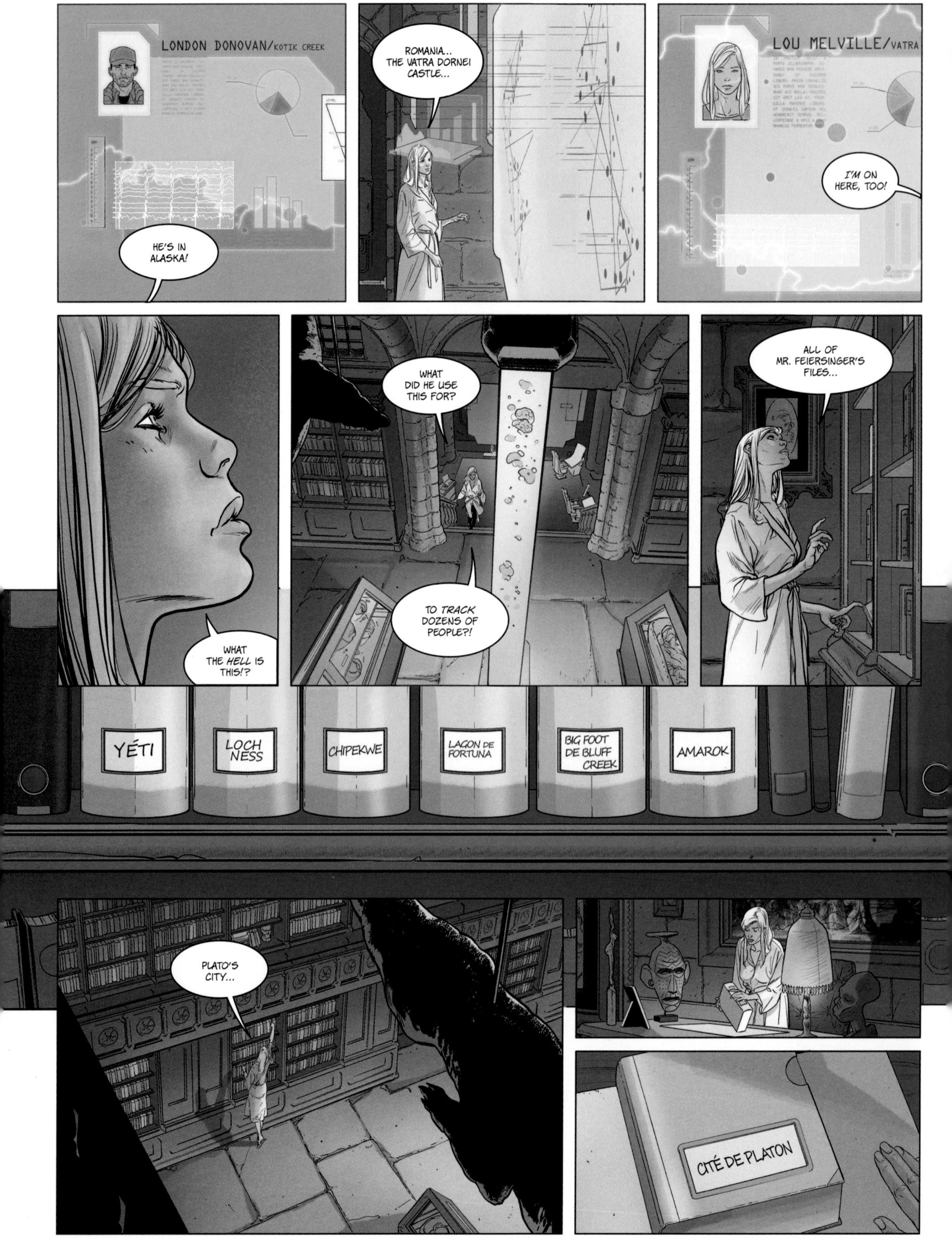

LONDON DONOVAN/KOTIK CREEK
HE'S IN ALASKA!
ROMANIA.. THE VATRA DORNEI CASTLE...
LOU MELVILLE/VATRA
I'M ON HERE, TOO!
WHAT THE HELL IS THIS!?
WHAT DID HE USE THIS FOR?
TO TRACK DOZENS OF PEOPLE?!
ALL OF MR. FEIERSINGER'S FILES...
YÉTI
LOCH NESS
CHIPEKWE
LAGON DE FORTUNA
BIG FOOT DE BLUFF CREEK
AMAROK
PLATO'S CITY...
CITÉ DE PLATON

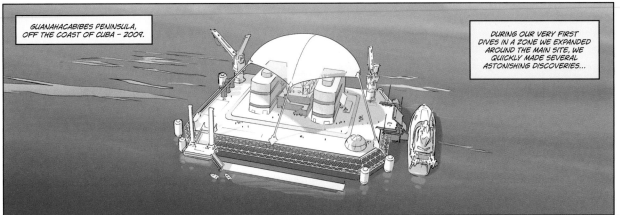

GUANAHACABIBES PENINSULA, OFF THE COAST OF CUBA – 2009.

DURING OUR VERY FIRST DIVES IN A ZONE WE EXPANDED AROUND THE MAIN SITE, WE QUICKLY MADE SEVERAL ASTONISHING DISCOVERIES...

...THREE SUNKEN HISTORICAL SPANISH SHIPS.

THANKS TO NEW GENERATION UNDERWATER DRONES AND A WHOLE ARSENAL OF DEEPWATER EQUIPMENT...

...SUCH AS A HIGH PRECISION DUAL FREQUENCY SONAR AND POSITIONING SYSTEM INTEGRATED INTO THE OCEAN BED BY SATELLITE, HD CAMERAS, 3D LIDAR SCANNERS...

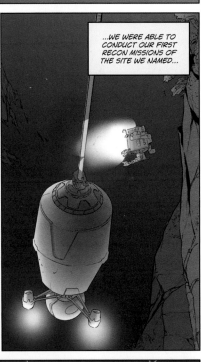

...WE WERE ABLE TO CONDUCT OUR FIRST RECON MISSIONS OF THE SITE WE NAMED...

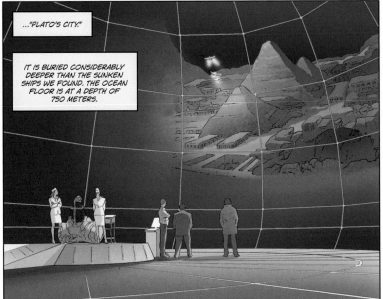

..."PLATO'S CITY."

IT IS BURIED CONSIDERABLY DEEPER THAN THE SUNKEN SHIPS WE FOUND. THE OCEAN FLOOR IS AT A DEPTH OF 750 METERS.

AFTER STUDYING THE READINGS, PROFESSOR NOBUAKI ESTIMATED THAT THE LARGEST OF THE THREE PYRAMIDS IS 128 METERS HIGH, WITH A BASE OF 164 METERS.

IT THEREFORE BEARS A STRONG RESEMBLANCE TO THE GREAT PYRAMID OF GIZA IN EGYPT, WHICH STANDS A LITTLE OVER 146 METERS HIGH.

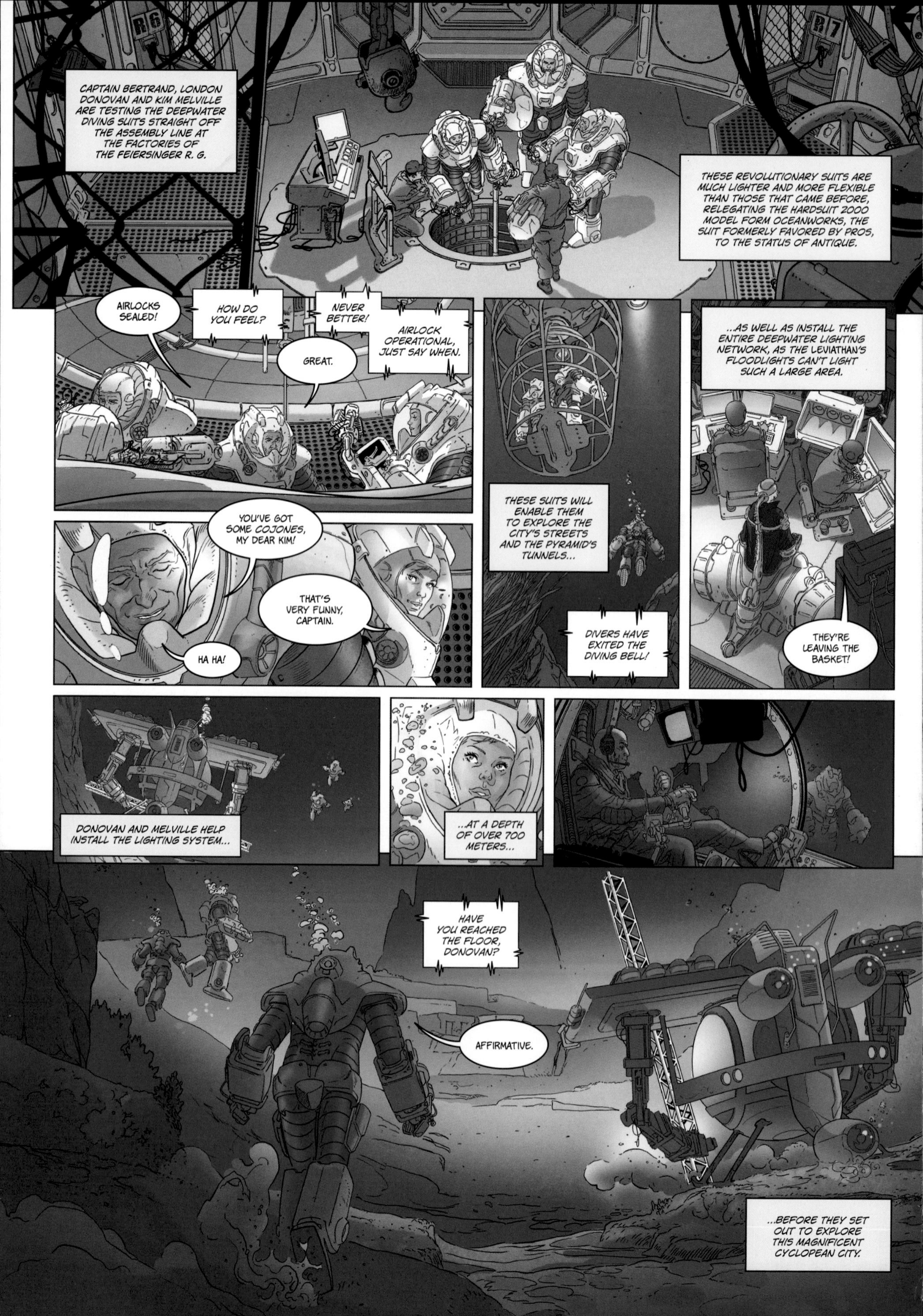
CAPTAIN BERTRAND, LONDON DONOVAN AND KIM MELVILLE ARE TESTING THE DEEPWATER DIVING SUITS STRAIGHT OFF THE ASSEMBLY LINE AT THE FACTORIES OF THE FEIERSINGER R. G.
R6
R7
THESE REVOLUTIONARY SUITS ARE MUCH LIGHTER AND MORE FLEXIBLE THAN THOSE THAT CAME BEFORE, RELEGATING THE HARDSUIT 2000 MODEL FORM OCEANWORKS, THE SUIT FORMERLY FAVORED BY PROS, TO THE STATUS OF ANTIQUE.
AIRLOCKS SEALED!
HOW DO YOU FEEL?
NEVER BETTER!
GREAT.
AIRLOCK OPERATIONAL, JUST SAY WHEN.
YOU'VE GOT SOME COJONES, MY DEAR KIM!
THAT'S VERY FUNNY, CAPTAIN.
HA HA!
THESE SUITS WILL ENABLE THEM TO EXPLORE THE CITY'S STREETS AND THE PYRAMID'S TUNNELS...
DIVERS HAVE EXITED THE DIVING BELL!
...AS WELL AS INSTALL THE ENTIRE DEEPWATER LIGHTING NETWORK, AS THE LEVIATHAN'S FLOODLIGHTS CAN'T LIGHT SUCH A LARGE AREA.
THEY'RE LEAVING THE BASKET!
DONOVAN AND MELVILLE HELP INSTALL THE LIGHTING SYSTEM...
...AT A DEPTH OF OVER 700 METERS...
HAVE YOU REACHED THE FLOOR, DONOVAN?
AFFIRMATIVE.
...BEFORE THEY SET OUT TO EXPLORE THIS MAGNIFICENT CYCLOPEAN CITY.

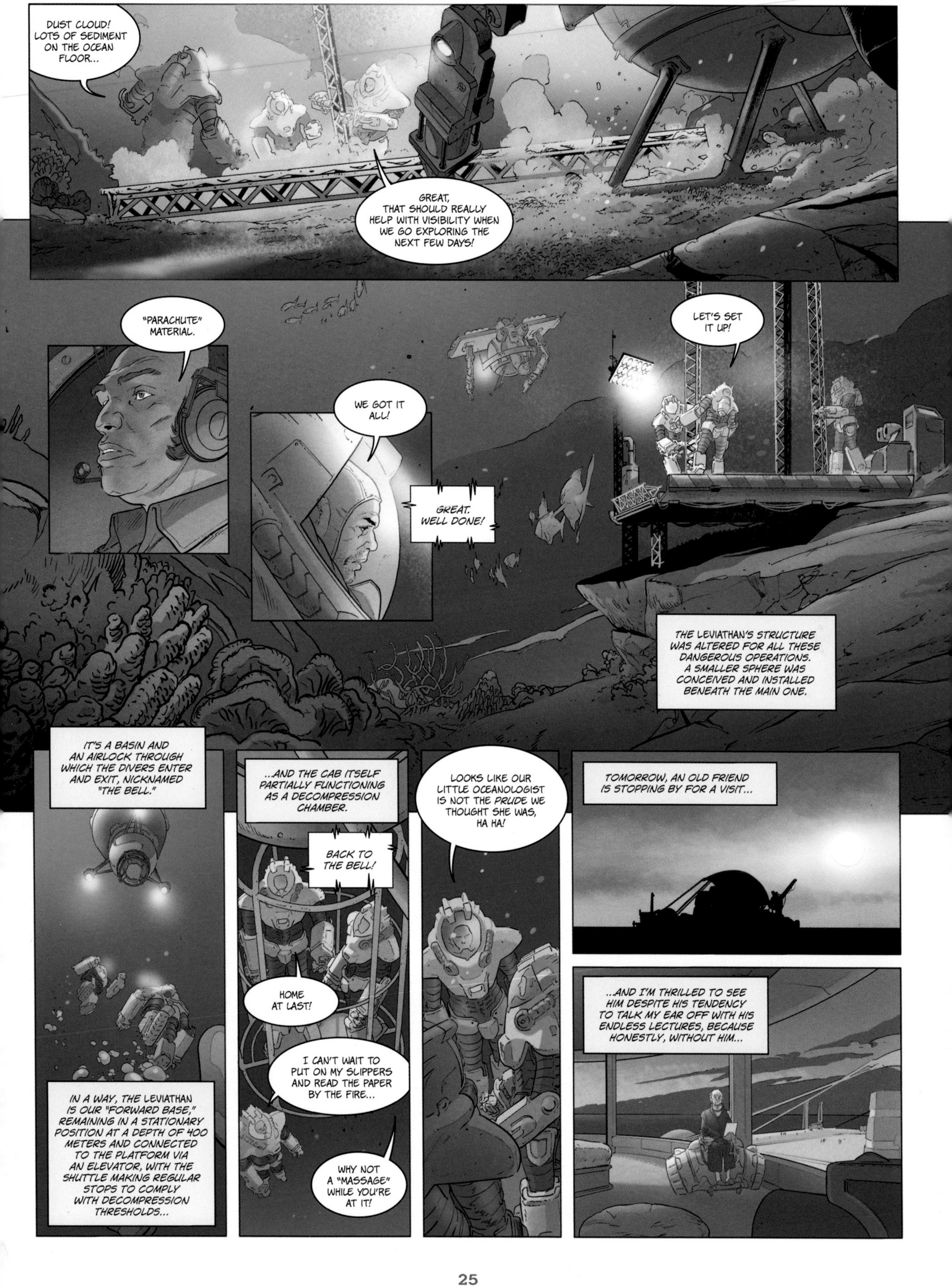
DUST CLOUD! LOTS OF SEDIMENT ON THE OCEAN FLOOR...
GREAT, THAT SHOULD REALLY HELP WITH VISIBILITY WHEN WE GO EXPLORING THE NEXT FEW DAYS!
"PARACHUTE" MATERIAL.
WE GOT IT ALL!
GREAT. WELL DONE!
LET'S SET IT UP!
THE LEVIATHAN'S STRUCTURE WAS ALTERED FOR ALL THESE DANGEROUS OPERATIONS. A SMALLER SPHERE WAS CONCEIVED AND INSTALLED BENEATH THE MAIN ONE.
IT'S A BASIN AND AN AIRLOCK THROUGH WHICH THE DIVERS ENTER AND EXIT, NICKNAMED "THE BELL."
IN A WAY, THE LEVIATHAN IS OUR "FORWARD BASE," REMAINING IN A STATIONARY POSITION AT A DEPTH OF 400 METERS AND CONNECTED TO THE PLATFORM VIA AN ELEVATOR, WITH THE SHUTTLE MAKING REGULAR STOPS TO COMPLY WITH DECOMPRESSION THRESHOLDS...
...AND THE CAB ITSELF PARTIALLY FUNCTIONING AS A DECOMPRESSION CHAMBER.
BACK TO THE BELL!
HOME AT LAST!
I CAN'T WAIT TO PUT ON MY SLIPPERS AND READ THE PAPER BY THE FIRE...
WHY NOT A "MASSAGE" WHILE YOU'RE AT IT!
LOOKS LIKE OUR LITTLE OCEANOLOGIST IS NOT THE PRUDE WE THOUGHT SHE WAS, HA HA!
TOMORROW, AN OLD FRIEND IS STOPPING BY FOR A VISIT...
...AND I'M THRILLED TO SEE HIM DESPITE HIS TENDENCY TO TALK MY EAR OFF WITH HIS ENDLESS LECTURES, BECAUSE HONESTLY, WITHOUT HIM...

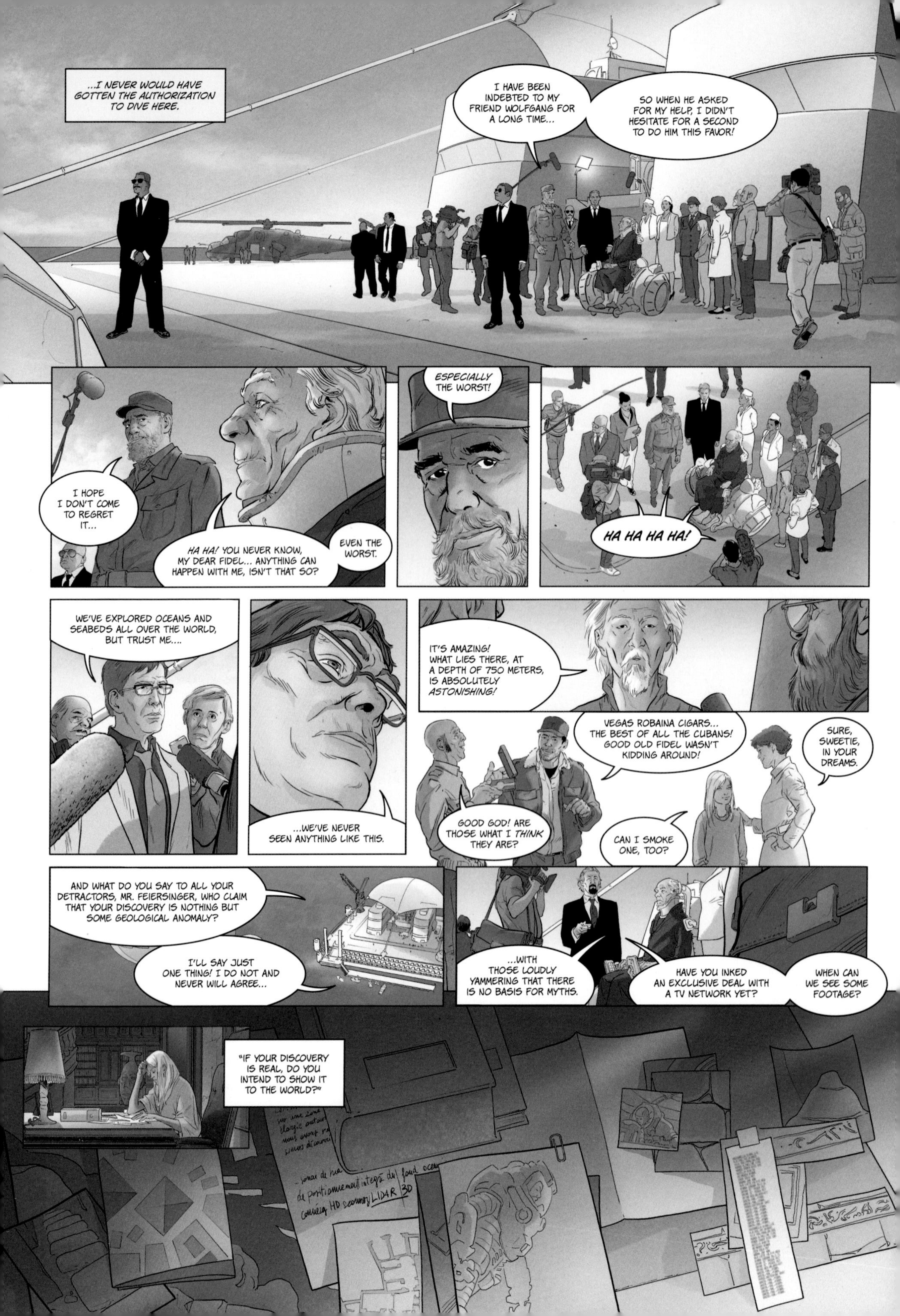
...I NEVER WOULD HAVE GOTTEN THE AUTHORIZATION TO DIVE HERE.
I HAVE BEEN INDEBTED TO MY FRIEND WOLFGANG FOR A LONG TIME...
SO WHEN HE ASKED FOR MY HELP, I DIDN'T HESITATE FOR A SECOND TO DO HIM THIS FAVOR!
I HOPE I DON'T COME TO REGRET IT...
HA HA! YOU NEVER KNOW, MY DEAR FIDEL... ANYTHING CAN HAPPEN WITH ME, ISN'T THAT SO?
EVEN THE WORST.
ESPECIALLY THE WORST!
HA HA HA HA!
WE'VE EXPLORED OCEANS AND SEABEDS ALL OVER THE WORLD, BUT TRUST ME....
...WE'VE NEVER SEEN ANYTHING LIKE THIS.
IT'S AMAZING! WHAT LIES THERE, AT A DEPTH OF 750 METERS, IS ABSOLUTELY ASTONISHING!
GOOD GOD! ARE THOSE WHAT I THINK THEY ARE?
VEGAS ROBAINA CIGARS... THE BEST OF ALL THE CUBANS! GOOD OLD FIDEL WASN'T KIDDING AROUND!
CAN I SMOKE ONE, TOO?
SURE, SWEETIE, IN YOUR DREAMS.
AND WHAT DO YOU SAY TO ALL YOUR DETRACTORS, MR. FEIERSINGER, WHO CLAIM THAT YOUR DISCOVERY IS NOTHING BUT SOME GEOLOGICAL ANOMALY?
I'LL SAY JUST ONE THING! I DO NOT AND NEVER WILL AGREE...
...WITH THOSE LOUDLY YAMMERING THAT THERE IS NO BASIS FOR MYTHS.
HAVE YOU INKED AN EXCLUSIVE DEAL WITH A TV NETWORK YET?
WHEN CAN WE SEE SOME FOOTAGE?
"IF YOUR DISCOVERY IS REAL, DO YOU INTEND TO SHOW IT TO THE WORLD?"
LIDAR 3D

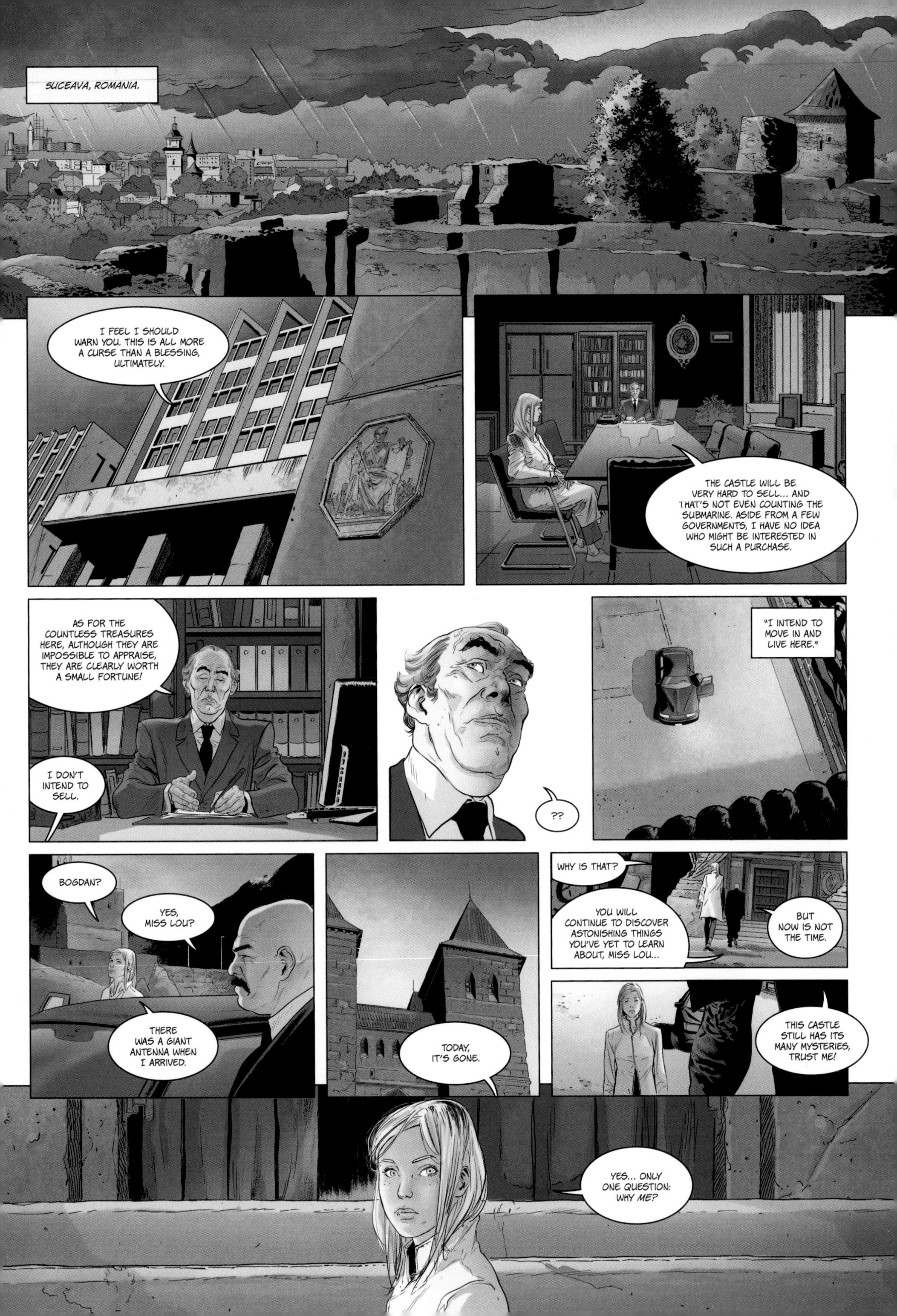
SUCEAVA, ROMANIA.
I FEEL I SHOULD WARN YOU. THIS IS ALL MORE A CURSE THAN A BLESSING, ULTIMATELY.
THE CASTLE WILL BE VERY HARD TO SELL... AND THAT'S NOT EVEN COUNTING THE SUBMARINE. ASIDE FROM A FEW GOVERNMENTS, I HAVE NO IDEA WHO MIGHT BE INTERESTED IN SUCH A PURCHASE.
AS FOR THE COUNTLESS TREASURES HERE, ALTHOUGH THEY ARE IMPOSSIBLE TO APPRAISE, THEY ARE CLEARLY WORTH A SMALL FORTUNE!
I DON'T INTEND TO SELL.
??
"I INTEND TO MOVE IN AND LIVE HERE."
BOGDAN?
YES, MISS LOU?
THERE WAS A GIANT ANTENNA WHEN I ARRIVED.
TODAY, IT'S GONE.
WHY IS THAT?
YOU WILL CONTINUE TO DISCOVER ASTONISHING THINGS YOU'VE YET TO LEARN ABOUT, MISS LOU...
BUT NOW IS NOT THE TIME.
THIS CASTLE STILL HAS ITS MANY MYSTERIES, TRUST ME!
YES... ONLY ONE QUESTION: WHY ME?

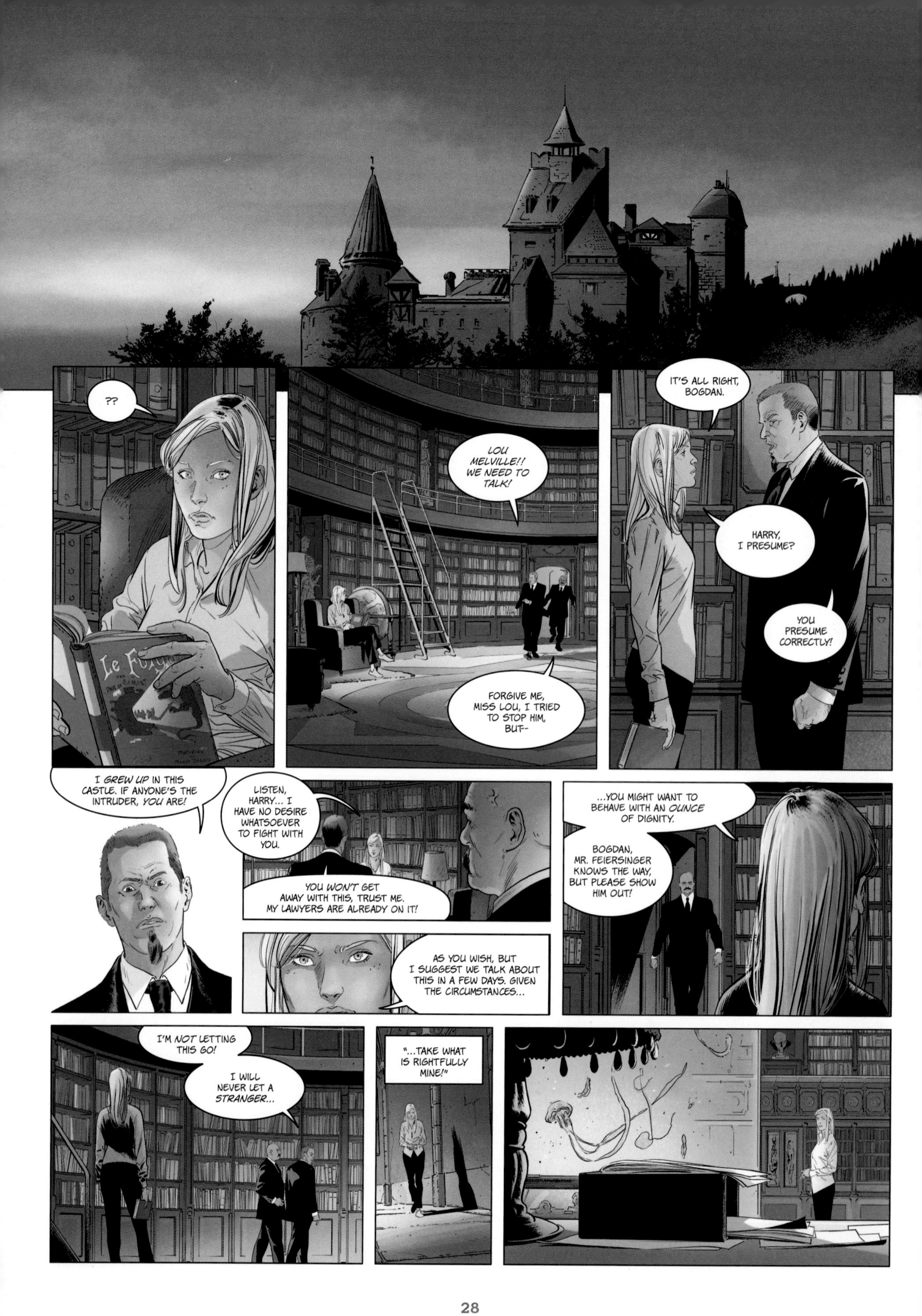
??
LOU MELVILLE!! WE NEED TO TALK!
FORGIVE ME, MISS LOU, I TRIED TO STOP HIM, BUT-
IT'S ALL RIGHT, BOGDAN.
HARRY, I PRESUME?
YOU PRESUME CORRECTLY!
I GREW UP IN THIS CASTLE. IF ANYONE'S THE INTRUDER, YOU ARE!
LISTEN, HARRY... I HAVE NO DESIRE WHATSOEVER TO FIGHT WITH YOU.
YOU WON'T GET AWAY WITH THIS, TRUST ME. MY LAWYERS ARE ALREADY ON IT!
AS YOU WISH, BUT I SUGGEST WE TALK ABOUT THIS IN A FEW DAYS. GIVEN THE CIRCUMSTANCES...
...YOU MIGHT WANT TO BEHAVE WITH AN OUNCE OF DIGNITY.
BOGDAN, MR. FEIERSINGER KNOWS THE WAY, BUT PLEASE SHOW HIM OUT!
I'M NOT LETTING THIS GO!
I WILL NEVER LET A STRANGER...
"...TAKE WHAT IS RIGHTFULLY MINE!"

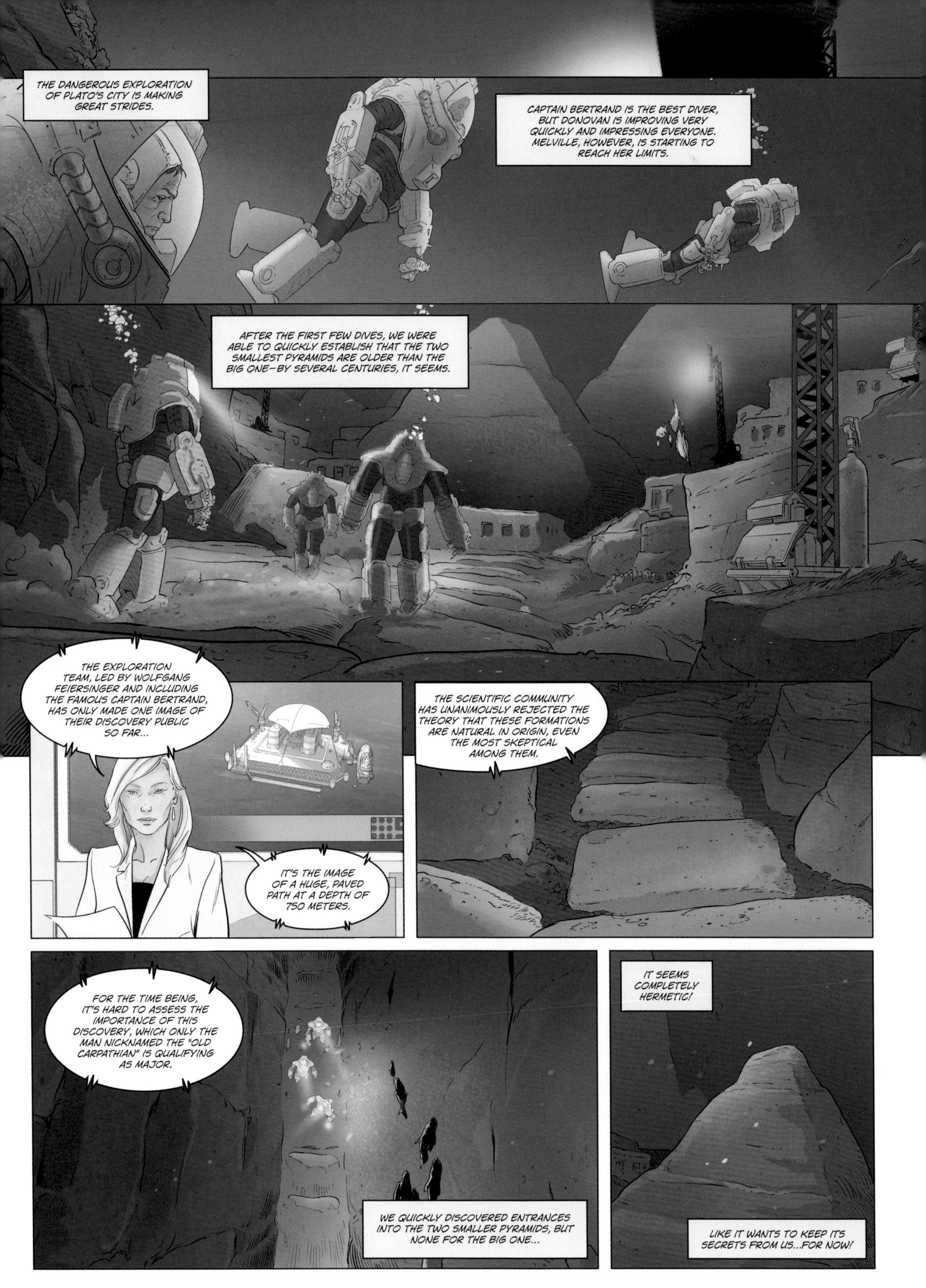
THE DANGEROUS EXPLORATION OF PLATO'S CITY IS MAKING GREAT STRIDES.
CAPTAIN BERTRAND IS THE BEST DIVER, BUT DONOVAN IS IMPROVING VERY QUICKLY AND IMPRESSING EVERYONE. MELVILLE, HOWEVER, IS STARTING TO REACH HER LIMITS.
AFTER THE FIRST FEW DIVES, WE WERE ABLE TO QUICKLY ESTABLISH THAT THE TWO SMALLEST PYRAMIDS ARE OLDER THAN THE BIG ONE—BY SEVERAL CENTURIES, IT SEEMS.
THE EXPLORATION TEAM, LED BY WOLFGANG FEIERSINGER AND INCLUDING THE FAMOUS CAPTAIN BERTRAND, HAS ONLY MADE ONE IMAGE OF THEIR DISCOVERY PUBLIC SO FAR...
IT'S THE IMAGE OF A HUGE, PAVED PATH AT A DEPTH OF 750 METERS.
THE SCIENTIFIC COMMUNITY HAS UNANIMOUSLY REJECTED THE THEORY THAT THESE FORMATIONS ARE NATURAL IN ORIGIN, EVEN THE MOST SKEPTICAL AMONG THEM.
FOR THE TIME BEING, IT'S HARD TO ASSESS THE IMPORTANCE OF THIS DISCOVERY, WHICH ONLY THE MAN NICKNAMED THE "OLD CARPATHIAN" IS QUALIFYING AS MAJOR.
WE QUICKLY DISCOVERED ENTRANCES INTO THE TWO SMALLER PYRAMIDS, BUT NONE FOR THE BIG ONE...
IT SEEMS COMPLETELY HERMETIC!
LIKE IT WANTS TO KEEP ITS SECRETS FROM US...FOR NOW!

SPEAKING OF STRANGE THINGS, FOR SEVERAL DAYS WE'VE BEEN EXPERIENCING FREQUENT ELECTROMAGNETIC DISTURBANCES ABOVE THE SITE, WHICH ARE MESSING WITH OUR MEASURING INSTRUMENTS.

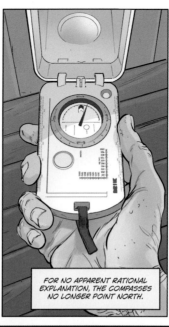

FOR NO APPARENT RATIONAL EXPLANATION, THE COMPASSES NO LONGER POINT NORTH.

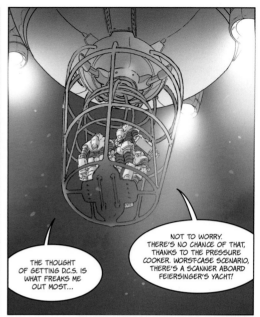

THE THOUGHT OF GETTING D.C.S. IS WHAT FREAKS ME OUT MOST...

NOT TO WORRY. THERE'S NO CHANCE OF THAT, THANKS TO THE PRESSURE COOKER. WORST-CASE SCENARIO, THERE'S A SCANNER ABOARD FEIERSINGER'S YACHT!

TIME FOR ANOTHER "DIVE"!

INTERNAL PRESSURE: 1,000 KILOPASCALS...

INTERNAL PRESSURE: 1,000 KILOPASCALS...

RELAX, KIM...

THE ELECTROENCEPHALOGRAMS LOOK GOOD FOR ALL THREE.

NO TINGLING IN YOUR EXTREMITIES?

NO.

WE'LL LET YOU OUT, THEN...

NOW YOU CAN START THE ASCENT TOWARDS "BASE CAMP."

THANKS, DOC! WE'RE COOKED ALL THE WAY THROUGH!

UGH... I DON'T FEEL SO GOOD... I'M FREEZING AND EXHAUSTED!

IT'S NOTHING, MELVILLE. JUST YOUR SECOND ROUND IN THE CHAMBER!

THINK OF THE NICE HOT BATH WAITING FOR YOU IN YOUR CABIN, KIM.

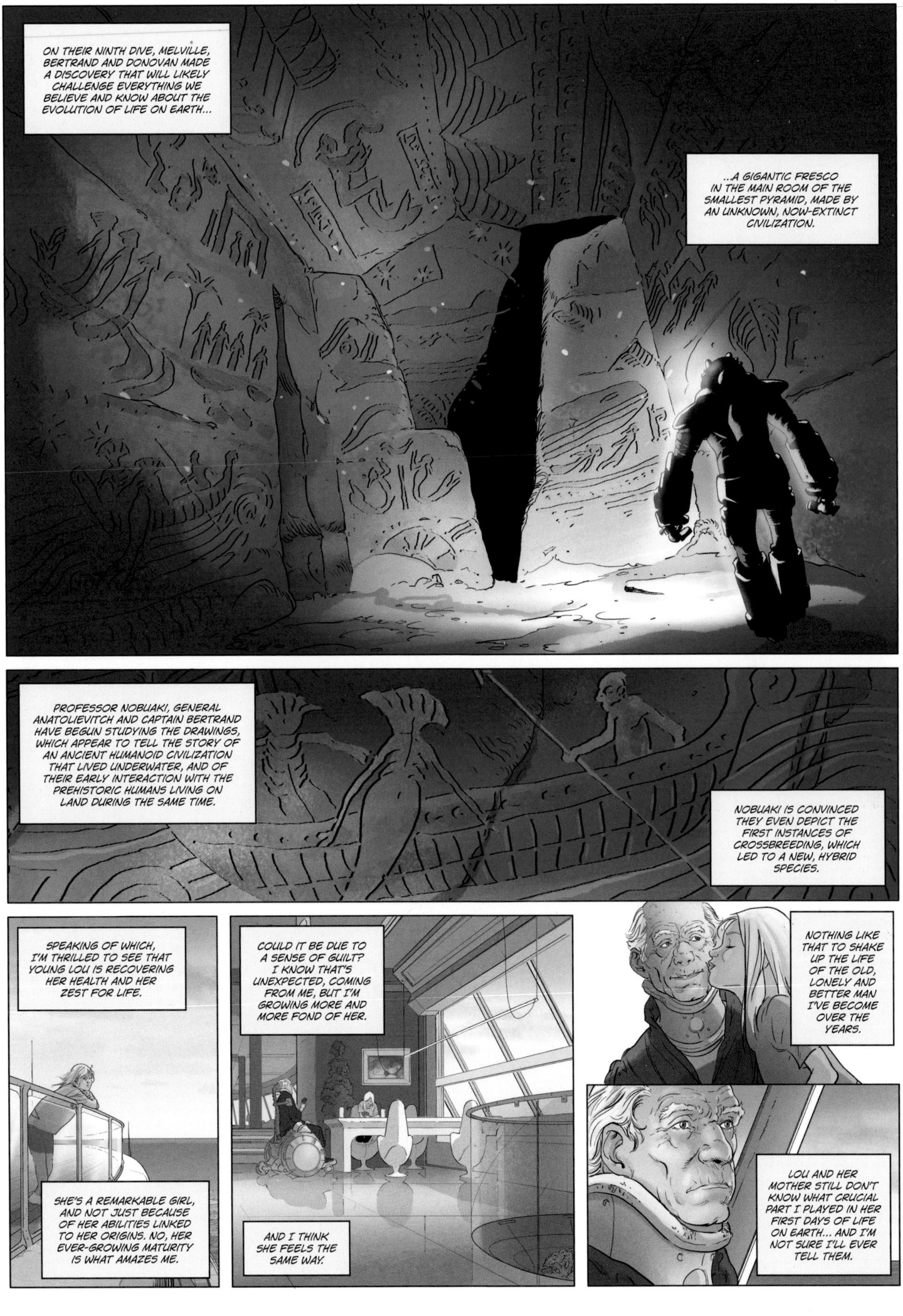
ON THEIR NINTH DIVE, MELVILLE, BERTRAND AND DONOVAN MADE A DISCOVERY THAT WILL LIKELY CHALLENGE EVERYTHING WE BELIEVE AND KNOW ABOUT THE EVOLUTION OF LIFE ON EARTH...
...A GIGANTIC FRESCO IN THE MAIN ROOM OF THE SMALLEST PYRAMID, MADE BY AN UNKNOWN, NOW-EXTINCT CIVILIZATION.
PROFESSOR NOBUAKI, GENERAL ANATOLIEVITCH AND CAPTAIN BERTRAND HAVE BEGUN STUDYING THE DRAWINGS, WHICH APPEAR TO TELL THE STORY OF AN ANCIENT HUMANOID CIVILIZATION THAT LIVED UNDERWATER, AND OF THEIR EARLY INTERACTION WITH THE PREHISTORIC HUMANS LIVING ON LAND DURING THE SAME TIME.
NOBUAKI IS CONVINCED THEY EVEN DEPICT THE FIRST INSTANCES OF CROSSBREEDING, WHICH LED TO A NEW, HYBRID SPECIES.
SPEAKING OF WHICH, I'M THRILLED TO SEE THAT YOUNG LOU IS RECOVERING HER HEALTH AND HER ZEST FOR LIFE.
SHE'S A REMARKABLE GIRL, AND NOT JUST BECAUSE OF HER ABILITIES LINKED TO HER ORIGINS. NO, HER EVER-GROWING MATURITY IS WHAT AMAZES ME.
COULD IT BE DUE TO A SENSE OF GUILT? I KNOW THAT'S UNEXPECTED, COMING FROM ME, BUT I'M GROWING MORE AND MORE FOND OF HER.
AND I THINK SHE FEELS THE SAME WAY.
NOTHING LIKE THAT TO SHAKE UP THE LIFE OF THE OLD, LONELY AND BETTER MAN I'VE BECOME OVER THE YEARS.
LOU AND HER MOTHER STILL DON'T KNOW WHAT CRUCIAL PART I PLAYED IN HER FIRST DAYS OF LIFE ON EARTH... AND I'M NOT SURE I'LL EVER TELL THEM.

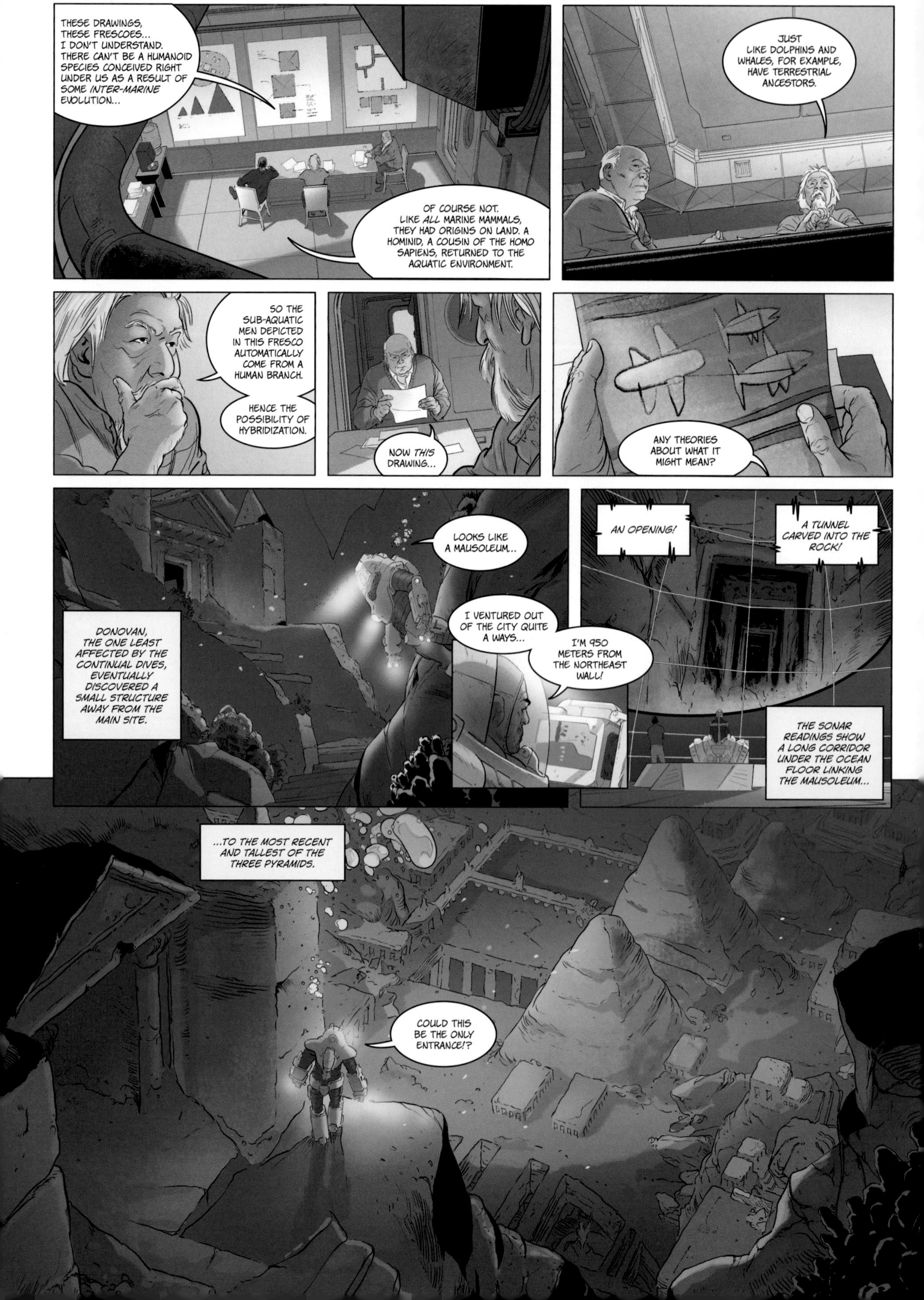
THESE DRAWINGS, THESE FRESCOES... I DON'T UNDERSTAND. THERE CAN'T BE A HUMANOID SPECIES CONCEIVED RIGHT UNDER US AS A RESULT OF SOME *INTER-MARINE* EVOLUTION...
OF COURSE NOT. LIKE *ALL* MARINE MAMMALS, THEY HAD ORIGINS ON LAND. A HOMINID, A COUSIN OF THE HOMO SAPIENS, RETURNED TO THE AQUATIC ENVIRONMENT.
JUST LIKE DOLPHINS AND WHALES, FOR EXAMPLE, HAVE TERRESTRIAL ANCESTORS.
SO THE SUB-AQUATIC MEN DEPICTED IN THIS FRESCO AUTOMATICALLY COME FROM A HUMAN BRANCH.
HENCE THE POSSIBILITY OF HYBRIDIZATION.
NOW *THIS* DRAWING...
ANY THEORIES ABOUT WHAT IT MIGHT MEAN?
LOOKS LIKE A MAUSOLEUM...
DONOVAN, THE ONE LEAST AFFECTED BY THE CONTINUAL DIVES, EVENTUALLY DISCOVERED A SMALL STRUCTURE AWAY FROM THE MAIN SITE.
I VENTURED OUT OF THE CITY QUITE A WAYS...
I'M 950 METERS FROM THE NORTHEAST WALL!
AN OPENING!
A TUNNEL CARVED INTO THE ROCK!
THE SONAR READINGS SHOW A LONG CORRIDOR UNDER THE OCEAN FLOOR LINKING THE MAUSOLEUM...
...TO THE MOST RECENT AND TALLEST OF THE THREE PYRAMIDS.
COULD THIS BE THE ONLY ENTRANCE!?

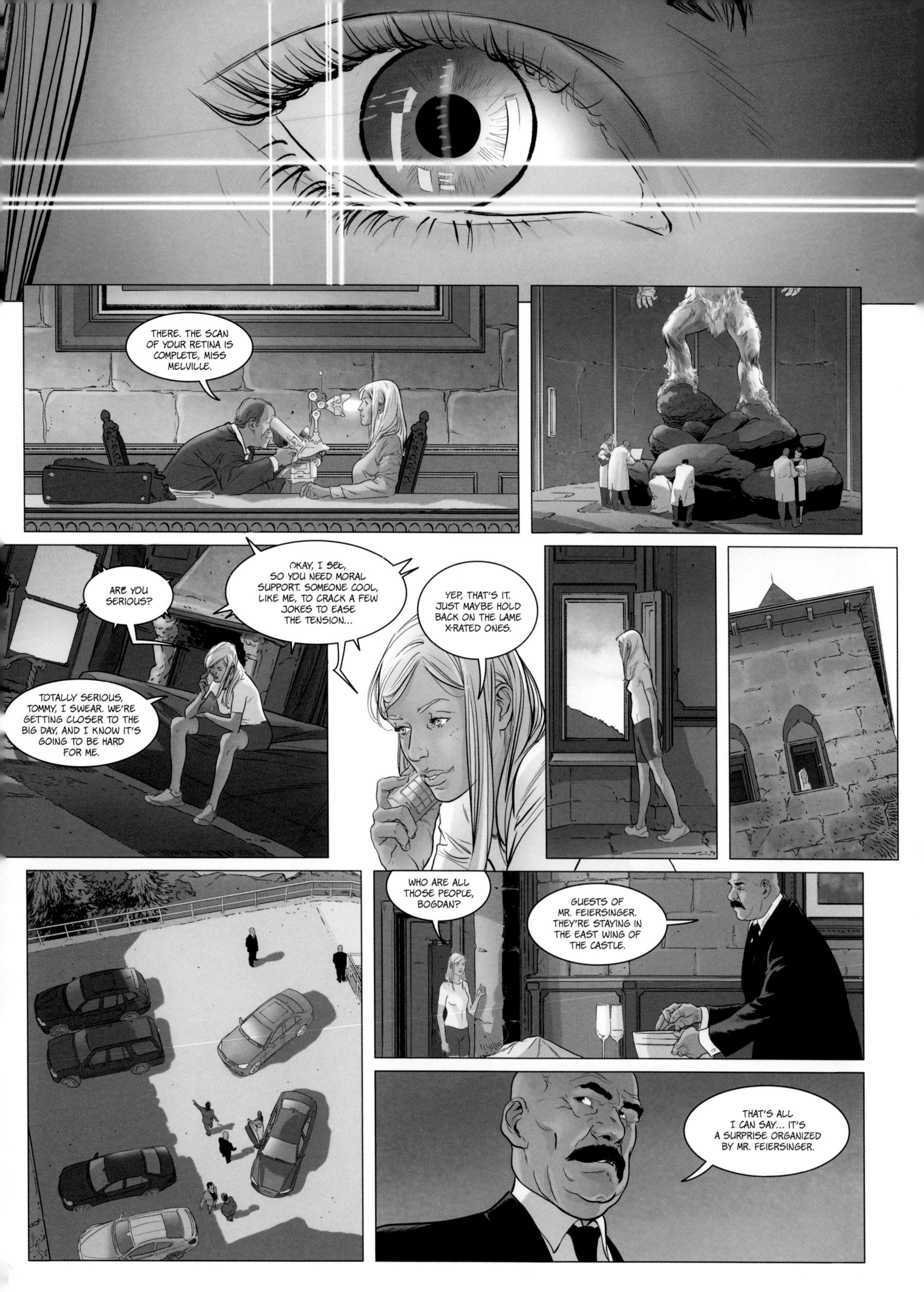
THERE. THE SCAN OF YOUR RETINA IS COMPLETE, MISS MELVILLE.
ARE YOU SERIOUS?
TOTALLY SERIOUS, TOMMY, I SWEAR. WE'RE GETTING CLOSER TO THE BIG DAY, AND I KNOW IT'S GOING TO BE HARD FOR ME.
OKAY, I SEE, SO YOU NEED MORAL SUPPORT. SOMEONE COOL, LIKE ME, TO CRACK A FEW JOKES TO EASE THE TENSION...
YEP, THAT'S IT. JUST MAYBE HOLD BACK ON THE LAME X-RATED ONES.
WHO ARE ALL THOSE PEOPLE, BOGDAN?
GUESTS OF MR. FEIERSINGER. THEY'RE STAYING IN THE EAST WING OF THE CASTLE.
THAT'S ALL I CAN SAY... IT'S A SURPRISE ORGANIZED BY MR. FEIERSINGER.

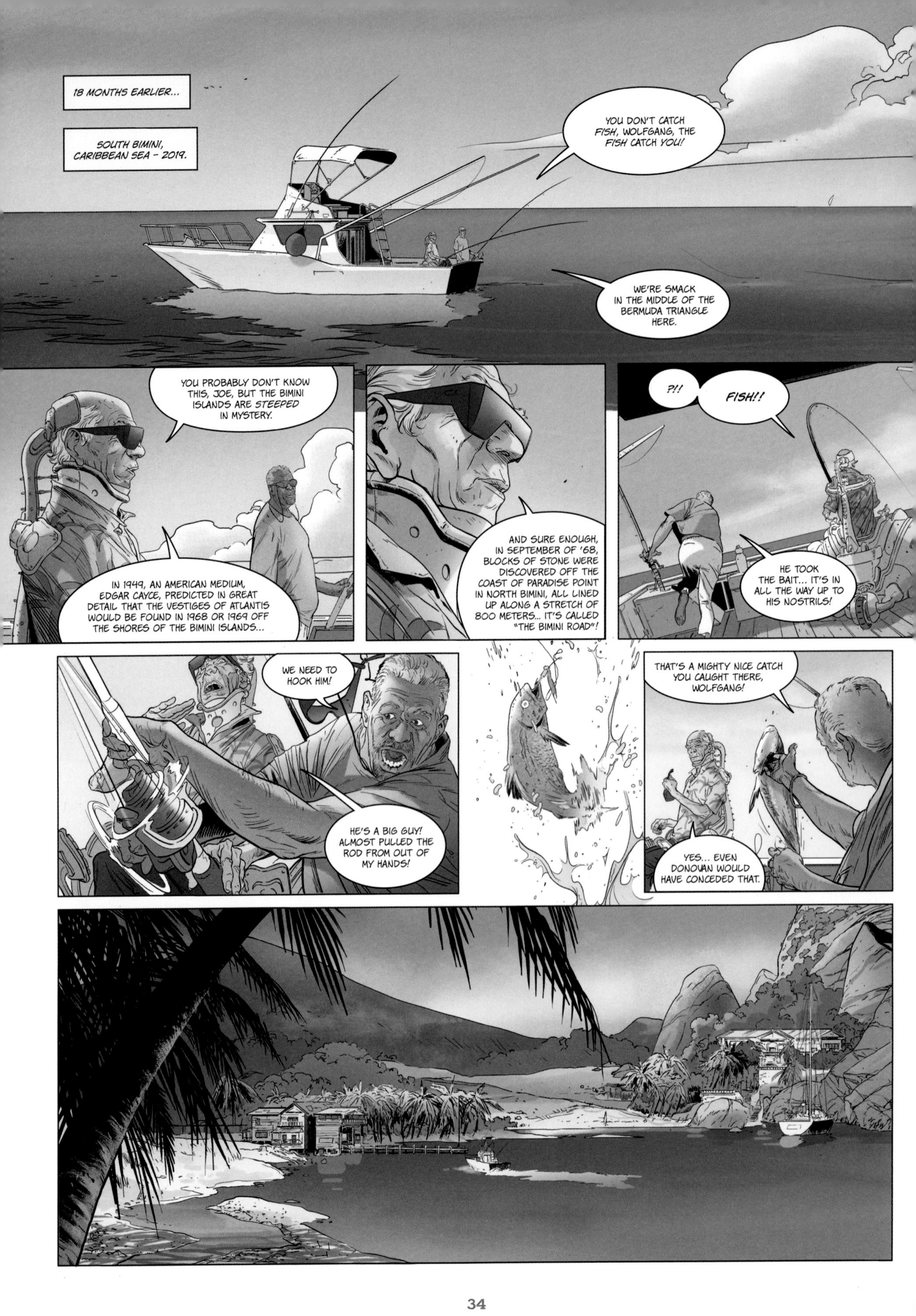
18 MONTHS EARLIER...
SOUTH BIMINI, CARIBBEAN SEA - 2019.
YOU DON'T CATCH FISH, WOLFGANG, THE FISH CATCH YOU!
WE'RE SMACK IN THE MIDDLE OF THE BERMUDA TRIANGLE HERE.
YOU PROBABLY DON'T KNOW THIS, JOE, BUT THE BIMINI ISLANDS ARE STEEPED IN MYSTERY.
IN 1949, AN AMERICAN MEDIUM, EDGAR CAYCE, PREDICTED IN GREAT DETAIL THAT THE VESTIGES OF ATLANTIS WOULD BE FOUND IN 1968 OR 1969 OFF THE SHORES OF THE BIMINI ISLANDS...
AND SURE ENOUGH, IN SEPTEMBER OF '68, BLOCKS OF STONE WERE DISCOVERED OFF THE COAST OF PARADISE POINT IN NORTH BIMINI, ALL LINED UP ALONG A STRETCH OF 800 METERS... IT'S CALLED "THE BIMINI ROAD"!
?!!
FISH!!
HE TOOK THE BAIT... IT'S IN ALL THE WAY UP TO HIS NOSTRILS!
WE NEED TO HOOK HIM!
HE'S A BIG GUY! ALMOST PULLED THE ROD FROM OUT OF MY HANDS!
THAT'S A MIGHTY NICE CATCH YOU CAUGHT THERE, WOLFGANG!
YES... EVEN DONOVAN WOULD HAVE CONCEDED THAT.

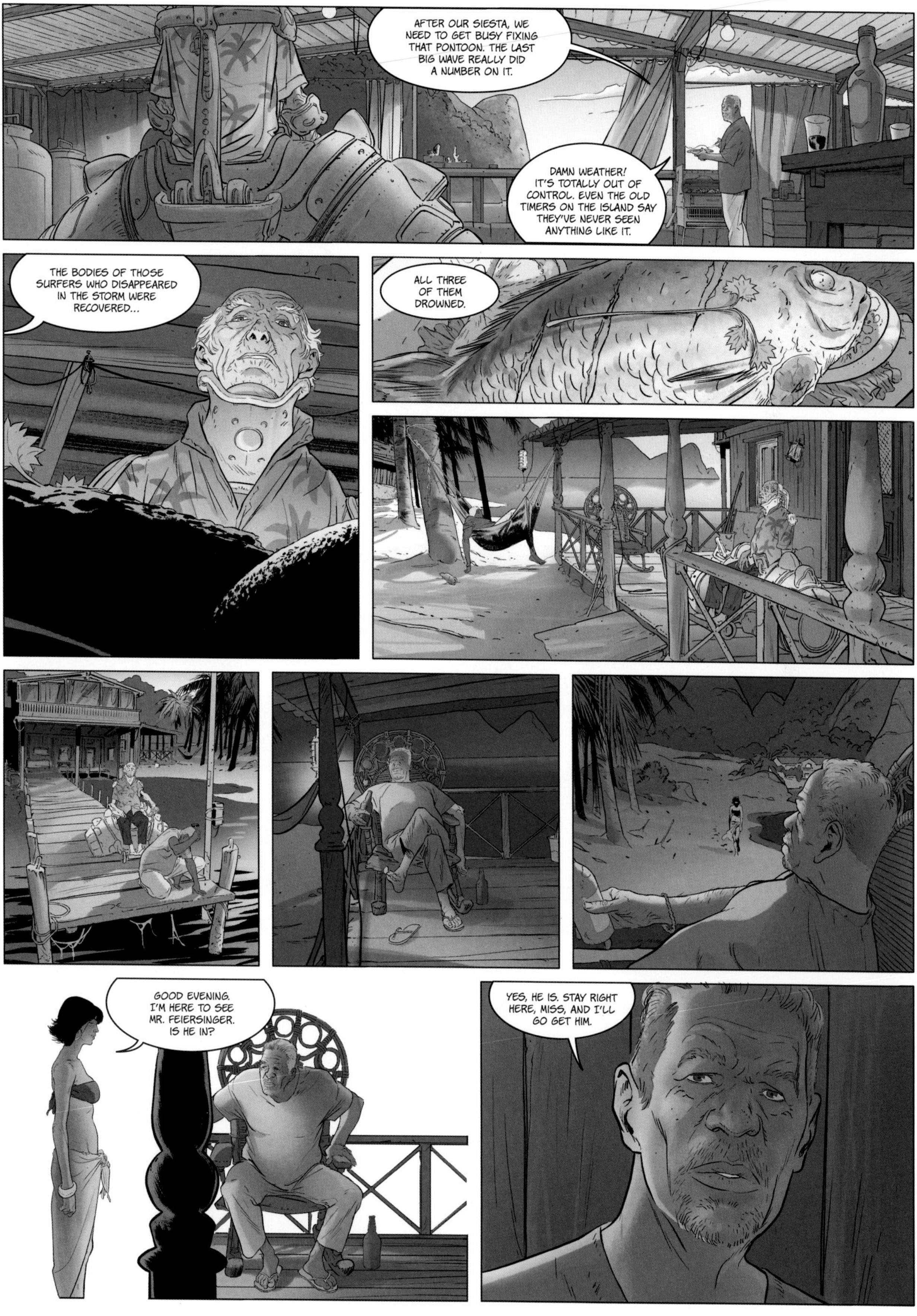
AFTER OUR SIESTA, WE NEED TO GET BUSY FIXING THAT PONTOON. THE LAST BIG WAVE REALLY DID A NUMBER ON IT.
DAMN WEATHER! IT'S TOTALLY OUT OF CONTROL. EVEN THE OLD TIMERS ON THE ISLAND SAY THEY'VE NEVER SEEN ANYTHING LIKE IT.
THE BODIES OF THOSE SURFERS WHO DISAPPEARED IN THE STORM WERE RECOVERED...
ALL THREE OF THEM DROWNED.
GOOD EVENING. I'M HERE TO SEE MR. FEIERSINGER. IS HE IN?
YES, HE IS. STAY RIGHT HERE, MISS, AND I'LL GO GET HIM.

HELLO. I'M MELANIE BRESON, YOUR NEIGHBOR.

I LIVE ON THE BIG PROPERTY NEXT DOOR. I JUST BOUGHT IT.

I MOVED IN TWO DAYS AGO, AND I CAME TO INVITE YOU TO A LITTLE HOUSEWARMING RECEPTION I'M HAVING TOMORROW NIGHT. IT WOULD BE AN HONOR TO HAVE YOU AMONG US!

GLADLY. I ACCEPT, MS. BRESON.

PLEASE, CALL ME MELANIE.

UNTIL TOMORROW THEN. DON'T LET ME DOWN!

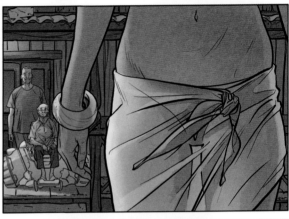

JOE...

I DIDN'T SAY ANYTHING, WOLFGANG.

I'M JUST OBSERVING.

OF COURSE YOU ARE... GOOD NIGHT. AND TAKE IT EASY ON THE BOOZE.

IT GIVES YOU CRAZY IDEAS.

AUSCHWITZ-BIRKENAU, POLAND – JANUARY 27, 1945.

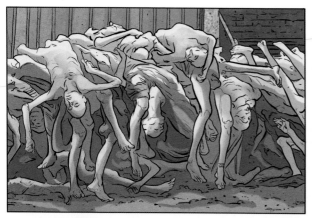

I HAVE TO CONFESS SOMETHING... I INVITED YOU HERE WITH AN AGENDA. YOUR REPUTATION PRECEDES YOU...

MY GRANDFATHER AND MY GREAT-GRANDFATHER TOLD ME ABOUT YOU...

??

YOUR GREAT-GRANDFATHER TOLD YOU ABOUT ME?

YOU SURE KNOW HOW TO MAKE A MAN FEEL YOUNG!

I'M SORRY, THAT WAS NOT MY INTENTION...

COME, MEET SOME OF MY FRIENDS.

YOU'VE NO DOUBT HEARD OF GEORGE BERNSTEIN, A MAJOR PRODUCER OF ACTION FILMS.

YES, WE'VE CROSSED PATHS A COUPLE OF TIMES.

WOLFGANG... I'M SO GLAD YOU COULD MAKE IT!

MR. FEIERSINGER... I'M A BIT SURPRISED TO SEE YOU HERE IN THE CARIBBEAN. I DIDN'T THINK YOU *VACATIONED* IN THESE PARTS.

ME, NO, BUT A LOT OF WEALTHY AMERICANS DO. THEY COME TO BIMINI TO FISH.

AND IS *THAT* WHY *YOU'RE* HERE, FEIERSINGER?

YES, BUT NOT JUST THAT. I BOUGHT A HOUSE HERE. JUST NEXT DOOR, ON THE BEACH.

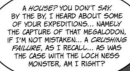

A *HOUSE?* YOU DON'T SAY. BY THE BY, I HEARD ABOUT SOME OF YOUR EXPEDITIONS... NAMELY THE CAPTURE OF THAT MEGALODON, IF I'M NOT MISTAKEN... A *CRUSHING FAILURE*, AS I RECALL... AS WAS THE CASE WITH THE LOCH NESS MONSTER, AM I RIGHT?

SUCH A *SHAME*... THOSE WOULD HAVE MADE GREAT FILMS!

INDEED. PROVIDED THERE'S A GOOD PRODUCER AT THE HELM.

I SEE YOU TWO ALREADY KNOW EACH OTHER... A LITTLE TOO WELL, PERHAPS.

WOLFGANG, I'M STEALING YOU FOR A MINUTE. I HAVE SOMETHING I WANT TO SHOW YOU... A SPECIAL SPOT ON MY PROPERTY. YOU DON'T MIND, GEORGE, DO YOU?

NOT AT ALL, MELANIE.

MR. FEIERSINGER AND I WILL RESUME THIS *RIVETING* DISCUSSION A LITTLE LATER.

I CAN *HARDLY* WAIT.

THIS WHEELCHAIR IS MOTORIZED, YOU KNOW. THERE'S NO NEED FOR YOU TO PUSH ME.

BUT THANKS FOR GETTING ME AWAY FROM HIM.

I HATE TO KEEP APOLOGIZING, BUT AGAIN, I'M SORRY... I HAD NO IDEA YOU TWO KNEW EACH OTHER.

BERNSTEIN IS ONE GRUMPY OLD MAN!

I'M AFRAID WE DON'T BELONG TO THE SAME SPECIES.

NO, I DON'T THINK SO.

IS THIS WHAT YOU WANTED TO SHOW ME? IT'S BEAUTIFUL.

ISN'T IT?

A GLASS OF BOLLINGER 2002?

GLADLY. IT'S ONE OF THE BEST YEARS!

YOU WOULDN'T, BY CHANCE, BE TRYING TO *SEDUCE* ME, WOULD YOU, MISS BRESON? I'M JUST AN OLD CRIPPLE...

I TOLD YOU, PLEASE CALL ME MELANIE!

RUMOR HAS IT YOU HAD HUNDREDS OF CONQUESTS, NAMELY FAMOUS HOLLYWOOD ACTRESSES... I WOULD ONLY BE ONE MORE NOTCH ON YOUR BEDPOST...

THAT'S JUST *LEGEND*.

BUT YOU *ARE* A LEGEND, MR. FEIERSINGER!

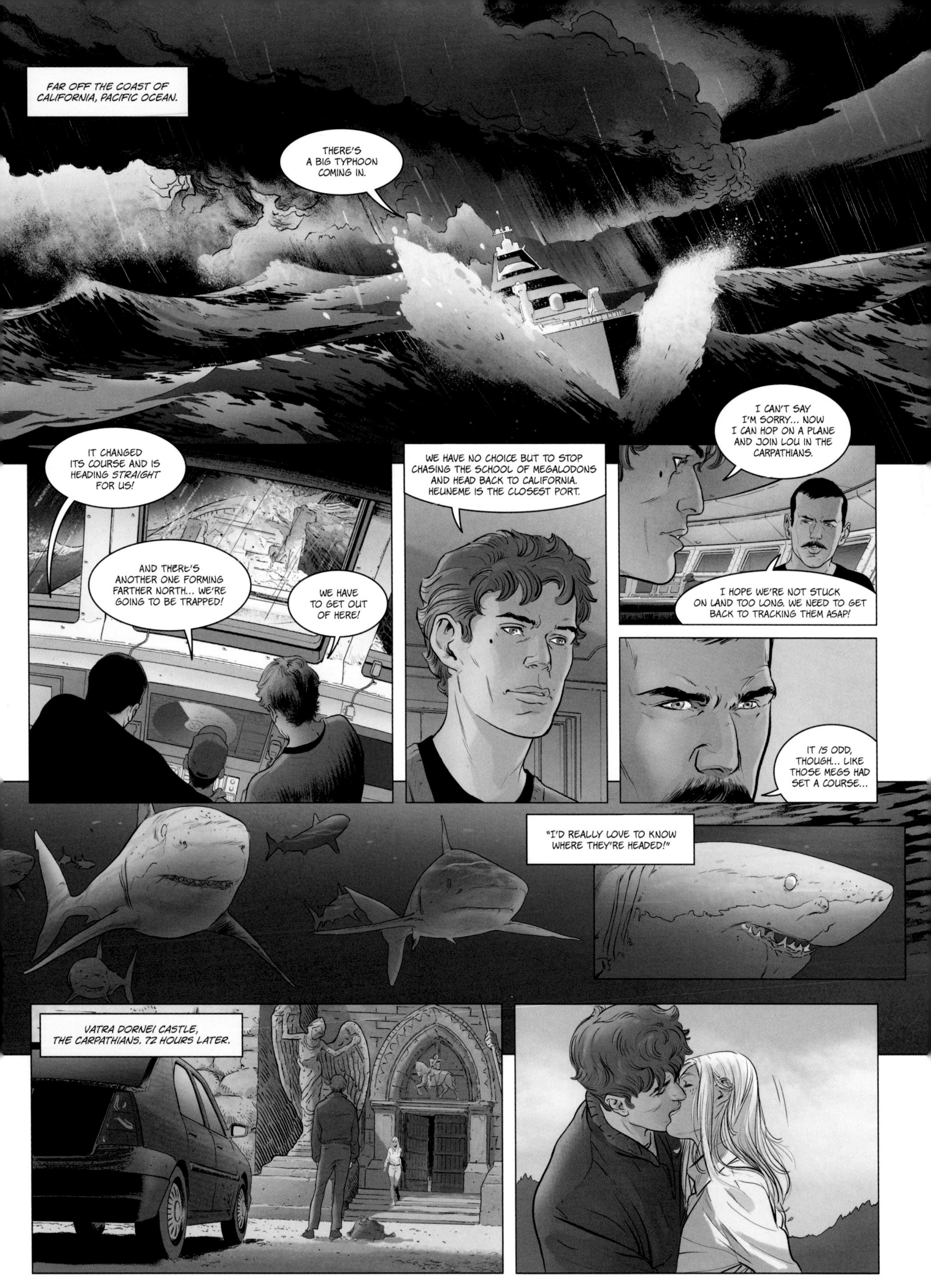
FAR OFF THE COAST OF CALIFORNIA, PACIFIC OCEAN.
THERE'S A BIG TYPHOON COMING IN.
IT CHANGED ITS COURSE AND IS HEADING STRAIGHT FOR US!
AND THERE'S ANOTHER ONE FORMING FARTHER NORTH... WE'RE GOING TO BE TRAPPED!
WE HAVE TO GET OUT OF HERE!
WE HAVE NO CHOICE BUT TO STOP CHASING THE SCHOOL OF MEGALODONS AND HEAD BACK TO CALIFORNIA. HEUNEME IS THE CLOSEST PORT.
I CAN'T SAY I'M SORRY... NOW I CAN HOP ON A PLANE AND JOIN LOU IN THE CARPATHIANS.
I HOPE WE'RE NOT STUCK ON LAND TOO LONG. WE NEED TO GET BACK TO TRACKING THEM ASAP!
IT IS ODD, THOUGH... LIKE THOSE MEGS HAD SET A COURSE...
"I'D REALLY LOVE TO KNOW WHERE THEY'RE HEADED!"
VATRA DORNEI CASTLE, THE CARPATHIANS. 72 HOURS LATER.

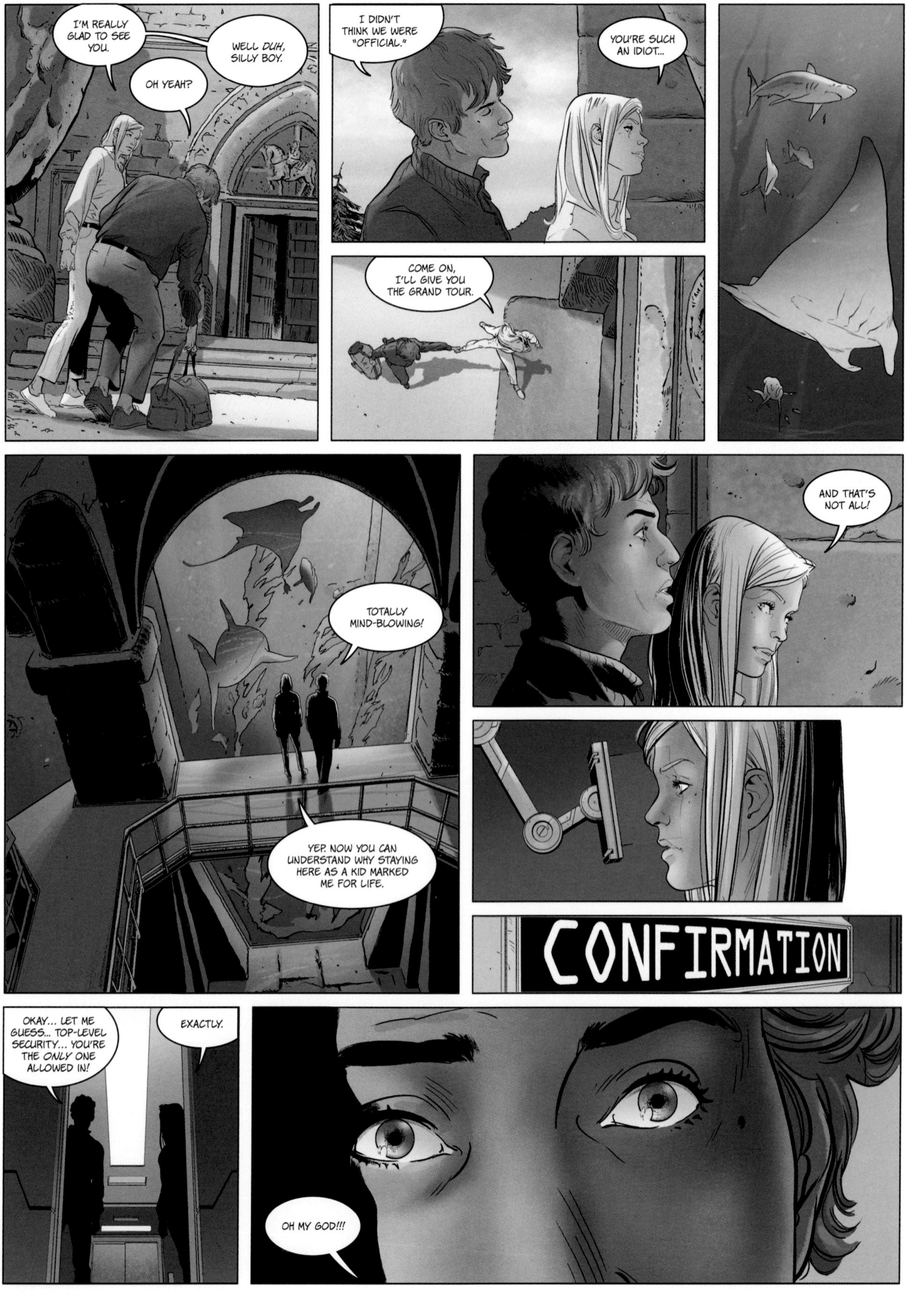

I'M REALLY GLAD TO SEE YOU.
WELL *DUH*, SILLY BOY.
OH YEAH?
I DIDN'T THINK WE WERE "OFFICIAL."
YOU'RE SUCH AN IDIOT...
COME ON, I'LL GIVE YOU THE GRAND TOUR.
TOTALLY MIND-BLOWING!
YEP. NOW YOU CAN UNDERSTAND WHY STAYING HERE AS A KID MARKED ME FOR LIFE.
AND THAT'S NOT ALL!
CONFIRMATION
OKAY... LET ME GUESS... TOP-LEVEL SECURITY... YOU'RE THE *ONLY* ONE ALLOWED IN!
EXACTLY.
OH MY GOD!!!

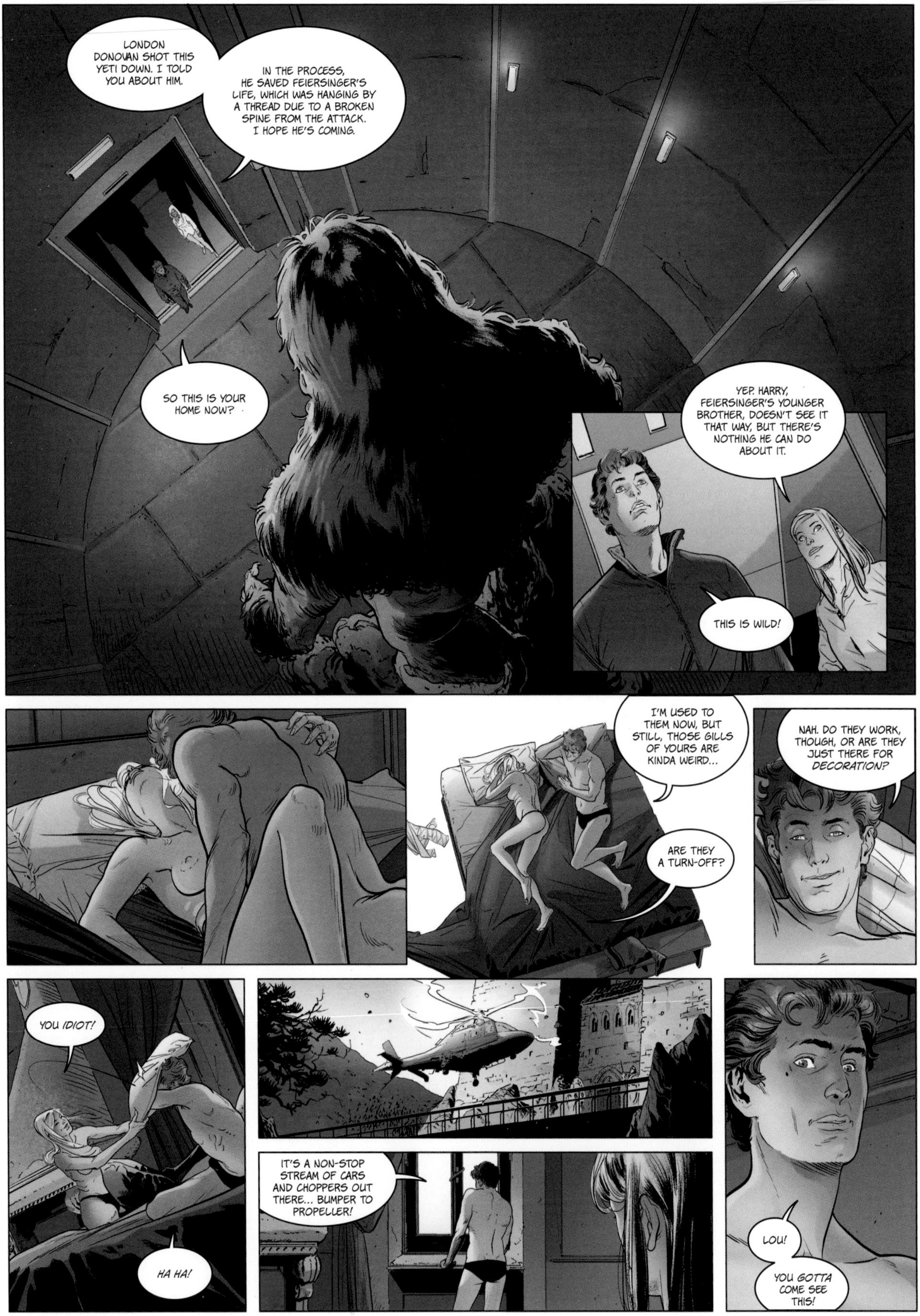
LONDON DONOVAN SHOT THIS YETI DOWN. I TOLD YOU ABOUT HIM.
IN THE PROCESS, HE SAVED FEIERSINGER'S LIFE, WHICH WAS HANGING BY A THREAD DUE TO A BROKEN SPINE FROM THE ATTACK. I HOPE HE'S COMING.
SO THIS IS YOUR HOME NOW?
YEP. HARRY, FEIERSINGER'S YOUNGER BROTHER, DOESN'T SEE IT THAT WAY, BUT THERE'S NOTHING HE CAN DO ABOUT IT.
THIS IS WILD!
I'M USED TO THEM NOW, BUT STILL, THOSE GILLS OF YOURS ARE KINDA WEIRD...
ARE THEY A TURN-OFF?
NAH. DO THEY WORK, THOUGH, OR ARE THEY JUST THERE FOR *DECORATION?*
YOU IDIOT!
HA HA!
IT'S A NON-STOP STREAM OF CARS AND CHOPPERS OUT THERE... BUMPER TO PROPELLER!
LOU!
YOU GOTTA COME SEE THIS!

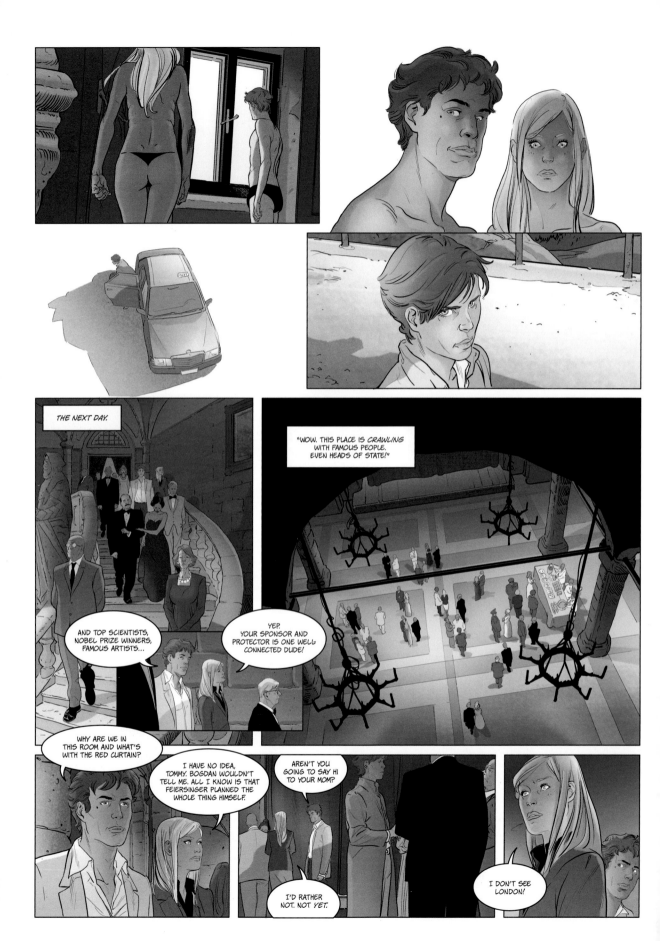

THE NEXT DAY.

"WOW. THIS PLACE IS CRAWLING WITH FAMOUS PEOPLE. EVEN HEADS OF STATE!"

AND TOP SCIENTISTS, NOBEL PRIZE WINNERS, FAMOUS ARTISTS...

YEP. YOUR SPONSOR AND PROTECTOR IS ONE WELL CONNECTED DUDE!

WHY ARE WE IN THIS ROOM AND WHAT'S WITH THE RED CURTAIN?

I HAVE NO IDEA, TOMMY. BOGDAN WOULDN'T TELL ME. ALL I KNOW IS THAT FEIERSINGER PLANNED THE WHOLE THING HIMSELF.

AREN'T YOU GOING TO SAY HI TO YOUR MOM?

I'D RATHER NOT. NOT YET.

I DON'T SEE LONDON!

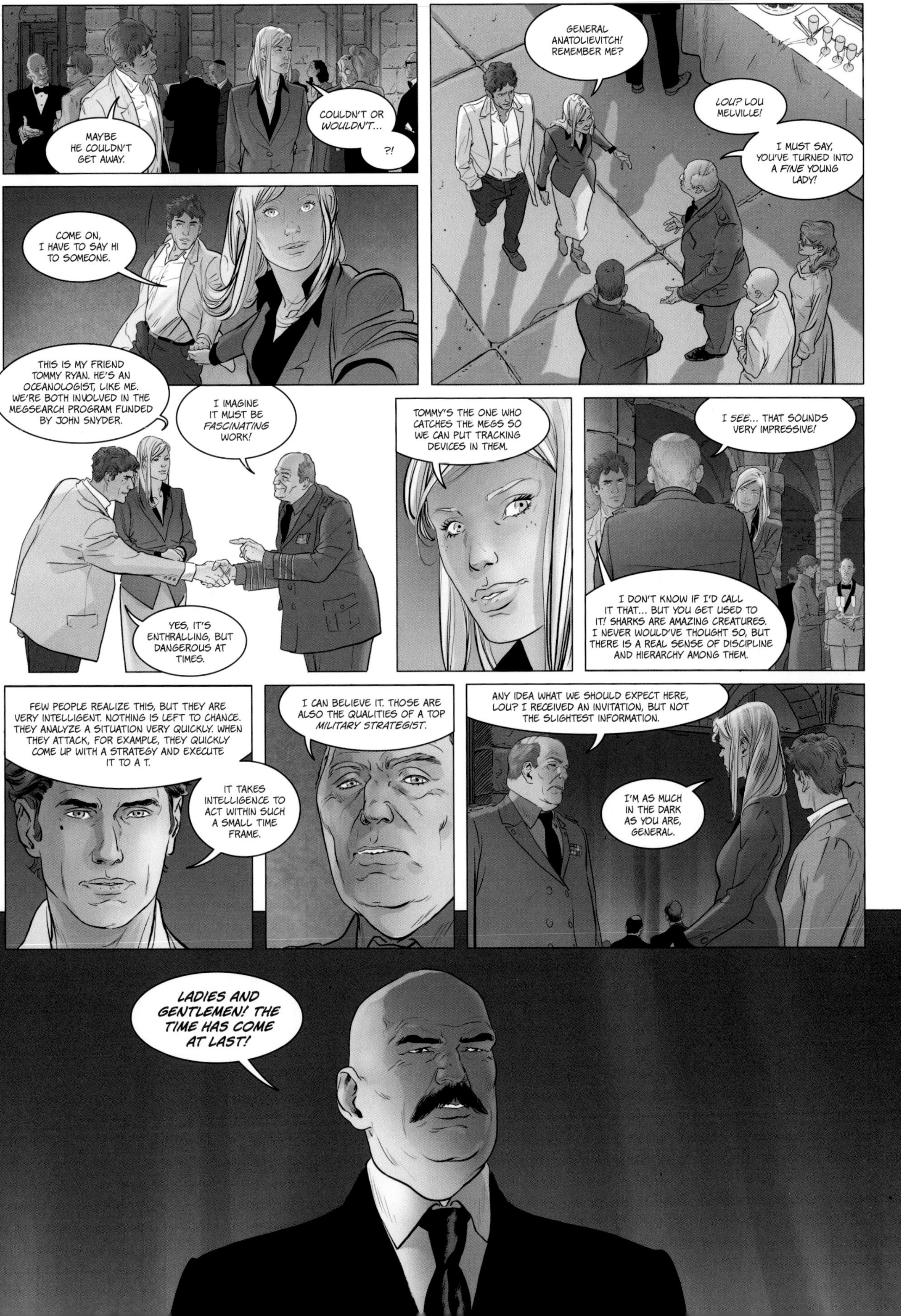
MAYBE HE COULDN'T GET AWAY.
COULDN'T OR *WOULDN'T*...
?!
COME ON, I HAVE TO SAY HI TO SOMEONE.
GENERAL ANATOLIEVITCH! REMEMBER ME?
LOU? LOU MELVILLE!
I MUST SAY, YOU'VE TURNED INTO A *FINE* YOUNG LADY!
THIS IS MY FRIEND TOMMY RYAN. HE'S AN OCEANOLOGIST, LIKE ME. WE'RE BOTH INVOLVED IN THE MEGSEARCH PROGRAM FUNDED BY JOHN SNYDER.
I IMAGINE IT MUST BE *FASCINATING* WORK!
YES, IT'S ENTHRALLING, BUT DANGEROUS AT TIMES.
TOMMY'S THE ONE WHO CATCHES THE MEGS SO WE CAN PUT TRACKING DEVICES IN THEM.
I *SEE*... THAT SOUNDS VERY IMPRESSIVE!
I DON'T KNOW IF I'D CALL IT THAT... BUT YOU GET USED TO IT! SHARKS ARE AMAZING CREATURES. I NEVER WOULD'VE THOUGHT SO, BUT THERE IS A REAL SENSE OF DISCIPLINE AND HIERARCHY AMONG THEM.
FEW PEOPLE REALIZE THIS, BUT THEY ARE VERY INTELLIGENT. NOTHING IS LEFT TO CHANCE. THEY ANALYZE A SITUATION VERY QUICKLY. WHEN THEY ATTACK, FOR EXAMPLE, THEY QUICKLY COME UP WITH A STRATEGY AND EXECUTE IT TO A T.
IT TAKES INTELLIGENCE TO ACT WITHIN SUCH A SMALL TIME FRAME.
I CAN BELIEVE IT. THOSE ARE ALSO THE QUALITIES OF A TOP *MILITARY STRATEGIST*.
ANY IDEA WHAT WE SHOULD EXPECT HERE, LOU? I RECEIVED AN INVITATION, BUT NOT THE SLIGHTEST INFORMATION.
I'M AS MUCH IN THE DARK AS YOU ARE, GENERAL.
LADIES AND GENTLEMEN! THE TIME HAS COME AT LAST!

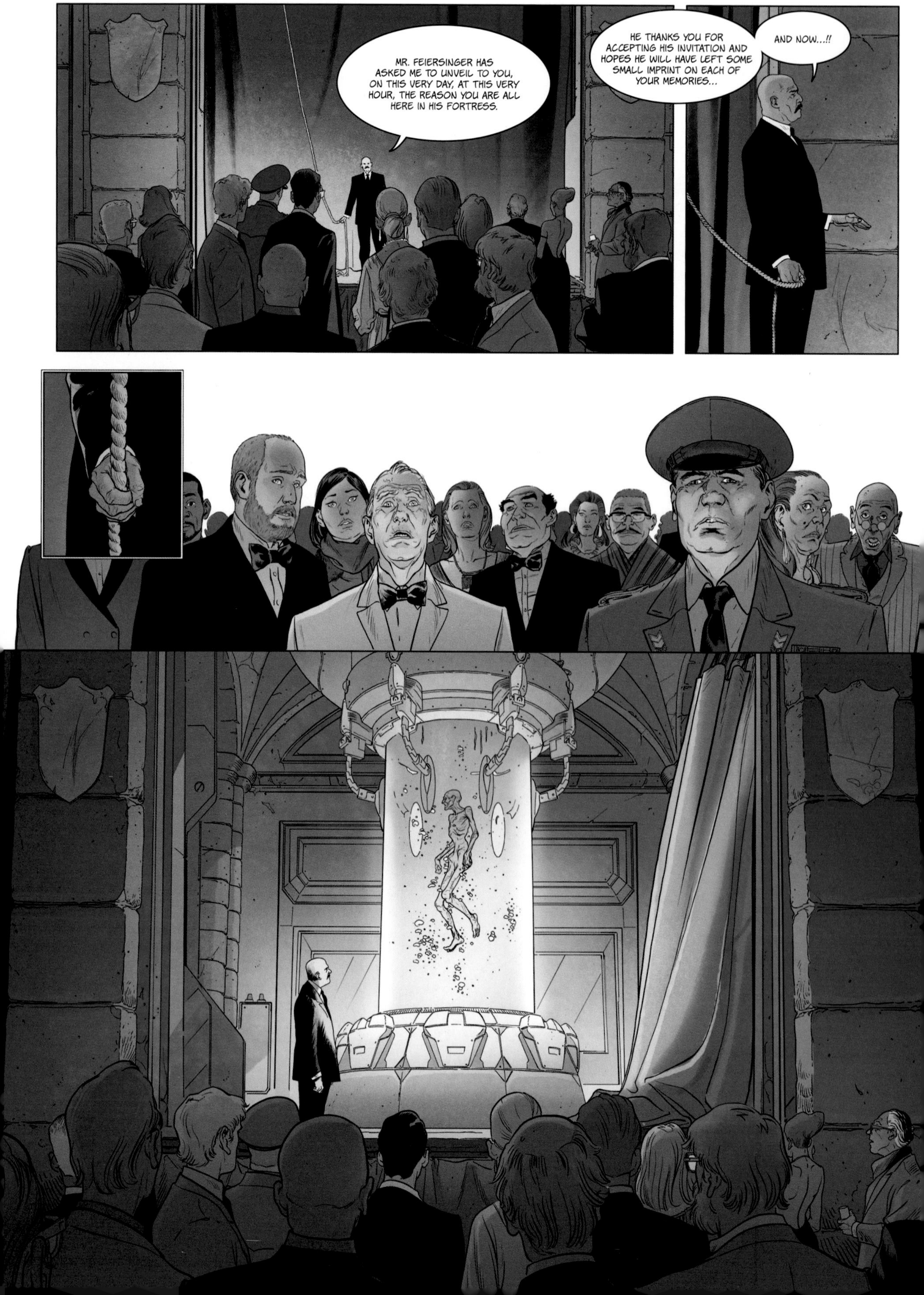
MR. FEIERSINGER HAS ASKED ME TO UNVEIL TO YOU, ON THIS VERY DAY, AT THIS VERY HOUR, THE REASON YOU ARE ALL HERE IN HIS FORTRESS.
HE THANKS YOU FOR ACCEPTING HIS INVITATION AND HOPES HE WILL HAVE LEFT SOME SMALL IMPRINT ON EACH OF YOUR MEMORIES...
AND NOW...!!

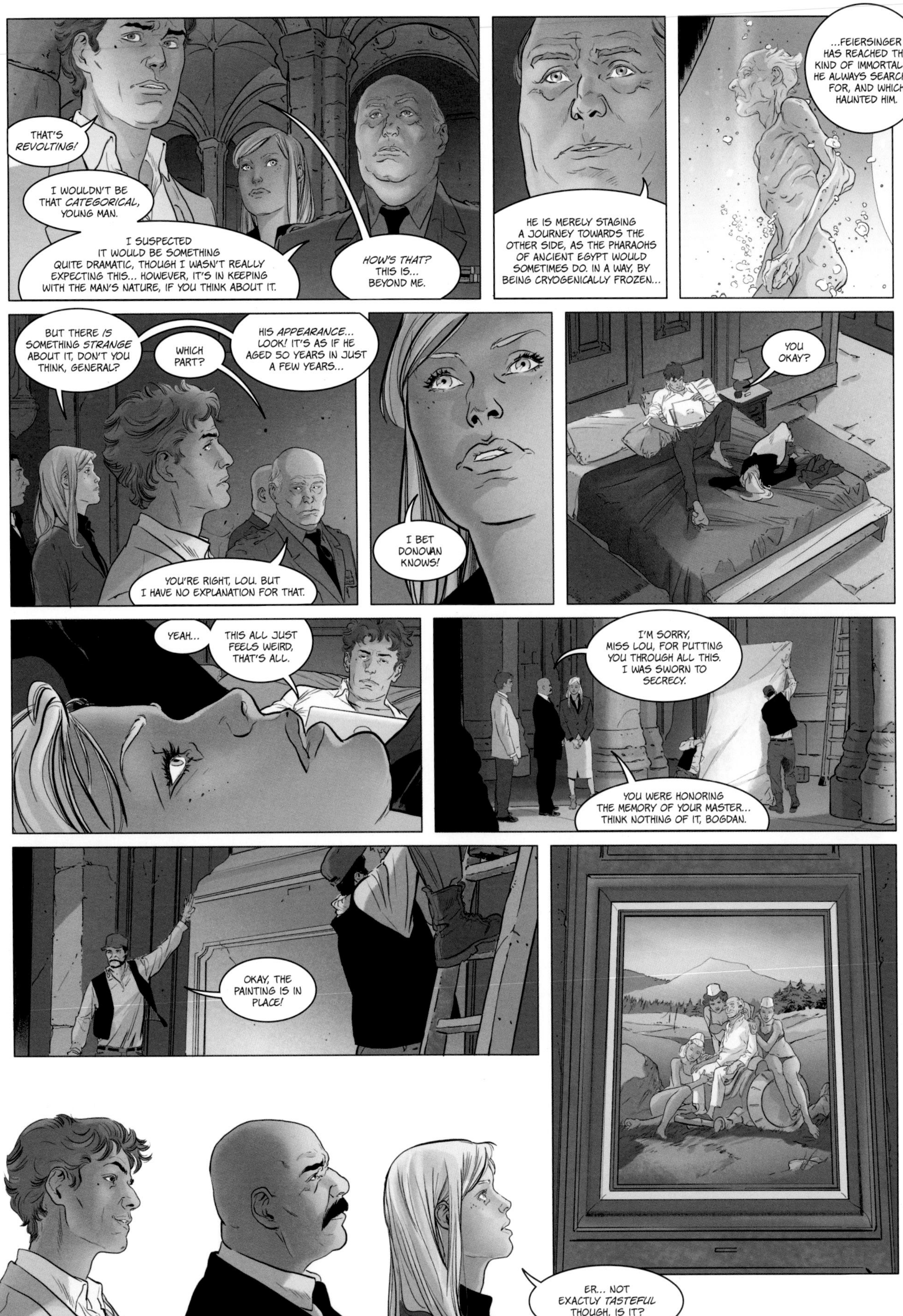
THAT'S REVOLTING!
I WOULDN'T BE THAT CATEGORICAL, YOUNG MAN.
I SUSPECTED IT WOULD BE SOMETHING QUITE DRAMATIC, THOUGH I WASN'T REALLY EXPECTING THIS... HOWEVER, IT'S IN KEEPING WITH THE MAN'S NATURE, IF YOU THINK ABOUT IT.
HOW'S THAT? THIS IS... BEYOND ME.
HE IS MERELY STAGING A JOURNEY TOWARDS THE OTHER SIDE, AS THE PHARAOHS OF ANCIENT EGYPT WOULD SOMETIMES DO. IN A WAY, BY BEING CRYOGENICALLY FROZEN...
...FEIERSINGER HAS REACHED THE KIND OF IMMORTALITY HE ALWAYS SEARCHED FOR, AND WHICH HAUNTED HIM.
BUT THERE IS SOMETHING STRANGE ABOUT IT, DON'T YOU THINK, GENERAL?
WHICH PART?
HIS APPEARANCE... LOOK! IT'S AS IF HE AGED 50 YEARS IN JUST A FEW YEARS...
YOU'RE RIGHT, LOU. BUT I HAVE NO EXPLANATION FOR THAT.
I BET DONOVAN KNOWS!
YOU OKAY?
YEAH...
THIS ALL JUST FEELS WEIRD, THAT'S ALL.
I'M SORRY, MISS LOU, FOR PUTTING YOU THROUGH ALL THIS. I WAS SWORN TO SECRECY.
YOU WERE HONORING THE MEMORY OF YOUR MASTER... THINK NOTHING OF IT, BOGDAN.
OKAY, THE PAINTING IS IN PLACE!
ER... NOT EXACTLY TASTEFUL THOUGH, IS IT?

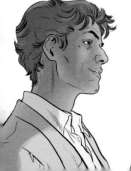

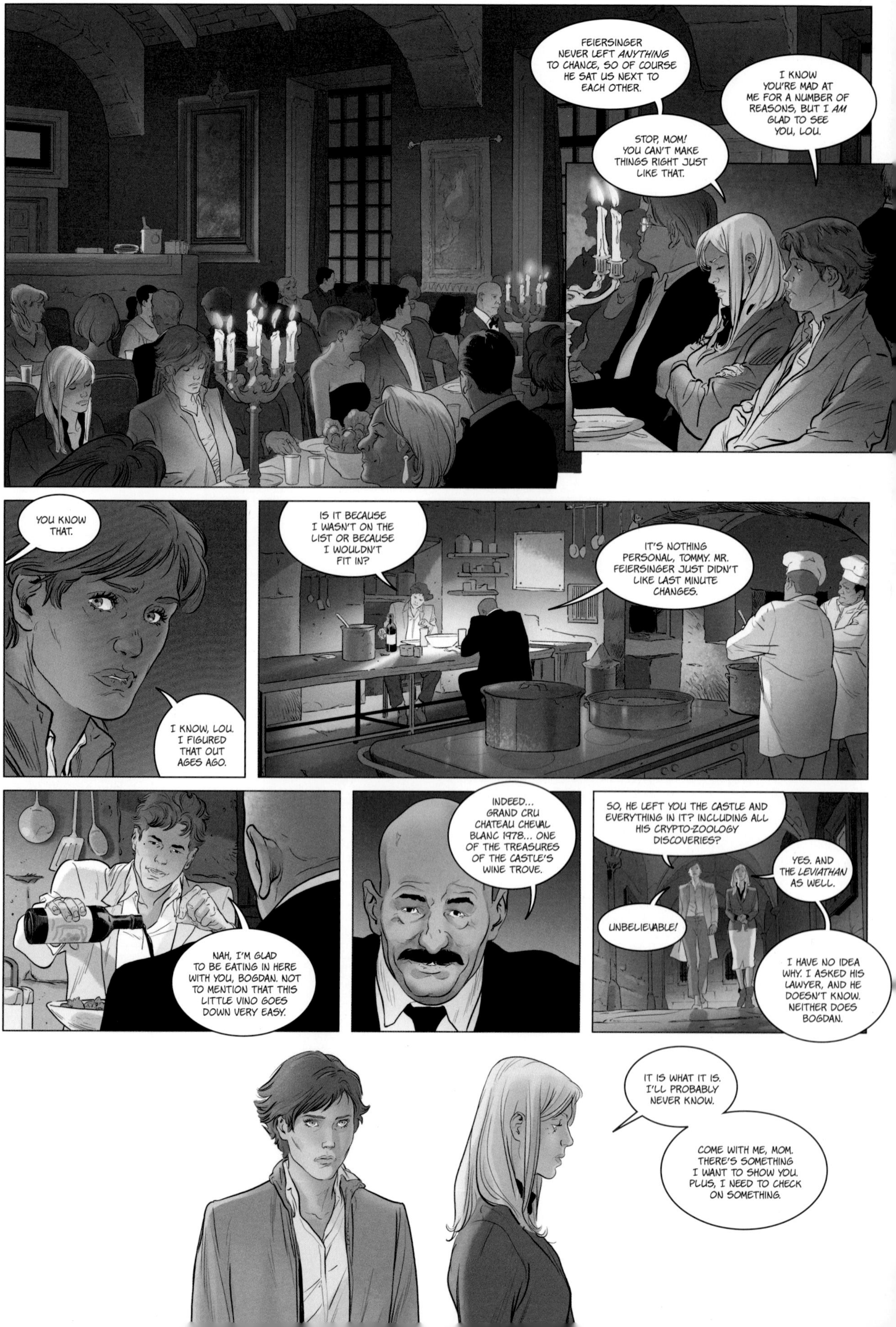
FEIERSINGER NEVER LEFT *ANYTHING* TO CHANCE, SO OF COURSE HE SAT US NEXT TO EACH OTHER.
I KNOW YOU'RE MAD AT ME FOR A NUMBER OF REASONS, BUT I *AM* GLAD TO SEE YOU, LOU.
STOP, MOM! YOU CAN'T MAKE THINGS RIGHT JUST LIKE THAT.
YOU KNOW THAT.
I KNOW, LOU. I FIGURED THAT OUT AGES AGO.
IS IT BECAUSE I WASN'T ON THE LIST OR BECAUSE I WOULDN'T FIT IN?
IT'S NOTHING PERSONAL, TOMMY. MR. FEIERSINGER JUST DIDN'T LIKE LAST MINUTE CHANGES.
NAH, I'M GLAD TO BE EATING IN HERE WITH YOU, BOGDAN. NOT TO MENTION THAT THIS LITTLE VINO GOES DOWN VERY EASY.
INDEED... GRAND CRU CHATEAU CHEVAL BLANC 1978... ONE OF THE TREASURES OF THE CASTLE'S WINE TROVE.
SO, HE LEFT YOU THE CASTLE AND EVERYTHING IN IT? INCLUDING ALL HIS CRYPTO-ZOOLOGY DISCOVERIES?
YES. AND THE *LEVIATHAN* AS WELL.
UNBELIEVABLE!
I HAVE NO IDEA WHY. I ASKED HIS LAWYER, AND HE DOESN'T KNOW. NEITHER DOES BOGDAN.
IT IS WHAT IT IS. I'LL PROBABLY NEVER KNOW.
COME WITH ME, MOM. THERE'S SOMETHING I WANT TO SHOW YOU. PLUS, I NEED TO CHECK ON SOMETHING.

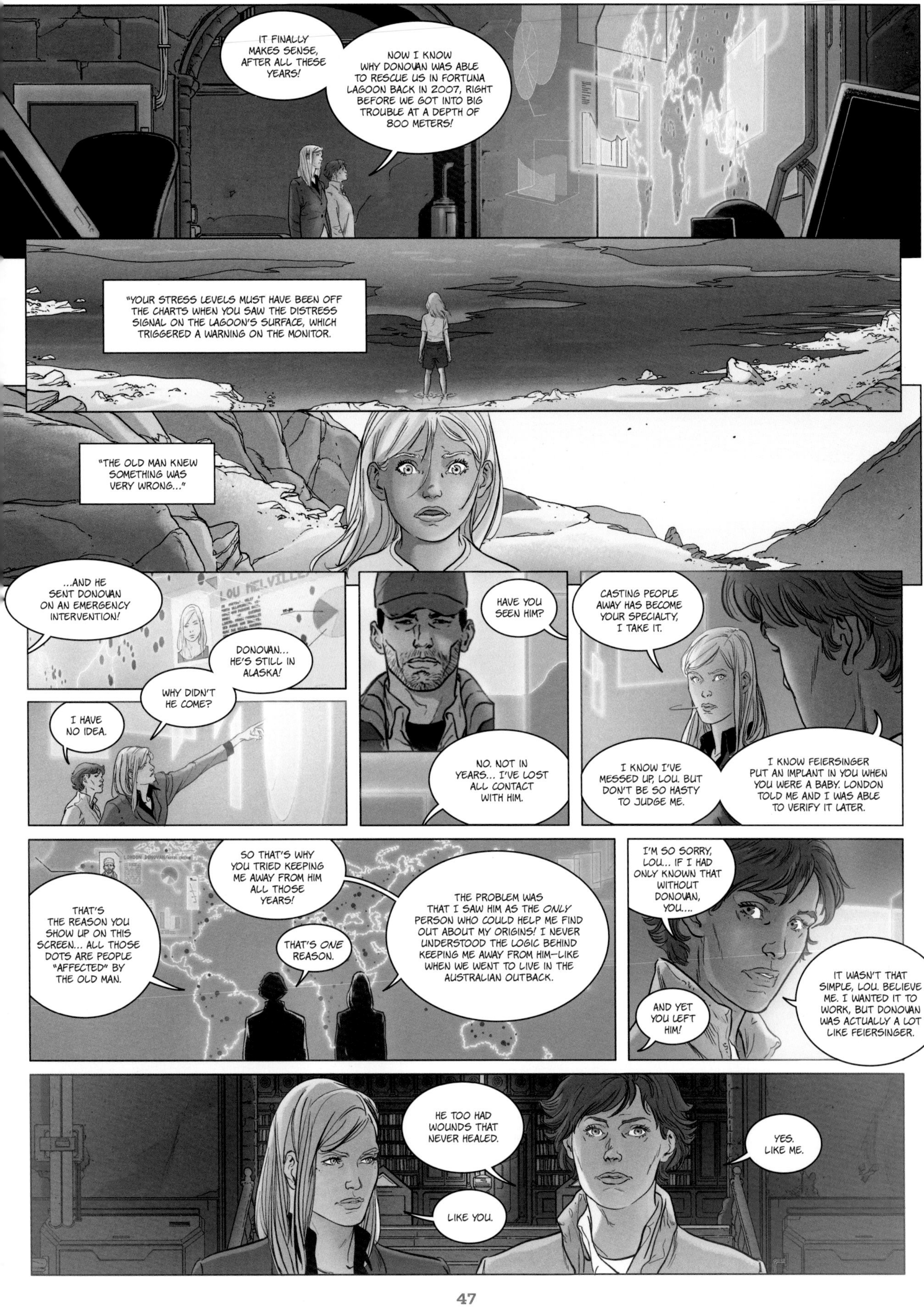
IT FINALLY MAKES SENSE, AFTER ALL THESE YEARS!
NOW I KNOW WHY DONOVAN WAS ABLE TO RESCUE US IN FORTUNA LAGOON BACK IN 2007, RIGHT BEFORE WE GOT INTO BIG TROUBLE AT A DEPTH OF 800 METERS!
"YOUR STRESS LEVELS MUST HAVE BEEN OFF THE CHARTS WHEN YOU SAW THE DISTRESS SIGNAL ON THE LAGOON'S SURFACE, WHICH TRIGGERED A WARNING ON THE MONITOR.
"THE OLD MAN KNEW SOMETHING WAS VERY WRONG..."
...AND HE SENT DONOVAN ON AN EMERGENCY INTERVENTION!
DONOVAN... HE'S STILL IN ALASKA!
WHY DIDN'T HE COME?
I HAVE NO IDEA.
HAVE YOU SEEN HIM?
NO. NOT IN YEARS... I'VE LOST ALL CONTACT WITH HIM.
CASTING PEOPLE AWAY HAS BECOME YOUR SPECIALTY, I TAKE IT.
I KNOW I'VE MESSED UP, LOU. BUT DON'T BE SO HASTY TO JUDGE ME.
I KNOW FEIERSINGER PUT AN IMPLANT IN YOU WHEN YOU WERE A BABY. LONDON TOLD ME AND I WAS ABLE TO VERIFY IT LATER.
THAT'S THE REASON YOU SHOW UP ON THIS SCREEN... ALL THOSE DOTS ARE PEOPLE "AFFECTED" BY THE OLD MAN.
SO THAT'S WHY YOU TRIED KEEPING ME AWAY FROM HIM ALL THOSE YEARS!
THAT'S *ONE* REASON.
THE PROBLEM WAS THAT I SAW HIM AS THE *ONLY* PERSON WHO COULD HELP ME FIND OUT ABOUT MY ORIGINS! I NEVER UNDERSTOOD THE LOGIC BEHIND KEEPING ME AWAY FROM HIM—LIKE WHEN WE WENT TO LIVE IN THE AUSTRALIAN OUTBACK.
I'M SO SORRY, LOU... IF I HAD ONLY KNOWN THAT WITHOUT DONOVAN, YOU....
AND YET YOU LEFT HIM!
IT WASN'T THAT SIMPLE, LOU. BELIEVE ME. I WANTED IT TO WORK, BUT DONOVAN WAS ACTUALLY A LOT LIKE FEIERSINGER.
HE TOO HAD WOUNDS THAT NEVER HEALED.
LIKE YOU.
YES. LIKE ME.

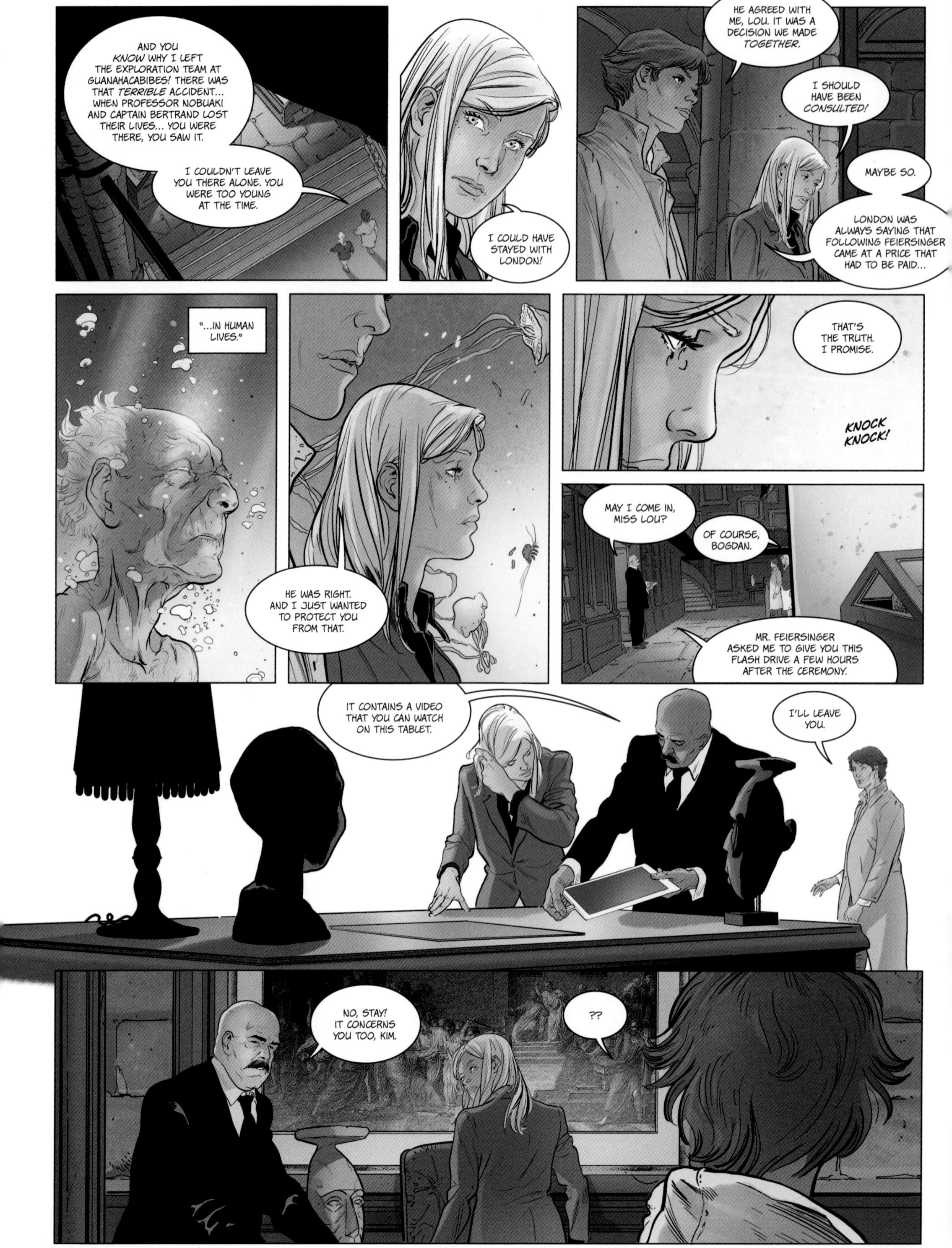
AND YOU KNOW WHY I LEFT THE EXPLORATION TEAM AT GUANAHACABIBES! THERE WAS THAT TERRIBLE ACCIDENT... WHEN PROFESSOR NOBUAKI AND CAPTAIN BERTRAND LOST THEIR LIVES... YOU WERE THERE, YOU SAW IT.
I COULDN'T LEAVE YOU THERE ALONE. YOU WERE TOO YOUNG AT THE TIME.
I COULD HAVE STAYED WITH LONDON!
HE AGREED WITH ME, LOU. IT WAS A DECISION WE MADE TOGETHER.
I SHOULD HAVE BEEN CONSULTED!
MAYBE SO.
LONDON WAS ALWAYS SAYING THAT FOLLOWING FEIERSINGER CAME AT A PRICE THAT HAD TO BE PAID...
"...IN HUMAN LIVES."
HE WAS RIGHT. AND I JUST WANTED TO PROTECT YOU FROM THAT.
THAT'S THE TRUTH. I PROMISE.
KNOCK KNOCK!
MAY I COME IN, MISS LOU?
OF COURSE, BOGDAN.
MR. FEIERSINGER ASKED ME TO GIVE YOU THIS FLASH DRIVE A FEW HOURS AFTER THE CEREMONY.
IT CONTAINS A VIDEO THAT YOU CAN WATCH ON THIS TABLET.
I'LL LEAVE YOU.
NO, STAY! IT CONCERNS YOU TOO, KIM.
??

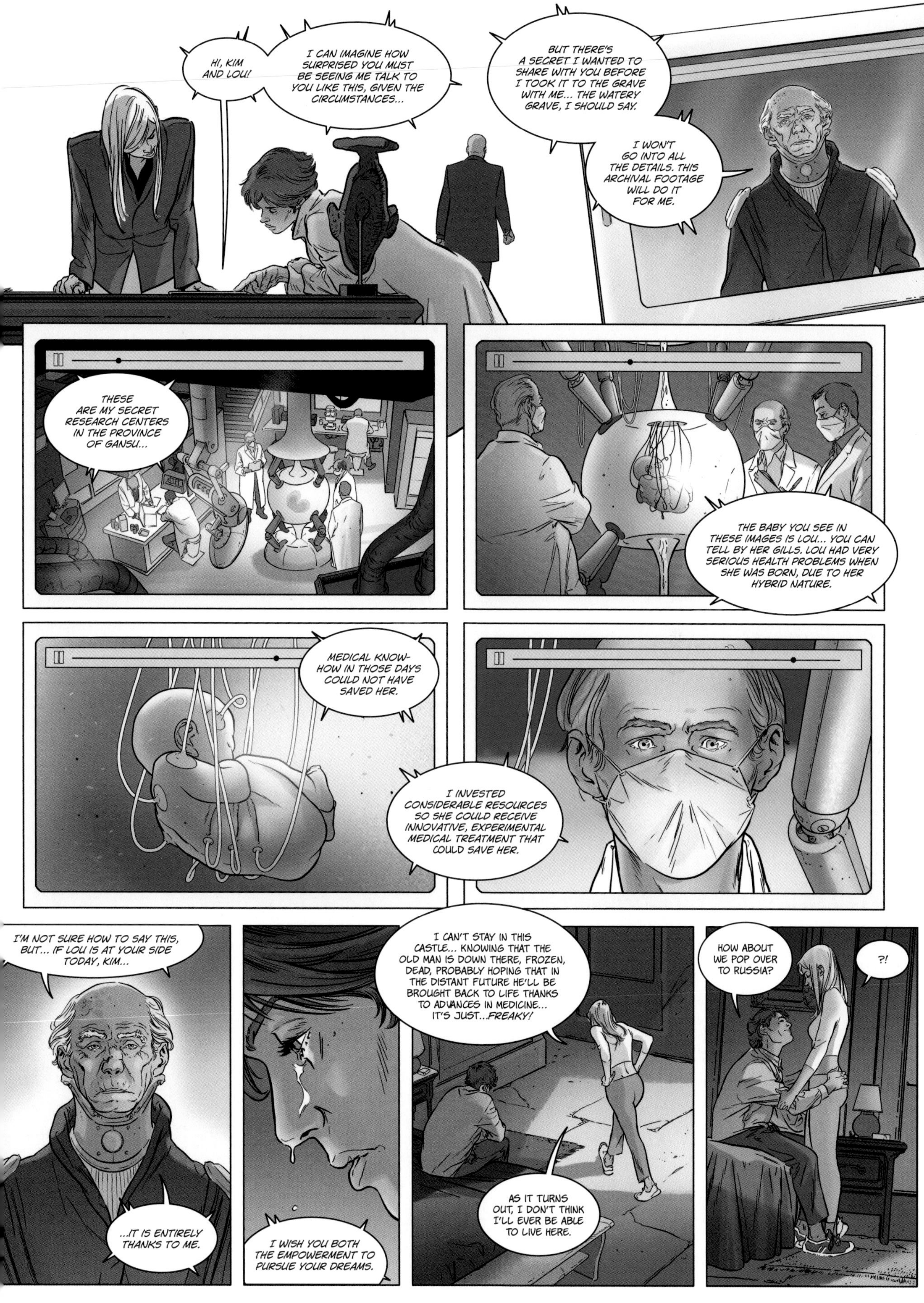
HI, KIM AND LOU!
I CAN IMAGINE HOW SURPRISED YOU MUST BE SEEING ME TALK TO YOU LIKE THIS, GIVEN THE CIRCUMSTANCES...
BUT THERE'S A SECRET I WANTED TO SHARE WITH YOU BEFORE I TOOK IT TO THE GRAVE WITH ME... THE WATERY GRAVE, I SHOULD SAY.
I WON'T GO INTO ALL THE DETAILS. THIS ARCHIVAL FOOTAGE WILL DO IT FOR ME.
THESE ARE MY SECRET RESEARCH CENTERS IN THE PROVINCE OF GANSU...
THE BABY YOU SEE IN THESE IMAGES IS LOU... YOU CAN TELL BY HER GILLS. LOU HAD VERY SERIOUS HEALTH PROBLEMS WHEN SHE WAS BORN, DUE TO HER HYBRID NATURE.
MEDICAL KNOW-HOW IN THOSE DAYS COULD NOT HAVE SAVED HER.
I INVESTED CONSIDERABLE RESOURCES SO SHE COULD RECEIVE INNOVATIVE, EXPERIMENTAL MEDICAL TREATMENT THAT COULD SAVE HER.
I'M NOT SURE HOW TO SAY THIS, BUT... IF LOU IS AT YOUR SIDE TODAY, KIM...
...IT IS ENTIRELY THANKS TO ME.
I WISH YOU BOTH THE EMPOWERMENT TO PURSUE YOUR DREAMS.
I CAN'T STAY IN THIS CASTLE... KNOWING THAT THE OLD MAN IS DOWN THERE, FROZEN, DEAD, PROBABLY HOPING THAT IN THE DISTANT FUTURE HE'LL BE BROUGHT BACK TO LIFE THANKS TO ADVANCES IN MEDICINE... IT'S JUST...FREAKY!
AS IT TURNS OUT, I DON'T THINK I'LL EVER BE ABLE TO LIVE HERE.
HOW ABOUT WE POP OVER TO RUSSIA?
?!

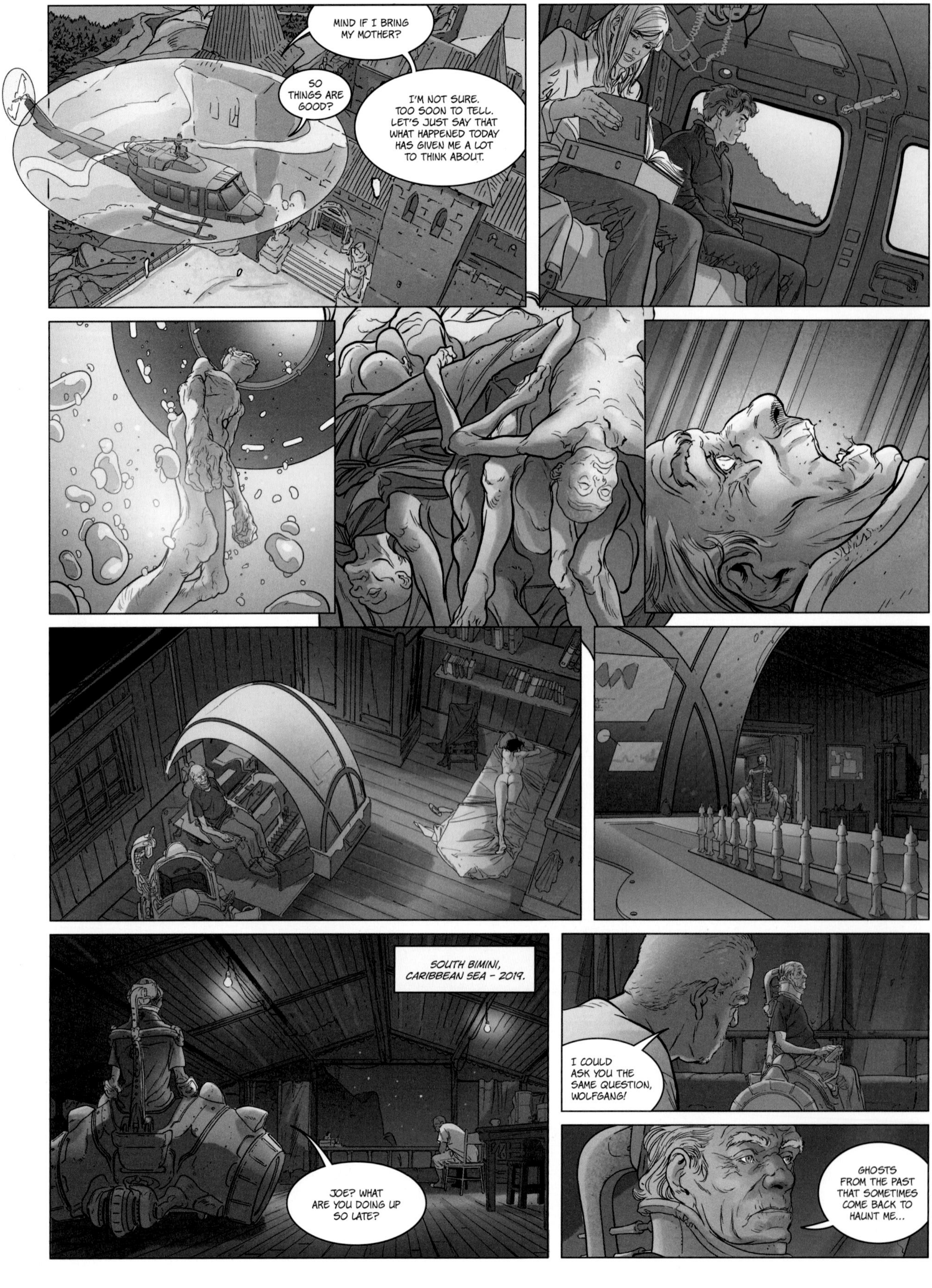

MIND IF I BRING MY MOTHER?
SO THINGS ARE GOOD?
I'M NOT SURE. TOO SOON TO TELL. LET'S JUST SAY THAT WHAT HAPPENED TODAY HAS GIVEN ME A LOT TO THINK ABOUT.
SOUTH BIMINI, CARIBBEAN SEA - 2019.
JOE? WHAT ARE YOU DOING UP SO LATE?
I COULD ASK YOU THE SAME QUESTION, WOLFGANG!
GHOSTS FROM THE PAST THAT SOMETIMES COME BACK TO HAUNT ME...

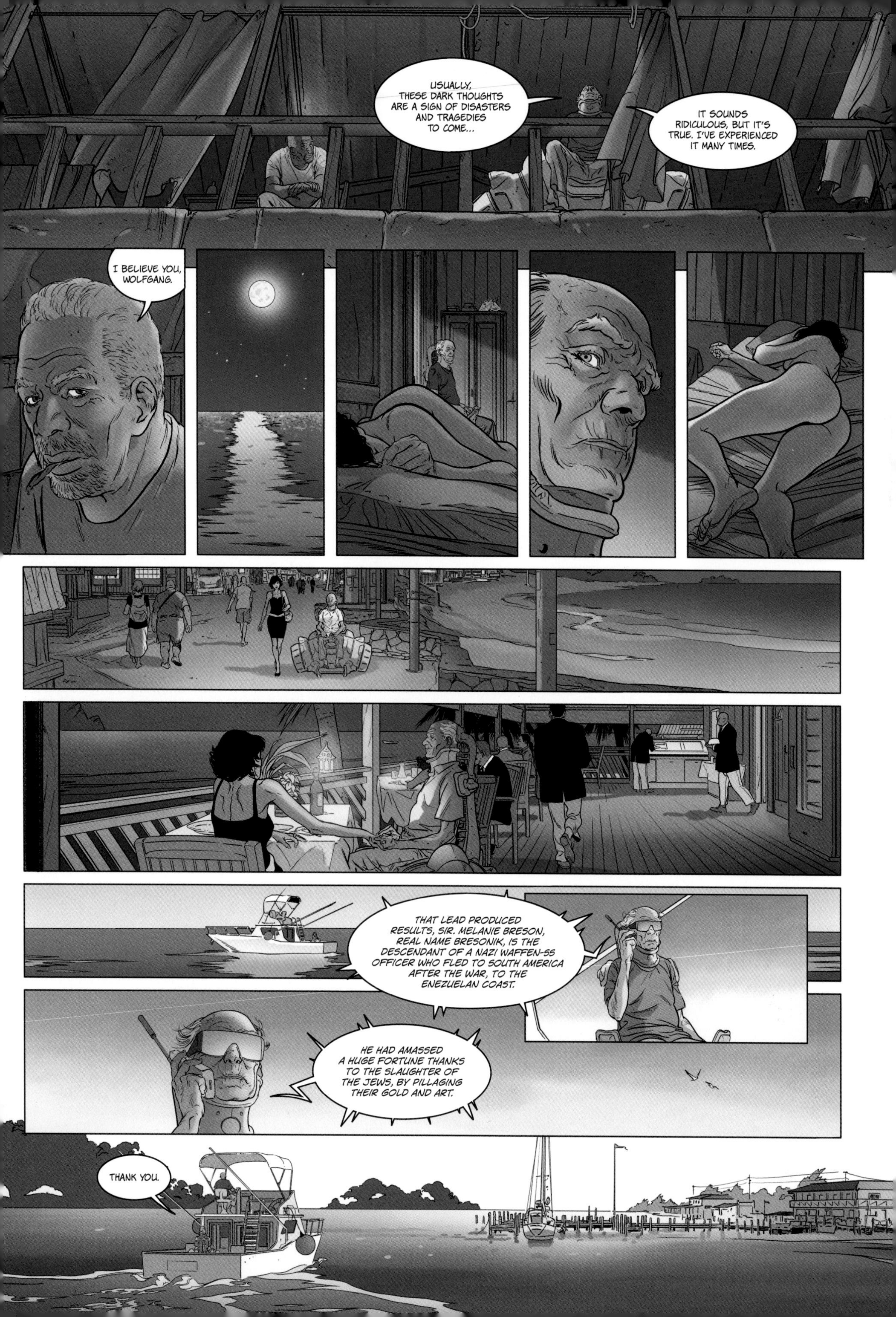
USUALLY, THESE DARK THOUGHTS ARE A SIGN OF DISASTERS AND TRAGEDIES TO COME...
IT SOUNDS RIDICULOUS, BUT IT'S TRUE. I'VE EXPERIENCED IT MANY TIMES.
I BELIEVE YOU, WOLFGANG.
THAT LEAD PRODUCED RESULTS, SIR. MELANIE BRESON, REAL NAME BRESONIK, IS THE DESCENDANT OF A NAZI WAFFEN-SS OFFICER WHO FLED TO SOUTH AMERICA AFTER THE WAR, TO THE ENEZUELAN COAST.
HE HAD AMASSED A HUGE FORTUNE THANKS TO THE SLAUGHTER OF THE JEWS, BY PILLAGING THEIR GOLD AND ART.
THANK YOU.

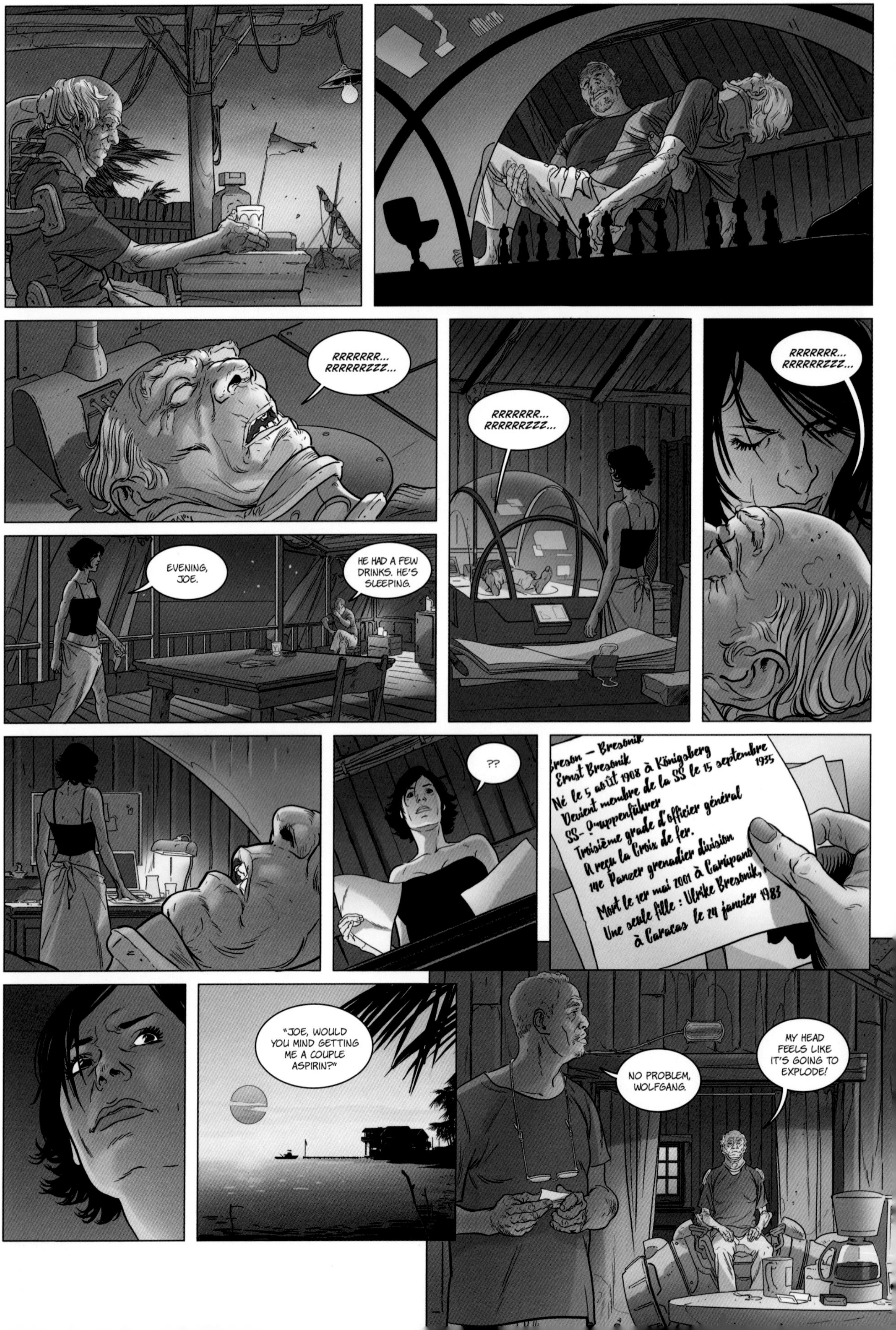
RRRRRRR... RRRRRRZZZ...
RRRRRRR... RRRRRRZZZ...
RRRRRRR... RRRRRRZZZ...
EVENING, JOE.
HE HAD A FEW DRINKS. HE'S SLEEPING.
??
reson — Bresonik
Ernst Bresonik
Né le 5 août 1908 à Königsberg
Devient membre de la SS le 15 septembre 1935
SS- Gruppenführer
Troisième grade d'officier général
A reçu la Croix de fer.
14e Panzer grenadier division
Mort le 1er mai 2001 à Carúpan
Une seule fille : Ulrike Bresonik,
à Caracas le 24 janvier 1983
"JOE, WOULD YOU MIND GETTING ME A COUPLE ASPIRIN?"
NO PROBLEM, WOLFGANG.
MY HEAD FEELS LIKE IT'S GOING TO EXPLODE!

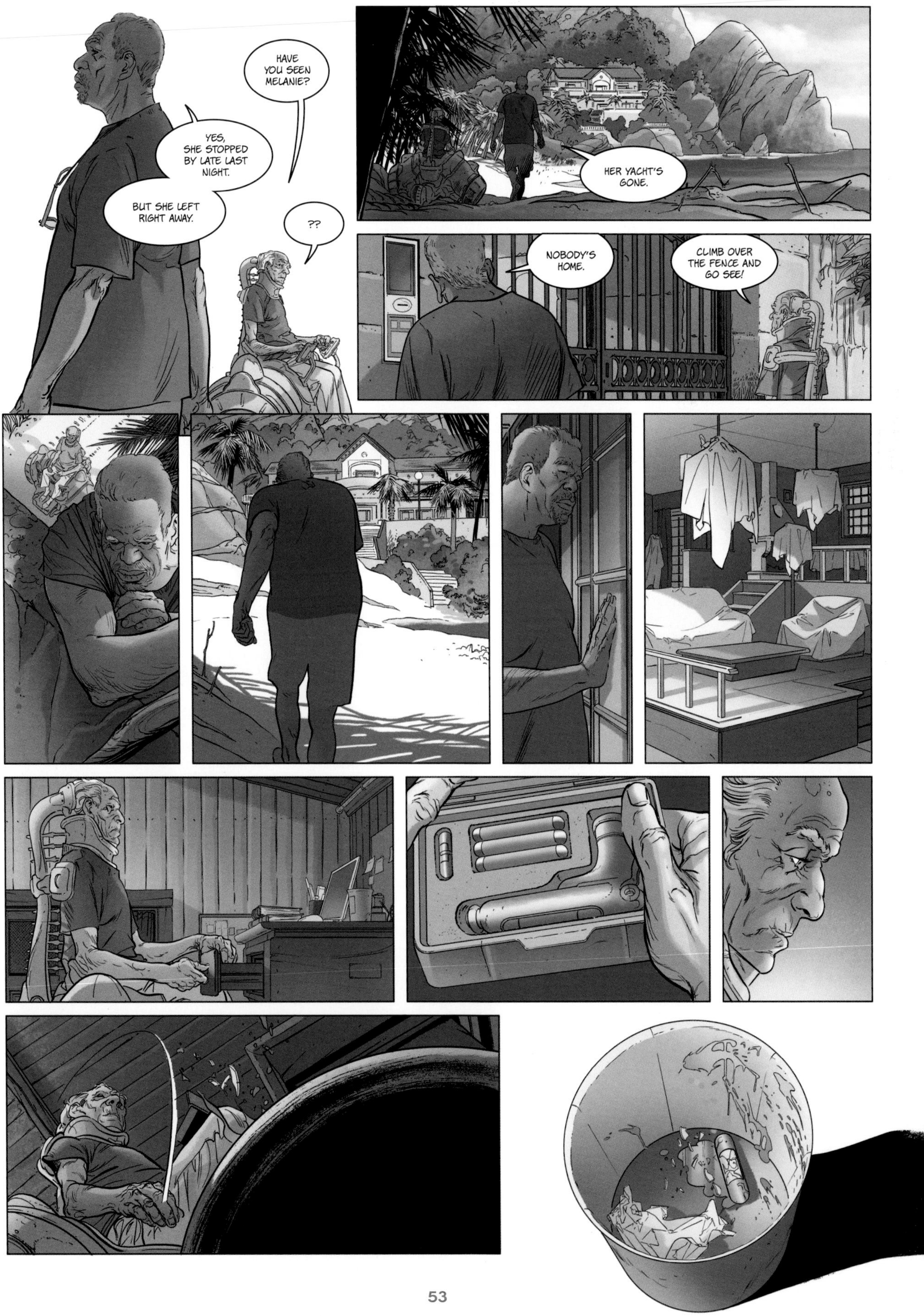
HAVE YOU SEEN MELANIE?
YES, SHE STOPPED BY LATE LAST NIGHT.
BUT SHE LEFT RIGHT AWAY.
??
HER YACHT'S GONE.
NOBODY'S HOME.
CLIMB OVER THE FENCE AND GO SEE!

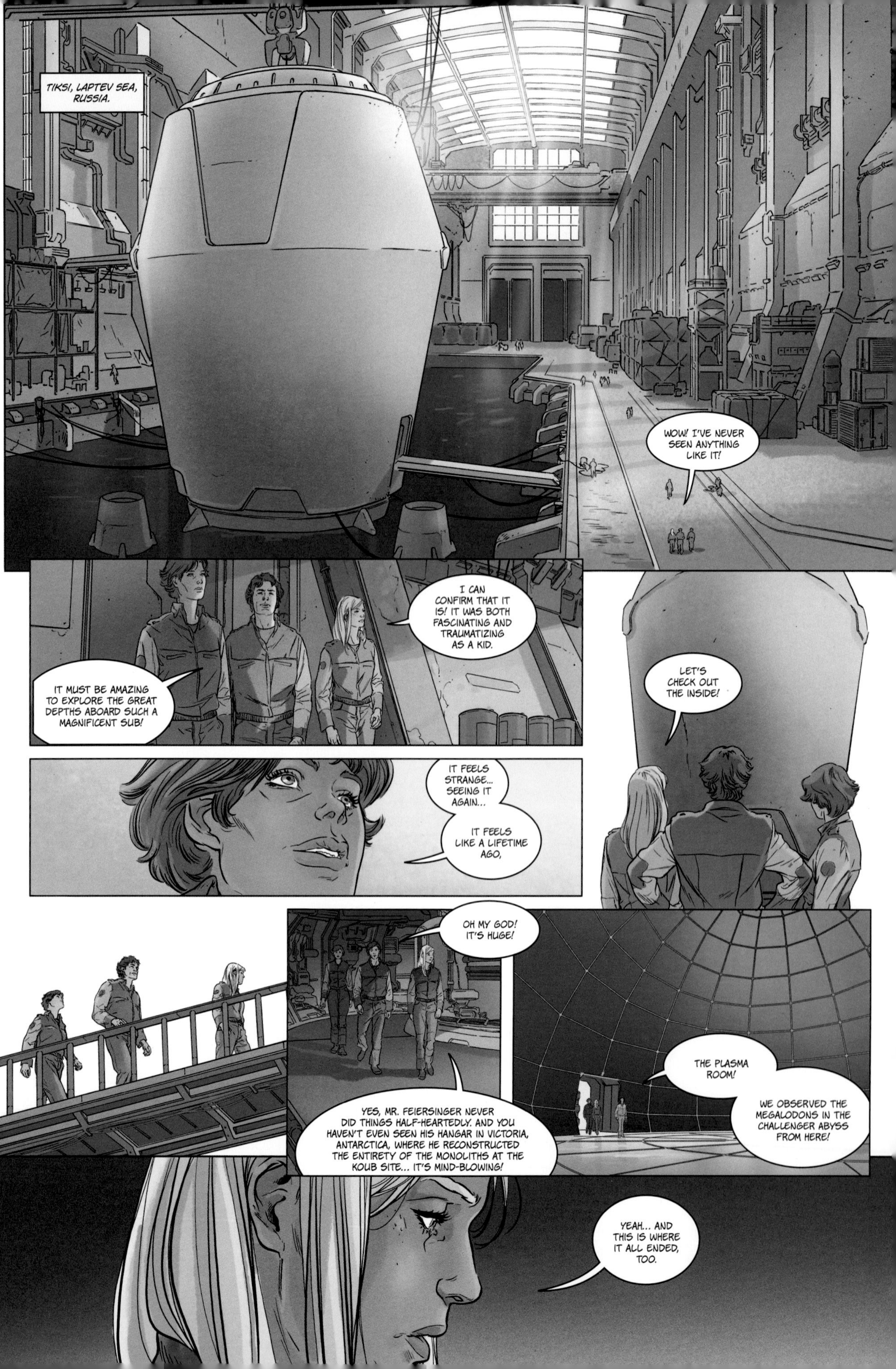
TIKSI, LAPTEV SEA, RUSSIA.
WOW! I'VE NEVER SEEN ANYTHING LIKE IT!
I CAN CONFIRM THAT IT IS! IT WAS BOTH FASCINATING AND TRAUMATIZING AS A KID.
IT MUST BE AMAZING TO EXPLORE THE GREAT DEPTHS ABOARD SUCH A MAGNIFICENT SUB!
LET'S CHECK OUT THE INSIDE!
IT FEELS STRANGE... SEEING IT AGAIN...
IT FEELS LIKE A LIFETIME AGO,
OH MY GOD! IT'S HUGE!
YES, MR. FEIERSINGER NEVER DID THINGS HALF-HEARTEDLY. AND YOU HAVEN'T EVEN SEEN HIS HANGAR IN VICTORIA, ANTARCTICA, WHERE HE RECONSTRUCTED THE ENTIRETY OF THE MONOLITHS AT THE KOUB SITE... IT'S MIND-BLOWING!
THE PLASMA ROOM!
WE OBSERVED THE MEGALODONS IN THE CHALLENGER ABYSS FROM HERE!
YEAH... AND THIS IS WHERE IT ALL ENDED, TOO.

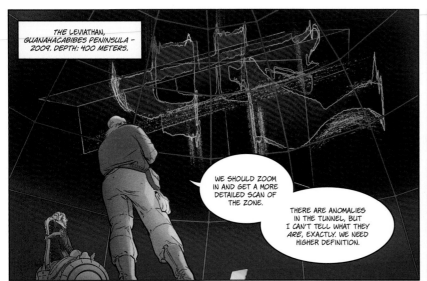

THE LEVIATHAN, GUANAHACABIBES PENINSULA – 2009. DEPTH: 400 METERS.

WE SHOULD ZOOM IN AND GET A MORE DETAILED SCAN OF THE ZONE.

THERE ARE ANOMALIES IN THE TUNNEL, BUT I CAN'T TELL WHAT THEY *ARE*, EXACTLY. WE NEED HIGHER DEFINITION.

IT COULD BE CROSS-TUNNELS... AND THERE'S A STRANGE DARK AREA, WHICH LOOKS EXPANSIVE...

THAT WOULD TAKE WAY TOO LONG, DONOVAN. MY FRIEND CASTRO GAVE US PERMISSION TO STAY IN THIS ZONE, BUT NOT INDEFINITELY.

IT COULD BE DANGEROUS.

"WHY? NOTHING HAPPENED DURING THE EXPLORATION OF THE FIRST TWO PYRAMIDS."

"CORRECT, BUT THIS IS A MUCH NEWER ONE. YOU CAN'T COMPARE IT WITH THE OTHER TWO."

"THE SCAN IS OUT OF THE QUESTION. SO WHAT DO YOU SUGGEST, DONOVAN?"

I'M GOING IN FIRST... ALONE!

NO. *THAT* HONOR GOES TO CAPTAIN BERTRAND AND PROFESSOR NOBUAKI. I PROMISED THEM AND THEY DESERVE IT!

THEN WE NEED TO TAKE THE TIME TO DO A FULL LIDAR SCAN!

YOU'RE GETTING ON MY *NERVES*, DONOVAN. I SAID NO!

I DON'T GIVE A HOOT ABOUT YOUR *DAMN* PRECAUTIONS!

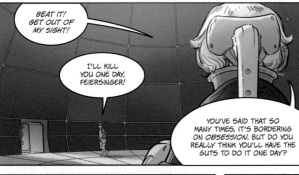

BEAT IT! GET OUT OF MY SIGHT!

I'LL KILL YOU ONE DAY, FEIERSINGER!

YOU'VE SAID THAT SO MANY TIMES, IT'S BORDERING ON *OBSESSION*. BUT DO YOU REALLY THINK YOU'LL HAVE THE GUTS TO DO IT ONE DAY?

YES, YOU *WILL*. I KNOW YOU WILL, DONOVAN.

AND I FIND THAT REASSURING.

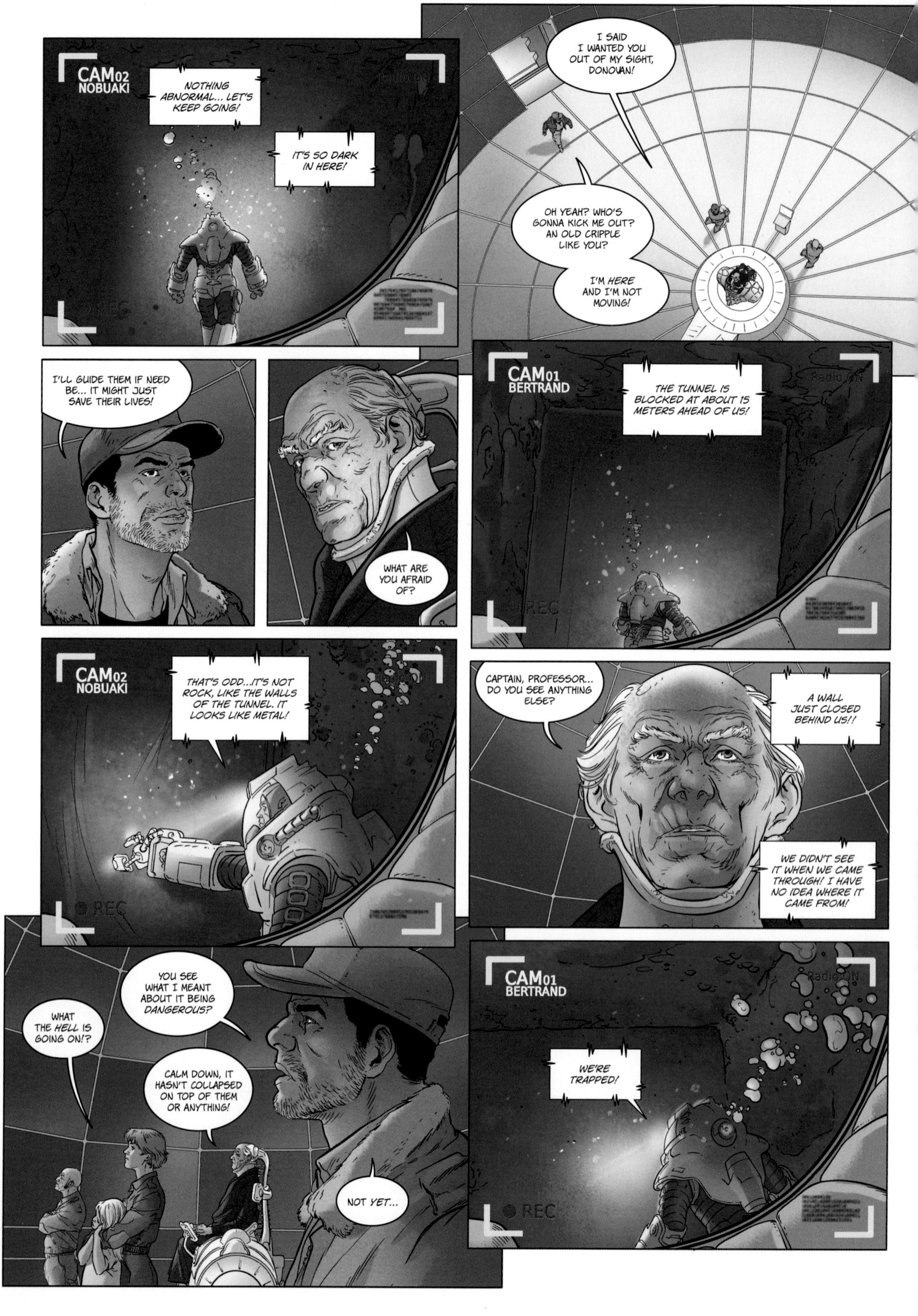
CAM02
NOBUAKI
NOTHING ABNORMAL... LET'S KEEP GOING!
IT'S SO DARK IN HERE!
REC
I SAID I WANTED YOU OUT OF MY SIGHT, DONOVAN!
OH YEAH? WHO'S GONNA KICK ME OUT? AN OLD CRIPPLE LIKE YOU?
I'M HERE AND I'M NOT MOVING!
I'LL GUIDE THEM IF NEED BE... IT MIGHT JUST SAVE THEIR LIVES!
WHAT ARE YOU AFRAID OF?
CAM01
BERTRAND
THE TUNNEL IS BLOCKED AT ABOUT 15 METERS AHEAD OF US!
CAM02
NOBUAKI
THAT'S ODD...IT'S NOT ROCK, LIKE THE WALLS OF THE TUNNEL. IT LOOKS LIKE METAL!
REC
CAPTAIN, PROFESSOR... DO YOU SEE ANYTHING ELSE?
A WALL JUST CLOSED BEHIND US!!
WE DIDN'T SEE IT WHEN WE CAME THROUGH! I HAVE NO IDEA WHERE IT CAME FROM!
WHAT THE HELL IS GOING ON!?
YOU SEE WHAT I MEANT ABOUT IT BEING DANGEROUS?
CALM DOWN, IT HASN'T COLLAPSED ON TOP OF THEM OR ANYTHING!
NOT YET...
CAM01
BERTRAND
Radio ON
WE'RE TRAPPED!
REC

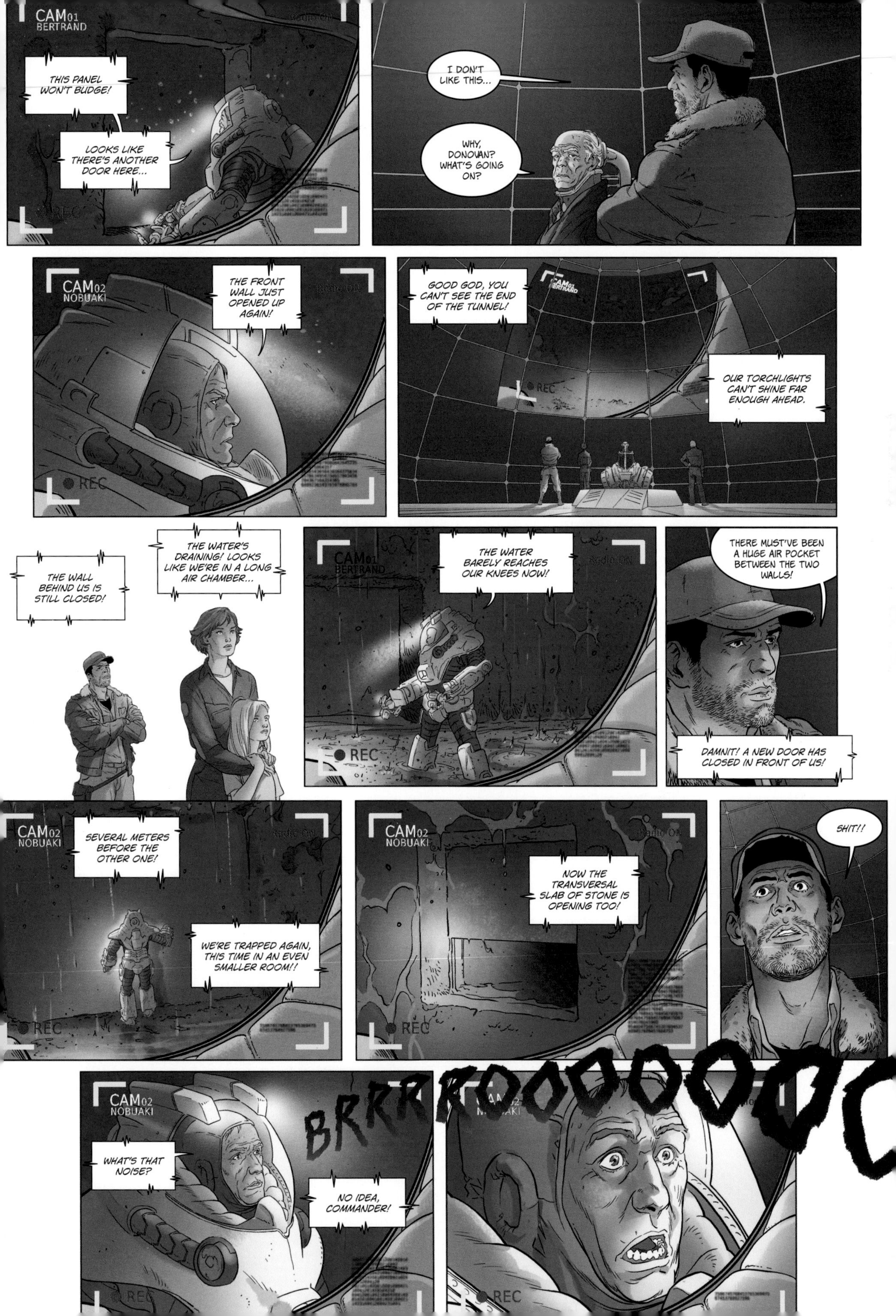
CAM01
BERTRAND
THIS PANEL WON'T BUDGE!
LOOKS LIKE THERE'S ANOTHER DOOR HERE...
REC
I DON'T LIKE THIS...
WHY, DONOVAN? WHAT'S GOING ON?
CAM02
NOBUAKI
THE FRONT WALL JUST OPENED UP AGAIN!
REC
GOOD GOD, YOU CAN'T SEE THE END OF THE TUNNEL!
CAM01
BERTRAND
REC
OUR TORCHLIGHTS CAN'T SHINE FAR ENOUGH AHEAD.
THE WALL BEHIND US IS STILL CLOSED!
THE WATER'S DRAINING! LOOKS LIKE WE'RE IN A LONG AIR CHAMBER...
CAM01
BERTRAND
THE WATER BARELY REACHES OUR KNEES NOW!
REC
THERE MUST'VE BEEN A HUGE AIR POCKET BETWEEN THE TWO WALLS!
DAMNIT! A NEW DOOR HAS CLOSED IN FRONT OF US!
CAM02
NOBUAKI
SEVERAL METERS BEFORE THE OTHER ONE!
WE'RE TRAPPED AGAIN, THIS TIME IN AN EVEN SMALLER ROOM!!
REC
CAM02
NOBUAKI
NOW THE TRANSVERSAL SLAB OF STONE IS OPENING TOO!
REC
SHIT!!
CAM02
NOBUAKI
WHAT'S THAT NOISE?
NO IDEA, COMMANDER!
BRRRROOOOOOC
REC

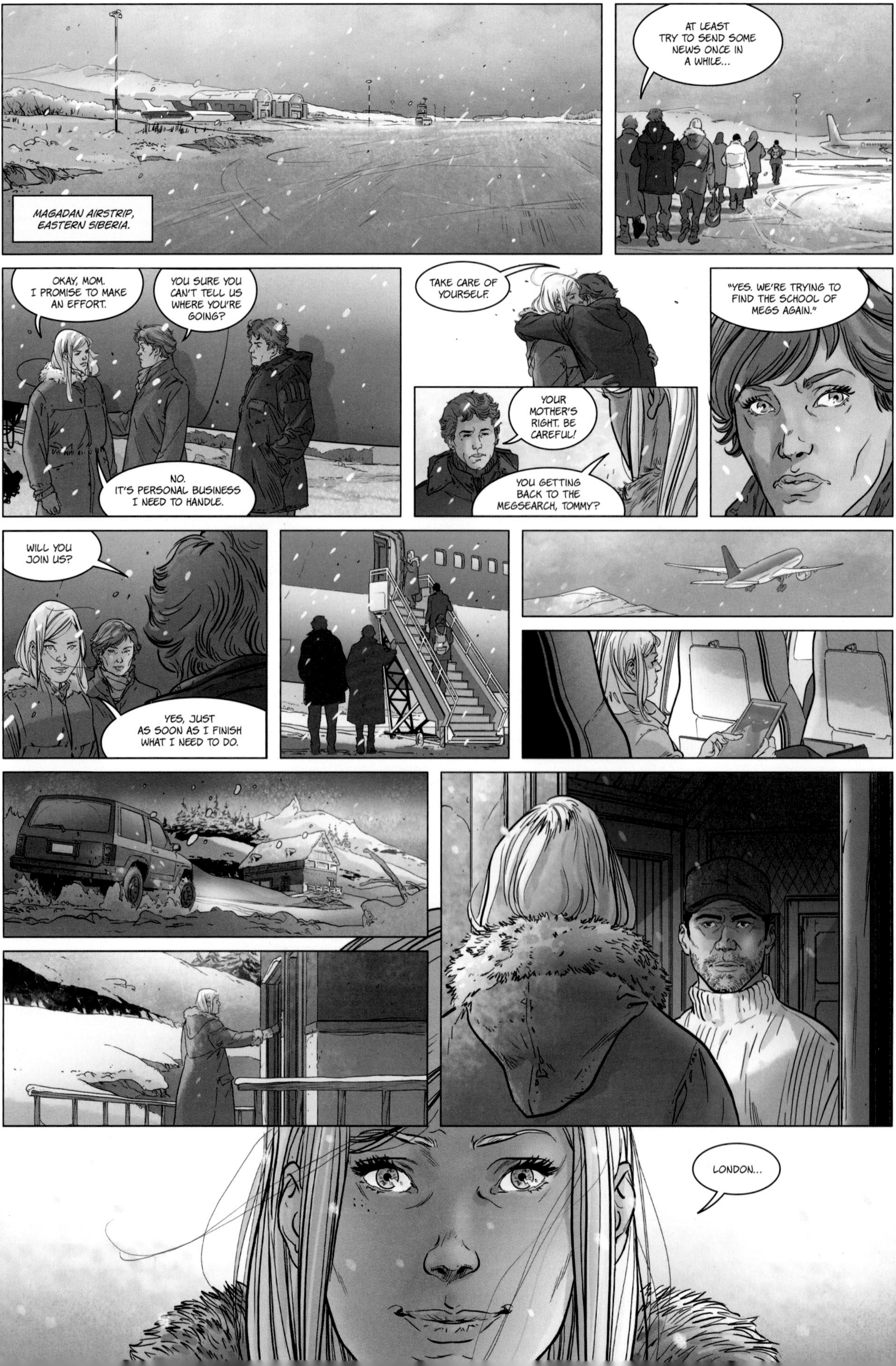
MAGADAN AIRSTRIP, EASTERN SIBERIA.
AT LEAST TRY TO SEND SOME NEWS ONCE IN A WHILE...
OKAY, MOM. I PROMISE TO MAKE AN EFFORT.
YOU SURE YOU CAN'T TELL US WHERE YOU'RE GOING?
NO. IT'S PERSONAL BUSINESS I NEED TO HANDLE.
TAKE CARE OF YOURSELF.
YOUR MOTHER'S RIGHT. BE CAREFUL!
YOU GETTING BACK TO THE MEGSEARCH, TOMMY?
"YES. WE'RE TRYING TO FIND THE SCHOOL OF MEGS AGAIN."
WILL YOU JOIN US?
YES, JUST AS SOON AS I FINISH WHAT I NEED TO DO.
LONDON...

Book 7:
THE KAMCHATKA TRENCH

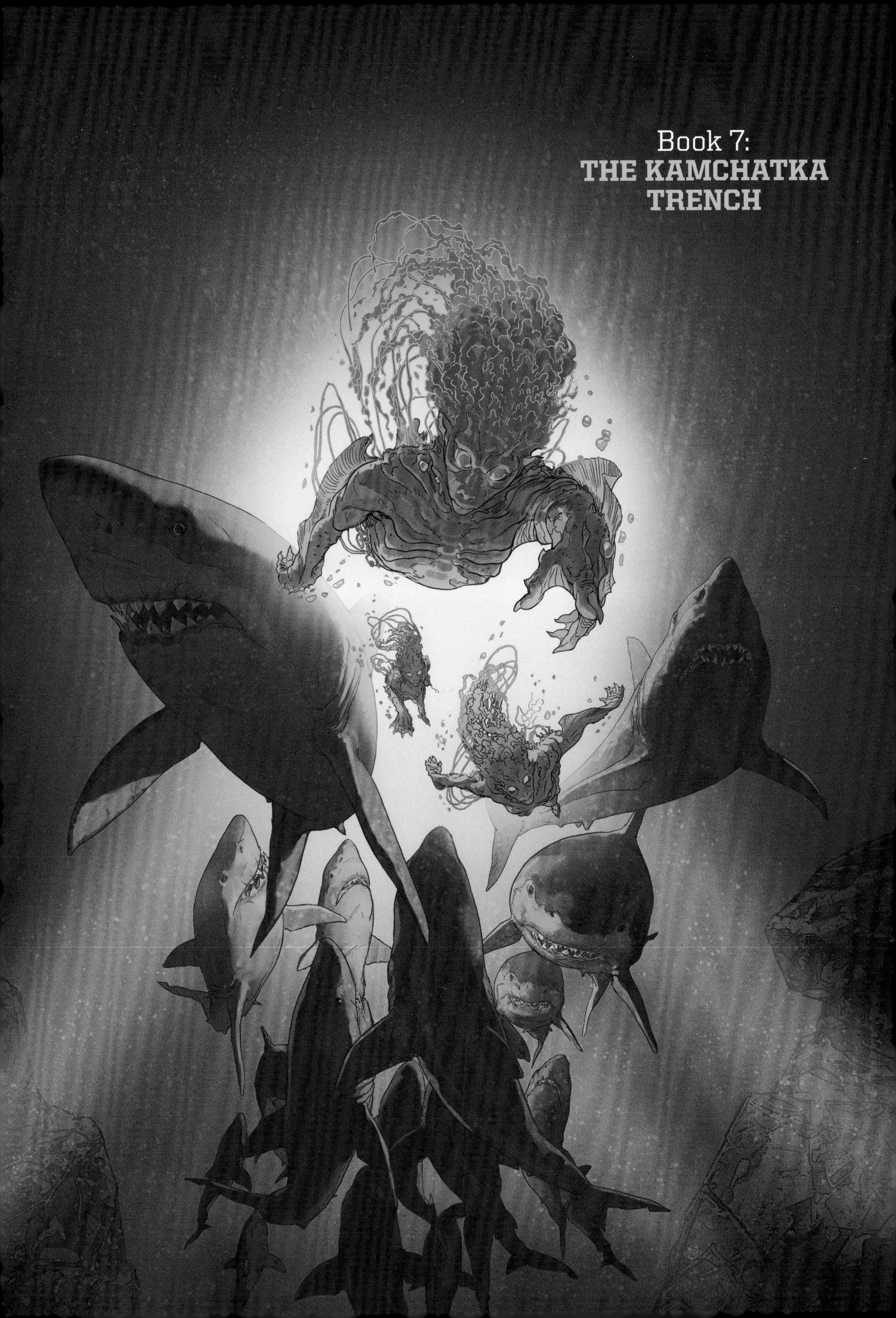

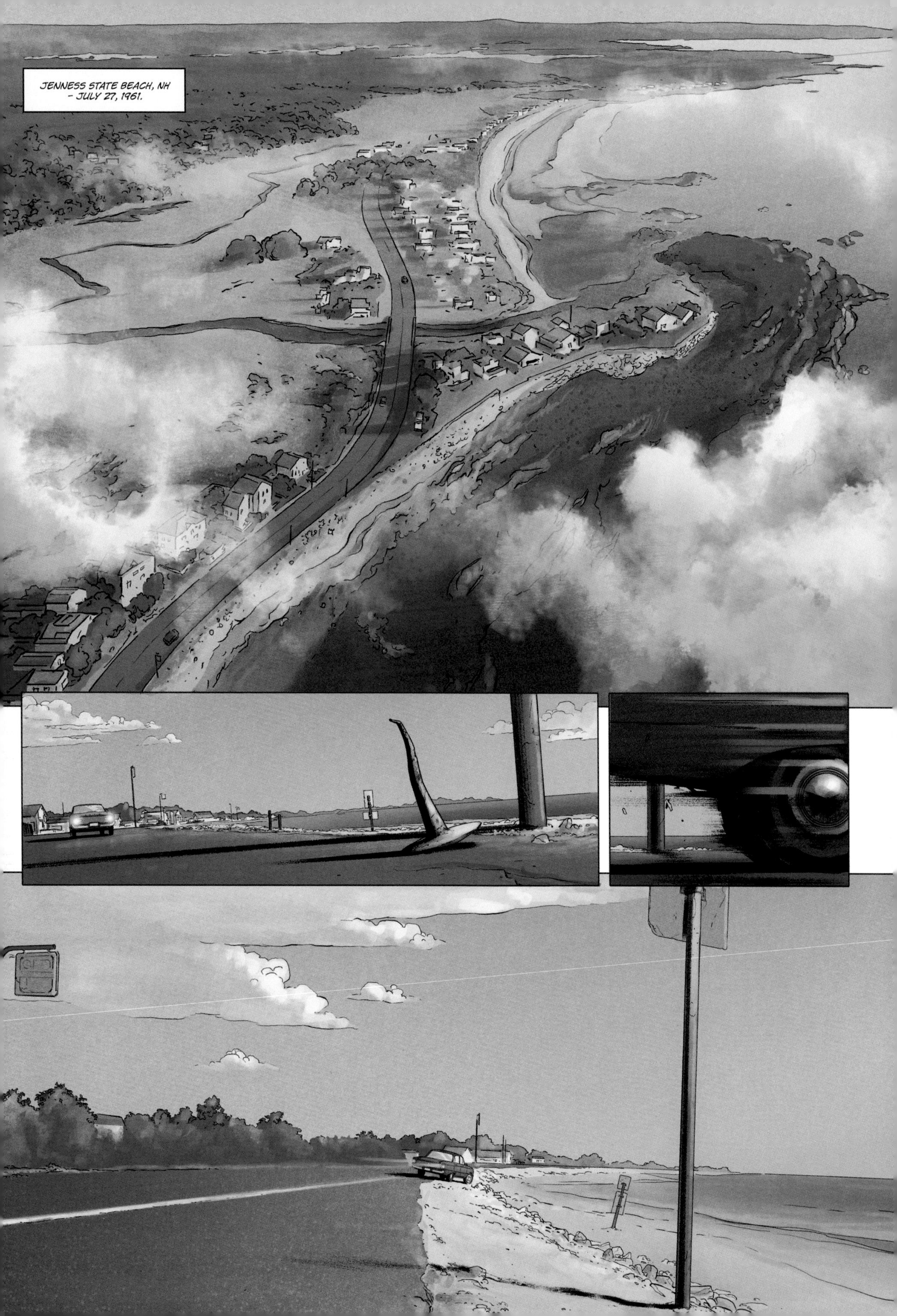
JENNESS STATE BEACH, NH
– JULY 27, 1961.

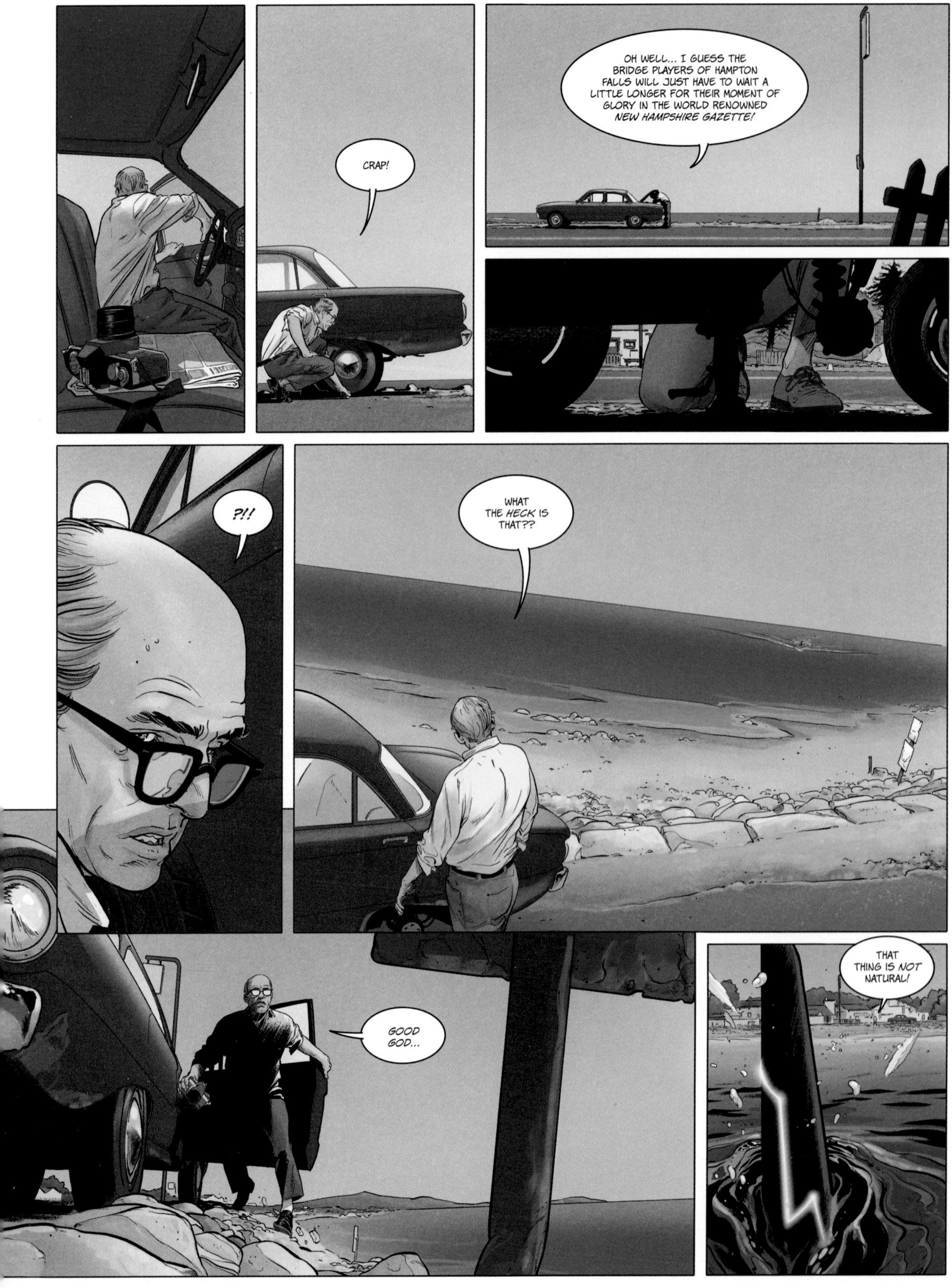
CRAP!
OH WELL... I GUESS THE BRIDGE PLAYERS OF HAMPTON FALLS WILL JUST HAVE TO WAIT A LITTLE LONGER FOR THEIR MOMENT OF GLORY IN THE WORLD RENOWNED NEW HAMPSHIRE GAZETTE!
?!!
WHAT THE HECK IS THAT??
GOOD GOD...
THAT THING IS NOT NATURAL!

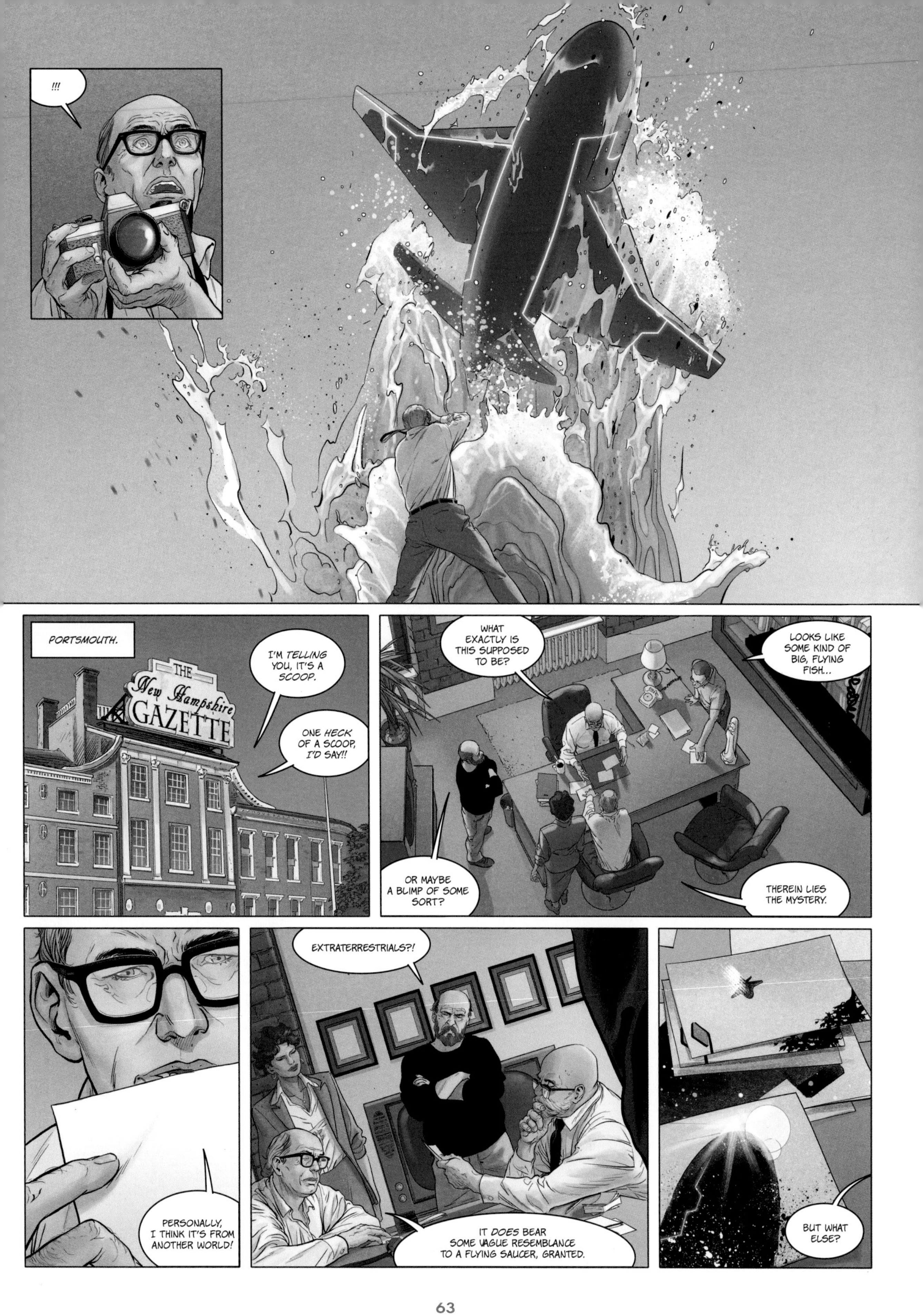
!!!
PORTSMOUTH.
THE New Hampshire GAZETTE
I'M TELLING YOU, IT'S A SCOOP.
ONE HECK OF A SCOOP, I'D SAY!!
WHAT EXACTLY IS THIS SUPPOSED TO BE?
LOOKS LIKE SOME KIND OF BIG, FLYING FISH...
OR MAYBE A BLIMP OF SOME SORT?
THEREIN LIES THE MYSTERY.
PERSONALLY, I THINK IT'S FROM ANOTHER WORLD!
EXTRATERRESTRIALS?!
IT DOES BEAR SOME VAGUE RESEMBLANCE TO A FLYING SAUCER, GRANTED.
BUT WHAT ELSE?

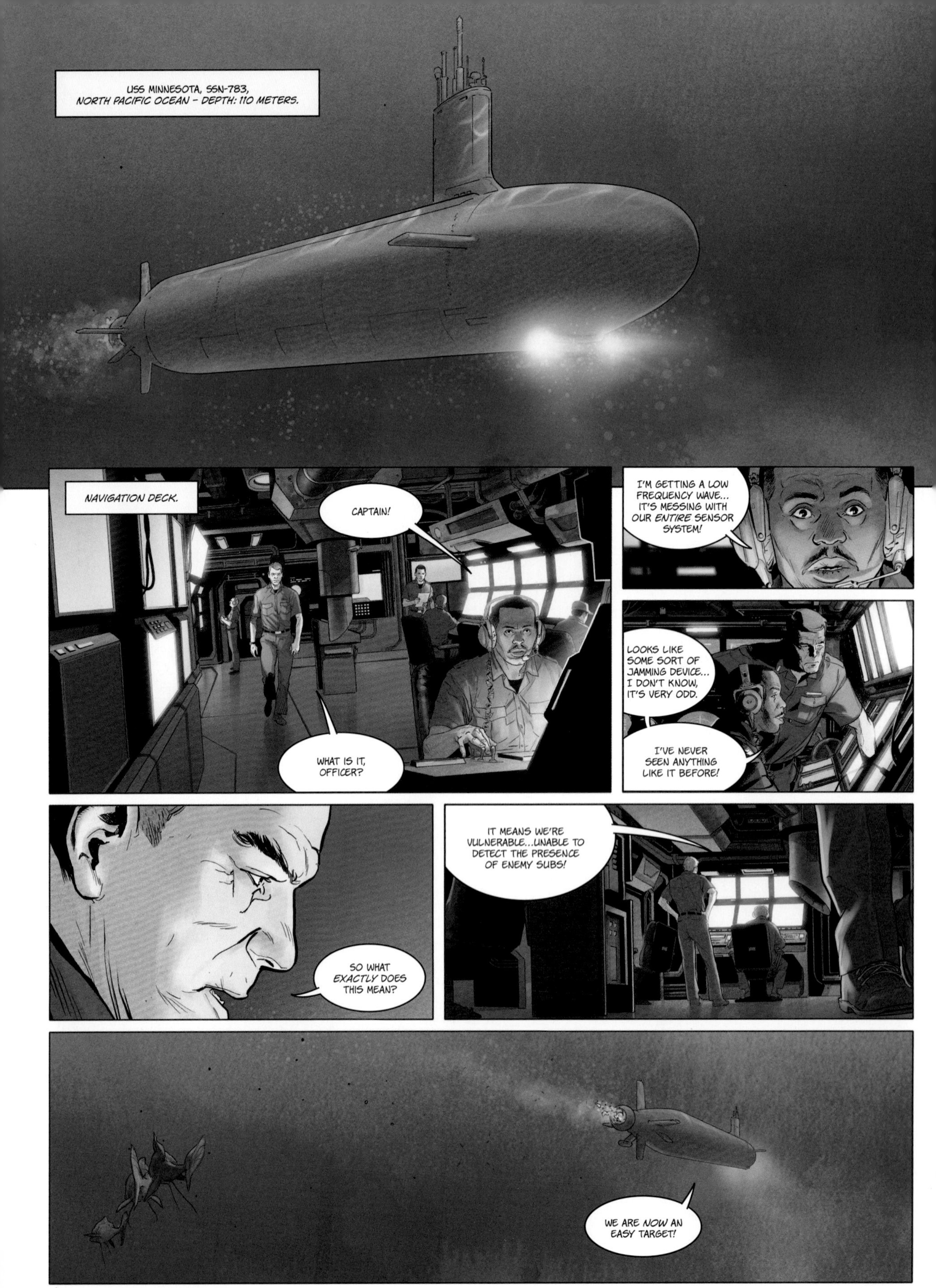
USS MINNESOTA, SSN-783,
NORTH PACIFIC OCEAN – DEPTH: 110 METERS.
NAVIGATION DECK.
CAPTAIN!
WHAT IS IT, OFFICER?
I'M GETTING A LOW FREQUENCY WAVE... IT'S MESSING WITH OUR ENTIRE SENSOR SYSTEM!
LOOKS LIKE SOME SORT OF JAMMING DEVICE... I DON'T KNOW, IT'S VERY ODD.
I'VE NEVER SEEN ANYTHING LIKE IT BEFORE!
SO WHAT EXACTLY DOES THIS MEAN?
IT MEANS WE'RE VULNERABLE...UNABLE TO DETECT THE PRESENCE OF ENEMY SUBS!
WE ARE NOW AN EASY TARGET!

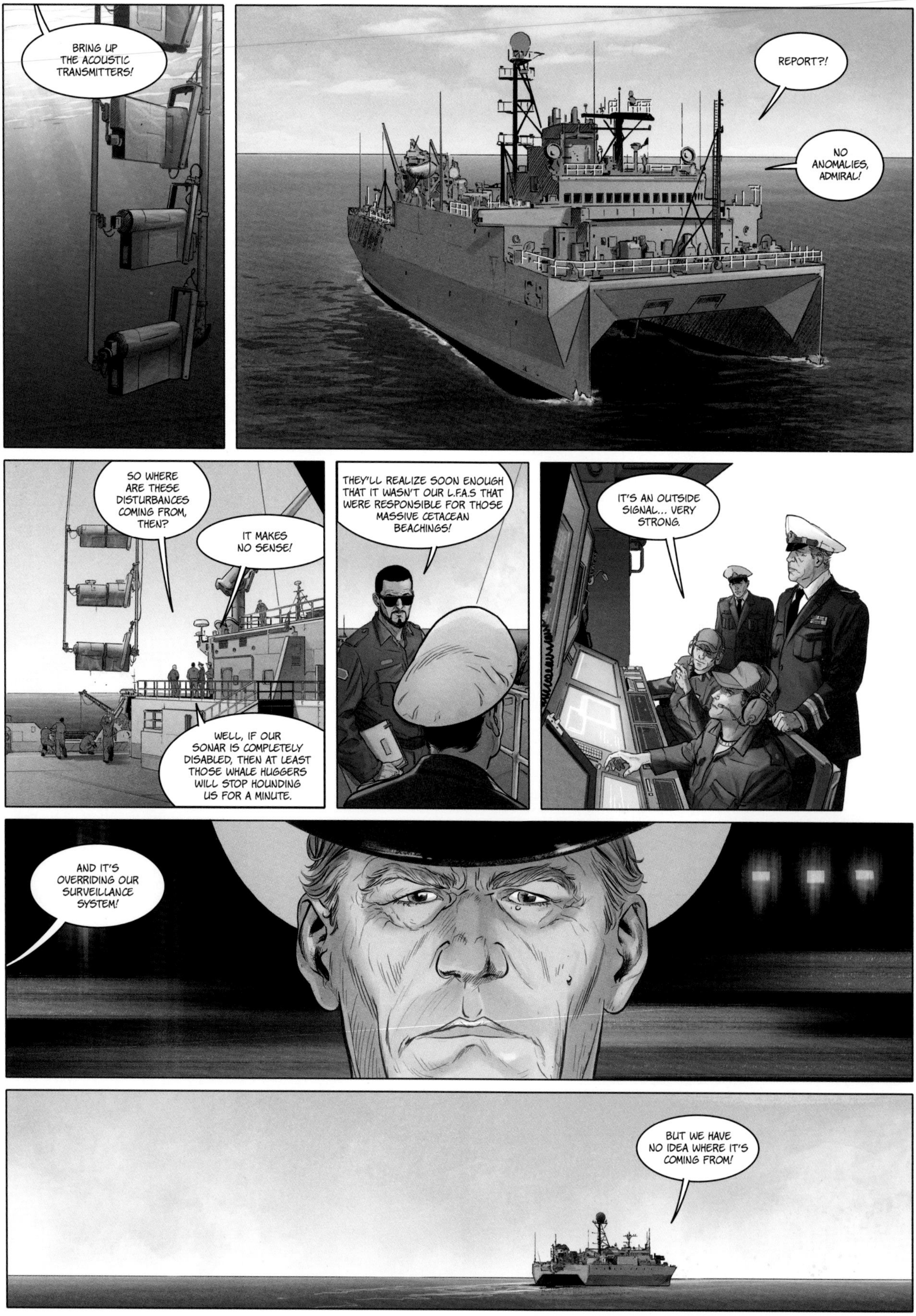
BRING UP THE ACOUSTIC TRANSMITTERS!
REPORT?!
NO ANOMALIES, ADMIRAL!
SO WHERE ARE THESE DISTURBANCES COMING FROM, THEN?
IT MAKES NO SENSE!
WELL, IF OUR SONAR IS COMPLETELY DISABLED, THEN AT LEAST THOSE WHALE HUGGERS WILL STOP HOUNDING US FOR A MINUTE.
THEY'LL REALIZE SOON ENOUGH THAT IT WASN'T OUR L.F.A.S THAT WERE RESPONSIBLE FOR THOSE MASSIVE CETACEAN BEACHINGS!
IT'S AN OUTSIDE SIGNAL... VERY STRONG.
AND IT'S OVERRIDING OUR SURVEILLANCE SYSTEM!
BUT WE HAVE NO IDEA WHERE IT'S COMING FROM!

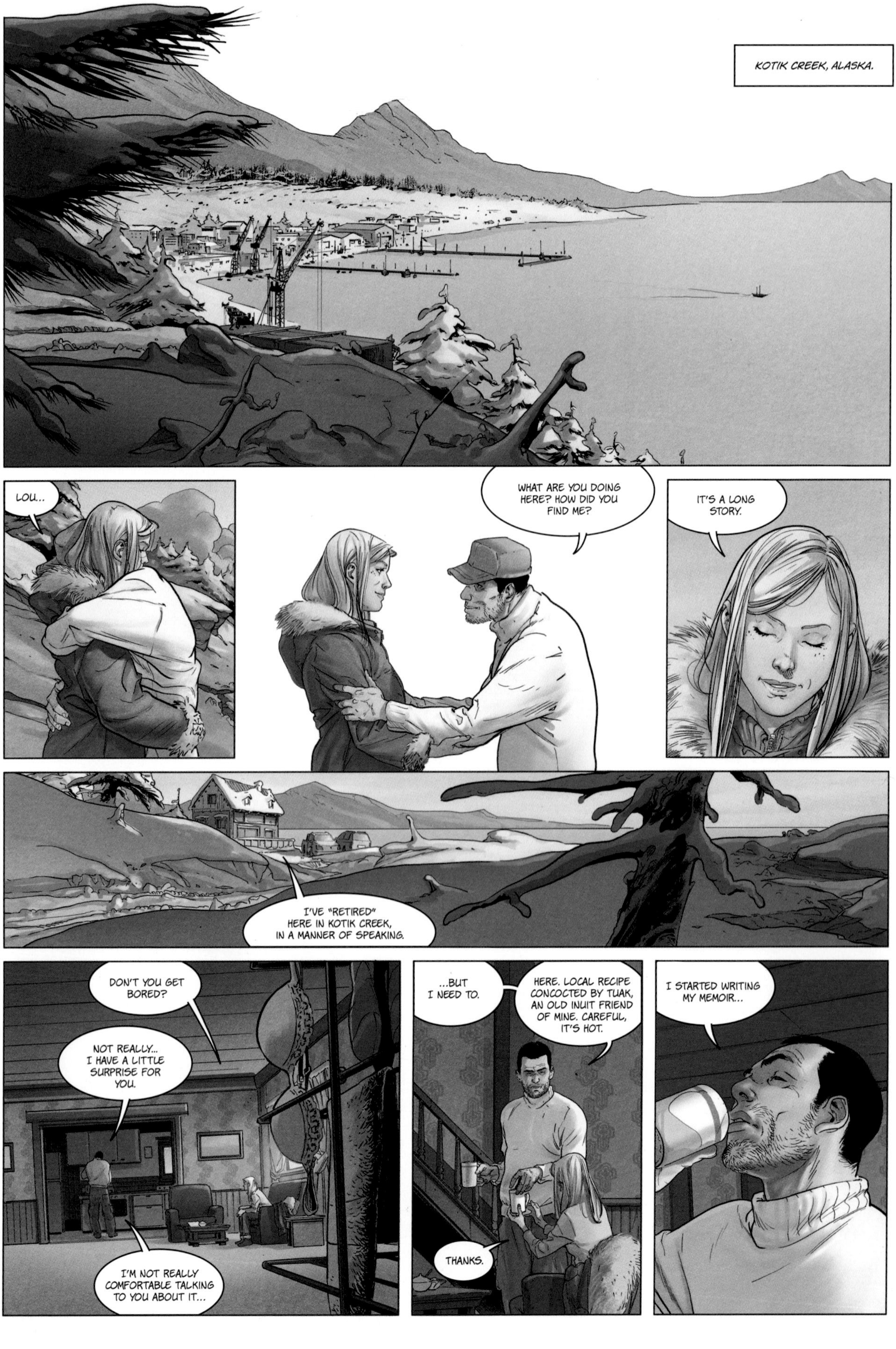
KOTIK CREEK, ALASKA.
LOU...
WHAT ARE YOU DOING HERE? HOW DID YOU FIND ME?
IT'S A LONG STORY.
I'VE "RETIRED" HERE IN KOTIK CREEK, IN A MANNER OF SPEAKING.
DON'T YOU GET BORED?
NOT REALLY... I HAVE A LITTLE SURPRISE FOR YOU.
I'M NOT REALLY COMFORTABLE TALKING TO YOU ABOUT IT...
...BUT I NEED TO.
HERE. LOCAL RECIPE CONCOCTED BY TUAK, AN OLD INUIT FRIEND OF MINE. CAREFUL, IT'S HOT.
THANKS.
I STARTED WRITING MY MEMOIR...

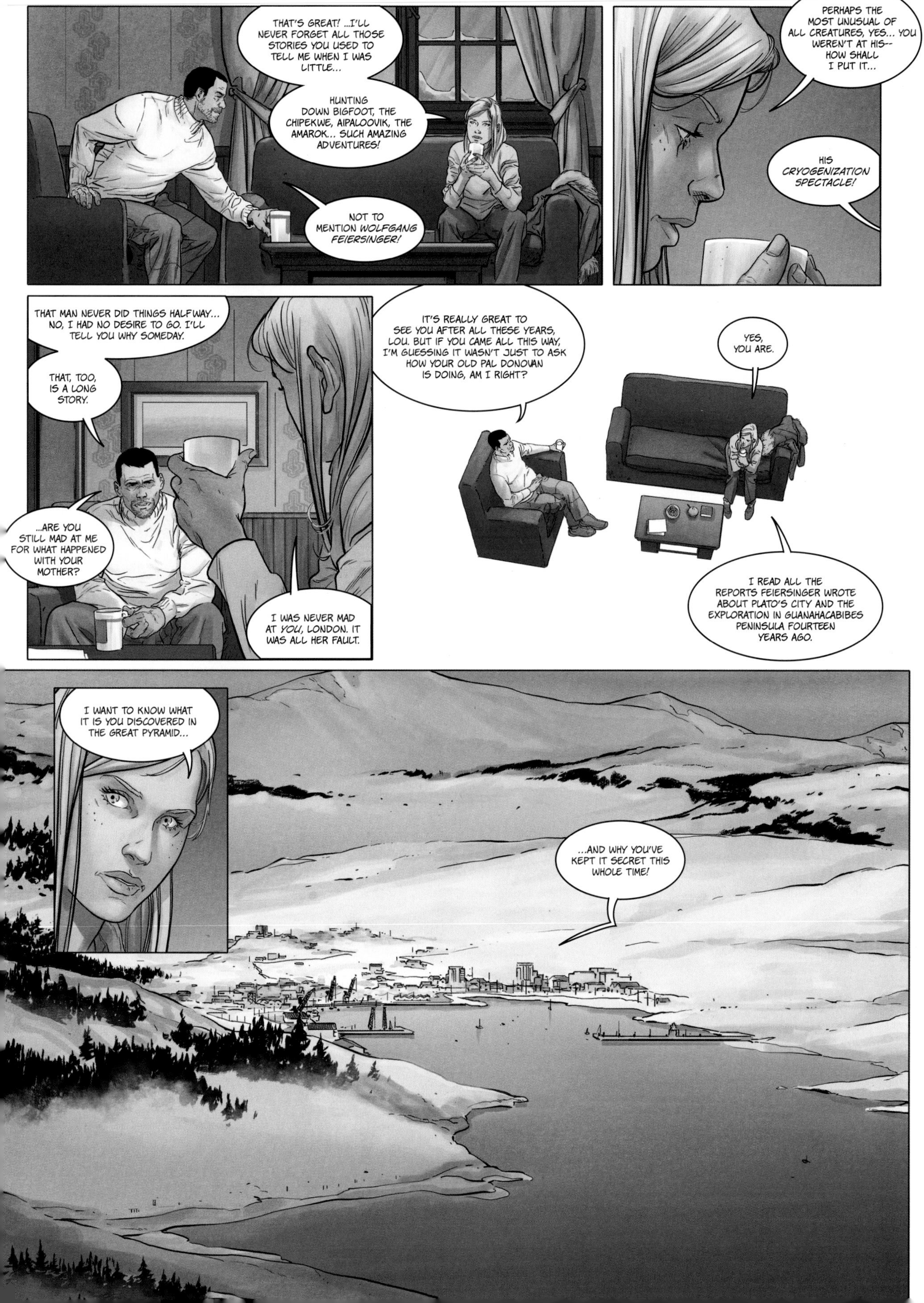
THAT'S GREAT! ...I'LL NEVER FORGET ALL THOSE STORIES YOU USED TO TELL ME WHEN I WAS LITTLE...
HUNTING DOWN BIGFOOT, THE CHIPEKWE, AIPALOOVIK, THE AMAROK... SUCH AMAZING ADVENTURES!
NOT TO MENTION WOLFGANG FEIERSINGER!
PERHAPS THE MOST UNUSUAL OF ALL CREATURES, YES... YOU WEREN'T AT HIS-- HOW SHALL I PUT IT...
HIS CRYOGENIZATION SPECTACLE!
THAT MAN NEVER DID THINGS HALFWAY... NO, I HAD NO DESIRE TO GO. I'LL TELL YOU WHY SOMEDAY.
THAT, TOO, IS A LONG STORY.
...ARE YOU STILL MAD AT ME FOR WHAT HAPPENED WITH YOUR MOTHER?
I WAS NEVER MAD AT YOU, LONDON. IT WAS ALL HER FAULT.
IT'S REALLY GREAT TO SEE YOU AFTER ALL THESE YEARS, LOU. BUT IF YOU CAME ALL THIS WAY, I'M GUESSING IT WASN'T JUST TO ASK HOW YOUR OLD PAL DONOVAN IS DOING, AM I RIGHT?
YES, YOU ARE.
I READ ALL THE REPORTS FEIERSINGER WROTE ABOUT PLATO'S CITY AND THE EXPLORATION IN GUANAHACABIBES PENINSULA FOURTEEN YEARS AGO.
I WANT TO KNOW WHAT IT IS YOU DISCOVERED IN THE GREAT PYRAMID...
...AND WHY YOU'VE KEPT IT SECRET THIS WHOLE TIME!

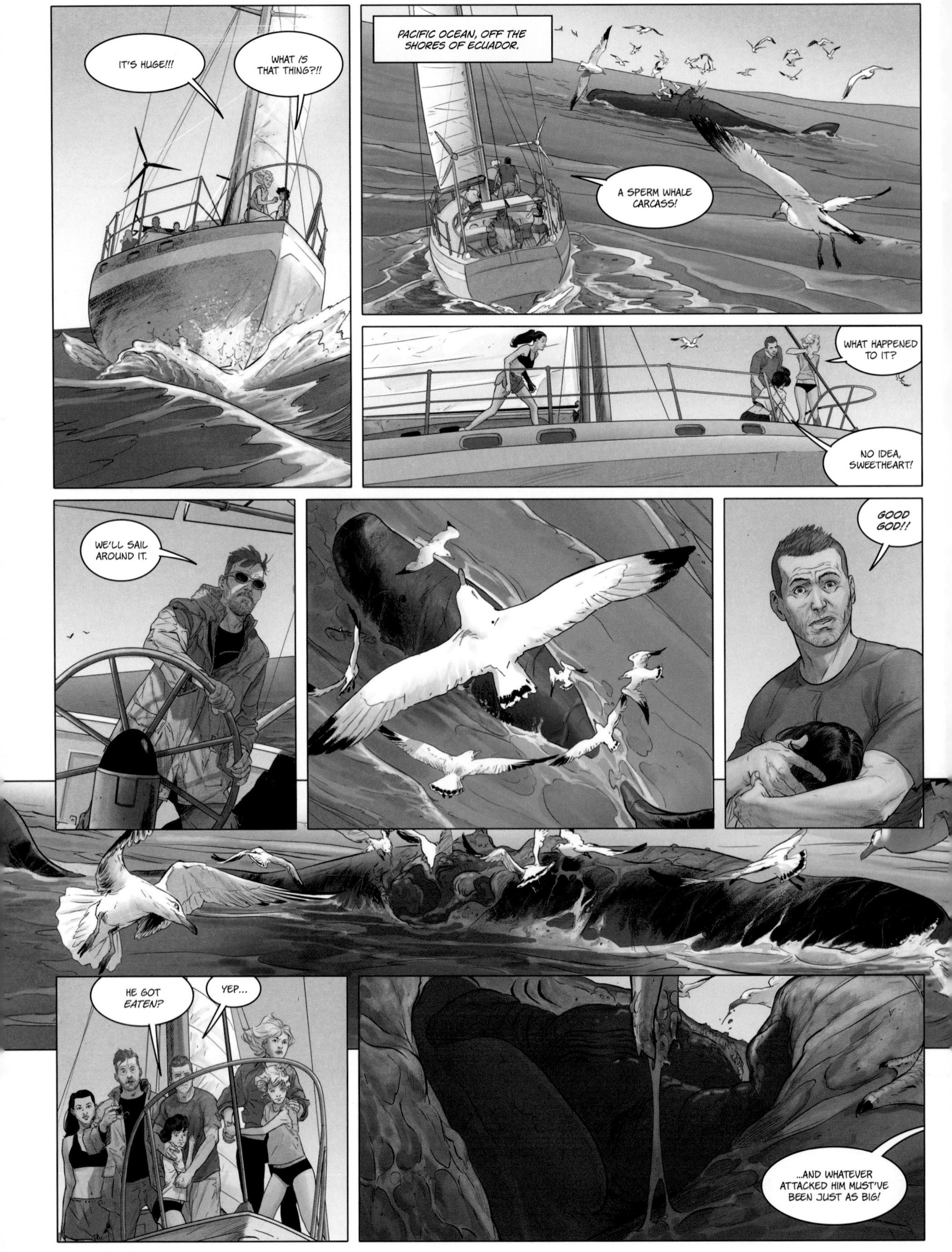
IT'S HUGE!!!
WHAT IS THAT THING?!!
PACIFIC OCEAN, OFF THE SHORES OF ECUADOR.
A SPERM WHALE CARCASS!
WHAT HAPPENED TO IT?
NO IDEA, SWEETHEART!
WE'LL SAIL AROUND IT.
GOOD GOD!!
HE GOT EATEN?
YEP...
...AND WHATEVER ATTACKED HIM MUST'VE BEEN JUST AS BIG!

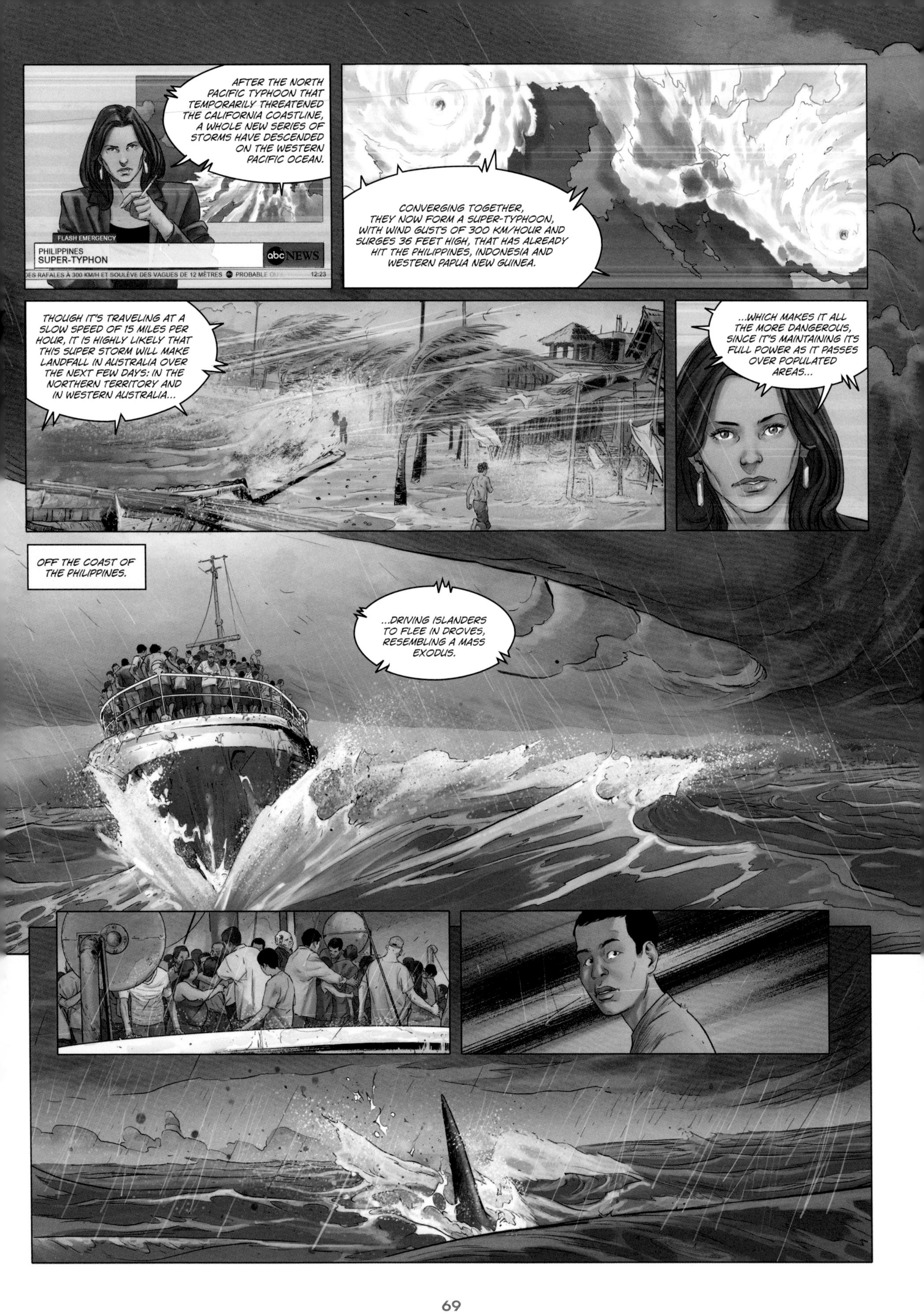
FLASH EMERGENCY
PHILIPPINES
SUPER-TYPHON
abc NEWS
DES RAFALES À 300 KM/H ET SOULÈVE DES VAGUES DE 12 MÈTRES PROBABLE
12:23
AFTER THE NORTH PACIFIC TYPHOON THAT TEMPORARILY THREATENED THE CALIFORNIA COASTLINE, A WHOLE NEW SERIES OF STORMS HAVE DESCENDED ON THE WESTERN PACIFIC OCEAN.
CONVERGING TOGETHER, THEY NOW FORM A SUPER-TYPHOON, WITH WIND GUSTS OF 300 KM/HOUR AND SURGES 36 FEET HIGH, THAT HAS ALREADY HIT THE PHILIPPINES, INDONESIA AND WESTERN PAPUA NEW GUINEA.
THOUGH IT'S TRAVELING AT A SLOW SPEED OF 15 MILES PER HOUR, IT IS HIGHLY LIKELY THAT THIS SUPER STORM WILL MAKE LANDFALL IN AUSTRALIA OVER THE NEXT FEW DAYS: IN THE NORTHERN TERRITORY AND IN WESTERN AUSTRALIA...
...WHICH MAKES IT ALL THE MORE DANGEROUS, SINCE IT'S MAINTAINING ITS FULL POWER AS IT PASSES OVER POPULATED AREAS...
OFF THE COAST OF THE PHILIPPINES.
...DRIVING ISLANDERS TO FLEE IN DROVES, RESEMBLING A MASS EXODUS.

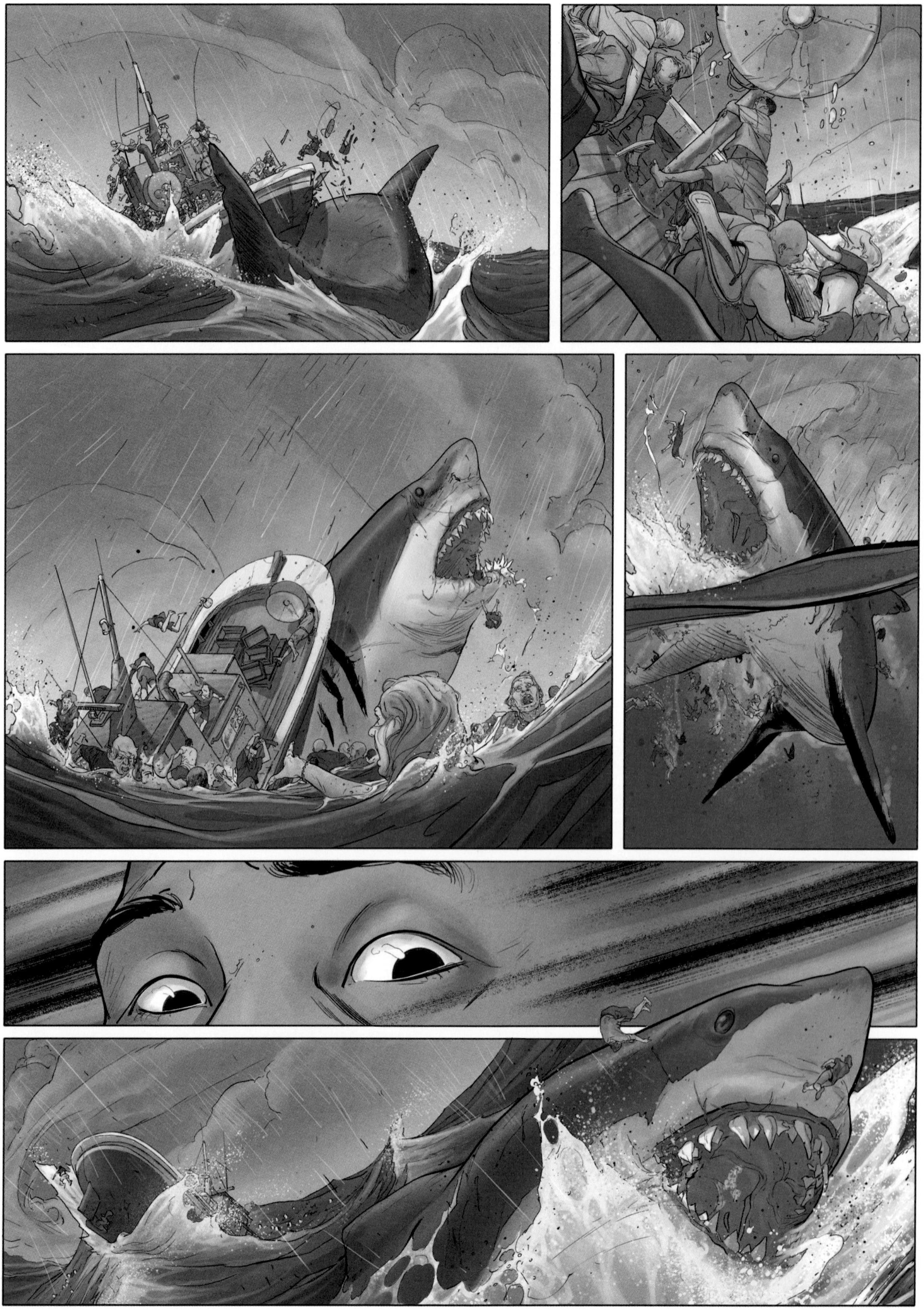

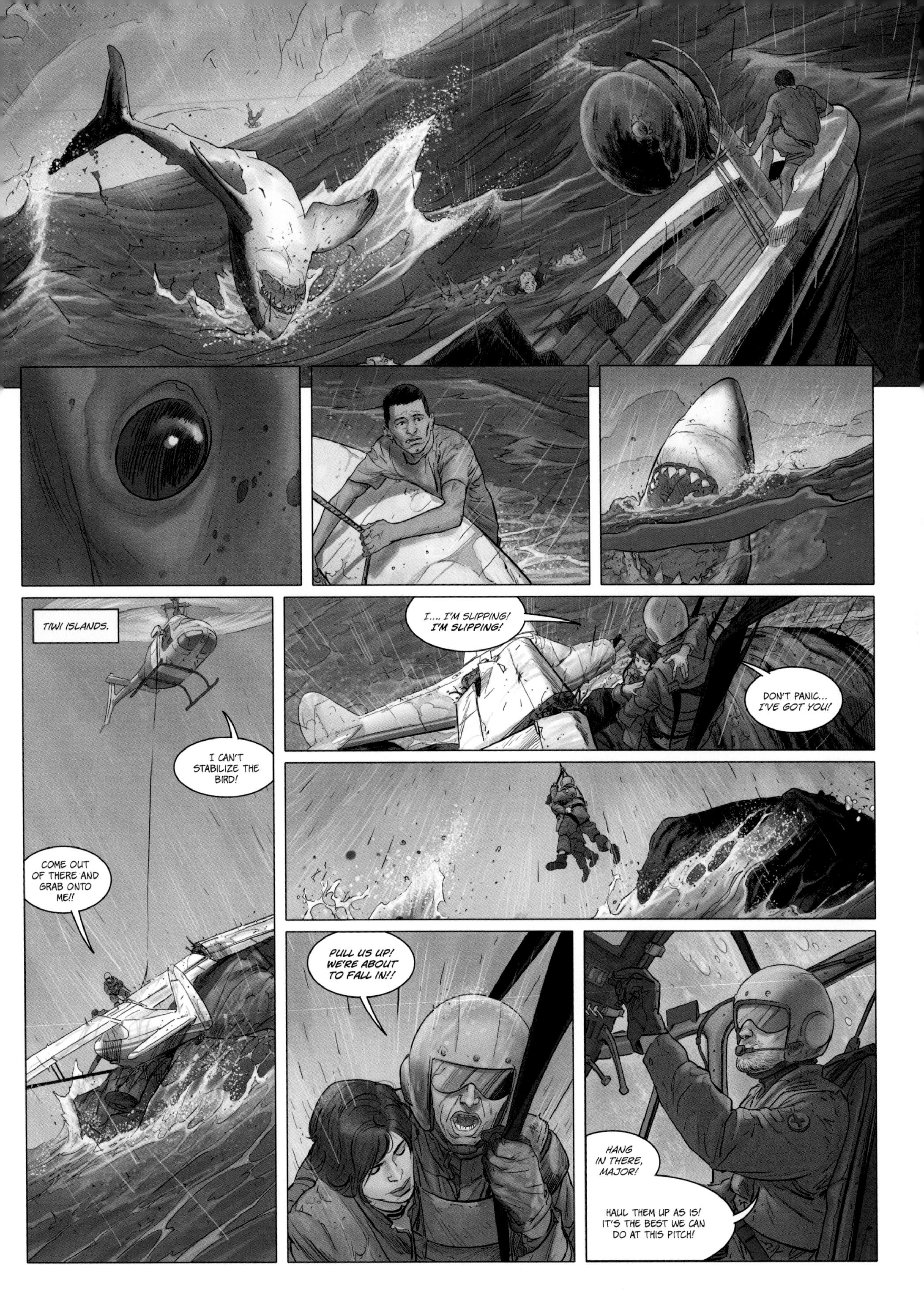

TIWI ISLANDS.
I CAN'T STABILIZE THE BIRD!
COME OUT OF THERE AND GRAB ONTO ME!!
I.... I'M SLIPPING! I'M SLIPPING!
DON'T PANIC... I'VE GOT YOU!
PULL US UP! WE'RE ABOUT TO FALL IN!!
HANG IN THERE, MAJOR!
HAUL THEM UP AS IS! IT'S THE BEST WE CAN DO AT THIS PITCH!

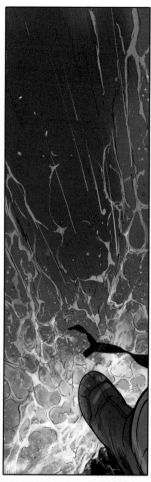

!!!

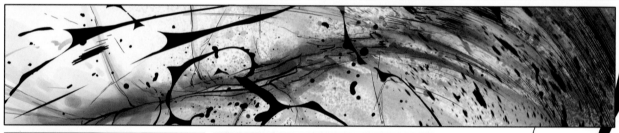

YES!
WE MADE IT!

WE'RE IN THE
SAFE ZONE!

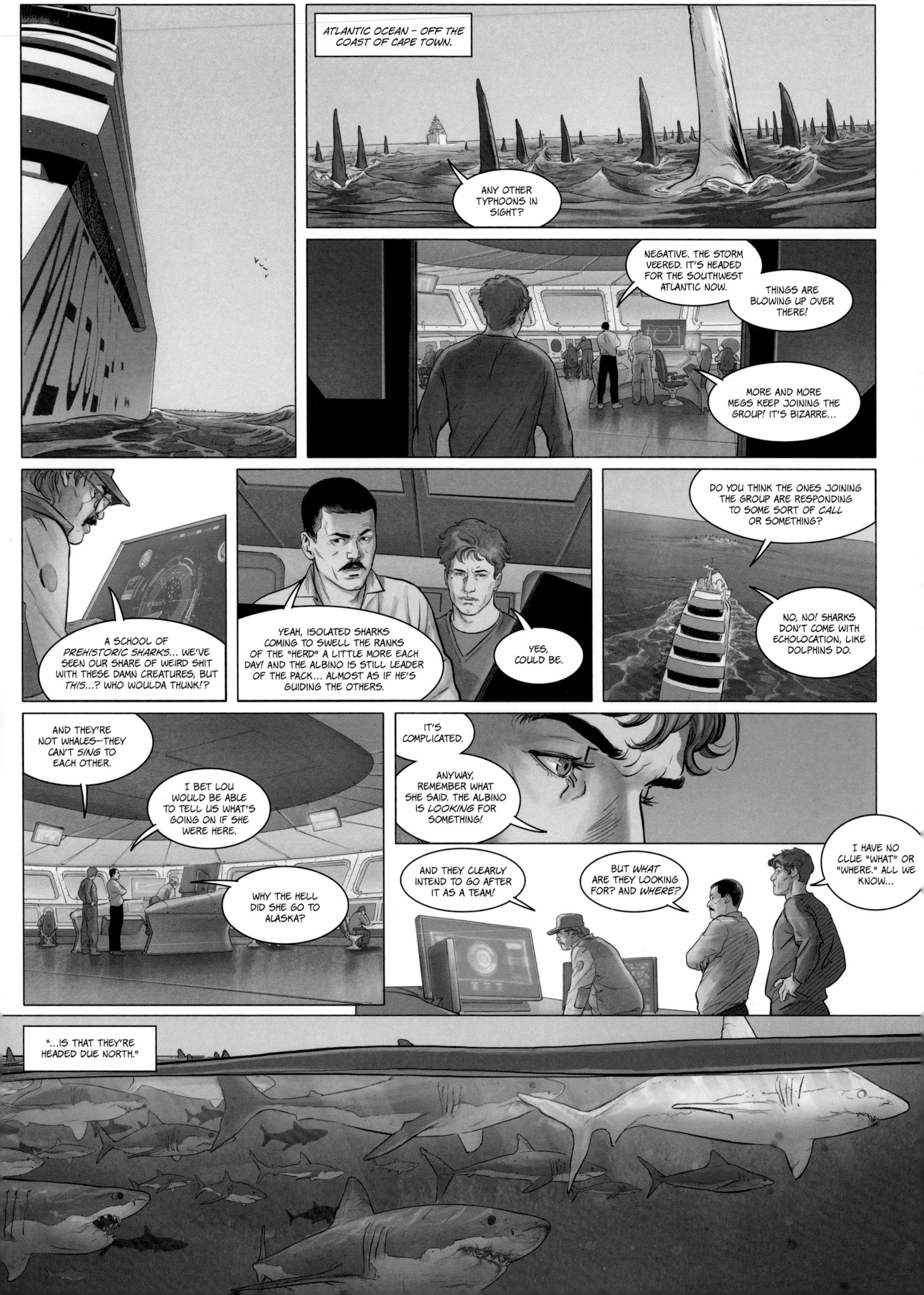

ATLANTIC OCEAN – OFF THE COAST OF CAPE TOWN.
ANY OTHER TYPHOONS IN SIGHT?
NEGATIVE. THE STORM VEERED. IT'S HEADED FOR THE SOUTHWEST ATLANTIC NOW.
THINGS ARE BLOWING UP OVER THERE!
MORE AND MORE MEGS KEEP JOINING THE GROUP! IT'S BIZARRE...
A SCHOOL OF *PREHISTORIC SHARKS*... WE'VE SEEN OUR SHARE OF WEIRD SHIT WITH THESE DAMN CREATURES, BUT *THIS*...? WHO WOULDA THUNK!?
YEAH, ISOLATED SHARKS COMING TO SWELL THE RANKS OF THE "HERD" A LITTLE MORE EACH DAY! AND THE ALBINO IS STILL LEADER OF THE PACK... ALMOST AS IF HE'S GUIDING THE OTHERS.
YES, COULD BE.
DO YOU THINK THE ONES JOINING THE GROUP ARE RESPONDING TO SOME SORT OF *CALL* OR SOMETHING?
NO, NO! SHARKS DON'T COME WITH ECHOLOCATION, LIKE DOLPHINS DO.
AND THEY'RE NOT WHALES—THEY CAN'T *SING* TO EACH OTHER.
I BET LOU WOULD BE ABLE TO TELL US WHAT'S GOING ON IF SHE WERE HERE.
WHY THE HELL DID SHE GO TO ALASKA?
IT'S COMPLICATED.
ANYWAY, REMEMBER WHAT SHE SAID. THE ALBINO IS *LOOKING* FOR SOMETHING!
AND THEY CLEARLY INTEND TO GO AFTER IT AS A TEAM!
BUT *WHAT* ARE THEY LOOKING FOR? AND *WHERE?*
I HAVE NO CLUE "WHAT" OR "WHERE." ALL WE KNOW...
"...IS THAT THEY'RE HEADED DUE NORTH."

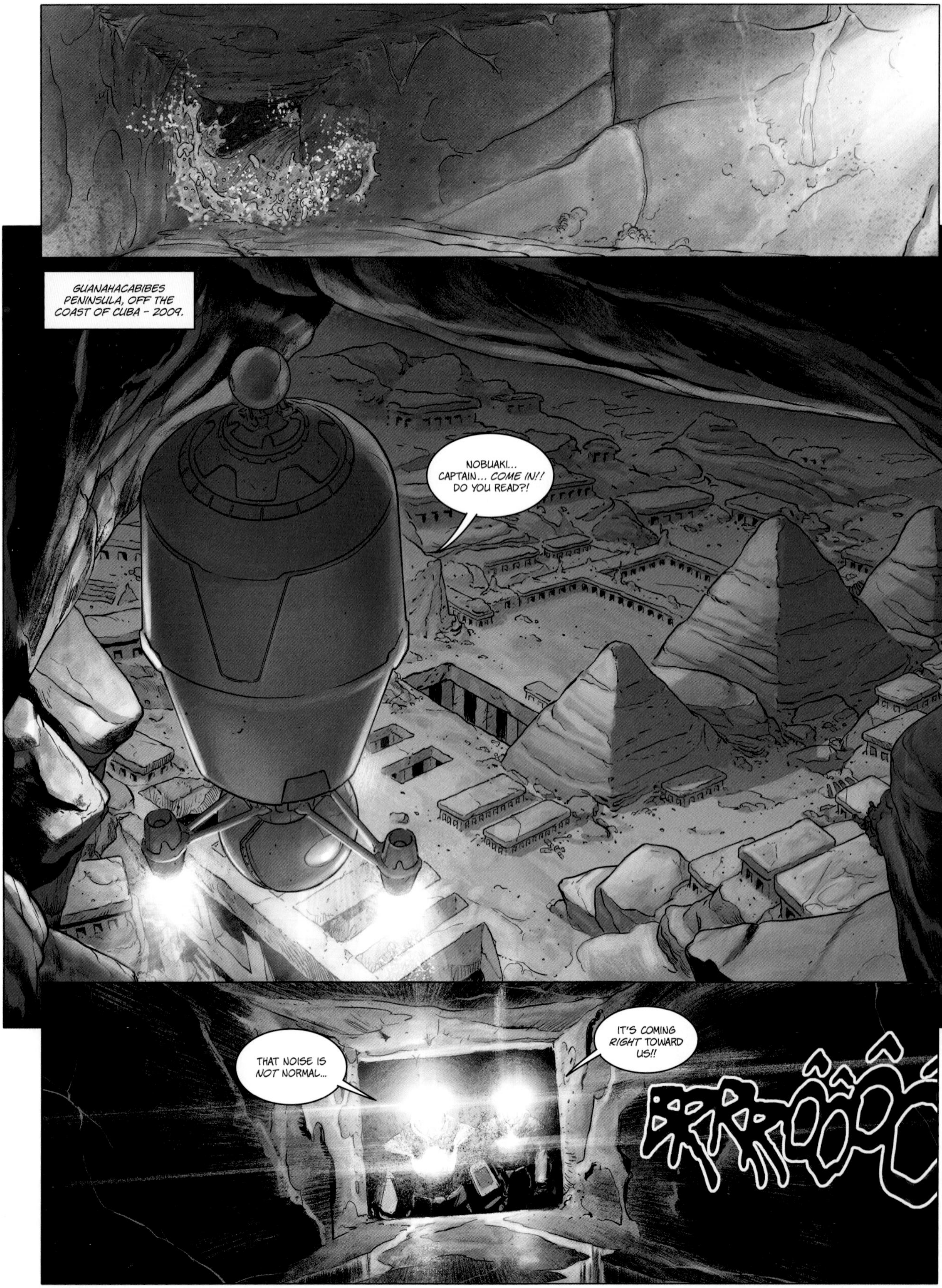
GUANAHACABIBES PENINSULA, OFF THE COAST OF CUBA - 2009.
NOBUAKI... CAPTAIN... COME IN!! DO YOU READ?!
THAT NOISE IS NOT NORMAL...
IT'S COMING RIGHT TOWARD US!!

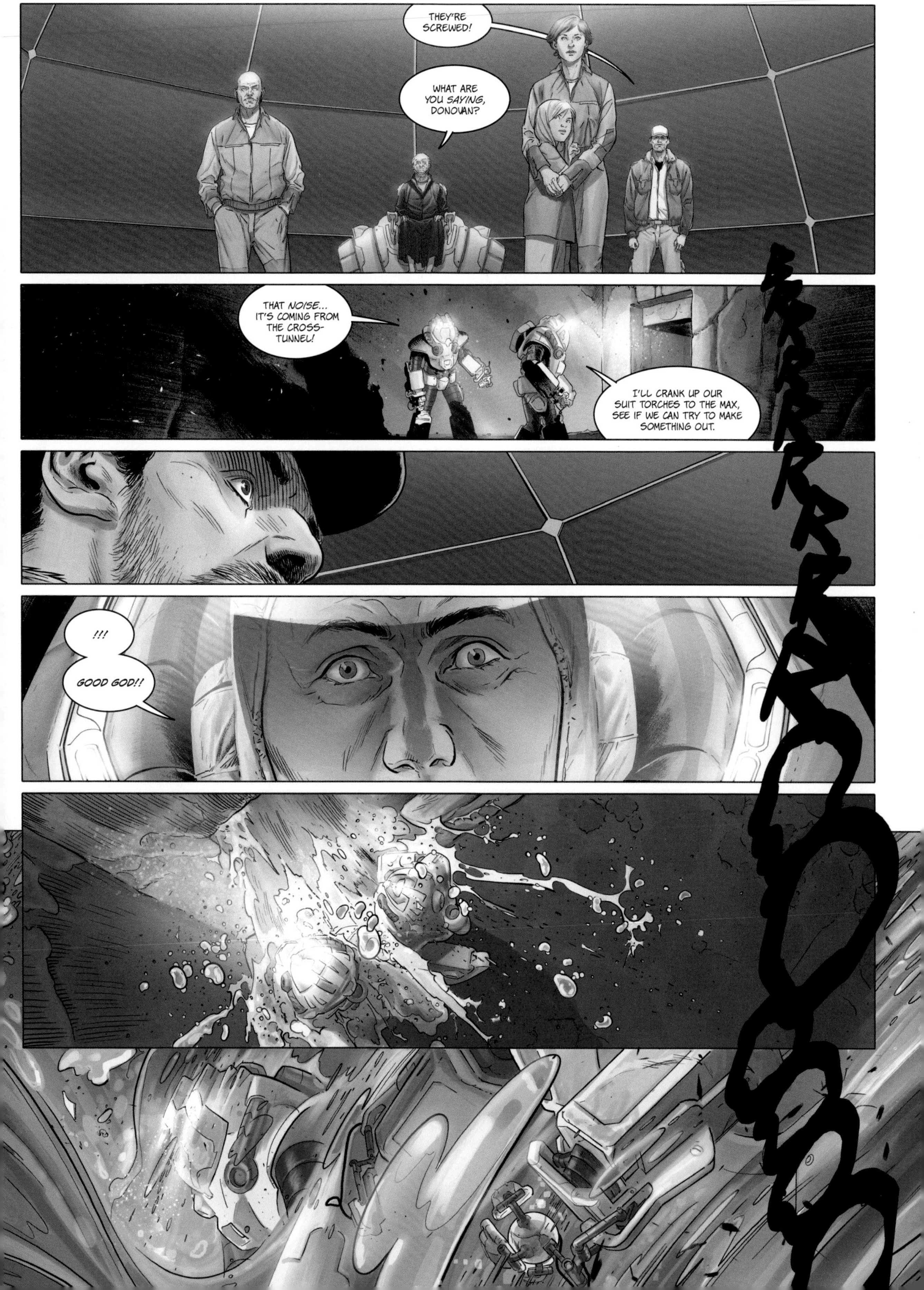
THEY'RE SCREWED!
WHAT ARE YOU SAYING, DONOVAN?
THAT NOISE... IT'S COMING FROM THE CROSS-TUNNEL!
I'LL CRANK UP OUR SUIT TORCHES TO THE MAX, SEE IF WE CAN TRY TO MAKE SOMETHING OUT.
!!!
GOOD GOD!!

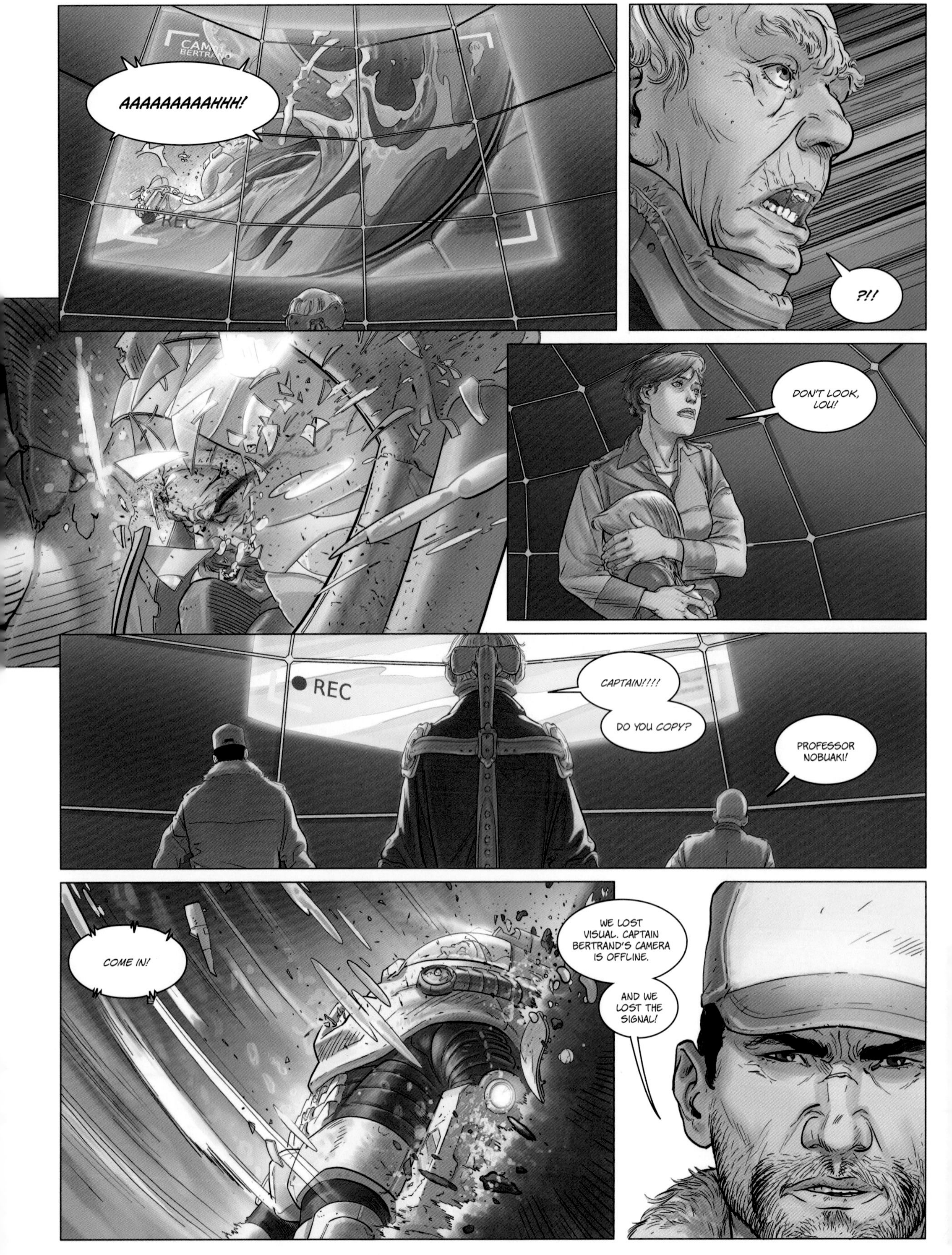
CAM01
BERTRAND
REC
AAAAAAAAAHHH!
?!!
DON'T LOOK, LOU!
REC
CAPTAIN!!!!
DO YOU COPY?
PROFESSOR NOBUAKI!
COME IN!
WE LOST VISUAL. CAPTAIN BERTRAND'S CAMERA IS OFFLINE.
AND WE LOST THE SIGNAL!

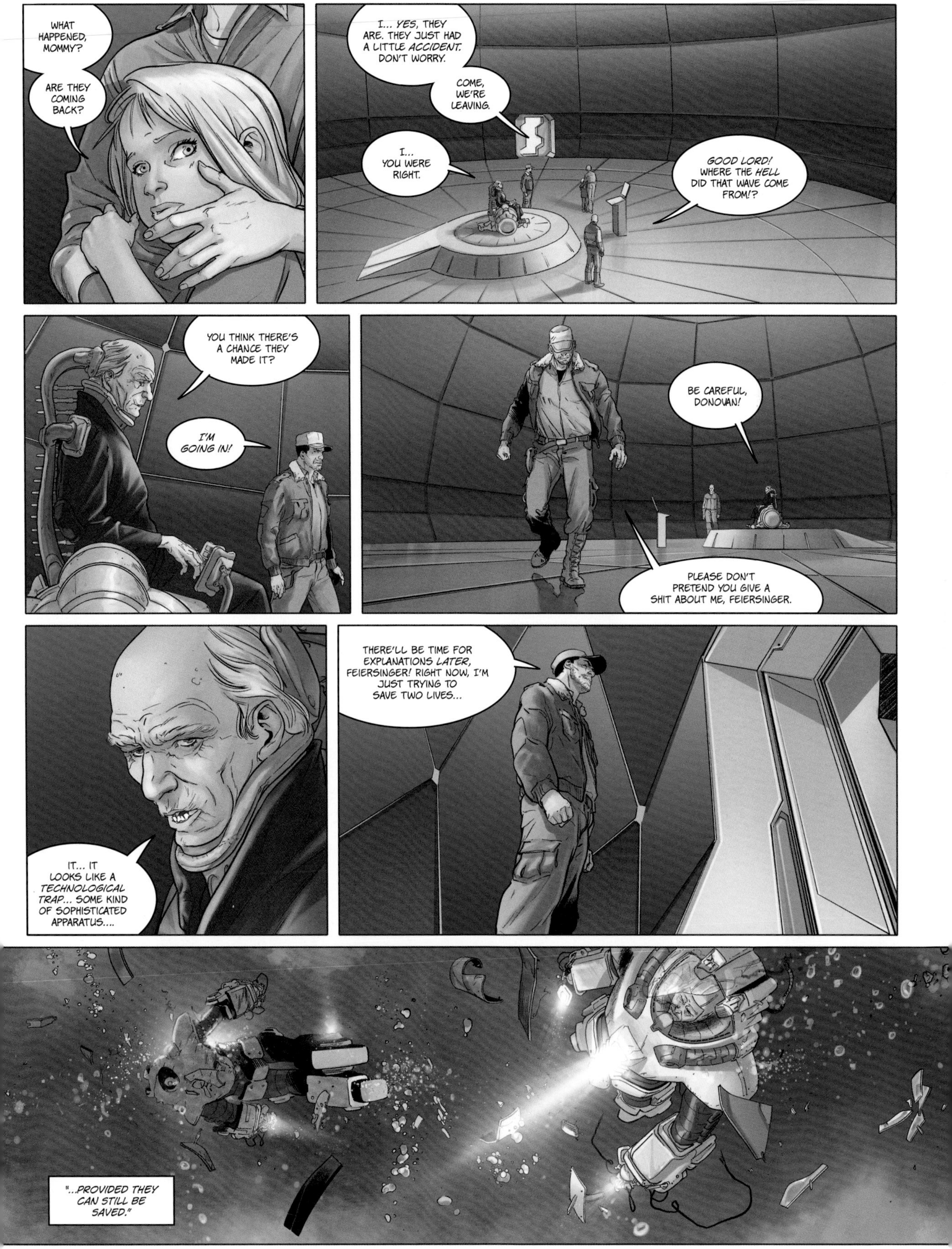

WHAT HAPPENED, MOMMY?
ARE THEY COMING BACK?
I... *YES*, THEY ARE. THEY JUST HAD A LITTLE *ACCIDENT*. DON'T WORRY.
COME, WE'RE LEAVING.
I... YOU WERE RIGHT.
GOOD LORD! WHERE THE *HELL* DID THAT WAVE COME FROM!?
YOU THINK THERE'S A CHANCE THEY MADE IT?
I'M GOING IN!
BE CAREFUL, DONOVAN!
PLEASE DON'T PRETEND YOU GIVE A SHIT ABOUT ME, FEIERSINGER.
IT... IT LOOKS LIKE A *TECHNOLOGICAL TRAP*... SOME KIND OF SOPHISTICATED APPARATUS....
THERE'LL BE TIME FOR EXPLANATIONS *LATER*, FEIERSINGER*!* RIGHT NOW, I'M JUST TRYING TO SAVE TWO LIVES...
"...PROVIDED THEY CAN STILL BE SAVED."

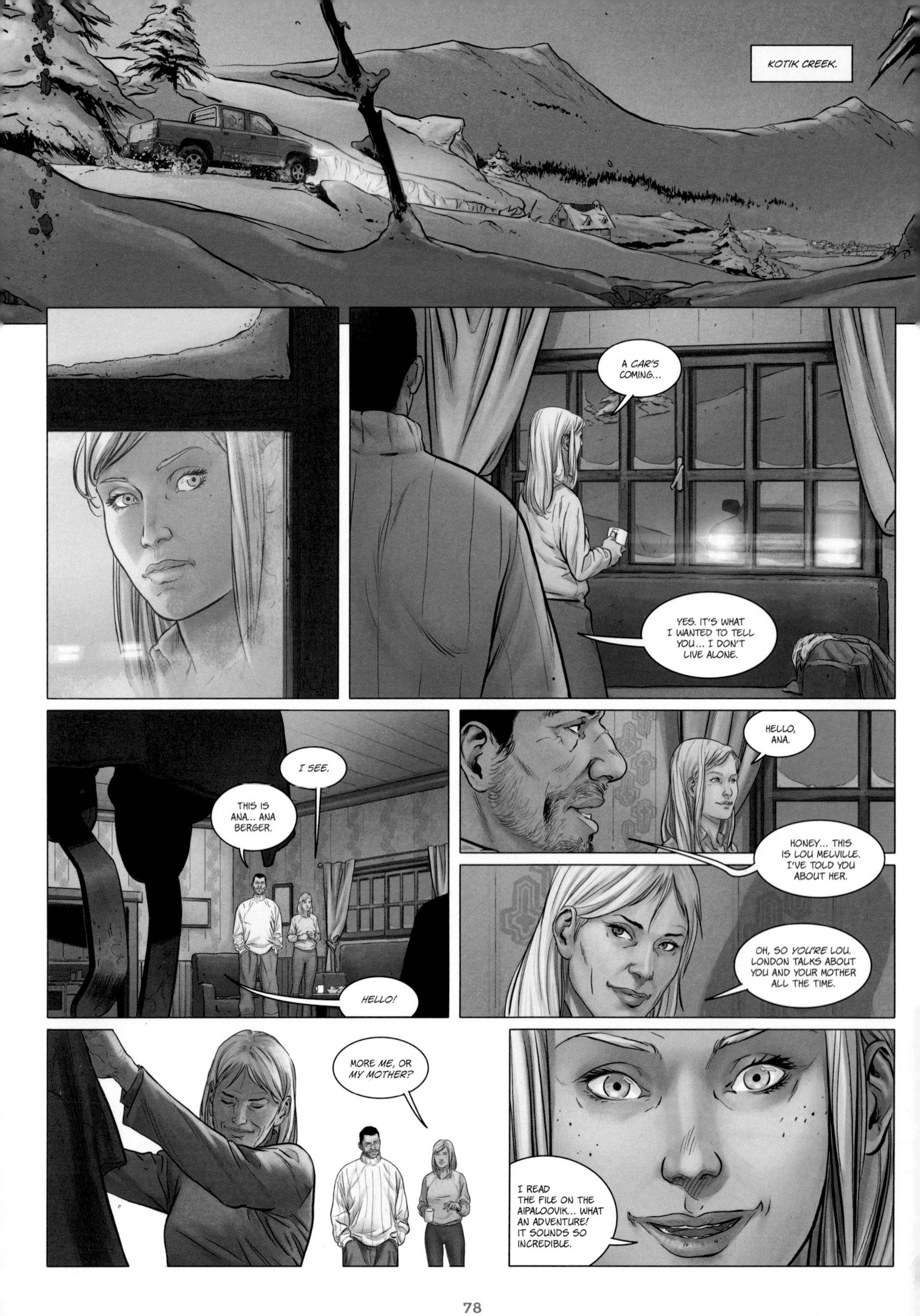
KOTIK CREEK.
A CAR'S COMING...
YES. IT'S WHAT I WANTED TO TELL YOU... I DON'T LIVE ALONE.
THIS IS ANA... ANA BERGER.
I SEE.
HELLO!
HELLO, ANA.
HONEY... THIS IS LOU MELVILLE. I'VE TOLD YOU ABOUT HER.
OH, SO YOU'RE LOU. LONDON TALKS ABOUT YOU AND YOUR MOTHER ALL THE TIME.
MORE ME, OR MY MOTHER?
I READ THE FILE ON THE AIPALOOVIK... WHAT AN ADVENTURE! IT SOUNDS SO INCREDIBLE.

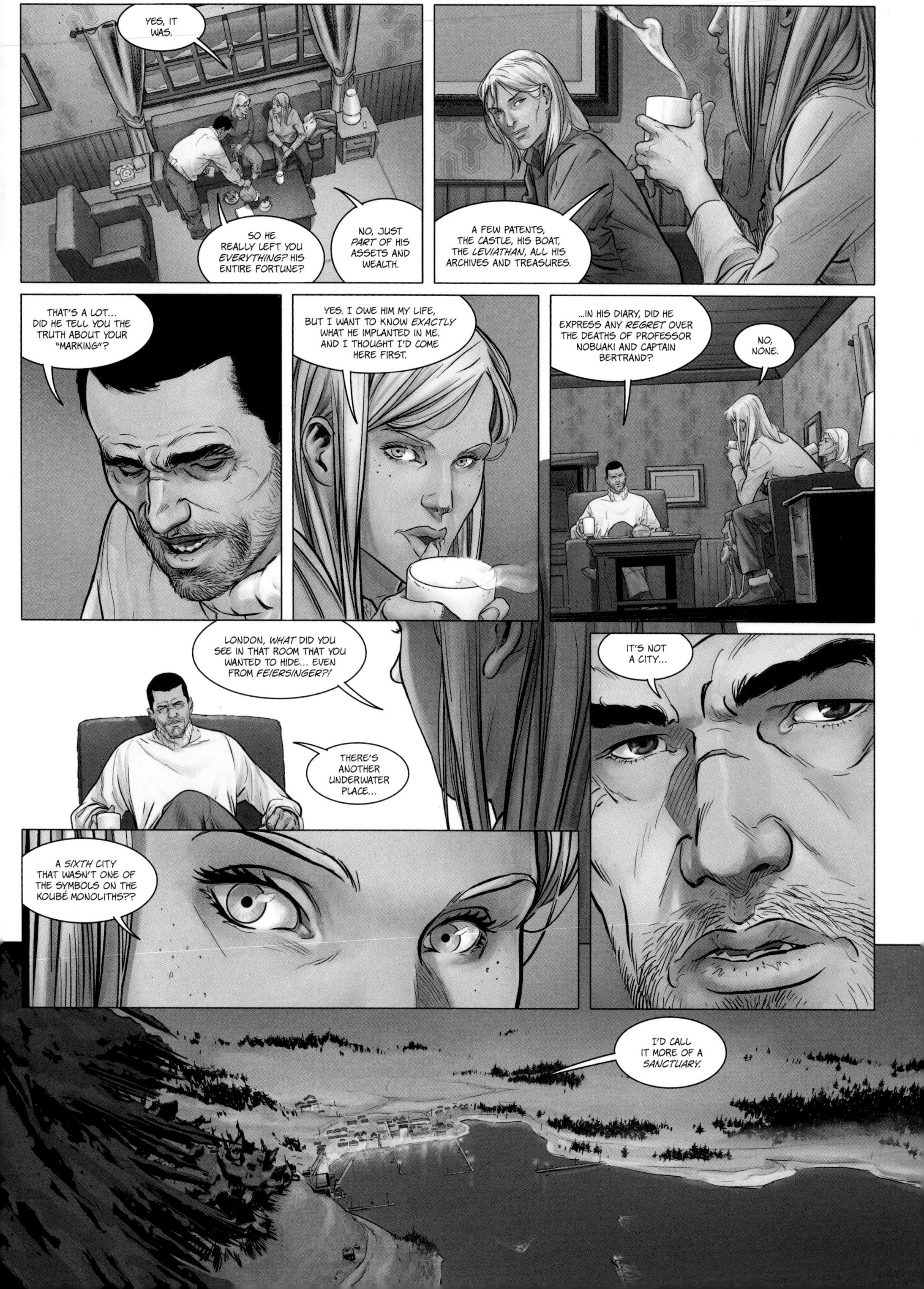
YES, IT WAS.
SO HE REALLY LEFT YOU *EVERYTHING?* HIS ENTIRE FORTUNE?
NO, JUST *PART* OF HIS ASSETS AND WEALTH.
A FEW PATENTS, THE CASTLE, HIS BOAT, THE *LEVIATHAN*, ALL HIS ARCHIVES AND TREASURES.
THAT'S A LOT... DID HE TELL YOU THE TRUTH ABOUT YOUR "MARKING"?
YES. I OWE HIM MY LIFE, BUT I WANT TO KNOW *EXACTLY* WHAT HE IMPLANTED IN ME. AND I THOUGHT I'D COME HERE FIRST.
...IN HIS DIARY, DID HE EXPRESS ANY *REGRET* OVER THE DEATHS OF PROFESSOR NOBUAKI AND CAPTAIN BERTRAND?
NO, NONE.
LONDON, *WHAT* DID YOU SEE IN THAT ROOM THAT YOU WANTED TO HIDE... EVEN FROM *FEIERSINGER?!*
THERE'S ANOTHER UNDERWATER PLACE...
IT'S NOT A CITY...
A *SIXTH* CITY THAT WASN'T ONE OF THE SYMBOLS ON THE KOUBÉ MONOLITHS??
I'D CALL IT MORE OF A *SANCTUARY.*

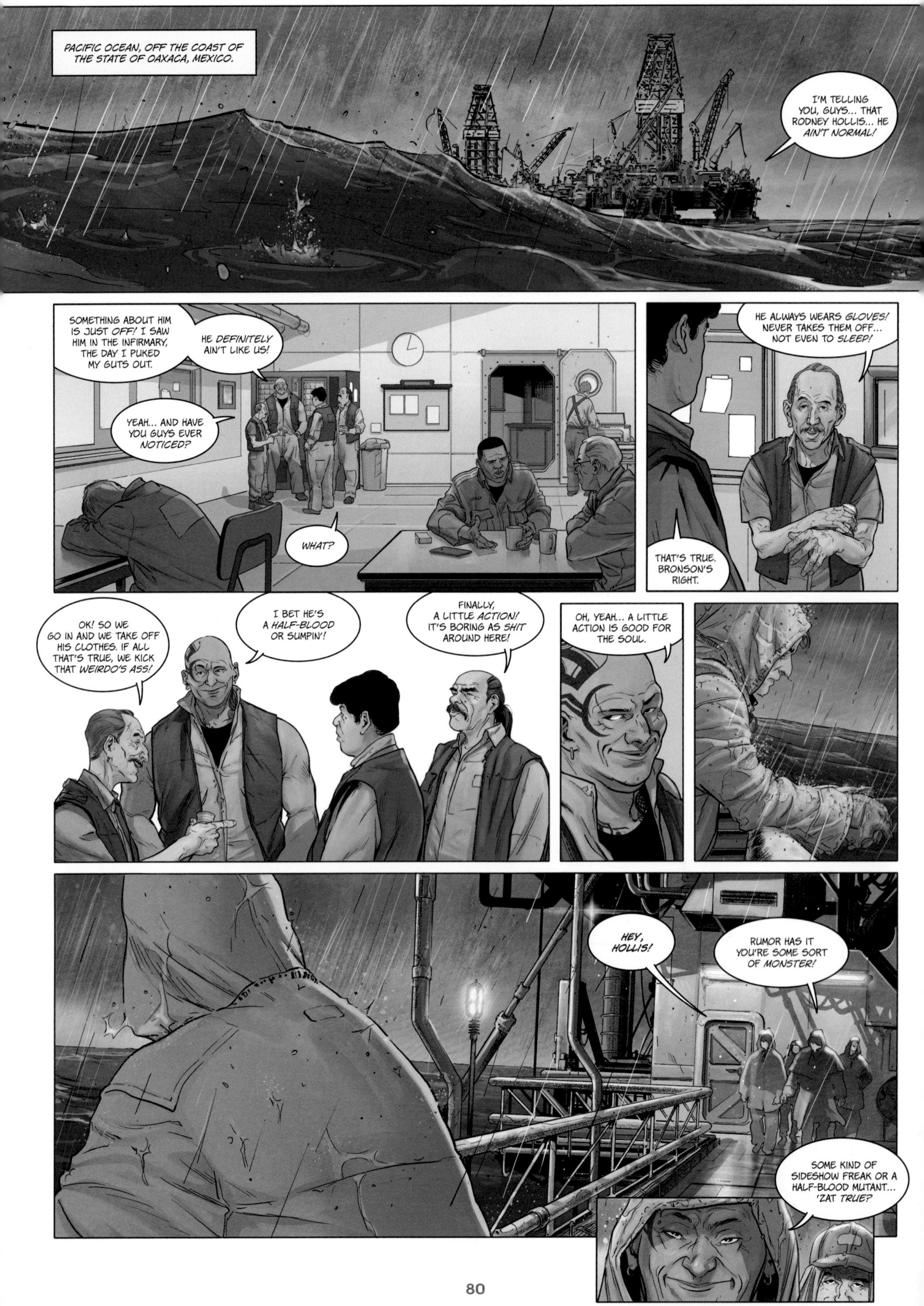
PACIFIC OCEAN, OFF THE COAST OF THE STATE OF OAXACA, MEXICO.
I'M TELLING YOU, GUYS... THAT RODNEY HOLLIS... HE *AIN'T NORMAL!*
SOMETHING ABOUT HIM IS JUST *OFF!* I SAW HIM IN THE INFIRMARY, THE DAY I PUKED MY GUTS OUT.
HE *DEFINITELY* AIN'T LIKE US!
YEAH... AND HAVE YOU GUYS EVER *NOTICED?*
WHAT?
HE ALWAYS WEARS *GLOVES!* NEVER TAKES THEM OFF... NOT EVEN TO *SLEEP!*
THAT'S TRUE. BRONSON'S RIGHT.
OK! SO WE GO IN AND WE TAKE OFF HIS CLOTHES. IF ALL THAT'S TRUE, WE KICK THAT *WEIRDO'S ASS!*
I BET HE'S A *HALF-BLOOD* OR SUMPIN'!
FINALLY, A LITTLE *ACTION!* IT'S BORING AS *SHIT* AROUND HERE!
OH, YEAH... A LITTLE ACTION IS GOOD FOR THE SOUL.
HEY, HOLLIS!
RUMOR HAS IT YOU'RE SOME SORT OF *MONSTER!*
SOME KIND OF SIDESHOW FREAK OR A HALF-BLOOD MUTANT... 'ZAT *TRUE?*

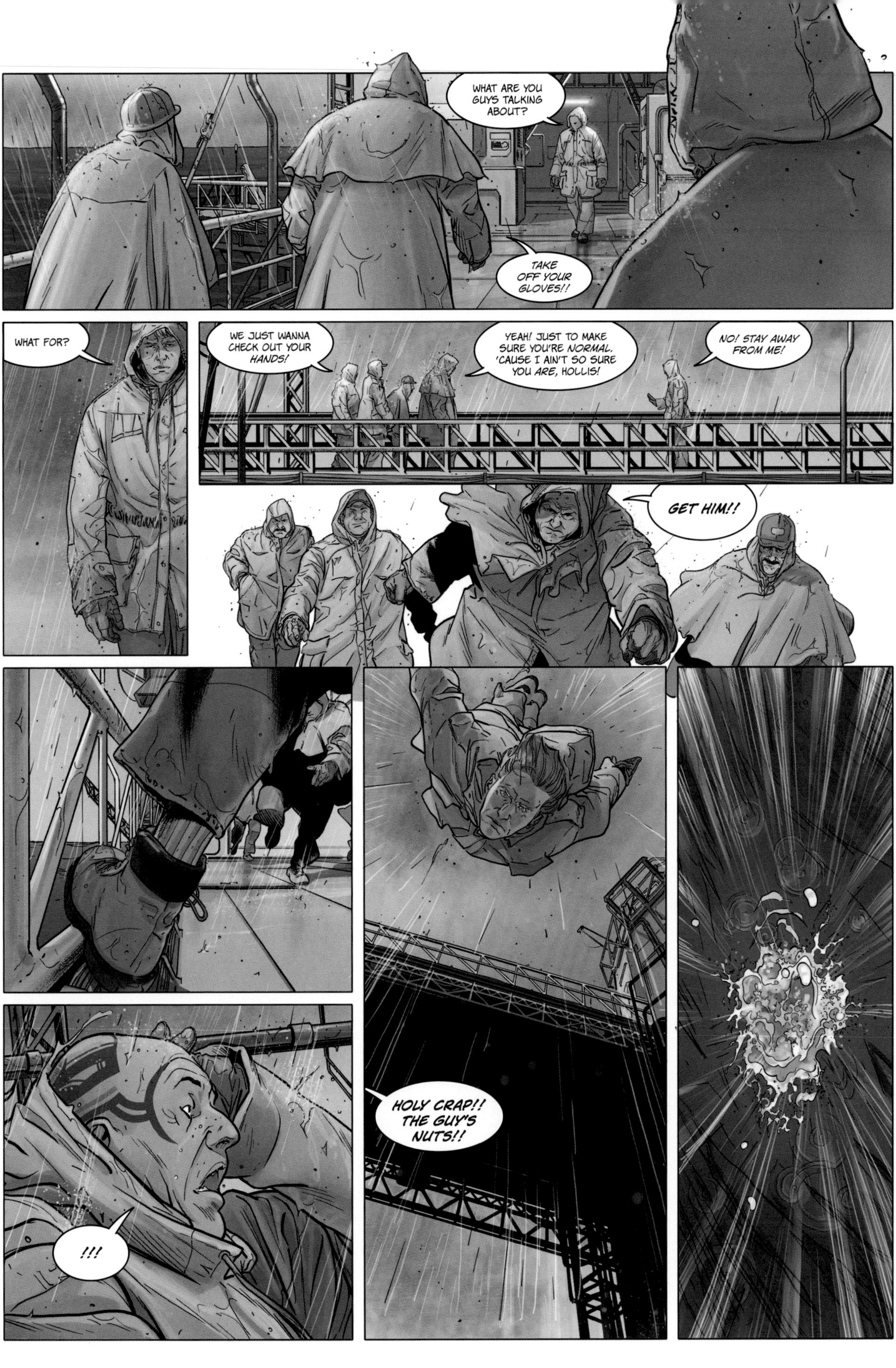
WHAT ARE YOU GUYS TALKING ABOUT?
TAKE OFF YOUR GLOVES!!
WHAT FOR?
WE JUST WANNA CHECK OUT YOUR HANDS!
YEAH! JUST TO MAKE SURE YOU'RE NORMAL. 'CAUSE I AIN'T SO SURE YOU ARE, HOLLIS!
NO! STAY AWAY FROM ME!
GET HIM!!
!!!
HOLY CRAP!! THE GUY'S NUTS!!

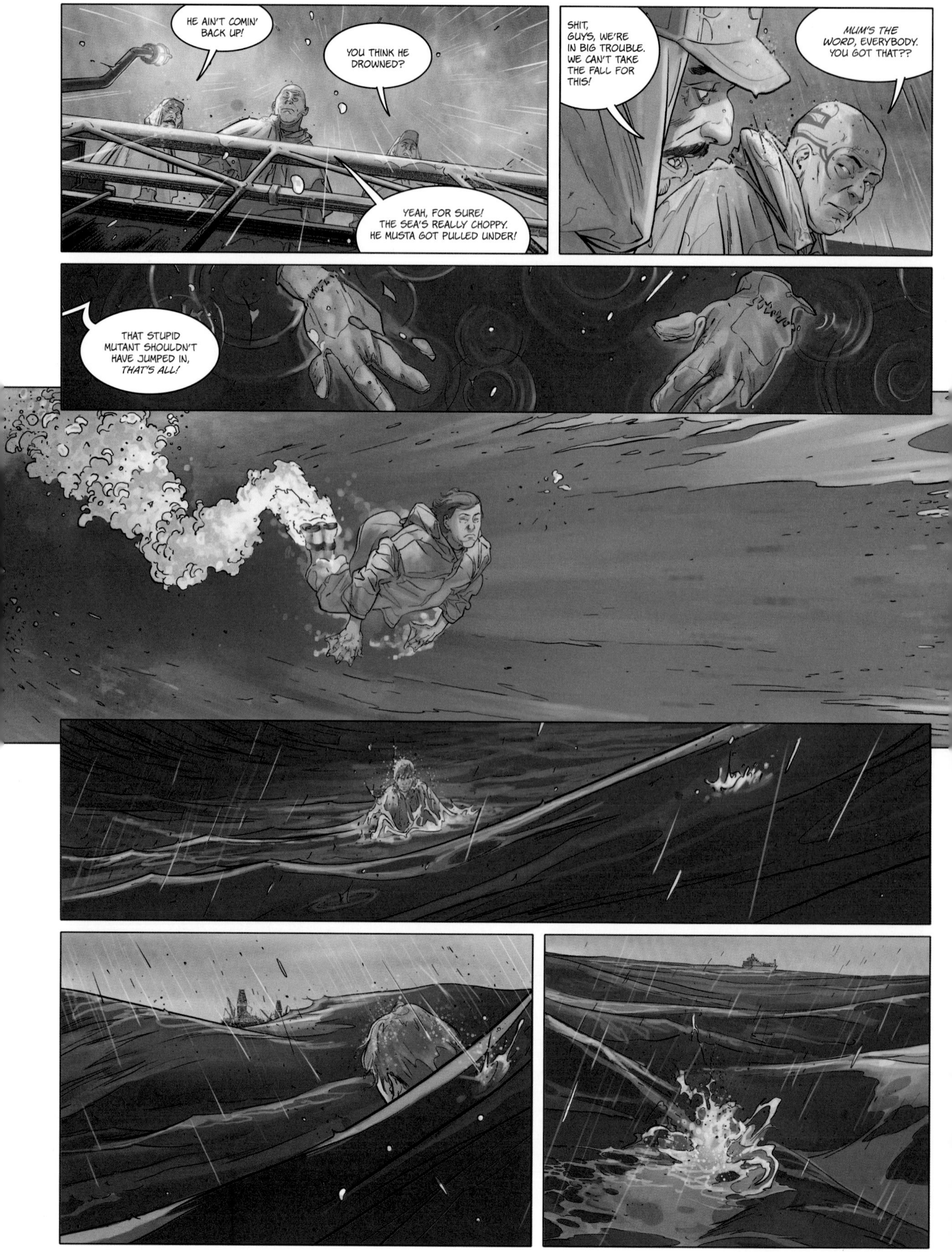
HE AIN'T COMIN' BACK UP!
YOU THINK HE DROWNED?
YEAH, FOR SURE! THE SEA'S REALLY CHOPPY. HE MUSTA GOT PULLED UNDER!
SHIT, GUYS, WE'RE IN BIG TROUBLE. WE CAN'T TAKE THE FALL FOR THIS!
MUM'S THE WORD, EVERYBODY. YOU GOT THAT??
THAT STUPID MUTANT SHOULDN'T HAVE JUMPED IN, THAT'S ALL!

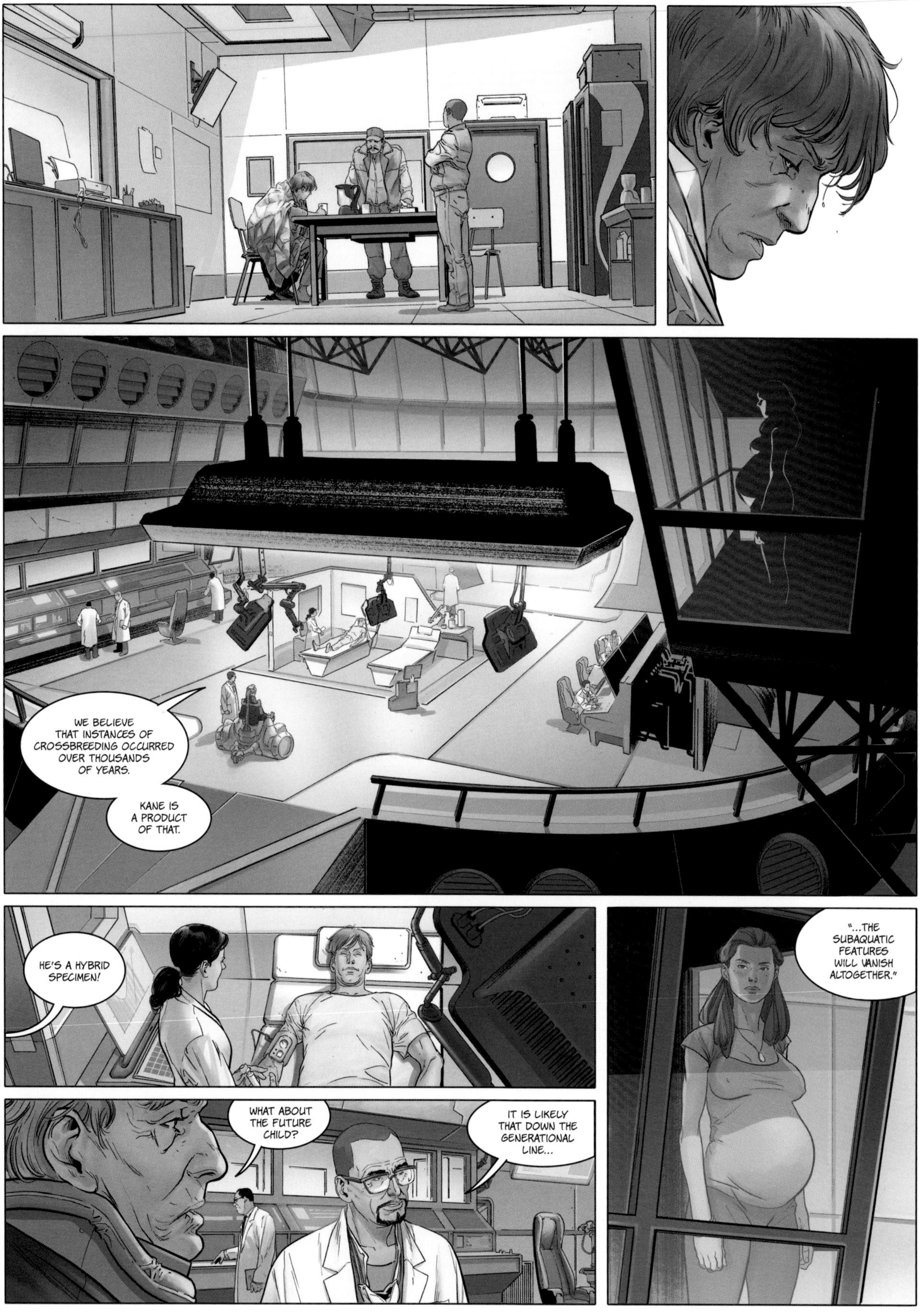
WE BELIEVE THAT INSTANCES OF CROSSBREEDING OCCURRED OVER THOUSANDS OF YEARS.
KANE IS A PRODUCT OF THAT.
HE'S A HYBRID SPECIMEN!
WHAT ABOUT THE FUTURE CHILD?
IT IS LIKELY THAT DOWN THE GENERATIONAL LINE...
"...THE SUBAQUATIC FEATURES WILL VANISH ALTOGETHER."

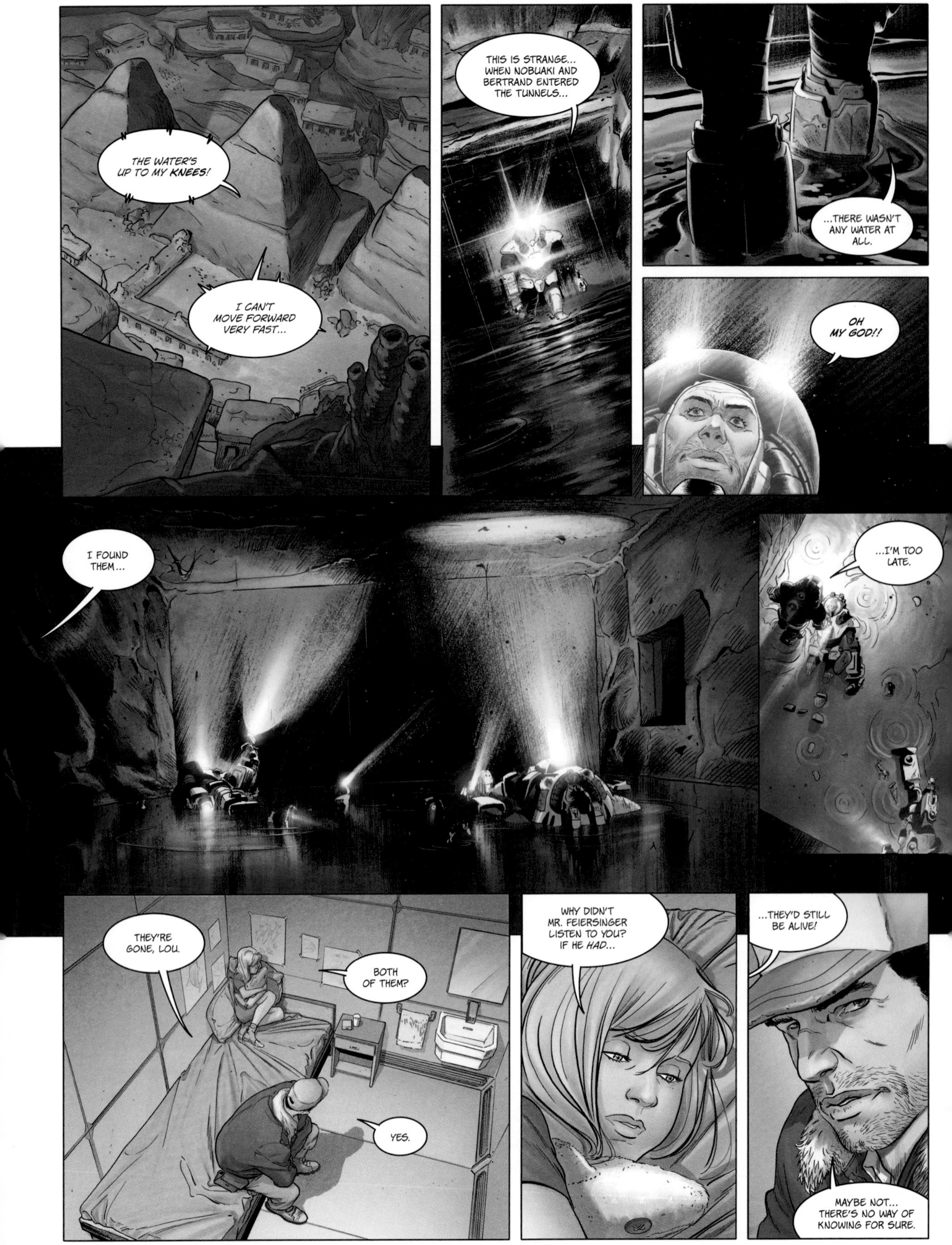
THE WATER'S UP TO MY KNEES!
I CAN'T MOVE FORWARD VERY FAST...
THIS IS STRANGE... WHEN NOBUAKI AND BERTRAND ENTERED THE TUNNELS...
...THERE WASN'T ANY WATER AT ALL.
OH MY GOD!!
I FOUND THEM...
...I'M TOO LATE.
THEY'RE GONE, LOU.
BOTH OF THEM?
YES.
WHY DIDN'T MR. FEIERSINGER LISTEN TO YOU? IF HE HAD...
...THEY'D STILL BE ALIVE!
MAYBE NOT... THERE'S NO WAY OF KNOWING FOR SURE.

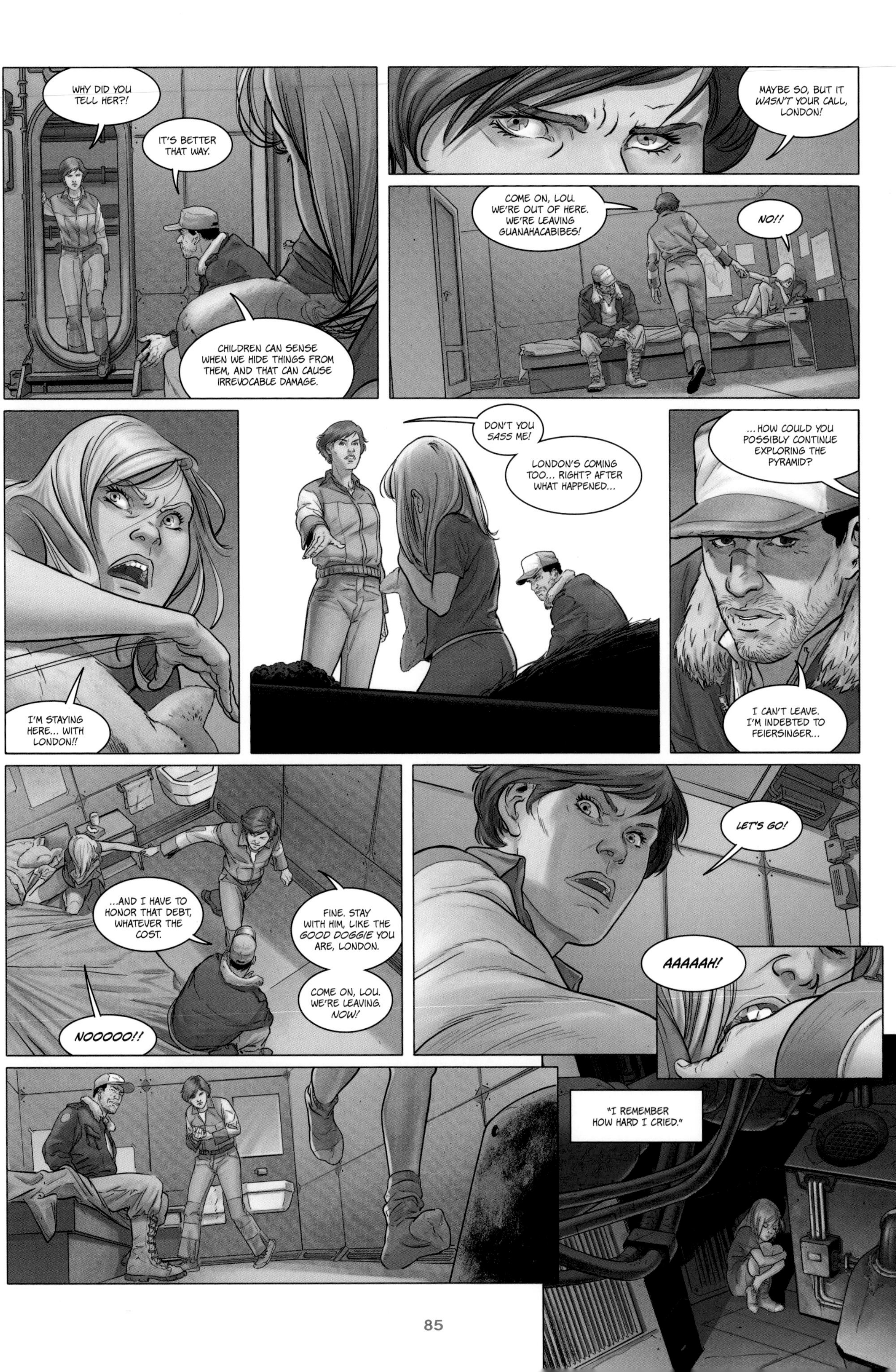

WHY DID YOU TELL HER?!
IT'S BETTER THAT WAY.
CHILDREN CAN SENSE WHEN WE HIDE THINGS FROM THEM, AND THAT CAN CAUSE IRREVOCABLE DAMAGE.
MAYBE SO, BUT IT *WASN'T* YOUR CALL, LONDON!
COME ON, LOU. WE'RE OUT OF HERE. WE'RE LEAVING GUANAHACABIBES!
NO!!
I'M STAYING HERE... WITH LONDON!!
DON'T YOU *SASS* ME!
LONDON'S COMING TOO... RIGHT? AFTER WHAT HAPPENED...
...HOW COULD YOU POSSIBLY CONTINUE EXPLORING THE PYRAMID?
I CAN'T LEAVE. I'M INDEBTED TO FEIERSINGER...
...AND I HAVE TO HONOR THAT DEBT, WHATEVER THE COST.
FINE. STAY WITH HIM, LIKE THE *GOOD DOGGIE* YOU ARE, LONDON.
COME ON, LOU. WE'RE LEAVING. *NOW!*
NOOOOO!!
LET'S GO!
AAAAAH!
"I REMEMBER HOW HARD I CRIED."

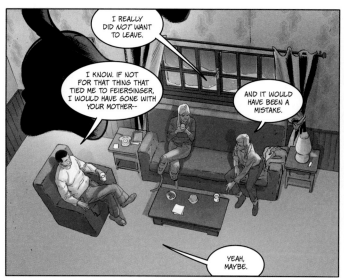

I REALLY DID *NOT* WANT TO LEAVE.

I KNOW. IF NOT FOR THAT THING THAT TIED ME TO FEIERSINGER, I WOULD HAVE GONE WITH YOUR MOTHER--

AND IT WOULD HAVE BEEN A MISTAKE.

YEAH, MAYBE.

IT TOOK YOU GUYS TWO HOURS TO FIND ME. I HAD A GOOD HIDING PLACE.

TRUE. WE SEARCHED THE ENTIRE *LEVIATHAN*, TWICE!

BUT TO GET BACK TO WHAT HAPPENED... THE TRAP, AS CLEVER AS IT WAS, ONLY HAD THE CAPACITY OF WORKING ONCE. THAT WAS THE ONLY ONE THERE WAS.

"WE WERE ABLE TO CONFIRM THAT BY PERSUADING FEIERSINGER TO DO A COMPLETE DYNAMIC LIDAR 3D SCAN THIS TIME AROUND."

IT'S A COMMUNICATING VESSELS PRINCIPLE!

EXACTLY. A CLOSED AND CONFINED ENVIRONMENT IN WHICH DEPRESSURIZATION IS CREATED.

WATER FROM A HUGE WATER RETENTION BASIN FLOWS THROUGH TO THIS ROOM VIA A CROSS-TUNNEL.

THE IMPACT WAS TREMENDOUS.

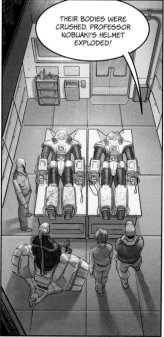

THEIR BODIES WERE CRUSHED. PROFESSOR NOBUAKI'S HELMET EXPLODED!

WITH A TRAP LIKE THAT, THEY DIDN'T STAND A CHANCE.

I WENT BACK INSIDE THE BIG PYRAMID THE VERY NEXT DAY.

"I HAD PASSED THE TRAP, WHICH WAS OPEN AGAIN..."

I'M MAKING MY WAY INTO A LARGER TUNNEL NOW... IT SLOPES GENTLY UPWARD.

BINGO! NO MORE WATER.

IT'S NOT JUST ROCK AND SCULPTURES HERE, AS IT IS INSIDE THE TWO OLDER PYRAMIDS...

WHAT DO YOU MEAN, DONOVAN?

THERE ARE METALLIC PARTS...

SHOW US, WE CAN'T SEE VERY WELL ON THE MONITORS!

LOOK AT THIS BIG DOOR BEFORE ME...

IT'S MADE OF METAL!

OH MY GOD!!

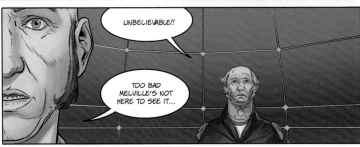

UNBELIEVABLE!!

TOO BAD MELVILLE'S NOT HERE TO SEE IT...

"YES, SHE WOULDN'T BELIEVE HER EYES!"

GO IN, DONOVAN... GO THROUGH THAT DOOR! YOU'RE SO CLOSE...

BEHIND IT IS THE LARGEST OF THE CHAMBERS THAT WE SAW ON THE SCAN.

THE DOOR'S LOCKED!

I SEE TECHNOLOGY ON THE DOOR.... THERE'S SOME SORT OF LEVER.

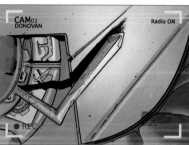

CAM01 DONOVAN   Radio ON

● REC

YOU THINK IT COULD BE A TRAP, DONOVAN?

NO, CHIEF KAZINSKY... I ANALYZED THE STRUCTURE OF THE ROCK AND THE NOTCHED WHEELS...

IT DEFINITELY LOOKS LIKE AN OPENING MECHANISM.

I'M GOING FOR IT!

YES! IT'S OPENING!

I'M ENTERING THE CHAMBER!

CAM01 DONOVAN   Radio ON

● REC

DONOVAN, CHECK YOUR CAMERA!

WE LOST THE FEED!

SO FAR, SO GOOD...

IT'S VERY DARK IN HERE. THE WALLS ARE ALL MADE OF METAL.

MAYBE THAT'S WHY THE VIDEO...GZZZ... FEED ISN'T GETTING THROUGH.

AND THE WALLS ARE... GZZ... THERE'S GZZZ... EVERYWHERE!

IT'S UNBELIEVABLE!!

WHAT?? WHAT IS IT, DONOVAN? WE DON'T COPY!

WHAT DO YOU SEE?

WE LOST RADIO COMM, TOO!

THAT'S STRANGE... THERE WERE INTERFERENCES, BUT IT WAS WORKING UP UNTIL NOW.

UNLESS...

I DELIBERATELY CUT OFF RADIO COMMUNICATION.

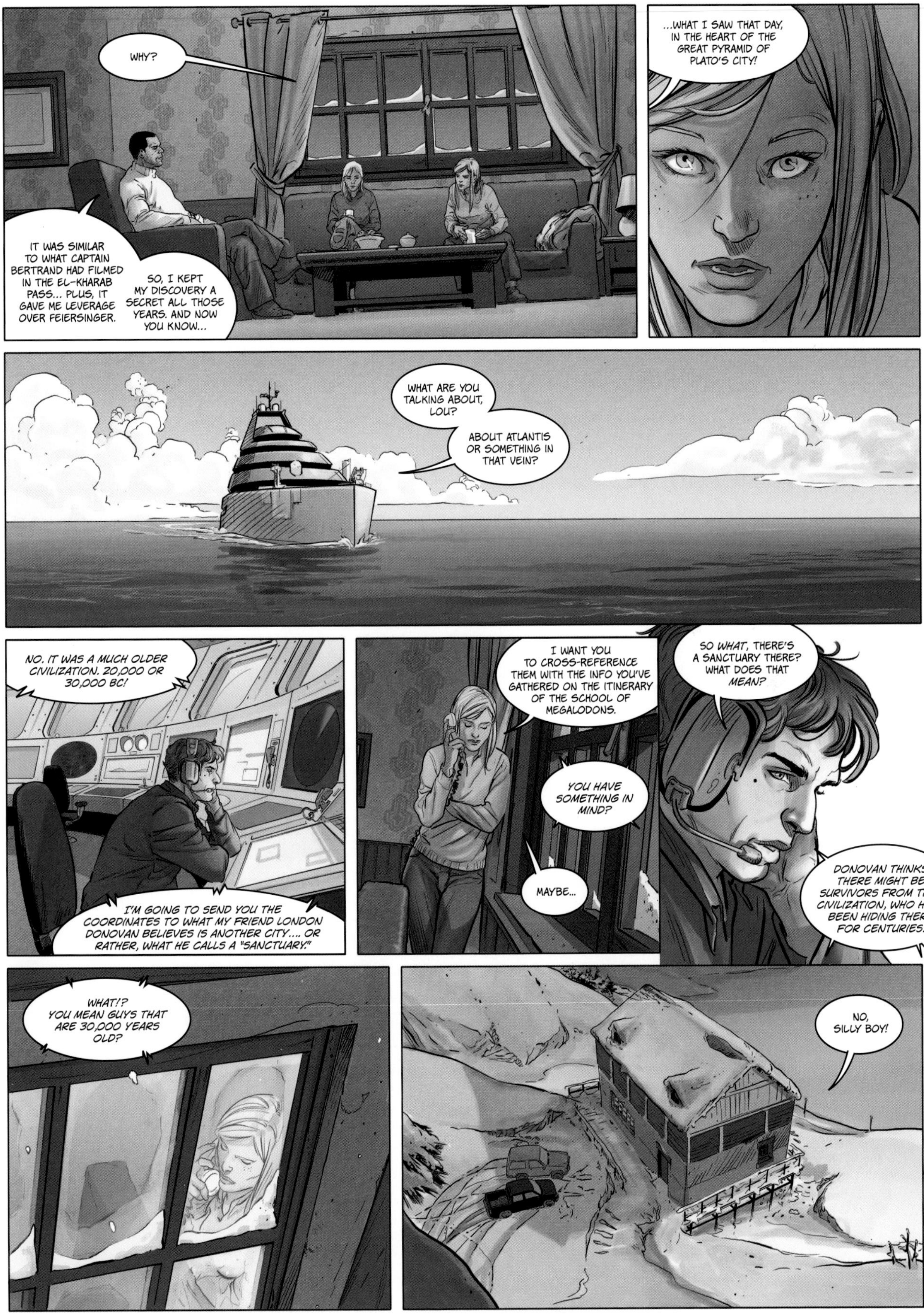
WHY?
IT WAS SIMILAR TO WHAT CAPTAIN BERTRAND HAD FILMED IN THE EL-KHARAB PASS... PLUS, IT GAVE ME LEVERAGE OVER FEIERSINGER.
SO, I KEPT MY DISCOVERY A SECRET ALL THOSE YEARS. AND NOW YOU KNOW...
...WHAT I SAW THAT DAY, IN THE HEART OF THE GREAT PYRAMID OF PLATO'S CITY!
WHAT ARE YOU TALKING ABOUT, LOU?
ABOUT ATLANTIS OR SOMETHING IN THAT VEIN?
NO. IT WAS A MUCH OLDER CIVILIZATION. 20,000 OR 30,000 BC!
I'M GOING TO SEND YOU THE COORDINATES TO WHAT MY FRIEND LONDON DONOVAN BELIEVES IS ANOTHER CITY.... OR RATHER, WHAT HE CALLS A "SANCTUARY."
I WANT YOU TO CROSS-REFERENCE THEM WITH THE INFO YOU'VE GATHERED ON THE ITINERARY OF THE SCHOOL OF MEGALODONS.
YOU HAVE SOMETHING IN MIND?
MAYBE...
SO WHAT, THERE'S A SANCTUARY THERE? WHAT DOES THAT MEAN?
DONOVAN THINKS THERE MIGHT BE SURVIVORS FROM THAT CIVILIZATION, WHO HAVE BEEN HIDING THERE FOR CENTURIES.
WHAT!? YOU MEAN GUYS THAT ARE 30,000 YEARS OLD?
NO, SILLY BOY!

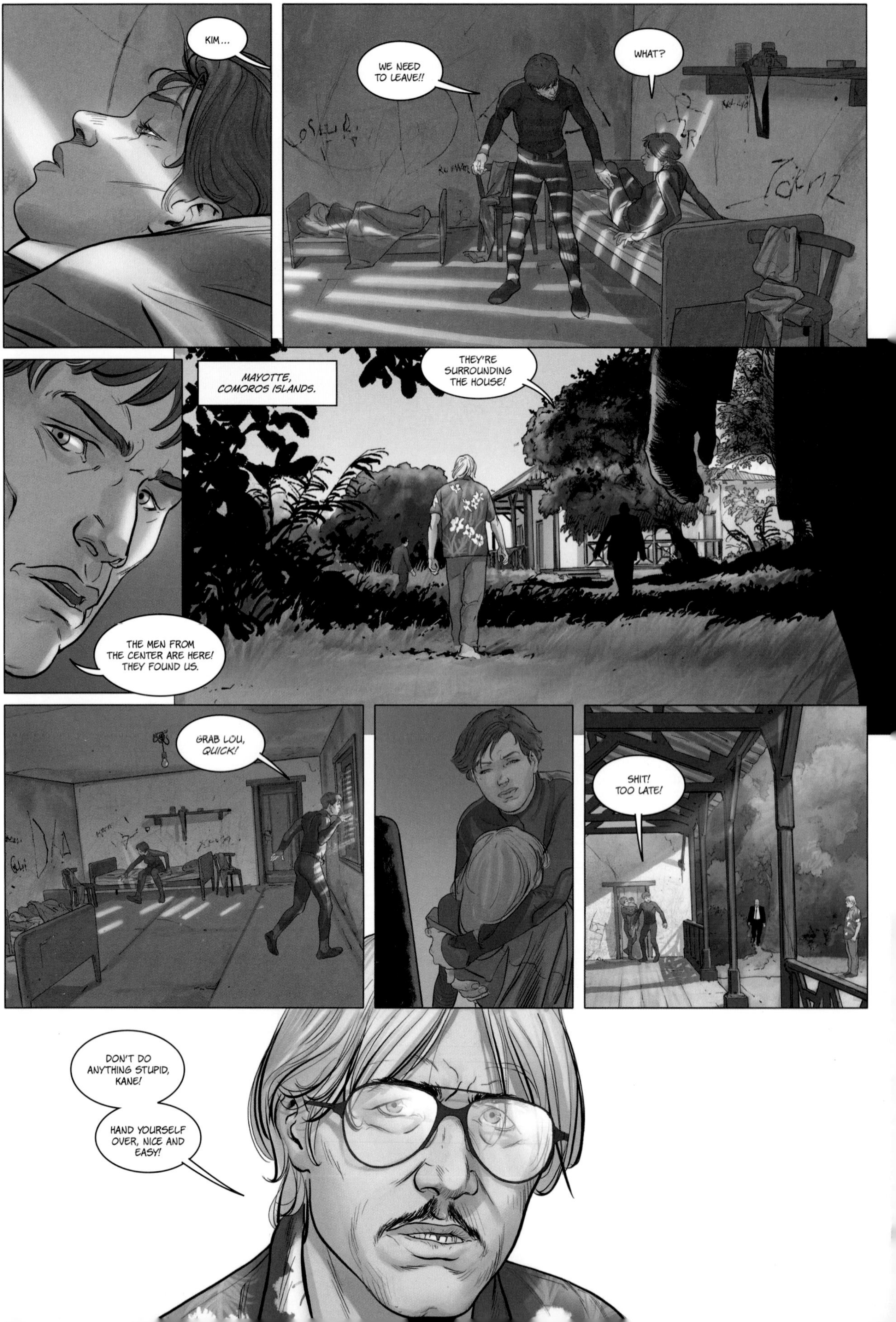
KIM...
WE NEED TO LEAVE!!
WHAT?
MAYOTTE, COMOROS ISLANDS.
THEY'RE SURROUNDING THE HOUSE!
THE MEN FROM THE CENTER ARE HERE! THEY FOUND US.
GRAB LOU, QUICK!
SHIT! TOO LATE!
DON'T DO ANYTHING STUPID, KANE!
HAND YOURSELF OVER, NICE AND EASY!

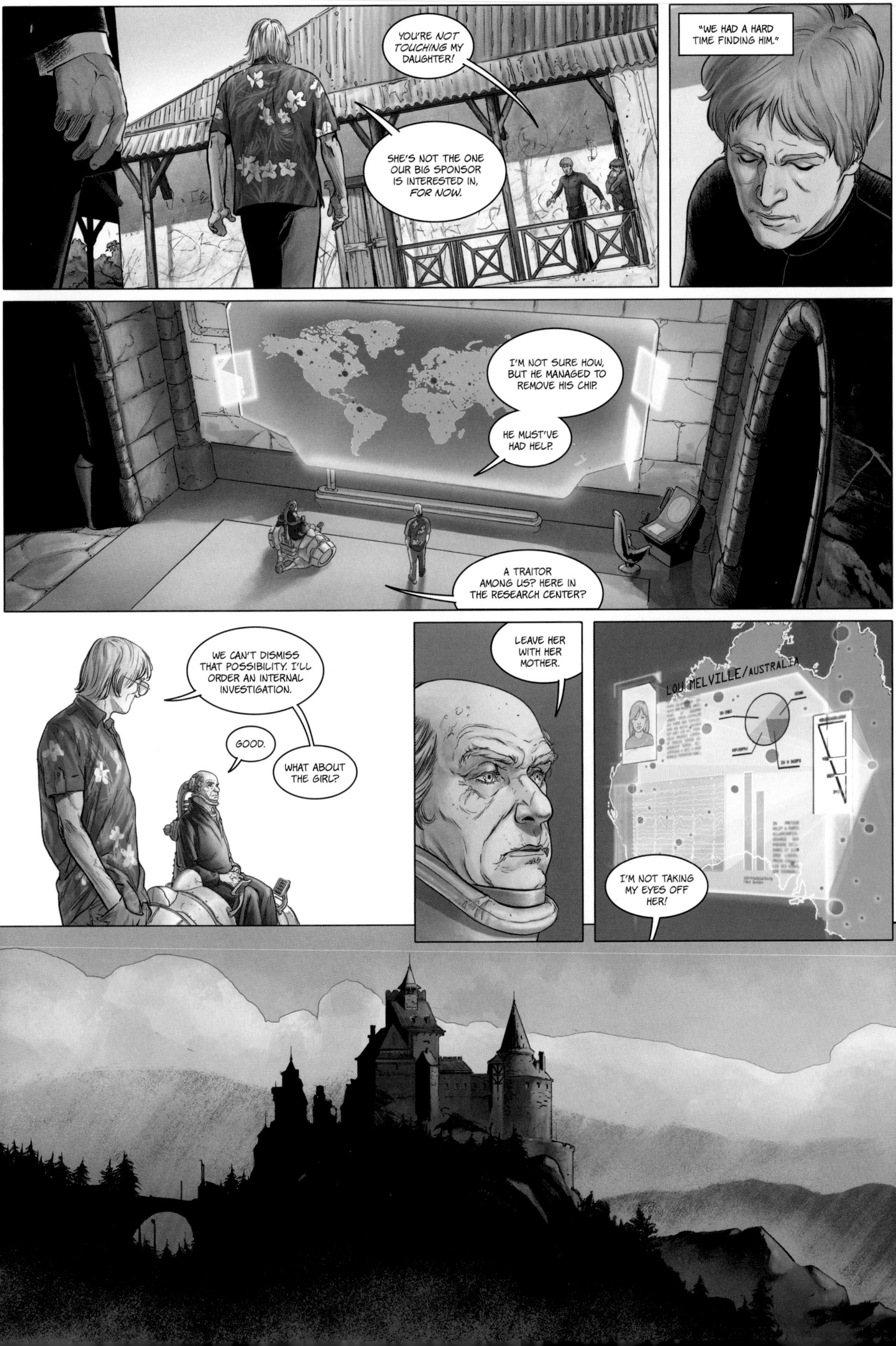
YOU'RE NOT TOUCHING MY DAUGHTER!
SHE'S NOT THE ONE OUR BIG SPONSOR IS INTERESTED IN, FOR NOW.
"WE HAD A HARD TIME FINDING HIM."
I'M NOT SURE HOW, BUT HE MANAGED TO REMOVE HIS CHIP.
HE MUST'VE HAD HELP.
A TRAITOR AMONG US? HERE IN THE RESEARCH CENTER?
WE CAN'T DISMISS THAT POSSIBILITY. I'LL ORDER AN INTERNAL INVESTIGATION.
GOOD.
WHAT ABOUT THE GIRL?
LEAVE HER WITH HER MOTHER.
LOU MELVILLE/AUSTRALIA
I'M NOT TAKING MY EYES OFF HER!

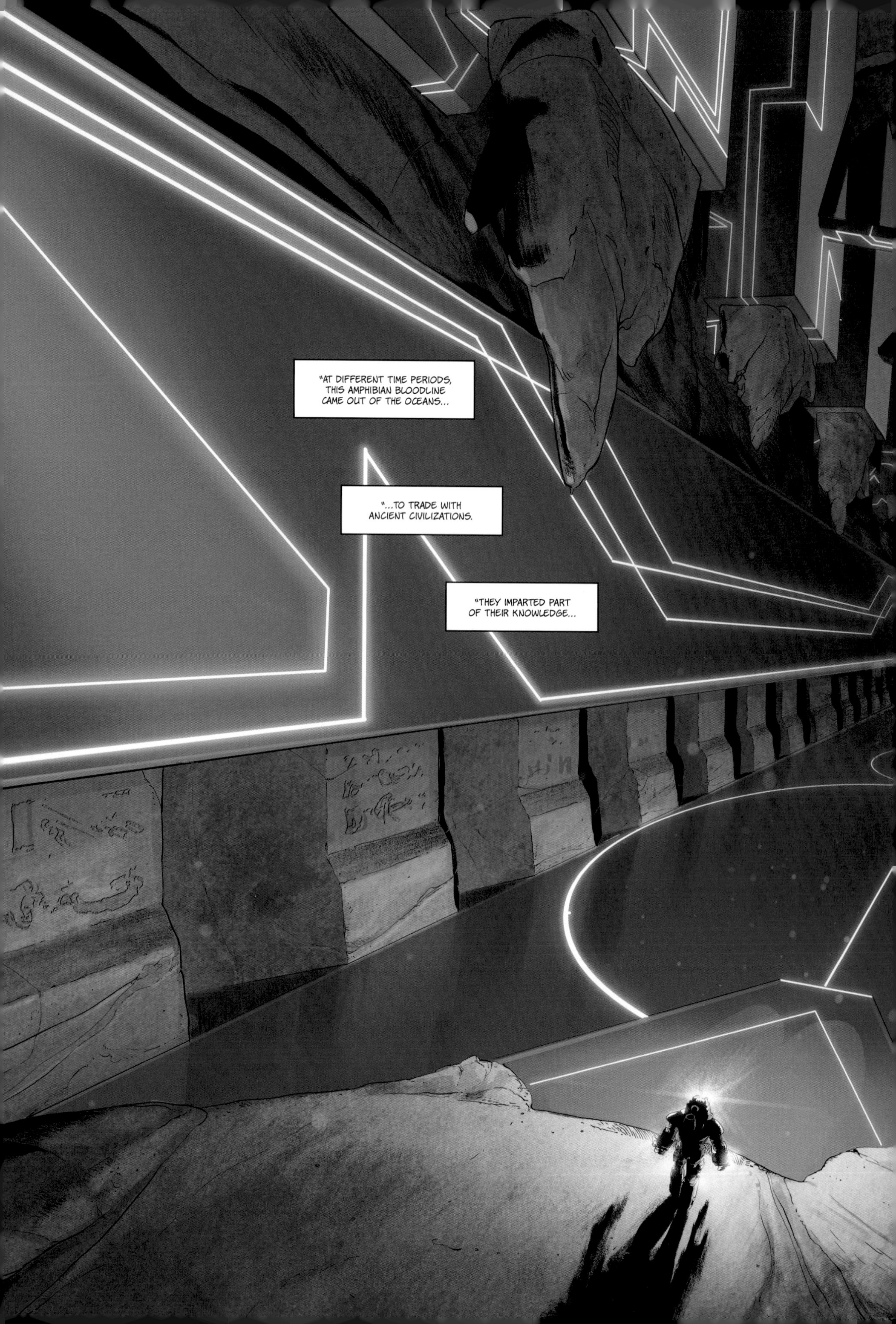
"AT DIFFERENT TIME PERIODS, THIS AMPHIBIAN BLOODLINE CAME OUT OF THE OCEANS...
"...TO TRADE WITH ANCIENT CIVILIZATIONS.
"THEY IMPARTED PART OF THEIR KNOWLEDGE...

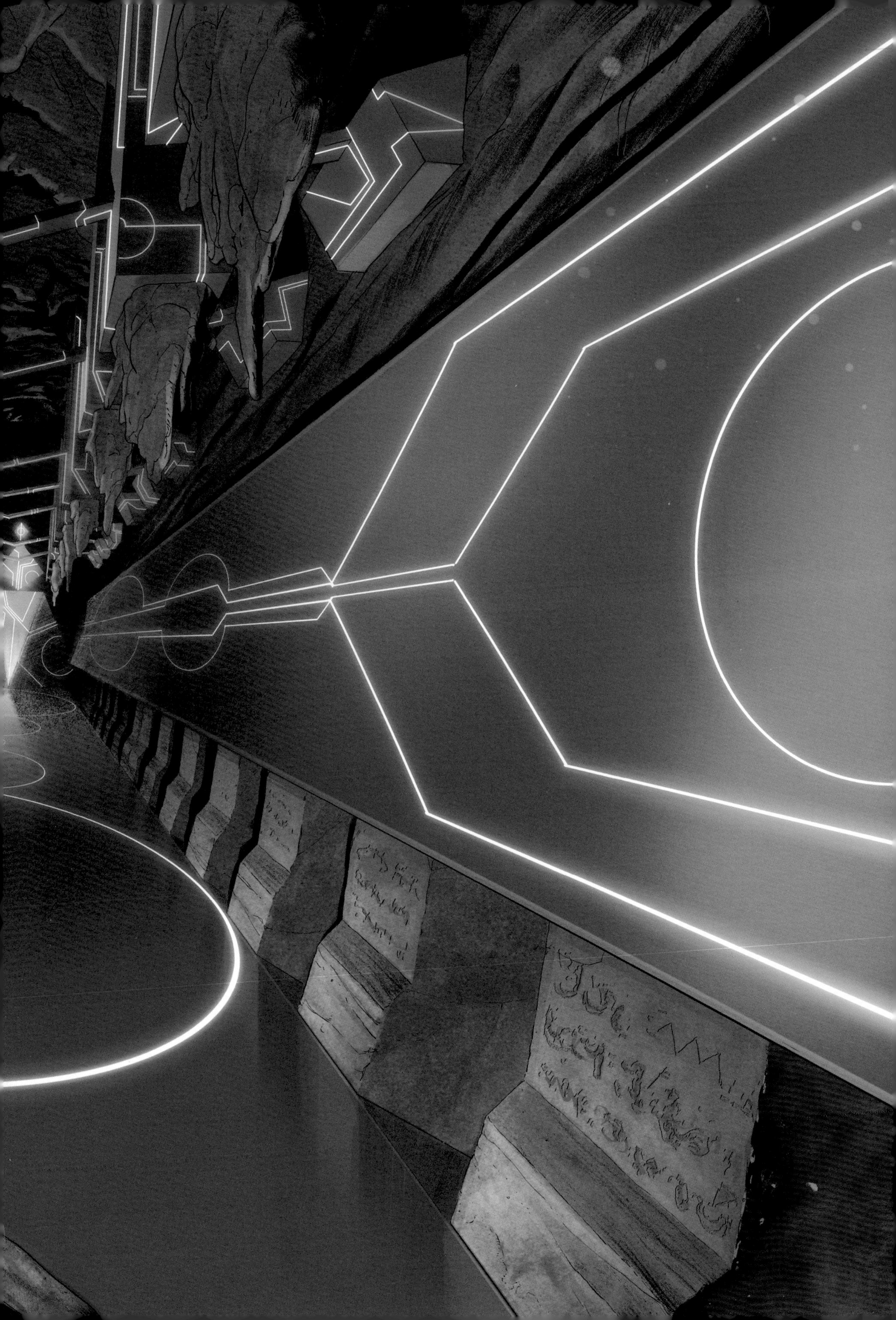

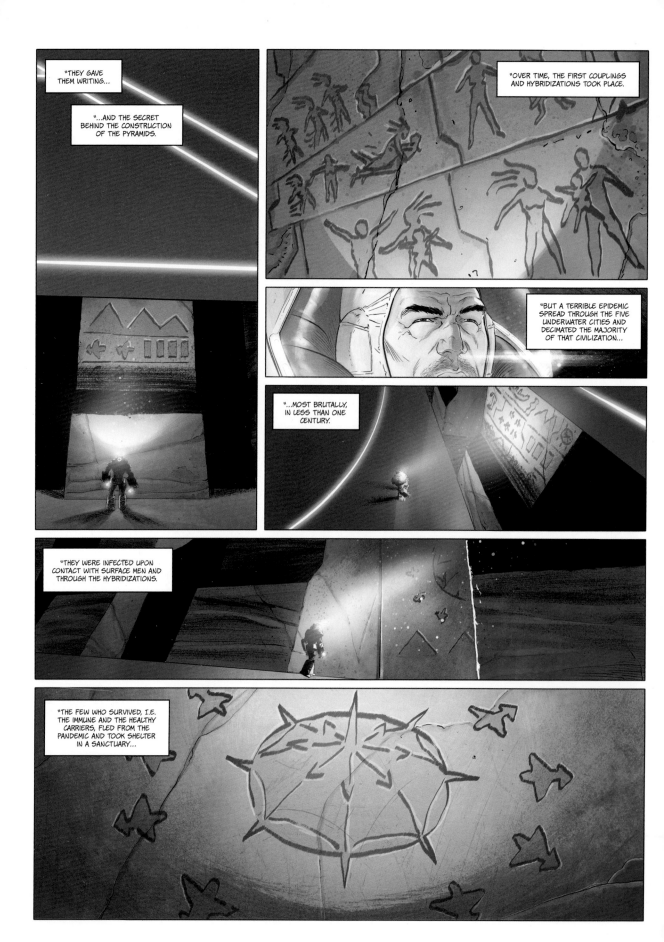

"THEY GAVE THEM WRITING...

"...AND THE SECRET BEHIND THE CONSTRUCTION OF THE PYRAMIDS.

"OVER TIME, THE FIRST COUPLINGS AND HYBRIDIZATIONS TOOK PLACE.

"BUT A TERRIBLE EPIDEMIC SPREAD THROUGH THE FIVE UNDERWATER CITIES AND DECIMATED THE MAJORITY OF THAT CIVILIZATION...

"...MOST BRUTALLY, IN LESS THAN ONE CENTURY.

"THEY WERE INFECTED UPON CONTACT WITH SURFACE MEN AND THROUGH THE HYBRIDIZATIONS.

"THE FEW WHO SURVIVED, I.E. THE IMMUNE AND THE HEALTHY CARRIERS, FLED FROM THE PANDEMIC AND TOOK SHELTER IN A SANCTUARY...

"...WHICH, ACCORDING TO DONOVAN, IS LOCATED SOMEWHERE IN THE BERING SEA."

GIVE ME A BREAK! I'VE NEVER BOUGHT INTO ALL THAT EXOTIC NONSENSE!

I SWEAR, PHILIP, I SAW THE OLD MAN'S COLLECTION WITH MY OWN TWO EYES!

THERE WAS A GIANT STUFFED YETI!... I MEAN, WHO WOULD BELIEVE IT EXISTED!?

THE GUY LOU'S TALKING ABOUT, LONDON DONOVAN, HE'S HUNTED LEGENDARY CREATURES ALL ACROSS THE GLOBE!

SO IT'S "NONSENSE," HUH?

LISTEN, WE'RE TALKING ABOUT UNDERWATER CITIES AND A CIVILIZATION OF FISHMEN, HERE!

IT'S ECCENTRIC HOGWASH!

FINE! I HAVE SOMETHING TO SHOW YOU...

WHAT THE...?

ER, LOU... NOT THAT WE MIND OR ANYTHING, BUT WHY ARE YOU STRIPPING FOR US?

BECAUSE!

LOOK!

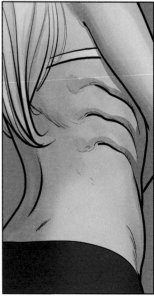

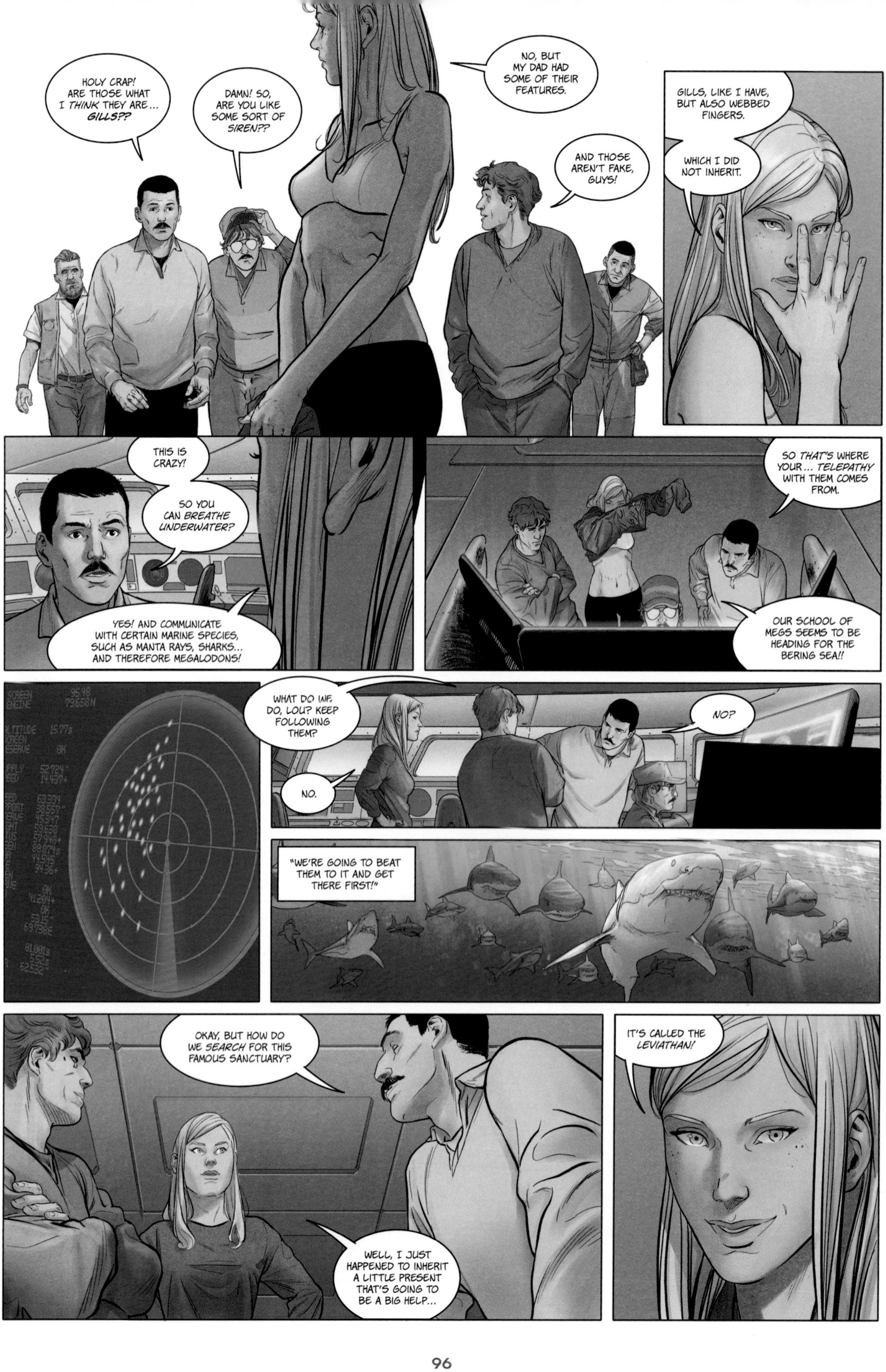
HOLY CRAP! ARE THOSE WHAT I THINK THEY ARE... GILLS??
DAMN! SO, ARE YOU LIKE SOME SORT OF SIREN??
NO, BUT MY DAD HAD SOME OF THEIR FEATURES.
AND THOSE AREN'T FAKE, GUYS!
GILLS, LIKE I HAVE, BUT ALSO WEBBED FINGERS.
WHICH I DID NOT INHERIT.
THIS IS CRAZY!
SO YOU CAN BREATHE UNDERWATER?
YES! AND COMMUNICATE WITH CERTAIN MARINE SPECIES, SUCH AS MANTA RAYS, SHARKS... AND THEREFORE MEGALODONS!
SO THAT'S WHERE YOUR... TELEPATHY WITH THEM COMES FROM.
OUR SCHOOL OF MEGS SEEMS TO BE HEADING FOR THE BERING SEA!!
WHAT DO WE DO, LOU? KEEP FOLLOWING THEM?
NO.
NO?
"WE'RE GOING TO BEAT THEM TO IT AND GET THERE FIRST!"
OKAY, BUT HOW DO WE SEARCH FOR THIS FAMOUS SANCTUARY?
WELL, I JUST HAPPENED TO INHERIT A LITTLE PRESENT THAT'S GOING TO BE A BIG HELP...
IT'S CALLED THE LEVIATHAN!

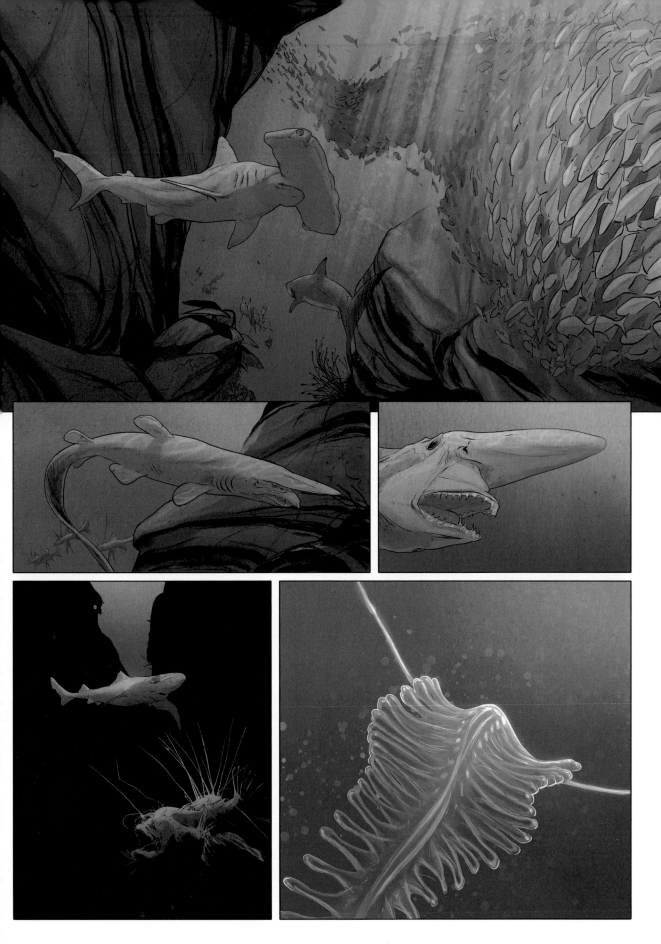

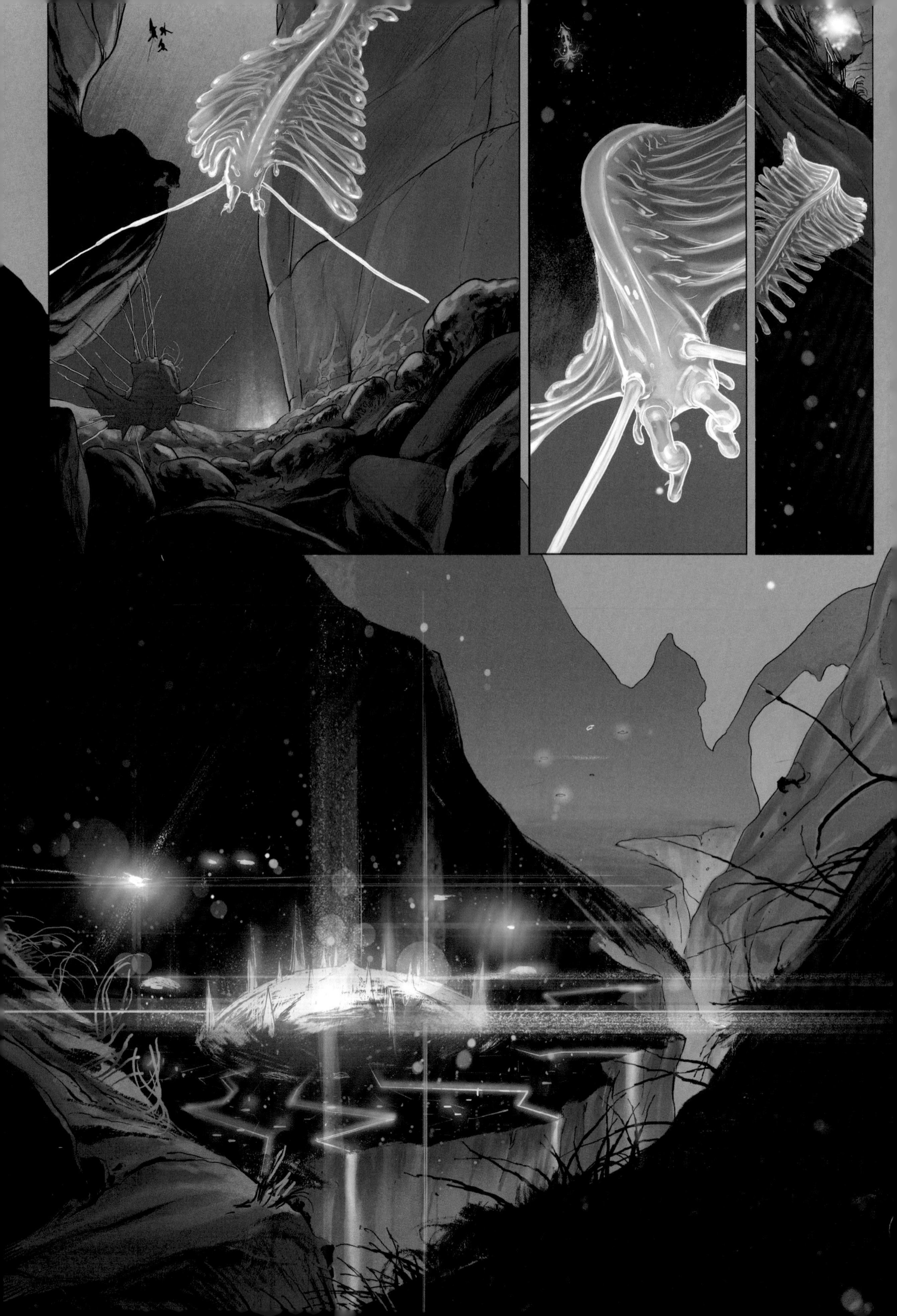

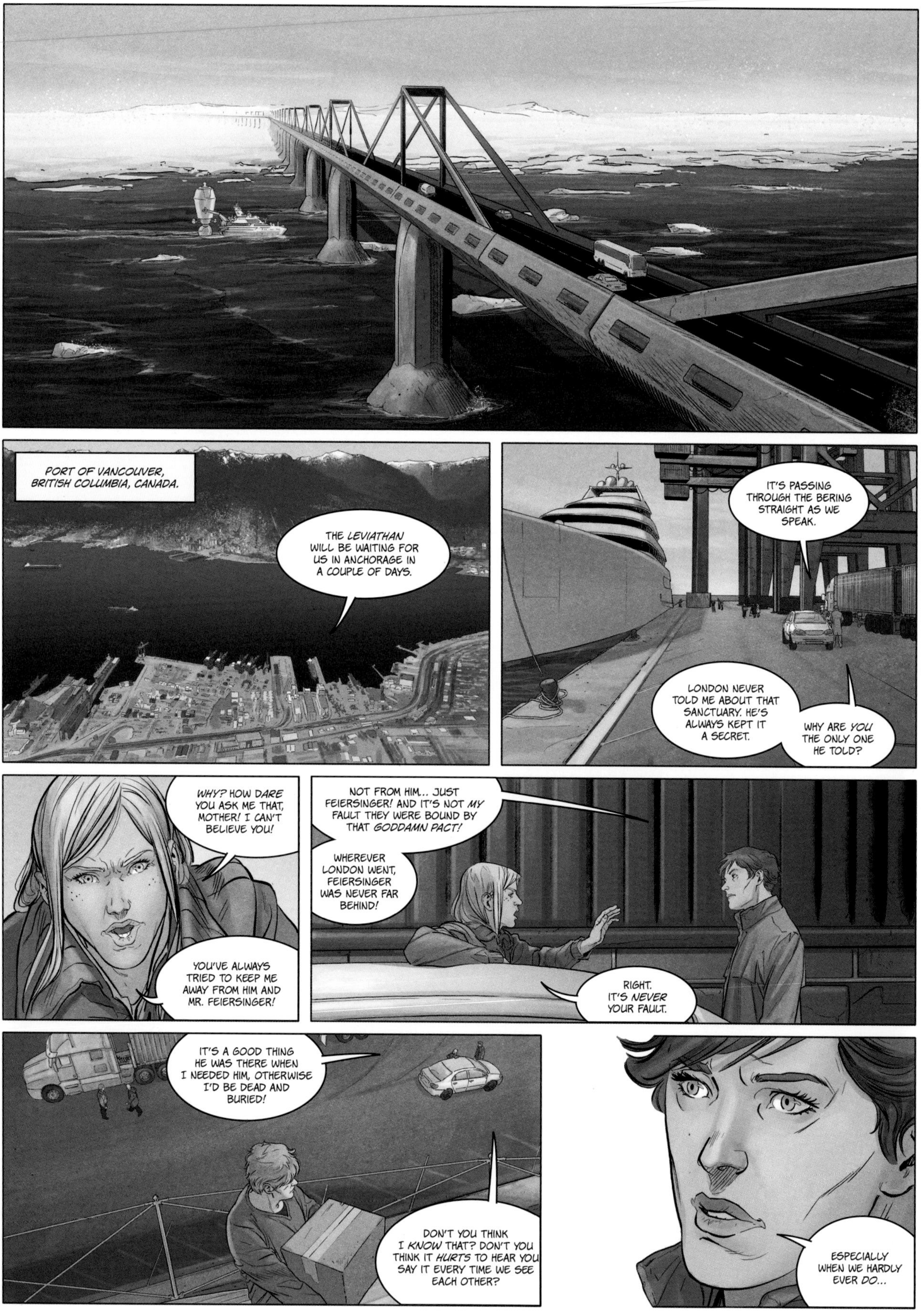

PORT OF VANCOUVER, BRITISH COLUMBIA, CANADA.
THE LEVIATHAN WILL BE WAITING FOR US IN ANCHORAGE IN A COUPLE OF DAYS.
IT'S PASSING THROUGH THE BERING STRAIGHT AS WE SPEAK.
LONDON NEVER TOLD ME ABOUT THAT SANCTUARY. HE'S ALWAYS KEPT IT A SECRET.
WHY ARE YOU THE ONLY ONE HE TOLD?
WHY? HOW DARE YOU ASK ME THAT, MOTHER! I CAN'T BELIEVE YOU!
YOU'VE ALWAYS TRIED TO KEEP ME AWAY FROM HIM AND MR. FEIERSINGER!
NOT FROM HIM... JUST FEIERSINGER! AND IT'S NOT MY FAULT THEY WERE BOUND BY THAT GODDAMN PACT!
WHEREVER LONDON WENT, FEIERSINGER WAS NEVER FAR BEHIND!
RIGHT. IT'S NEVER YOUR FAULT.
IT'S A GOOD THING HE WAS THERE WHEN I NEEDED HIM, OTHERWISE I'D BE DEAD AND BURIED!
DON'T YOU THINK I KNOW THAT? DON'T YOU THINK IT HURTS TO HEAR YOU SAY IT EVERY TIME WE SEE EACH OTHER?
ESPECIALLY WHEN WE HARDLY EVER DO...

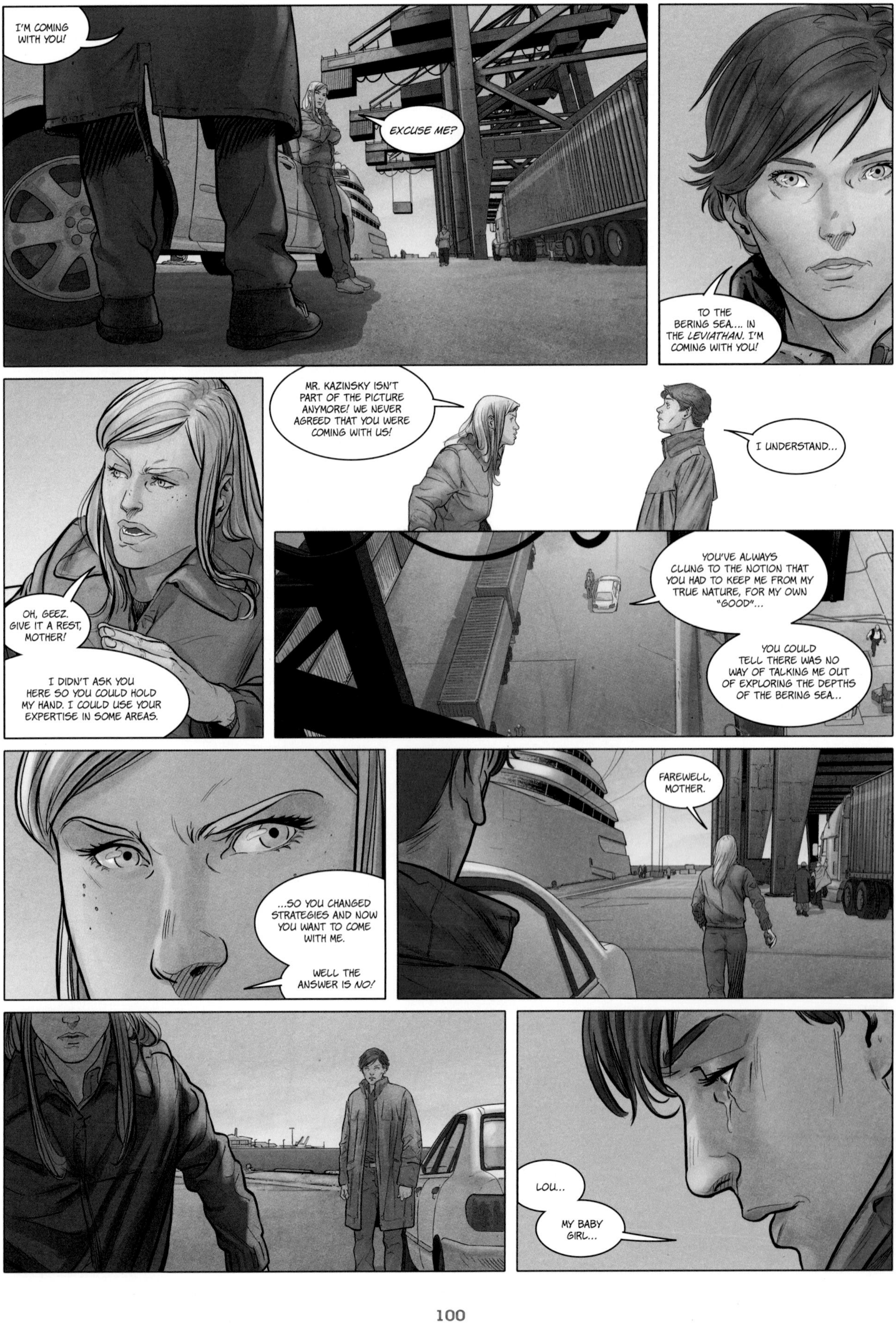
I'M COMING WITH YOU!
EXCUSE ME?
TO THE BERING SEA... IN THE LEVIATHAN. I'M COMING WITH YOU!
MR. KAZINSKY ISN'T PART OF THE PICTURE ANYMORE! WE NEVER AGREED THAT YOU WERE COMING WITH US!
I UNDERSTAND...
OH, GEEZ. GIVE IT A REST, MOTHER!
I DIDN'T ASK YOU HERE SO YOU COULD HOLD MY HAND. I COULD USE YOUR EXPERTISE IN SOME AREAS.
YOU'VE ALWAYS CLUNG TO THE NOTION THAT YOU HAD TO KEEP ME FROM MY TRUE NATURE, FOR MY OWN "GOOD"...
YOU COULD TELL THERE WAS NO WAY OF TALKING ME OUT OF EXPLORING THE DEPTHS OF THE BERING SEA...
...SO YOU CHANGED STRATEGIES AND NOW YOU WANT TO COME WITH ME.
WELL THE ANSWER IS NO!
FAREWELL, MOTHER.
LOU...
MY BABY GIRL...

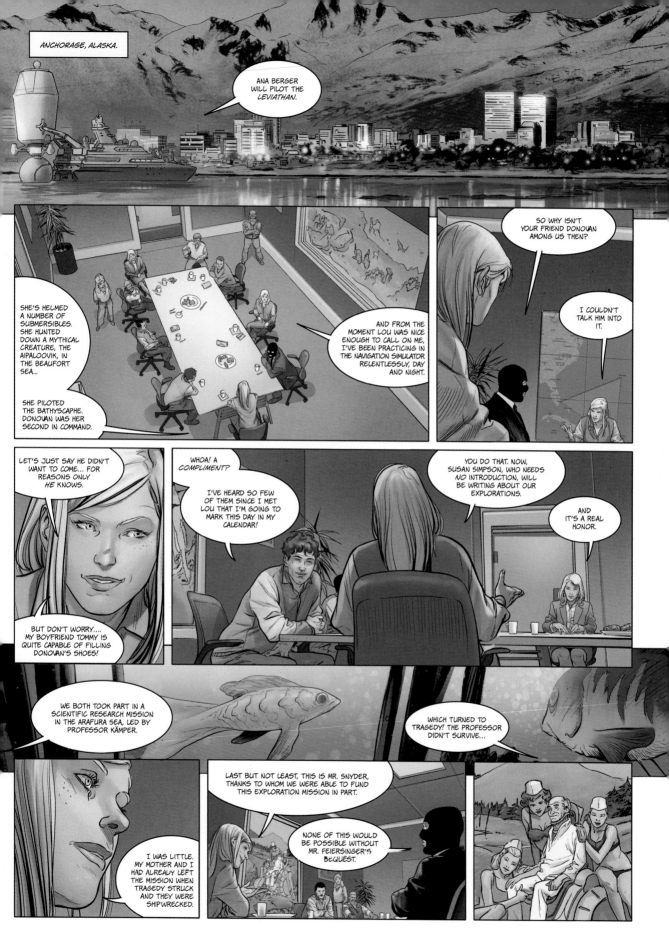

ANCHORAGE, ALASKA.

ANA BERGER WILL PILOT THE LEVIATHAN.

SO WHY ISN'T YOUR FRIEND DONOVAN AMONG US THEN?

I COULDN'T TALK HIM INTO IT.

SHE'S HELMED A NUMBER OF SUBMERSIBLES. SHE HUNTED DOWN A MYTHICAL CREATURE, THE AIPALOOVIK, IN THE BEAUFORT SEA...

SHE PILOTED THE BATHYSCAPHE. DONOVAN WAS HER SECOND IN COMMAND.

AND FROM THE MOMENT LOU WAS NICE ENOUGH TO CALL ON ME, I'VE BEEN PRACTICING IN THE NAVIGATION SIMULATOR RELENTLESSLY, DAY AND NIGHT.

LET'S JUST SAY HE DIDN'T WANT TO COME... FOR REASONS ONLY HE KNOWS.

WHOA! A COMPLIMENT?

I'VE HEARD SO FEW OF THEM SINCE I MET LOU THAT I'M GOING TO MARK THIS DAY IN MY CALENDAR!

YOU DO THAT. NOW, SUSAN SIMPSON, WHO NEEDS NO INTRODUCTION, WILL BE WRITING ABOUT OUR EXPLORATIONS.

AND IT'S A REAL HONOR.

BUT DON'T WORRY.... MY BOYFRIEND TOMMY IS QUITE CAPABLE OF FILLING DONOVAN'S SHOES!

WE BOTH TOOK PART IN A SCIENTIFIC RESEARCH MISSION IN THE ARAFURA SEA, LED BY PROFESSOR KÄMPER.

WHICH TURNED TO TRAGEDY! THE PROFESSOR DIDN'T SURVIVE...

LAST BUT NOT LEAST, THIS IS MR. SNYDER, THANKS TO WHOM WE WERE ABLE TO FUND THIS EXPLORATION MISSION IN PART.

I WAS LITTLE. MY MOTHER AND I HAD ALREADY LEFT THE MISSION WHEN TRAGEDY STRUCK AND THEY WERE SHIPWRECKED.

NONE OF THIS WOULD BE POSSIBLE WITHOUT MR. FEIERSINGER'S BEQUEST.

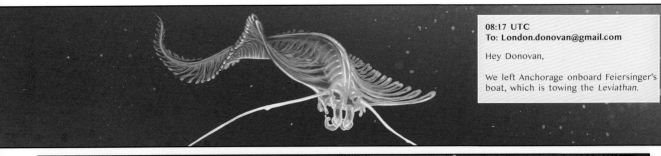

08:17 UTC
To: London.donovan@gmail.com

Hey Donovan,

We left Anchorage onboard Feiersinger's boat, which is towing the *Leviathan*.

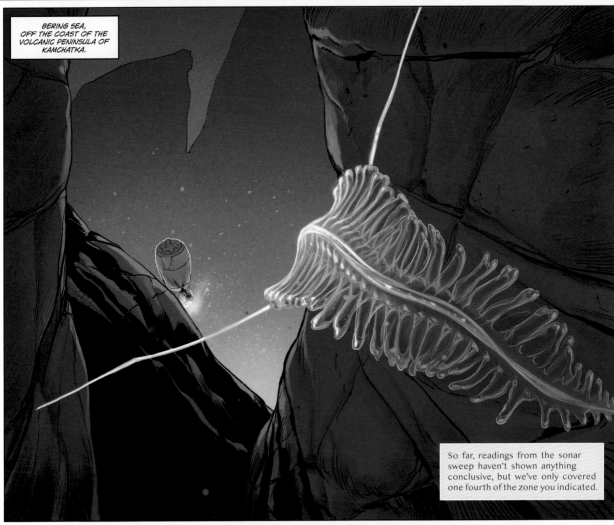

BERING SEA,
OFF THE COAST OF THE
VOLCANIC PENINSULA OF
KAMCHATKA.

So far, readings from the sonar sweep haven't shown anything conclusive, but we've only covered one fourth of the zone you indicated.

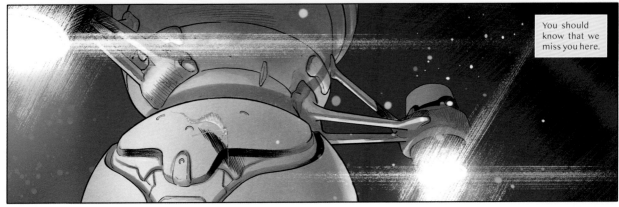

You should know that we miss you here.

I hope it's not too hard being separated from Ana.

I promise I'll return her ASAP!

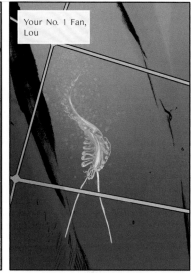

Your No. 1 Fan,
Lou

THERE. AN ANOMALY DISTURBING THE ENVIRONMENT.

IT SHOWS UP VERY CLEARLY ON THE SONAR, AND IT'S VERY DEEP... 4,700 METERS!

AND EXTREMELY LARGE...

IS IT CIRCULAR?

YOU THINK IT COULD BE WHAT WE'RE LOOKING FOR?

YES! WITH A DIAMETER CLOSE TO 500 METERS.

...THERE'S DEFINITELY SOMETHING UNDERNEATH US!

THE SANCTUARY DONOVAN DESCRIBED?

I DON'T KNOW, SUSAN. BUT ONE THING IS CERTAIN...

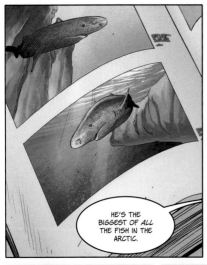

HE'S THE BIGGEST OF ALL THE FISH IN THE ARCTIC.

MOST OF ALL, HE'S THE ONLY SHARK WHO CAN LIVE YEAR-ROUND IN THOSE FREEZING WATERS.

BUT THE GREENLAND SHARK ISN'T POPULAR WITH ZOOLOGISTS.

WE KNOW THEY EAT JUST ABOUT ANYTHING...

...INCLUDING CARCASSES THEY FIND IN THE SEA. BUT WHAT'S REMAINED A MYSTERY ALL THIS TIME IS THEIR LONGEVITY!

THE ADULTS CAN GROW TO MORE THAN FIVE METERS LONG. THEY DEVELOP VERY SLOWLY, BY ONLY ONE CENTIMETER PER YEAR, MAYBE LESS.

SO SCIENTISTS LIKE MYSELF BELIEVE THEY MIGHT BE THE VERTEBRATES WITH THE LONGEST LIFESPAN...

...THEREFORE BEATING ANOTHER MARINE HEAVYWEIGHT, THE BOWHEAD WHALE!

WITH A RECORD AGE OF 211 YEARS!

EXACTLY. VERY GOOD, LOU.

SO AN INTERNATIONAL TEAM OF SCIENTISTS STARTED TAKING A CLOSER LOOK.

THEY STUDIED AND ANALYZED THE CARBON-14 CONTENT IN THE CRYSTALLINE LENS OF TWENTY GREENLAND SHARKS...

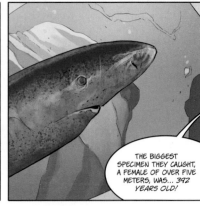

THE BIGGEST SPECIMEN THEY CAUGHT, A FEMALE OF OVER FIVE METERS, WAS... 392 YEARS OLD!

WHICH MEANS SHE WAS BORN WHILE LOUIS XIII WAS KING!

AUSTRALIA HADN'T EVEN BEEN DISCOVERED YET!

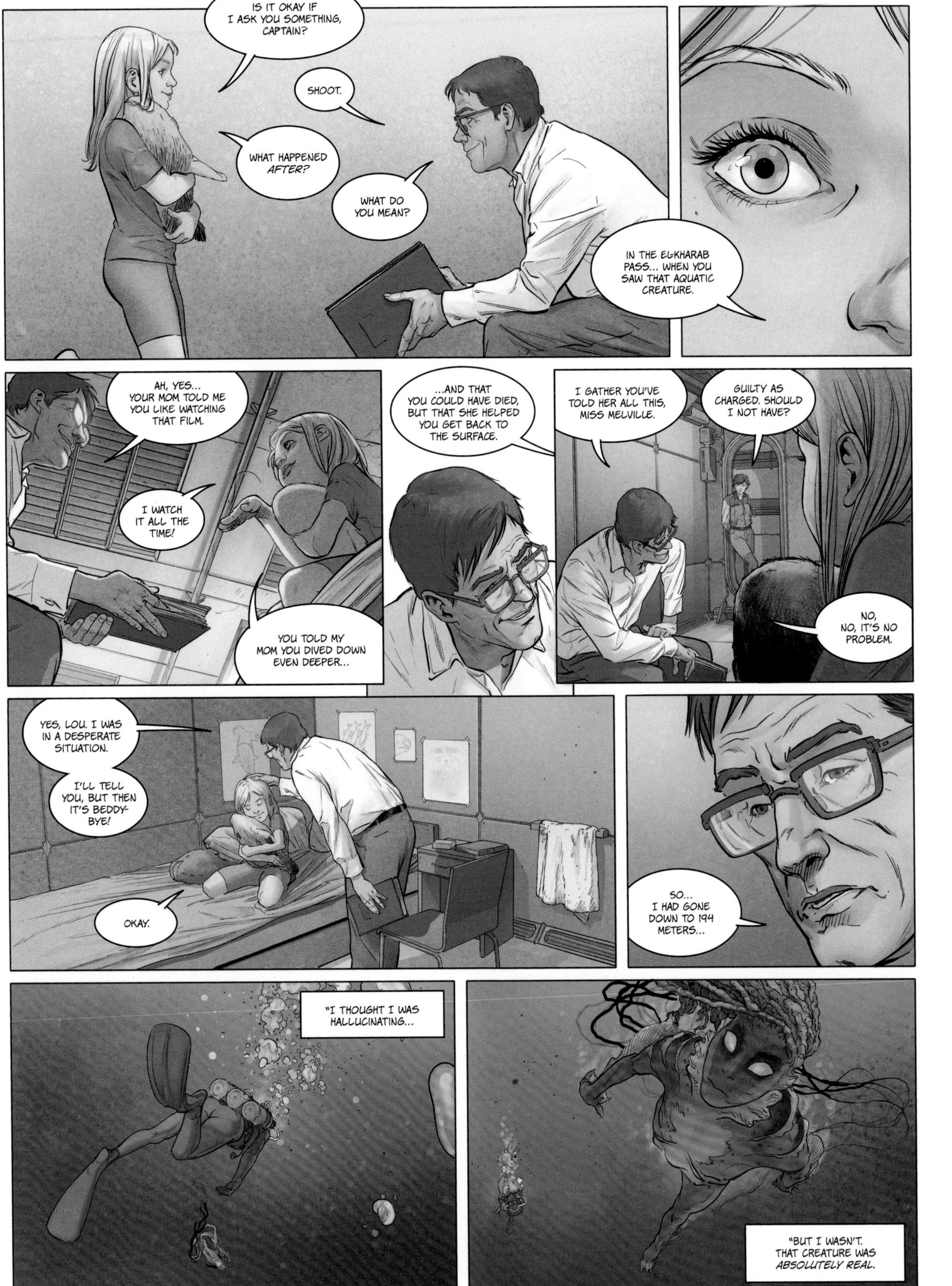

IS IT OKAY IF I ASK YOU SOMETHING, CAPTAIN?
SHOOT.
WHAT HAPPENED *AFTER?*
WHAT DO YOU MEAN?
IN THE EL-KHARAB PASS... WHEN YOU SAW THAT AQUATIC CREATURE.
AH, YES... YOUR MOM TOLD ME YOU LIKE WATCHING THAT FILM.
I WATCH IT ALL THE TIME!
YOU TOLD MY MOM YOU DIVED DOWN EVEN DEEPER...
...AND THAT YOU COULD HAVE DIED, BUT THAT SHE HELPED YOU GET BACK TO THE SURFACE.
I GATHER YOU'VE TOLD HER ALL THIS, MISS MELVILLE.
GUILTY AS CHARGED. SHOULD I NOT HAVE?
NO, NO, IT'S NO PROBLEM.
YES, LOU. I WAS IN A DESPERATE SITUATION.
I'LL TELL YOU, BUT THEN IT'S BEDDY-BYE!
OKAY.
SO... I HAD GONE DOWN TO 194 METERS...
"I THOUGHT I WAS HALLUCINATING...
"BUT I WASN'T. THAT CREATURE WAS *ABSOLUTELY REAL.*

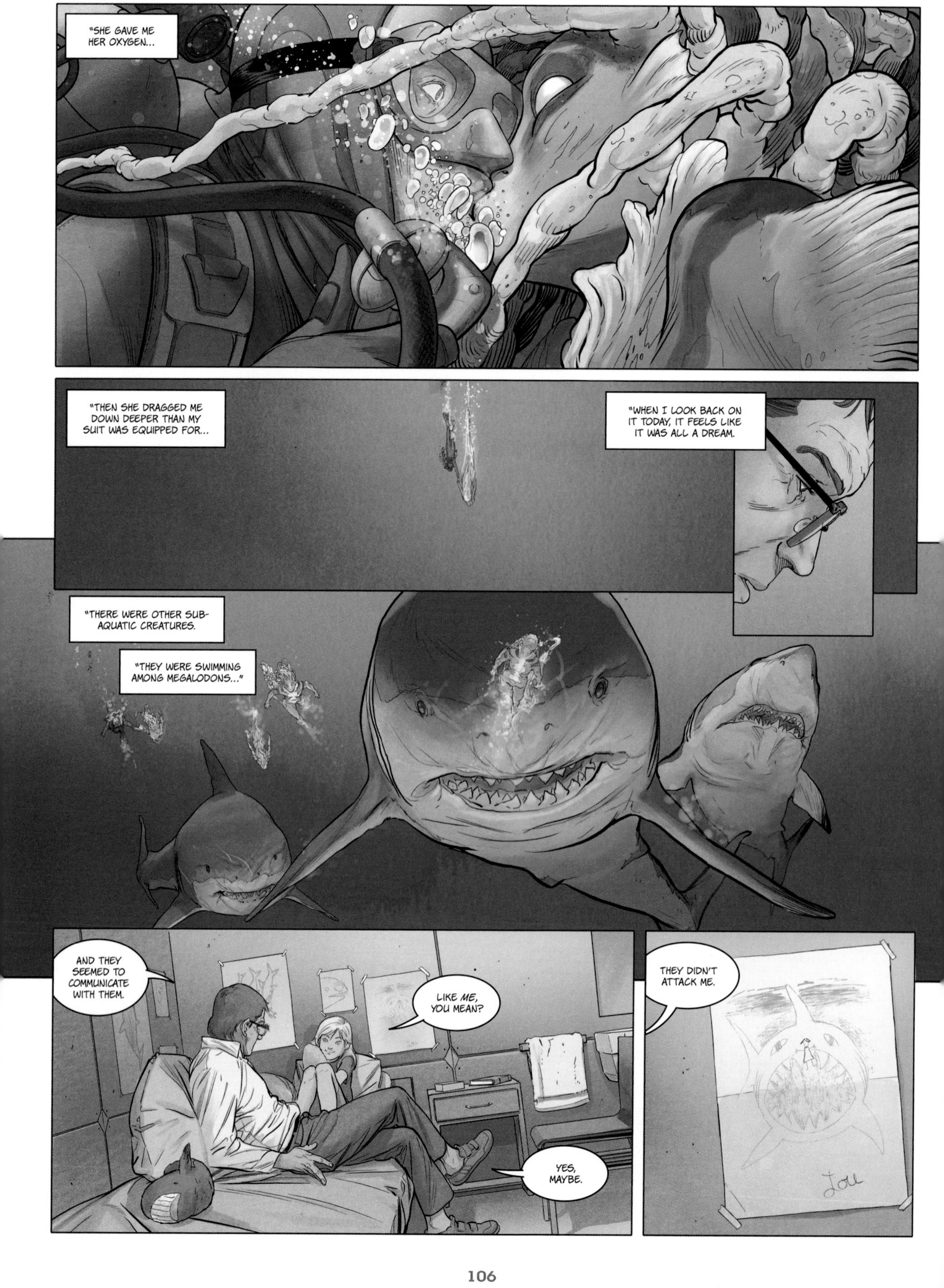
"SHE GAVE ME HER OXYGEN...
"THEN SHE DRAGGED ME DOWN DEEPER THAN MY SUIT WAS EQUIPPED FOR...
"WHEN I LOOK BACK ON IT TODAY, IT FEELS LIKE IT WAS ALL A DREAM.
"THERE WERE OTHER SUB-AQUATIC CREATURES.
"THEY WERE SWIMMING AMONG MEGALODONS...
AND THEY SEEMED TO COMMUNICATE WITH THEM.
LIKE *ME*, YOU MEAN?
YES, MAYBE.
THEY DIDN'T ATTACK ME.
Lou

"THERE WERE THE FOUR MONOLITHS THERE...

"AND A STRANGE VOICE ECHOING IN MY HEAD.

"SORT OF LIKE TELEPATHY, KNOW WHAT I MEAN?

"THIS VOICE SPOKE OF ANOTHER PLACE..."

NOT A CITY. IT WAS SOMETHING ELSE.

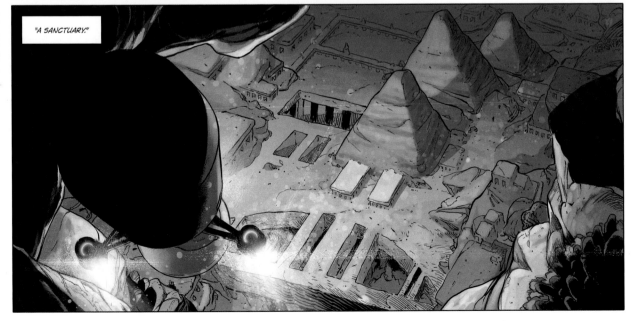

"A SANCTUARY."

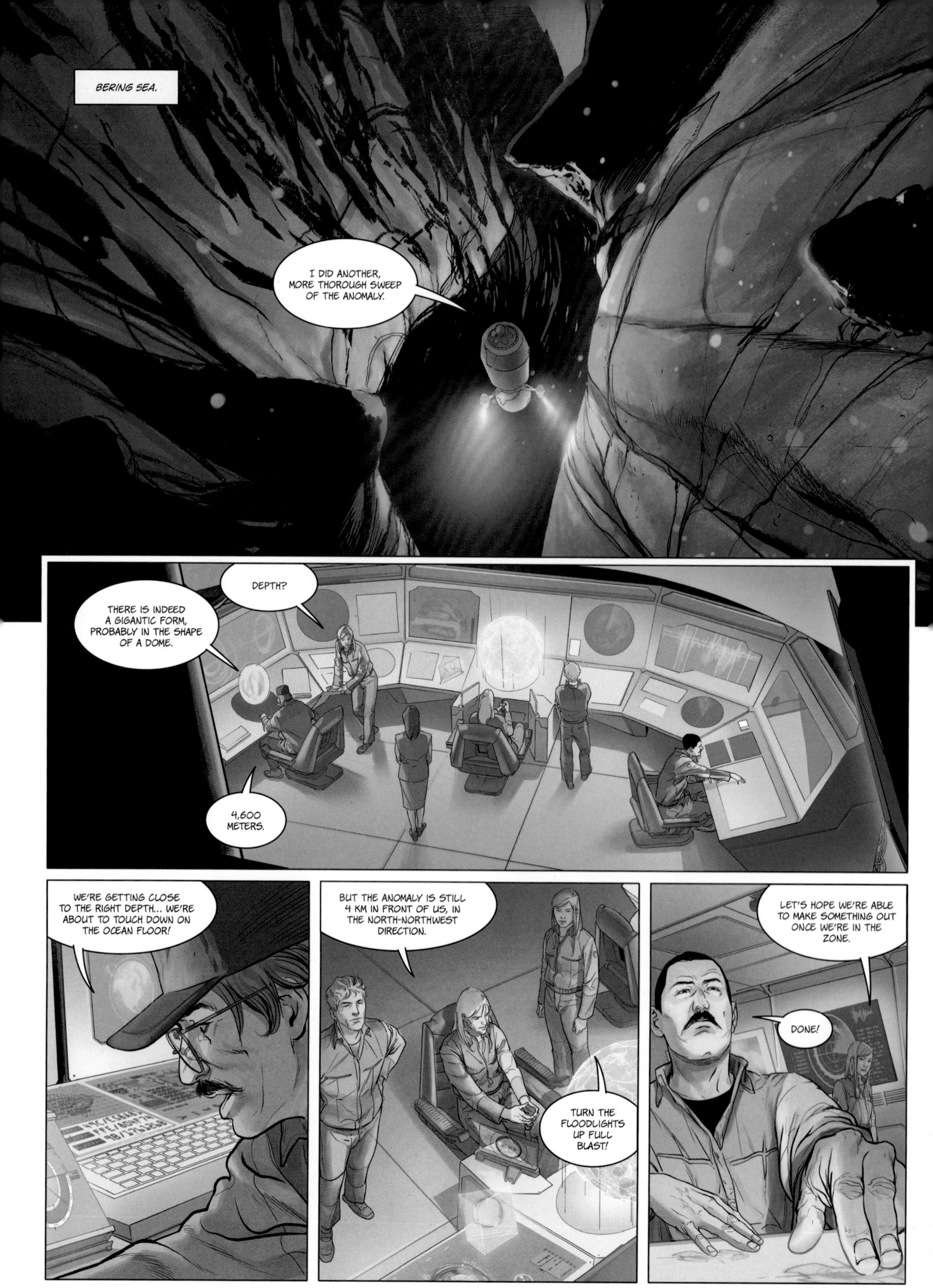
BERING SEA.
I DID ANOTHER, MORE THOROUGH SWEEP OF THE ANOMALY.
THERE IS INDEED A GIGANTIC FORM, PROBABLY IN THE SHAPE OF A DOME.
DEPTH?
4,600 METERS.
WE'RE GETTING CLOSE TO THE RIGHT DEPTH... WE'RE ABOUT TO TOUCH DOWN ON THE OCEAN FLOOR!
BUT THE ANOMALY IS STILL 4 KM IN FRONT OF US, IN THE NORTH-NORTHWEST DIRECTION.
TURN THE FLOODLIGHTS UP FULL BLAST!
LET'S HOPE WE'RE ABLE TO MAKE SOMETHING OUT ONCE WE'RE IN THE ZONE.
DONE!

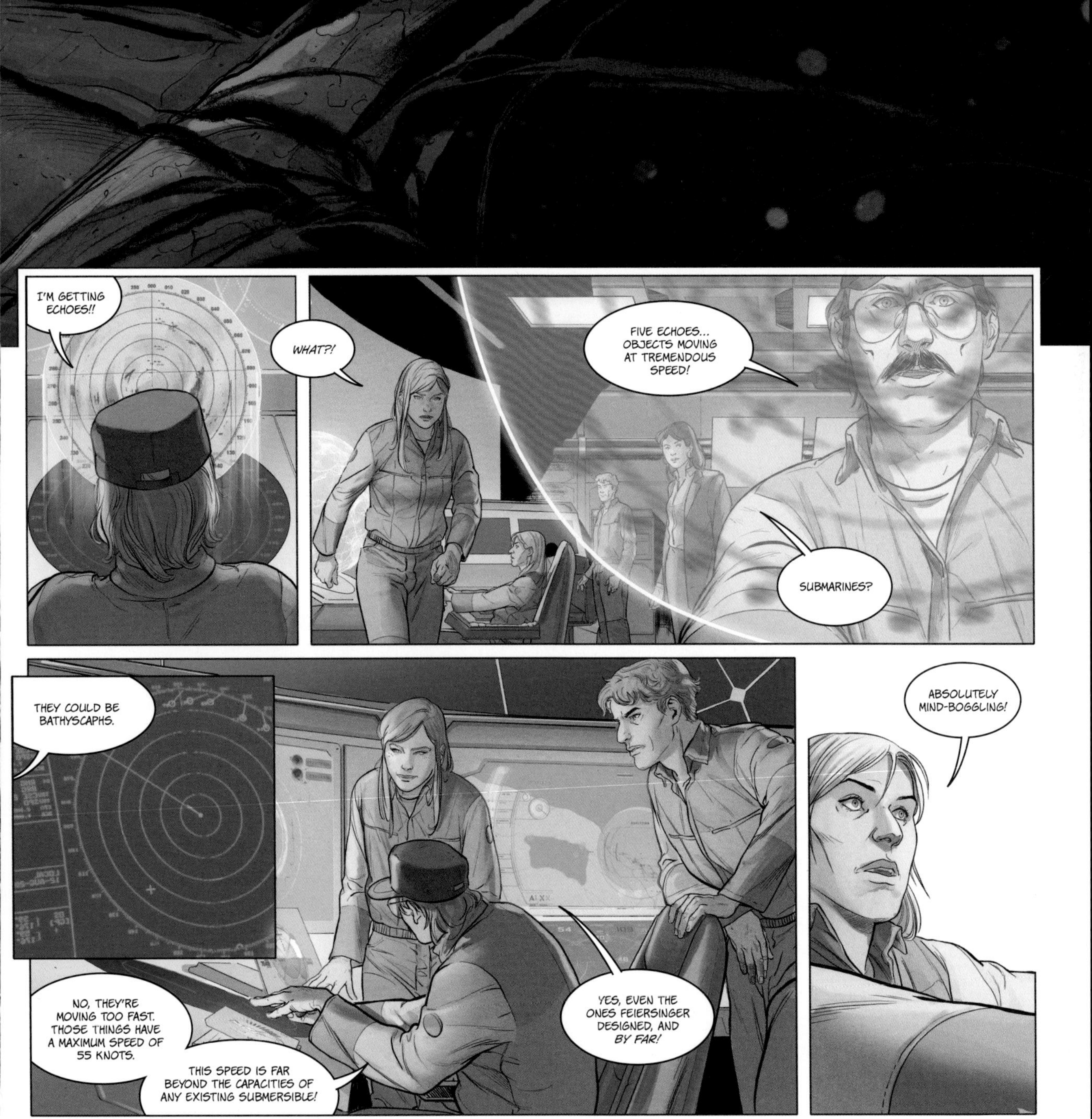
I'M GETTING ECHOES!!
WHAT?!
FIVE ECHOES... OBJECTS MOVING AT TREMENDOUS SPEED!
SUBMARINES?
THEY COULD BE BATHYSCAPHS.
NO, THEY'RE MOVING TOO FAST. THOSE THINGS HAVE A MAXIMUM SPEED OF 55 KNOTS.
THIS SPEED IS FAR BEYOND THE CAPACITIES OF ANY EXISTING SUBMERSIBLE!
YES, EVEN THE ONES FEIERSINGER DESIGNED, AND *BY FAR!*
ABSOLUTELY MIND-BOGGLING!

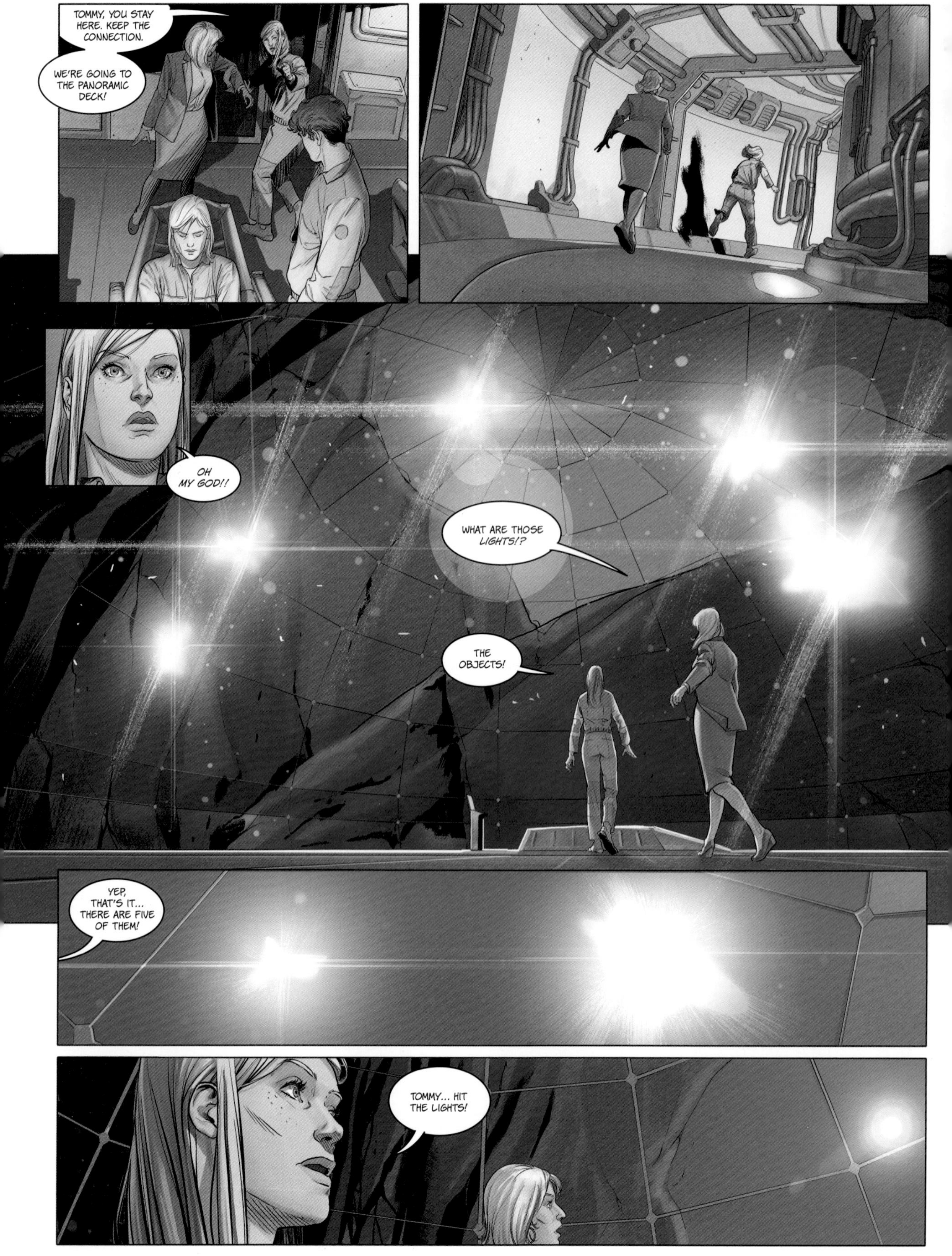
TOMMY, YOU STAY HERE. KEEP THE CONNECTION.
WE'RE GOING TO THE PANORAMIC DECK!
OH MY GOD!!
WHAT ARE THOSE LIGHTS!?
THE OBJECTS!
YEP, THAT'S IT... THERE ARE FIVE OF THEM!
TOMMY... HIT THE LIGHTS!

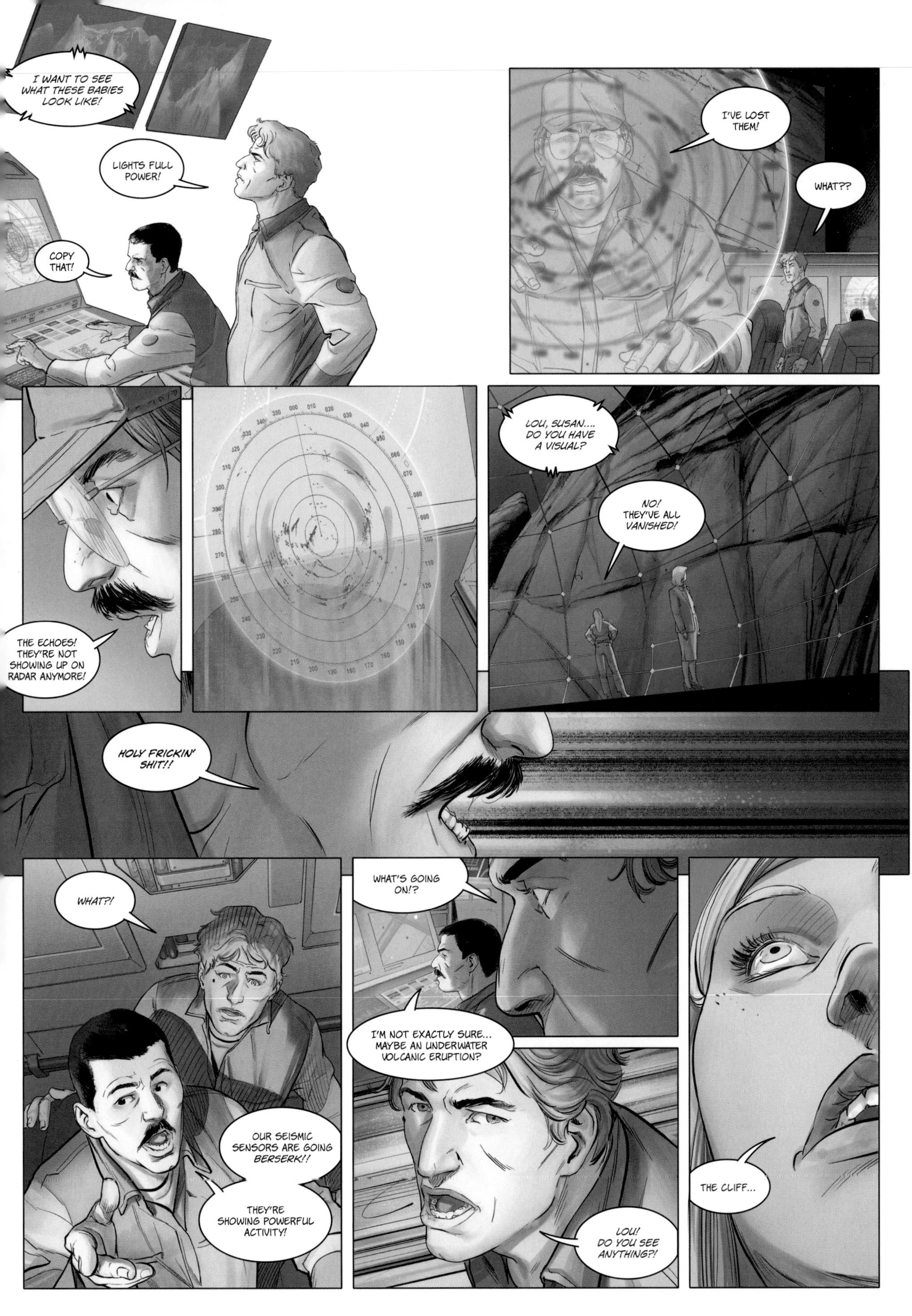
I WANT TO SEE WHAT THESE BABIES LOOK LIKE!
LIGHTS FULL POWER!
COPY THAT!
I'VE LOST THEM!
WHAT??
THE ECHOES! THEY'RE NOT SHOWING UP ON RADAR ANYMORE!
LOU, SUSAN.... DO YOU HAVE A VISUAL?
NO! THEY'VE ALL VANISHED!
HOLY FRICKIN' SHIT!!
WHAT?!
OUR SEISMIC SENSORS ARE GOING BERSERK!!
THEY'RE SHOWING POWERFUL ACTIVITY!
WHAT'S GOING ON!?
I'M NOT EXACTLY SURE... MAYBE AN UNDERWATER VOLCANIC ERUPTION?
LOU! DO YOU SEE ANYTHING?!
THE CLIFF...

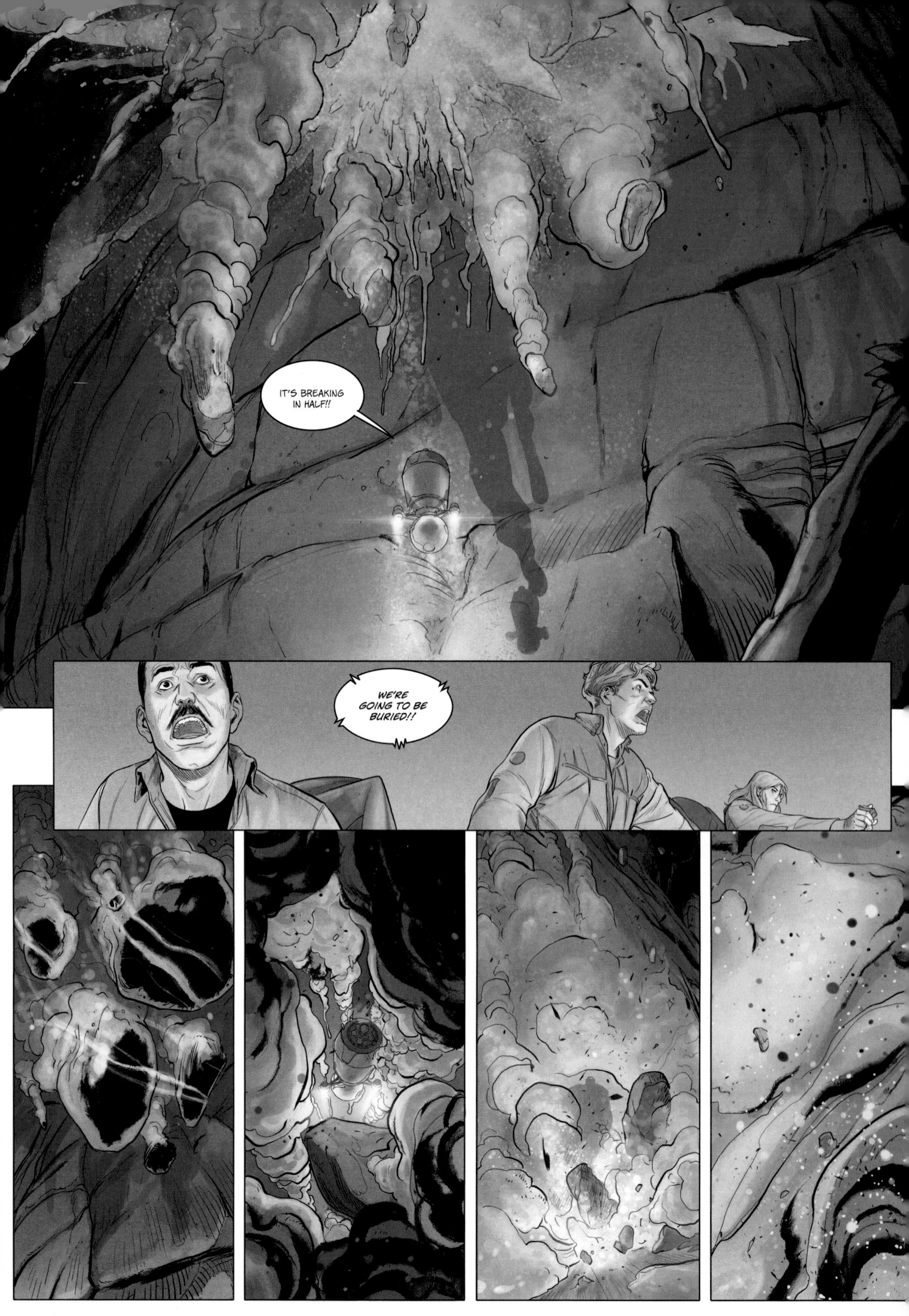
IT'S BREAKING IN HALF!!
WE'RE GOING TO BE BURIED!!

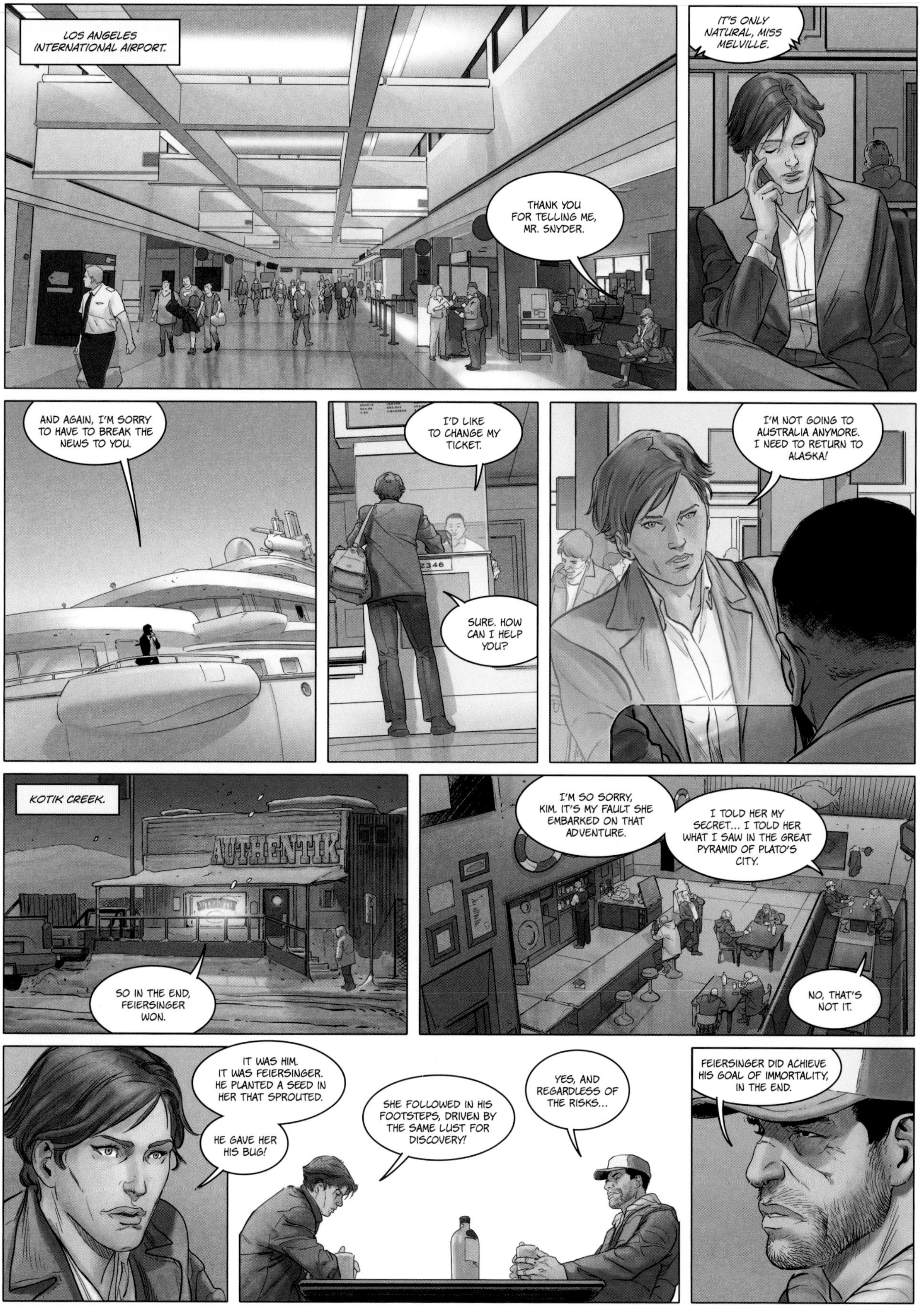
LOS ANGELES INTERNATIONAL AIRPORT.
THANK YOU FOR TELLING ME, MR. SNYDER.
IT'S ONLY NATURAL, MISS MELVILLE.
AND AGAIN, I'M SORRY TO HAVE TO BREAK THE NEWS TO YOU.
I'D LIKE TO CHANGE MY TICKET.
SURE. HOW CAN I HELP YOU?
I'M NOT GOING TO AUSTRALIA ANYMORE. I NEED TO RETURN TO ALASKA!
KOTIK CREEK.
AUTHENTIK
SO IN THE END, FEIERSINGER WON.
I'M SO SORRY, KIM. IT'S MY FAULT SHE EMBARKED ON THAT ADVENTURE.
I TOLD HER MY SECRET... I TOLD HER WHAT I SAW IN THE GREAT PYRAMID OF PLATO'S CITY.
NO, THAT'S NOT IT.
IT WAS HIM. IT WAS FEIERSINGER. HE PLANTED A SEED IN HER THAT SPROUTED.
HE GAVE HER HIS BUG!
SHE FOLLOWED IN HIS FOOTSTEPS, DRIVEN BY THE SAME LUST FOR DISCOVERY!
YES, AND REGARDLESS OF THE RISKS...
FEIERSINGER DID ACHIEVE HIS GOAL OF IMMORTALITY, IN THE END.

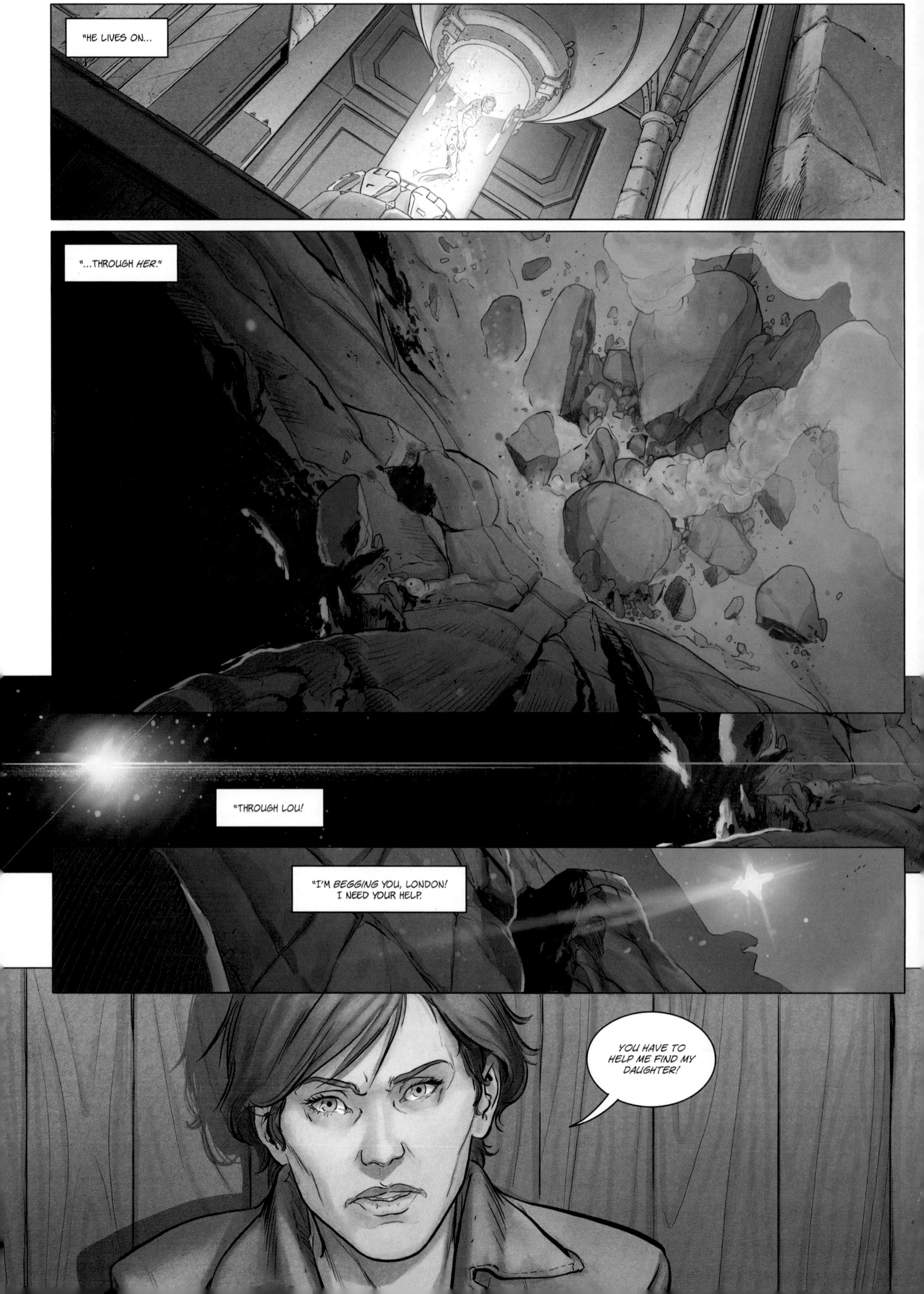
"HE LIVES ON...
"...THROUGH *HER*."
"THROUGH LOU!
"I'M *BEGGING* YOU, LONDON! I NEED YOUR HELP.
YOU HAVE TO HELP ME FIND MY DAUGHTER!

Book 8:
LEVIATHAN

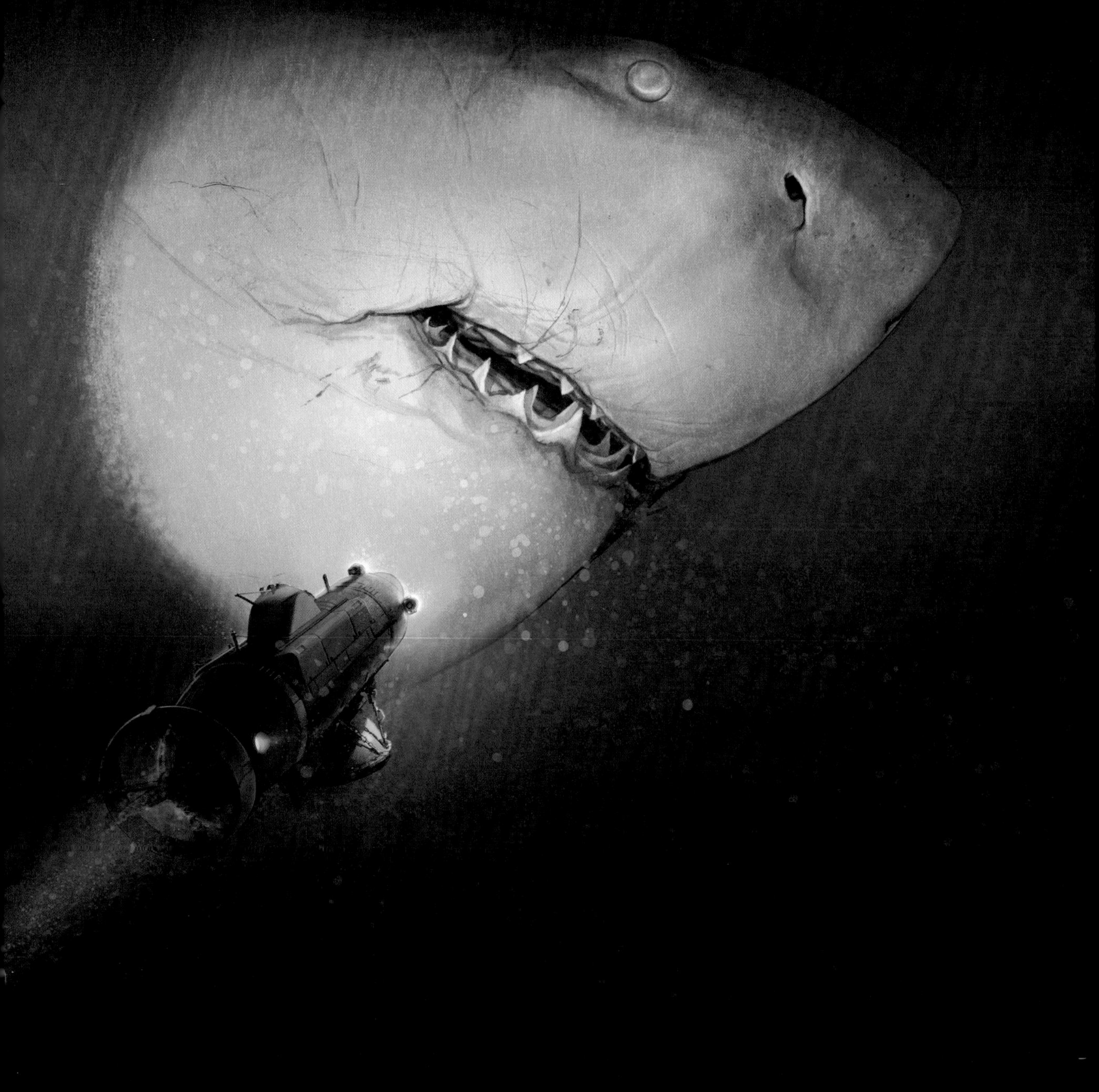

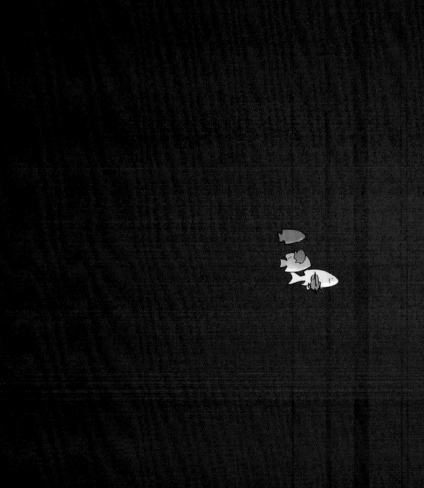

BOULDER CITY, NEVADA - 1988.

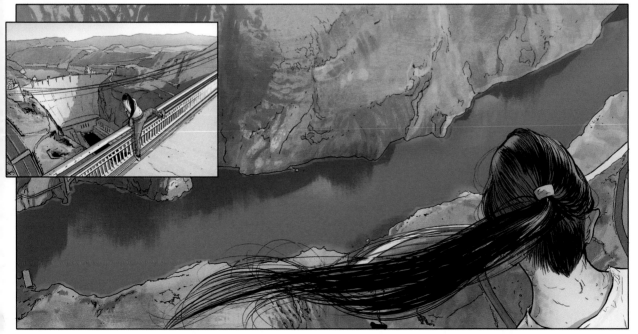

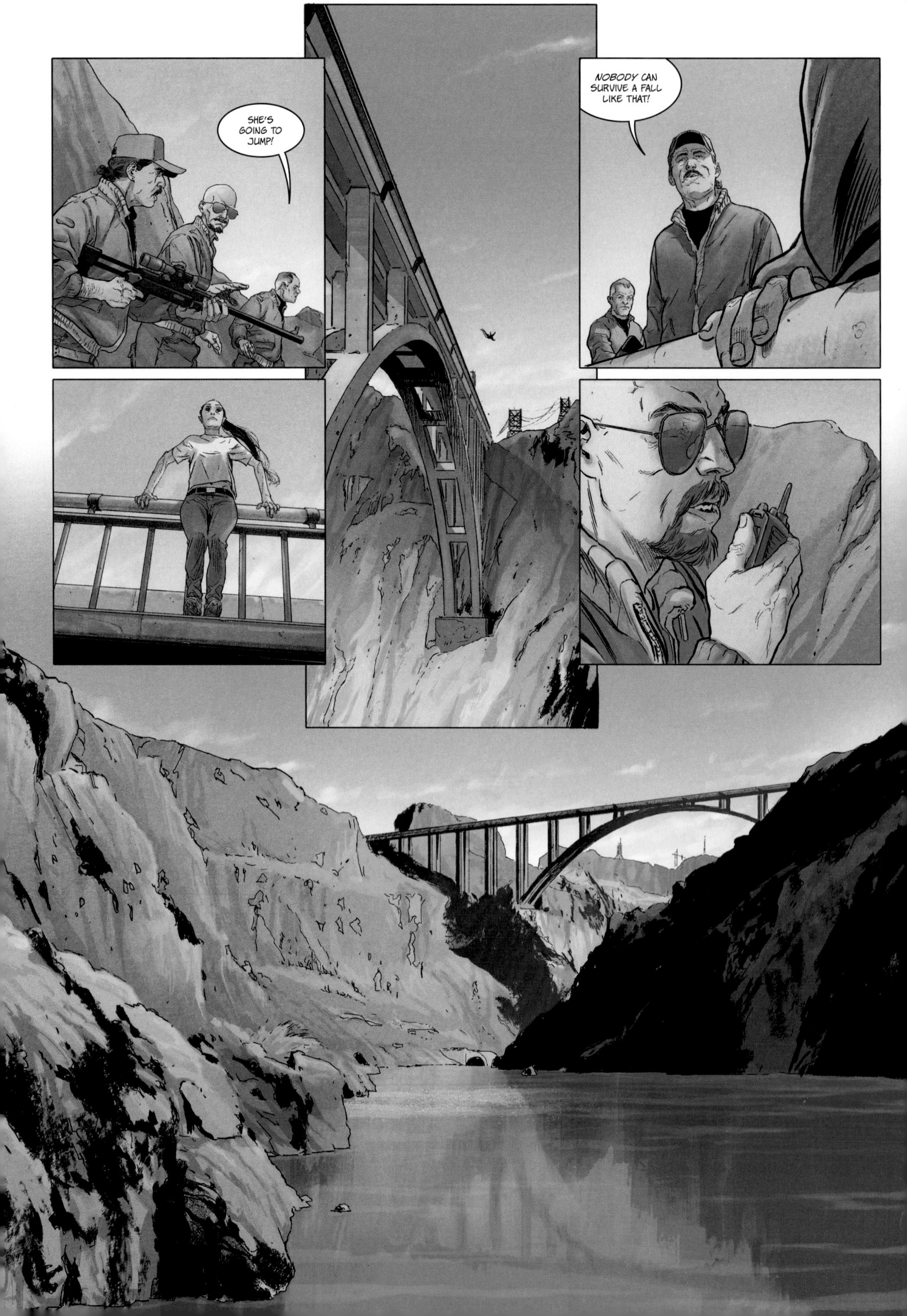
SHE'S GOING TO JUMP!
NOBODY CAN SURVIVE A FALL LIKE THAT!

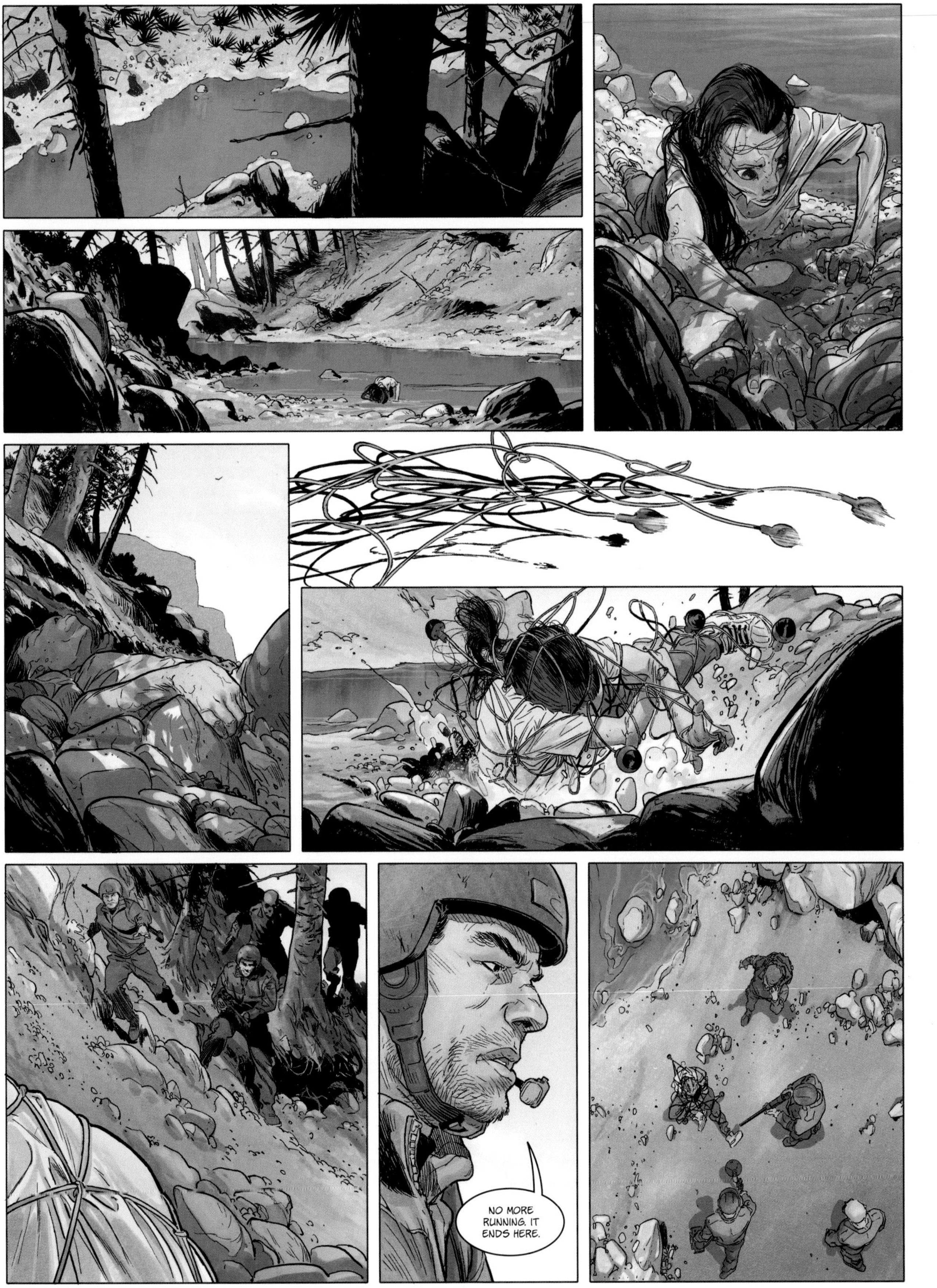
NO MORE RUNNING. IT ENDS HERE.

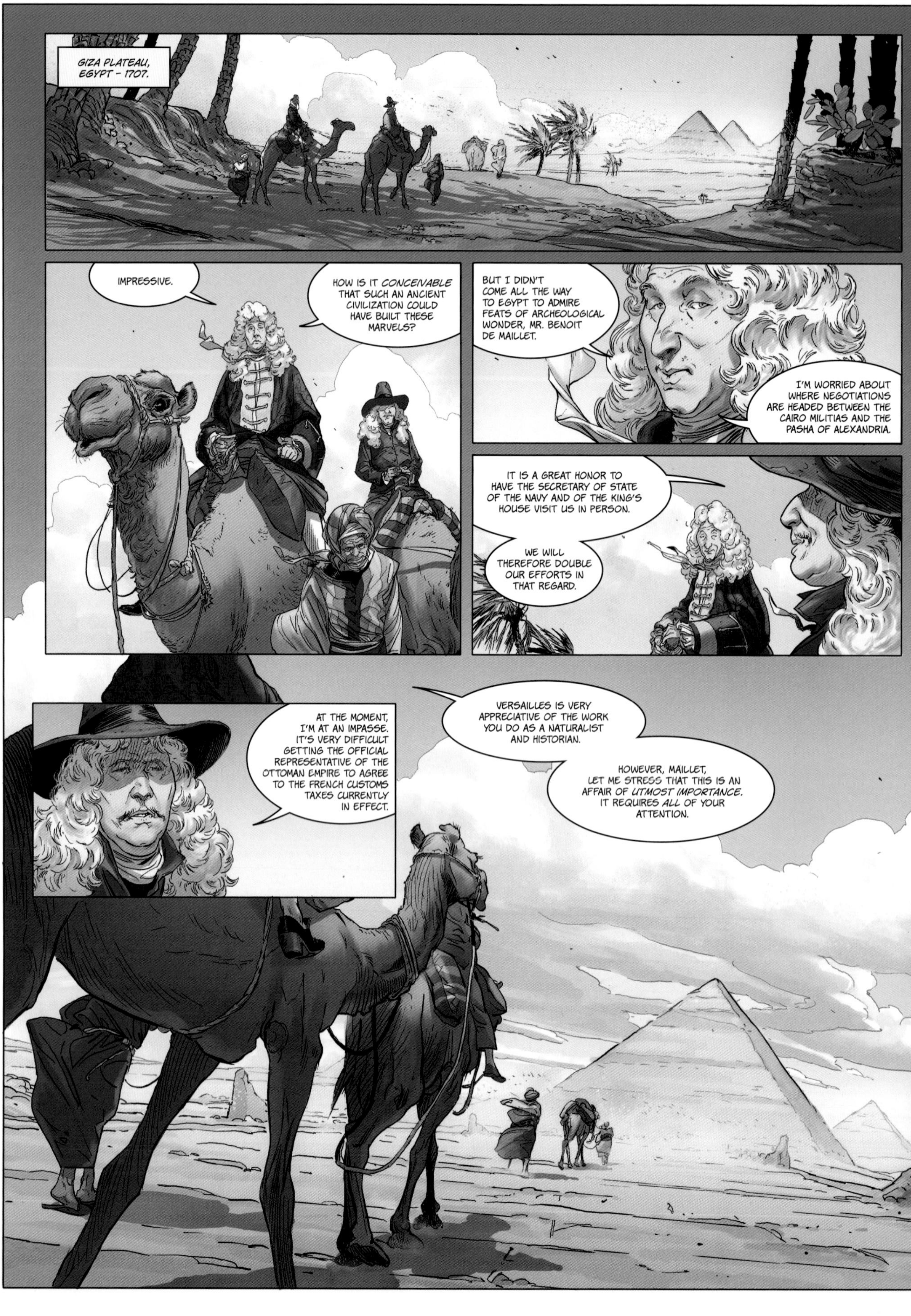
GIZA PLATEAU, EGYPT - 1707.
IMPRESSIVE.
HOW IS IT *CONCEIVABLE* THAT SUCH AN ANCIENT CIVILIZATION COULD HAVE BUILT THESE MARVELS?
BUT I DIDN'T COME ALL THE WAY TO EGYPT TO ADMIRE FEATS OF ARCHEOLOGICAL WONDER, MR. BENOIT DE MAILLET.
I'M WORRIED ABOUT WHERE NEGOTIATIONS ARE HEADED BETWEEN THE CAIRO MILITIAS AND THE PASHA OF ALEXANDRIA.
IT IS A GREAT HONOR TO HAVE THE SECRETARY OF STATE OF THE NAVY AND OF THE KING'S HOUSE VISIT US IN PERSON.
WE WILL THEREFORE DOUBLE OUR EFFORTS IN THAT REGARD.
AT THE MOMENT, I'M AT AN IMPASSE. IT'S VERY DIFFICULT GETTING THE OFFICIAL REPRESENTATIVE OF THE OTTOMAN EMPIRE TO AGREE TO THE FRENCH CUSTOMS TAXES CURRENTLY IN EFFECT.
VERSAILLES IS VERY APPRECIATIVE OF THE WORK YOU DO AS A NATURALIST AND HISTORIAN.
HOWEVER, MAILLET, LET ME STRESS THAT THIS IS AN AFFAIR OF *UTMOST IMPORTANCE.* IT REQUIRES *ALL* OF YOUR ATTENTION.

I UNDERSTOOD IT AS SUCH, MR. SECRETARY. YOU CAN COUNT ON MY DEVOTION. I SHAN'T GIVE IN ON ANY TERMS AND I SHALL ABANDON MY WORK AND MY WRITING FOR A TIME.

SPEAKING OF WHICH, NOW THAT I'VE COME ALL THIS WAY, PRAY TELL ME MORE ABOUT YOUR THEORY.

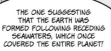

THE ONE SUGGESTING THAT THE EARTH WAS FORMED FOLLOWING RECEDING SEAWATERS, WHICH ONCE COVERED THE ENTIRE PLANET!

I KNOW IT IS NOT UNANIMOUSLY ACCEPTED AND I COULDN'T CARE LESS ABOUT VOLTAIRE'S SCATHING REMARKS!

I HAVE BECOME CONVINCED THAT ALL ANIMALS WERE ONCE AQUATIC AND THAT MAN COMES FROM FISH!

WHAT PROOF DO YOU HAVE?

I'VE OBSERVED THAT THE CHILD INSIDE THE WOMB BREATHES IN THROUGH TWO CAVITIES THAT CORRESPOND TO THE FOUR VESSELS THROUGH WHICH THE BLOOD FLOWS, WITHOUT ENTERING THE LUNGS.

ONE OF THESE OPENINGS IS CALLED THE FORAMEN OVALE; THE OTHER, THE ARTERIAL CANAL.

BEFORE HE'S BORN, THE CHILD LIVES IN A LIQUID ENVIRONMENT. WHEN HE'S BORN, AIR ENTERS HIS LUNGS FOR THE FIRST TIME, WHERE THE BLOOD NOW FLOWS.

THE FORAMEN OVALE THEN CLOSES UP.

DO YOU SEE WHERE I'M GOING WITH THIS, MR. SECRETARY?

NO, NOT EXACTLY.

IF THE FORAMEN OVALE DIDN'T COMPLETELY CLOSE UP, IT WOULD MEAN THAT THE CHILD...

...COULD LIVE AS AN AMPHIBIAN!

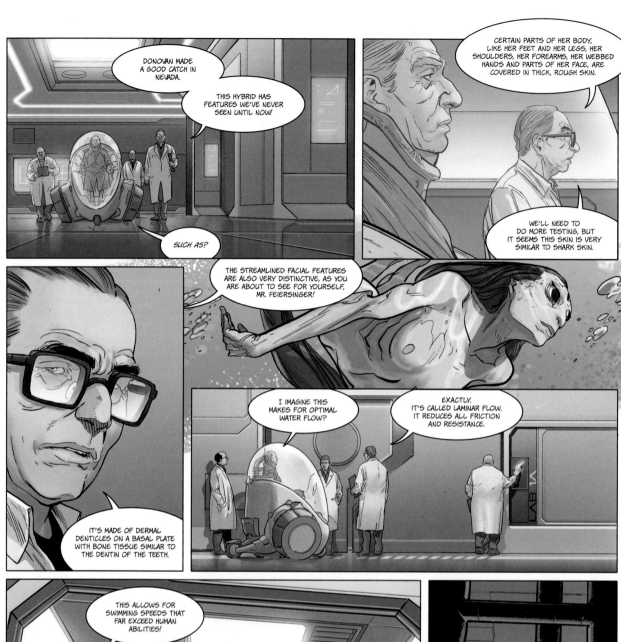

DONOVAN MADE A GOOD CATCH IN NEVADA.

THIS HYBRID HAS FEATURES WE'VE NEVER SEEN UNTIL NOW!

SUCH AS?

CERTAIN PARTS OF HER BODY, LIKE HER FEET AND HER LEGS, HER SHOULDERS, HER FOREARMS, HER WEBBED HANDS AND PARTS OF HER FACE, ARE COVERED IN THICK, ROUGH SKIN.

WE'LL NEED TO DO MORE TESTING, BUT IT SEEMS THIS SKIN IS VERY SIMILAR TO SHARK SKIN.

THE STREAMLINED FACIAL FEATURES ARE ALSO VERY DISTINCTIVE, AS YOU ARE ABOUT TO SEE FOR YOURSELF, MR. FEIERSINGER!

IT'S MADE OF DERMAL DENTICLES ON A BASAL PLATE WITH BONE TISSUE SIMILAR TO THE DENTIN OF THE TEETH.

I IMAGINE THIS MAKES FOR OPTIMAL WATER FLOW?

EXACTLY. IT'S CALLED LAMINAR FLOW. IT REDUCES ALL FRICTION AND RESISTANCE.

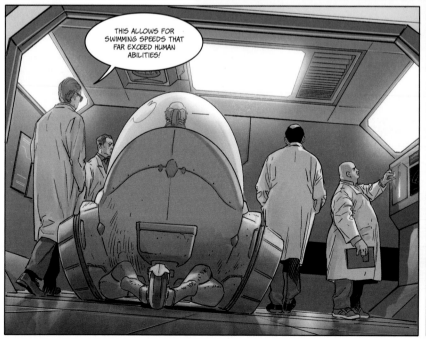

THIS ALLOWS FOR SWIMMING SPEEDS THAT FAR EXCEED HUMAN ABILITIES!

WE ALREADY KNEW THAT, AS AMPHIBIANS, THESE HYBRIDS COULD ONLY BREATHE UNDERWATER FOR A LIMITED TIME.

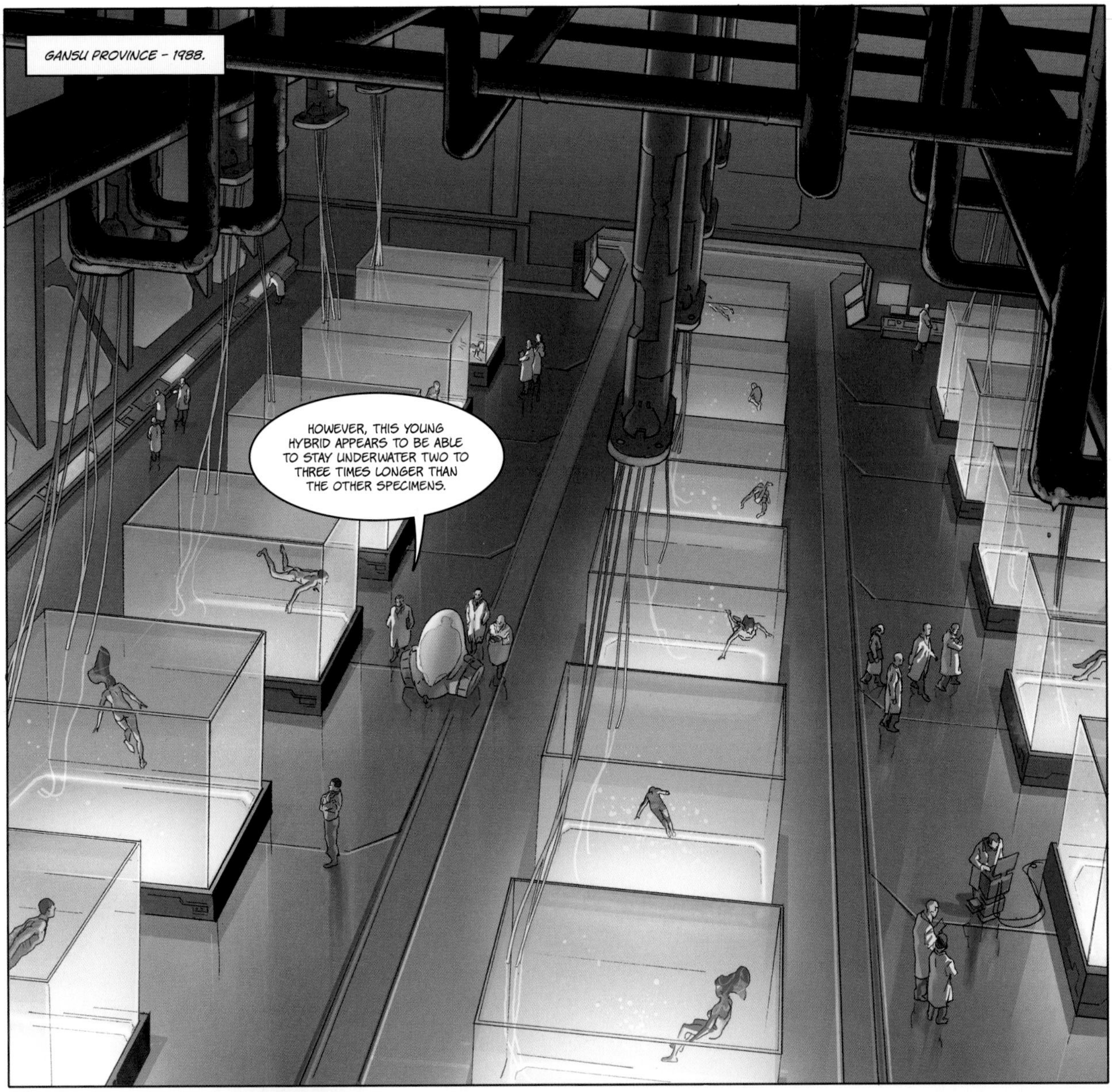
GANSU PROVINCE - 1988.
HOWEVER, THIS YOUNG HYBRID APPEARS TO BE ABLE TO STAY UNDERWATER TWO TO THREE TIMES LONGER THAN THE OTHER SPECIMENS.

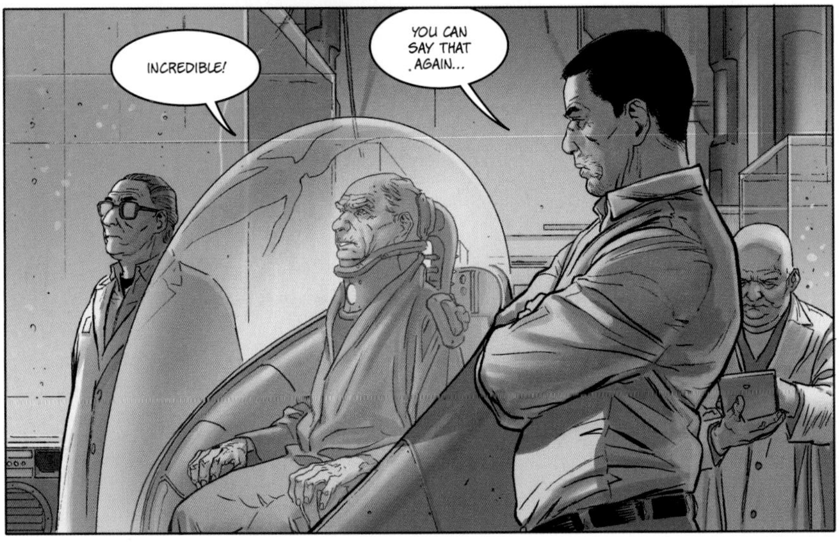
INCREDIBLE!
YOU CAN SAY THAT AGAIN...

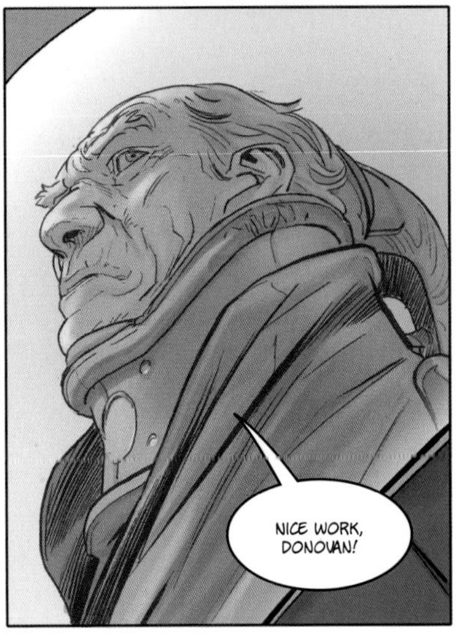
NICE WORK, DONOVAN!

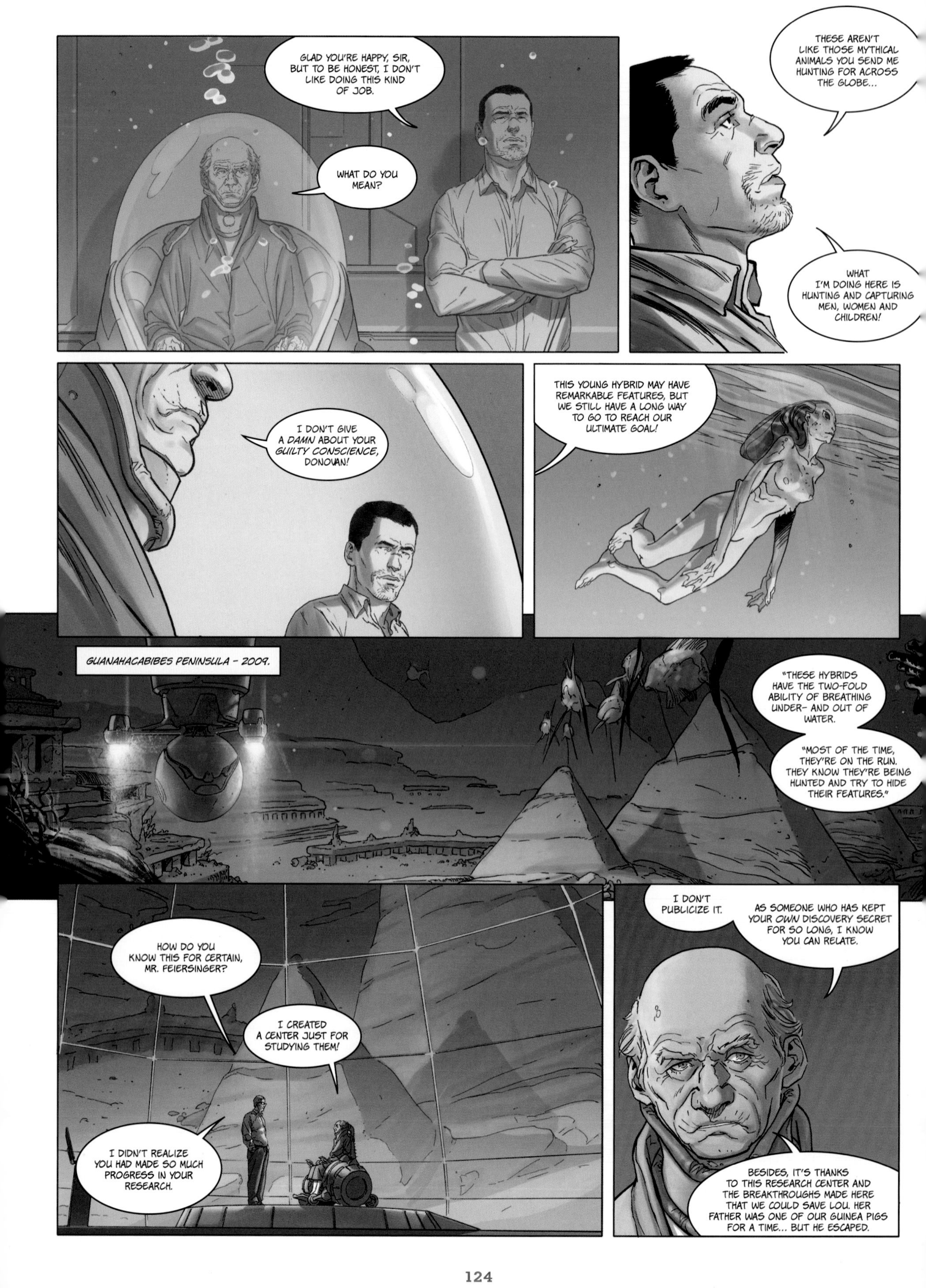
GLAD YOU'RE HAPPY, SIR, BUT TO BE HONEST, I DON'T LIKE DOING THIS KIND OF JOB.
WHAT DO YOU MEAN?
THESE AREN'T LIKE THOSE MYTHICAL ANIMALS YOU SEND ME HUNTING FOR ACROSS THE GLOBE...
WHAT I'M DOING HERE IS HUNTING AND CAPTURING MEN, WOMEN AND CHILDREN!
I DON'T GIVE A DAMN ABOUT YOUR GUILTY CONSCIENCE, DONOVAN!
THIS YOUNG HYBRID MAY HAVE REMARKABLE FEATURES, BUT WE STILL HAVE A LONG WAY TO GO TO REACH OUR ULTIMATE GOAL!
GUANAHACABIBES PENINSULA - 2009.
"THESE HYBRIDS HAVE THE TWO-FOLD ABILITY OF BREATHING UNDER- AND OUT OF WATER.
"MOST OF THE TIME, THEY'RE ON THE RUN. THEY KNOW THEY'RE BEING HUNTED AND TRY TO HIDE THEIR FEATURES."
HOW DO YOU KNOW THIS FOR CERTAIN, MR. FEIERSINGER?
I CREATED A CENTER JUST FOR STUDYING THEM!
I DIDN'T REALIZE YOU HAD MADE SO MUCH PROGRESS IN YOUR RESEARCH.
I DON'T PUBLICIZE IT.
AS SOMEONE WHO HAS KEPT YOUR OWN DISCOVERY SECRET FOR SO LONG, I KNOW YOU CAN RELATE.
BESIDES, IT'S THANKS TO THIS RESEARCH CENTER AND THE BREAKTHROUGHS MADE HERE THAT WE COULD SAVE LOU. HER FATHER WAS ONE OF OUR GUINEA PIGS FOR A TIME... BUT HE ESCAPED.

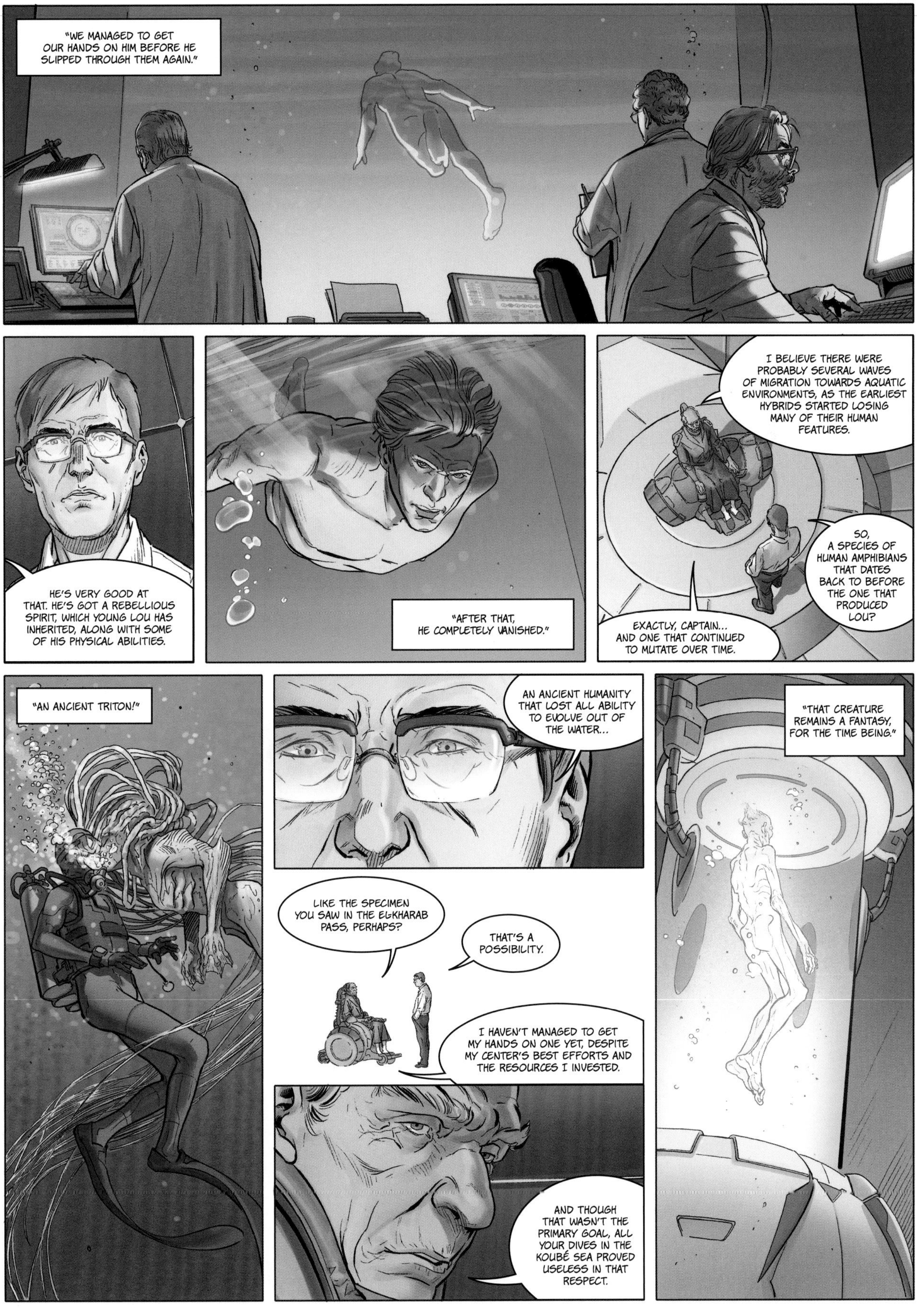
"WE MANAGED TO GET OUR HANDS ON HIM BEFORE HE SLIPPED THROUGH THEM AGAIN."
HE'S VERY GOOD AT THAT. HE'S GOT A REBELLIOUS SPIRIT, WHICH YOUNG LOU HAS INHERITED, ALONG WITH SOME OF HIS PHYSICAL ABILITIES.
"AFTER THAT, HE COMPLETELY VANISHED."
I BELIEVE THERE WERE PROBABLY SEVERAL WAVES OF MIGRATION TOWARDS AQUATIC ENVIRONMENTS, AS THE EARLIEST HYBRIDS STARTED LOSING MANY OF THEIR HUMAN FEATURES.
SO, A SPECIES OF HUMAN AMPHIBIANS THAT DATES BACK TO BEFORE THE ONE THAT PRODUCED LOU?
EXACTLY, CAPTAIN... AND ONE THAT CONTINUED TO MUTATE OVER TIME.
"AN ANCIENT TRITON!"
AN ANCIENT HUMANITY THAT LOST ALL ABILITY TO EVOLVE OUT OF THE WATER...
LIKE THE SPECIMEN YOU SAW IN THE EL-KHARAB PASS, PERHAPS?
THAT'S A POSSIBILITY.
I HAVEN'T MANAGED TO GET MY HANDS ON ONE YET, DESPITE MY CENTER'S BEST EFFORTS AND THE RESOURCES I INVESTED.
AND THOUGH THAT WASN'T THE PRIMARY GOAL, ALL YOUR DIVES IN THE KOUBÉ SEA PROVED USELESS IN THAT RESPECT.
"THAT CREATURE REMAINS A FANTASY, FOR THE TIME BEING."

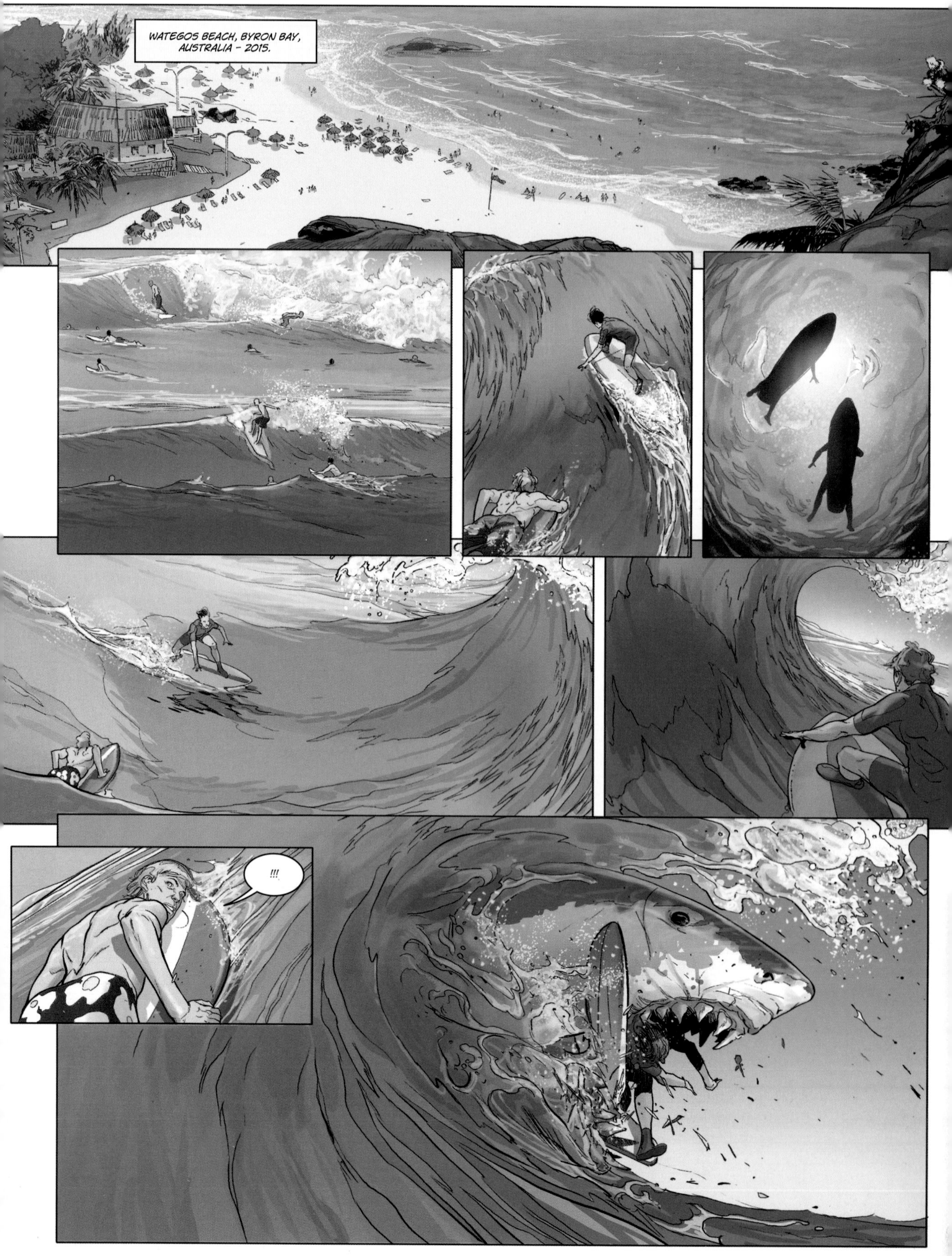
WATEGOS BEACH, BYRON BAY, AUSTRALIA – 2015.
!!!

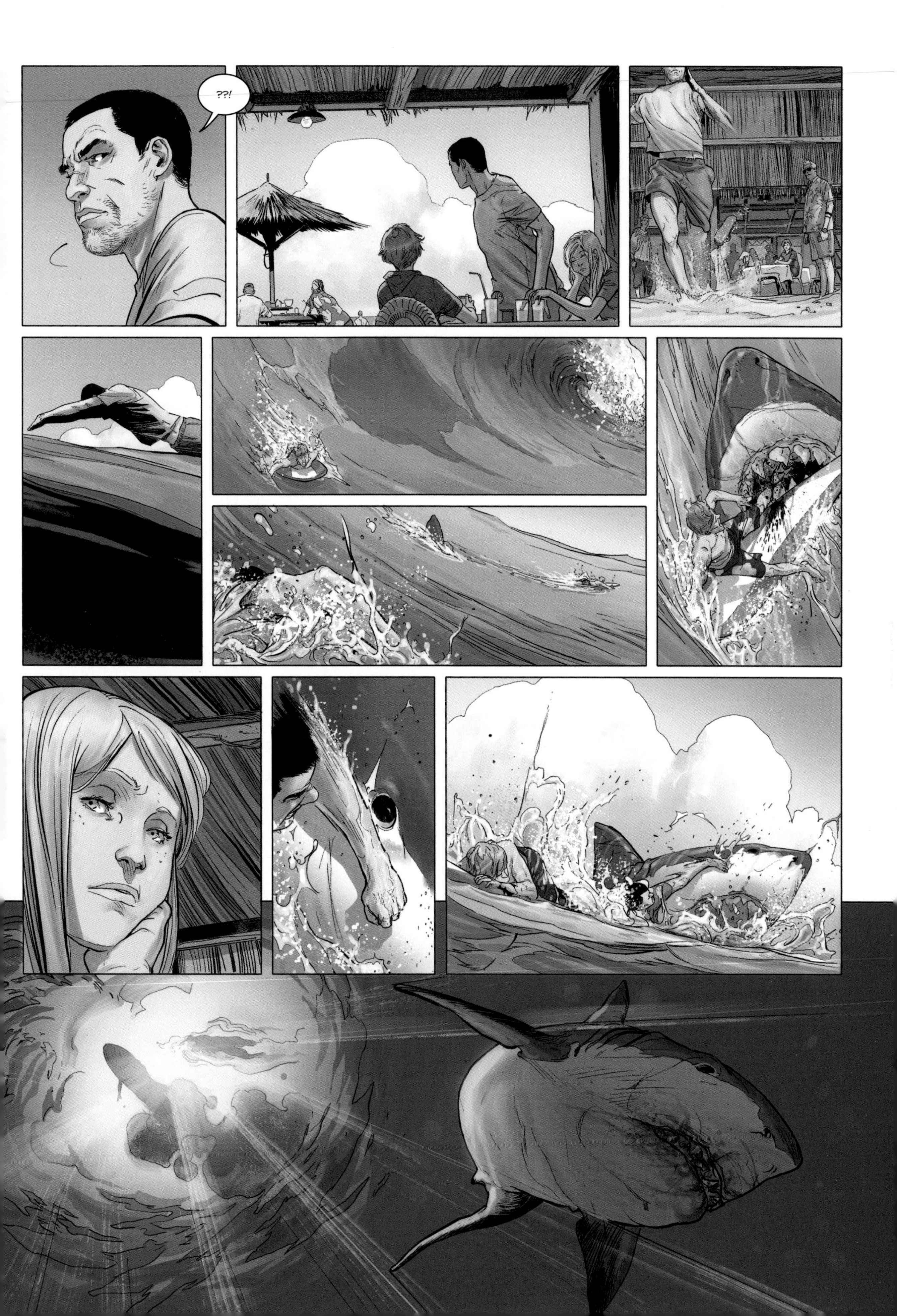
??!

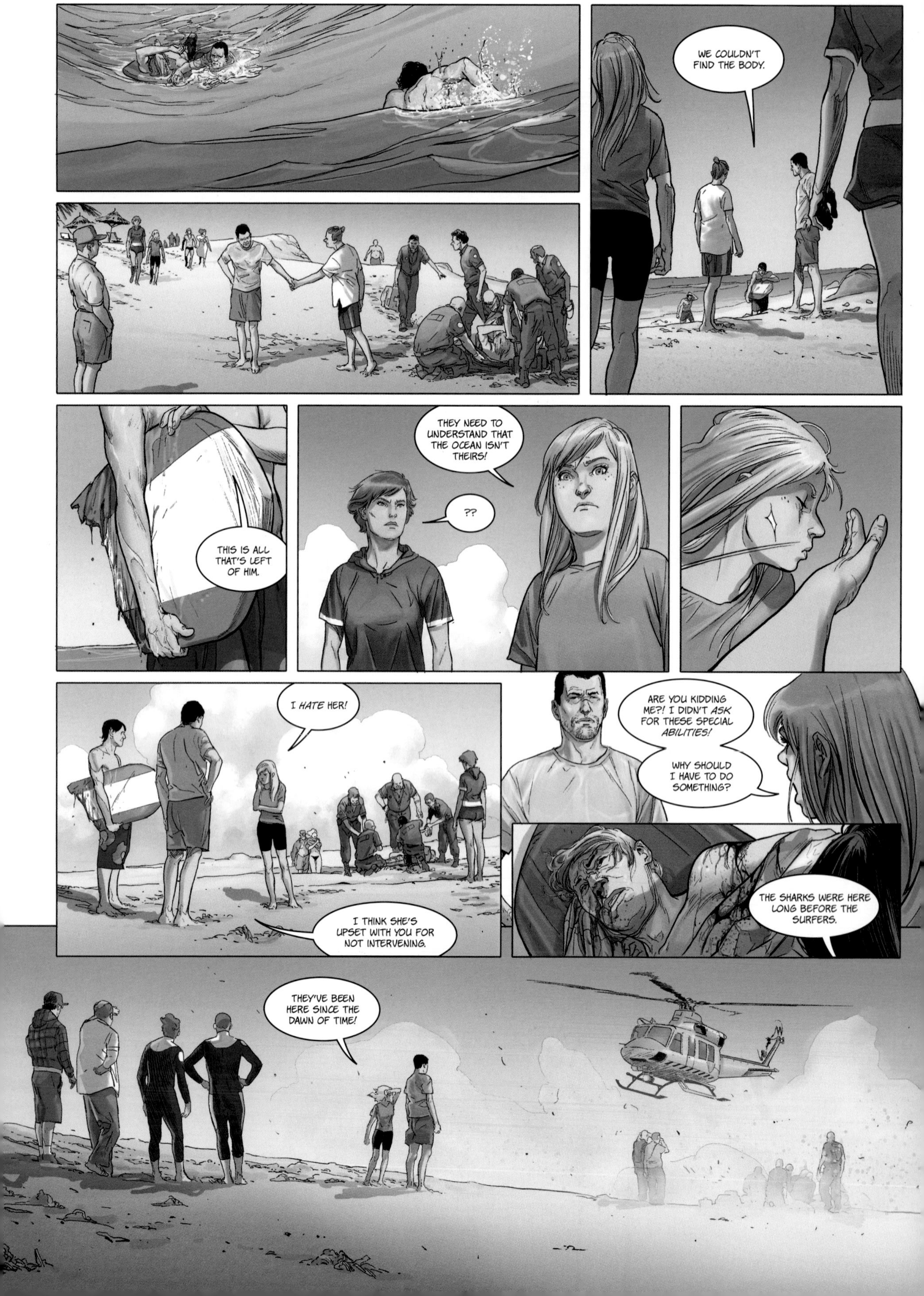
WE COULDN'T FIND THE BODY.
THIS IS ALL THAT'S LEFT OF HIM.
THEY NEED TO UNDERSTAND THAT THE OCEAN ISN'T THEIRS!
??
I HATE HER!
I THINK SHE'S UPSET WITH YOU FOR NOT INTERVENING.
ARE YOU KIDDING ME?! I DIDN'T ASK FOR THESE SPECIAL ABILITIES!
WHY SHOULD I HAVE TO DO SOMETHING?
THE SHARKS WERE HERE LONG BEFORE THE SURFERS.
THEY'VE BEEN HERE SINCE THE DAWN OF TIME!

KOTIK CREEK, ALASKA – 2021.

I NEED YOU, THIS IS AN EMERGENCY!

A MATTER OF LIFE AND DEATH!!

WE HAVE TO LOCATE LOU AT ALL COSTS, AND THERE'S ONLY ONE WAY TO DO THAT: GET HER G.P.S. COORDINATES FROM FEIERSINGER'S MONITOR!

MR. DONOVAN... AT MY MASTER'S INSISTENCE, I GAVE THE ONLY EXISTING KEY TO LOU. AND SHE APPEARS TO HAVE TAKEN IT WITH HER.

BOGDAN, WHO DO YOU THINK YOU'RE TALKING TO?!

DON'T TRY TO TELL ME FEIERSINGER DIDN'T HIDE A DOUBLE SOMEWHERE IN THE CASTLE!

VERY WELL... I'LL SEE WHAT I CAN DO, SIR.

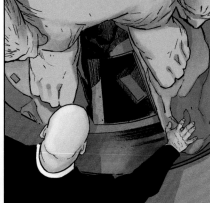

129

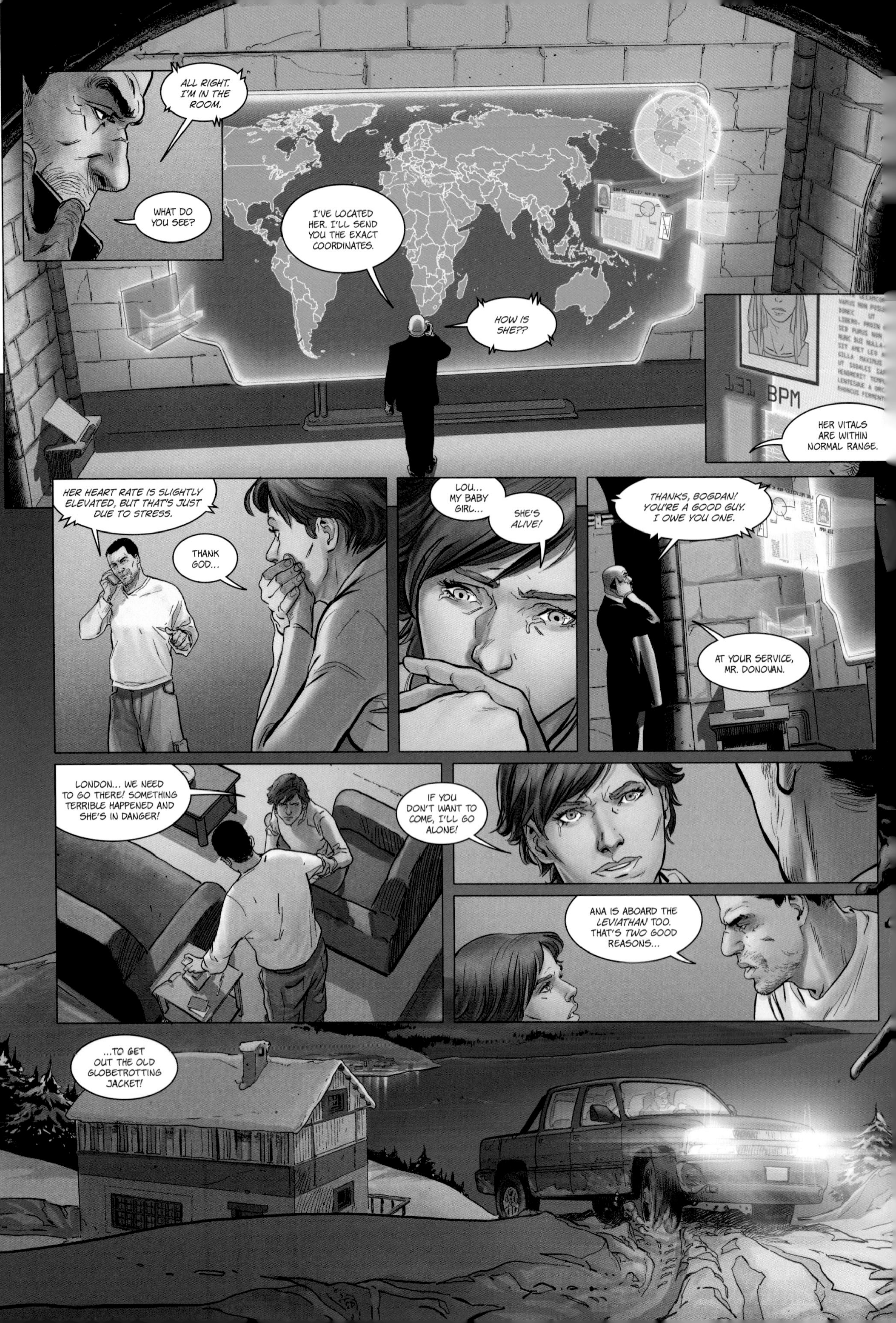

ALL RIGHT. I'M IN THE ROOM.
WHAT DO YOU SEE?
I'VE LOCATED HER. I'LL SEND YOU THE EXACT COORDINATES.
HOW IS SHE??
131 BPM
HER VITALS ARE WITHIN NORMAL RANGE.
HER HEART RATE IS SLIGHTLY ELEVATED, BUT THAT'S JUST DUE TO STRESS.
THANK GOD...
LOU... MY BABY GIRL...
SHE'S ALIVE!
THANKS, BOGDAN! YOU'RE A GOOD GUY. I OWE YOU ONE.
AT YOUR SERVICE, MR. DONOVAN.
LONDON... WE NEED TO GO THERE! SOMETHING TERRIBLE HAPPENED AND SHE'S IN DANGER!
IF YOU DON'T WANT TO COME, I'LL GO ALONE!
ANA IS ABOARD THE LEVIATHAN TOO. THAT'S TWO GOOD REASONS...
...TO GET OUT THE OLD GLOBETROTTING JACKET!

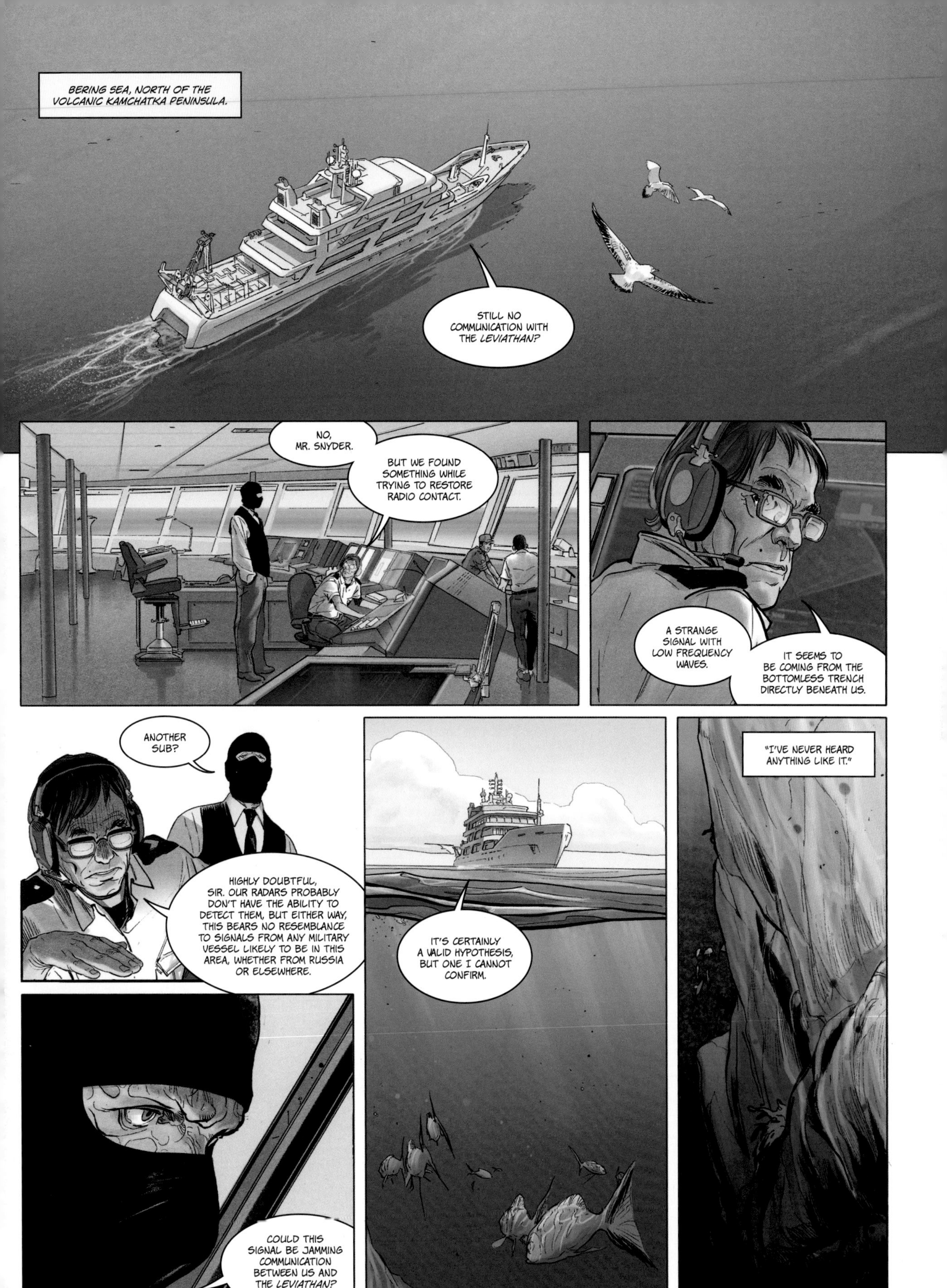
BERING SEA, NORTH OF THE VOLCANIC KAMCHATKA PENINSULA.
STILL NO COMMUNICATION WITH THE *LEVIATHAN?*
NO, MR. SNYDER.
BUT WE FOUND SOMETHING WHILE TRYING TO RESTORE RADIO CONTACT.
A STRANGE SIGNAL WITH LOW FREQUENCY WAVES.
IT SEEMS TO BE COMING FROM THE BOTTOMLESS TRENCH DIRECTLY BENEATH US.
ANOTHER SUB?
HIGHLY DOUBTFUL, SIR. OUR RADARS PROBABLY DON'T HAVE THE ABILITY TO DETECT THEM, BUT EITHER WAY, THIS BEARS NO RESEMBLANCE TO SIGNALS FROM ANY MILITARY VESSEL LIKELY TO BE IN THIS AREA, WHETHER FROM RUSSIA OR ELSEWHERE.
COULD THIS SIGNAL BE JAMMING COMMUNICATION BETWEEN US AND THE *LEVIATHAN?*
IT'S CERTAINLY A VALID HYPOTHESIS, BUT ONE I CANNOT CONFIRM.
"I'VE NEVER HEARD ANYTHING LIKE IT."

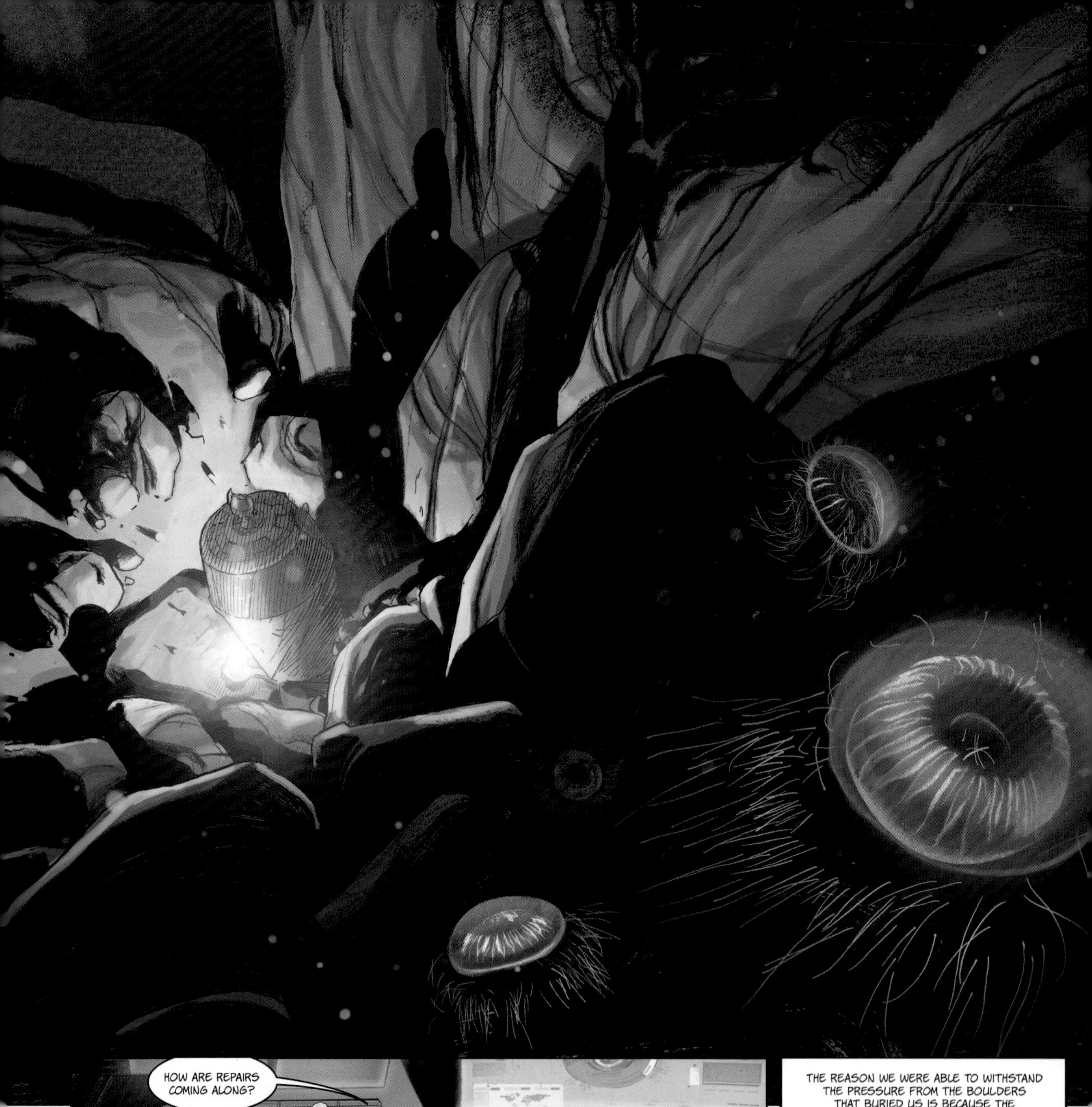

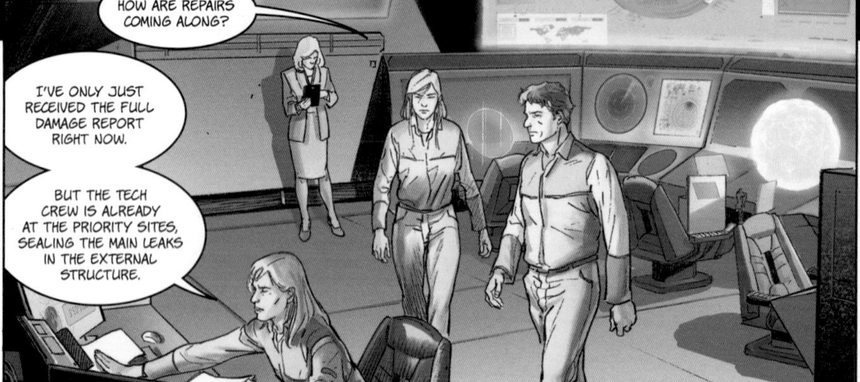
HOW ARE REPAIRS COMING ALONG?
I'VE ONLY JUST RECEIVED THE FULL DAMAGE REPORT RIGHT NOW.
BUT THE TECH CREW IS ALREADY AT THE PRIORITY SITES, SEALING THE MAIN LEAKS IN THE EXTERNAL STRUCTURE.

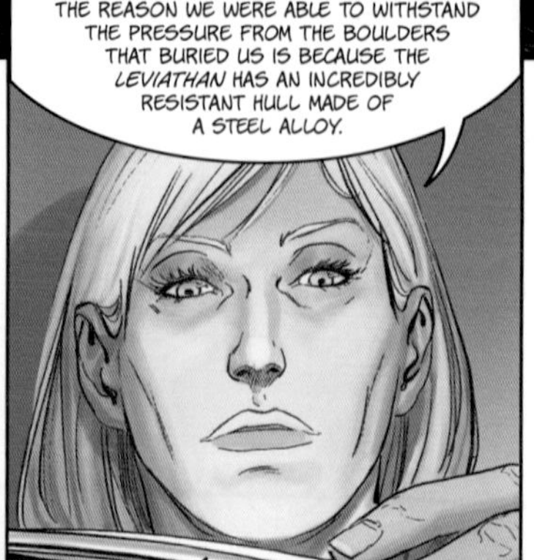
THE REASON WE WERE ABLE TO WITHSTAND THE PRESSURE FROM THE BOULDERS THAT BURIED US IS BECAUSE THE *LEVIATHAN* HAS AN INCREDIBLY RESISTANT HULL MADE OF A STEEL ALLOY.
WITHOUT IT, WE'D ALL BE DEAD!

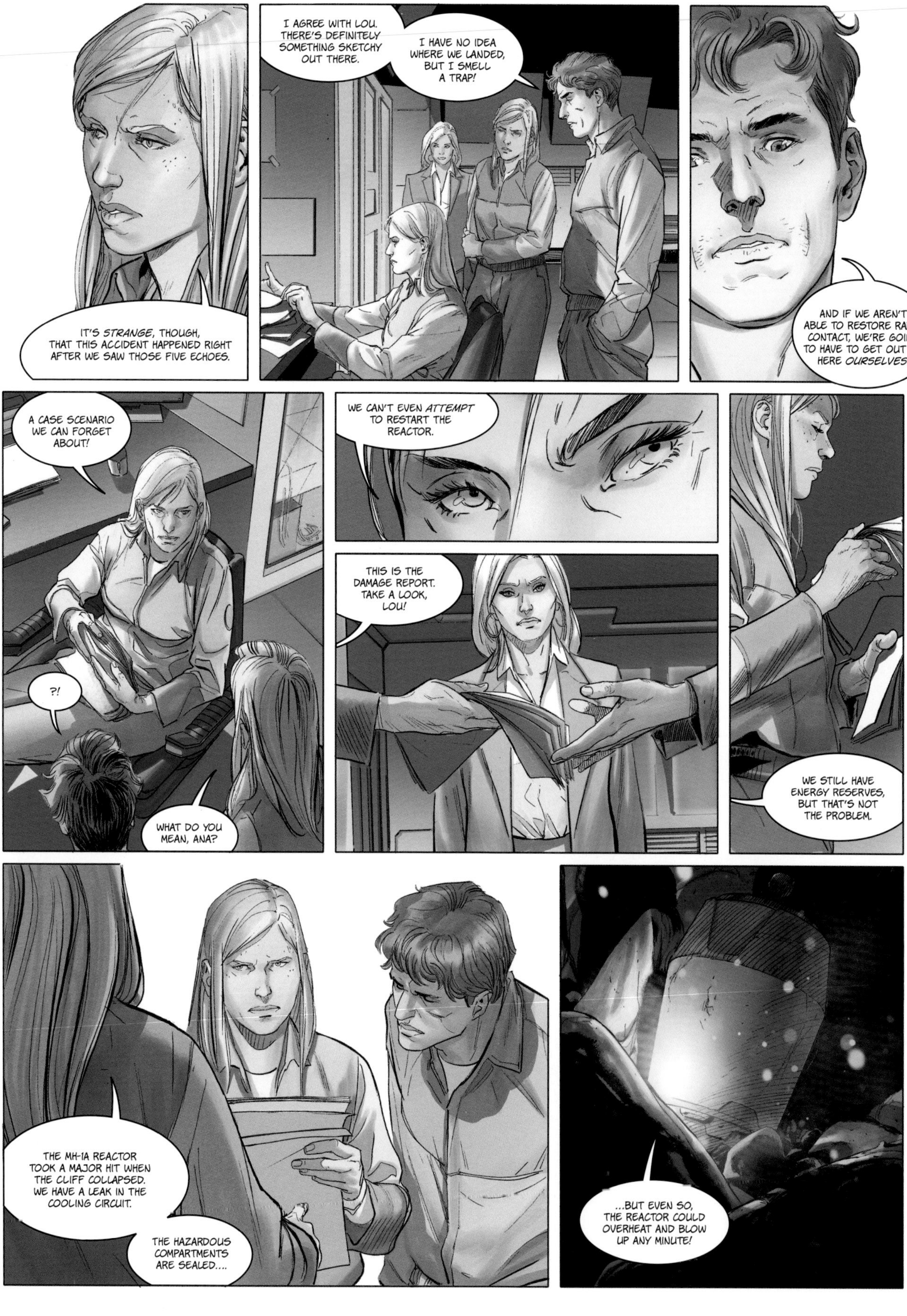
IT'S STRANGE, THOUGH, THAT THIS ACCIDENT HAPPENED RIGHT AFTER WE SAW THOSE FIVE ECHOES.
I AGREE WITH LOU. THERE'S DEFINITELY SOMETHING SKETCHY OUT THERE.
I HAVE NO IDEA WHERE WE LANDED, BUT I SMELL A TRAP!
AND IF WE AREN'T ABLE TO RESTORE RADIO CONTACT, WE'RE GOING TO HAVE TO GET OUT OF HERE OURSELVES.
A CASE SCENARIO WE CAN FORGET ABOUT!
?!
WHAT DO YOU MEAN, ANA?
WE CAN'T EVEN ATTEMPT TO RESTART THE REACTOR.
THIS IS THE DAMAGE REPORT. TAKE A LOOK, LOU!
WE STILL HAVE ENERGY RESERVES, BUT THAT'S NOT THE PROBLEM.
THE MH-1A REACTOR TOOK A MAJOR HIT WHEN THE CLIFF COLLAPSED. WE HAVE A LEAK IN THE COOLING CIRCUIT.
THE HAZARDOUS COMPARTMENTS ARE SEALED....
...BUT EVEN SO, THE REACTOR COULD OVERHEAT AND BLOW UP ANY MINUTE!

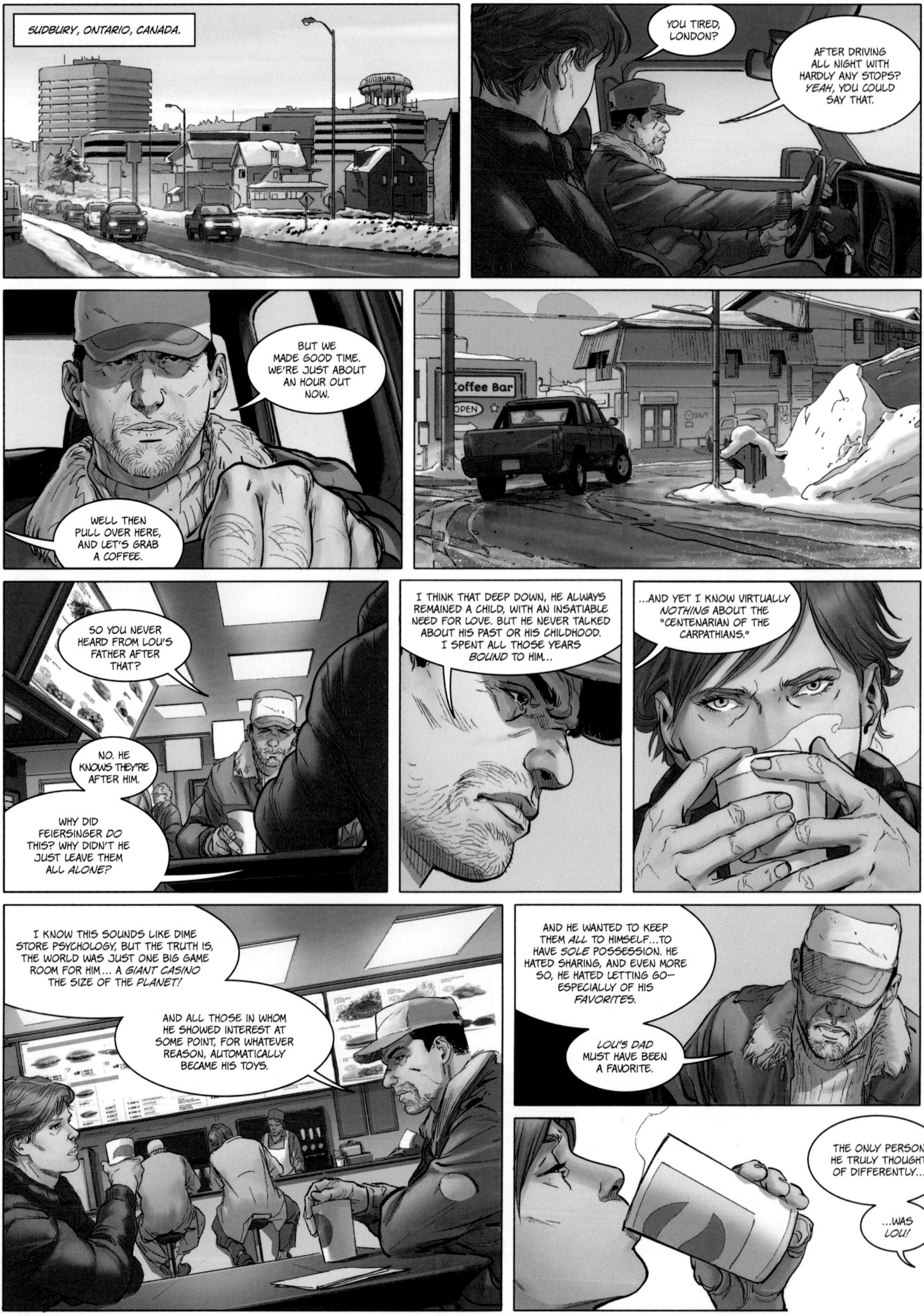
SUDBURY, ONTARIO, CANADA.
YOU TIRED, LONDON?
AFTER DRIVING ALL NIGHT WITH HARDLY ANY STOPS? YEAH, YOU COULD SAY THAT.
BUT WE MADE GOOD TIME. WE'RE JUST ABOUT AN HOUR OUT NOW.
WELL THEN PULL OVER HERE, AND LET'S GRAB A COFFEE.
Coffee Bar
OPEN
SO YOU NEVER HEARD FROM LOU'S FATHER AFTER THAT?
NO. HE KNOWS THEY'RE AFTER HIM.
WHY DID FEIERSINGER DO THIS? WHY DIDN'T HE JUST LEAVE THEM ALL ALONE?
I THINK THAT DEEP DOWN, HE ALWAYS REMAINED A CHILD, WITH AN INSATIABLE NEED FOR LOVE. BUT HE NEVER TALKED ABOUT HIS PAST OR HIS CHILDHOOD. I SPENT ALL THOSE YEARS BOUND TO HIM...
...AND YET I KNOW VIRTUALLY NOTHING ABOUT THE "CENTENARIAN OF THE CARPATHIANS."
I KNOW THIS SOUNDS LIKE DIME STORE PSYCHOLOGY, BUT THE TRUTH IS, THE WORLD WAS JUST ONE BIG GAME ROOM FOR HIM... A GIANT CASINO THE SIZE OF THE PLANET!
AND ALL THOSE IN WHOM HE SHOWED INTEREST AT SOME POINT, FOR WHATEVER REASON, AUTOMATICALLY BECAME HIS TOYS.
AND HE WANTED TO KEEP THEM ALL TO HIMSELF...TO HAVE SOLE POSSESSION. HE HATED SHARING, AND EVEN MORE SO, HE HATED LETTING GO—ESPECIALLY OF HIS FAVORITES.
LOU'S DAD MUST HAVE BEEN A FAVORITE.
THE ONLY PERSON HE TRULY THOUGHT OF DIFFERENTLY...
...WAS LOU!

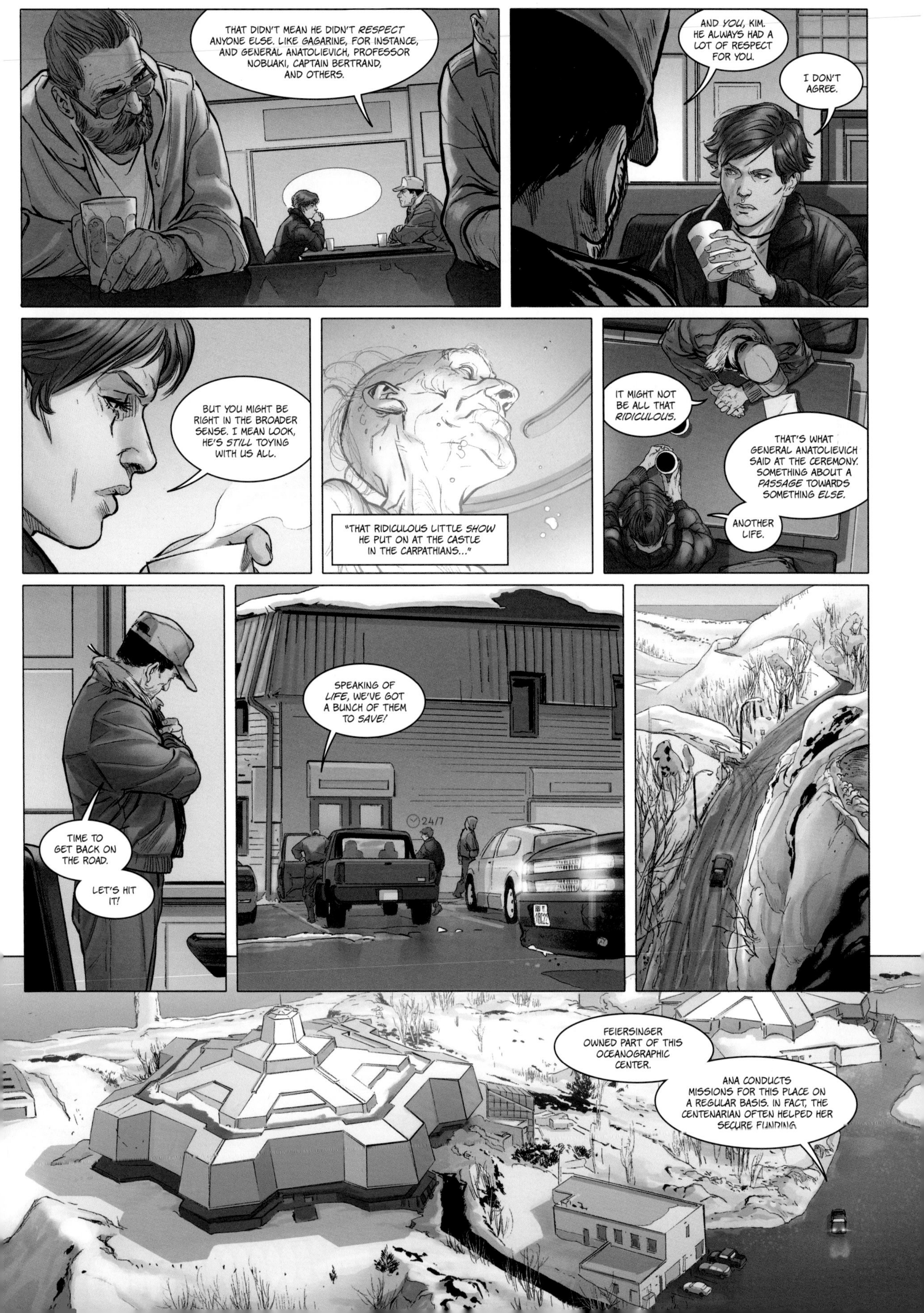
THAT DIDN'T MEAN HE DIDN'T *RESPECT* ANYONE ELSE. LIKE GAGARINE, FOR INSTANCE, AND GENERAL ANATOLIEVICH, PROFESSOR NOBUAKI, CAPTAIN BERTRAND, AND OTHERS.
AND *YOU*, KIM. HE ALWAYS HAD A LOT OF RESPECT FOR YOU.
I DON'T AGREE.
BUT YOU MIGHT BE RIGHT IN THE BROADER SENSE. I MEAN LOOK, HE'S *STILL* TOYING WITH US ALL.
"THAT RIDICULOUS LITTLE *SHOW* HE PUT ON AT THE CASTLE IN THE CARPATHIANS..."
IT MIGHT NOT BE ALL THAT *RIDICULOUS*.
THAT'S WHAT GENERAL ANATOLIEVICH SAID AT THE CEREMONY. SOMETHING ABOUT A *PASSAGE* TOWARDS SOMETHING *ELSE*.
ANOTHER LIFE.
TIME TO GET BACK ON THE ROAD.
LET'S HIT IT!
SPEAKING OF *LIFE*, WE'VE GOT A BUNCH OF THEM TO *SAVE!*
24/7
FEIERSINGER OWNED PART OF THIS OCEANOGRAPHIC CENTER.
ANA CONDUCTS MISSIONS FOR THIS PLACE ON A REGULAR BASIS. IN FACT, THE CENTENARIAN OFTEN HELPED HER SECURE FUNDING.

I'M SO SORRY ABOUT ANA... NOT KNOWING IS THE WORST PART.

BUT AS I SAID, ALL OUR SUBS ARE OUT ON MISSIONS, AND FAR AWAY FROM HERE, TO BOOT.

IT WOULD BE VERY DIFFICULT TO CALL THEM BACK IN ON SUCH SHORT NOTICE AND GET THEM BACK TO THE BERING SEA. THE ONLY FEASIBLE OPTION IS THE OLD D.S.R.V.* I TOLD YOU ABOUT OVER THE PHONE, DONOVAN.

BUT IT'S PRACTICALLY A WRECK.

I WANT TO SEE IT!

OKAY, I'LL TAKE YOU. WE PUT IN AN OLD HANGAR. WE HAVEN'T HAD A CHANCE TO DISMANTLE IT FOR PARTS YET.

HERE SHE IS!

IN PEAK CONDITION, IT COULD GO DOWN TO 6,000 METERS WITH A CREW OF FIVE ON BOARD.

GOOD BATTERY LIFE FOR DEEP-SEA WORK... FIVE FULL HOURS THANKS TO *LEAD* BATTERIES!

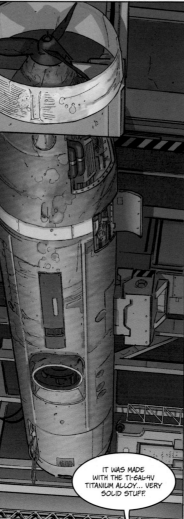

IT WAS MADE WITH THE TI-6AL-4V TITANIUM ALLOY... VERY SOLID STUFF.

THE MAIN CONCERNS ARE LEAKS IN THREE OF THE P.M.M.A. WINDOWS AND ISSUES WITH THE MERCURY TRANSFER FOR CONTROLLING THE TRIM.

THE DIVE RADIO WORKS BUT THE SURFACE V.H.F. TRANSMITTER-RECEIVER IS *CAPUT*, AS ARE THE DEPTH FINDER, THE DATA AND NAVIGATION PROCESSING SYSTEM, AND PARTS OF THE SECURITY SYSTEMS.

WE NEED TO KNOW IF THE MAIN FUNCTIONS CAN BE QUICKLY BROUGHT UP TO WORKING CONDITION FOR A DIVE.

FOR A *RESCUE* MISSION AT A DEPTH OF 4,700 METERS?

GOING DOW[N] THAT DEEP IN T[HE] WRECK IS *SUIC[IDE]* IF YOU ASK M[E].

YOU'RE GONNA NEED ONE *HELL* OF A PILOT!

DON'T YOU WORRY ABOUT THAT.

??

I KNOW JUST THE GUY.

*DEEP-SUBMERGENCE RESCUE VEHICLE.

136

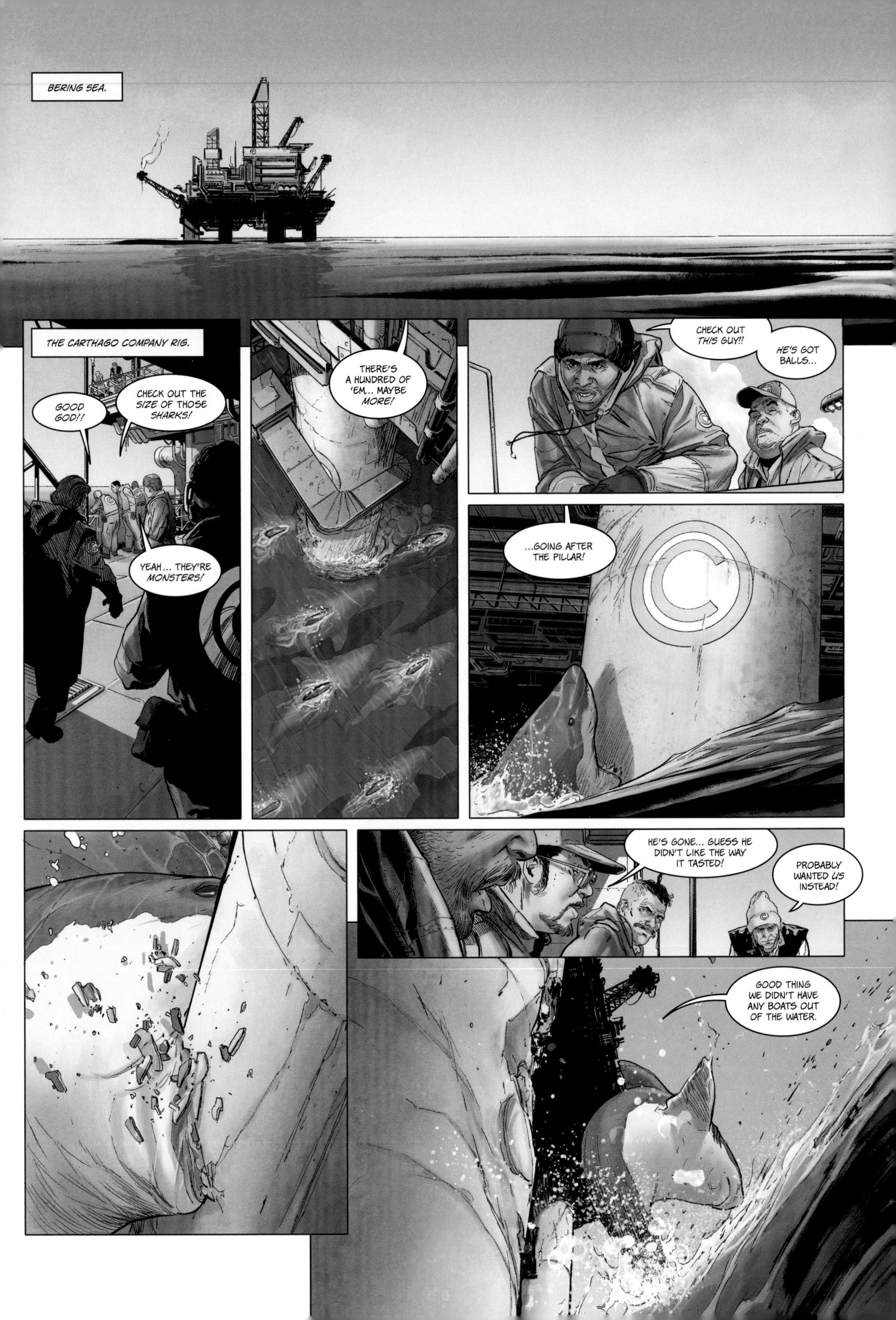
BERING SEA.
THE CARTHAGO COMPANY RIG.
GOOD GOD!!
CHECK OUT THE SIZE OF THOSE SHARKS!
YEAH... THEY'RE MONSTERS!
THERE'S A HUNDRED OF 'EM... MAYBE MORE!
CHECK OUT THIS GUY!!
HE'S GOT BALLS...
...GOING AFTER THE PILLAR!
HE'S GONE... GUESS HE DIDN'T LIKE THE WAY IT TASTED!
PROBABLY WANTED US INSTEAD!
GOOD THING WE DIDN'T HAVE ANY BOATS OUT OF THE WATER.

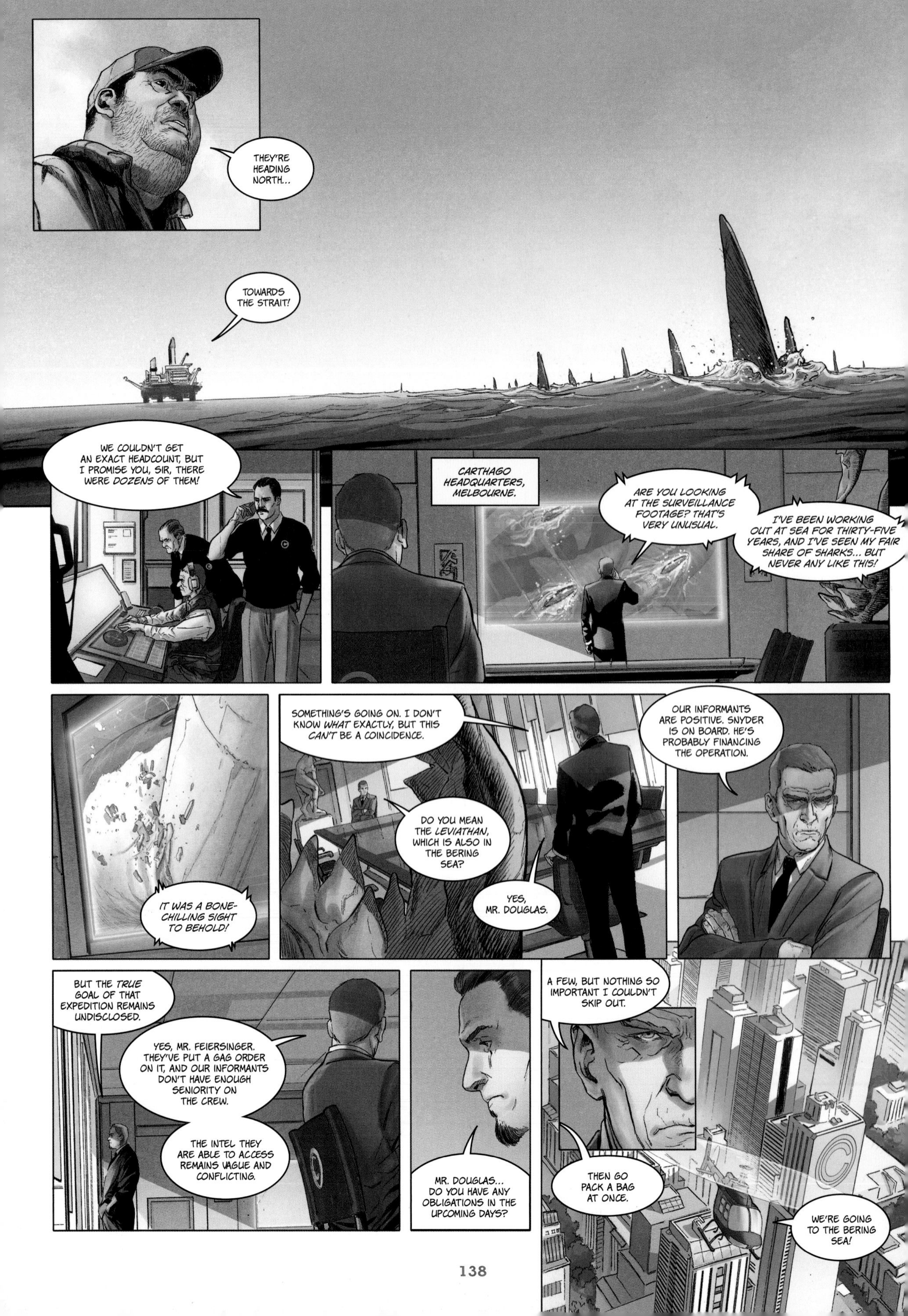
THEY'RE HEADING NORTH...
TOWARDS THE STRAIT!
WE COULDN'T GET AN EXACT HEADCOUNT, BUT I PROMISE YOU, SIR, THERE WERE DOZENS OF THEM!
CARTHAGO HEADQUARTERS, MELBOURNE.
ARE YOU LOOKING AT THE SURVEILLANCE FOOTAGE? THAT'S VERY UNUSUAL.
I'VE BEEN WORKING OUT AT SEA FOR THIRTY-FIVE YEARS, AND I'VE SEEN MY FAIR SHARE OF SHARKS... BUT NEVER ANY LIKE THIS!
IT WAS A BONE-CHILLING SIGHT TO BEHOLD!
SOMETHING'S GOING ON. I DON'T KNOW WHAT EXACTLY, BUT THIS CAN'T BE A COINCIDENCE.
DO YOU MEAN THE LEVIATHAN, WHICH IS ALSO IN THE BERING SEA?
YES, MR. DOUGLAS.
OUR INFORMANTS ARE POSITIVE. SNYDER IS ON BOARD. HE'S PROBABLY FINANCING THE OPERATION.
BUT THE TRUE GOAL OF THAT EXPEDITION REMAINS UNDISCLOSED.
YES, MR. FEIERSINGER. THEY'VE PUT A GAG ORDER ON IT, AND OUR INFORMANTS DON'T HAVE ENOUGH SENIORITY ON THE CREW.
THE INTEL THEY ARE ABLE TO ACCESS REMAINS VAGUE AND CONFLICTING.
MR. DOUGLAS... DO YOU HAVE ANY OBLIGATIONS IN THE UPCOMING DAYS?
A FEW, BUT NOTHING SO IMPORTANT I COULDN'T SKIP OUT.
THEN GO PACK A BAG AT ONCE.
WE'RE GOING TO THE BERING SEA!

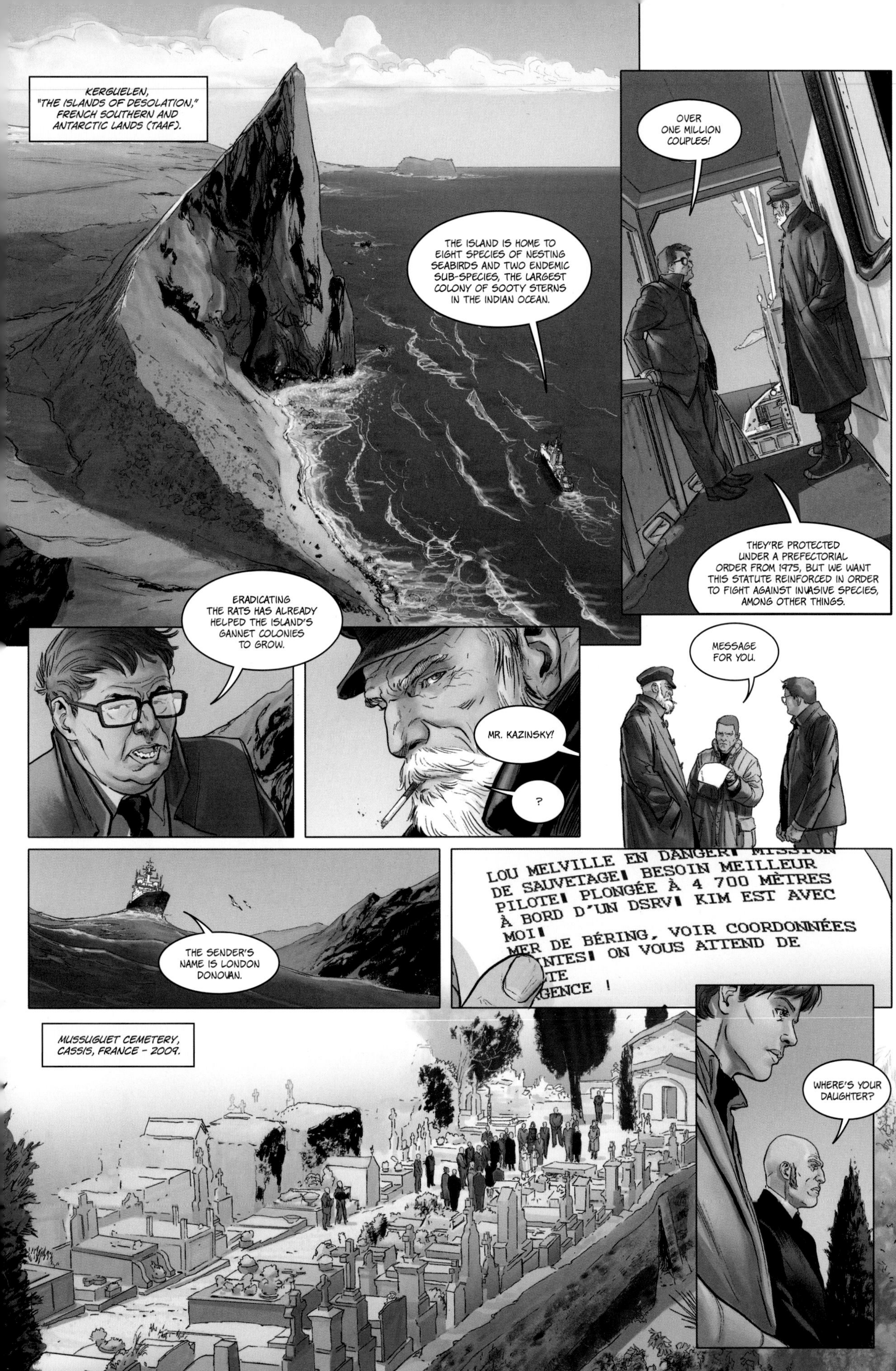
KERGUELEN, "THE ISLANDS OF DESOLATION," FRENCH SOUTHERN AND ANTARCTIC LANDS (TAAF).
THE ISLAND IS HOME TO EIGHT SPECIES OF NESTING SEABIRDS AND TWO ENDEMIC SUB-SPECIES, THE LARGEST COLONY OF SOOTY STERNS IN THE INDIAN OCEAN.
OVER ONE MILLION COUPLES!
THEY'RE PROTECTED UNDER A PREFECTORIAL ORDER FROM 1975, BUT WE WANT THIS STATUTE REINFORCED IN ORDER TO FIGHT AGAINST INVASIVE SPECIES, AMONG OTHER THINGS.
ERADICATING THE RATS HAS ALREADY HELPED THE ISLAND'S GANNET COLONIES TO GROW.
MR. KAZINSKY!
?
MESSAGE FOR YOU.
THE SENDER'S NAME IS LONDON DONOVAN.
LOU MELVILLE EN DANGER! MISSION
DE SAUVETAGE! BESOIN MEILLEUR
PILOTE! PLONGÉE À 4 700 MÈTRES
À BORD D'UN DSRV! KIM EST AVEC
MOI!
MER DE BÉRING, VOIR COORDONNÉES
INTES! ON VOUS ATTEND DE
TE
RGENCE !
MUSSUGUET CEMETERY, CASSIS, FRANCE - 2009.
WHERE'S YOUR DAUGHTER?

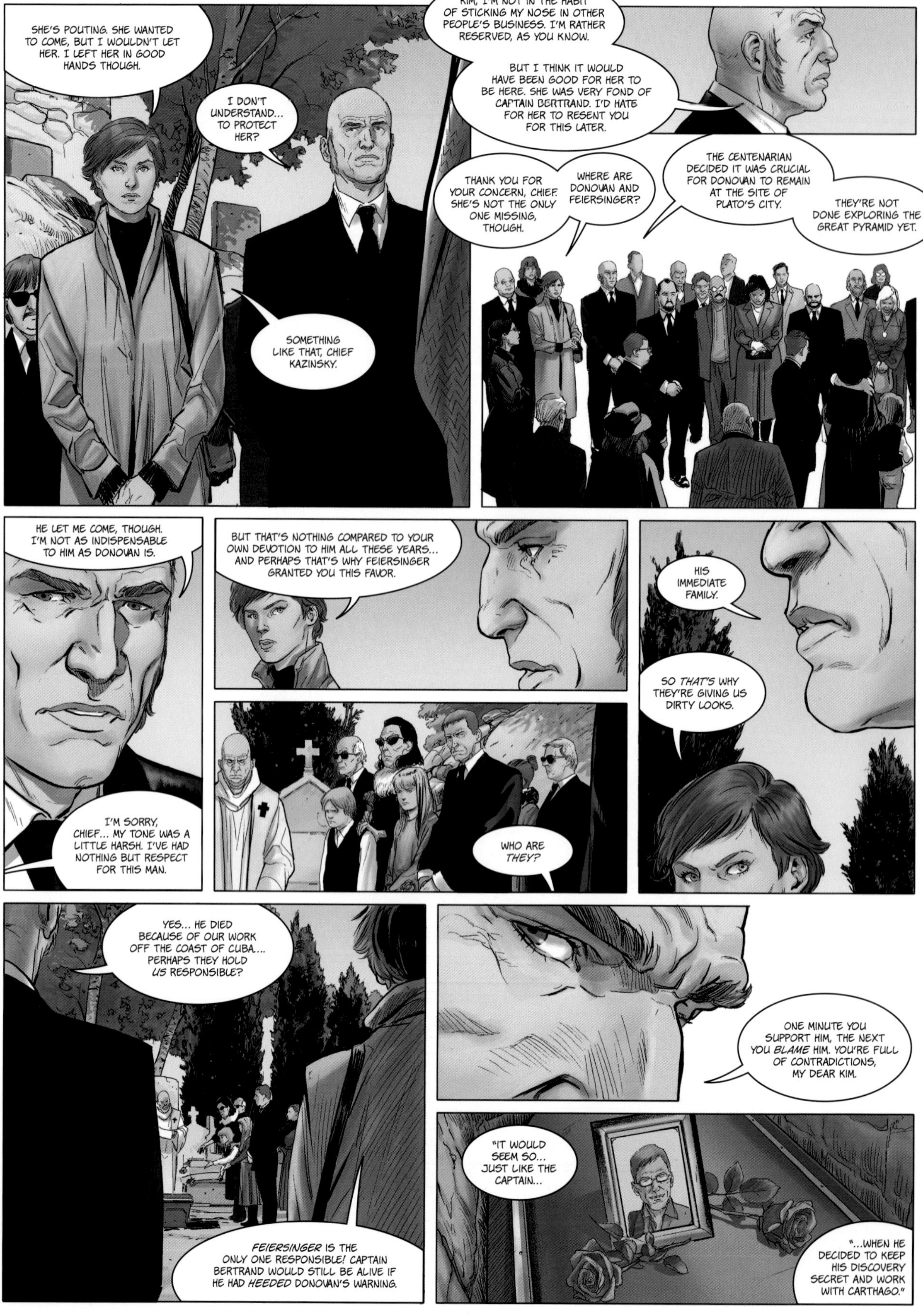
SHE'S POUTING. SHE WANTED TO COME, BUT I WOULDN'T LET HER. I LEFT HER IN GOOD HANDS THOUGH.
I DON'T UNDERSTAND... TO PROTECT HER?
SOMETHING LIKE THAT, CHIEF KAZINSKY.
KIM, I'M NOT IN THE HABIT OF STICKING MY NOSE IN OTHER PEOPLE'S BUSINESS. I'M RATHER RESERVED, AS YOU KNOW.
BUT I THINK IT WOULD HAVE BEEN GOOD FOR HER TO BE HERE. SHE WAS VERY FOND OF CAPTAIN BERTRAND. I'D HATE FOR HER TO RESENT YOU FOR THIS LATER.
THANK YOU FOR YOUR CONCERN, CHIEF. SHE'S NOT THE ONLY ONE MISSING, THOUGH.
WHERE ARE DONOVAN AND FEIERSINGER?
THE CENTENARIAN DECIDED IT WAS CRUCIAL FOR DONOVAN TO REMAIN AT THE SITE OF PLATO'S CITY.
THEY'RE NOT DONE EXPLORING THE GREAT PYRAMID YET.
HE LET ME COME, THOUGH. I'M NOT AS INDISPENSABLE TO HIM AS DONOVAN IS.
I'M SORRY, CHIEF... MY TONE WAS A LITTLE HARSH. I'VE HAD NOTHING BUT RESPECT FOR THIS MAN.
BUT THAT'S NOTHING COMPARED TO YOUR OWN DEVOTION TO HIM ALL THESE YEARS... AND PERHAPS THAT'S WHY FEIERSINGER GRANTED YOU THIS FAVOR.
WHO ARE *THEY*?
HIS IMMEDIATE FAMILY.
SO *THAT'S* WHY THEY'RE GIVING US DIRTY LOOKS.
YES... HE DIED BECAUSE OF OUR WORK OFF THE COAST OF CUBA... PERHAPS THEY HOLD *US* RESPONSIBLE?
FEIERSINGER IS THE ONLY ONE RESPONSIBLE! CAPTAIN BERTRAND WOULD STILL BE ALIVE IF HE HAD *HEEDED* DONOVAN'S WARNING.
ONE MINUTE YOU SUPPORT HIM, THE NEXT YOU *BLAME* HIM. YOU'RE FULL OF CONTRADICTIONS, MY DEAR KIM.
"IT WOULD SEEM SO... JUST LIKE THE CAPTAIN...
"...WHEN HE DECIDED TO KEEP HIS DISCOVERY SECRET AND WORK WITH CARTHAGO."

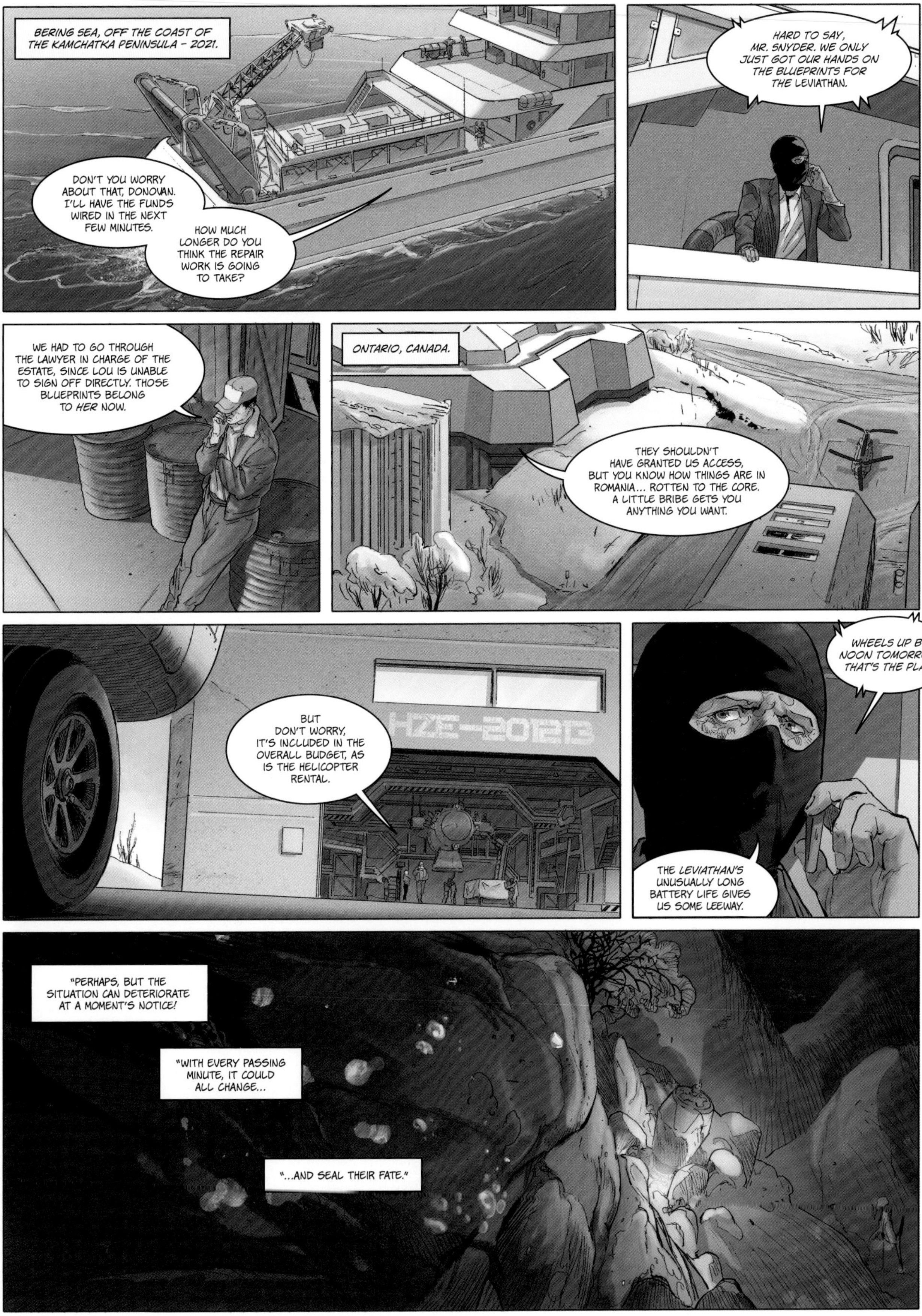
BERING SEA, OFF THE COAST OF THE KAMCHATKA PENINSULA - 2021.
HOW MUCH LONGER DO YOU THINK THE REPAIR WORK IS GOING TO TAKE?
HARD TO SAY, MR. SNYDER. WE ONLY JUST GOT OUR HANDS ON THE BLUEPRINTS FOR THE LEVIATHAN.
DON'T YOU WORRY ABOUT THAT, DONOVAN. I'LL HAVE THE FUNDS WIRED IN THE NEXT FEW MINUTES.
WE HAD TO GO THROUGH THE LAWYER IN CHARGE OF THE ESTATE, SINCE LOU IS UNABLE TO SIGN OFF DIRECTLY. THOSE BLUEPRINTS BELONG TO *HER* NOW.
ONTARIO, CANADA.
THEY SHOULDN'T HAVE GRANTED US ACCESS, BUT YOU KNOW HOW THINGS ARE IN ROMANIA... ROTTEN TO THE CORE. A LITTLE BRIBE GETS YOU ANYTHING YOU WANT.
HZE-20213
BUT DON'T WORRY, IT'S INCLUDED IN THE OVERALL BUDGET, AS IS THE HELICOPTER RENTAL.
WHEELS UP BY NOON TOMORROW. THAT'S THE PLAN.
THE *LEVIATHAN'S* UNUSUALLY LONG BATTERY LIFE GIVES US SOME LEEWAY.
"PERHAPS, BUT THE SITUATION CAN DETERIORATE AT A MOMENT'S NOTICE!
"WITH EVERY PASSING MINUTE, IT COULD ALL CHANGE...
"...AND SEAL THEIR FATE."

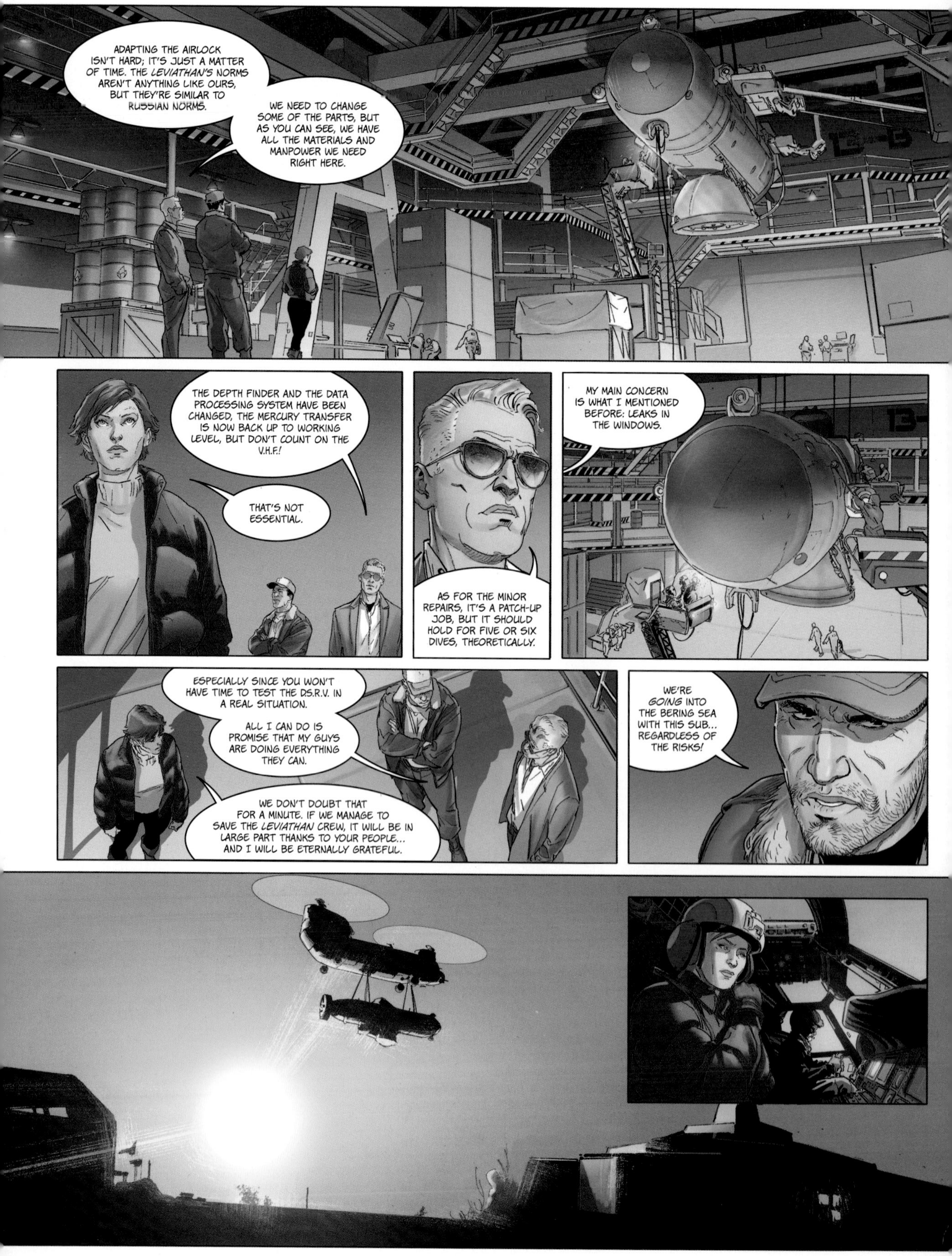
ADAPTING THE AIRLOCK ISN'T HARD; IT'S JUST A MATTER OF TIME. THE *LEVIATHAN'S* NORMS AREN'T ANYTHING LIKE OURS, BUT THEY'RE SIMILAR TO RUSSIAN NORMS.
WE NEED TO CHANGE SOME OF THE PARTS, BUT AS YOU CAN SEE, WE HAVE ALL THE MATERIALS AND MANPOWER WE NEED RIGHT HERE.
THE DEPTH FINDER AND THE DATA PROCESSING SYSTEM HAVE BEEN CHANGED, THE MERCURY TRANSFER IS NOW BACK UP TO WORKING LEVEL, BUT DON'T COUNT ON THE V.H.F.!
THAT'S NOT ESSENTIAL.
AS FOR THE MINOR REPAIRS, IT'S A PATCH-UP JOB, BUT IT SHOULD HOLD FOR FIVE OR SIX DIVES, THEORETICALLY.
MY MAIN CONCERN IS WHAT I MENTIONED BEFORE: LEAKS IN THE WINDOWS.
ESPECIALLY SINCE YOU WON'T HAVE TIME TO TEST THE D.S.R.V. IN A REAL SITUATION.
ALL I CAN DO IS PROMISE THAT MY GUYS ARE DOING EVERYTHING THEY CAN.
WE DON'T DOUBT THAT FOR A MINUTE. IF WE MANAGE TO SAVE THE *LEVIATHAN* CREW, IT WILL BE IN LARGE PART THANKS TO YOUR PEOPLE... AND I WILL BE ETERNALLY GRATEFUL.
WE'RE *GOING* INTO THE BERING SEA WITH THIS SUB... REGARDLESS OF THE RISKS!

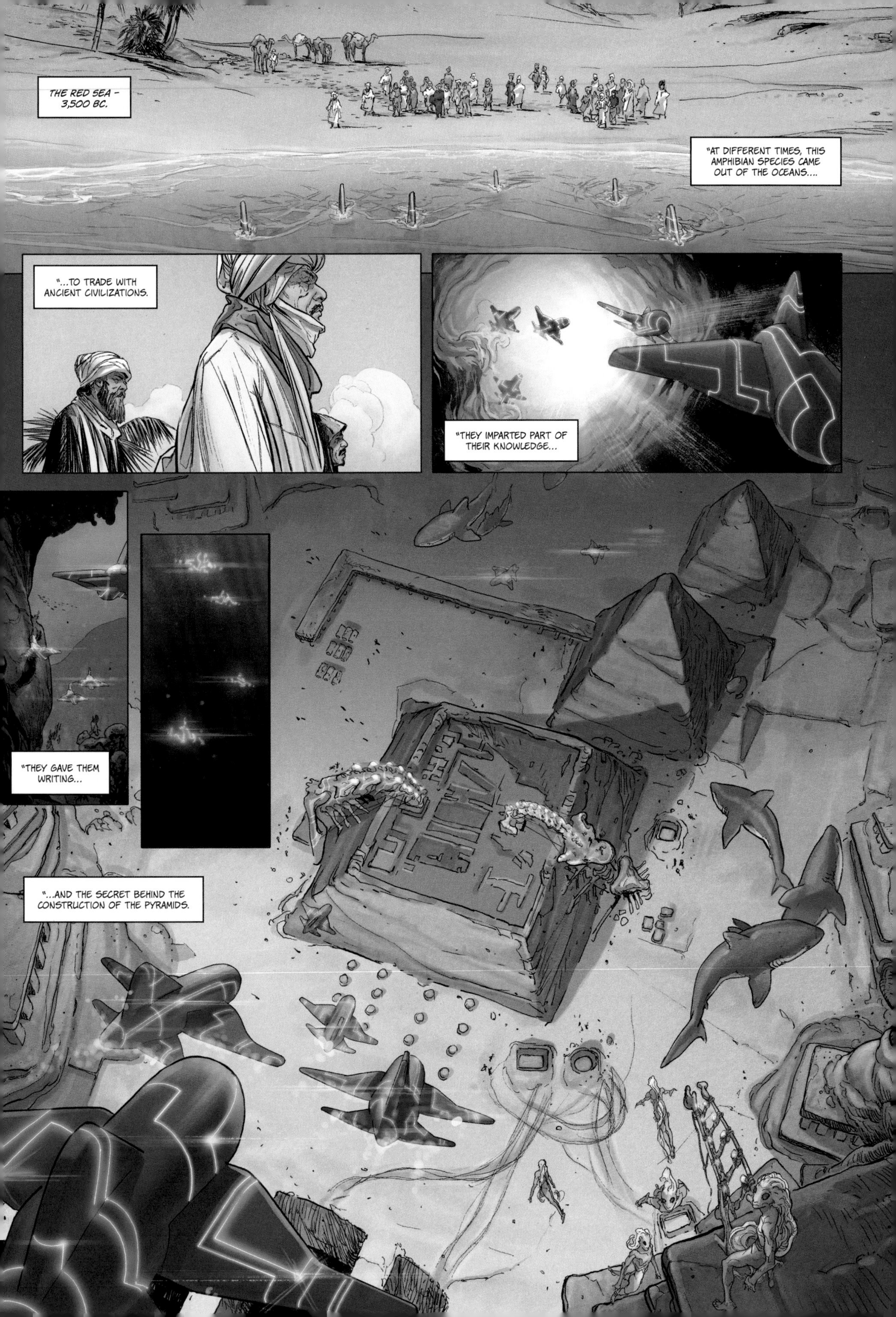
THE RED SEA – 3,500 BC.
"AT DIFFERENT TIMES, THIS AMPHIBIAN SPECIES CAME OUT OF THE OCEANS....
"...TO TRADE WITH ANCIENT CIVILIZATIONS.
"THEY IMPARTED PART OF THEIR KNOWLEDGE...
"THEY GAVE THEM WRITING...
"...AND THE SECRET BEHIND THE CONSTRUCTION OF THE PYRAMIDS.

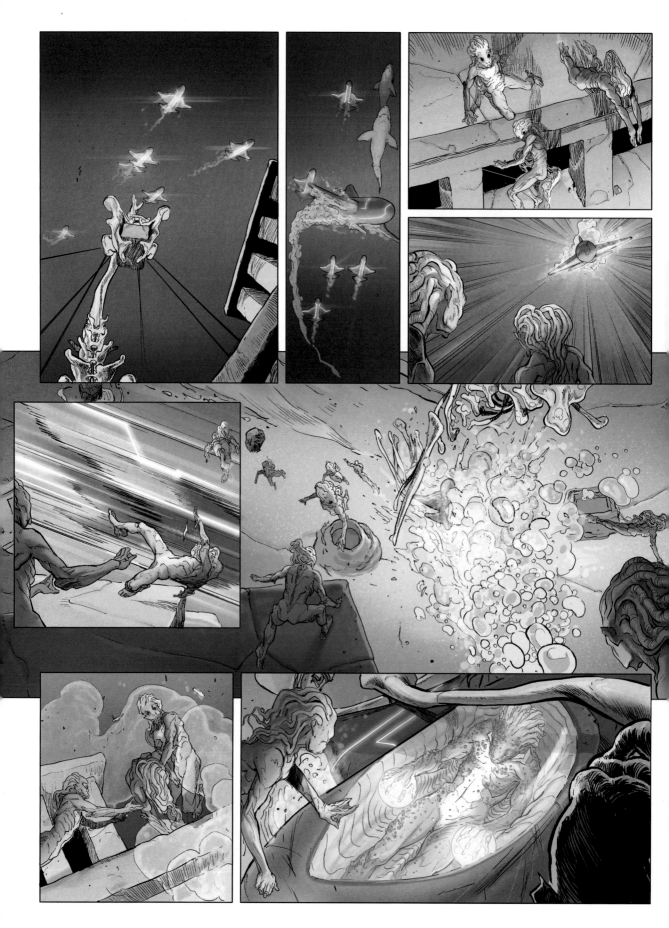

144

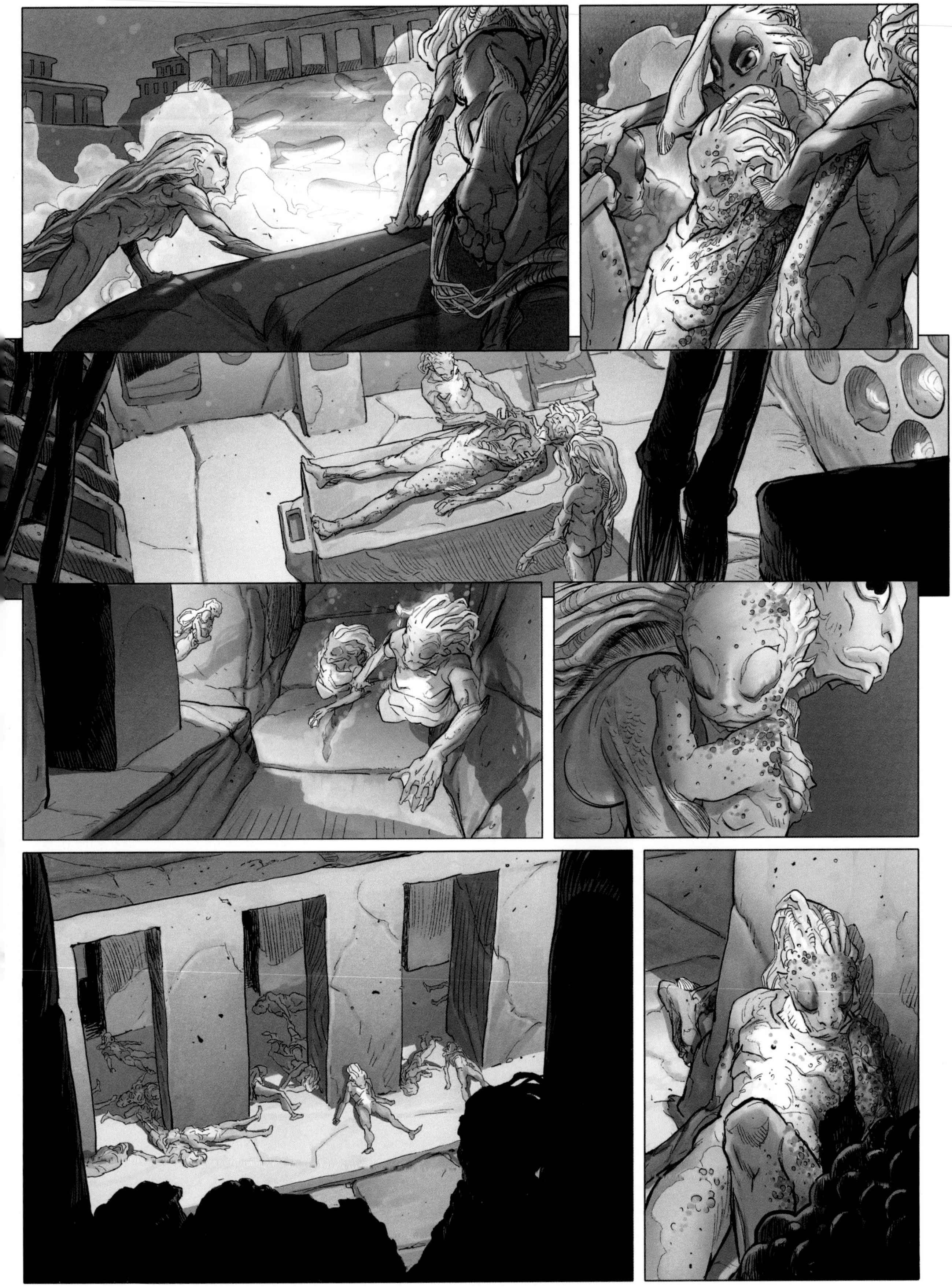

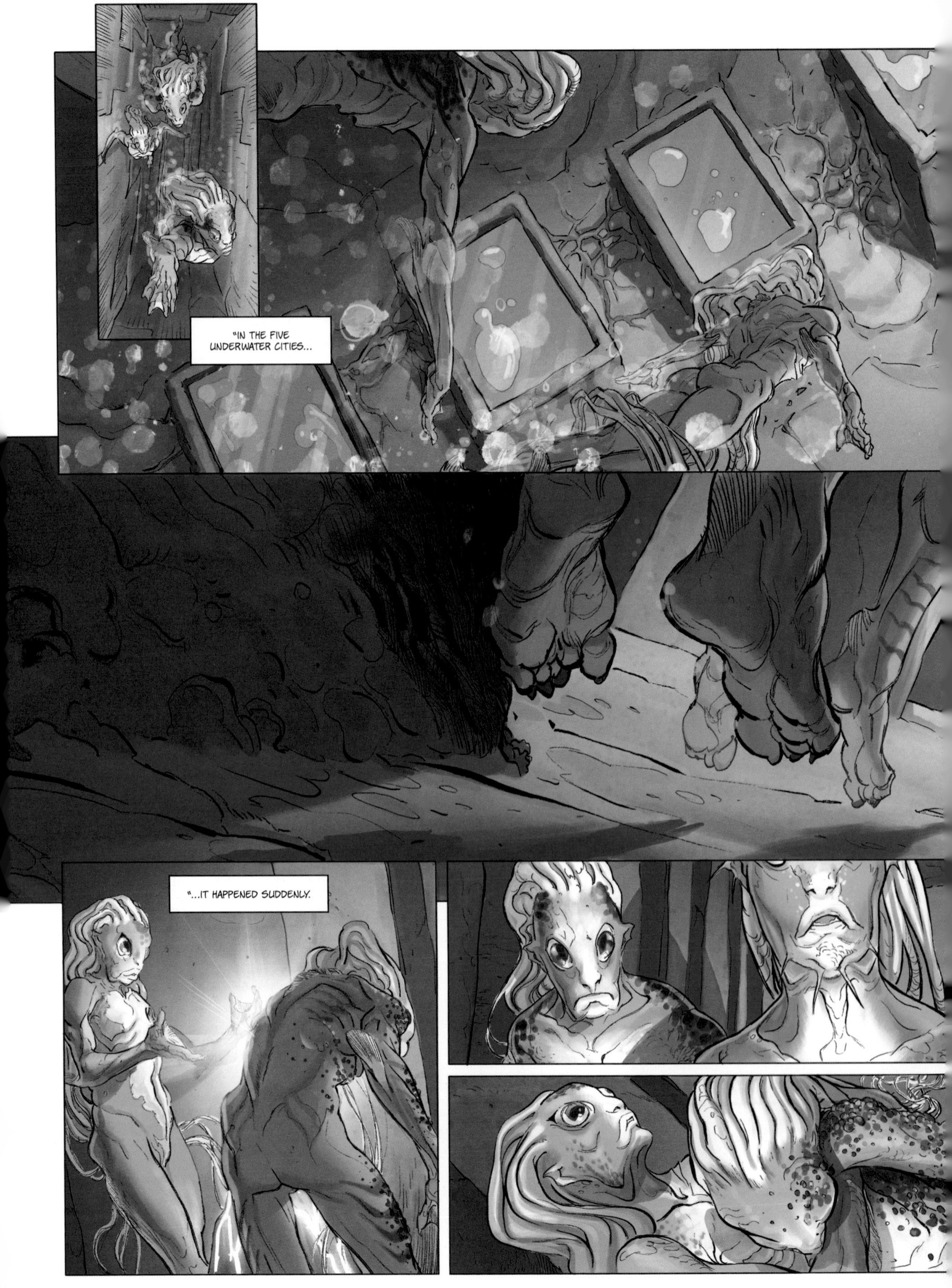
"IN THE FIVE UNDERWATER CITIES...
"...IT HAPPENED SUDDENLY.

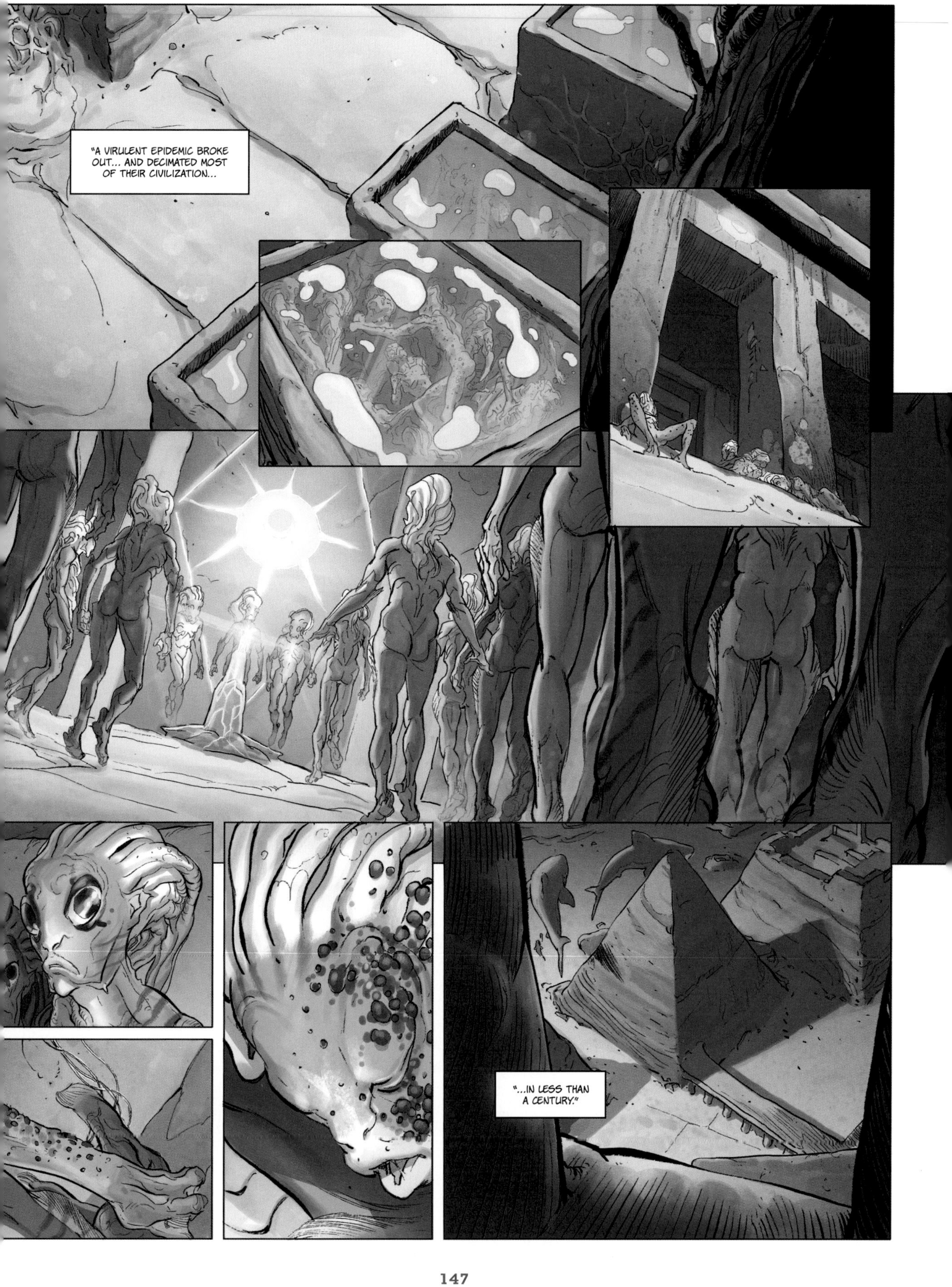
"A VIRULENT EPIDEMIC BROKE OUT... AND DECIMATED MOST OF THEIR CIVILIZATION...
"...IN LESS THAN A CENTURY."

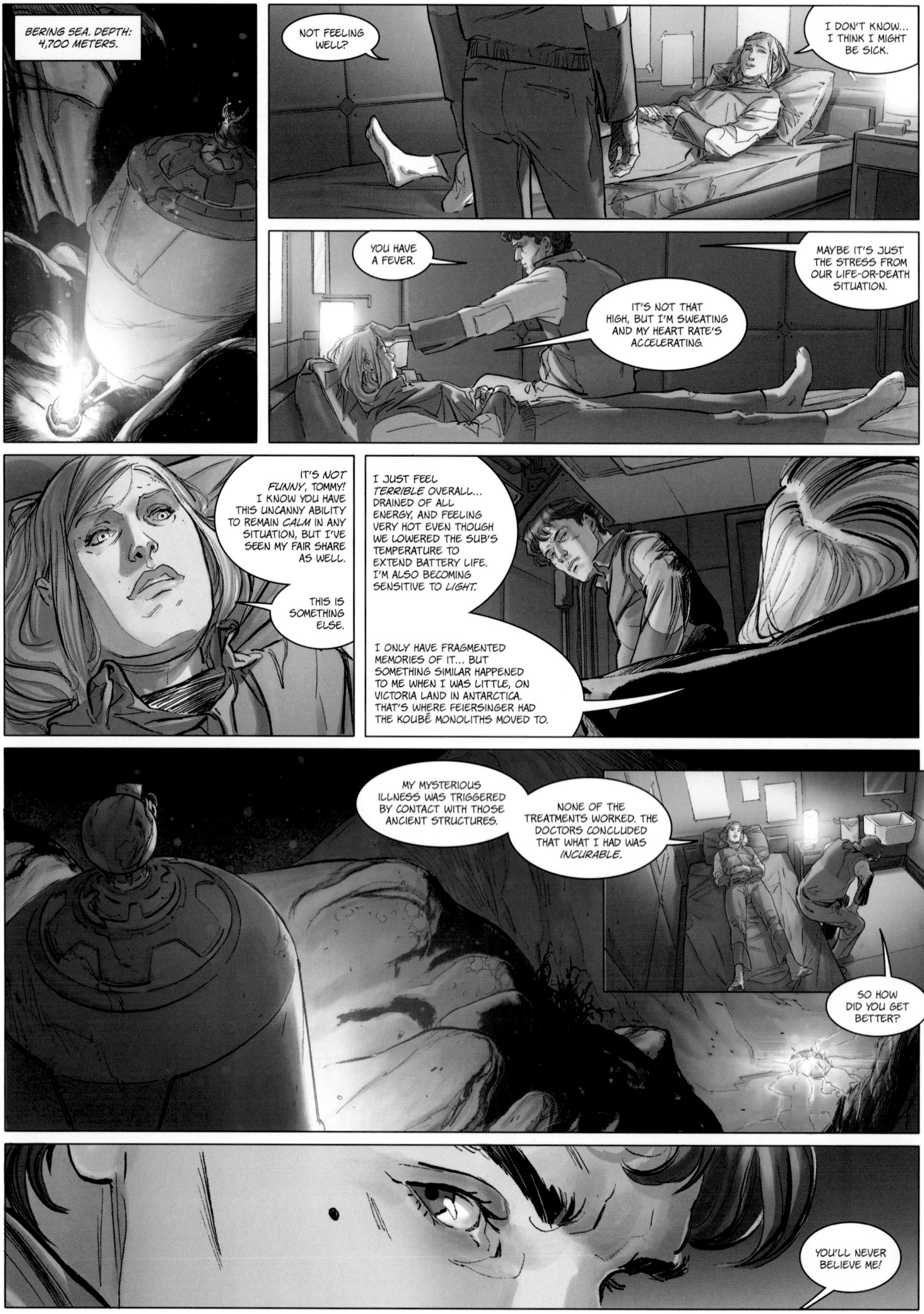
BERING SEA. DEPTH: 4,700 METERS.
NOT FEELING WELL?
I DON'T KNOW... I THINK I MIGHT BE SICK.
YOU HAVE A FEVER.
MAYBE IT'S JUST THE STRESS FROM OUR LIFE-OR-DEATH SITUATION.
IT'S NOT THAT HIGH, BUT I'M SWEATING AND MY HEART RATE'S ACCELERATING.
IT'S *NOT FUNNY*, TOMMY! I KNOW YOU HAVE THIS UNCANNY ABILITY TO REMAIN *CALM* IN ANY SITUATION, BUT I'VE SEEN MY FAIR SHARE AS WELL.
THIS IS SOMETHING ELSE.
I JUST FEEL *TERRIBLE OVERALL*... DRAINED OF ALL ENERGY, AND FEELING VERY HOT EVEN THOUGH WE LOWERED THE SUB'S TEMPERATURE TO EXTEND BATTERY LIFE. I'M ALSO BECOMING SENSITIVE TO *LIGHT.*
I ONLY HAVE FRAGMENTED MEMORIES OF IT... BUT SOMETHING SIMILAR HAPPENED TO ME WHEN I WAS LITTLE, ON VICTORIA LAND IN ANTARCTICA. THAT'S WHERE FEIERSINGER HAD THE KOUBÉ MONOLITHS MOVED TO.
MY MYSTERIOUS ILLNESS WAS TRIGGERED BY CONTACT WITH THOSE ANCIENT STRUCTURES.
NONE OF THE TREATMENTS WORKED. THE DOCTORS CONCLUDED THAT WHAT I HAD WAS *INCURABLE.*
SO HOW DID YOU GET BETTER?
YOU'LL NEVER BELIEVE ME!

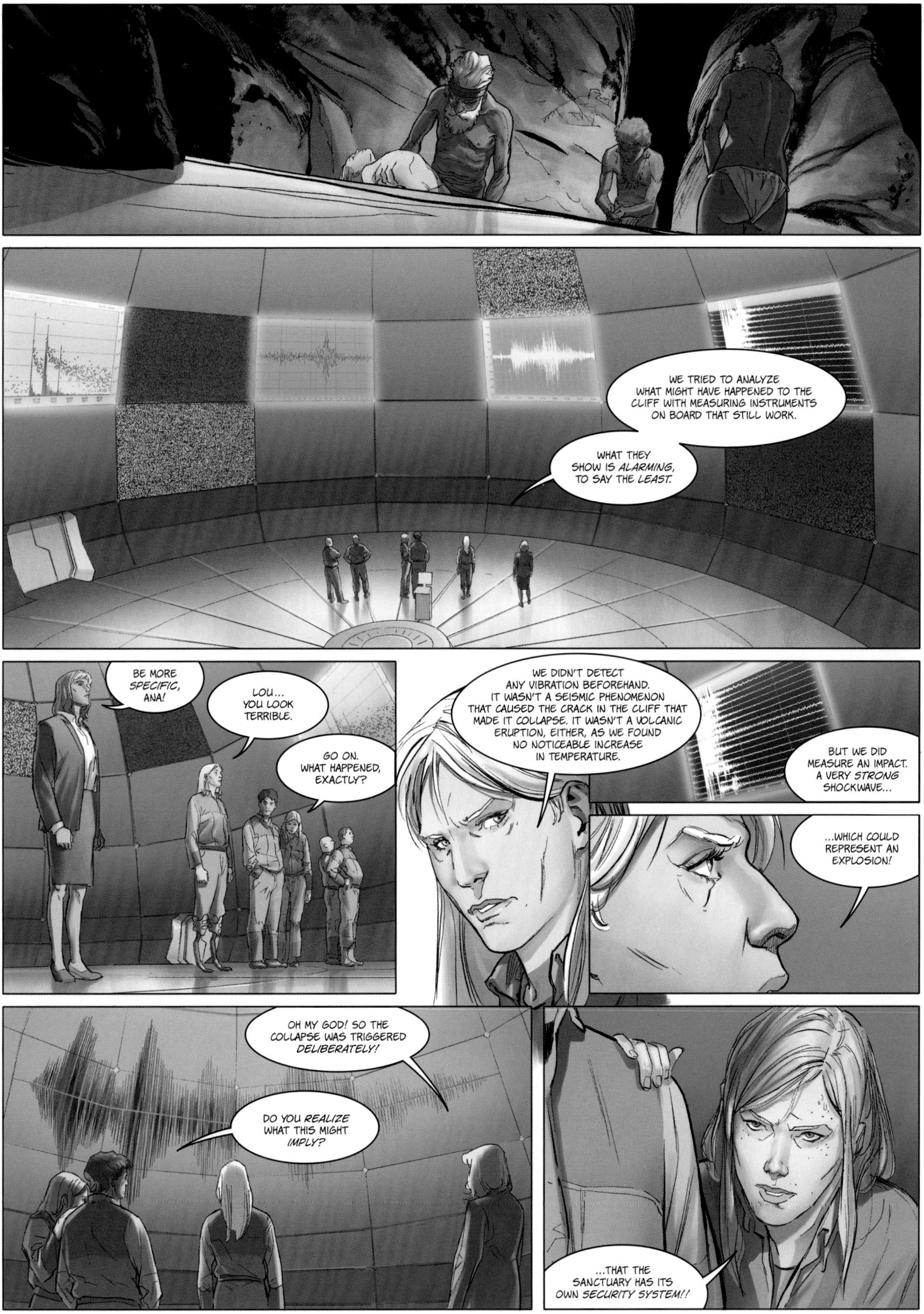
WE TRIED TO ANALYZE WHAT MIGHT HAVE HAPPENED TO THE CLIFF WITH MEASURING INSTRUMENTS ON BOARD THAT STILL WORK.
WHAT THEY SHOW IS *ALARMING*, TO SAY THE *LEAST*.
BE MORE *SPECIFIC*, ANA!
LOU... YOU LOOK TERRIBLE.
GO ON. WHAT HAPPENED, EXACTLY?
WE DIDN'T DETECT ANY VIBRATION BEFOREHAND. IT WASN'T A SEISMIC PHENOMENON THAT CAUSED THE CRACK IN THE CLIFF THAT MADE IT COLLAPSE. IT WASN'T A VOLCANIC ERUPTION, EITHER, AS WE FOUND NO NOTICEABLE INCREASE IN TEMPERATURE.
BUT WE DID MEASURE AN IMPACT. A VERY *STRONG* SHOCKWAVE...
...WHICH COULD REPRESENT AN EXPLOSION!
OH MY GOD! SO THE COLLAPSE WAS TRIGGERED *DELIBERATELY*!
DO YOU *REALIZE* WHAT THIS MIGHT *IMPLY*?
...THAT THE SANCTUARY HAS ITS OWN *SECURITY SYSTEM*!!

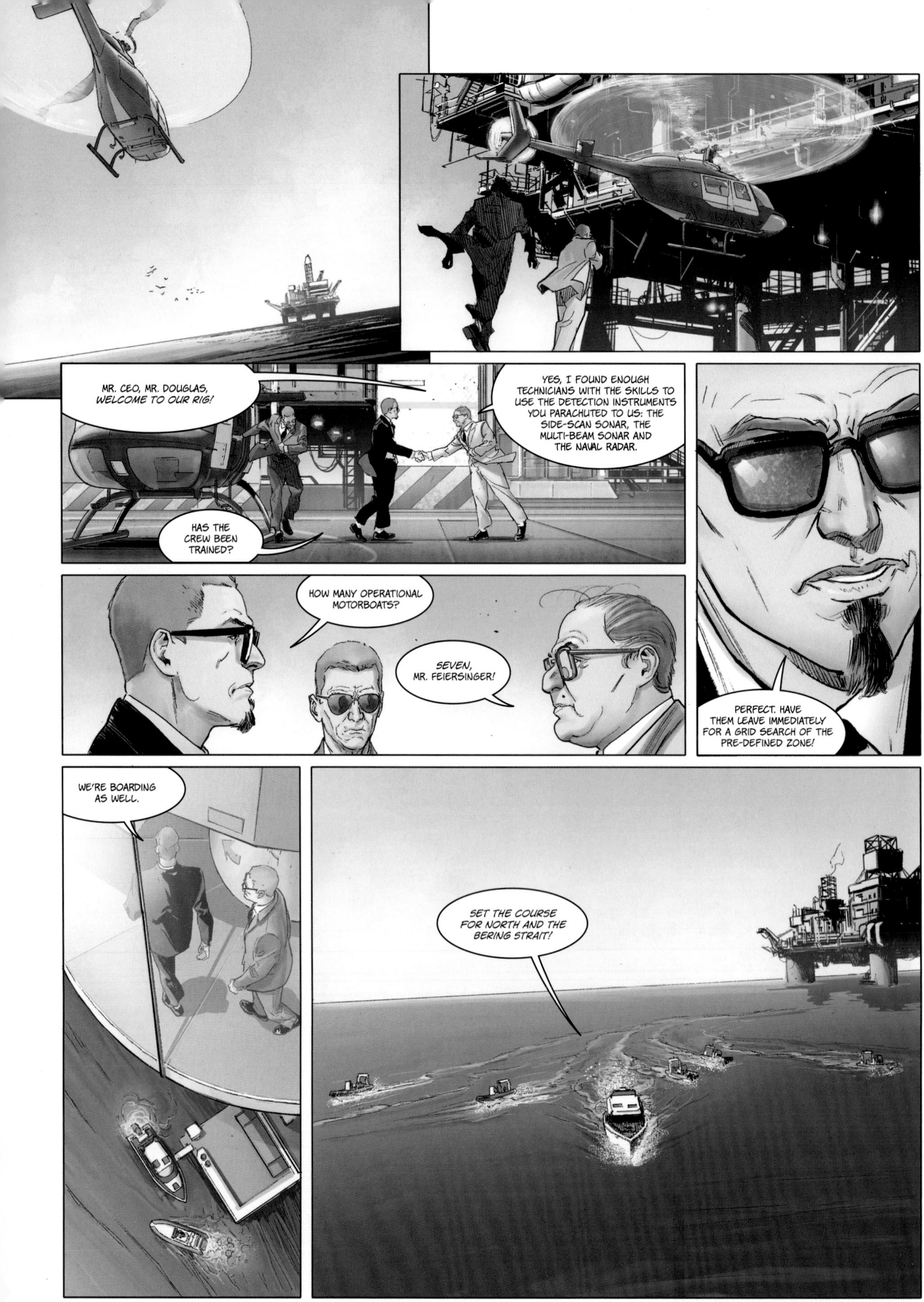
MR. CEO, MR. DOUGLAS, WELCOME TO OUR RIG!
HAS THE CREW BEEN TRAINED?
YES, I FOUND ENOUGH TECHNICIANS WITH THE SKILLS TO USE THE DETECTION INSTRUMENTS YOU PARACHUTED TO US: THE SIDE-SCAN SONAR, THE MULTI-BEAM SONAR AND THE NAVAL RADAR.
HOW MANY OPERATIONAL MOTORBOATS?
SEVEN, MR. FEIERSINGER!
PERFECT. HAVE THEM LEAVE IMMEDIATELY FOR A GRID SEARCH OF THE PRE-DEFINED ZONE!
WE'RE BOARDING AS WELL.
SET THE COURSE FOR NORTH AND THE BERING STRAIT!

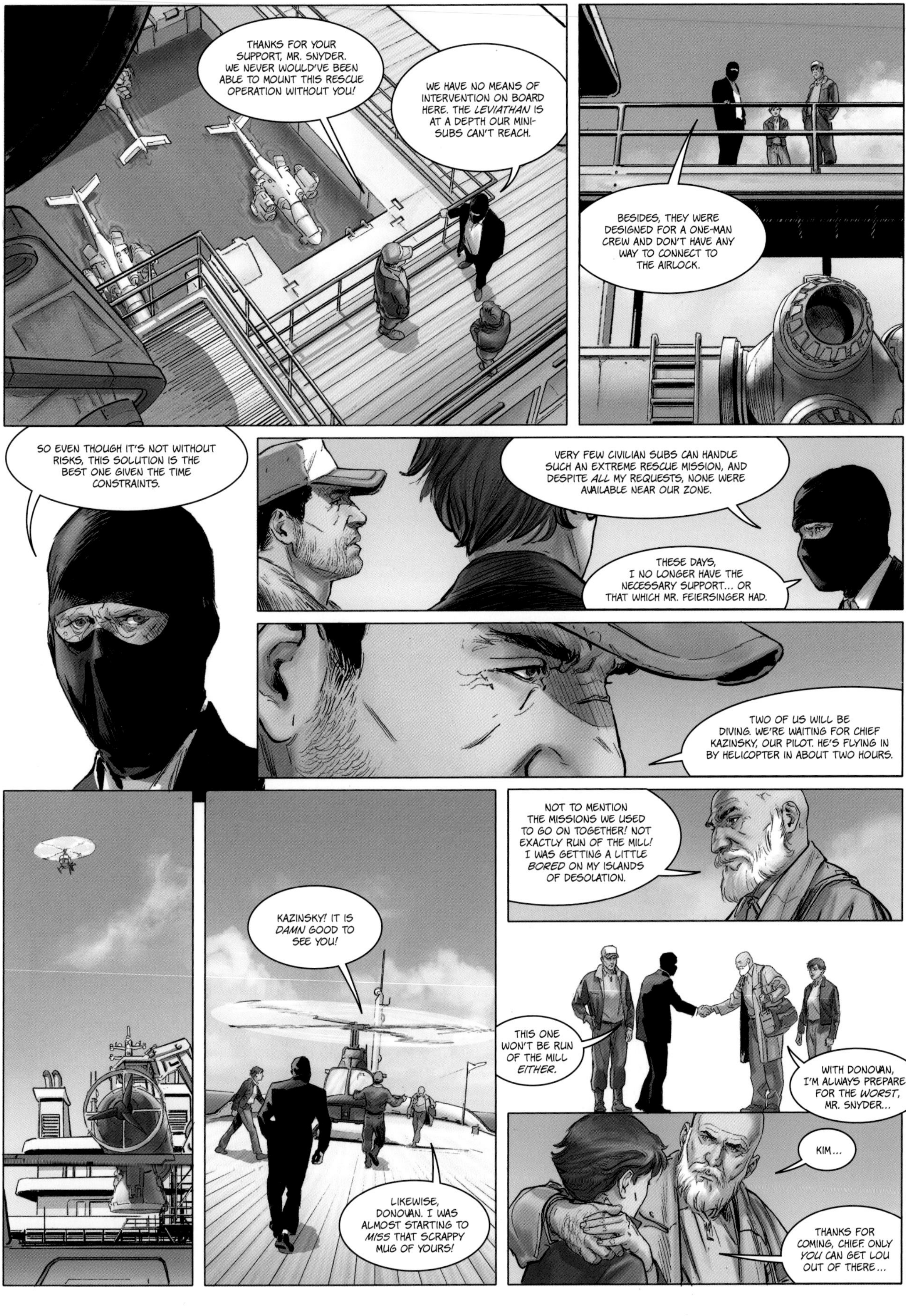
THANKS FOR YOUR SUPPORT, MR. SNYDER. WE NEVER WOULD'VE BEEN ABLE TO MOUNT THIS RESCUE OPERATION WITHOUT YOU!
WE HAVE NO MEANS OF INTERVENTION ON BOARD HERE. THE *LEVIATHAN* IS AT A DEPTH OUR MINI-SUBS CAN'T REACH.
BESIDES, THEY WERE DESIGNED FOR A ONE-MAN CREW AND DON'T HAVE ANY WAY TO CONNECT TO THE AIRLOCK.
SO EVEN THOUGH IT'S NOT WITHOUT RISKS, THIS SOLUTION IS THE BEST ONE GIVEN THE TIME CONSTRAINTS.
VERY FEW CIVILIAN SUBS CAN HANDLE SUCH AN EXTREME RESCUE MISSION, AND DESPITE *ALL* MY REQUESTS, NONE WERE AVAILABLE NEAR OUR ZONE.
THESE DAYS, I NO LONGER HAVE THE NECESSARY SUPPORT... OR THAT WHICH MR. FEIERSINGER HAD.
TWO OF US WILL BE DIVING. WE'RE WAITING FOR CHIEF KAZINSKY, OUR PILOT. HE'S FLYING IN BY HELICOPTER IN ABOUT TWO HOURS.
KAZINSKY! IT IS *DAMN* GOOD TO SEE YOU!
LIKEWISE, DONOVAN. I WAS ALMOST STARTING TO *MISS* THAT SCRAPPY MUG OF YOURS!
NOT TO MENTION THE MISSIONS WE USED TO GO ON TOGETHER! NOT EXACTLY RUN OF THE MILL! I WAS GETTING A LITTLE *BORED* ON MY ISLANDS OF DESOLATION.
THIS ONE WON'T BE RUN OF THE MILL *EITHER*.
WITH DONOVAN, I'M ALWAYS PREPARED FOR THE *WORST*, MR. SNYDER...
KIM...
THANKS FOR COMING, CHIEF. ONLY *YOU* CAN GET LOU OUT OF THERE...

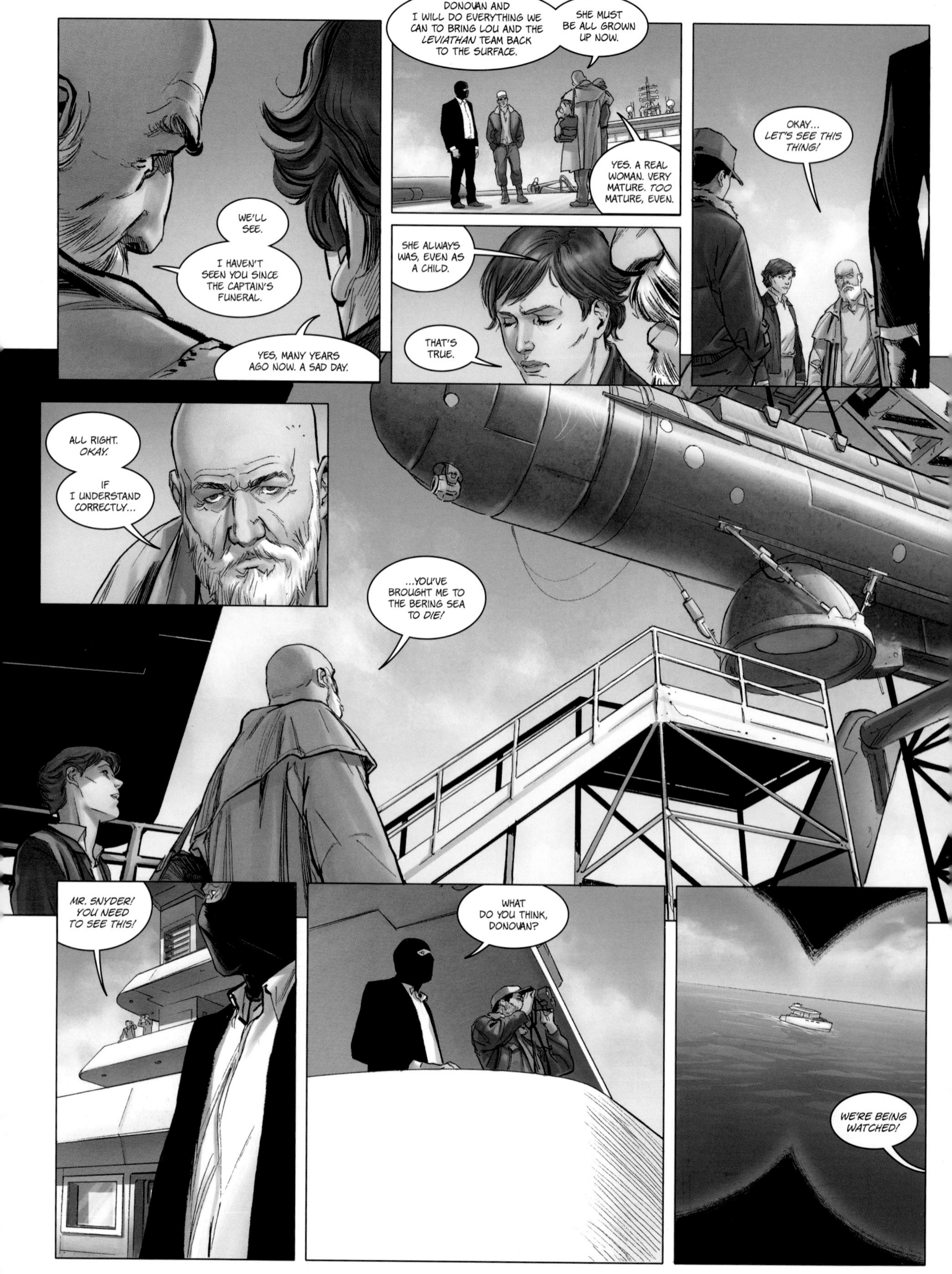
WE'LL SEE.
I HAVEN'T SEEN YOU SINCE THE CAPTAIN'S FUNERAL.
YES, MANY YEARS AGO NOW. A SAD DAY.
DONOVAN AND I WILL DO EVERYTHING WE CAN TO BRING LOU AND THE *LEVIATHAN* TEAM BACK TO THE SURFACE.
SHE MUST BE ALL GROWN UP NOW.
YES. A REAL WOMAN. VERY MATURE. *TOO* MATURE, EVEN.
SHE ALWAYS WAS, EVEN AS A CHILD.
THAT'S TRUE.
OKAY... *LET'S SEE THIS THING!*
ALL RIGHT. *OKAY.*
IF I UNDERSTAND CORRECTLY...
...YOU'VE BROUGHT ME TO THE BERING SEA TO *DIE!*
MR. SNYDER! YOU NEED TO SEE THIS!
WHAT DO YOU THINK, DONOVAN?
WE'RE BEING WATCHED!

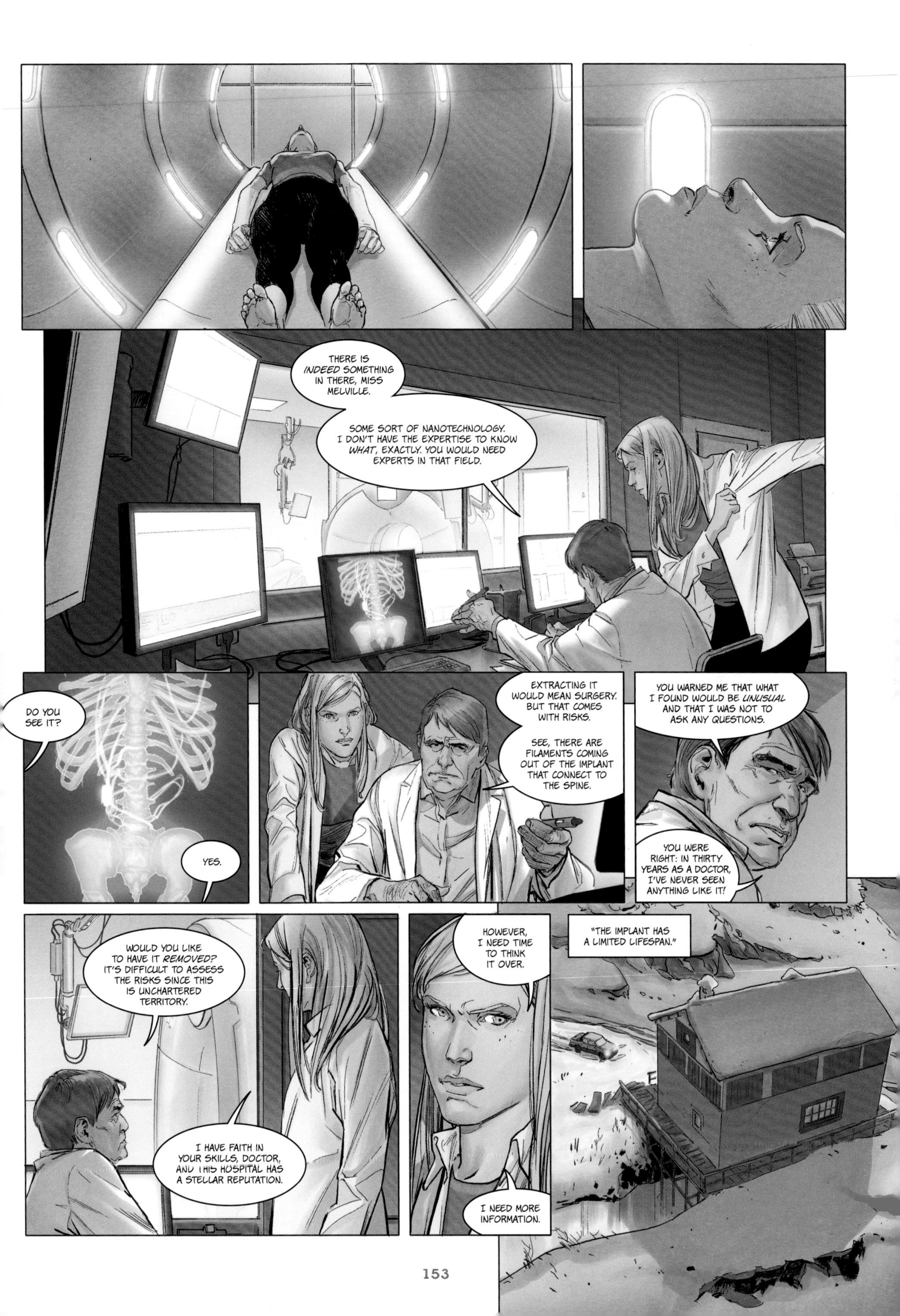

THERE IS *INDEED* SOMETHING IN THERE, MISS MELVILLE.
SOME SORT OF NANOTECHNOLOGY. I DON'T HAVE THE EXPERTISE TO KNOW *WHAT*, EXACTLY. YOU WOULD NEED EXPERTS IN THAT FIELD.
DO YOU SEE IT?
YES.
EXTRACTING IT WOULD MEAN SURGERY. BUT THAT COMES WITH RISKS.
SEE, THERE ARE FILAMENTS COMING OUT OF THE IMPLANT THAT CONNECT TO THE SPINE.
YOU WARNED ME THAT WHAT I FOUND WOULD BE *UNUSUAL* AND THAT I WAS NOT TO ASK ANY QUESTIONS.
YOU WERE RIGHT: IN THIRTY YEARS AS A DOCTOR, I'VE NEVER SEEN ANYTHING LIKE IT!
WOULD YOU LIKE TO HAVE IT *REMOVED?* IT'S DIFFICULT TO ASSESS THE RISKS SINCE THIS IS UNCHARTERED TERRITORY.
I HAVE FAITH IN YOUR SKILLS, DOCTOR, AND THIS HOSPITAL HAS A STELLAR REPUTATION.
HOWEVER, I NEED TIME TO THINK IT OVER.
I NEED MORE INFORMATION.
"THE IMPLANT HAS A LIMITED LIFESPAN."

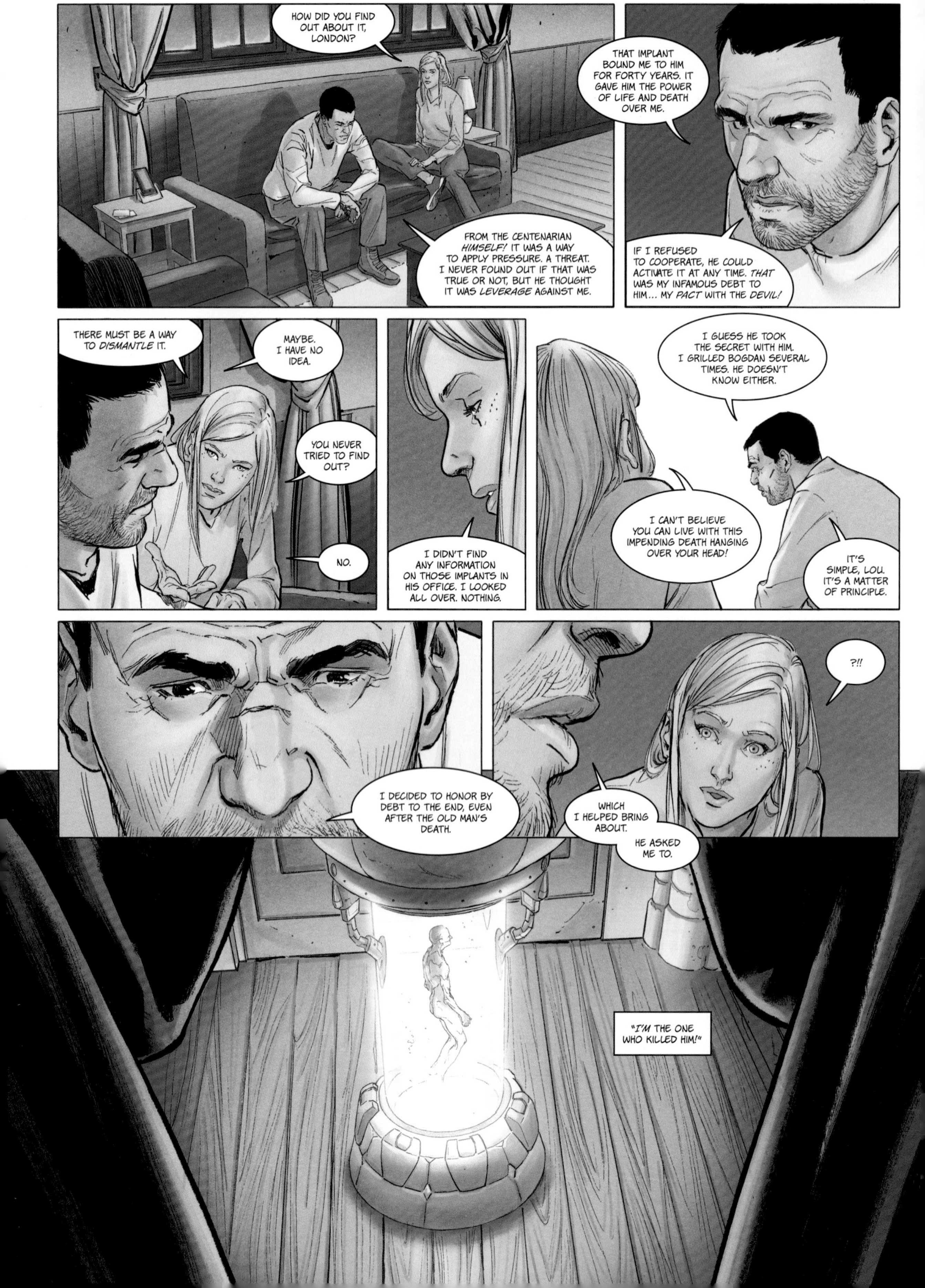

HOW DID YOU FIND OUT ABOUT IT, LONDON?
FROM THE CENTENARIAN *HIMSELF!* IT WAS A WAY TO APPLY PRESSURE. A THREAT. I NEVER FOUND OUT IF THAT WAS TRUE OR NOT, BUT HE THOUGHT IT WAS *LEVERAGE* AGAINST ME.
THAT IMPLANT BOUND ME TO HIM FOR FORTY YEARS. IT GAVE HIM THE POWER OF LIFE AND DEATH OVER ME.
IF I REFUSED TO COOPERATE, HE COULD ACTIVATE IT AT ANY TIME. *THAT* WAS MY INFAMOUS DEBT TO HIM... MY *PACT* WITH THE *DEVIL!*
THERE MUST BE A WAY TO *DISMANTLE* IT.
MAYBE. I HAVE NO IDEA.
YOU NEVER TRIED TO FIND OUT?
NO.
I DIDN'T FIND ANY INFORMATION ON THOSE IMPLANTS IN HIS OFFICE. I LOOKED ALL OVER. NOTHING.
I GUESS HE TOOK THE SECRET WITH HIM. I GRILLED BOGDAN SEVERAL TIMES. HE DOESN'T KNOW EITHER.
I CAN'T BELIEVE YOU CAN LIVE WITH THIS IMPENDING DEATH HANGING OVER YOUR HEAD!
IT'S SIMPLE, LOU. IT'S A MATTER OF PRINCIPLE.
I DECIDED TO HONOR BY DEBT TO THE END, EVEN AFTER THE OLD MAN'S DEATH.
?!!
WHICH I HELPED BRING ABOUT.
HE ASKED ME TO.
"*I'M* THE ONE WHO KILLED HIM!"

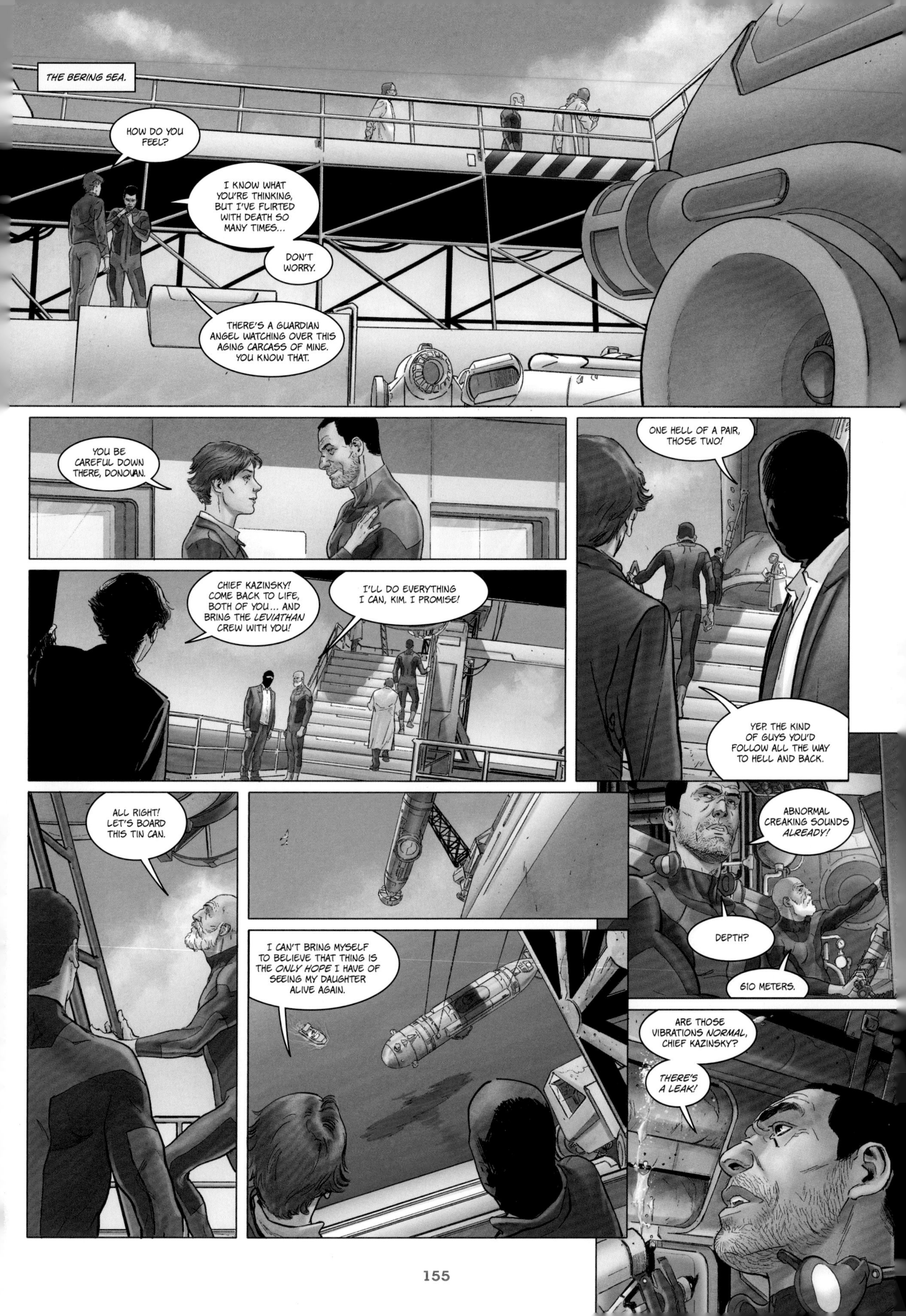
THE BERING SEA.
HOW DO YOU FEEL?
I KNOW WHAT YOU'RE THINKING, BUT I'VE FLIRTED WITH DEATH SO MANY TIMES...
DON'T WORRY.
THERE'S A GUARDIAN ANGEL WATCHING OVER THIS AGING CARCASS OF MINE. YOU KNOW THAT.
YOU BE CAREFUL DOWN THERE, DONOVAN.
CHIEF KAZINSKY! COME BACK TO LIFE, BOTH OF YOU... AND BRING THE *LEVIATHAN* CREW WITH YOU!
I'LL DO EVERYTHING I CAN, KIM. I PROMISE!
ONE HELL OF A PAIR, THOSE TWO!
YEP. THE KIND OF GUYS YOU'D FOLLOW ALL THE WAY TO HELL AND BACK.
ALL RIGHT! LET'S BOARD THIS TIN CAN.
I CAN'T BRING MYSELF TO BELIEVE THAT THING IS THE *ONLY HOPE* I HAVE OF SEEING MY DAUGHTER ALIVE AGAIN.
ABNORMAL CREAKING SOUNDS *ALREADY!*
DEPTH?
610 METERS.
ARE THOSE VIBRATIONS *NORMAL*, CHIEF KAZINSKY?
THERE'S A LEAK!

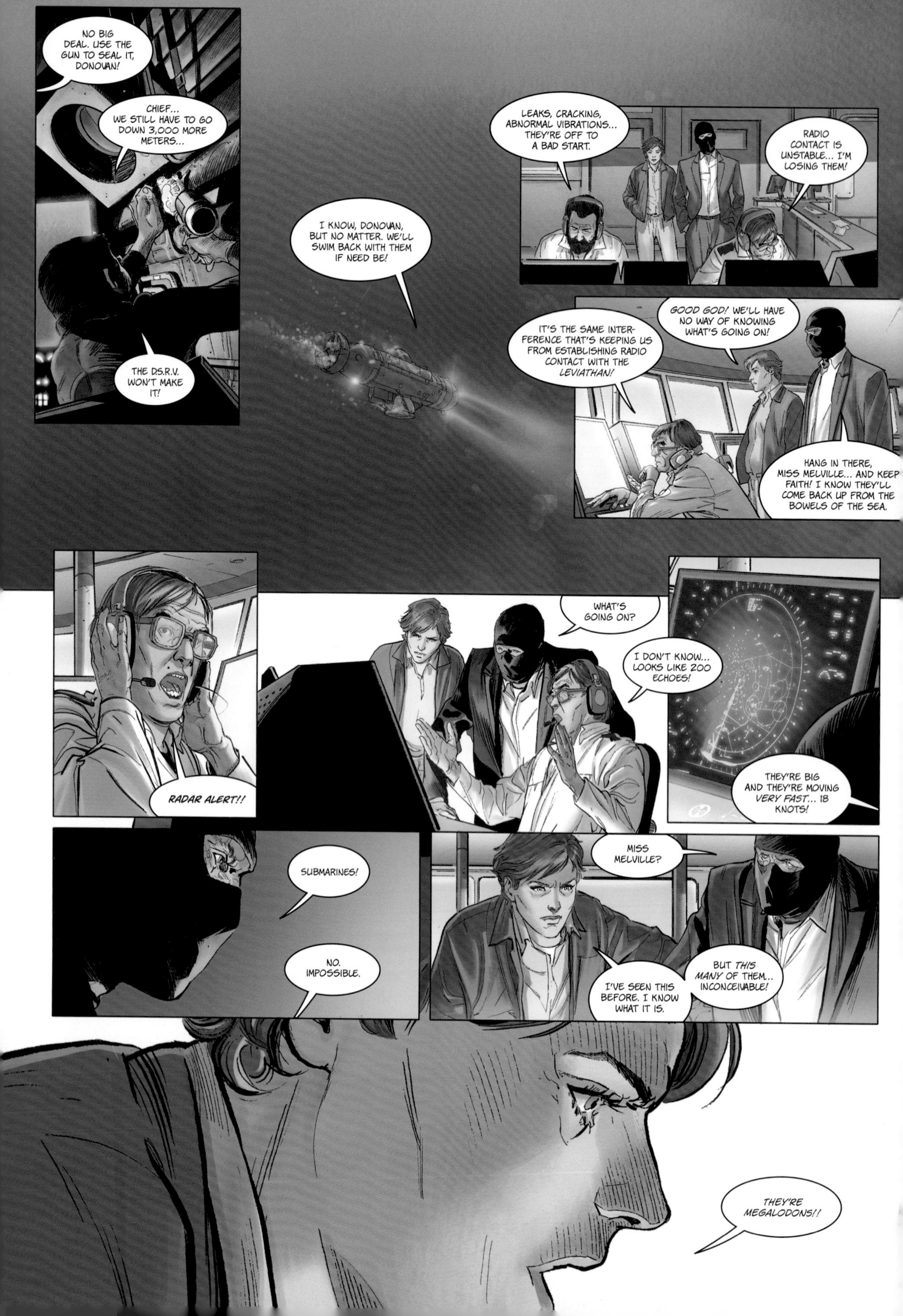
NO BIG DEAL. USE THE GUN TO SEAL IT, DONOVAN!
CHIEF... WE STILL HAVE TO GO DOWN 3,000 MORE METERS...
THE D.S.R.V. WON'T MAKE IT!
I KNOW, DONOVAN, BUT NO MATTER. WE'LL SWIM BACK WITH THEM IF NEED BE!
LEAKS, CRACKING, ABNORMAL VIBRATIONS... THEY'RE OFF TO A BAD START.
RADIO CONTACT IS UNSTABLE... I'M LOSING THEM!
GOOD GOD! WE'LL HAVE NO WAY OF KNOWING WHAT'S GOING ON!
IT'S THE SAME INTERFERENCE THAT'S KEEPING US FROM ESTABLISHING RADIO CONTACT WITH THE *LEVIATHAN!*
HANG IN THERE, MISS MELVILLE... AND KEEP FAITH! I KNOW THEY'LL COME BACK UP FROM THE BOWELS OF THE SEA.
RADAR ALERT!!
WHAT'S GOING ON?
I DON'T KNOW... LOOKS LIKE 200 ECHOES!
THEY'RE BIG AND THEY'RE MOVING *VERY FAST*... 18 KNOTS!
SUBMARINES!
NO. IMPOSSIBLE.
MISS MELVILLE?
BUT *THIS MANY* OF THEM... INCONCEIVABLE!
I'VE SEEN THIS BEFORE. I KNOW WHAT IT IS.
THEY'RE MEGALODONS!!

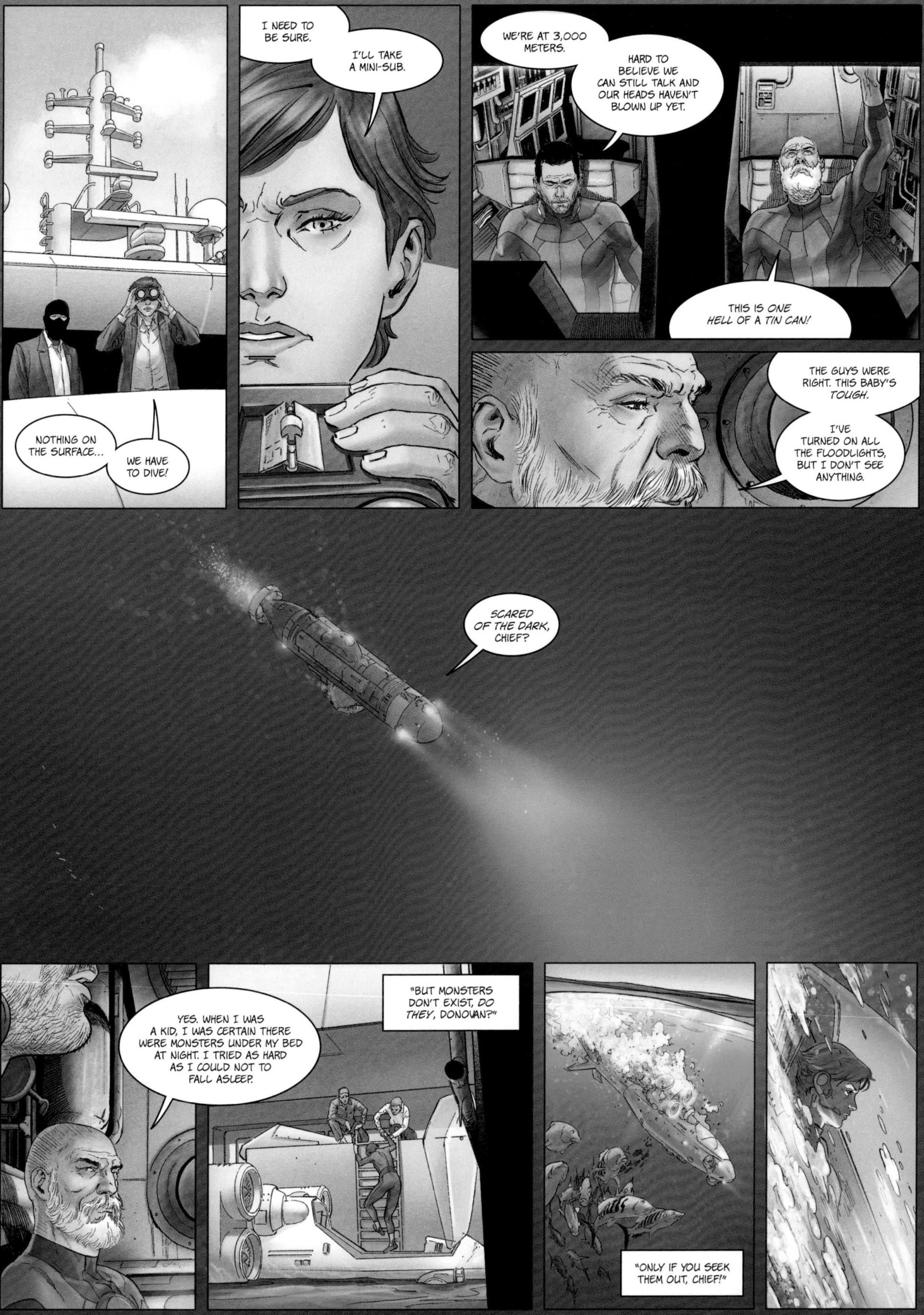
NOTHING ON THE SURFACE...
WE HAVE TO DIVE!
I NEED TO BE SURE.
I'LL TAKE A MINI-SUB.
WE'RE AT 3,000 METERS.
HARD TO BELIEVE WE CAN STILL TALK AND OUR HEADS HAVEN'T BLOWN UP YET.
THIS IS ONE HELL OF A TIN CAN!
THE GUYS WERE RIGHT. THIS BABY'S TOUGH.
I'VE TURNED ON ALL THE FLOODLIGHTS, BUT I DON'T SEE ANYTHING.
SCARED OF THE DARK, CHIEF?
YES. WHEN I WAS A KID, I WAS CERTAIN THERE WERE MONSTERS UNDER MY BED AT NIGHT. I TRIED AS HARD AS I COULD NOT TO FALL ASLEEP.
"BUT MONSTERS DON'T EXIST, DO THEY, DONOVAN?"
"ONLY IF YOU SEEK THEM OUT, CHIEF!"

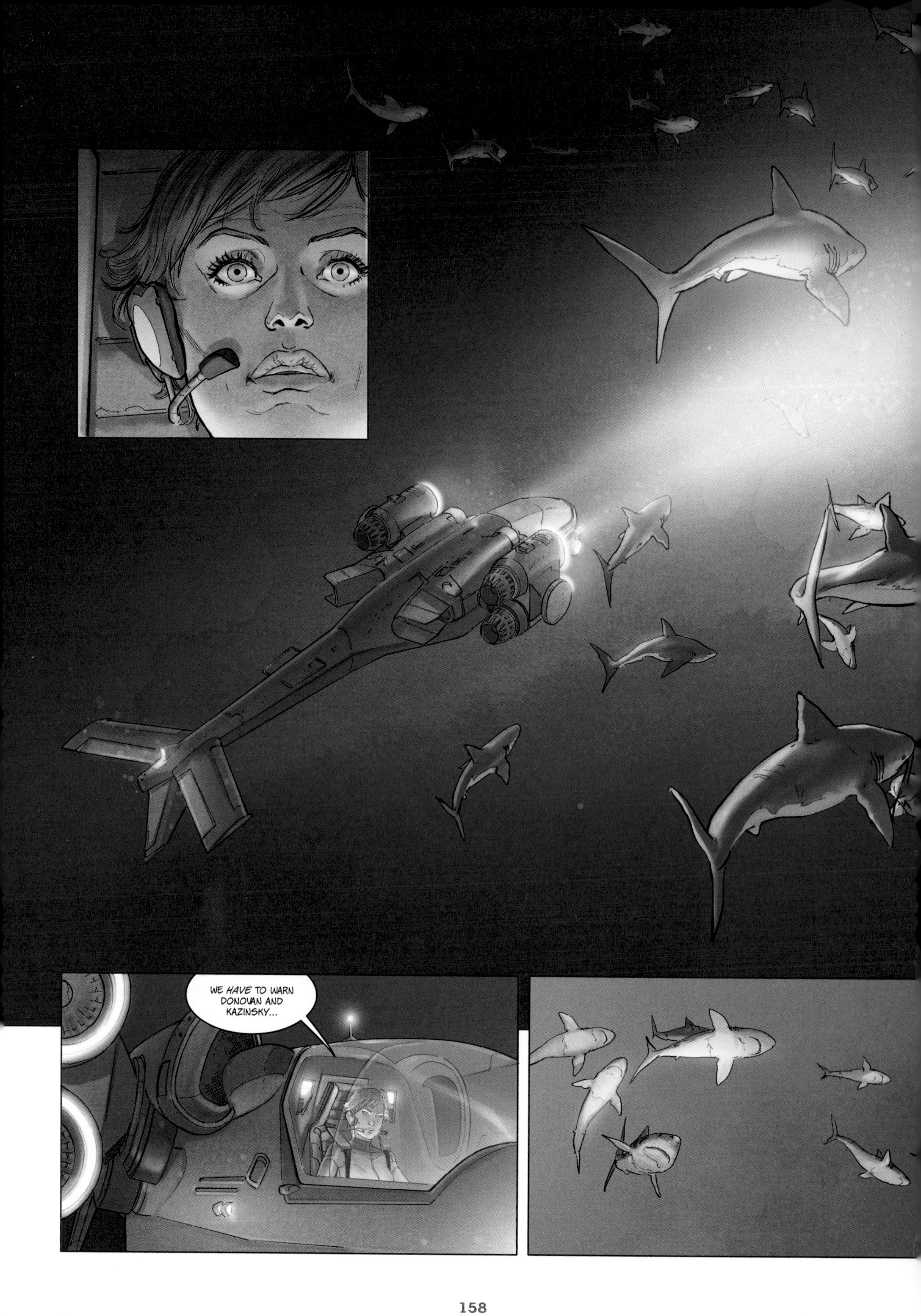
WE *HAVE* TO WARN DONOVAN AND KAZINSKY...

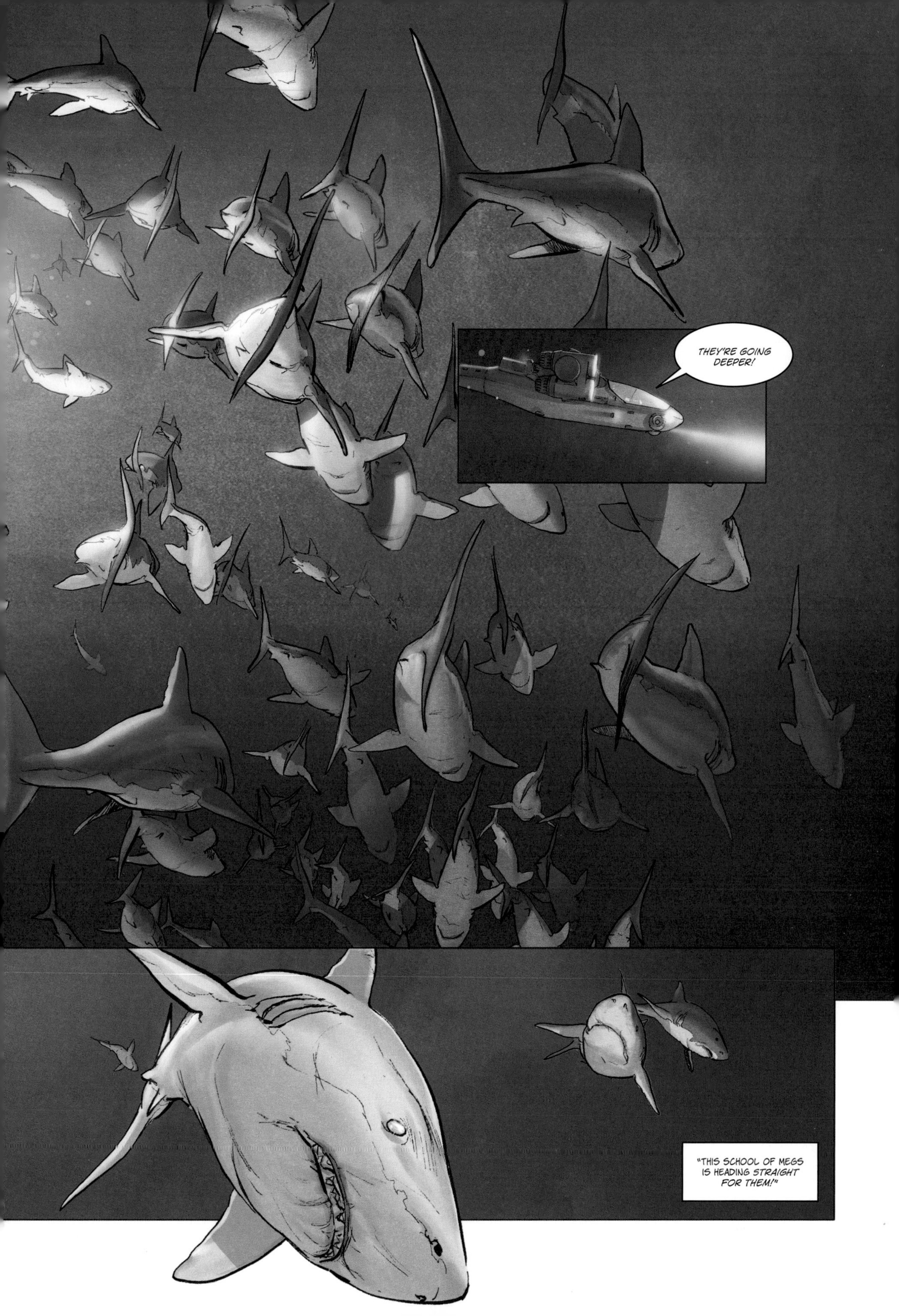
THEY'RE GOING DEEPER!
"THIS SCHOOL OF MEGS IS HEADING STRAIGHT FOR THEM!"

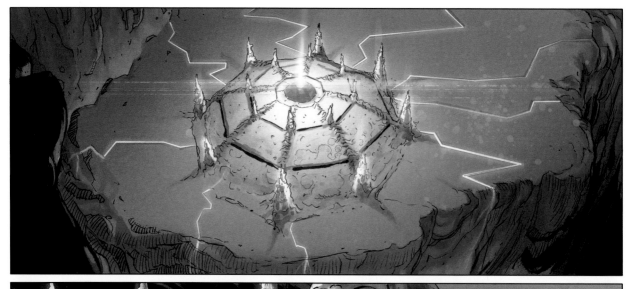

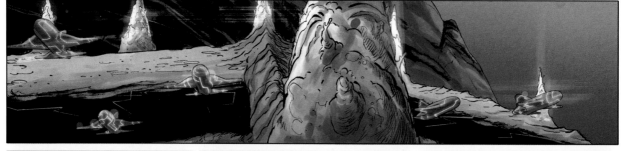

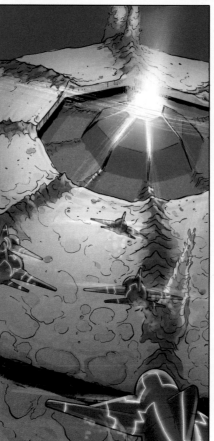

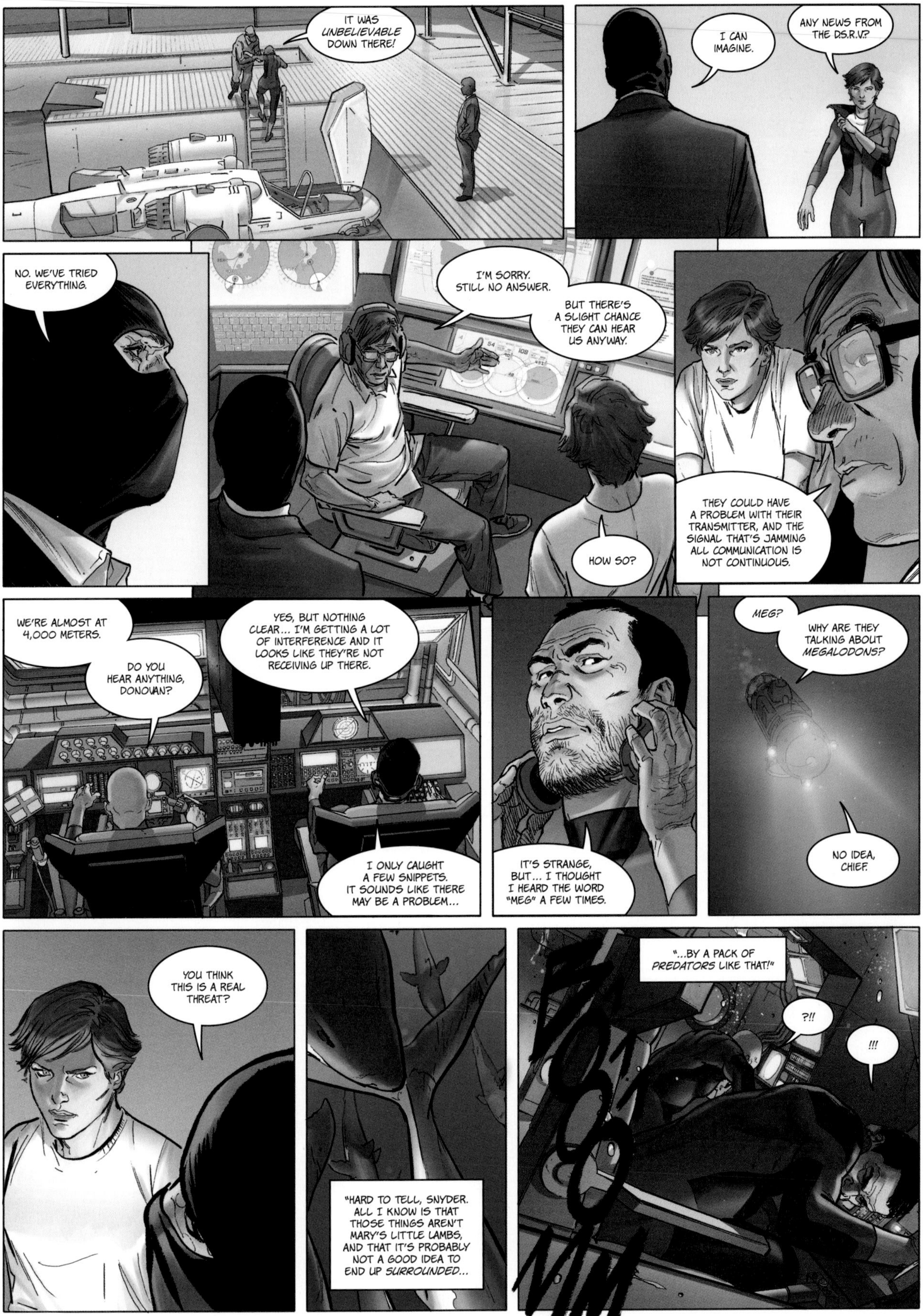

IT WAS *UNBELIEVABLE* DOWN THERE!
I CAN IMAGINE.
ANY NEWS FROM THE D.S.R.V.?
NO. WE'VE TRIED EVERYTHING.
I'M SORRY. STILL NO ANSWER.
BUT THERE'S A SLIGHT CHANCE THEY CAN HEAR US ANYWAY.
HOW SO?
THEY COULD HAVE A PROBLEM WITH THEIR TRANSMITTER, AND THE SIGNAL THAT'S JAMMING ALL COMMUNICATION IS NOT CONTINUOUS.
WE'RE ALMOST AT 4,000 METERS.
DO YOU HEAR ANYTHING, DONOVAN?
YES, BUT NOTHING CLEAR... I'M GETTING A LOT OF INTERFERENCE AND IT LOOKS LIKE THEY'RE NOT RECEIVING UP THERE.
I ONLY CAUGHT A FEW SNIPPETS. IT SOUNDS LIKE THERE MAY BE A PROBLEM...
IT'S STRANGE, BUT... I THOUGHT I HEARD THE WORD "MEG" A FEW TIMES.
MEG?
WHY ARE THEY TALKING ABOUT *MEGALODONS?*
NO IDEA, CHIEF.
YOU THINK THIS IS A REAL THREAT?
"HARD TO TELL, SNYDER. ALL I KNOW IS THAT THOSE THINGS AREN'T MARY'S LITTLE LAMBS, AND THAT IT'S PROBABLY NOT A GOOD IDEA TO END UP *SURROUNDED*...
"...BY A PACK OF *PREDATORS* LIKE THAT!"
?!!
!!!

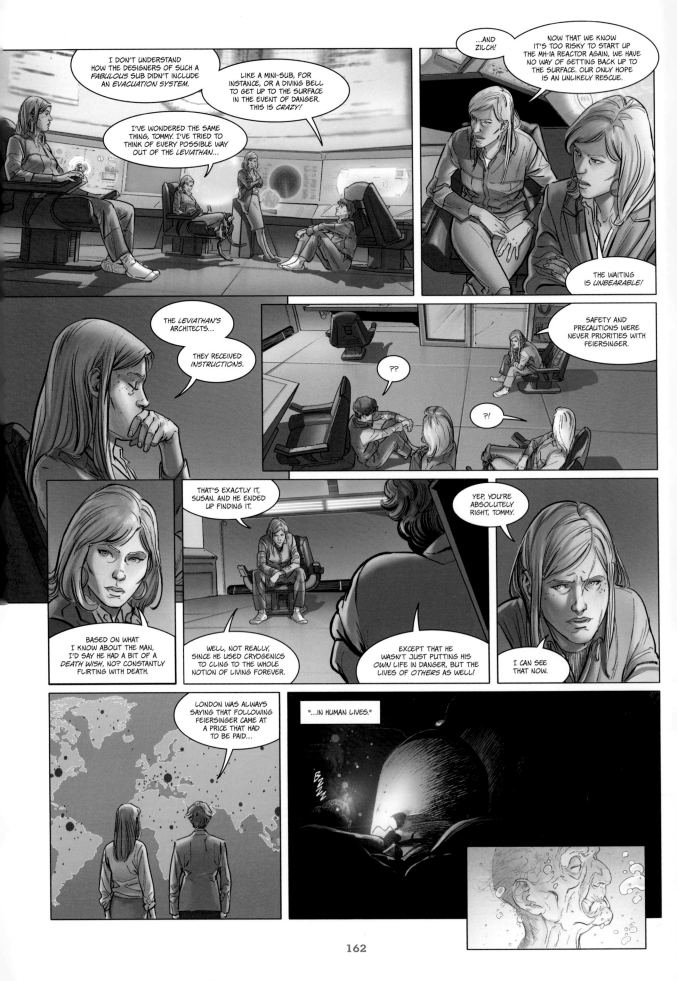

I DON'T UNDERSTAND HOW THE DESIGNERS OF SUCH A *FABULOUS* SUB DIDN'T INCLUDE AN EVACUATION SYSTEM.

LIKE A MINI-SUB, FOR INSTANCE, OR A DIVING BELL TO GET UP TO THE SURFACE IN THE EVENT OF DANGER. THIS IS *CRAZY!*

I'VE WONDERED THE SAME THING, TOMMY. I'VE TRIED TO THINK OF EVERY POSSIBLE WAY OUT OF THE *LEVIATHAN...*

...AND ZILCH!

NOW THAT WE KNOW IT'S TOO RISKY TO START UP THE MH-1A REACTOR AGAIN, WE HAVE NO WAY OF GETTING BACK UP TO THE SURFACE. OUR ONLY HOPE IS AN UNLIKELY RESCUE.

THE WAITING IS *UNBEARABLE!*

THE *LEVIATHAN'S* ARCHITECTS...

THEY RECEIVED INSTRUCTIONS.

??

?!

SAFETY AND PRECAUTIONS WERE NEVER PRIORITIES WITH FEIERSINGER.

BASED ON WHAT I KNOW ABOUT THE MAN, I'D SAY HE HAD A BIT OF A *DEATH WISH,* NO? CONSTANTLY FLIRTING WITH DEATH.

THAT'S EXACTLY IT, SUSAN. AND HE ENDED UP FINDING IT.

WELL, NOT REALLY, SINCE HE USED CRYOGENICS TO CLING TO THE WHOLE NOTION OF LIVING FOREVER.

EXCEPT THAT HE WASN'T JUST PUTTING HIS OWN LIFE IN DANGER, BUT THE LIVES OF *OTHERS* AS WELL!

YEP, YOU'RE ABSOLUTELY RIGHT, TOMMY.

I CAN SEE THAT NOW.

LONDON WAS ALWAYS SAYING THAT FOLLOWING FEIERSINGER CAME AT A PRICE THAT HAD TO BE PAID...

"...IN HUMAN LIVES."

BRMM

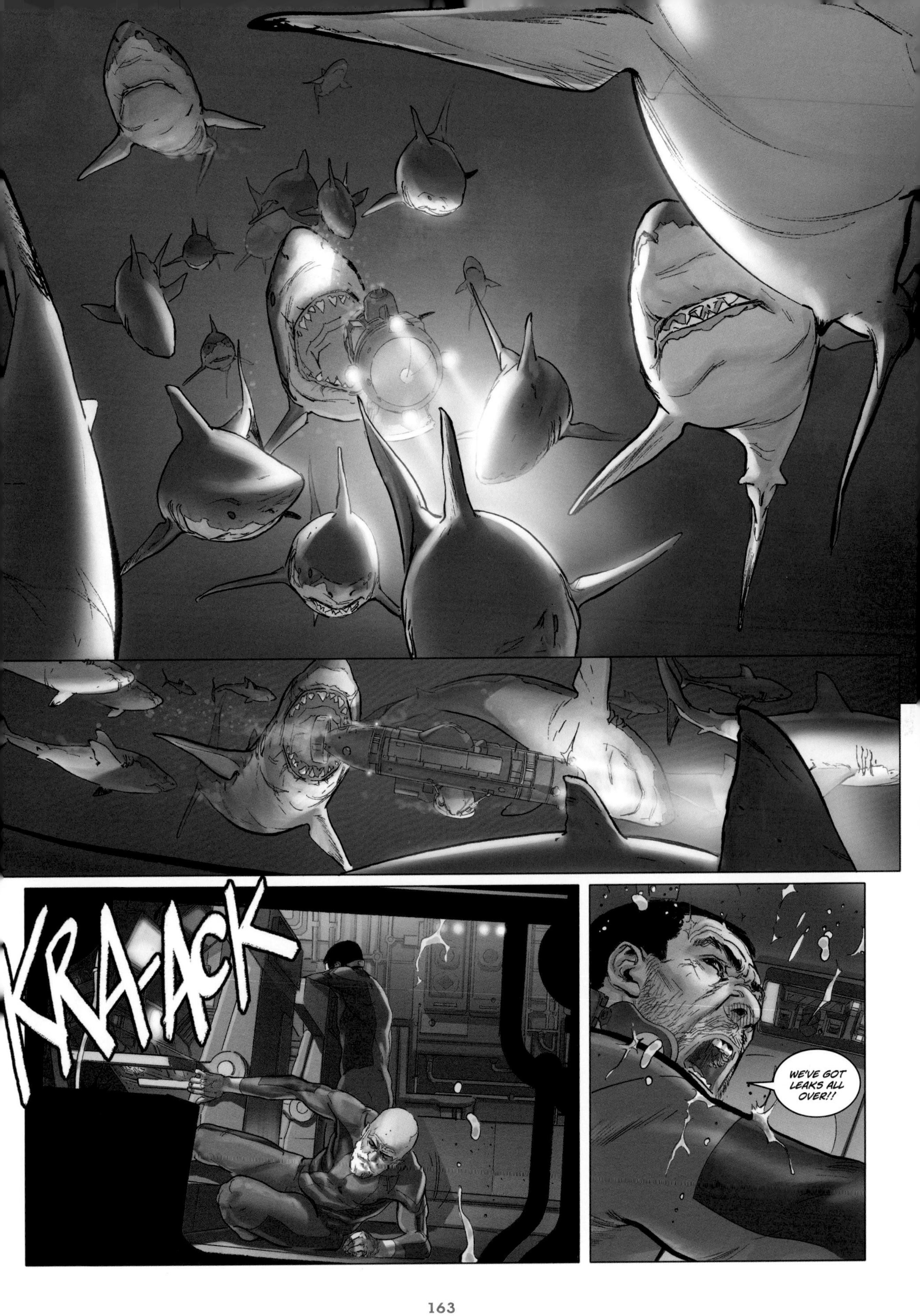
KRA-ACK
WE'VE GOT LEAKS ALL OVER!!

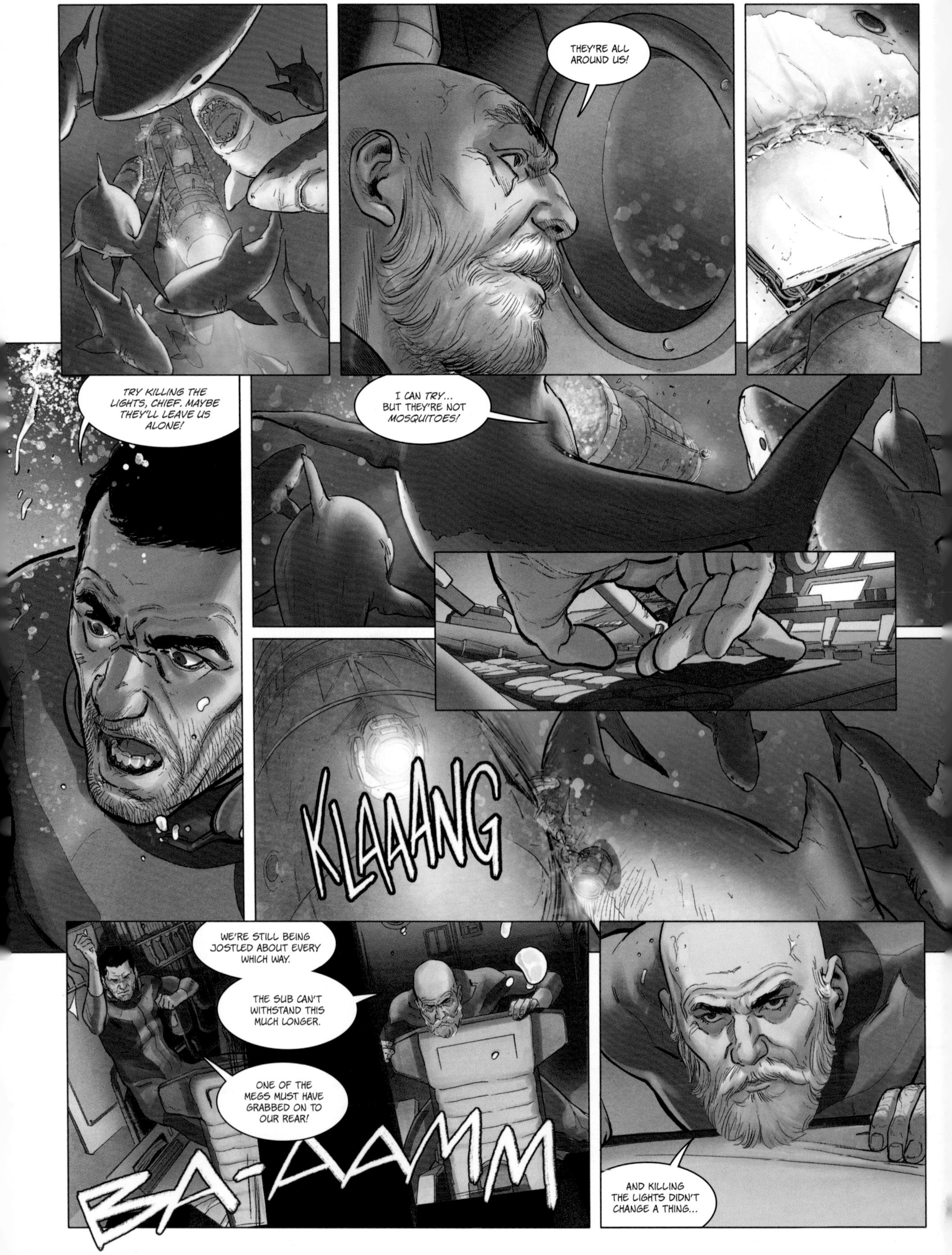
THEY'RE ALL AROUND US!
TRY KILLING THE LIGHTS, CHIEF. MAYBE THEY'LL LEAVE US ALONE!
I CAN TRY... BUT THEY'RE NOT MOSQUITOES!
KLAAANG
WE'RE STILL BEING JOSTLED ABOUT EVERY WHICH WAY.
THE SUB CAN'T WITHSTAND THIS MUCH LONGER.
ONE OF THE MEGS MUST HAVE GRABBED ON TO OUR REAR!
BA-AAMM
AND KILLING THE LIGHTS DIDN'T CHANGE A THING...

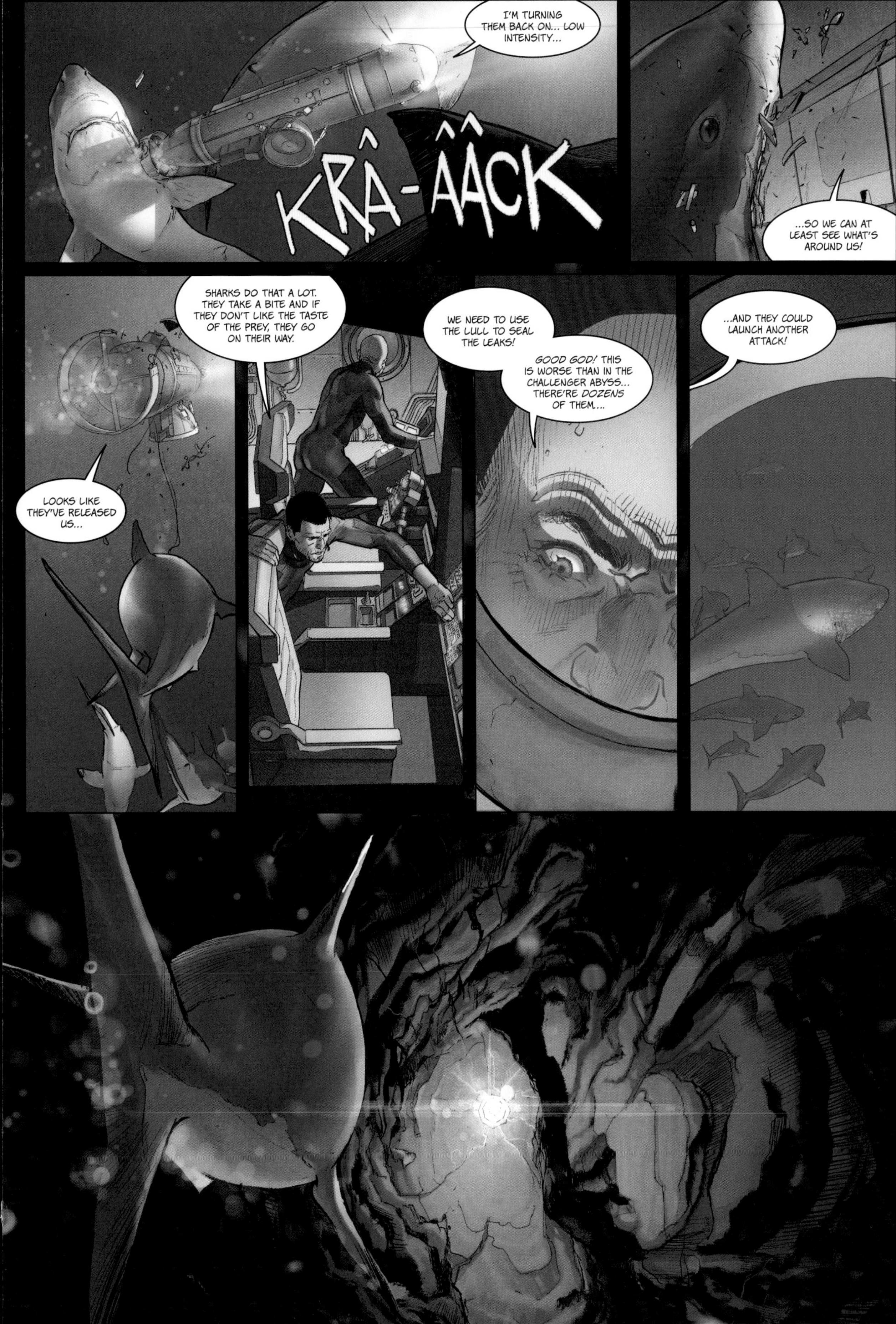
I'M TURNING THEM BACK ON... LOW INTENSITY...
KRÂ-ÂÂCK
...SO WE CAN AT LEAST SEE WHAT'S AROUND US!
LOOKS LIKE THEY'VE RELEASED US...
SHARKS DO THAT A LOT. THEY TAKE A BITE AND IF THEY DON'T LIKE THE TASTE OF THE PREY, THEY GO ON THEIR WAY.
WE NEED TO USE THE LULL TO SEAL THE LEAKS!
GOOD GOD! THIS IS WORSE THAN IN THE CHALLENGER ABYSS... THERE'RE *DOZENS* OF THEM...
...AND THEY COULD LAUNCH ANOTHER ATTACK!

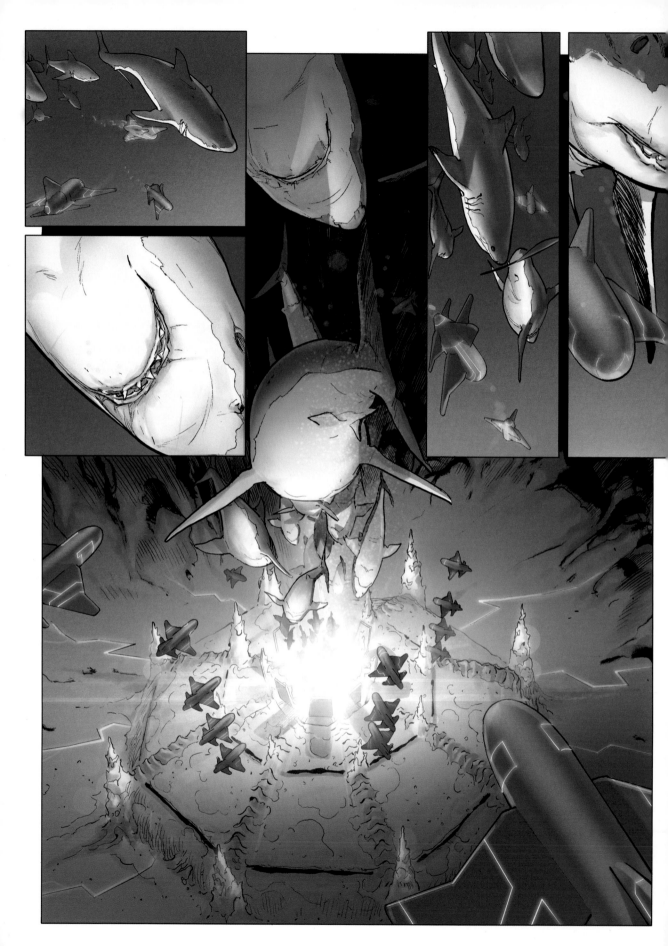

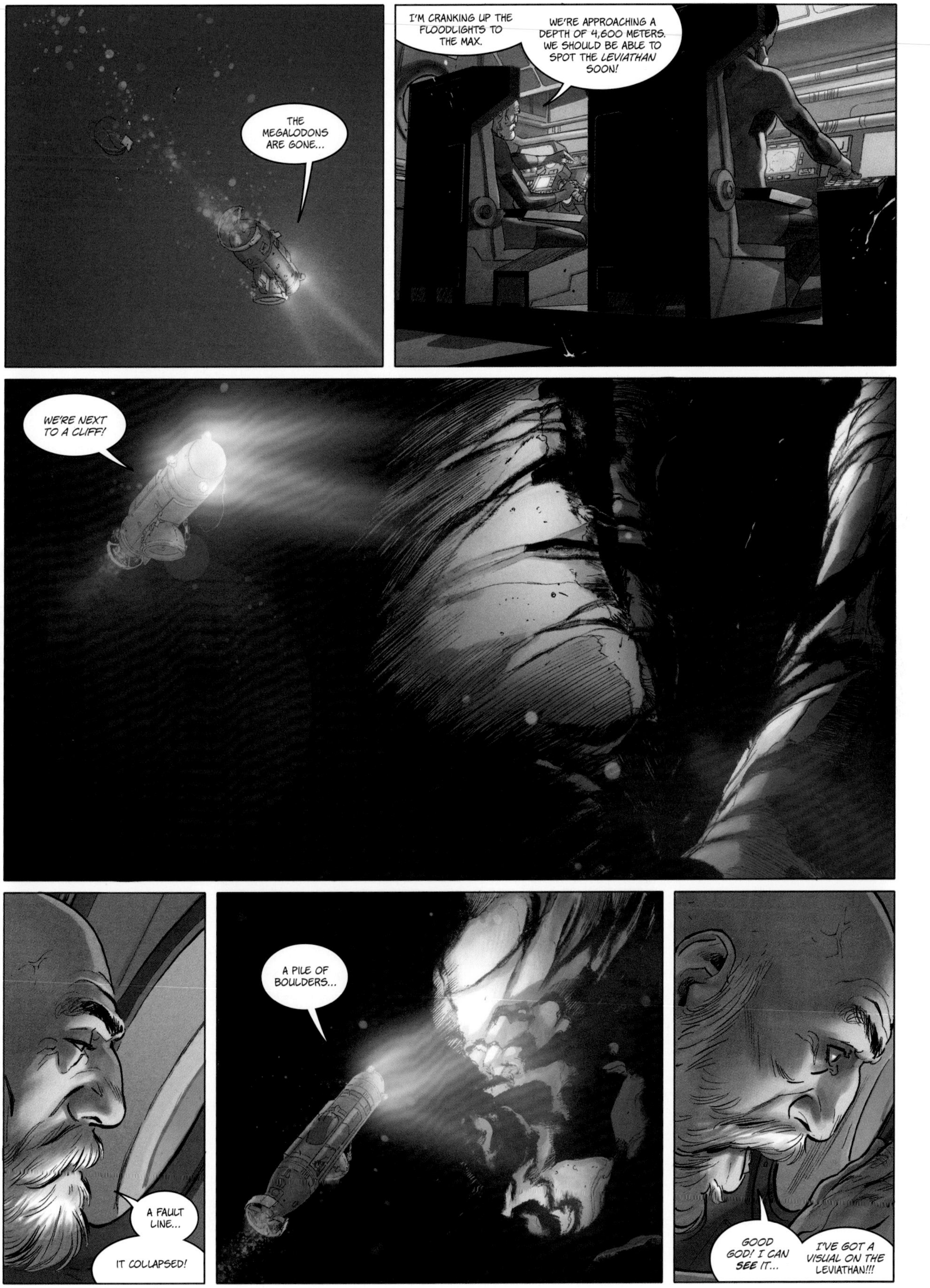
THE MEGALODONS ARE GONE...
I'M CRANKING UP THE FLOODLIGHTS TO THE MAX.
WE'RE APPROACHING A DEPTH OF 4,600 METERS. WE SHOULD BE ABLE TO SPOT THE *LEVIATHAN* SOON!
WE'RE NEXT TO A CLIFF!
A FAULT LINE...
IT COLLAPSED!
A PILE OF BOULDERS...
GOOD GOD! I CAN **SEE** *IT...*
I'VE GOT A VISUAL ON THE LEVIATHAN!!!

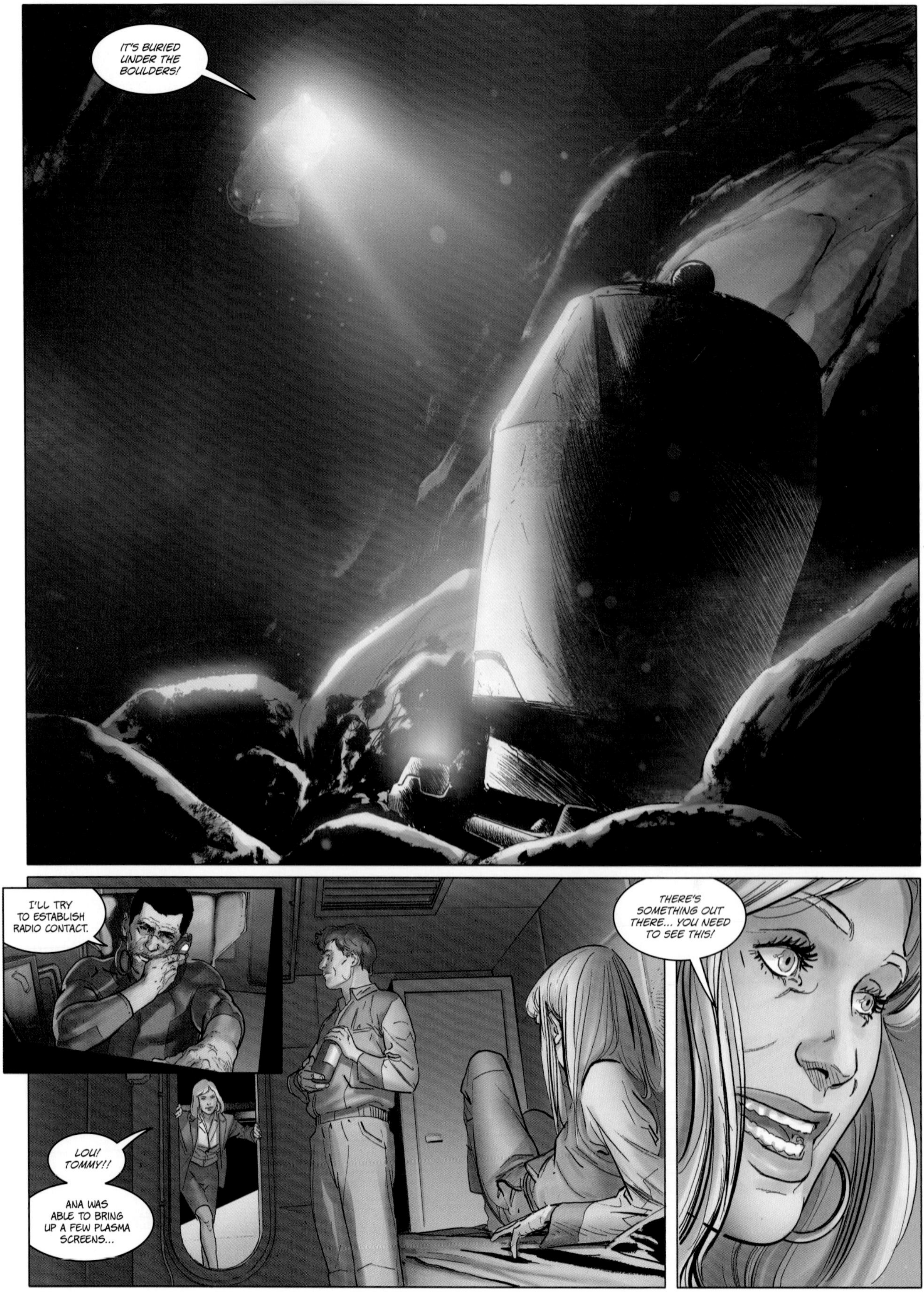
IT'S BURIED UNDER THE BOULDERS!
I'LL TRY TO ESTABLISH RADIO CONTACT.
LOU! TOMMY!!
ANA WAS ABLE TO BRING UP A FEW PLASMA SCREENS...
THERE'S SOMETHING OUT THERE... YOU NEED TO SEE THIS!

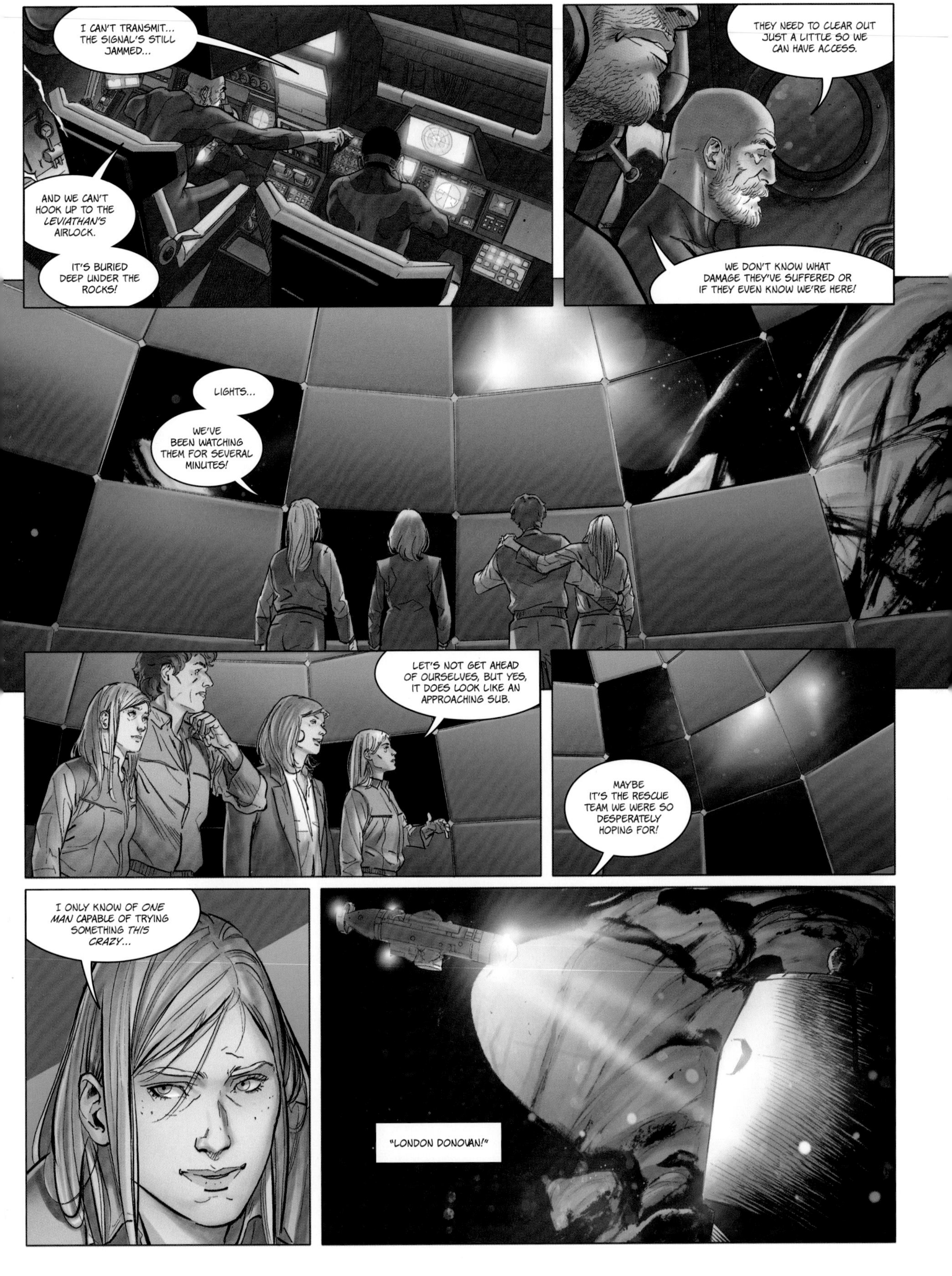

I CAN'T TRANSMIT... THE SIGNAL'S STILL JAMMED...
AND WE CAN'T HOOK UP TO THE *LEVIATHAN'S* AIRLOCK.
IT'S BURIED DEEP UNDER THE ROCKS!
THEY NEED TO CLEAR OUT JUST A LITTLE SO WE CAN HAVE ACCESS.
WE DON'T KNOW WHAT DAMAGE THEY'VE SUFFERED OR IF THEY EVEN KNOW WE'RE HERE!
LIGHTS...
WE'VE BEEN WATCHING THEM FOR SEVERAL MINUTES!
LET'S NOT GET AHEAD OF OURSELVES, BUT YES, IT DOES LOOK LIKE AN APPROACHING SUB.
MAYBE IT'S THE RESCUE TEAM WE WERE SO DESPERATELY HOPING FOR!
I ONLY KNOW OF *ONE MAN* CAPABLE OF TRYING SOMETHING *THIS CRAZY*...
"LONDON DONOVAN!"

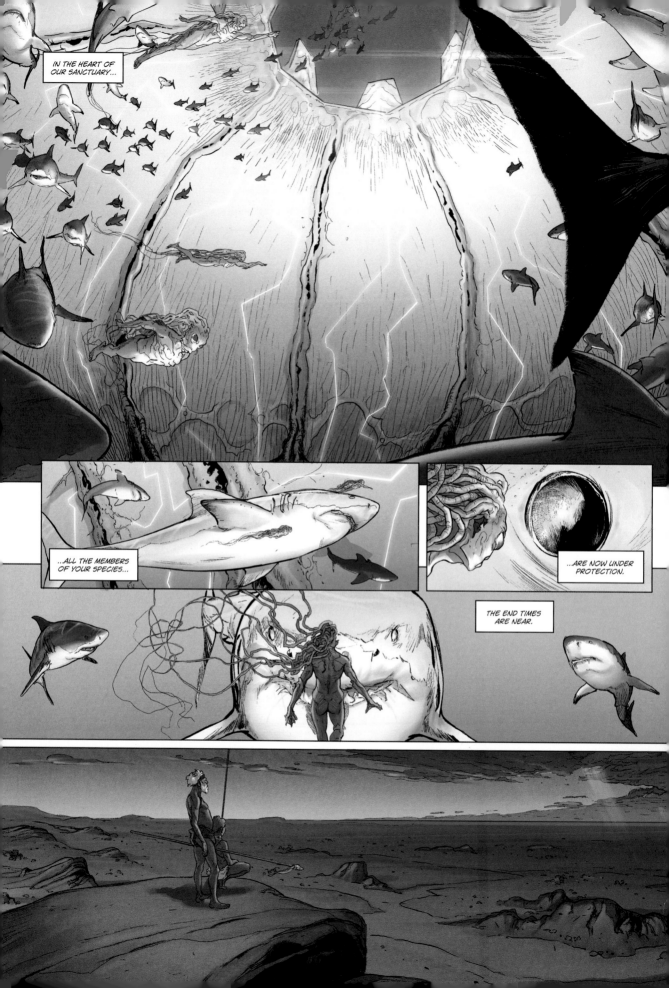

IN THE HEART OF
OUR SANCTUARY...

..ALL THE MEMBERS
OF YOUR SPECIES...

..ARE NOW UNDER
PROTECTION.

THE END TIMES
ARE NEAR.

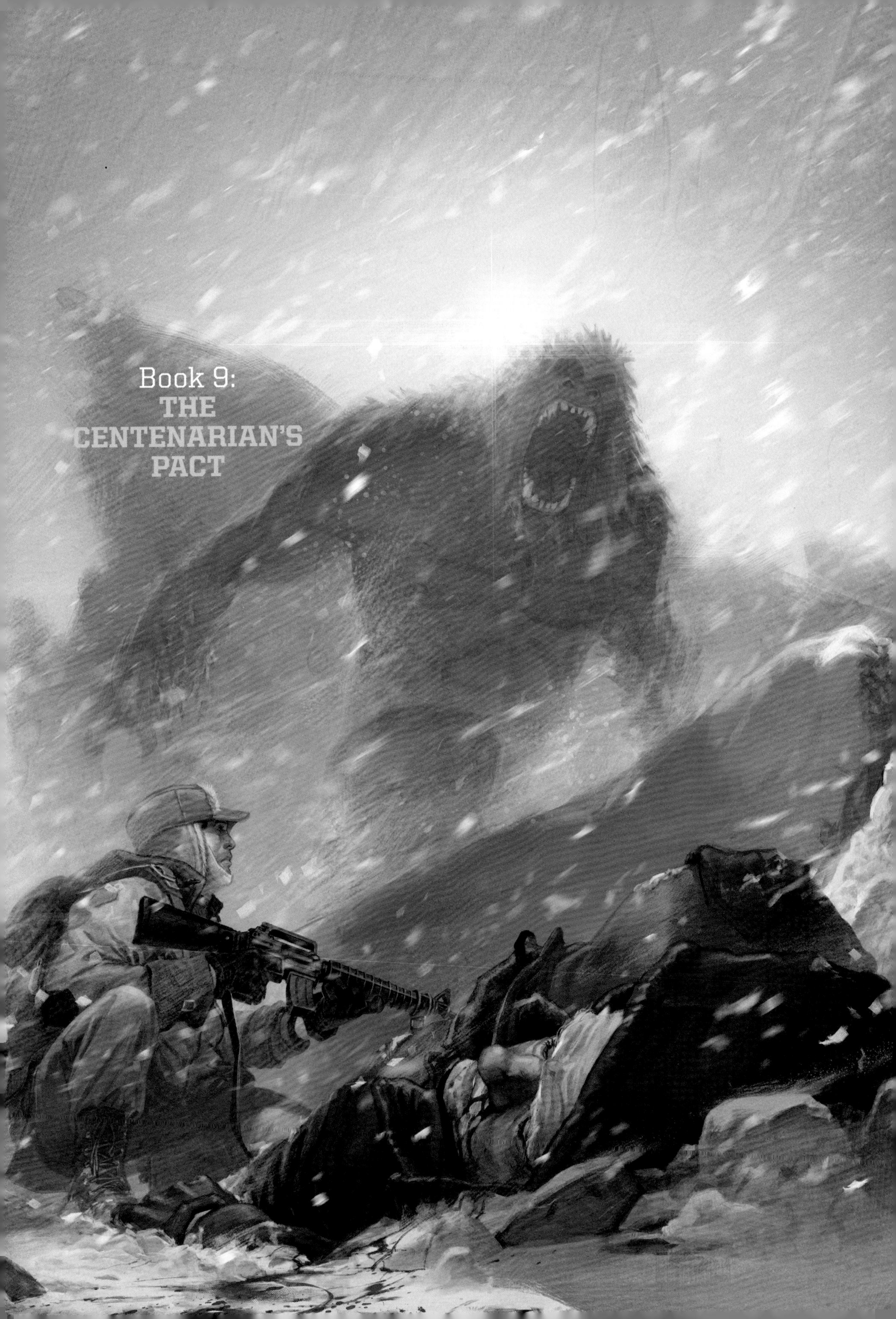
Book 9:
THE CENTENARIAN'S PACT

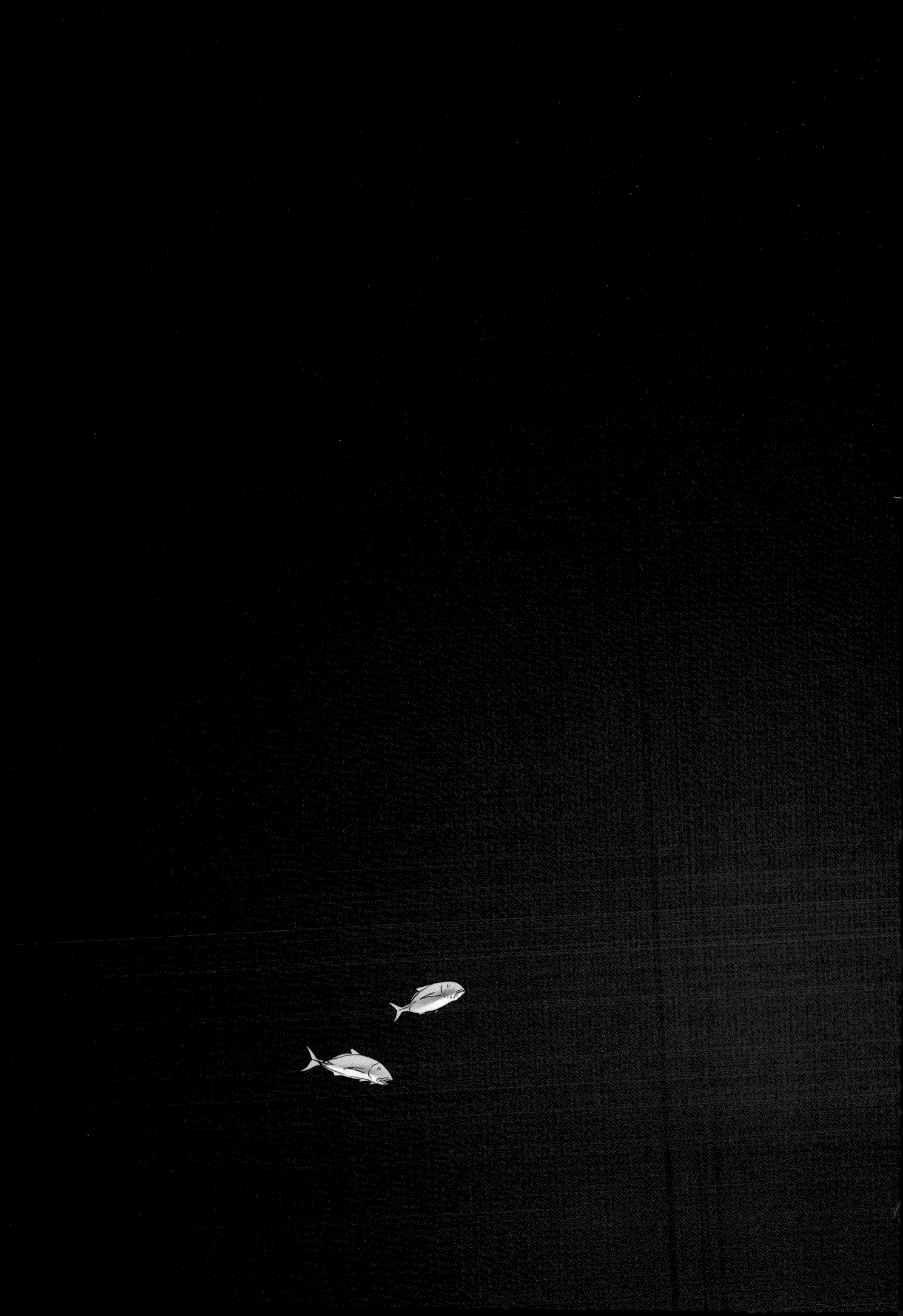

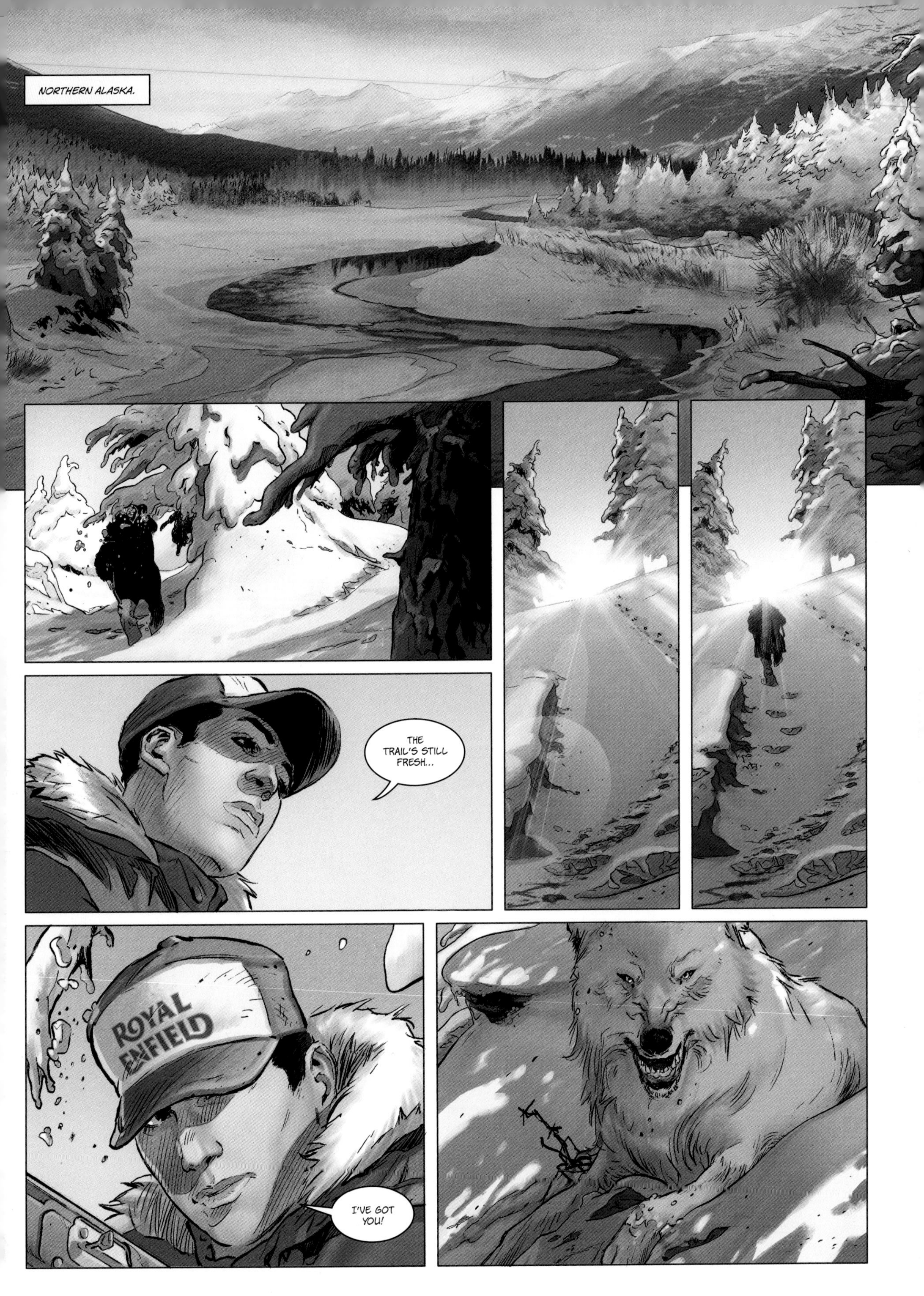
NORTHERN ALASKA.
THE TRAIL'S STILL FRESH...
ROYAL ENFIELD
I'VE GOT YOU!

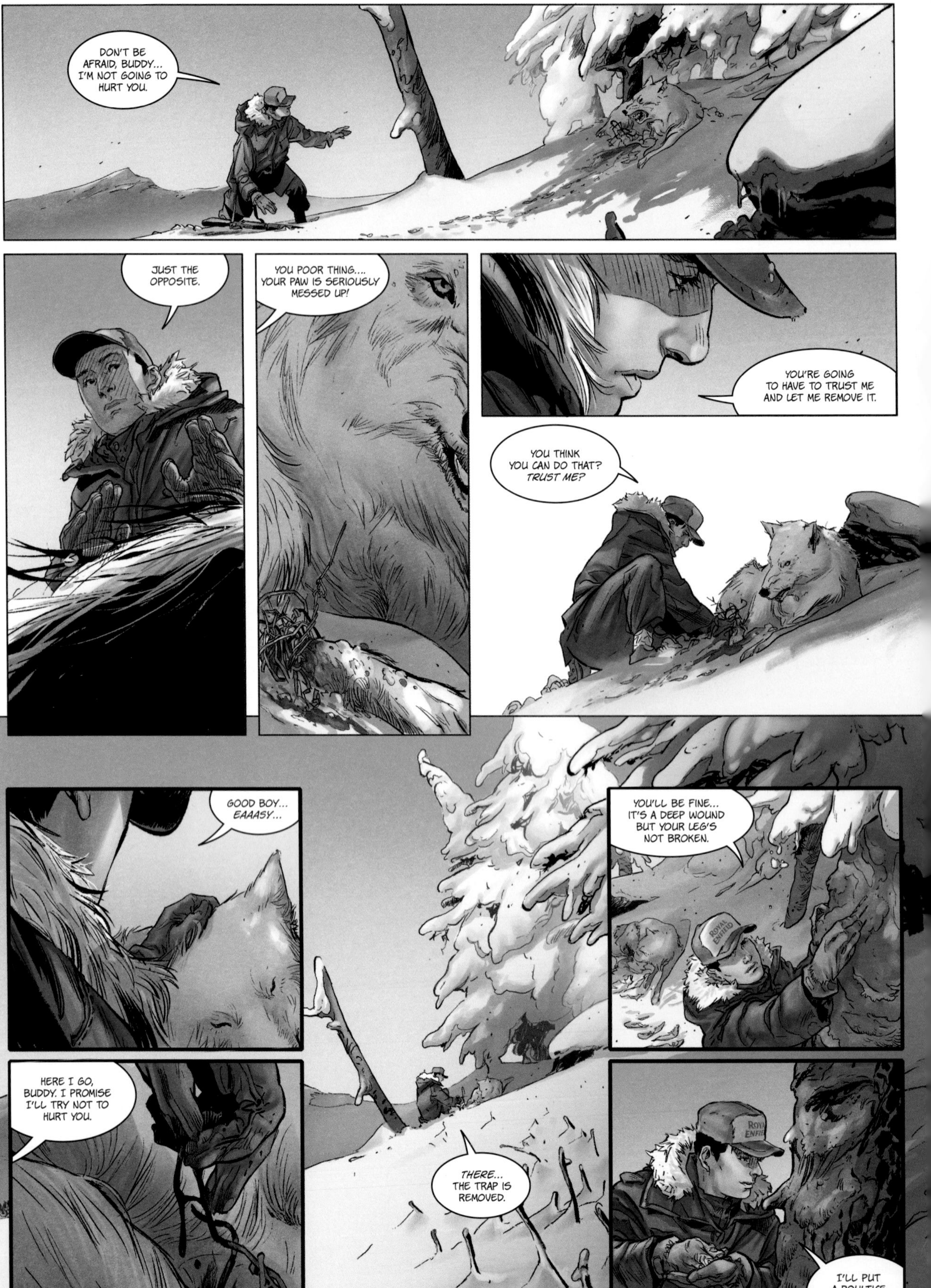
DON'T BE AFRAID, BUDDY... I'M NOT GOING TO HURT YOU.
JUST THE OPPOSITE.
YOU POOR THING.... YOUR PAW IS SERIOUSLY MESSED UP!
YOU'RE GOING TO HAVE TO TRUST ME AND LET ME REMOVE IT.
YOU THINK YOU CAN DO THAT? *TRUST ME?*
GOOD BOY... *EAAAASY...*
YOU'LL BE FINE... IT'S A DEEP WOUND BUT YOUR LEG'S NOT BROKEN.
HERE I GO, BUDDY. I PROMISE I'LL TRY NOT TO HURT YOU.
THERE... THE TRAP IS REMOVED.
I'LL PUT A POULTICE ON IT.

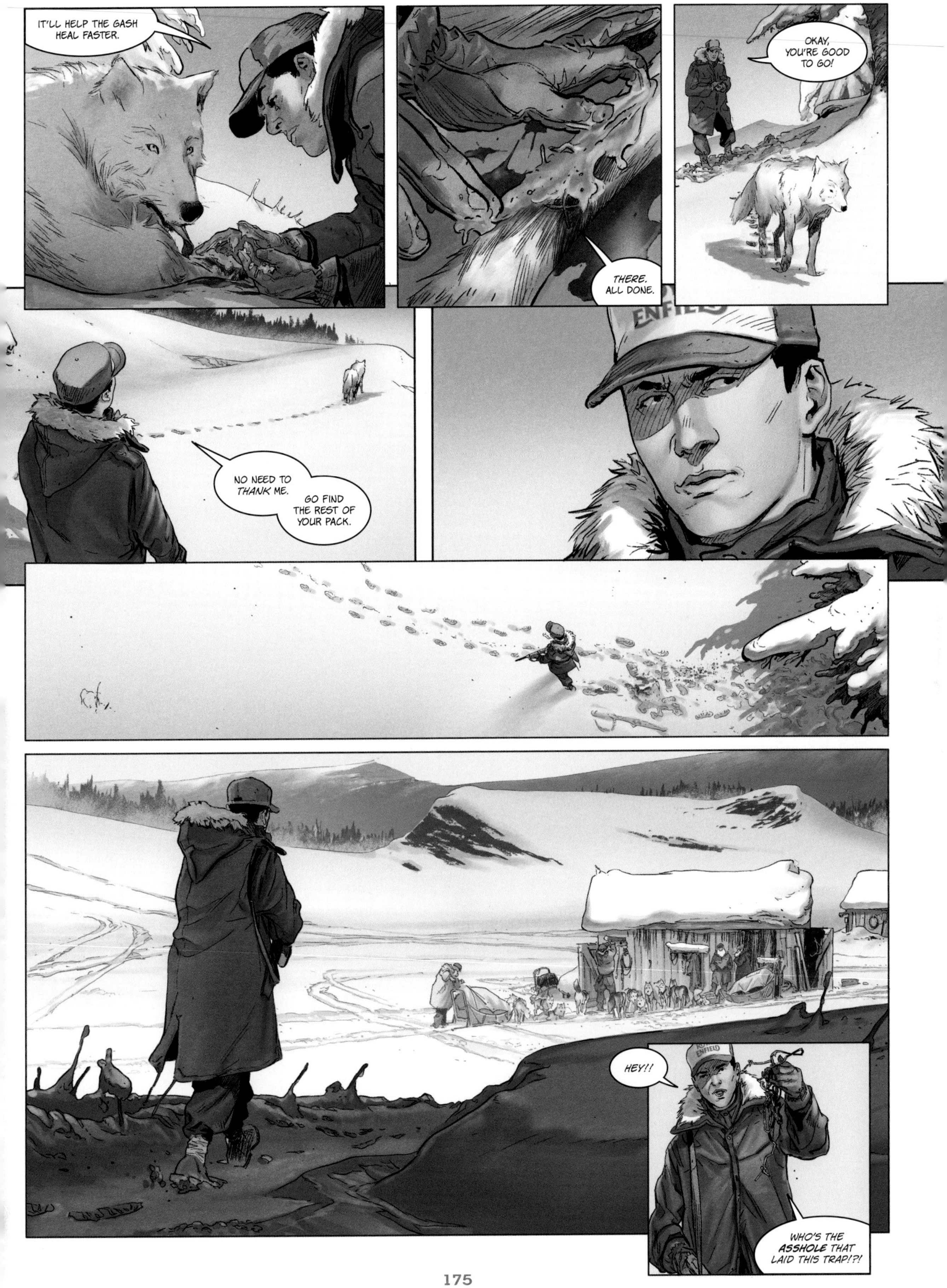
IT'LL HELP THE GASH HEAL FASTER.
THERE. ALL DONE.
OKAY, YOU'RE GOOD TO GO!
NO NEED TO *THANK* ME.
GO FIND THE REST OF YOUR PACK.
ENFIELD
HEY!!
ENFIELD
WHO'S THE ***ASSHOLE*** THAT LAID THIS TRAP!?!

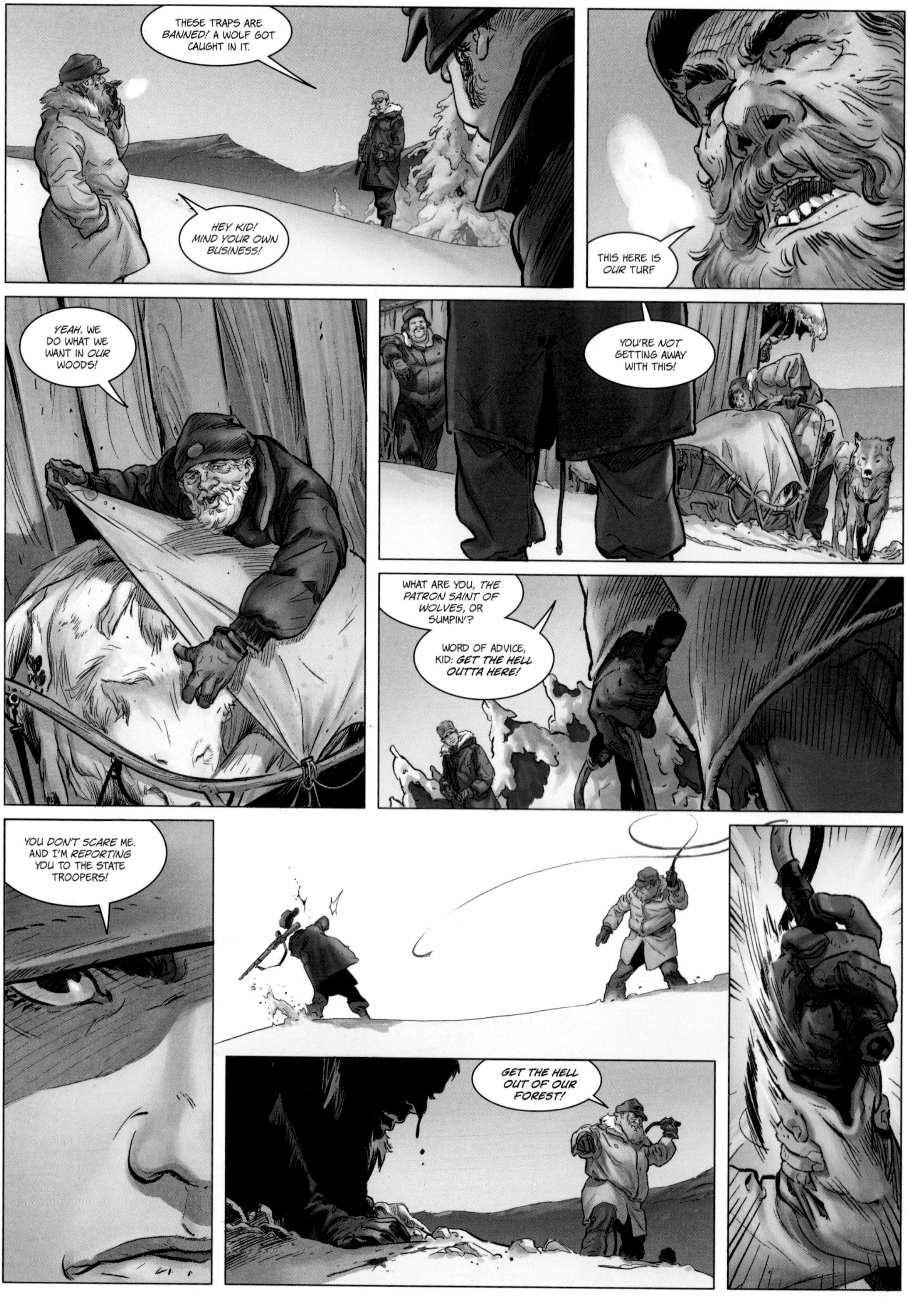
THESE TRAPS ARE BANNED! A WOLF GOT CAUGHT IN IT.
HEY KID! MIND YOUR OWN BUSINESS!
THIS HERE IS OUR TURF
YEAH. WE DO WHAT WE WANT IN OUR WOODS!
YOU'RE NOT GETTING AWAY WITH THIS!
WHAT ARE YOU, THE PATRON SAINT OF WOLVES, OR SUMPIN'?
WORD OF ADVICE, KID: GET THE HELL OUTTA HERE!
YOU DON'T SCARE ME. AND I'M REPORTING YOU TO THE STATE TROOPERS!
GET THE HELL OUT OF OUR FOREST!

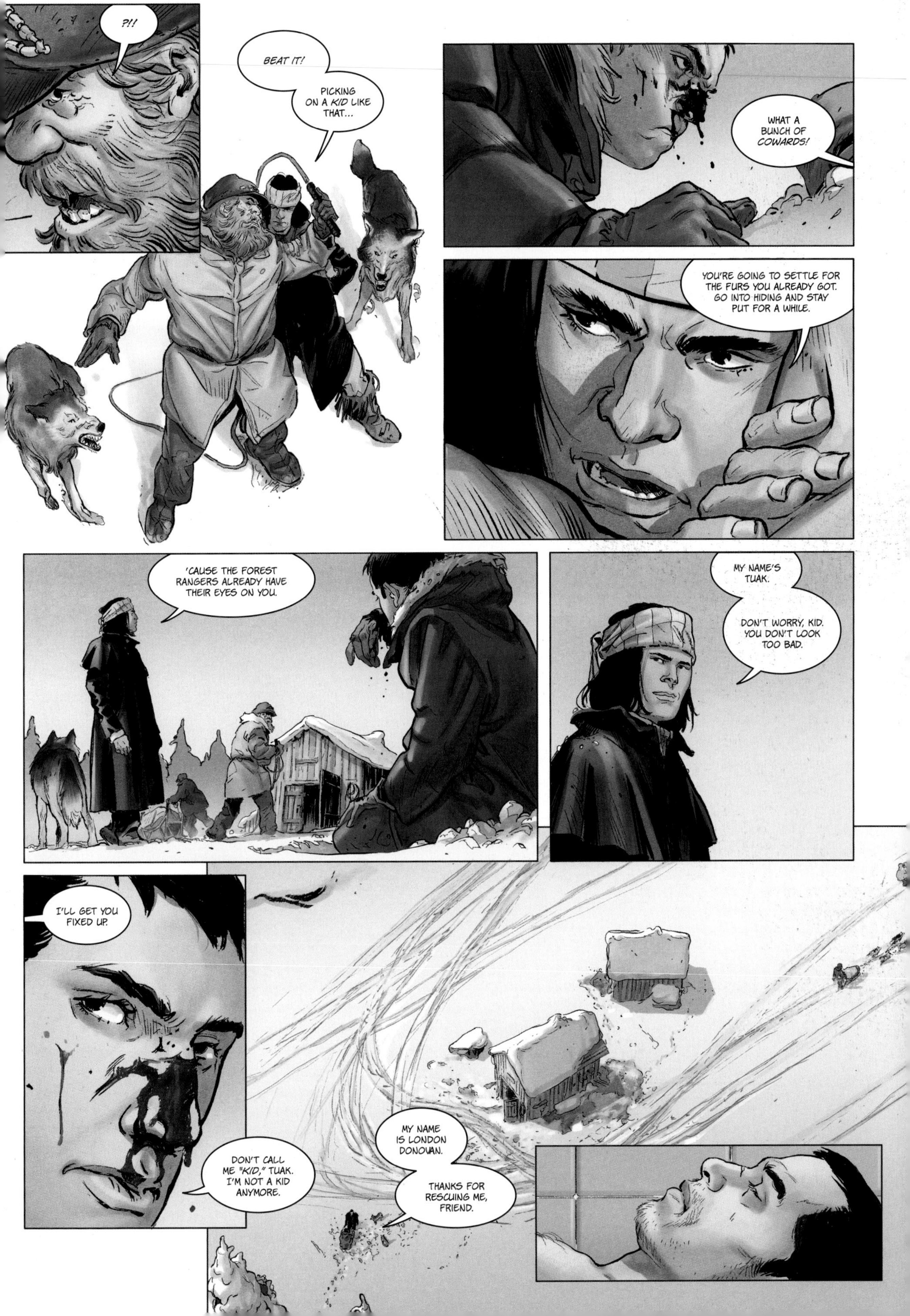
?!!
BEAT IT!
PICKING ON A *KID* LIKE THAT...
WHAT A BUNCH OF COWARDS!
YOU'RE GOING TO SETTLE FOR THE FURS YOU ALREADY GOT. GO INTO HIDING AND STAY PUT FOR A WHILE.
'CAUSE THE FOREST RANGERS ALREADY HAVE THEIR EYES ON YOU.
MY NAME'S TUAK.
DON'T WORRY, KID. YOU DON'T LOOK TOO BAD.
I'LL GET YOU FIXED UP.
DON'T CALL ME "*KID*," TUAK. I'M NOT A KID ANYMORE.
MY NAME IS LONDON DONOVAN.
THANKS FOR RESCUING ME, FRIEND.

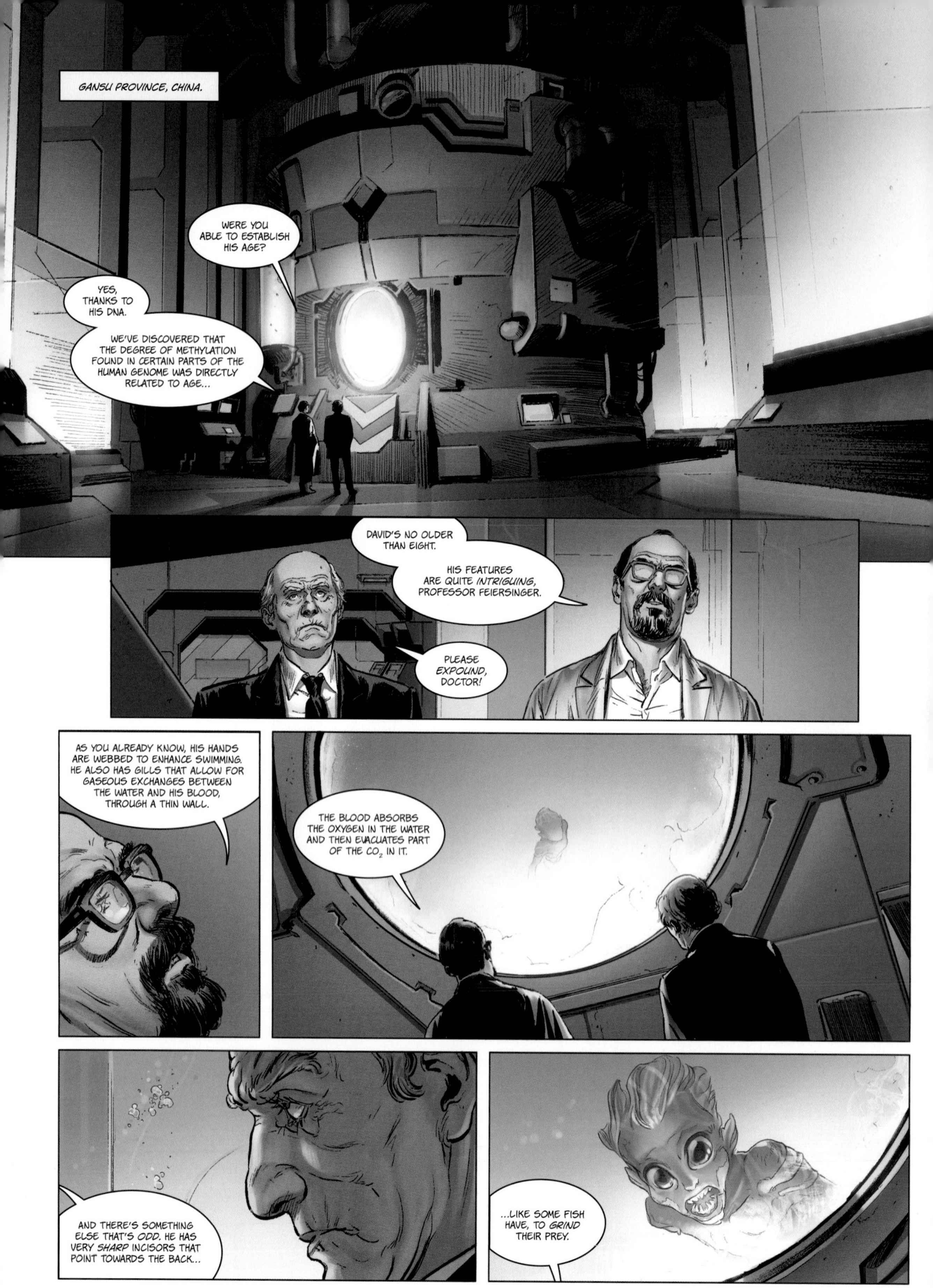
GANSU PROVINCE, CHINA.
WERE YOU ABLE TO ESTABLISH HIS AGE?
YES, THANKS TO HIS DNA.
WE'VE DISCOVERED THAT THE DEGREE OF METHYLATION FOUND IN CERTAIN PARTS OF THE HUMAN GENOME WAS DIRECTLY RELATED TO AGE...
DAVID'S NO OLDER THAN EIGHT.
HIS FEATURES ARE QUITE *INTRIGUING*, PROFESSOR FEIERSINGER.
PLEASE *EXPOUND*, DOCTOR!
AS YOU ALREADY KNOW, HIS HANDS ARE WEBBED TO ENHANCE SWIMMING. HE ALSO HAS GILLS THAT ALLOW FOR GASEOUS EXCHANGES BETWEEN THE WATER AND HIS BLOOD, THROUGH A THIN WALL.
THE BLOOD ABSORBS THE OXYGEN IN THE WATER AND THEN EVACUATES PART OF THE CO_2 IN IT.
AND THERE'S SOMETHING ELSE THAT'S *ODD*. HE HAS VERY *SHARP* INCISORS THAT POINT TOWARDS THE BACK...
...LIKE SOME FISH HAVE, TO *GRIND* THEIR PREY.

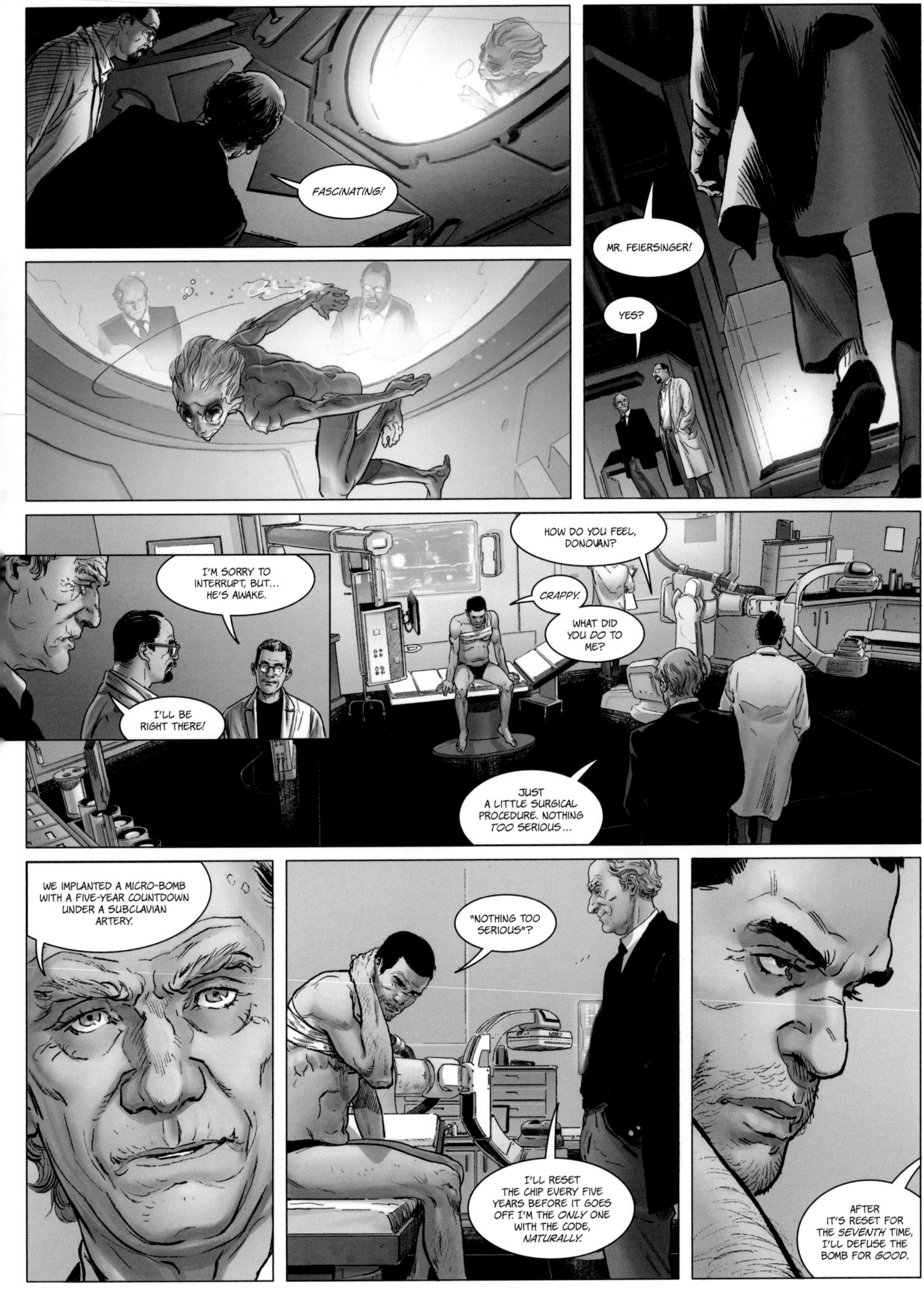
FASCINATING!
MR. FEIERSINGER!
YES?
I'M SORRY TO INTERRUPT, BUT... HE'S AWAKE.
I'LL BE RIGHT THERE!
HOW DO YOU FEEL, DONOVAN?
CRAPPY.
WHAT DID YOU DO TO ME?
JUST A LITTLE SURGICAL PROCEDURE. NOTHING TOO SERIOUS...
WE IMPLANTED A MICRO-BOMB WITH A FIVE-YEAR COUNTDOWN UNDER A SUBCLAVIAN ARTERY.
"NOTHING TOO SERIOUS"?
I'LL RESET THE CHIP EVERY FIVE YEARS BEFORE IT GOES OFF. I'M THE ONLY ONE WITH THE CODE, NATURALLY.
AFTER IT'S RESET FOR THE SEVENTH TIME, I'LL DEFUSE THE BOMB FOR GOOD.

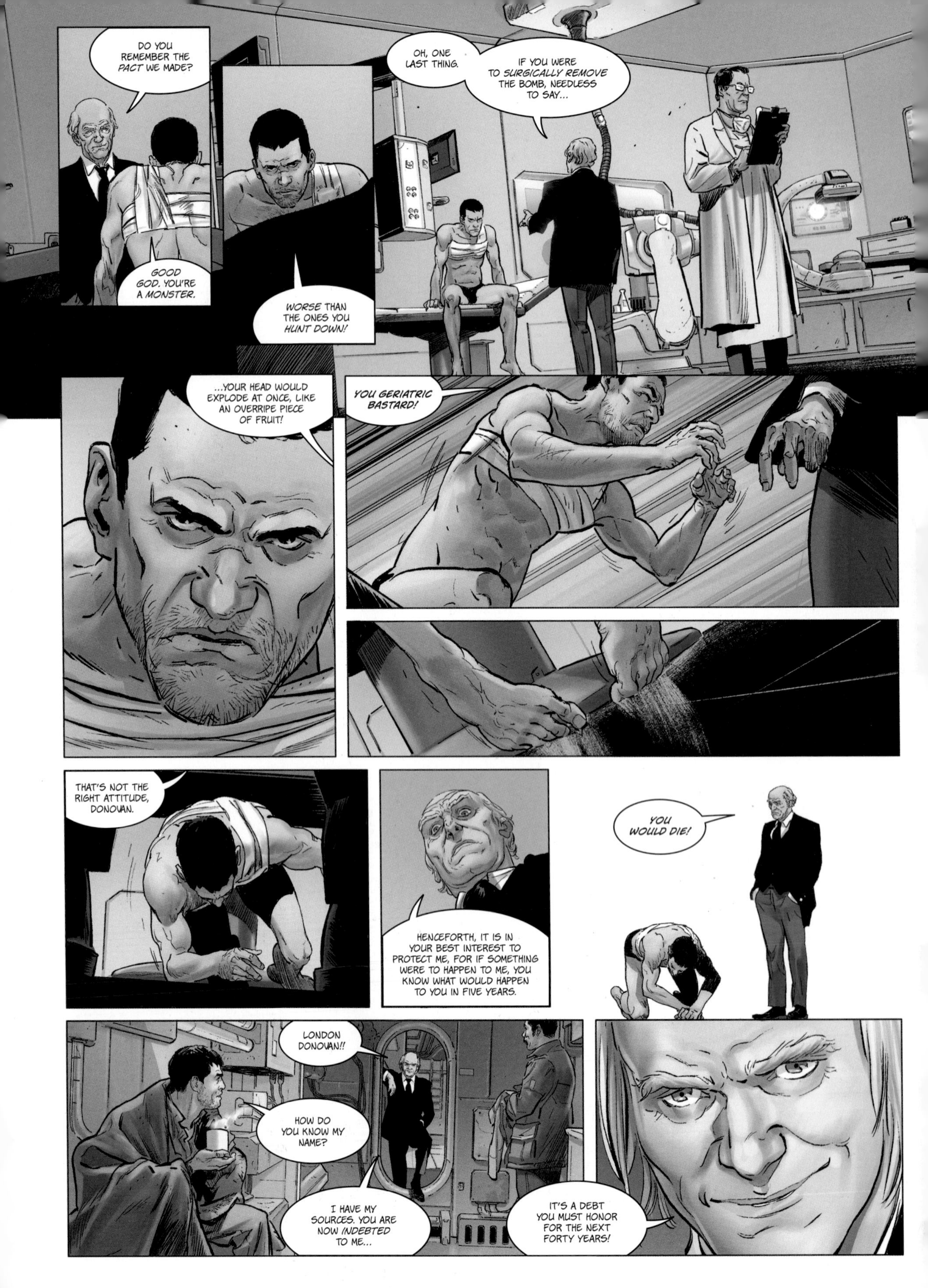
DO YOU REMEMBER THE PACT WE MADE?
GOOD GOD. YOU'RE A MONSTER.
WORSE THAN THE ONES YOU HUNT DOWN!
OH, ONE LAST THING.
IF YOU WERE TO SURGICALLY REMOVE THE BOMB, NEEDLESS TO SAY...
...YOUR HEAD WOULD EXPLODE AT ONCE, LIKE AN OVERRIPE PIECE OF FRUIT!
YOU GERIATRIC BASTARD!
THAT'S NOT THE RIGHT ATTITUDE, DONOVAN.
HENCEFORTH, IT IS IN YOUR BEST INTEREST TO PROTECT ME, FOR IF SOMETHING WERE TO HAPPEN TO ME, YOU KNOW WHAT WOULD HAPPEN TO YOU IN FIVE YEARS.
YOU WOULD DIE!
LONDON DONOVAN!!
HOW DO YOU KNOW MY NAME?
I HAVE MY SOURCES. YOU ARE NOW INDEBTED TO ME...
IT'S A DEBT YOU MUST HONOR FOR THE NEXT FORTY YEARS!

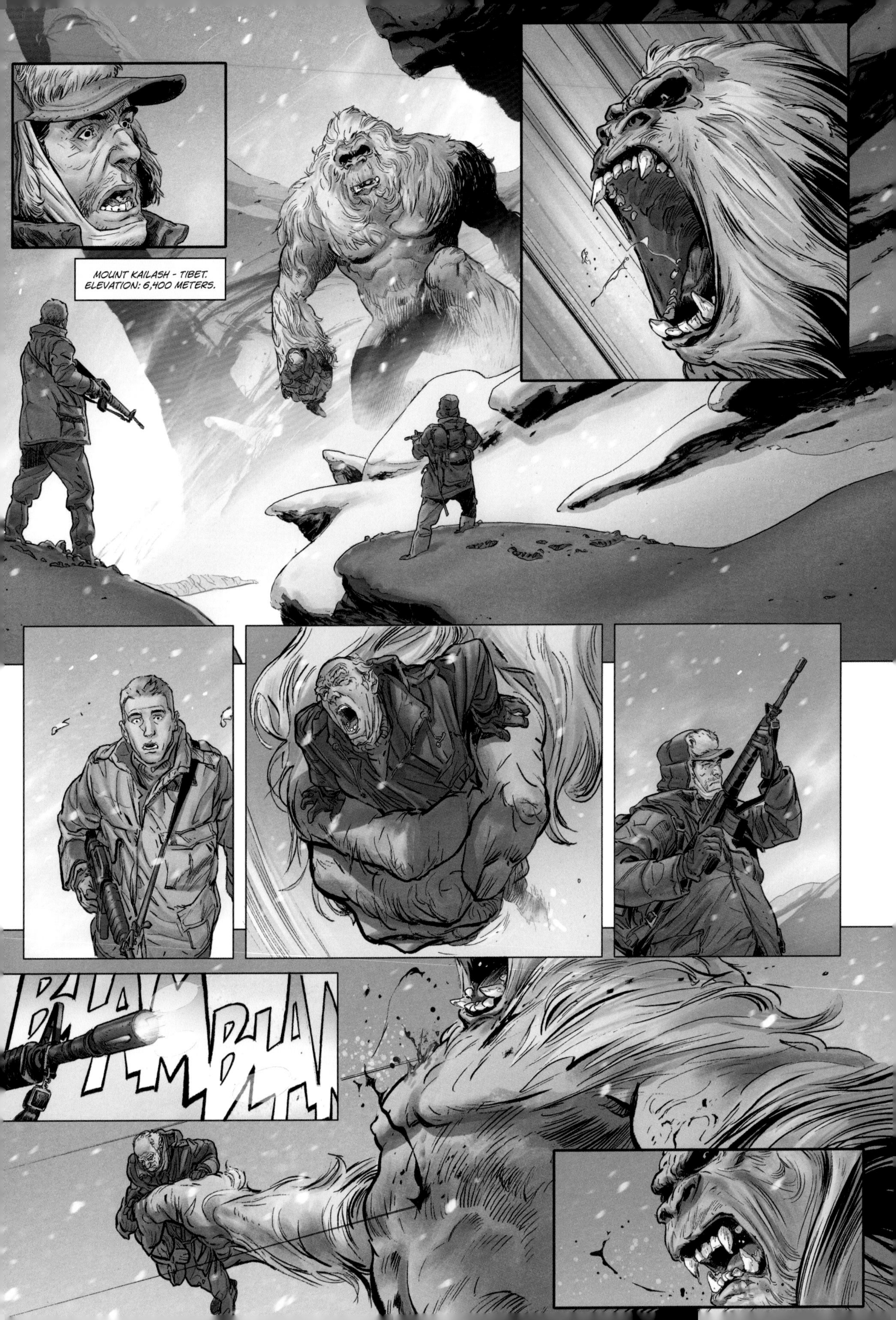
MOUNT KAILASH - TIBET.
ELEVATION: 6,400 METERS.

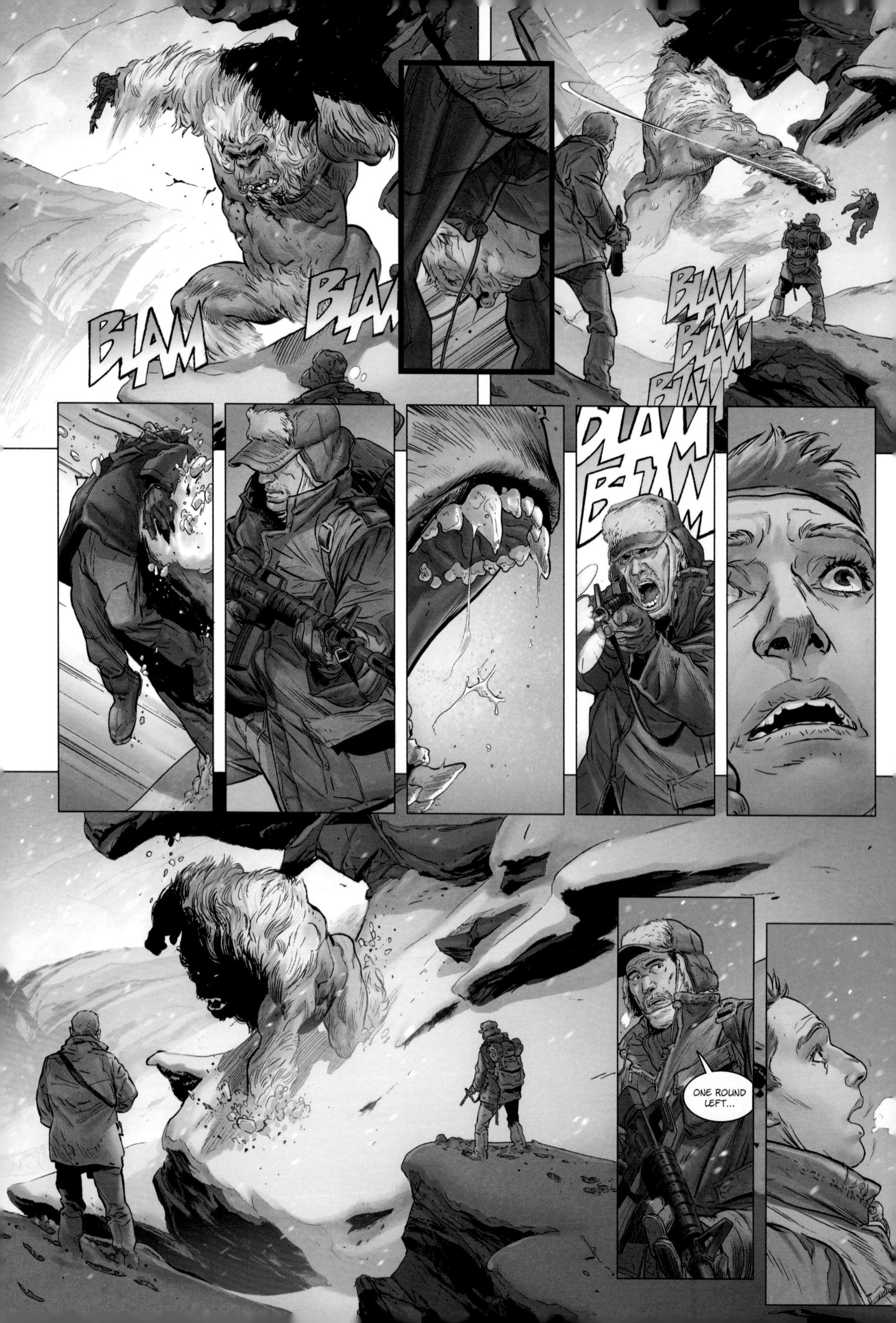
BLAM
BLAM
BLAM
BLAM
BLAM
BLAM
BLAM
BLAM
ONE ROUND LEFT...

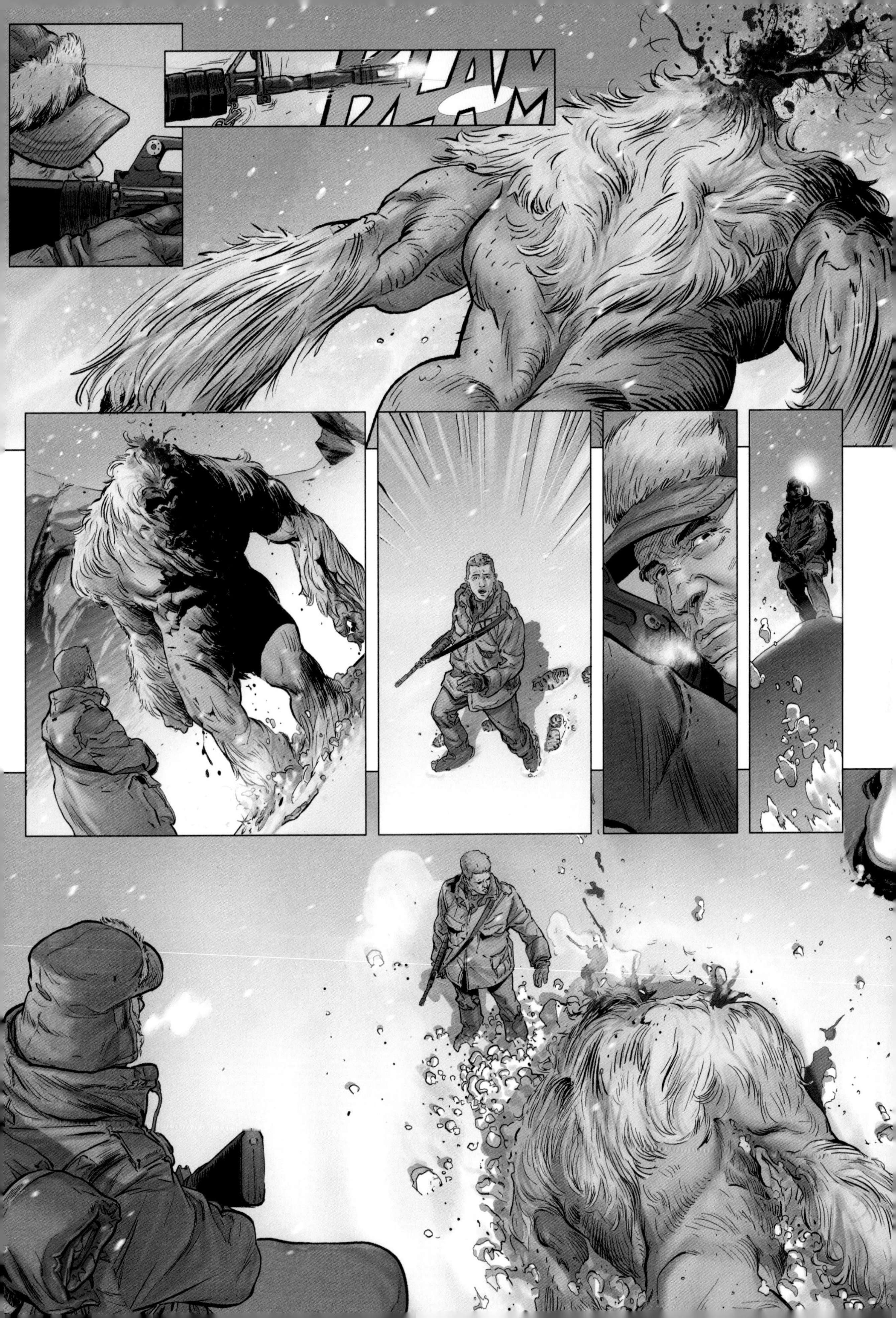

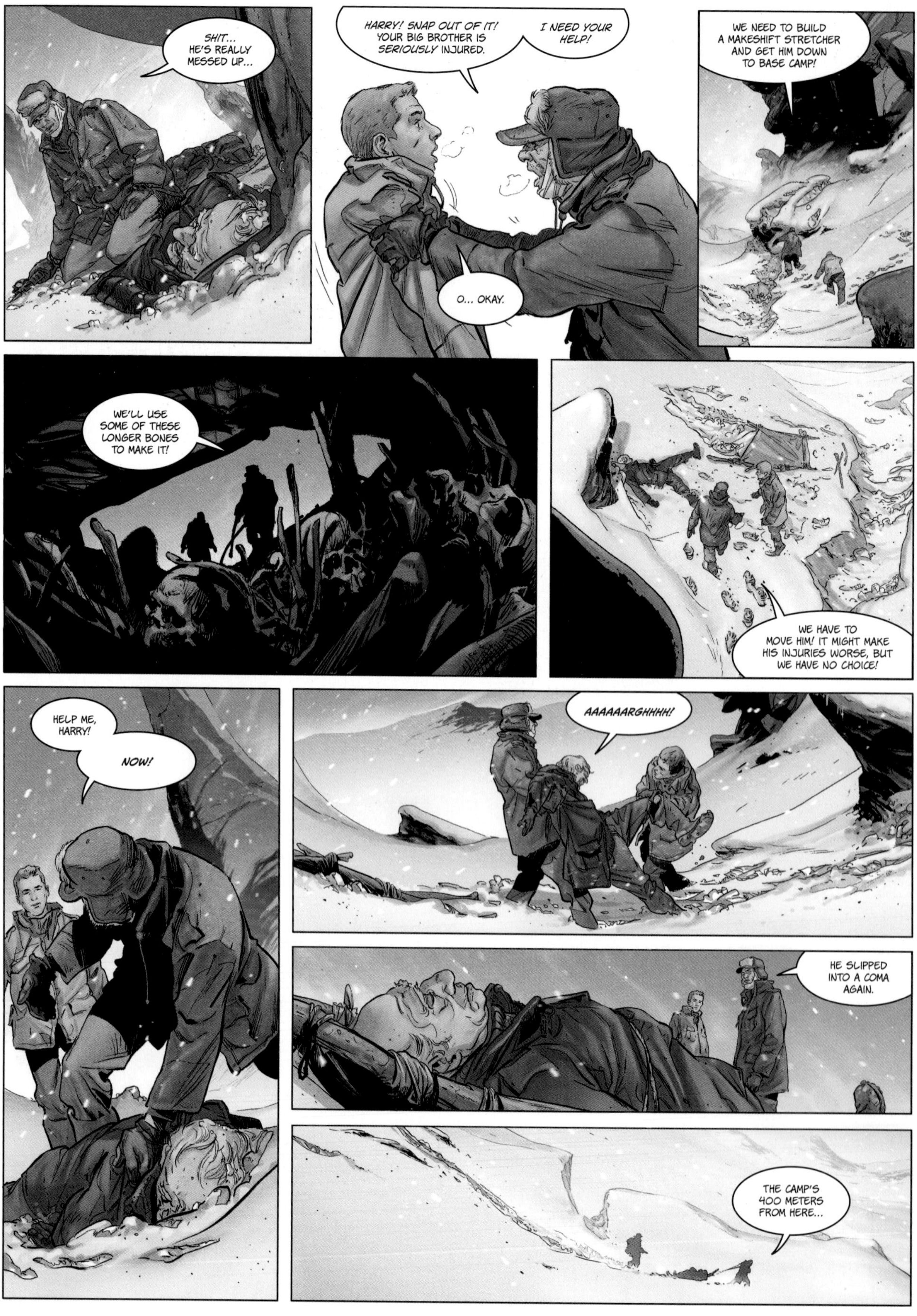
SHIT... HE'S REALLY MESSED UP...
HARRY! SNAP OUT OF IT! YOUR BIG BROTHER IS SERIOUSLY INJURED.
I NEED YOUR HELP!
O... OKAY.
WE NEED TO BUILD A MAKESHIFT STRETCHER AND GET HIM DOWN TO BASE CAMP!
WE'LL USE SOME OF THESE LONGER BONES TO MAKE IT!
WE HAVE TO MOVE HIM! IT MIGHT MAKE HIS INJURIES WORSE, BUT WE HAVE NO CHOICE!
HELP ME, HARRY!
NOW!
AAAAAARGHHHH!
HE SLIPPED INTO A COMA AGAIN.
THE CAMP'S 400 METERS FROM HERE...

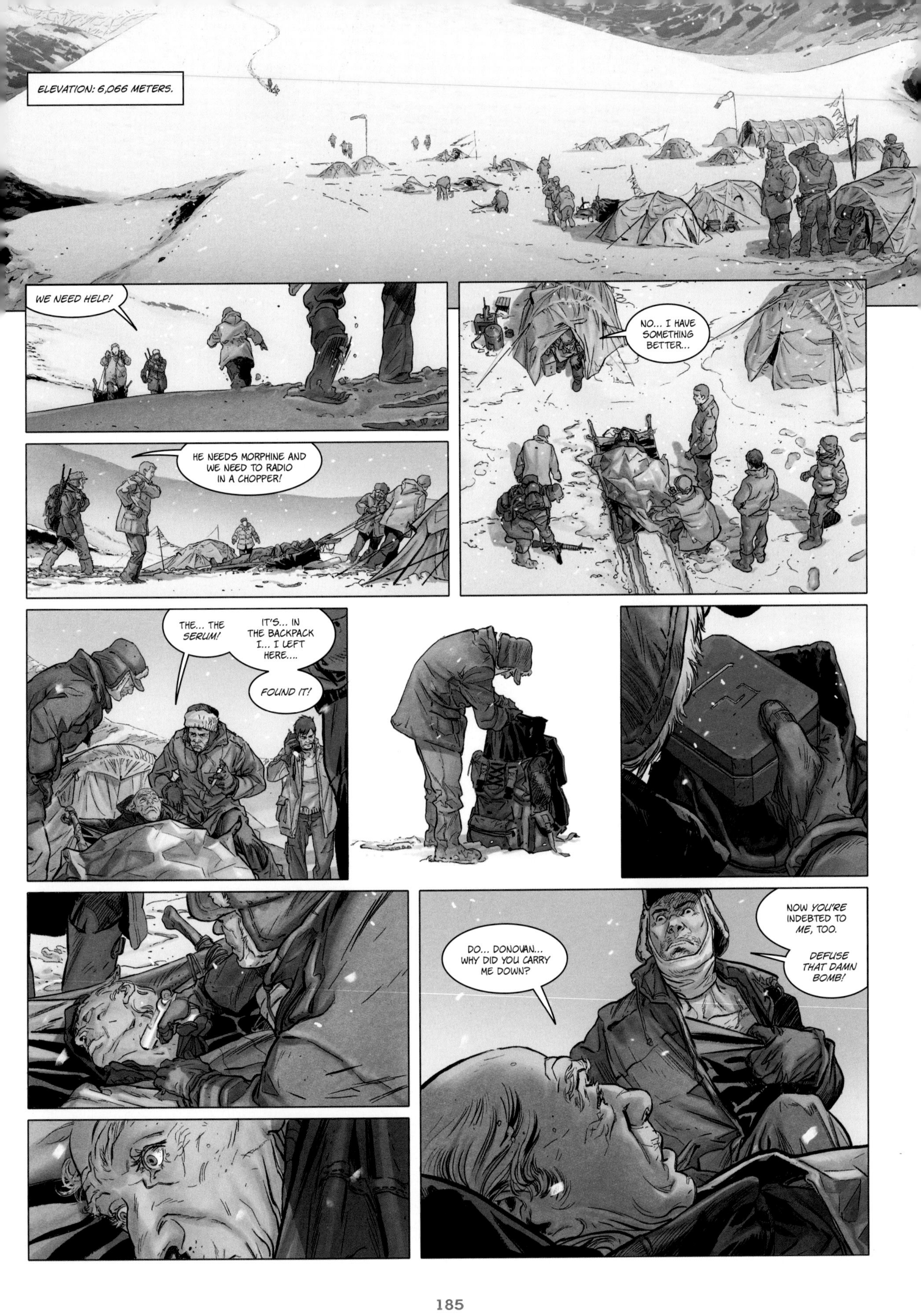
ELEVATION: 6,066 METERS.
WE NEED HELP!
HE NEEDS MORPHINE AND WE NEED TO RADIO IN A CHOPPER!
NO... I HAVE SOMETHING BETTER...
THE... THE SERUM!
IT'S... IN THE BACKPACK I... I LEFT HERE....
FOUND IT!
DO... DONOVAN... WHY DID YOU CARRY ME DOWN?
NOW YOU'RE INDEBTED TO ME, TOO.
DEFUSE THAT DAMN BOMB!

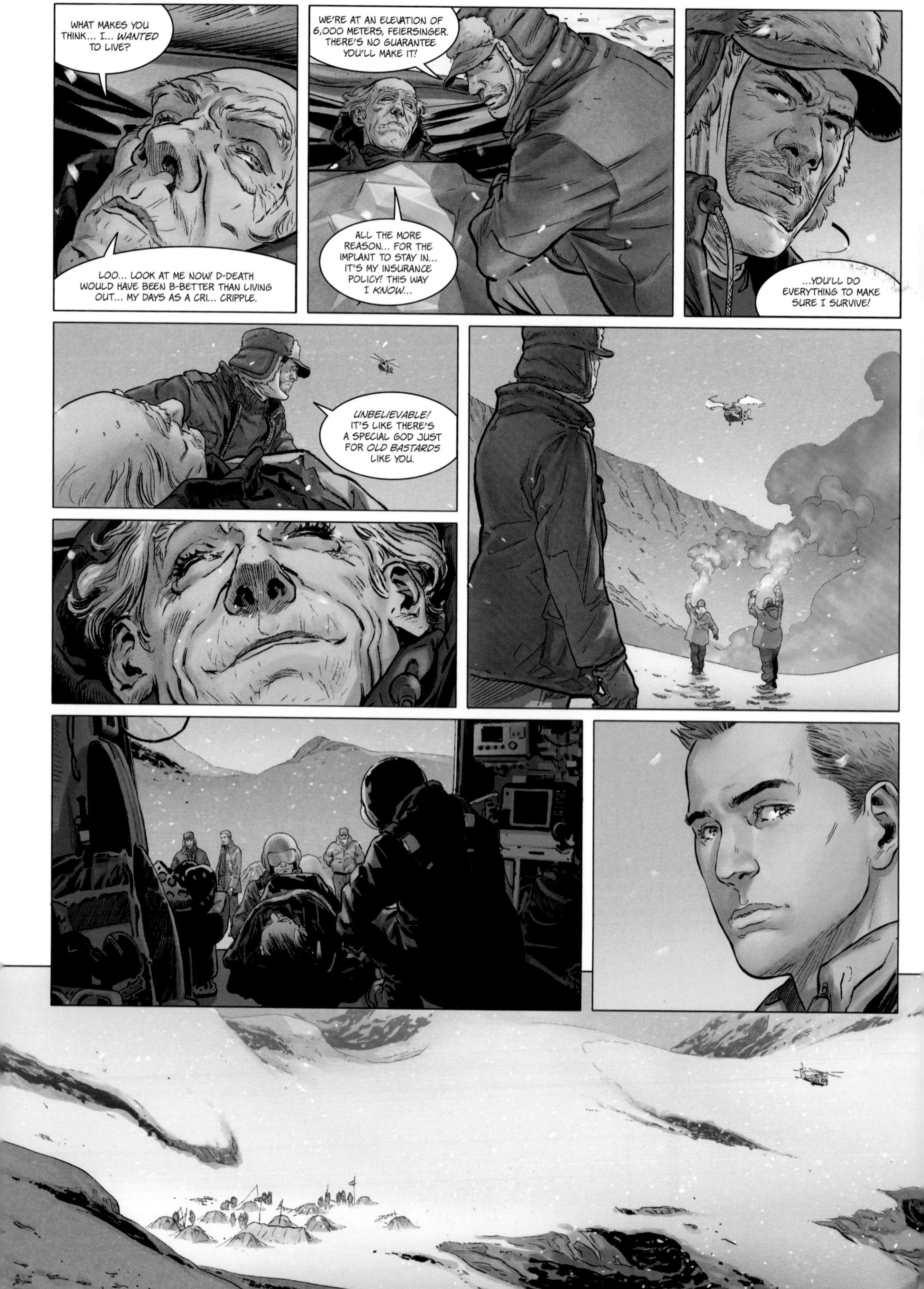
WHAT MAKES YOU THINK... I... WANTED TO LIVE?
LOO... LOOK AT ME NOW! D-DEATH WOULD HAVE BEEN B-BETTER THAN LIVING OUT... MY DAYS AS A CRI... CRIPPLE.
WE'RE AT AN ELEVATION OF 6,000 METERS, FEIERSINGER. THERE'S NO GUARANTEE YOU'LL MAKE IT!
ALL THE MORE REASON... FOR THE IMPLANT TO STAY IN... IT'S MY INSURANCE POLICY! THIS WAY I KNOW...
...YOU'LL DO EVERYTHING TO MAKE SURE I SURVIVE!
UNBELIEVABLE! IT'S LIKE THERE'S A SPECIAL GOD JUST FOR OLD BASTARDS LIKE YOU.

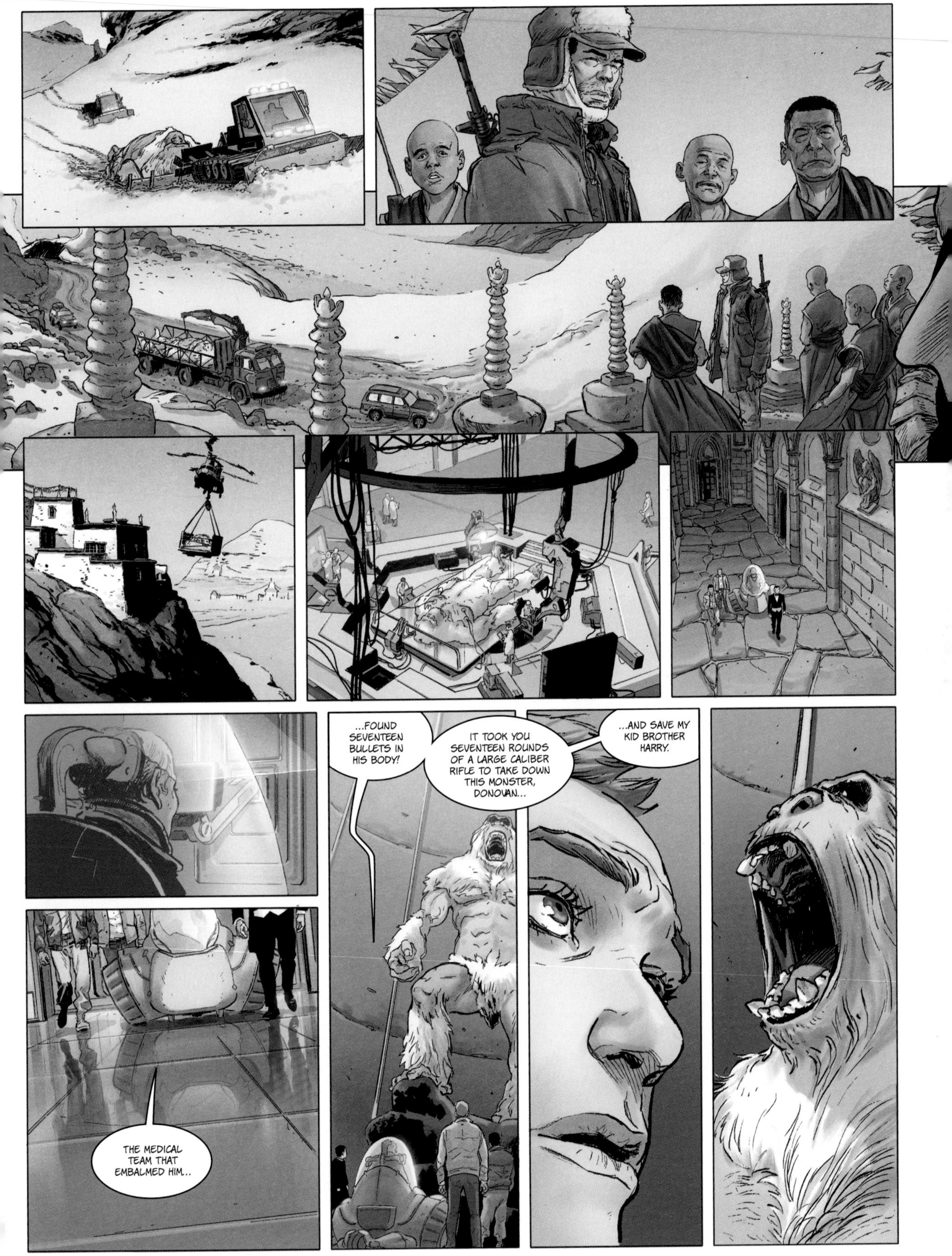
THE MEDICAL TEAM THAT EMBALMED HIM..
...FOUND SEVENTEEN BULLETS IN HIS BODY!
IT TOOK YOU SEVENTEEN ROUNDS OF A LARGE CALIBER RIFLE TO TAKE DOWN THIS MONSTER, DONOVAN...
...AND SAVE MY KID BROTHER HARRY.

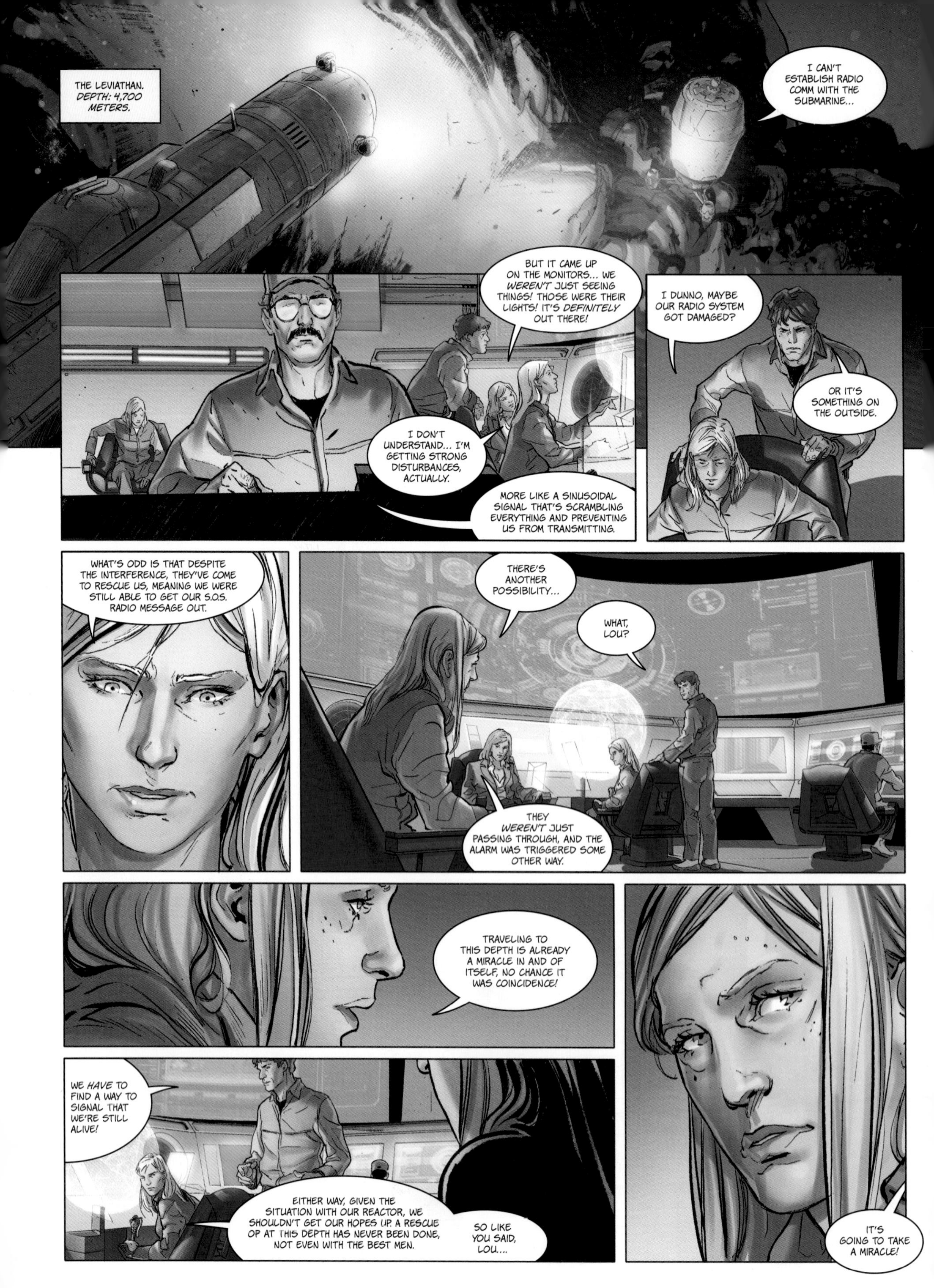

THE LEVIATHAN. *DEPTH: 4,700 METERS.*
I CAN'T ESTABLISH RADIO COMM WITH THE SUBMARINE...
BUT IT CAME UP ON THE MONITORS... WE *WEREN'T* JUST SEEING THINGS! THOSE WERE THEIR LIGHTS! IT'S *DEFINITELY* OUT THERE!
I DON'T UNDERSTAND... I'M GETTING STRONG DISTURBANCES, ACTUALLY.
MORE LIKE A SINUSOIDAL SIGNAL THAT'S SCRAMBLING EVERYTHING AND PREVENTING US FROM TRANSMITTING.
I DUNNO, MAYBE OUR RADIO SYSTEM GOT DAMAGED?
OR IT'S SOMETHING ON THE OUTSIDE.
WHAT'S ODD IS THAT DESPITE THE INTERFERENCE, THEY'VE COME TO RESCUE US, MEANING WE WERE STILL ABLE TO GET OUR S.O.S. RADIO MESSAGE OUT.
THERE'S ANOTHER POSSIBILITY...
WHAT, LOU?
THEY *WEREN'T* JUST PASSING THROUGH, AND THE ALARM WAS TRIGGERED SOME OTHER WAY.
TRAVELING TO THIS DEPTH IS ALREADY A MIRACLE IN AND OF ITSELF, NO CHANCE IT WAS COINCIDENCE!
WE *HAVE* TO FIND A WAY TO SIGNAL THAT WE'RE STILL ALIVE!
EITHER WAY, GIVEN THE SITUATION WITH OUR REACTOR, WE SHOULDN'T GET OUR HOPES UP. A RESCUE OP AT THIS DEPTH HAS NEVER BEEN DONE, NOT EVEN WITH THE BEST MEN.
SO LIKE YOU SAID, LOU...
IT'S GOING TO TAKE A MIRACLE!

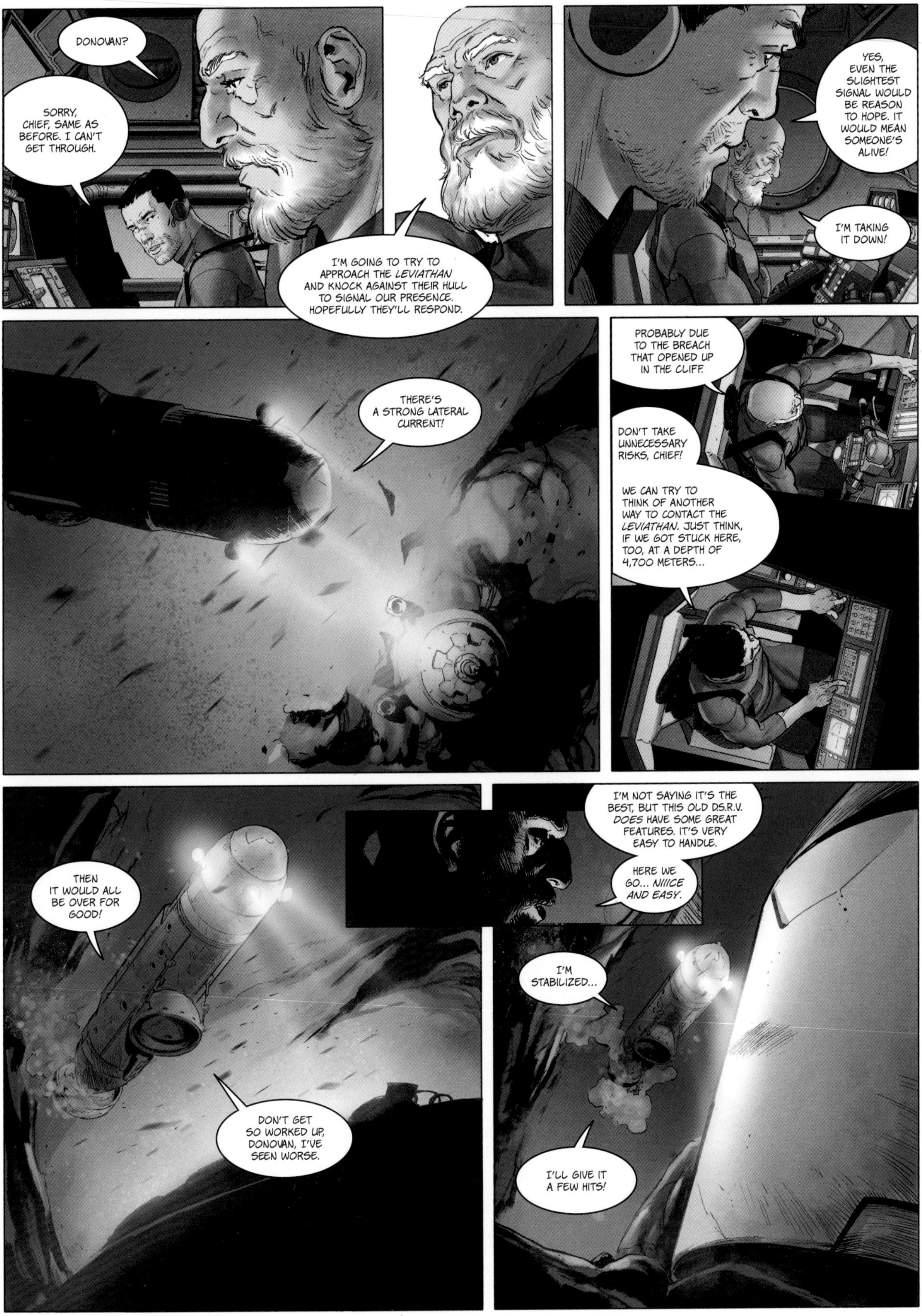
DONOVAN?
SORRY, CHIEF, SAME AS BEFORE. I CAN'T GET THROUGH.
I'M GOING TO TRY TO APPROACH THE *LEVIATHAN* AND KNOCK AGAINST THEIR HULL TO SIGNAL OUR PRESENCE. HOPEFULLY THEY'LL RESPOND.
YES, EVEN THE SLIGHTEST SIGNAL WOULD BE REASON TO HOPE. IT WOULD MEAN SOMEONE'S ALIVE!
I'M TAKING IT DOWN!
THERE'S A STRONG LATERAL CURRENT!
PROBABLY DUE TO THE BREACH THAT OPENED UP IN THE CLIFF.
DON'T TAKE UNNECESSARY RISKS, CHIEF!
WE CAN TRY TO THINK OF ANOTHER WAY TO CONTACT THE *LEVIATHAN*. JUST THINK, IF WE GOT STUCK HERE, TOO, AT A DEPTH OF 4,700 METERS...
THEN IT WOULD ALL BE OVER FOR GOOD!
DON'T GET SO WORKED UP, DONOVAN, I'VE SEEN WORSE.
I'M NOT SAYING IT'S THE BEST, BUT THIS OLD DS.R.V. *DOES* HAVE SOME GREAT FEATURES. IT'S VERY EASY TO HANDLE.
HERE WE GO... *NIIICE AND EASY*.
I'M STABILIZED...
I'LL GIVE IT A FEW HITS!

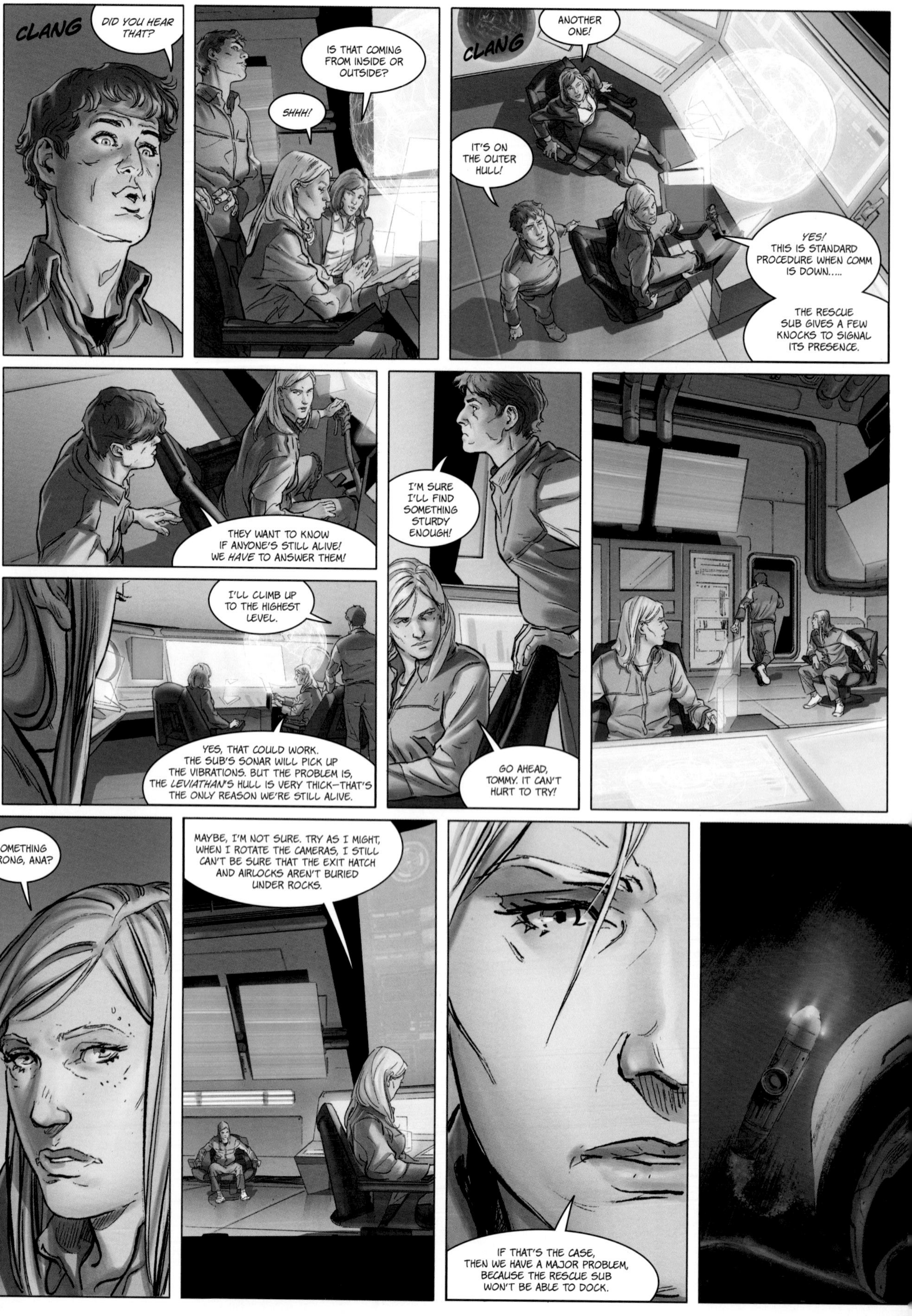
CLANG
DID YOU HEAR THAT?
IS THAT COMING FROM INSIDE OR OUTSIDE?
SHHH!
CLANG
ANOTHER ONE!
IT'S ON THE OUTER HULL!
YES! THIS IS STANDARD PROCEDURE WHEN COMM IS DOWN.....
THE RESCUE SUB GIVES A FEW KNOCKS TO SIGNAL ITS PRESENCE.
THEY WANT TO KNOW IF ANYONE'S STILL ALIVE! WE HAVE TO ANSWER THEM!
I'LL CLIMB UP TO THE HIGHEST LEVEL.
YES, THAT COULD WORK. THE SUB'S SONAR WILL PICK UP THE VIBRATIONS. BUT THE PROBLEM IS, THE LEVIATHAN'S HULL IS VERY THICK—THAT'S THE ONLY REASON WE'RE STILL ALIVE.
I'M SURE I'LL FIND SOMETHING STURDY ENOUGH!
GO AHEAD, TOMMY. IT CAN'T HURT TO TRY!
SOMETHING WRONG, ANA?
MAYBE, I'M NOT SURE. TRY AS I MIGHT, WHEN I ROTATE THE CAMERAS, I STILL CAN'T BE SURE THAT THE EXIT HATCH AND AIRLOCKS AREN'T BURIED UNDER ROCKS.
IF THAT'S THE CASE, THEN WE HAVE A MAJOR PROBLEM, BECAUSE THE RESCUE SUB WON'T BE ABLE TO DOCK.

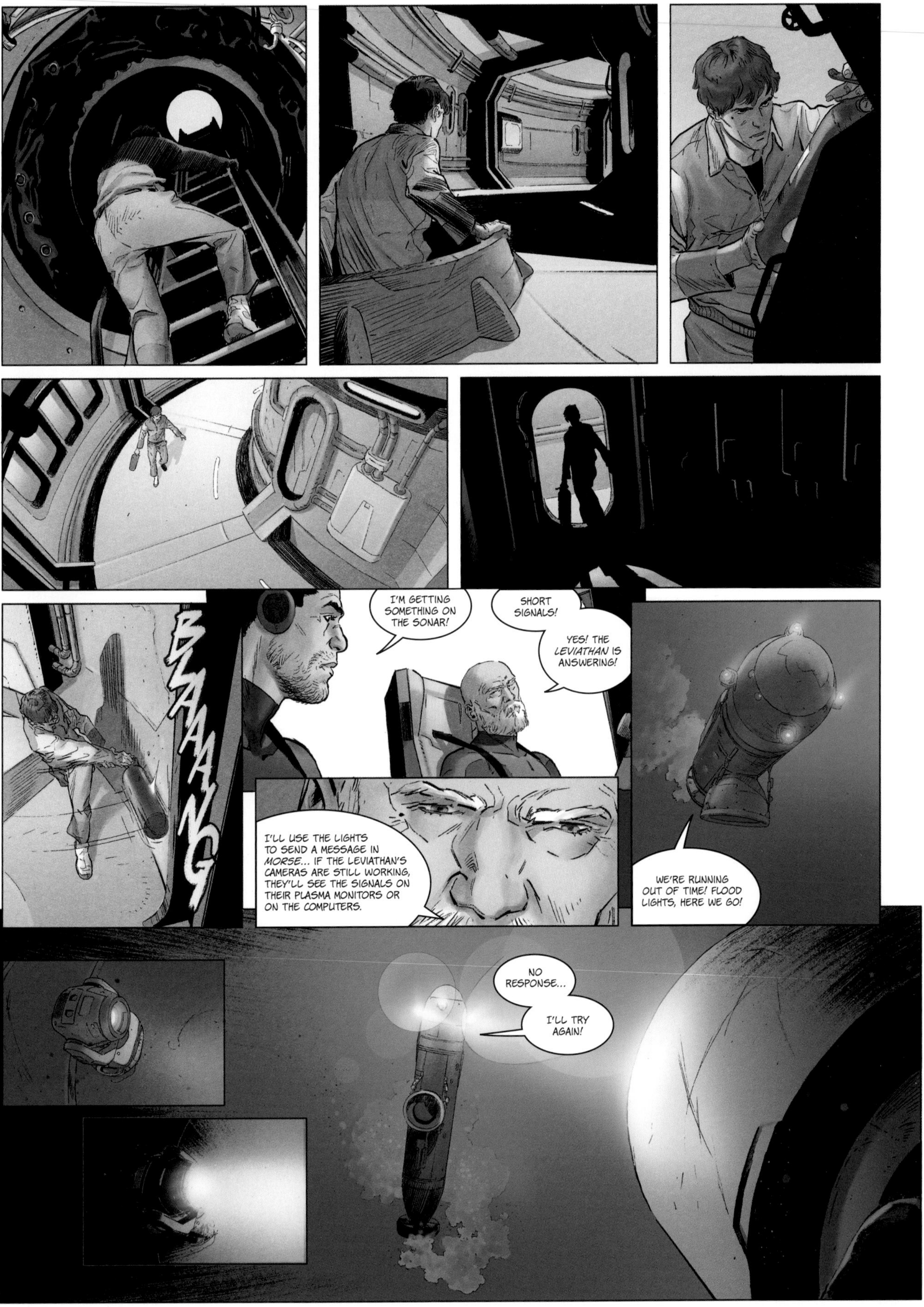
BLAAANG
I'M GETTING SOMETHING ON THE SONAR!
SHORT SIGNALS!
YES! THE *LEVIATHAN* IS ANSWERING!
I'LL USE THE LIGHTS TO SEND A MESSAGE IN *MORSE*... IF THE LEVIATHAN'S CAMERAS ARE STILL WORKING, THEY'LL SEE THE SIGNALS ON THEIR PLASMA MONITORS OR ON THE COMPUTERS.
WE'RE RUNNING OUT OF TIME! FLOOD LIGHTS, HERE WE GO!
NO RESPONSE...
I'LL TRY AGAIN!

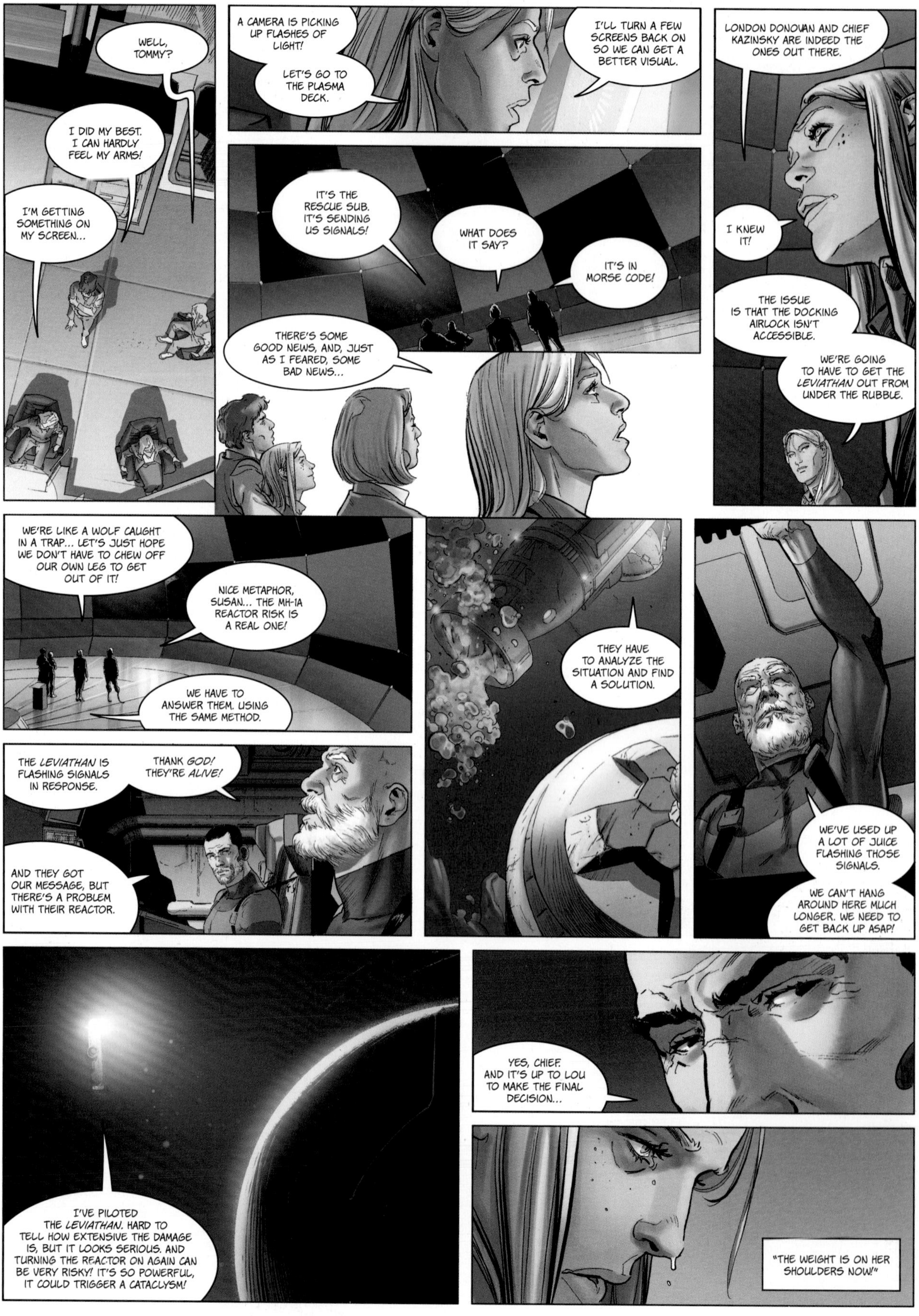

WELL, TOMMY?
I DID MY BEST. I CAN HARDLY FEEL MY ARMS!
I'M GETTING SOMETHING ON MY SCREEN...
A CAMERA IS PICKING UP FLASHES OF LIGHT!
LET'S GO TO THE PLASMA DECK.
I'LL TURN A FEW SCREENS BACK ON SO WE CAN GET A BETTER VISUAL.
LONDON DONOVAN AND CHIEF KAZINSKY ARE INDEED THE ONES OUT THERE.
IT'S THE RESCUE SUB. IT'S SENDING US SIGNALS!
WHAT DOES IT SAY?
IT'S IN MORSE CODE!
I KNEW IT!
THERE'S SOME GOOD NEWS, AND, JUST AS I FEARED, SOME BAD NEWS...
THE ISSUE IS THAT THE DOCKING AIRLOCK ISN'T ACCESSIBLE.
WE'RE GOING TO HAVE TO GET THE *LEVIATHAN* OUT FROM UNDER THE RUBBLE.
WE'RE LIKE A WOLF CAUGHT IN A TRAP... LET'S JUST HOPE WE DON'T HAVE TO CHEW OFF OUR OWN LEG TO GET OUT OF IT!
NICE METAPHOR, SUSAN... THE MH-1A REACTOR RISK IS A REAL ONE!
WE HAVE TO ANSWER THEM. USING THE SAME METHOD.
THEY HAVE TO ANALYZE THE SITUATION AND FIND A SOLUTION.
THE *LEVIATHAN* IS FLASHING SIGNALS IN RESPONSE.
THANK *GOD!* THEY'RE *ALIVE!*
AND THEY GOT OUR MESSAGE, BUT THERE'S A PROBLEM WITH THEIR REACTOR.
WE'VE USED UP A LOT OF JUICE FLASHING THOSE SIGNALS.
WE CAN'T HANG AROUND HERE MUCH LONGER. WE NEED TO GET BACK UP ASAP!
I'VE PILOTED THE *LEVIATHAN*. HARD TO TELL HOW EXTENSIVE THE DAMAGE IS, BUT IT LOOKS SERIOUS. AND TURNING THE REACTOR ON AGAIN CAN BE VERY RISKY! IT'S SO POWERFUL, IT COULD TRIGGER A CATACLYSM!
YES, CHIEF. AND IT'S UP TO LOU TO MAKE THE FINAL DECISION...
"THE WEIGHT IS ON HER SHOULDERS NOW!"

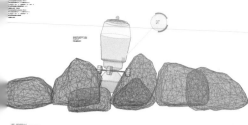

AND WITH THE MH-IA REACTOR, THAT'S TAKING A HUGE RISK, RIGHT?

THAT'S OUR NEXT STEP: TO EVALUATE THE RISK WITH OUR ONBOARD TECHNICIANS.

WE'VE RUN SOME SIMULATIONS.

THE ONLY WAY TO FREE THE ACCESS POINT IS TO JETTISON ALL THE BALLASTS AND START UP THE REACTOR AT FULL POWER SO WE CAN MOVE AWAY IN ONE QUICK BURST, HOPEFULLY DISLODGING THE ROCKS AND GETTING OUT FROM UNDER THE RUBBLE SOME.

BUT FIRST, WE NEED TO KNOW IF THIS MANEUVER TO FREE OURSELVES CAN ACTUALLY WORK.

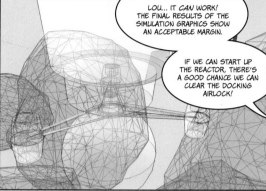

LOU... IT CAN WORK! THE FINAL RESULTS OF THE SIMULATION GRAPHICS SHOW AN ACCEPTABLE MARGIN.

IF WE CAN START UP THE REACTOR, THERE'S A GOOD CHANCE WE CAN CLEAR THE DOCKING AIRLOCK!

WE HAVE TO KNOW WHAT TO EXPECT FROM THE MH-IA, ANA!

WE'RE ON IT!

BUT DON'T GET YOUR HOPES UP... EITHER WAY, THERE'S A HIGH RISK OF NUCLEAR FUSION.

I KEEP GOING OVER IMAGES OF THE D.S.R.V.

IF YOU LOOK CLOSELY, THIS SUB IS TOTALLY OBSOLETE!

"...EVEN ABOARD A WRECK LIKE THAT!"

YES, AND LIKE I WAS SAYING, THERE HAS NEVER BEEN A SUCCESSFUL RESCUE OP BELOW 600 METERS!

SO HOW CAN IT BE FEASIBLE WITH AN ANTIQUE LIKE THIS?

BECAUSE CHIEF KAZINSKY'S AT THE COMMAND. THEY CAN DO IT! DONOVAN CAN DO IT!

IN FACT, THEY'RE PROBABLY THE ONLY TWO MEN IN THE WORLD ABLE TO PULL OFF SUCH A FEAT...

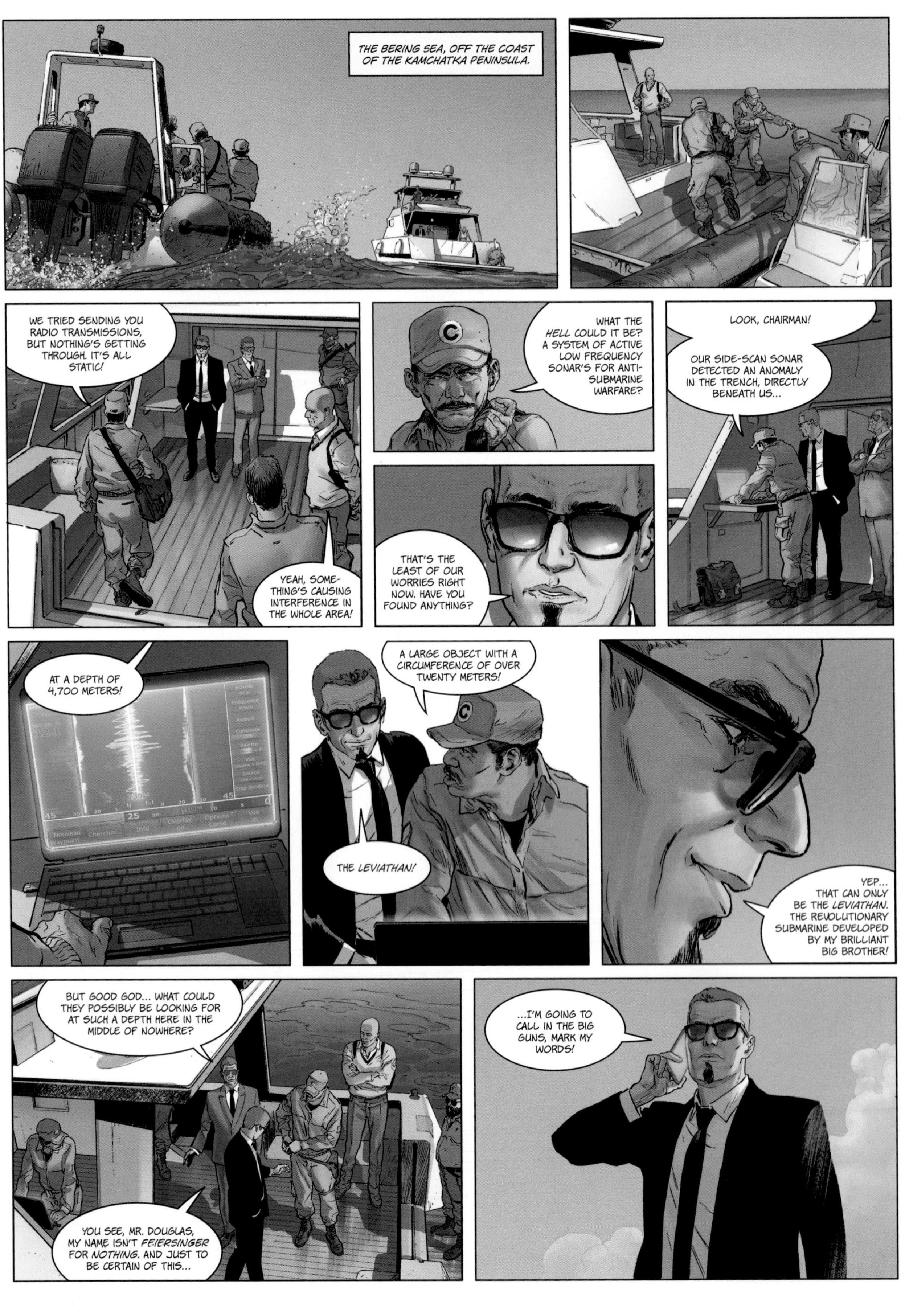
THE BERING SEA, OFF THE COAST OF THE KAMCHATKA PENINSULA.
WE TRIED SENDING YOU RADIO TRANSMISSIONS, BUT NOTHING'S GETTING THROUGH. IT'S ALL STATIC!
YEAH, SOME-THING'S CAUSING INTERFERENCE IN THE WHOLE AREA!
WHAT THE *HELL* COULD IT BE? A SYSTEM OF ACTIVE LOW FREQUENCY SONAR'S FOR ANTI-SUBMARINE WARFARE?
THAT'S THE LEAST OF OUR WORRIES RIGHT NOW. HAVE YOU FOUND ANYTHING?
LOOK, CHAIRMAN!
OUR SIDE-SCAN SONAR DETECTED AN ANOMALY IN THE TRENCH, DIRECTLY BENEATH US...
AT A DEPTH OF 4,700 METERS!
A LARGE OBJECT WITH A CIRCUMFERENCE OF OVER TWENTY METERS!
THE *LEVIATHAN!*
YEP... THAT CAN ONLY BE THE *LEVIATHAN.* THE REVOLUTIONARY SUBMARINE DEVELOPED BY MY BRILLIANT BIG BROTHER!
BUT GOOD GOD... WHAT COULD THEY POSSIBLY BE LOOKING FOR AT SUCH A DEPTH HERE IN THE MIDDLE OF NOWHERE?
YOU SEE, MR. DOUGLAS, MY NAME ISN'T *FEIERSINGER* FOR *NOTHING.* AND JUST TO BE CERTAIN OF THIS...
...I'M GOING TO CALL IN THE BIG GUNS, MARK MY WORDS!

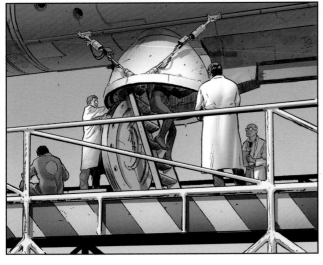

CHIEF KAZINSKY... LONDON...

THEY'RE ALONE...

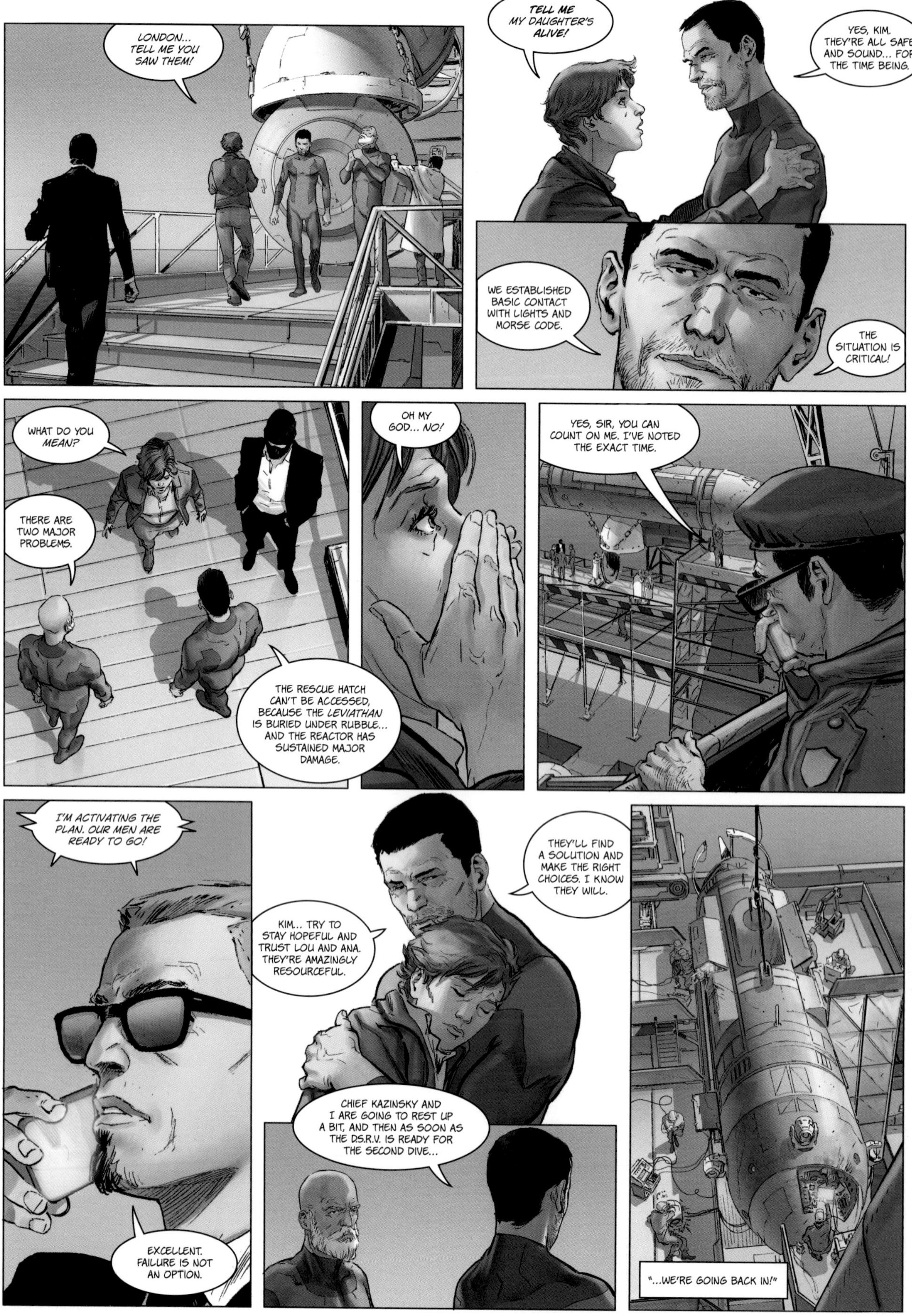

LONDON... TELL ME YOU SAW THEM!
TELL ME MY DAUGHTER'S ALIVE!
YES, KIM. THEY'RE ALL SAFE AND SOUND... FOR THE TIME BEING.
WE ESTABLISHED BASIC CONTACT WITH LIGHTS AND MORSE CODE.
THE SITUATION IS CRITICAL!
WHAT DO YOU MEAN?
THERE ARE TWO MAJOR PROBLEMS.
THE RESCUE HATCH CAN'T BE ACCESSED, BECAUSE THE LEVIATHAN IS BURIED UNDER RUBBLE... AND THE REACTOR HAS SUSTAINED MAJOR DAMAGE.
OH MY GOD... NO!
YES, SIR, YOU CAN COUNT ON ME. I'VE NOTED THE EXACT TIME.
I'M ACTIVATING THE PLAN. OUR MEN ARE READY TO GO!
EXCELLENT. FAILURE IS NOT AN OPTION.
KIM... TRY TO STAY HOPEFUL AND TRUST LOU AND ANA. THEY'RE AMAZINGLY RESOURCEFUL.
THEY'LL FIND A SOLUTION AND MAKE THE RIGHT CHOICES. I KNOW THEY WILL.
CHIEF KAZINSKY AND I ARE GOING TO REST UP A BIT, AND THEN AS SOON AS THE D.S.R.V. IS READY FOR THE SECOND DIVE...
"...WE'RE GOING BACK IN!"

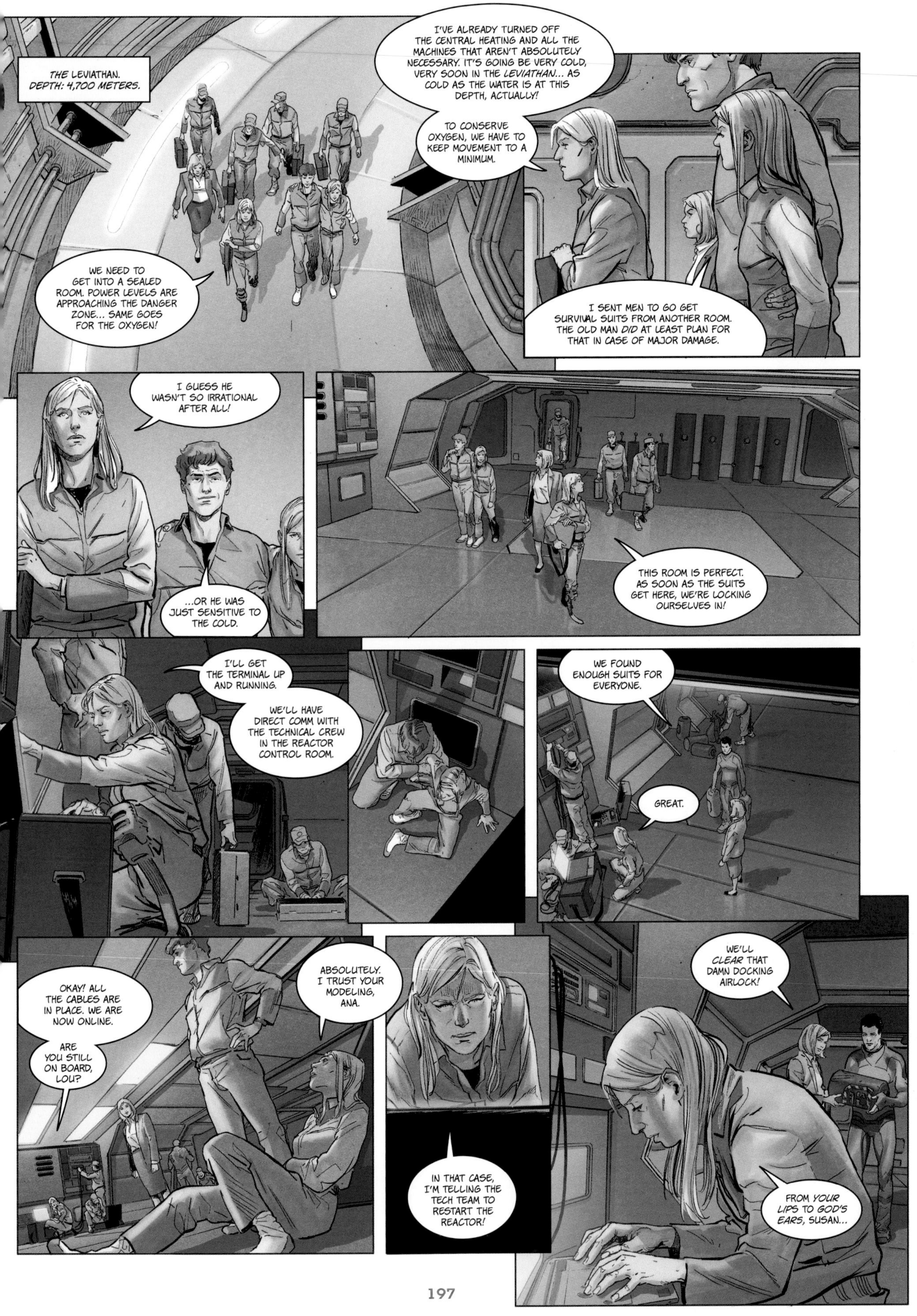
THE LEVIATHAN. DEPTH: 4,700 METERS.
I'VE ALREADY TURNED OFF THE CENTRAL HEATING AND ALL THE MACHINES THAT AREN'T ABSOLUTELY NECESSARY. IT'S GOING BE VERY COLD, VERY SOON IN THE LEVIATHAN... AS COLD AS THE WATER IS AT THIS DEPTH, ACTUALLY!
TO CONSERVE OXYGEN, WE HAVE TO KEEP MOVEMENT TO A MINIMUM.
WE NEED TO GET INTO A SEALED ROOM. POWER LEVELS ARE APPROACHING THE DANGER ZONE... SAME GOES FOR THE OXYGEN!
I SENT MEN TO GO GET SURVIVAL SUITS FROM ANOTHER ROOM. THE OLD MAN DID AT LEAST PLAN FOR THAT IN CASE OF MAJOR DAMAGE.
I GUESS HE WASN'T SO IRRATIONAL AFTER ALL!
...OR HE WAS JUST SENSITIVE TO THE COLD.
THIS ROOM IS PERFECT. AS SOON AS THE SUITS GET HERE, WE'RE LOCKING OURSELVES IN!
I'LL GET THE TERMINAL UP AND RUNNING.
WE'LL HAVE DIRECT COMM WITH THE TECHNICAL CREW IN THE REACTOR CONTROL ROOM.
WE FOUND ENOUGH SUITS FOR EVERYONE.
GREAT.
OKAY! ALL THE CABLES ARE IN PLACE. WE ARE NOW ONLINE.
ARE YOU STILL ON BOARD, LOU?
ABSOLUTELY. I TRUST YOUR MODELING, ANA.
IN THAT CASE, I'M TELLING THE TECH TEAM TO RESTART THE REACTOR!
WE'LL CLEAR THAT DAMN DOCKING AIRLOCK!
FROM YOUR LIPS TO GOD'S EARS, SUSAN...

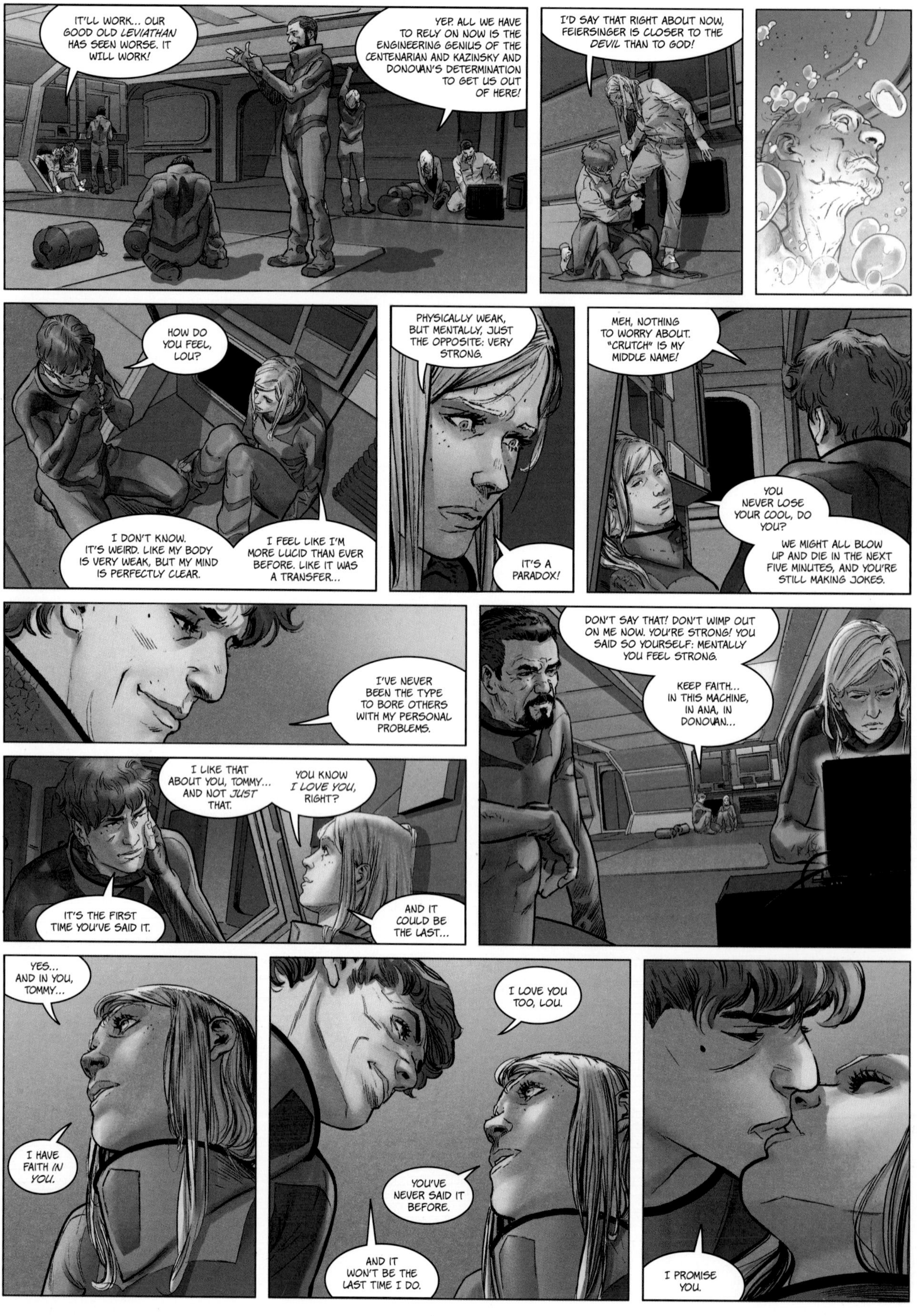
IT'LL WORK... OUR GOOD OLD LEVIATHAN HAS SEEN WORSE. IT WILL WORK!
YEP. ALL WE HAVE TO RELY ON NOW IS THE ENGINEERING GENIUS OF THE CENTENARIAN AND KAZINSKY AND DONOVAN'S DETERMINATION TO GET US OUT OF HERE!
I'D SAY THAT RIGHT ABOUT NOW, FEIERSINGER IS CLOSER TO THE DEVIL THAN TO GOD!
HOW DO YOU FEEL, LOU?
I DON'T KNOW. IT'S WEIRD. LIKE MY BODY IS VERY WEAK, BUT MY MIND IS PERFECTLY CLEAR.
I FEEL LIKE I'M MORE LUCID THAN EVER BEFORE. LIKE IT WAS A TRANSFER...
PHYSICALLY WEAK, BUT MENTALLY, JUST THE OPPOSITE: VERY STRONG.
IT'S A PARADOX!
MEH, NOTHING TO WORRY ABOUT. "CRUTCH" IS MY MIDDLE NAME!
YOU NEVER LOSE YOUR COOL, DO YOU?
WE MIGHT ALL BLOW UP AND DIE IN THE NEXT FIVE MINUTES, AND YOU'RE STILL MAKING JOKES.
I'VE NEVER BEEN THE TYPE TO BORE OTHERS WITH MY PERSONAL PROBLEMS.
I LIKE THAT ABOUT YOU, TOMMY... AND NOT JUST THAT.
YOU KNOW I LOVE YOU, RIGHT?
IT'S THE FIRST TIME YOU'VE SAID IT.
AND IT COULD BE THE LAST...
DON'T SAY THAT! DON'T WIMP OUT ON ME NOW. YOU'RE STRONG! YOU SAID SO YOURSELF: MENTALLY YOU FEEL STRONG.
KEEP FAITH... IN THIS MACHINE, IN ANA, IN DONOVAN...
YES... AND IN YOU, TOMMY...
I HAVE FAITH IN YOU.
I LOVE YOU TOO, LOU.
YOU'VE NEVER SAID IT BEFORE.
AND IT WON'T BE THE LAST TIME I DO.
I PROMISE YOU.

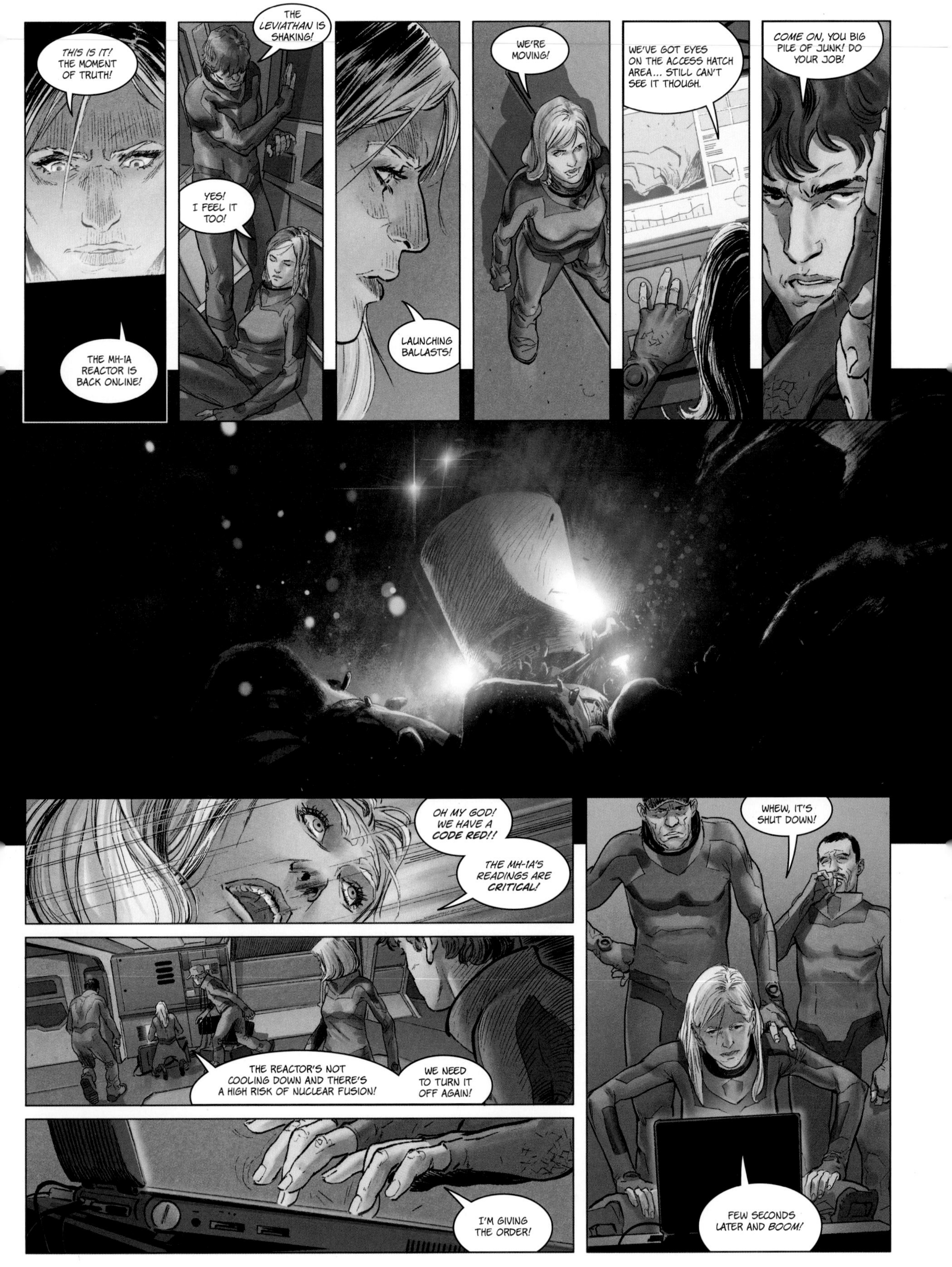
THIS IS IT! THE MOMENT OF TRUTH!
THE MH-1A REACTOR IS BACK ONLINE!
THE LEVIATHAN IS SHAKING!
YES! I FEEL IT TOO!
LAUNCHING BALLASTS!
WE'RE MOVING!
WE'VE GOT EYES ON THE ACCESS HATCH AREA... STILL CAN'T SEE IT THOUGH.
COME ON, YOU BIG PILE OF JUNK! DO YOUR JOB!
OH MY GOD! WE HAVE A CODE RED!!
THE MH-1A'S READINGS ARE CRITICAL!
THE REACTOR'S NOT COOLING DOWN AND THERE'S A HIGH RISK OF NUCLEAR FUSION!
WE NEED TO TURN IT OFF AGAIN!
I'M GIVING THE ORDER!
WHEW, IT'S SHUT DOWN!
FEW SECONDS LATER AND BOOM!

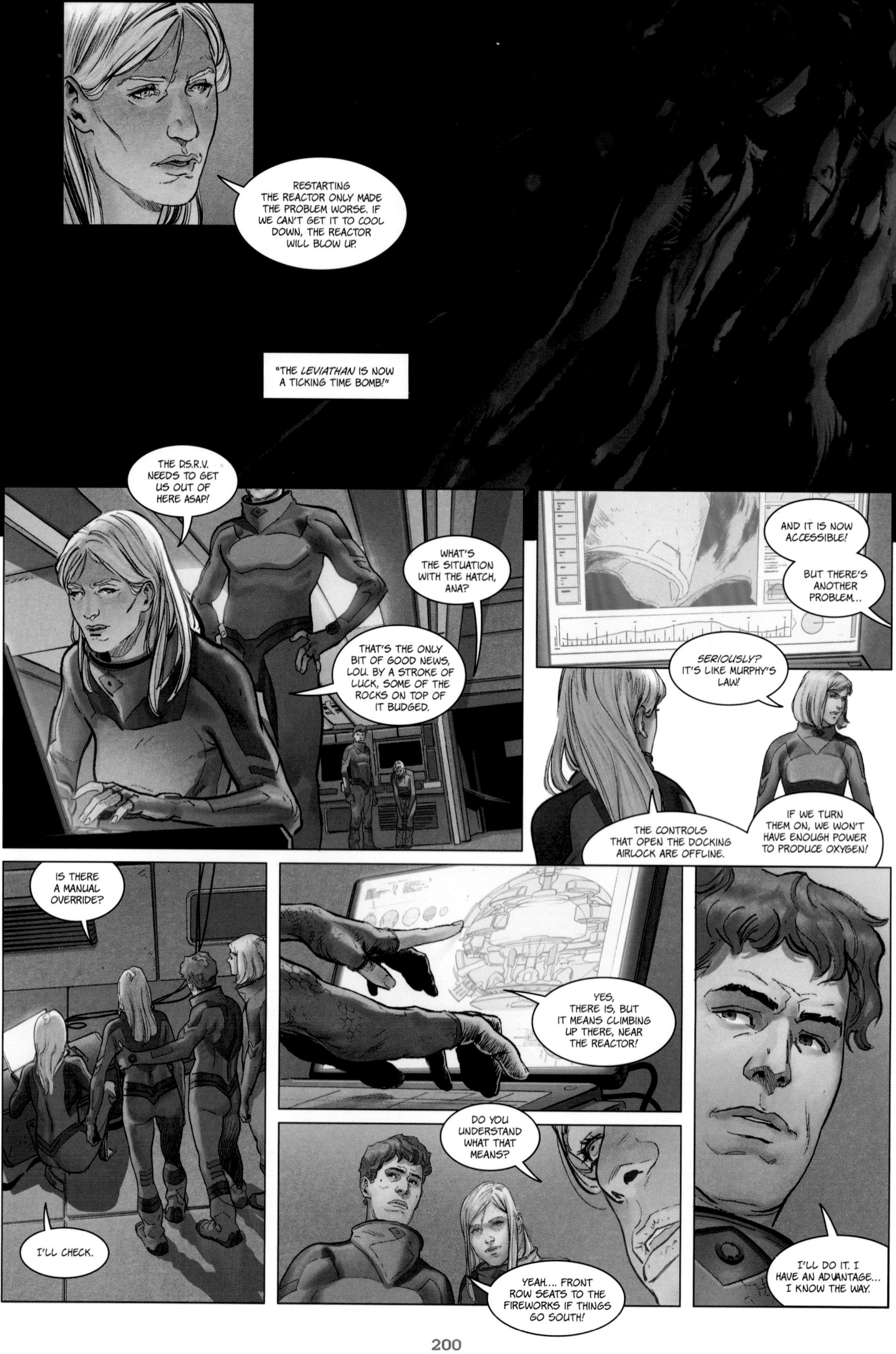
RESTARTING THE REACTOR ONLY MADE THE PROBLEM WORSE. IF WE CAN'T GET IT TO COOL DOWN, THE REACTOR WILL BLOW UP.
"THE *LEVIATHAN* IS NOW A TICKING TIME BOMB!"
THE D.S.R.V. NEEDS TO GET US OUT OF HERE ASAP!
WHAT'S THE SITUATION WITH THE HATCH, ANA?
THAT'S THE ONLY BIT OF GOOD NEWS, LOU. BY A STROKE OF LUCK, SOME OF THE ROCKS ON TOP OF IT BUDGED.
AND IT IS NOW ACCESSIBLE!
BUT THERE'S ANOTHER PROBLEM...
SERIOUSLY? IT'S LIKE MURPHY'S LAW!
THE CONTROLS THAT OPEN THE DOCKING AIRLOCK ARE OFFLINE.
IF WE TURN THEM ON, WE WON'T HAVE ENOUGH POWER TO PRODUCE OXYGEN!
IS THERE A MANUAL OVERRIDE?
I'LL CHECK.
YES, THERE IS, BUT IT MEANS CLIMBING UP THERE, NEAR THE REACTOR!
DO YOU UNDERSTAND WHAT THAT MEANS?
YEAH.... FRONT ROW SEATS TO THE FIREWORKS IF THINGS GO SOUTH!
I'LL DO IT. I HAVE AN ADVANTAGE... I KNOW THE WAY.

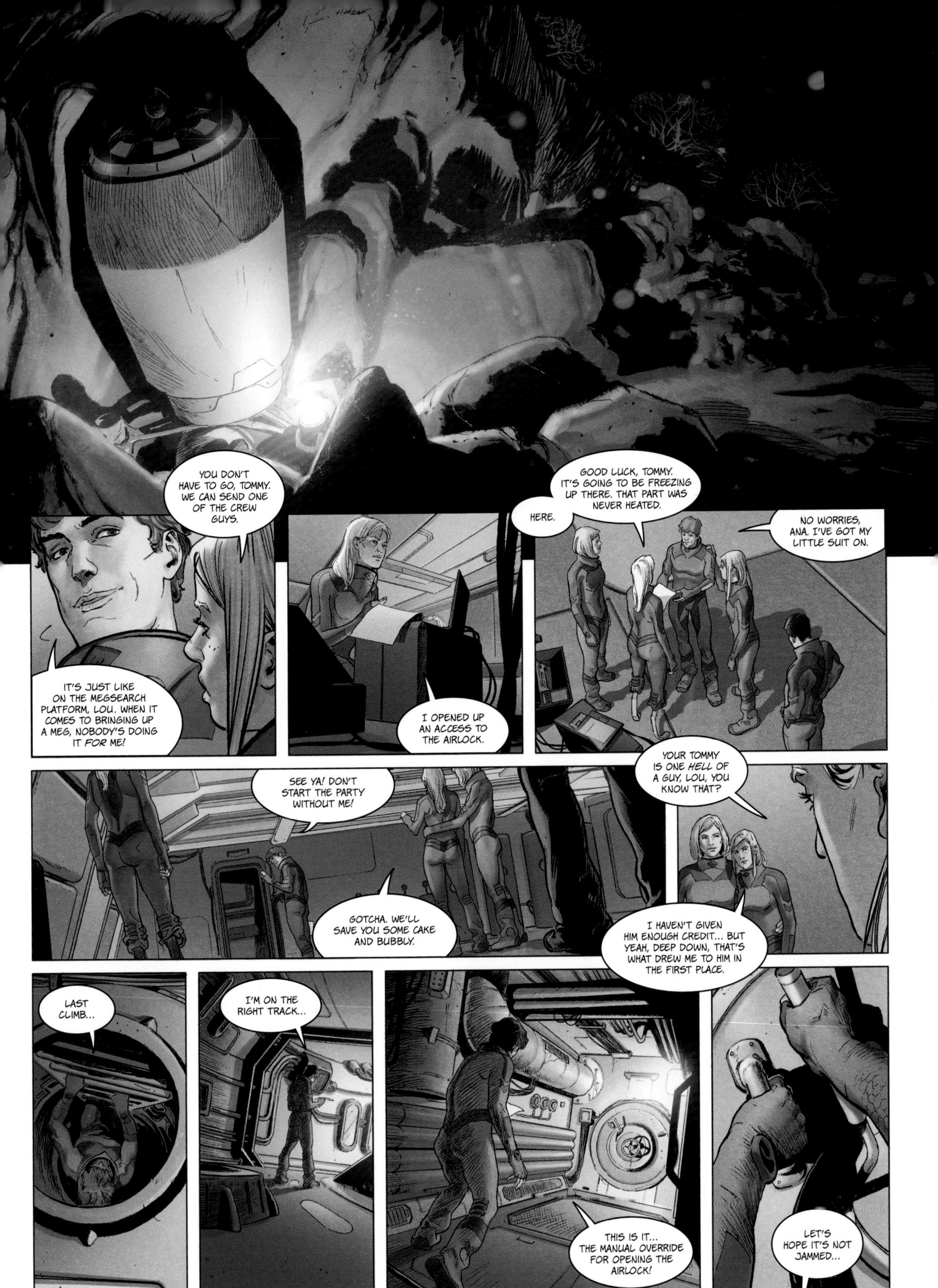
YOU DON'T HAVE TO GO, TOMMY. WE CAN SEND ONE OF THE CREW GUYS.
IT'S JUST LIKE ON THE MEGSEARCH PLATFORM, LOU. WHEN IT COMES TO BRINGING UP A MEG, NOBODY'S DOING IT *FOR* ME!
I OPENED UP AN ACCESS TO THE AIRLOCK.
HERE.
GOOD LUCK, TOMMY. IT'S GOING TO BE FREEZING UP THERE. THAT PART WAS NEVER HEATED.
NO WORRIES, ANA. I'VE GOT MY LITTLE SUIT ON.
SEE YA! DON'T START THE PARTY WITHOUT ME!
GOTCHA. WE'LL SAVE YOU SOME CAKE AND BUBBLY.
YOUR TOMMY IS ONE *HELL* OF A GUY, LOU, YOU KNOW THAT?
I HAVEN'T GIVEN HIM ENOUGH CREDIT... BUT YEAH, DEEP DOWN, THAT'S WHAT DREW ME TO HIM IN THE FIRST PLACE.
LAST CLIMB...
I'M ON THE RIGHT TRACK...
THIS IS IT... THE MANUAL OVERRIDE FOR OPENING THE AIRLOCK!
LET'S HOPE IT'S NOT JAMMED...

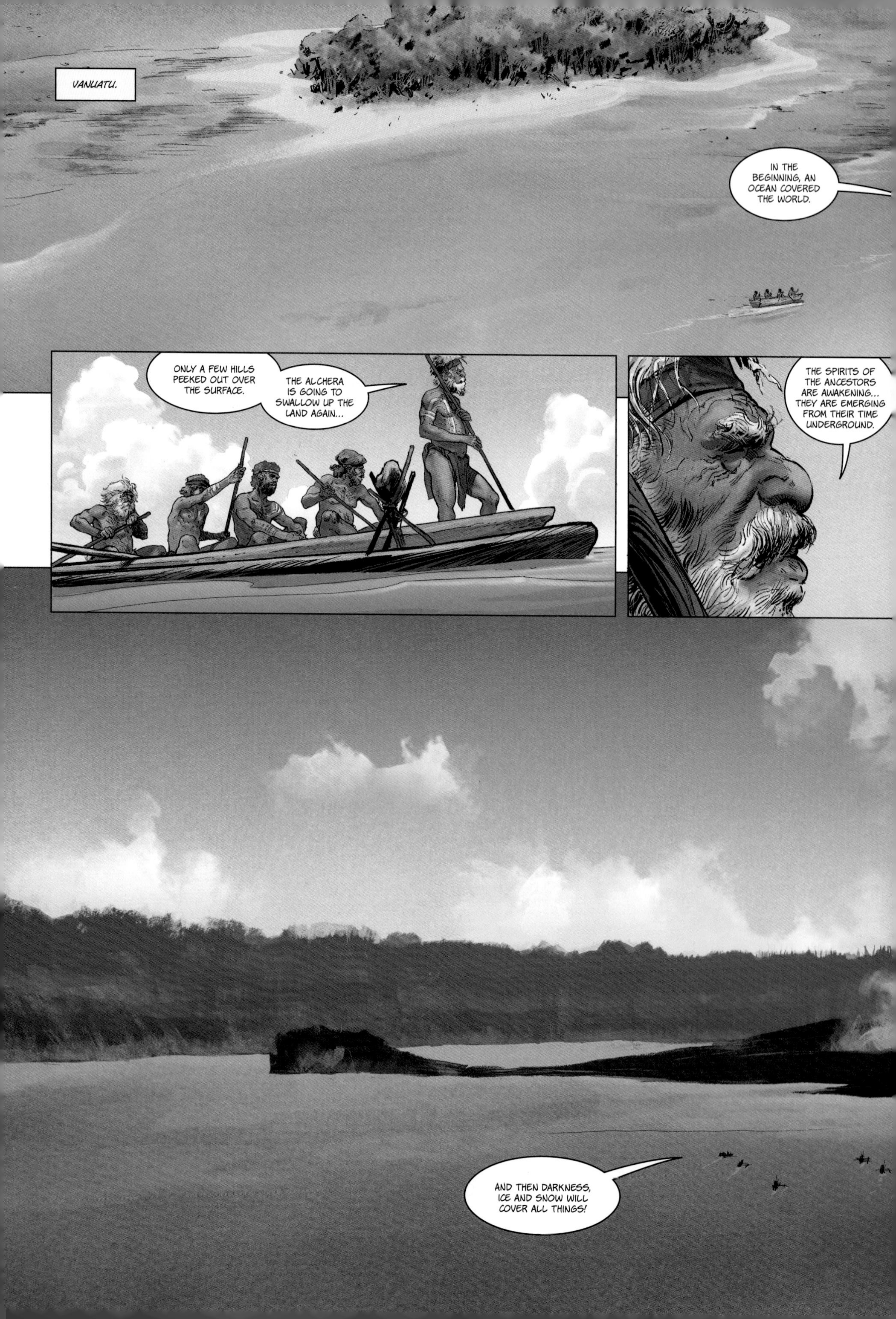
VANUATU.
IN THE BEGINNING, AN OCEAN COVERED THE WORLD.
ONLY A FEW HILLS PEEKED OUT OVER THE SURFACE.
THE ALCHERA IS GOING TO SWALLOW UP THE LAND AGAIN...
THE SPIRITS OF THE ANCESTORS ARE AWAKENING... THEY ARE EMERGING FROM THEIR TIME UNDERGROUND.
AND THEN DARKNESS, ICE AND SNOW WILL COVER ALL THINGS!

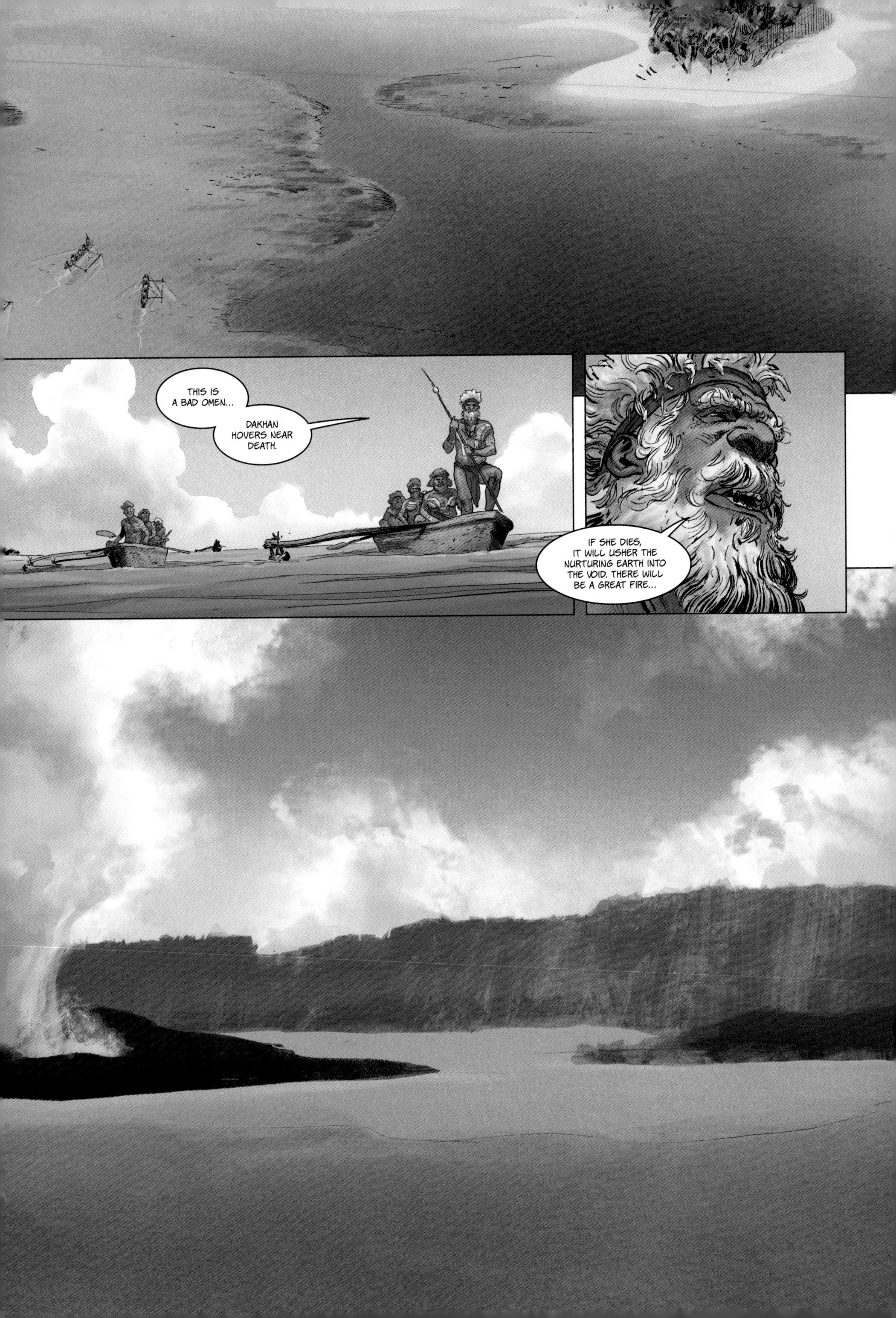
THIS IS A BAD OMEN...
DAKHAN HOVERS NEAR DEATH.
IF SHE DIES, IT WILL USHER THE NURTURING EARTH INTO THE VOID. THERE WILL BE A GREAT FIRE...

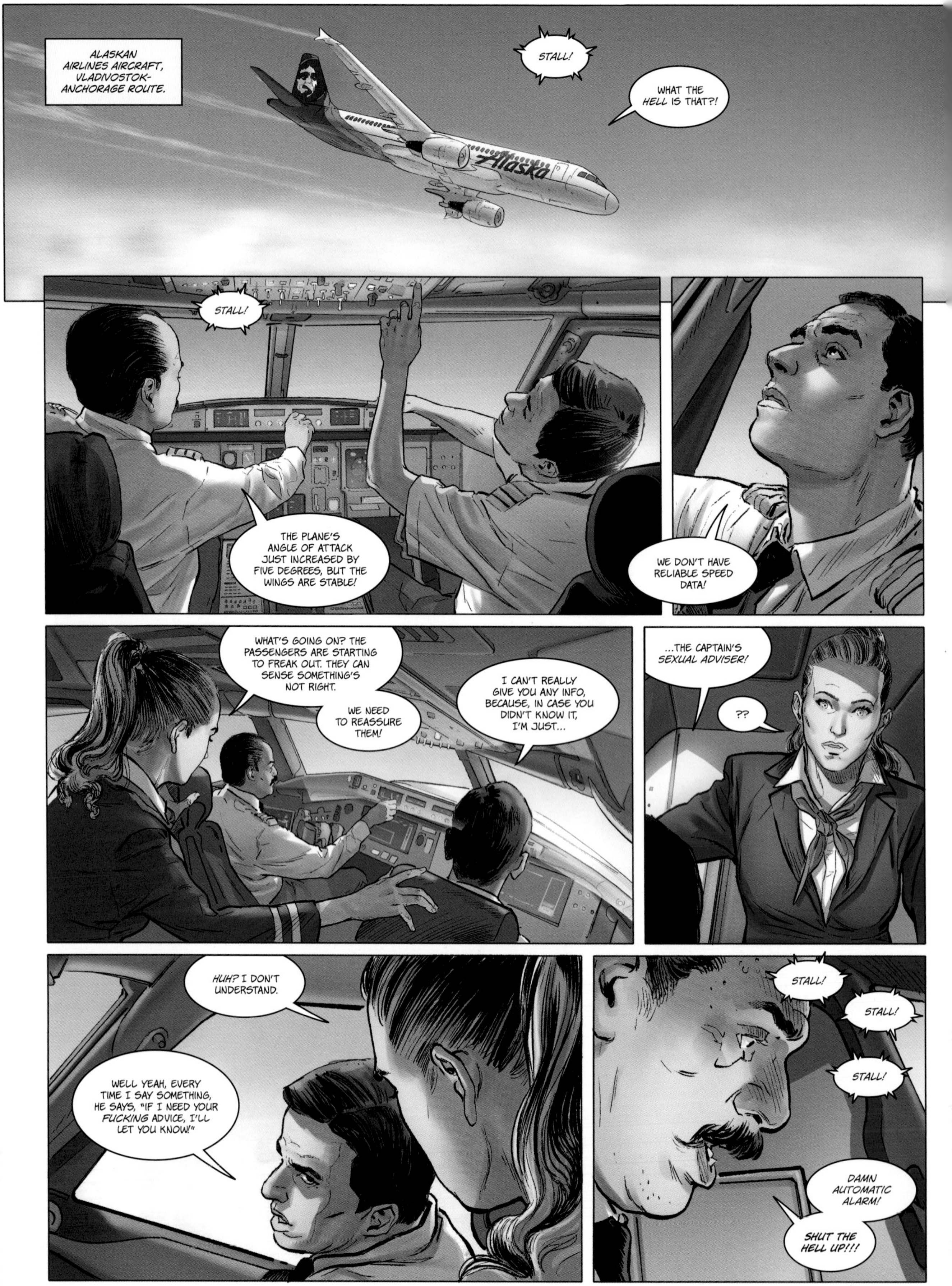

ALASKAN AIRLINES AIRCRAFT, VLADIVOSTOK-ANCHORAGE ROUTE.
Alaska
STALL!
WHAT THE HELL IS THAT?!
STALL!
THE PLANE'S ANGLE OF ATTACK JUST INCREASED BY FIVE DEGREES, BUT THE WINGS ARE STABLE!
WE DON'T HAVE RELIABLE SPEED DATA!
WHAT'S GOING ON? THE PASSENGERS ARE STARTING TO FREAK OUT. THEY CAN SENSE SOMETHING'S NOT RIGHT.
WE NEED TO REASSURE THEM!
I CAN'T REALLY GIVE YOU ANY INFO, BECAUSE, IN CASE YOU DIDN'T KNOW IT, I'M JUST...
...THE CAPTAIN'S SEXUAL ADVISER!
??
HUH? I DON'T UNDERSTAND.
WELL YEAH, EVERY TIME I SAY SOMETHING, HE SAYS, "IF I NEED YOUR FUCKING ADVICE, I'LL LET YOU KNOW!"
STALL!
STALL!
STALL!
DAMN AUTOMATIC ALARM!
SHUT THE HELL UP!!!

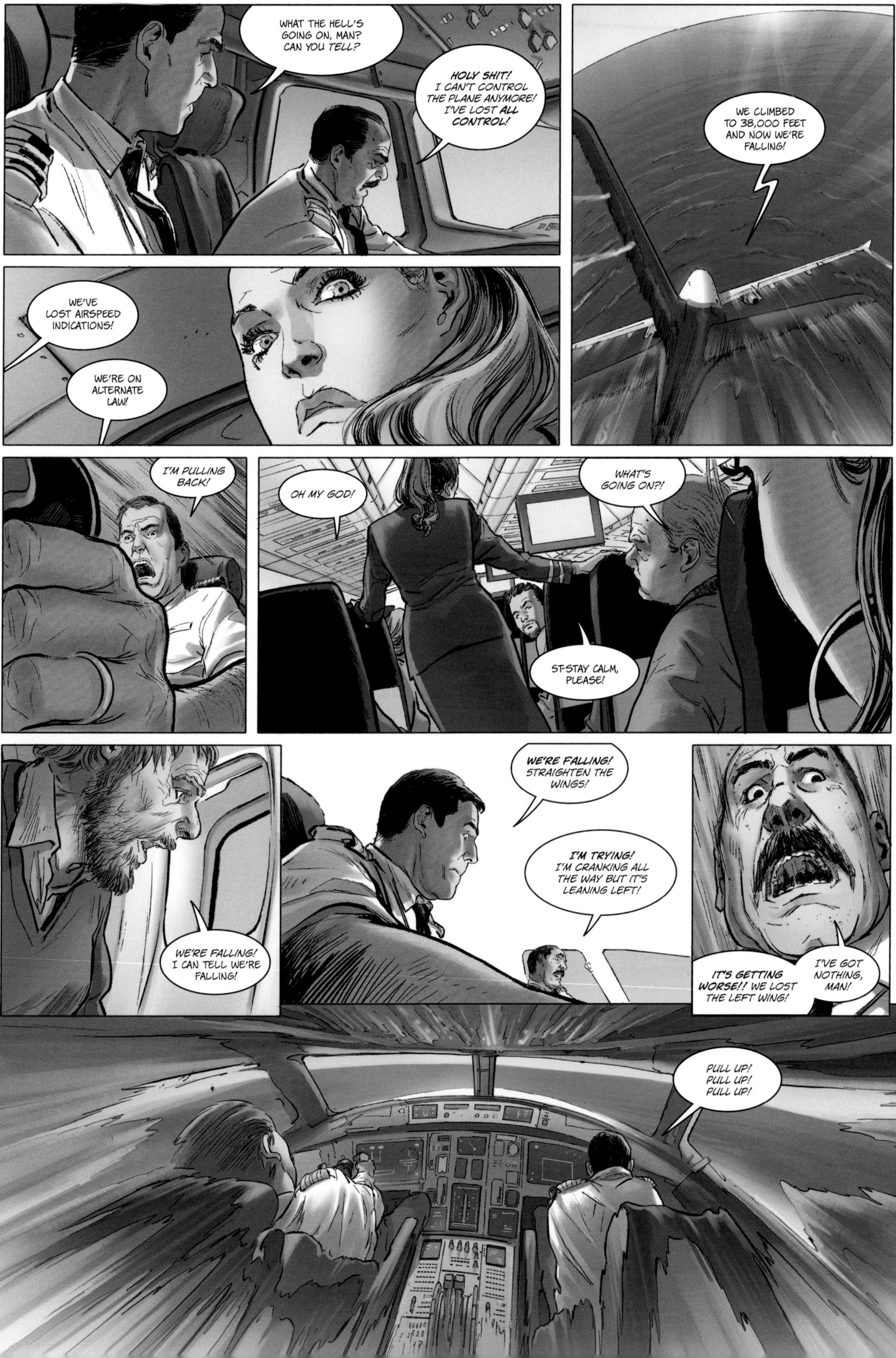
WHAT THE HELL'S GOING ON, MAN? CAN YOU TELL?
HOLY SHIT! I CAN'T CONTROL THE PLANE ANYMORE! I'VE LOST ALL CONTROL!
WE CLIMBED TO 38,000 FEET AND NOW WE'RE FALLING!
WE'VE LOST AIRSPEED INDICATIONS!
WE'RE ON ALTERNATE LAW!
I'M PULLING BACK!
OH MY GOD!
WHAT'S GOING ON?!
ST-STAY CALM, PLEASE!
WE'RE FALLING! I CAN TELL WE'RE FALLING!
WE'RE FALLING! STRAIGHTEN THE WINGS!
I'M TRYING! I'M CRANKING ALL THE WAY BUT IT'S LEANING LEFT!
I'VE GOT NOTHING, MAN!
IT'S GETTING WORSE!! WE LOST THE LEFT WING!
PULL UP! PULL UP! PULL UP!

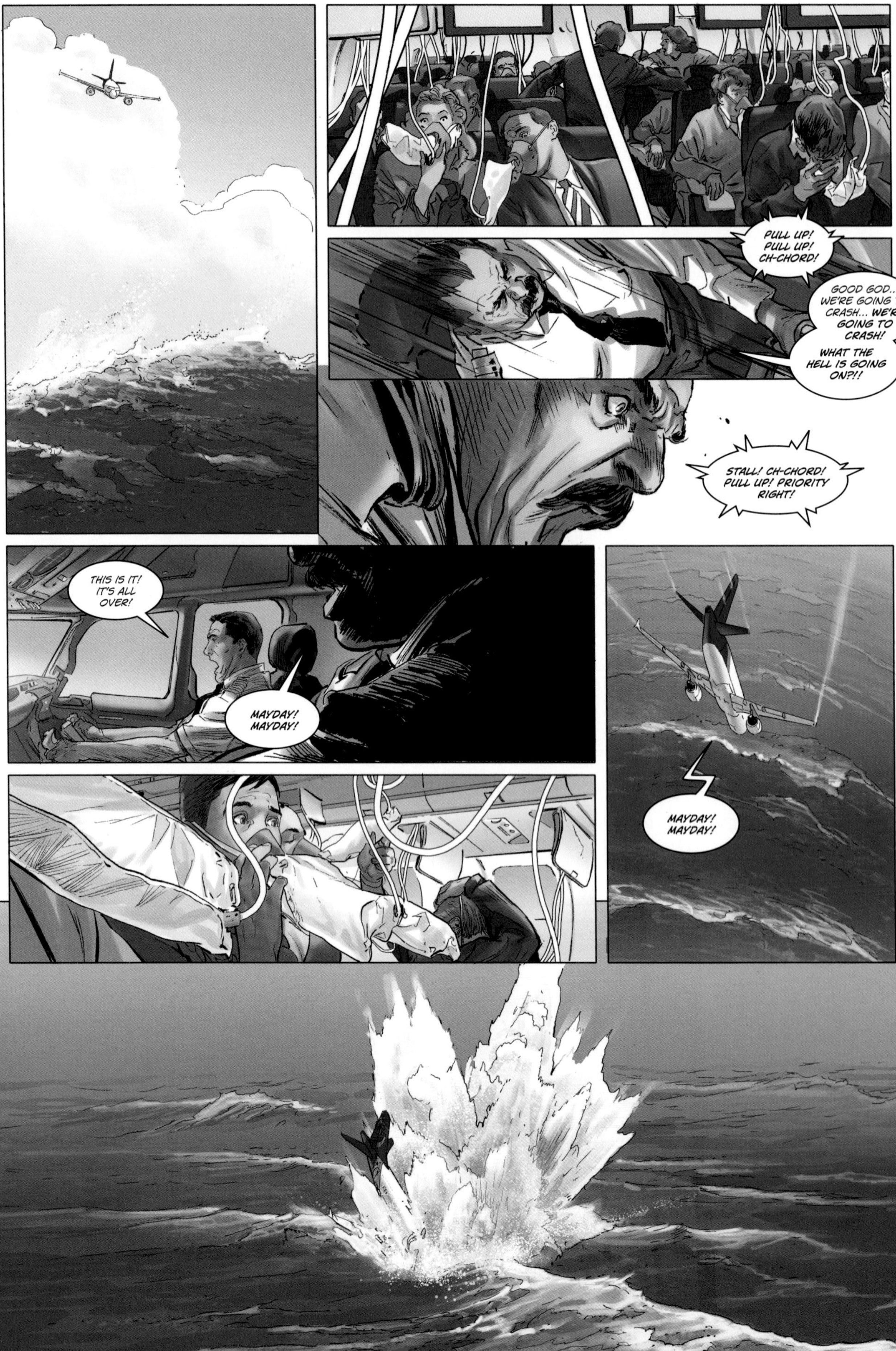
PULL UP! PULL UP! CH-CHORD!
GOOD GOD... WE'RE GOING TO CRASH... WE'RE GOING TO CRASH!
WHAT THE HELL IS GOING ON?!!
STALL! CH-CHORD! PULL UP! PRIORITY RIGHT!
THIS IS IT! IT'S ALL OVER!
MAYDAY! MAYDAY!
MAYDAY! MAYDAY!

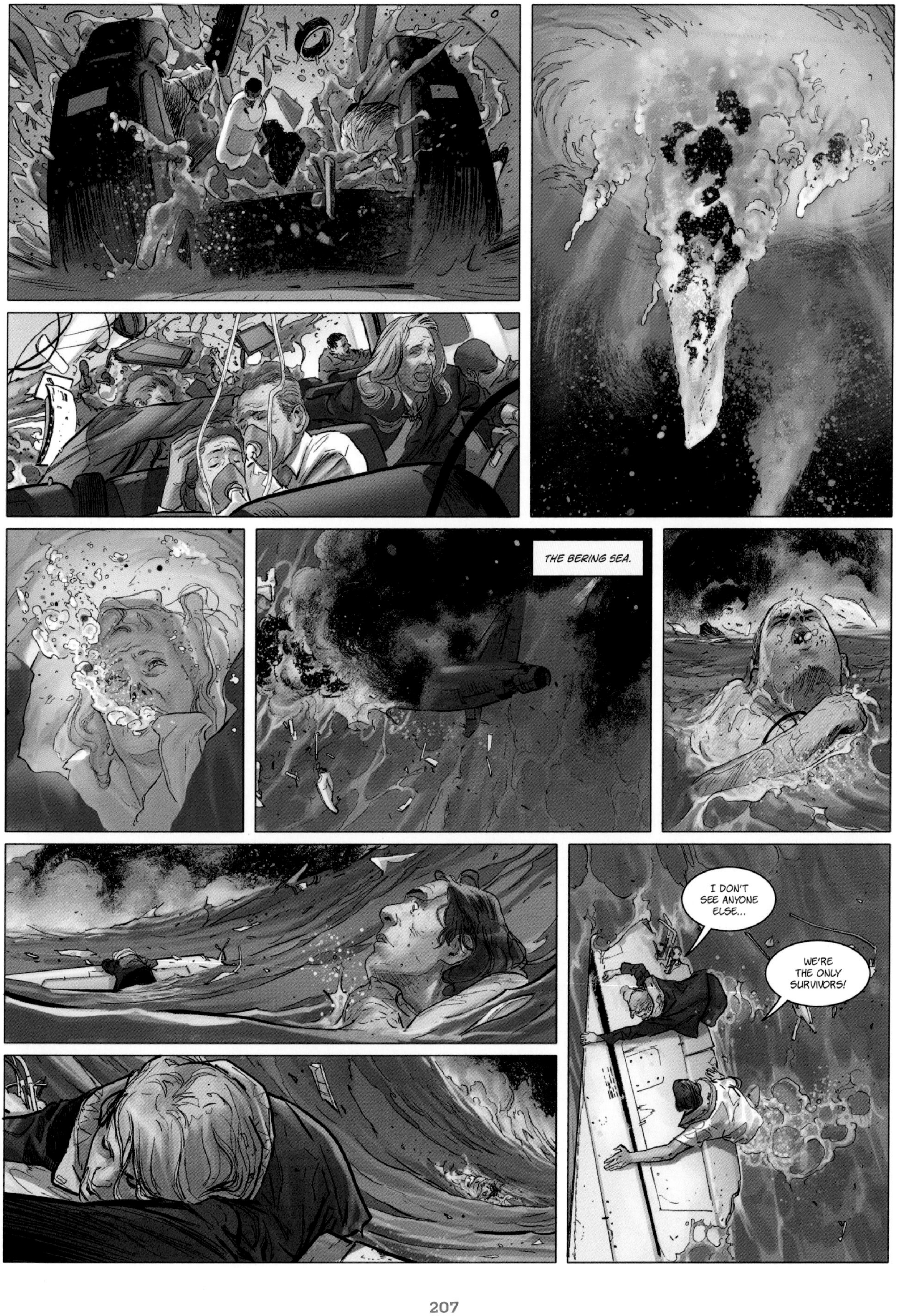
THE BERING SEA.
I DON'T SEE ANYONE ELSE...
WE'RE THE ONLY SURVIVORS!

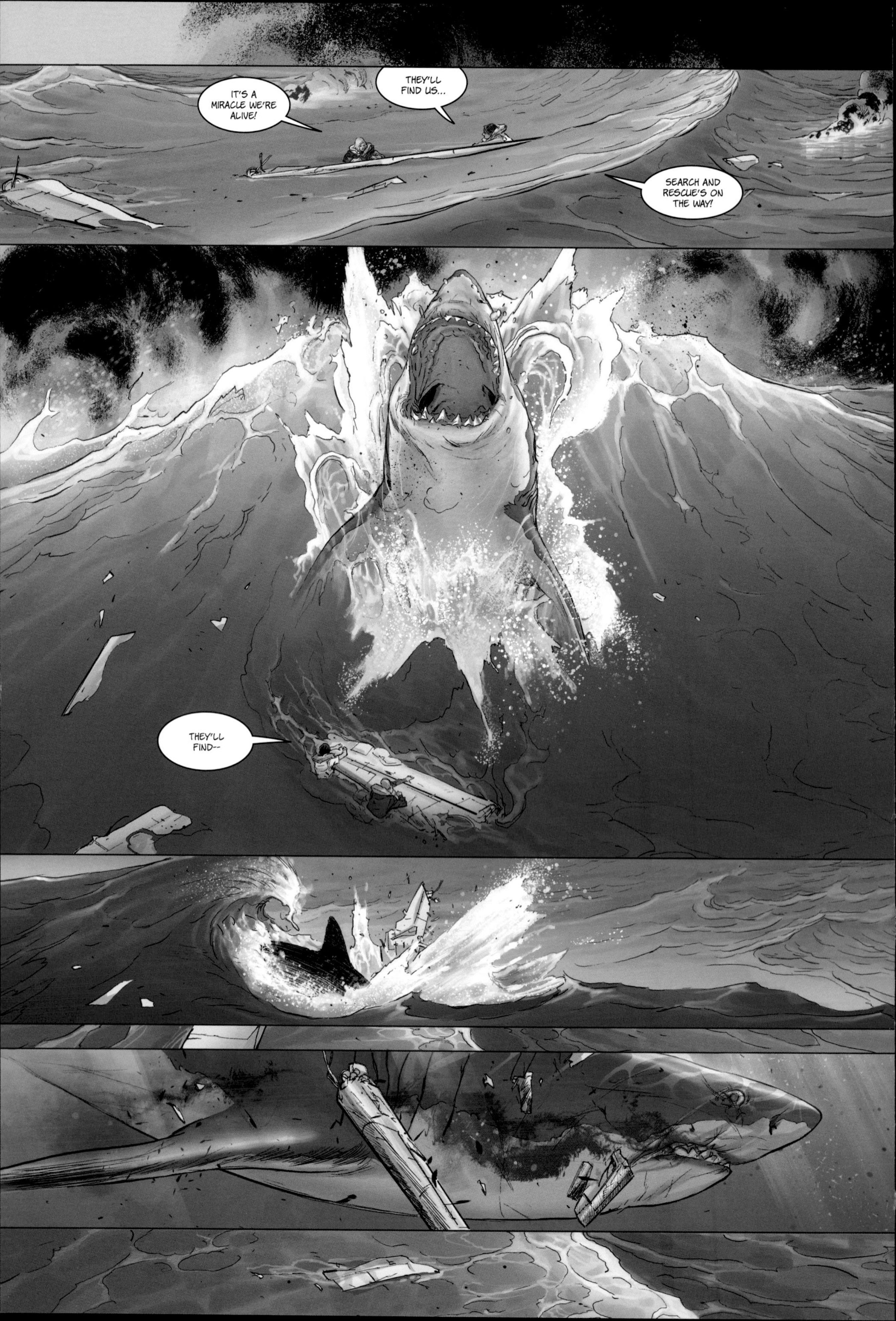
IT'S A MIRACLE WE'RE ALIVE!
THEY'LL FIND US...
SEARCH AND RESCUE'S ON THE WAY!
THEY'LL FIND--

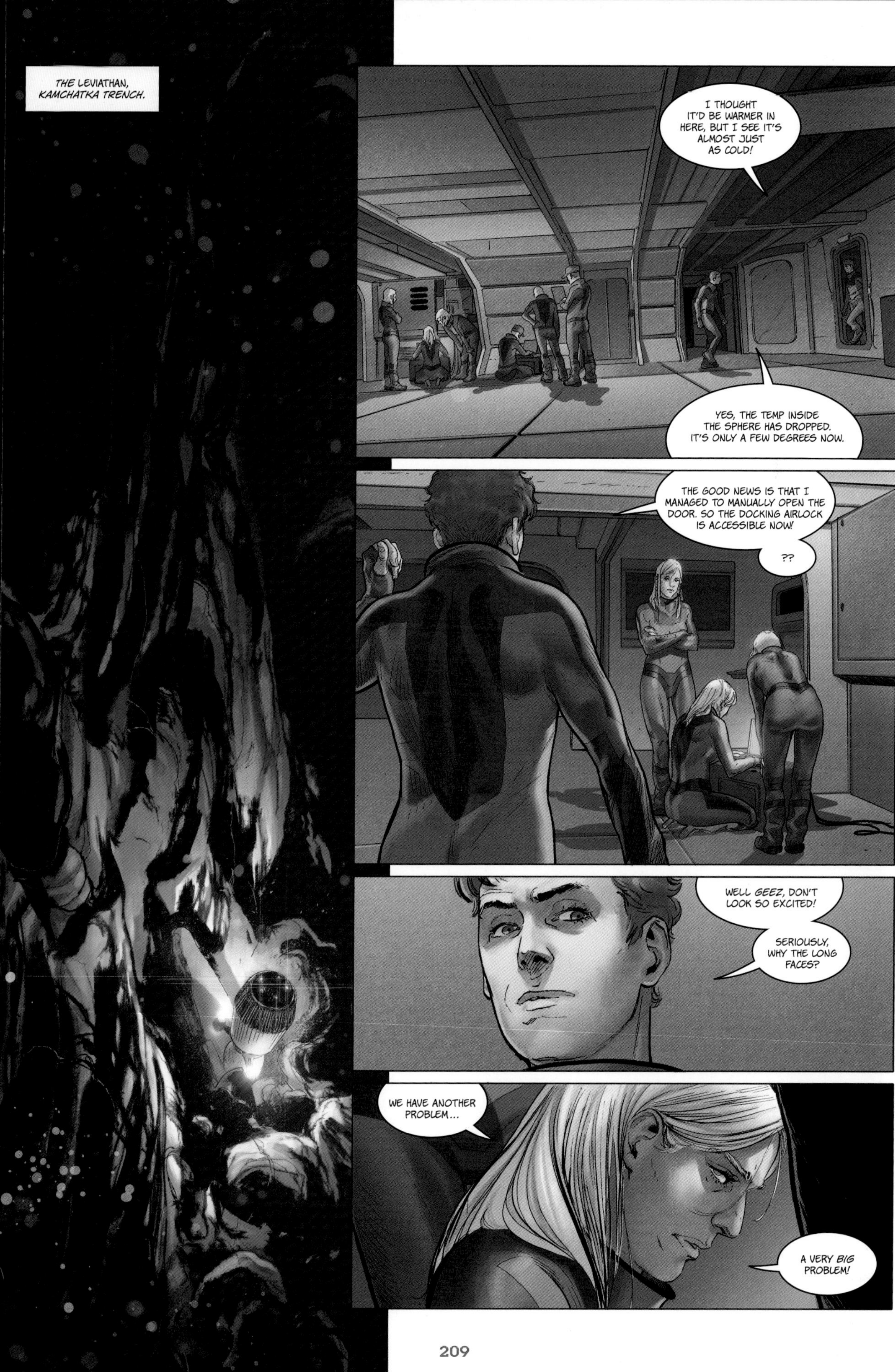
THE LEVIATHAN, KAMCHATKA TRENCH.
I THOUGHT IT'D BE WARMER IN HERE, BUT I SEE IT'S ALMOST JUST AS COLD!
YES, THE TEMP INSIDE THE SPHERE HAS DROPPED. IT'S ONLY A FEW DEGREES NOW.
THE GOOD NEWS IS THAT I MANAGED TO MANUALLY OPEN THE DOOR. SO THE DOCKING AIRLOCK IS ACCESSIBLE NOW!
??
WELL *GEEZ*, DON'T LOOK SO EXCITED!
SERIOUSLY, WHY THE LONG FACES?
WE HAVE ANOTHER PROBLEM...
A VERY *BIG* PROBLEM!

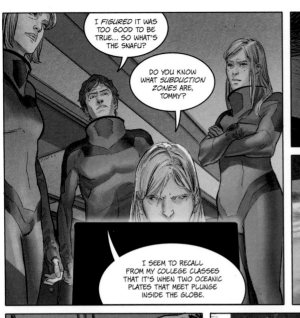

I *FIGURED* IT WAS TOO GOOD TO BE TRUE... SO WHAT'S THE SNAFU?

DO YOU KNOW WHAT *SUBDUCTION ZONES* ARE, TOMMY?

I SEEM TO RECALL FROM MY COLLEGE CLASSES THAT IT'S WHEN TWO OCEANIC PLATES THAT MEET PLUNGE INSIDE THE GLOBE.

THAT'S CORRECT. THE PLATE THAT PLUNGES INTO SUBDUCTION IS USUALLY AN OCEANIC PLATE, WHICH HAS A HIGH DENSITY. IT CAN PLUNGE UNDER A CONTINENTAL PLATE OR UNDER ANOTHER OCEANIC PLATE.

I'M NOT REALLY SURE WHAT YOU'RE GETTING AT, ANA.

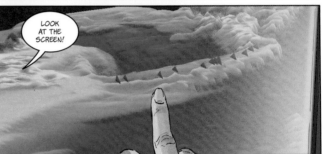

LOOK AT THE SCREEN!

WHAT AM I LOOKING AT?

IT'S A MODELING OF OCEANIC VOLCANIC ACTIVITY ON THE NORTH AMERICAN PLATE.

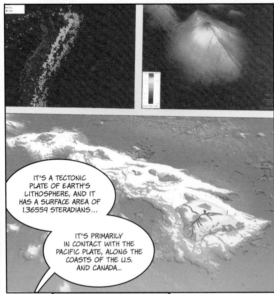

IT'S A TECTONIC PLATE OF EARTH'S LITHOSPHERE, AND IT HAS A SURFACE AREA OF 1.36559 STERADIANS...

IT'S PRIMARILY IN CONTACT WITH THE PACIFIC PLATE, ALONG THE COASTS OF THE U.S. AND CANADA...

THEN IT EXTENDS INTO THE ARCTIC OCEAN VIA THE GAKKEL RIDGE...

...AND ENDS WEST AT ITS BOUNDARY WITH THE OKHOTSK PLATE, WHICH WAS ONCE CONSIDERED PART OF THE NORTH AMERICAN PLATE.

I STILL DON'T FOLLOW...

THAT BOUNDARY IS FORMED BY THE *KAMCHATKA TRENCH!*

GOOD GOD!

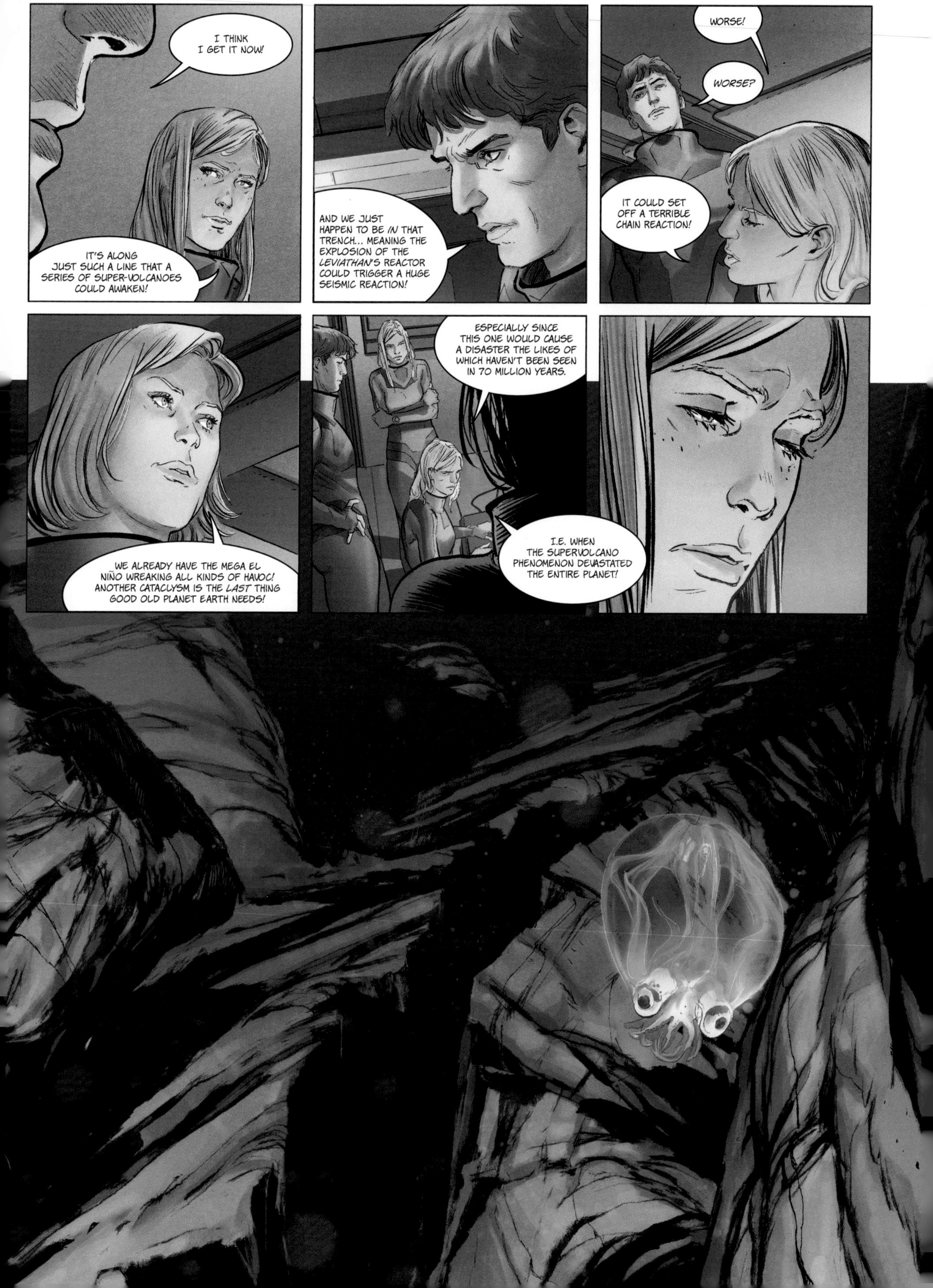
I THINK I GET IT NOW!
IT'S ALONG JUST SUCH A LINE THAT A SERIES OF SUPER-VOLCANOES COULD AWAKEN!
AND WE JUST HAPPEN TO BE *IN* THAT TRENCH... MEANING THE EXPLOSION OF THE *LEVIATHAN*'S REACTOR COULD TRIGGER A HUGE SEISMIC REACTION!
WORSE!
WORSE?
IT COULD SET OFF A TERRIBLE CHAIN REACTION!
WE ALREADY HAVE THE MEGA EL NIÑO WREAKING ALL KINDS OF HAVOC! ANOTHER CATACLYSM IS THE *LAST* THING GOOD OLD PLANET EARTH NEEDS!
ESPECIALLY SINCE THIS ONE WOULD CAUSE A DISASTER THE LIKES OF WHICH HAVEN'T BEEN SEEN IN 70 MILLION YEARS.
I.E. WHEN THE SUPERVOLCANO PHENOMENON DEVASTATED THE ENTIRE PLANET!

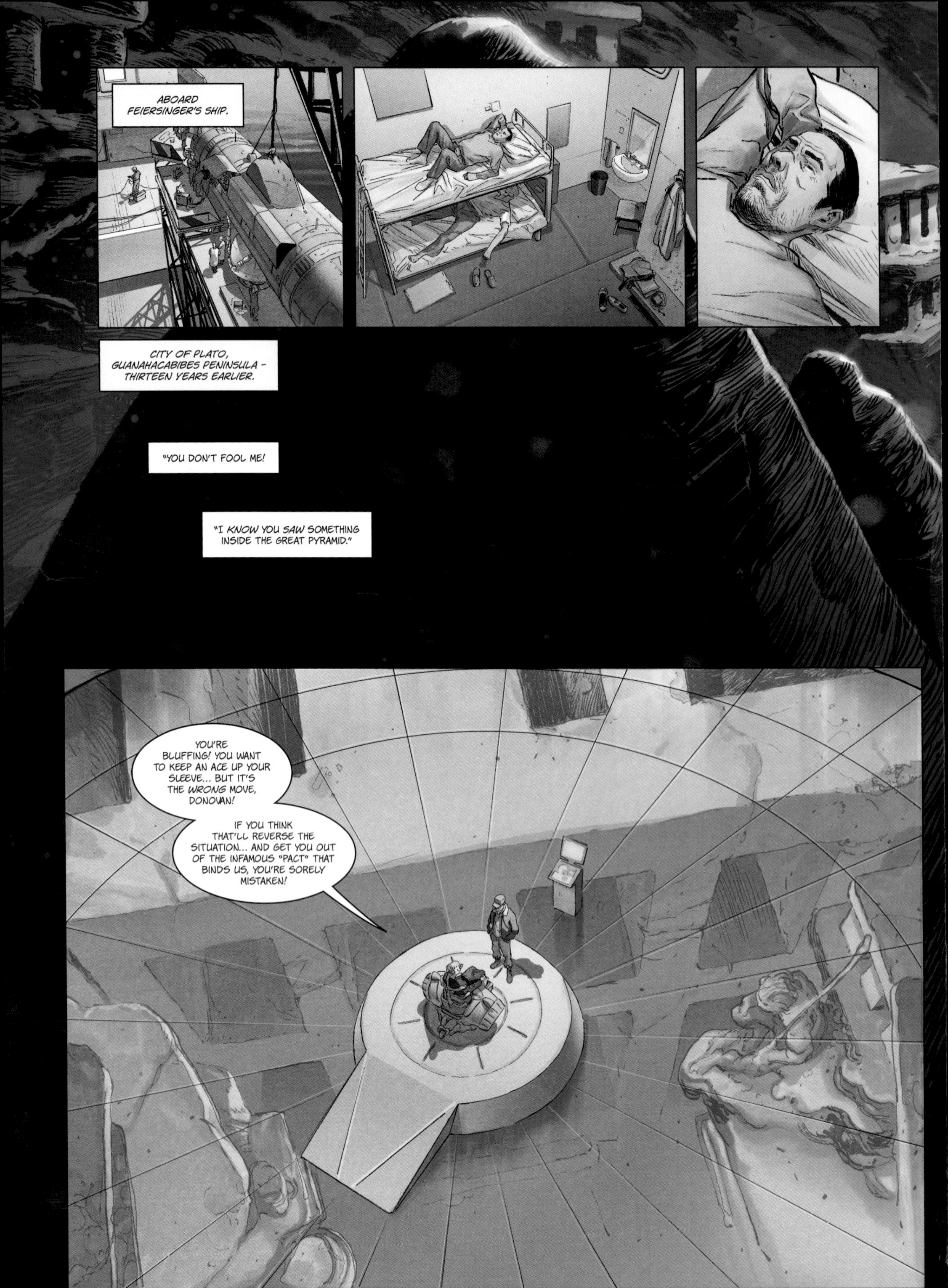
ABOARD FEIERSINGER'S SHIP.
CITY OF PLATO, GUANAHACABIBES PENINSULA – THIRTEEN YEARS EARLIER.
"YOU DON'T FOOL ME!
"I KNOW YOU SAW SOMETHING INSIDE THE GREAT PYRAMID."
YOU'RE BLUFFING! YOU WANT TO KEEP AN ACE UP YOUR SLEEVE... BUT IT'S THE WRONG MOVE, DONOVAN!
IF YOU THINK THAT'LL REVERSE THE SITUATION... AND GET YOU OUT OF THE INFAMOUS "PACT" THAT BINDS US, YOU'RE SORELY MISTAKEN!

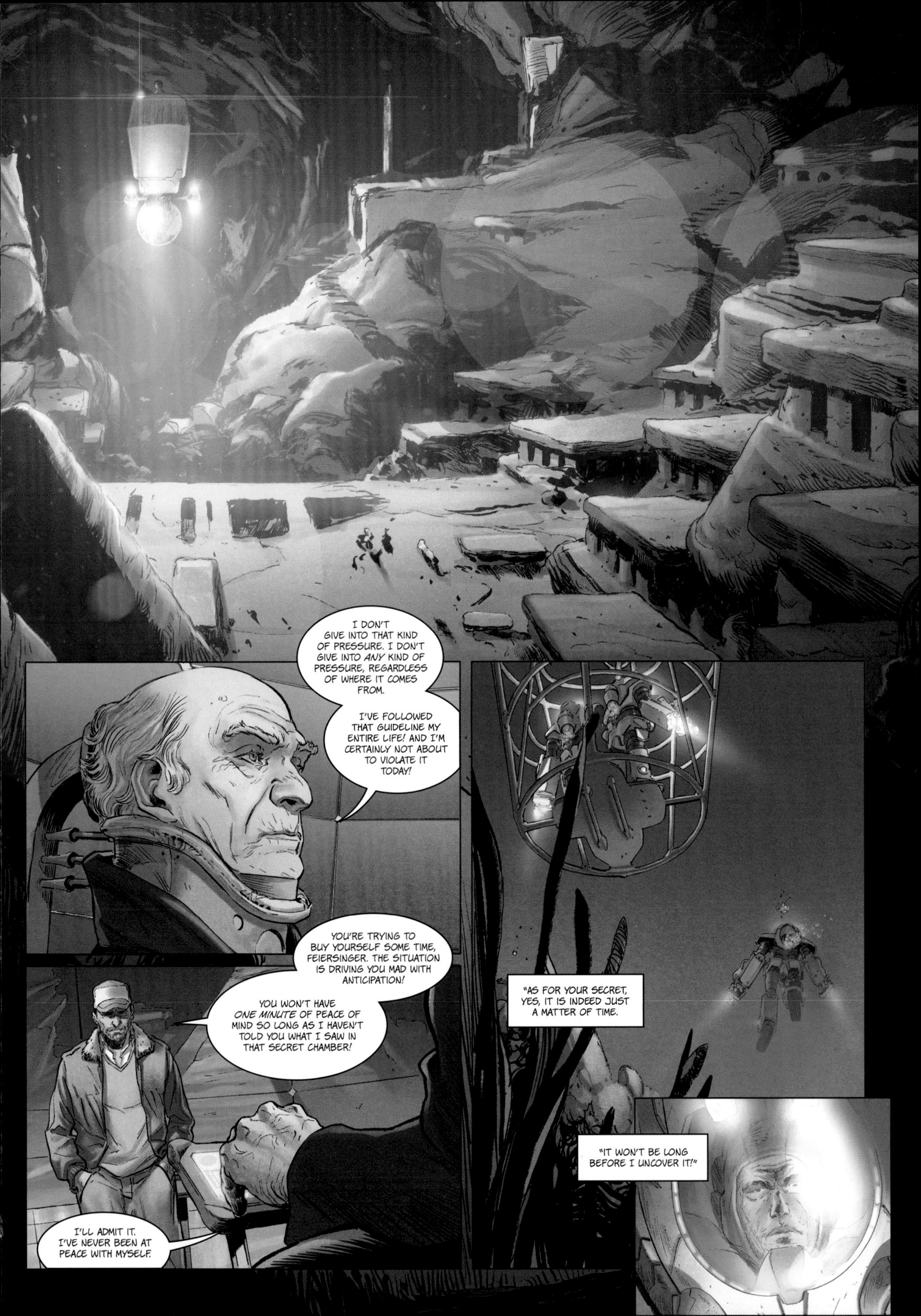
I DON'T GIVE INTO THAT KIND OF PRESSURE. I DON'T GIVE INTO *ANY* KIND OF PRESSURE, REGARDLESS OF WHERE IT COMES FROM.
I'VE FOLLOWED THAT GUIDELINE MY ENTIRE LIFE! AND I'M CERTAINLY NOT ABOUT TO VIOLATE IT TODAY!
YOU'RE TRYING TO BUY YOURSELF SOME TIME, FEIERSINGER. THE SITUATION IS DRIVING YOU MAD WITH ANTICIPATION!
YOU WON'T HAVE *ONE MINUTE* OF PEACE OF MIND SO LONG AS I HAVEN'T TOLD YOU WHAT I SAW IN THAT SECRET CHAMBER!
I'LL ADMIT IT. I'VE NEVER BEEN AT PEACE WITH MYSELF.
"AS FOR YOUR SECRET, YES, IT IS INDEED JUST A MATTER OF TIME.
"IT WON'T BE LONG BEFORE I UNCOVER IT!"

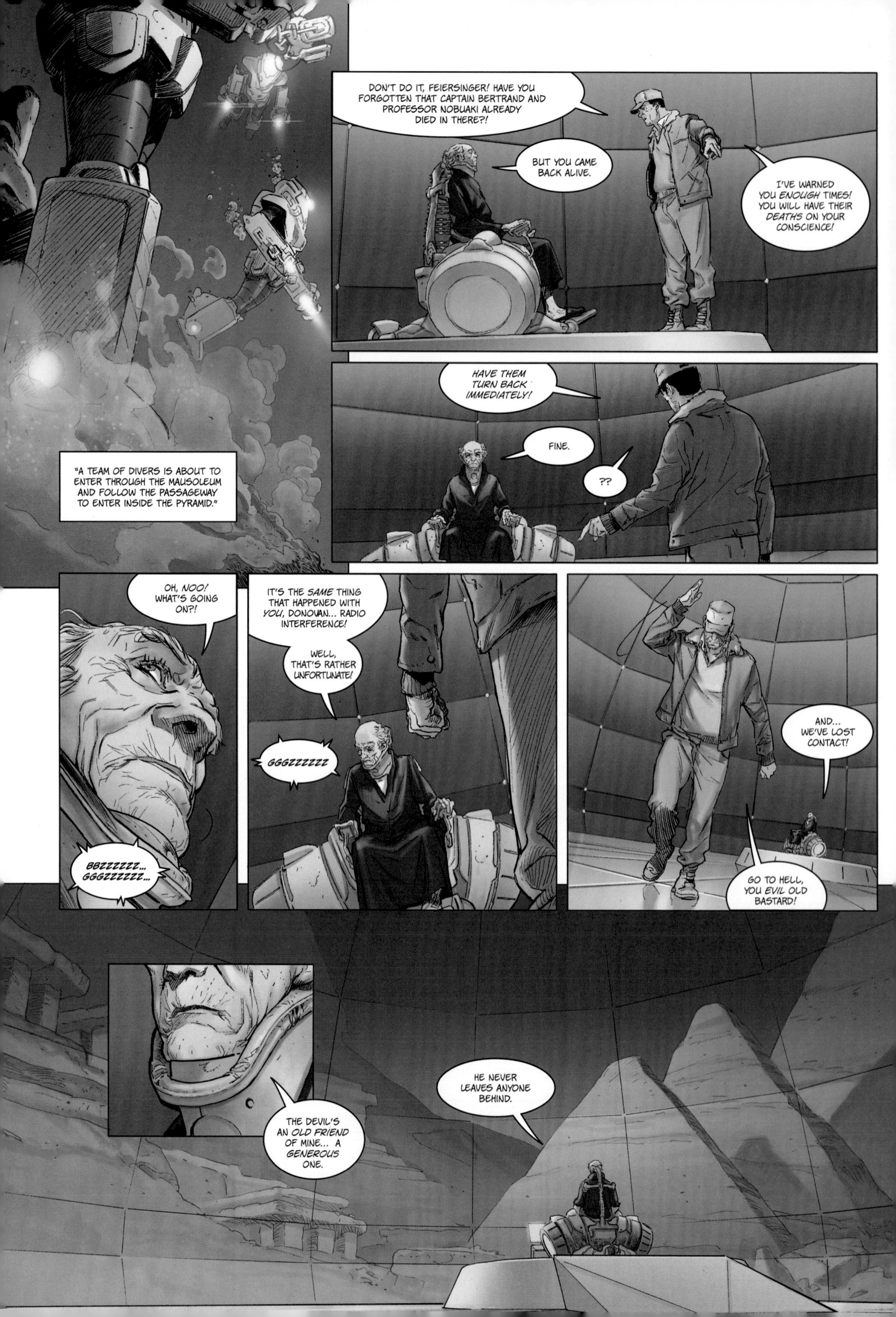
DON'T DO IT, FEIERSINGER! HAVE YOU FORGOTTEN THAT CAPTAIN BERTRAND AND PROFESSOR NOBUAKI ALREADY DIED IN THERE?!
BUT YOU CAME BACK ALIVE.
I'VE WARNED YOU *ENOUGH* TIMES! YOU WILL HAVE THEIR *DEATHS* ON YOUR CONSCIENCE!
"A TEAM OF DIVERS IS ABOUT TO ENTER THROUGH THE MAUSOLEUM AND FOLLOW THE PASSAGEWAY TO ENTER INSIDE THE PYRAMID."
HAVE THEM TURN BACK IMMEDIATELY!
FINE.
??
OH, *NOO!* WHAT'S GOING ON?!
BBZZZZZZ... GGGZZZZZZZ...
IT'S THE *SAME* THING THAT HAPPENED WITH *YOU*, DONOVAN... RADIO INTERFERENCE!
WELL, THAT'S RATHER UNFORTUNATE!
GGGZZZZZZ
AND... WE'VE LOST CONTACT!
GO TO HELL, YOU *EVIL* OLD BASTARD!
THE DEVIL'S AN *OLD FRIEND* OF MINE... A *GENEROUS* ONE.
HE NEVER LEAVES ANYONE BEHIND.

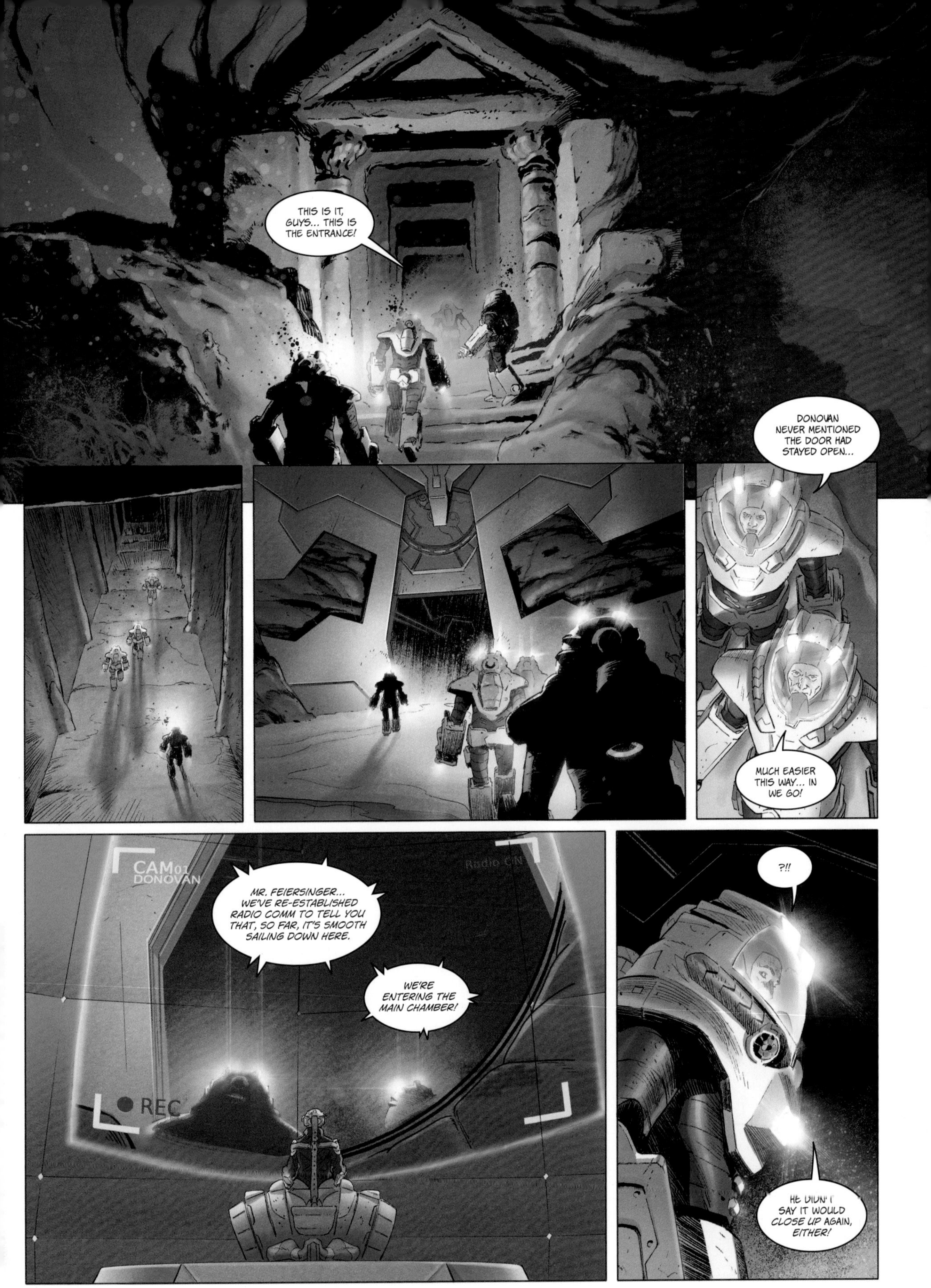
THIS IS IT, GUYS... THIS IS THE ENTRANCE!
DONOVAN NEVER MENTIONED THE DOOR HAD STAYED OPEN...
MUCH EASIER THIS WAY... IN WE GO!
CAM01 DONOVAN
Radio ON
MR. FEIERSINGER... WE'VE RE-ESTABLISHED RADIO COMM TO TELL YOU THAT, SO FAR, IT'S SMOOTH SAILING DOWN HERE.
WE'RE ENTERING THE MAIN CHAMBER!
REC
?!!
HE DIDN'T SAY IT WOULD CLOSE UP AGAIN, EITHER!

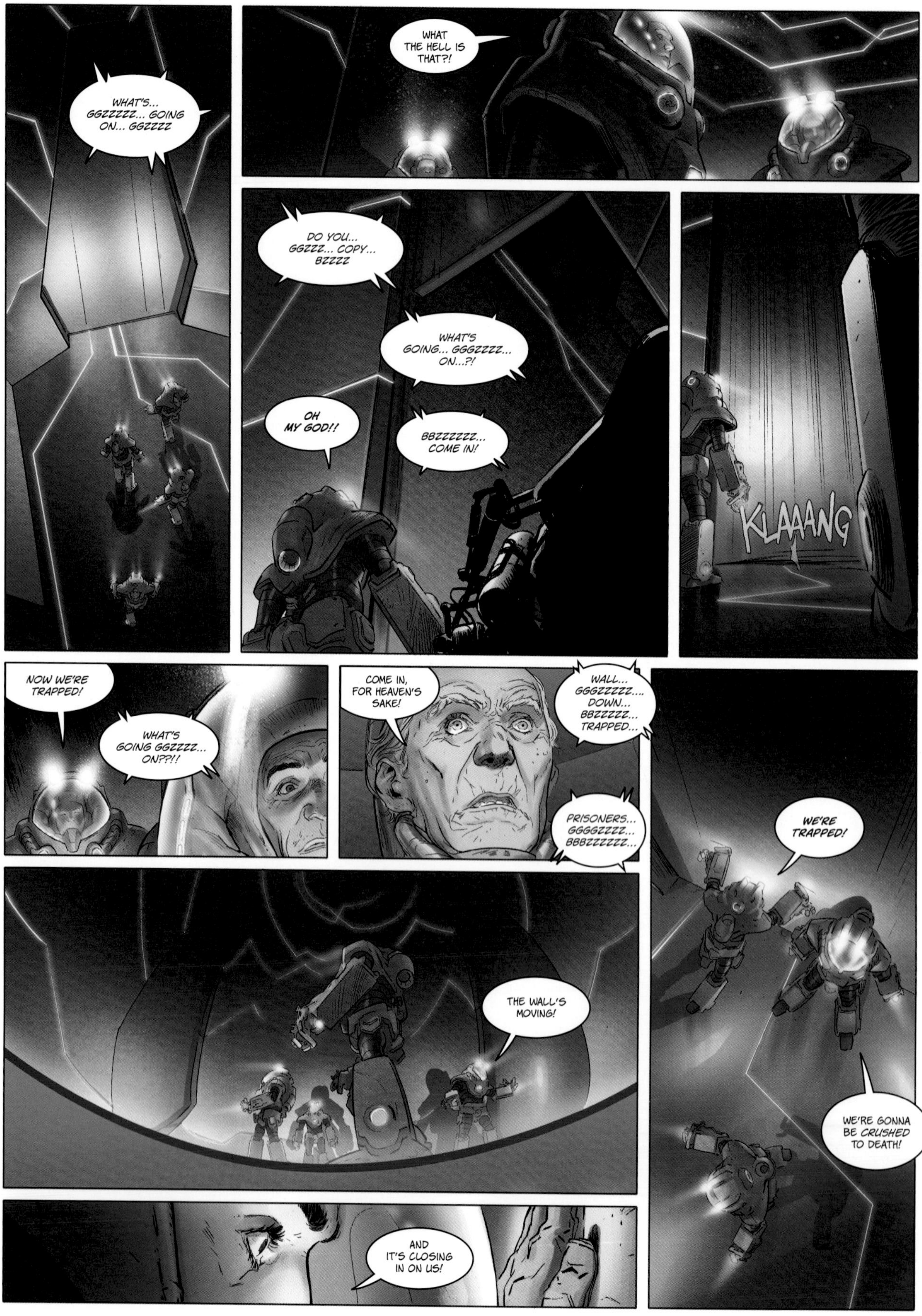
WHAT'S... GGZZZZZ... GOING ON... GGZZZZ
WHAT THE HELL IS THAT?!
DO YOU... GGZZZ... COPY... BZZZZ
WHAT'S GOING... GGGZZZZ... ON...?!
OH MY GOD!!
BBZZZZZZ... COME IN!
KLAAANG
NOW WE'RE TRAPPED!
WHAT'S GOING GGZZZZ... ON??!!
COME IN, FOR HEAVEN'S SAKE!
WALL... GGGZZZZZ.... DOWN... BBZZZZZ... TRAPPED...
PRISONERS... GGGGZZZZ... BBBZZZZZZZ...
WE'RE TRAPPED!
THE WALL'S MOVING!
WE'RE GONNA BE CRUSHED TO DEATH!
AND IT'S CLOSING IN ON US!

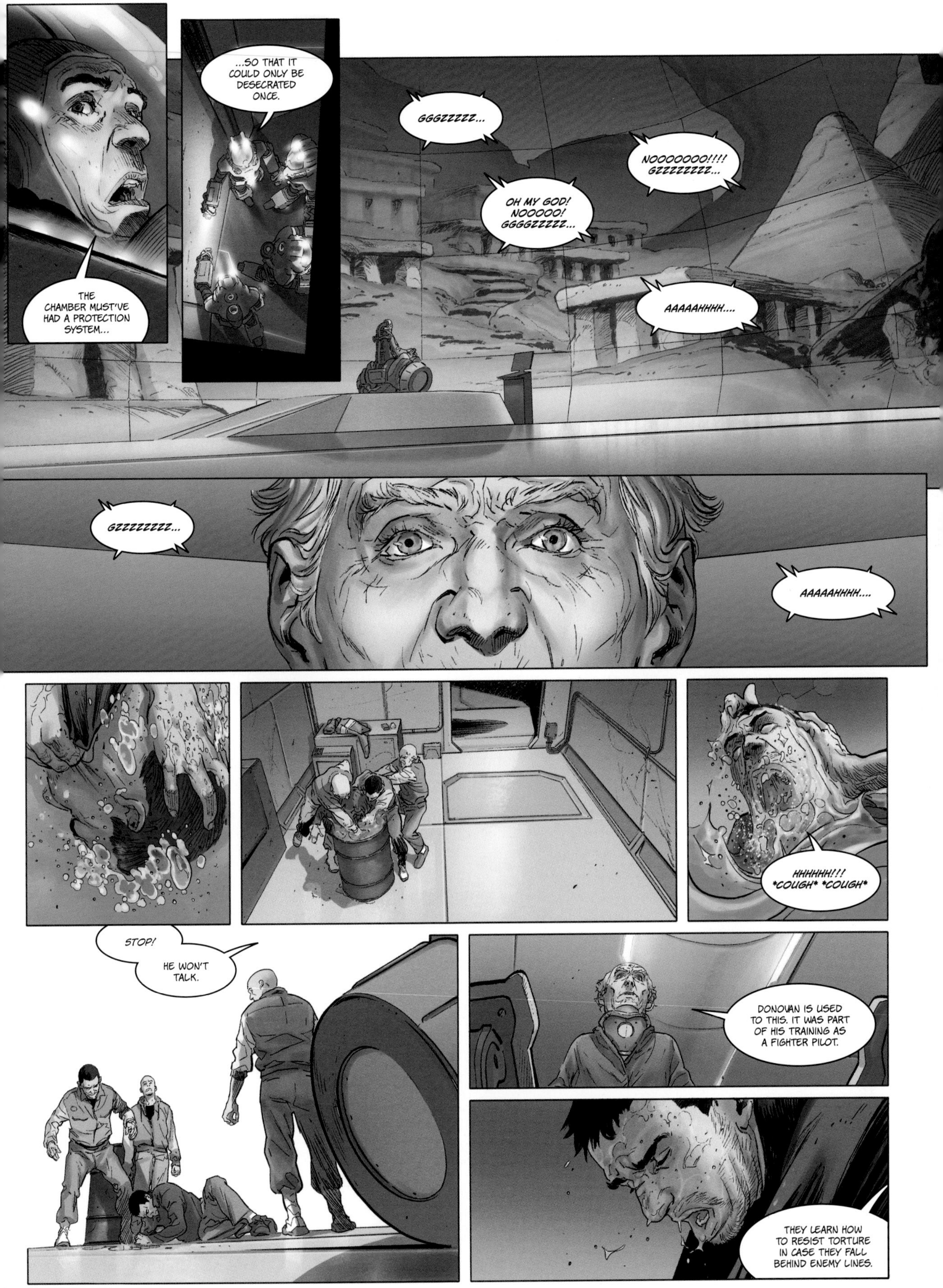
THE CHAMBER MUST'VE HAD A PROTECTION SYSTEM...
...SO THAT IT COULD ONLY BE DESECRATED ONCE.
GGGZZZZZ...
OH MY GOD! NOOOOO! GGGGZZZZZ...
NOOOOOOO!!!! GZZZZZZZZ...
AAAAAHHHH....
GZZZZZZZZ...
AAAAAHHHH....
HHHHHH!!! *COUGH* *COUGH*
STOP!
HE WON'T TALK.
DONOVAN IS USED TO THIS. IT WAS PART OF HIS TRAINING AS A FIGHTER PILOT.
THEY LEARN HOW TO RESIST TORTURE IN CASE THEY FALL BEHIND ENEMY LINES.

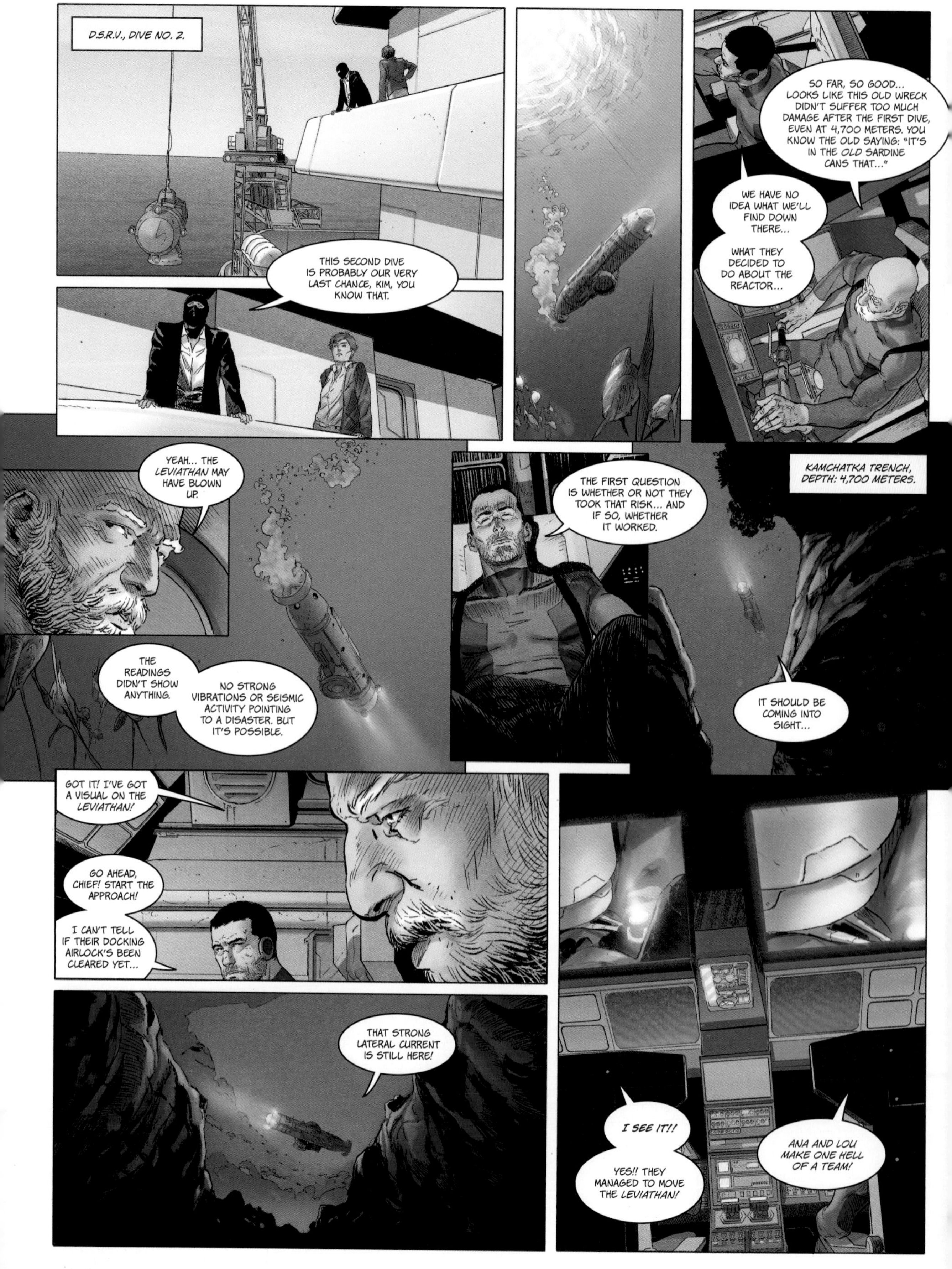
D.S.R.V., DIVE NO. 2.
THIS SECOND DIVE IS PROBABLY OUR VERY LAST CHANCE, KIM, YOU KNOW THAT.
SO FAR, SO GOOD... LOOKS LIKE THIS OLD WRECK DIDN'T SUFFER TOO MUCH DAMAGE AFTER THE FIRST DIVE, EVEN AT 4,700 METERS. YOU KNOW THE OLD SAYING: "IT'S IN THE OLD SARDINE CANS THAT..."
WE HAVE NO IDEA WHAT WE'LL FIND DOWN THERE...
WHAT THEY DECIDED TO DO ABOUT THE REACTOR...
YEAH... THE LEVIATHAN MAY HAVE BLOWN UP.
THE READINGS DIDN'T SHOW ANYTHING.
NO STRONG VIBRATIONS OR SEISMIC ACTIVITY POINTING TO A DISASTER. BUT IT'S POSSIBLE.
THE FIRST QUESTION IS WHETHER OR NOT THEY TOOK THAT RISK... AND IF SO, WHETHER IT WORKED.
KAMCHATKA TRENCH, DEPTH: 4,700 METERS.
IT SHOULD BE COMING INTO SIGHT...
GOT IT! I'VE GOT A VISUAL ON THE LEVIATHAN!
GO AHEAD, CHIEF! START THE APPROACH!
I CAN'T TELL IF THEIR DOCKING AIRLOCK'S BEEN CLEARED YET...
THAT STRONG LATERAL CURRENT IS STILL HERE!
I SEE IT!!
YES!! THEY MANAGED TO MOVE THE LEVIATHAN!
ANA AND LOU MAKE ONE HELL OF A TEAM!

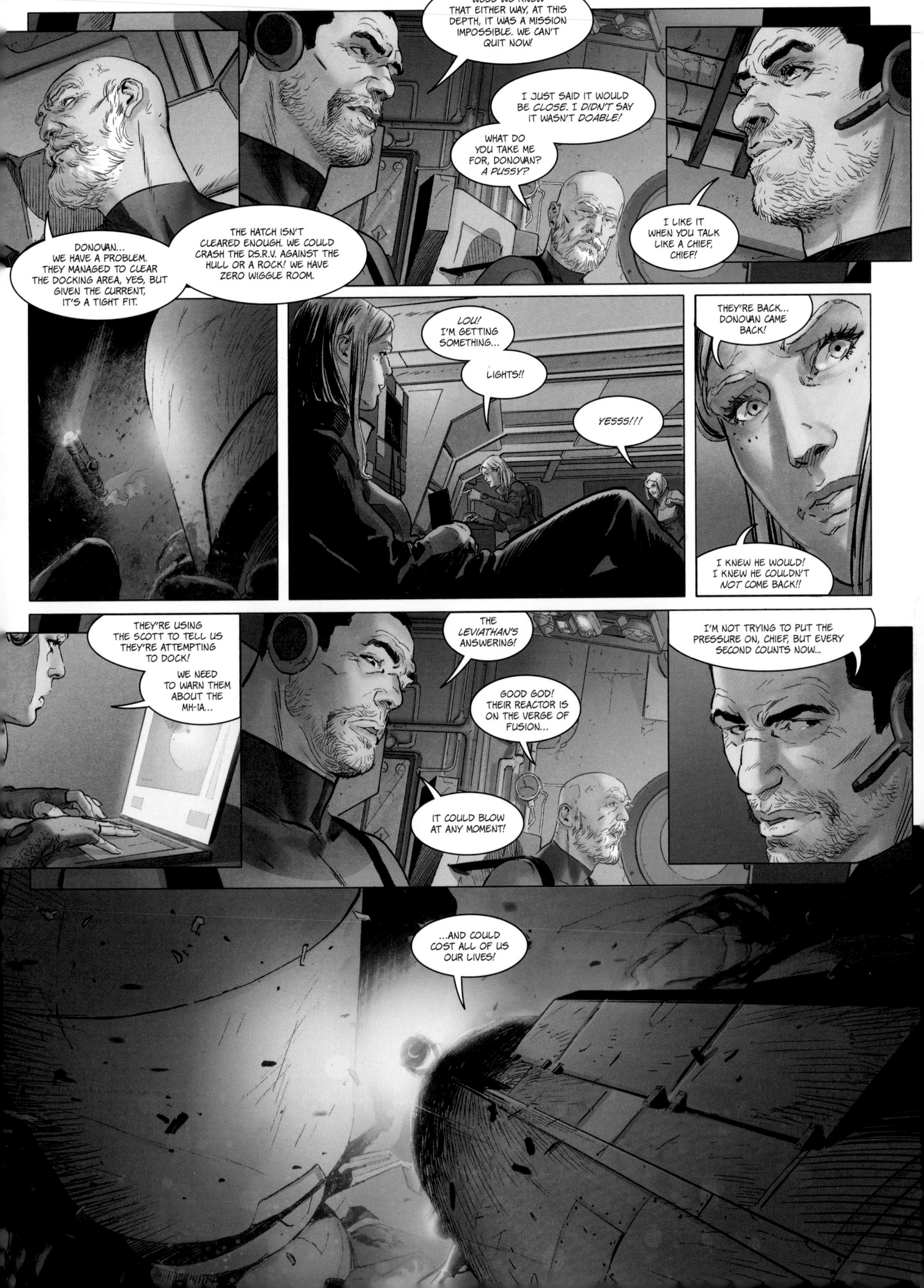
DONOVAN... WE HAVE A PROBLEM. THEY MANAGED TO CLEAR THE DOCKING AREA, YES, BUT GIVEN THE CURRENT, IT'S A TIGHT FIT.
THE HATCH ISN'T CLEARED ENOUGH. WE COULD CRASH THE DS.R.V. AGAINST THE HULL OR A ROCK! WE HAVE ZERO WIGGLE ROOM.
WELL WE KNEW THAT EITHER WAY, AT THIS DEPTH, IT WAS A MISSION IMPOSSIBLE. WE CAN'T QUIT NOW!
I JUST SAID IT WOULD BE CLOSE. I DIDN'T SAY IT WASN'T DOABLE!
WHAT DO YOU TAKE ME FOR, DONOVAN? A PUSSY?
I LIKE IT WHEN YOU TALK LIKE A CHIEF, CHIEF!
LOU! I'M GETTING SOMETHING...
LIGHTS!!
YESSS!!!
THEY'RE BACK... DONOVAN CAME BACK!
I KNEW HE WOULD! I KNEW HE COULDN'T NOT COME BACK!!
THEY'RE USING THE SCOTT TO TELL US THEY'RE ATTEMPTING TO DOCK!
WE NEED TO WARN THEM ABOUT THE MH-1A...
THE LEVIATHAN'S ANSWERING!
GOOD GOD! THEIR REACTOR IS ON THE VERGE OF FUSION...
IT COULD BLOW AT ANY MOMENT!
I'M NOT TRYING TO PUT THE PRESSURE ON, CHIEF, BUT EVERY SECOND COUNTS NOW...
...AND COULD COST ALL OF US OUR LIVES!

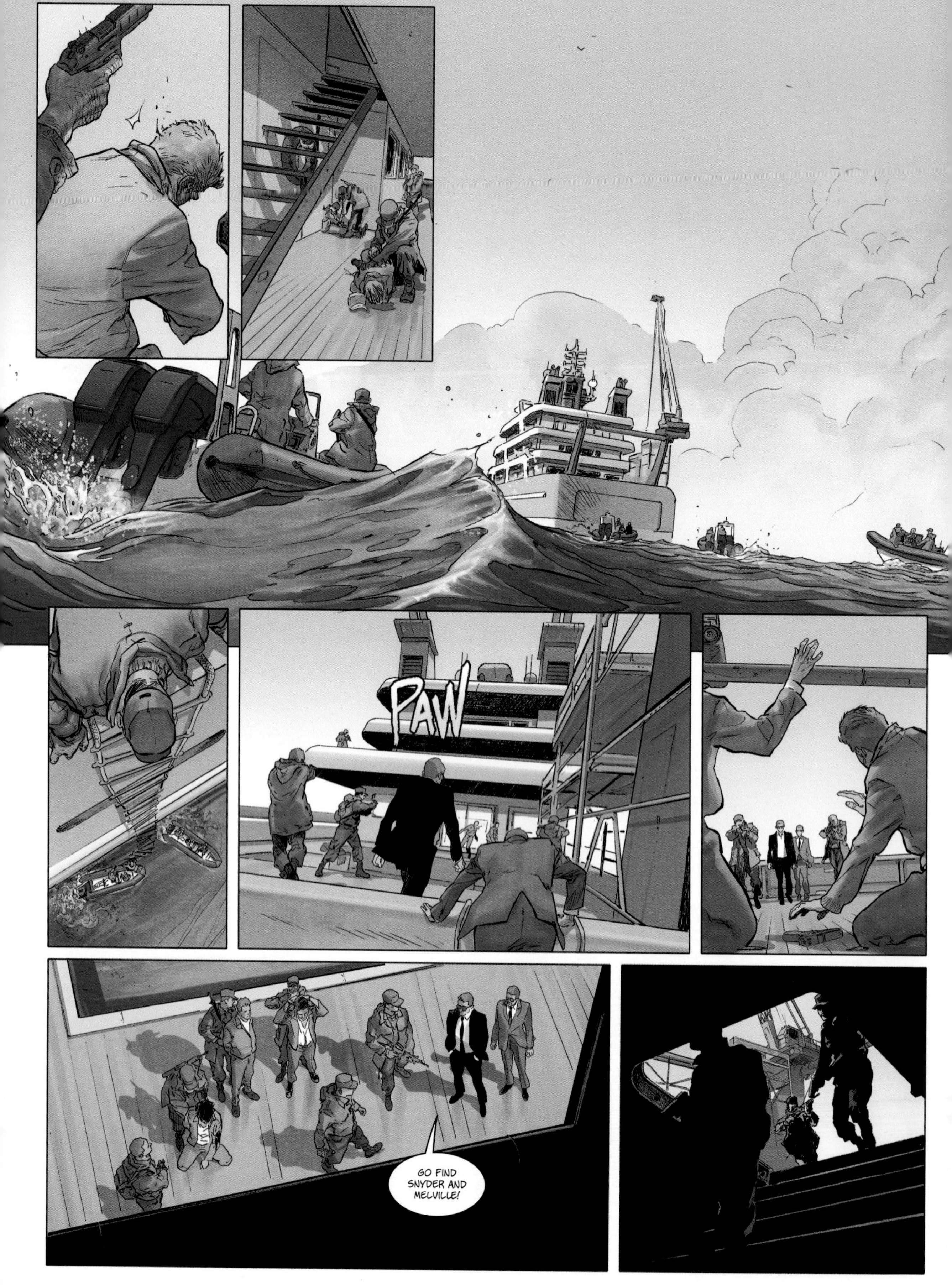
PAW
GO FIND SNYDER AND MELVILLE!

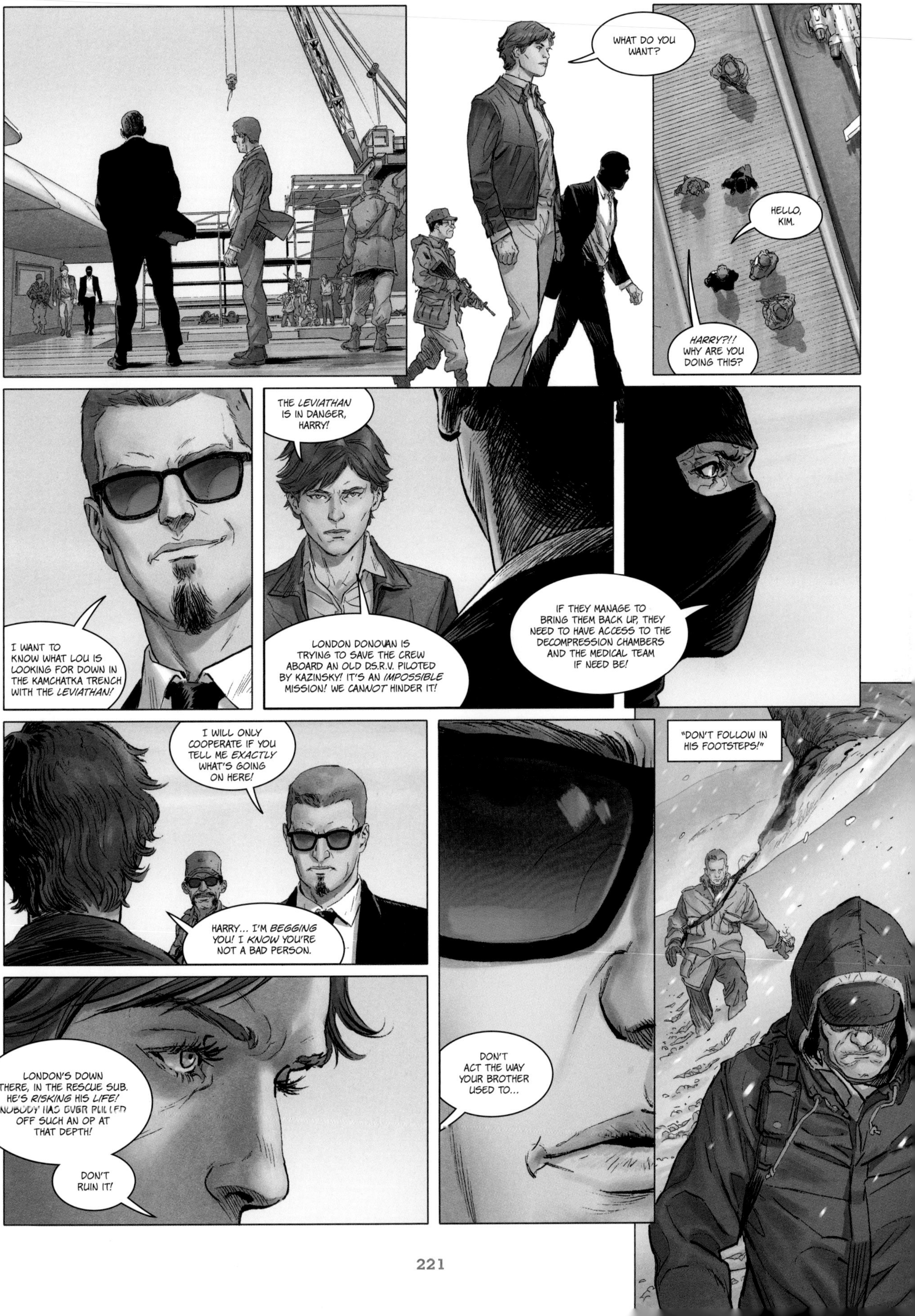
WHAT DO YOU WANT?
HELLO, KIM.
HARRY?!! WHY ARE YOU DOING THIS?
I WANT TO KNOW WHAT LOU IS LOOKING FOR DOWN IN THE KAMCHATKA TRENCH WITH THE LEVIATHAN!
THE LEVIATHAN IS IN DANGER, HARRY!
LONDON DONOVAN IS TRYING TO SAVE THE CREW ABOARD AN OLD D.S.R.V. PILOTED BY KAZINSKY! IT'S AN IMPOSSIBLE MISSION! WE CANNOT HINDER IT!
IF THEY MANAGE TO BRING THEM BACK UP, THEY NEED TO HAVE ACCESS TO THE DECOMPRESSION CHAMBERS AND THE MEDICAL TEAM IF NEED BE!
I WILL ONLY COOPERATE IF YOU TELL ME EXACTLY WHAT'S GOING ON HERE!
HARRY... I'M BEGGING YOU! I KNOW YOU'RE NOT A BAD PERSON.
"DON'T FOLLOW IN HIS FOOTSTEPS!"
LONDON'S DOWN THERE, IN THE RESCUE SUB. HE'S RISKING HIS LIFE! NOBODY HAS EVER PULLED OFF SUCH AN OP AT THAT DEPTH!
DON'T RUIN IT!
DON'T ACT THE WAY YOUR BROTHER USED TO...

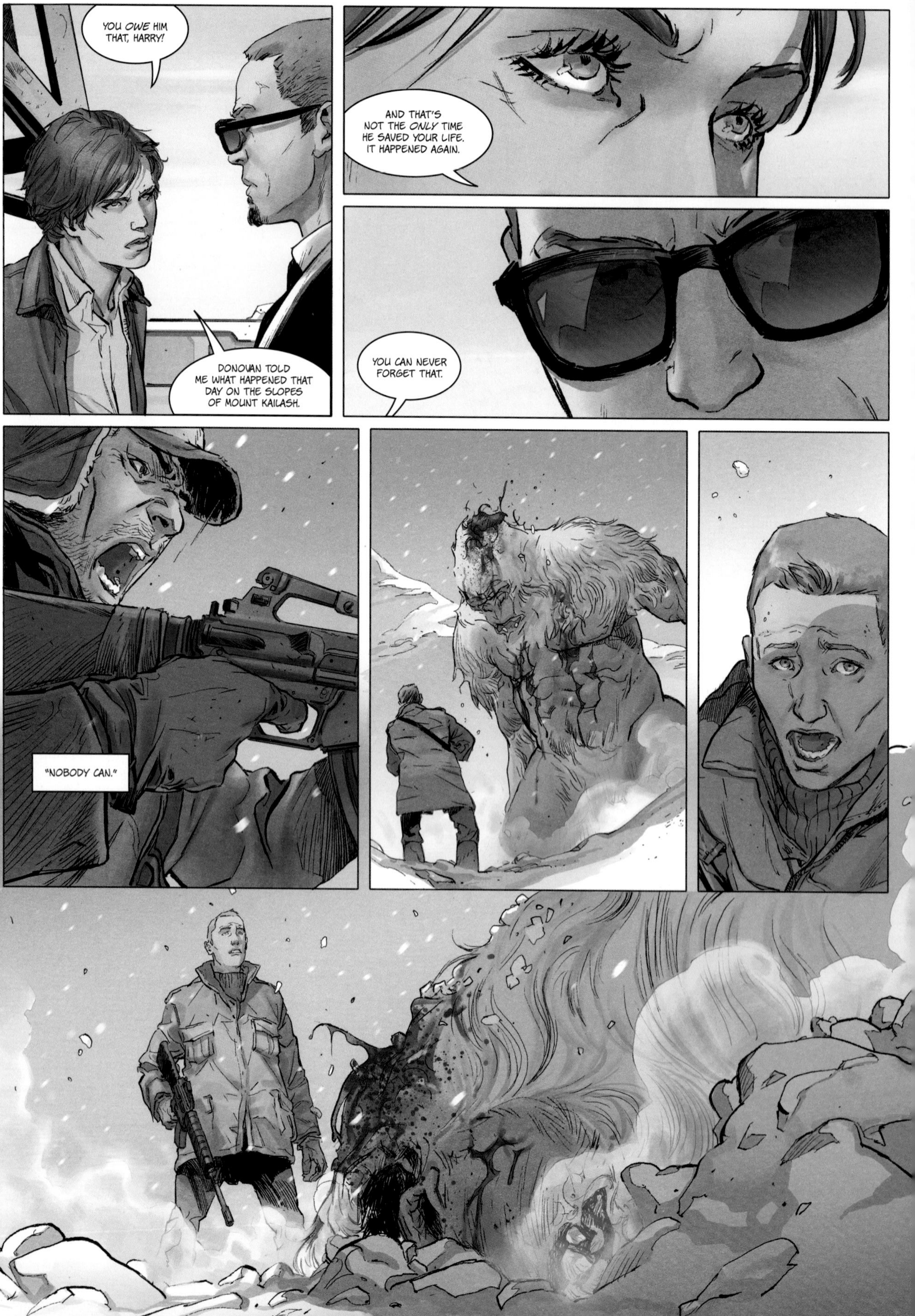
YOU OWE HIM THAT, HARRY!
DONOVAN TOLD ME WHAT HAPPENED THAT DAY ON THE SLOPES OF MOUNT KAILASH.
AND THAT'S NOT THE ONLY TIME HE SAVED YOUR LIFE. IT HAPPENED AGAIN.
YOU CAN NEVER FORGET THAT.
"NOBODY CAN."

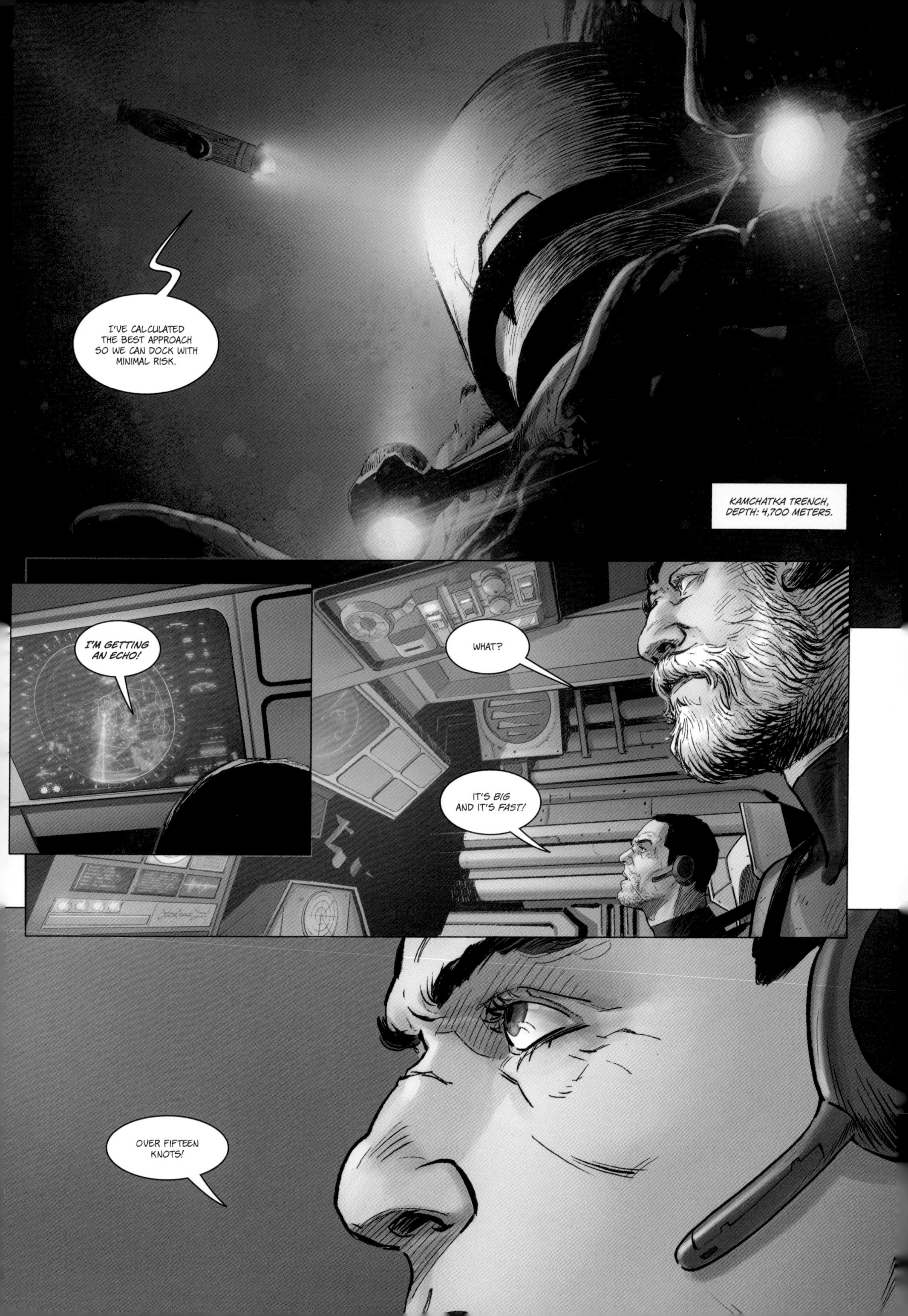
I'VE CALCULATED THE BEST APPROACH SO WE CAN DOCK WITH MINIMAL RISK.
KAMCHATKA TRENCH, DEPTH: 4,700 METERS.
I'M GETTING AN ECHO!
WHAT?
IT'S BIG AND IT'S FAST!
OVER FIFTEEN KNOTS!

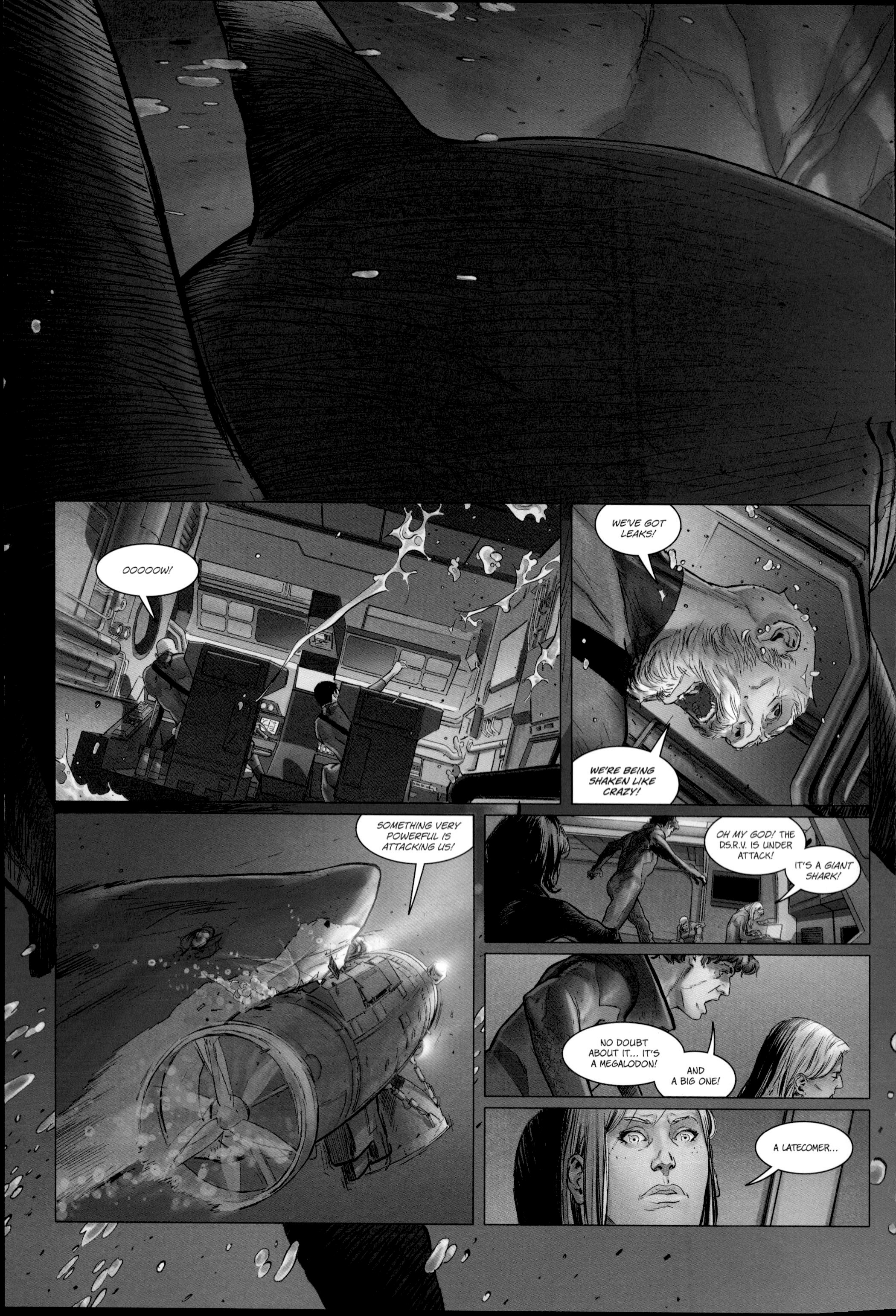
OOOOOW!
WE'VE GOT LEAKS!
WE'RE BEING SHAKEN LIKE CRAZY!
SOMETHING VERY POWERFUL IS ATTACKING US!
OH MY GOD! THE D.S.R.V. IS UNDER ATTACK!
IT'S A GIANT SHARK!
NO DOUBT ABOUT IT... IT'S A MEGALODON!
AND A BIG ONE!
A LATECOMER...

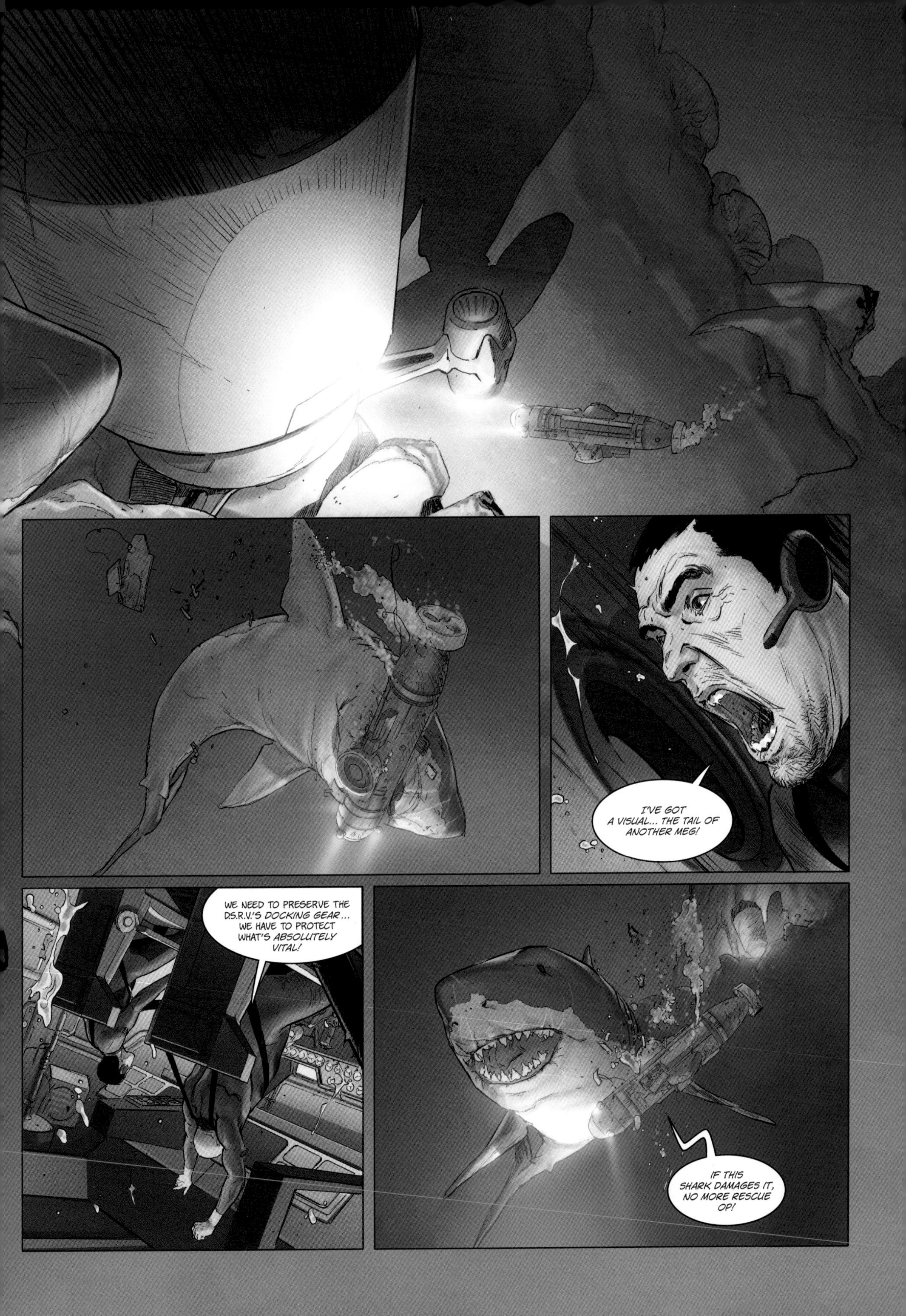
I'VE GOT A VISUAL... THE TAIL OF ANOTHER MEG!
WE NEED TO PRESERVE THE D.S.R.V.'S DOCKING GEAR... WE HAVE TO PROTECT WHAT'S ABSOLUTELY VITAL!
IF THIS SHARK DAMAGES IT, NO MORE RESCUE OP!

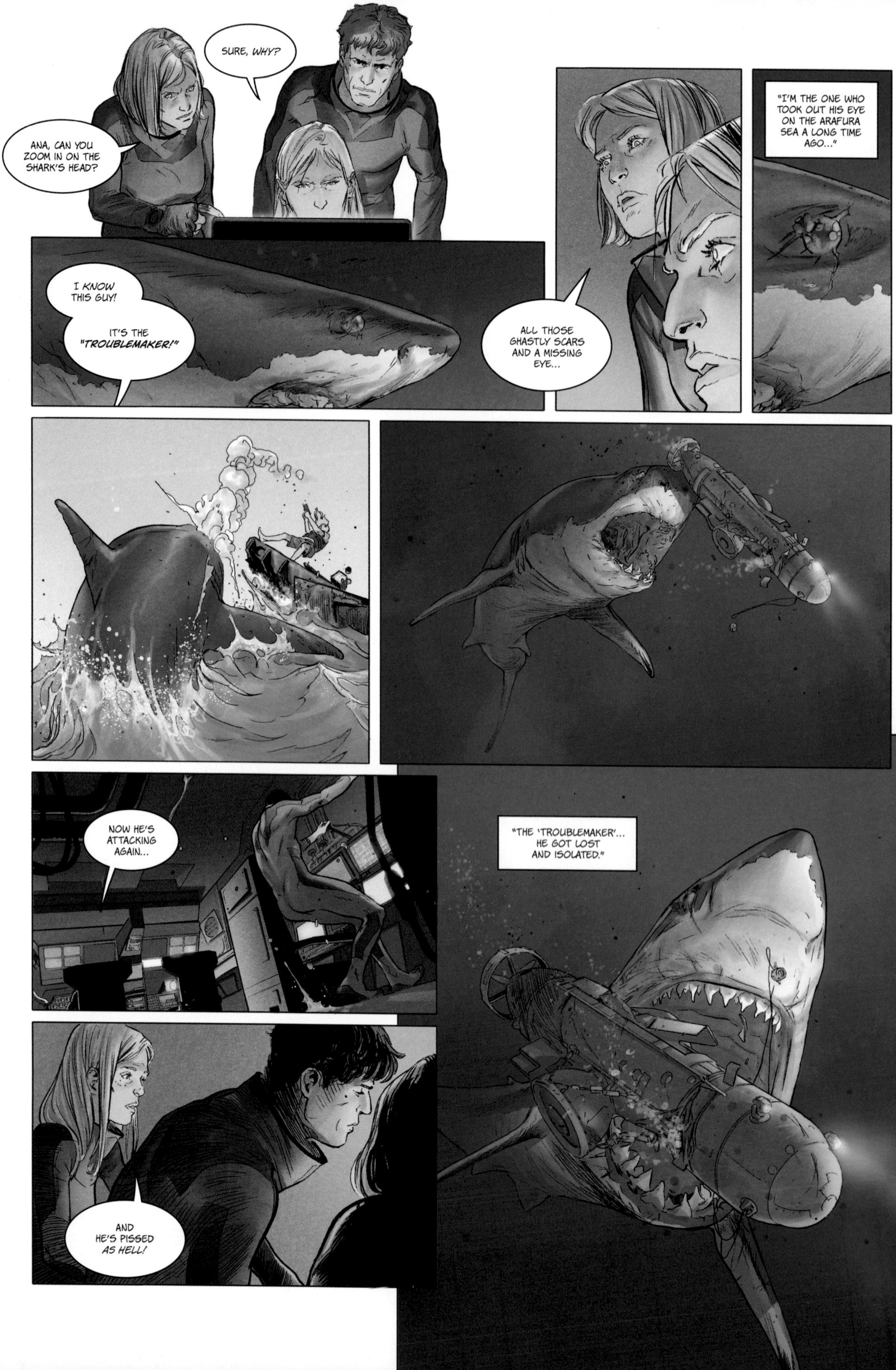
SURE, WHY?
ANA, CAN YOU ZOOM IN ON THE SHARK'S HEAD?
I KNOW THIS GUY!
IT'S THE "TROUBLEMAKER!"
ALL THOSE GHASTLY SCARS AND A MISSING EYE...
"I'M THE ONE WHO TOOK OUT HIS EYE ON THE ARAFURA SEA A LONG TIME AGO..."
NOW HE'S ATTACKING AGAIN...
AND HE'S PISSED AS HELL!
"THE 'TROUBLEMAKER'... HE GOT LOST AND ISOLATED."

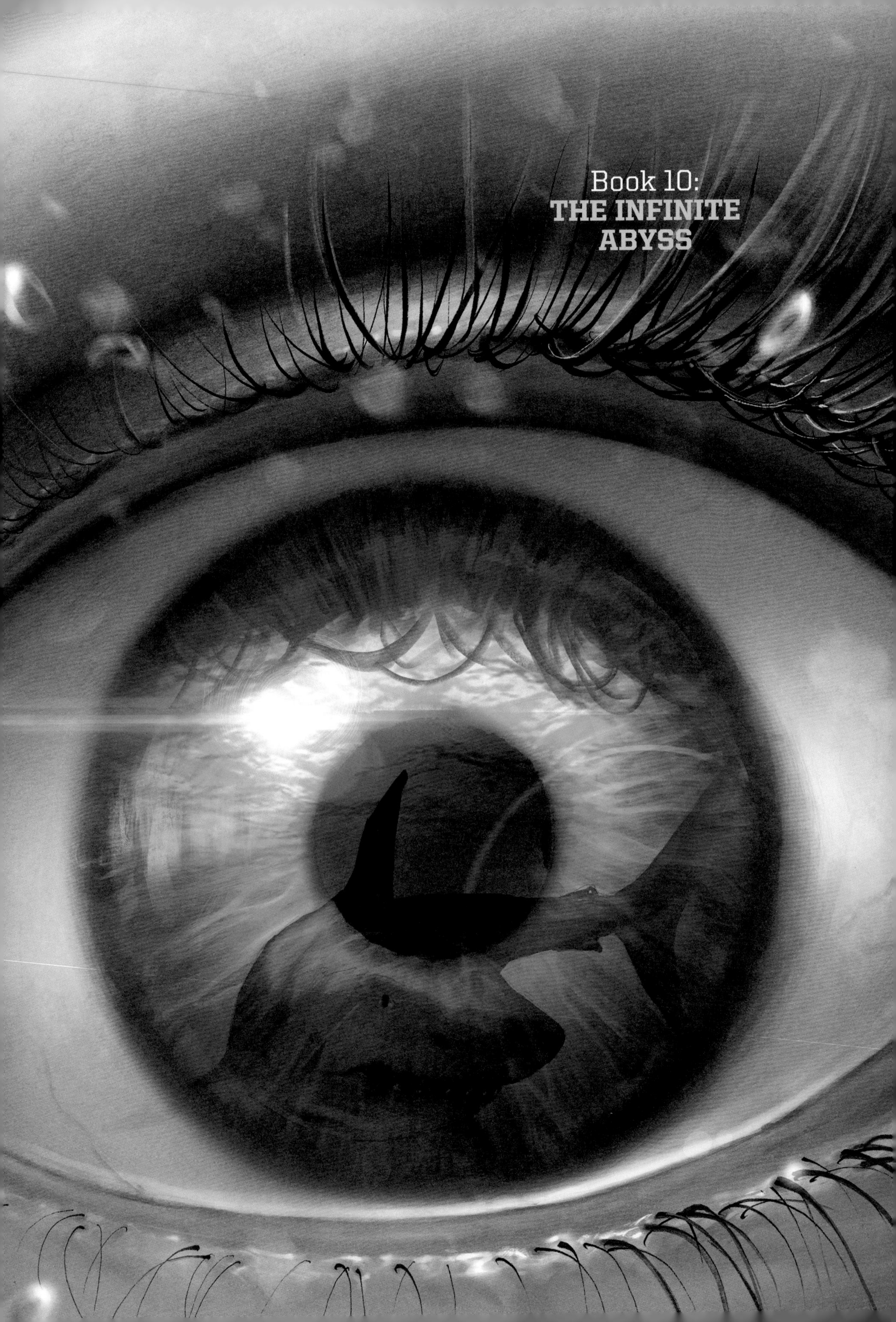

Book 10: THE INFINITE ABYSS

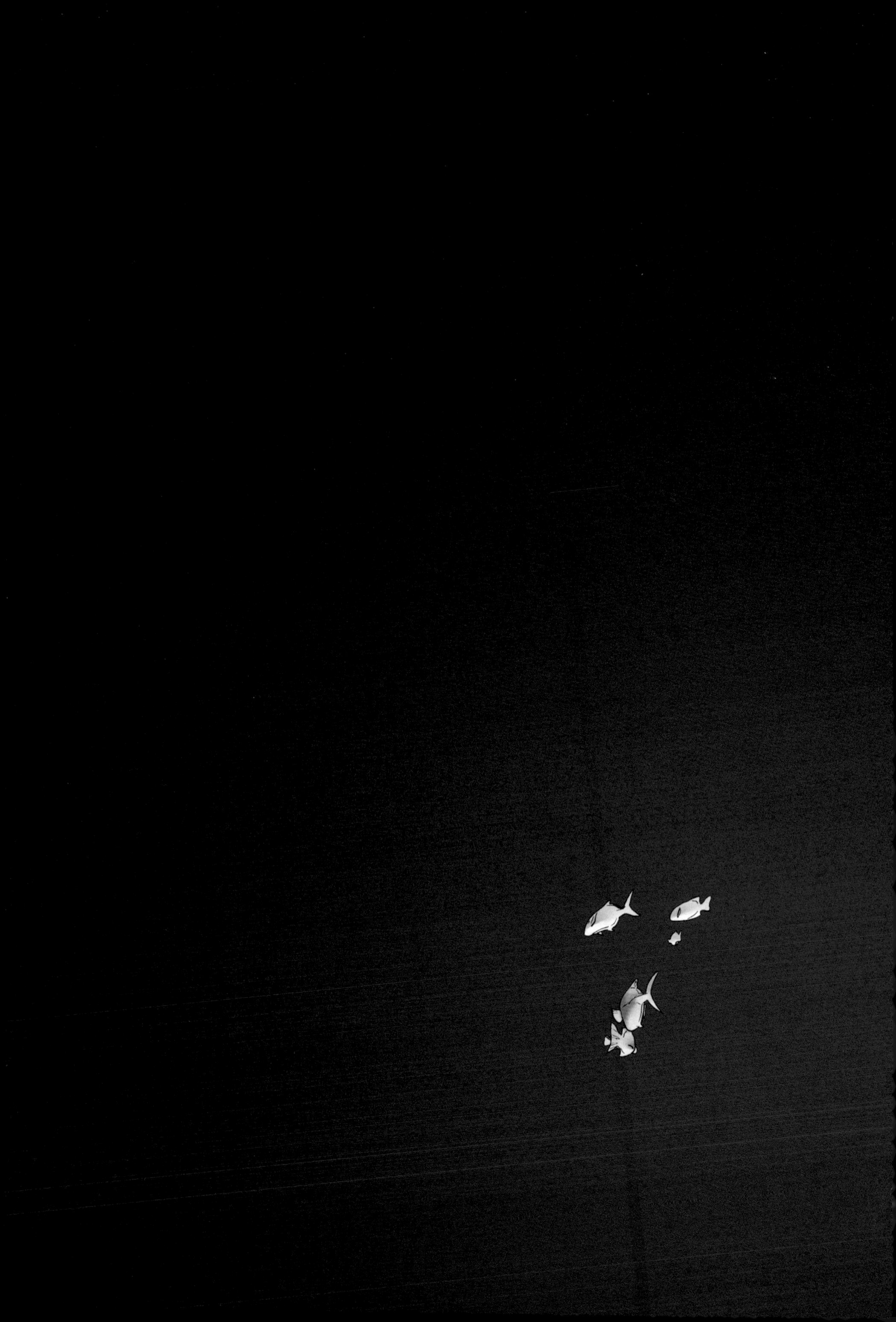

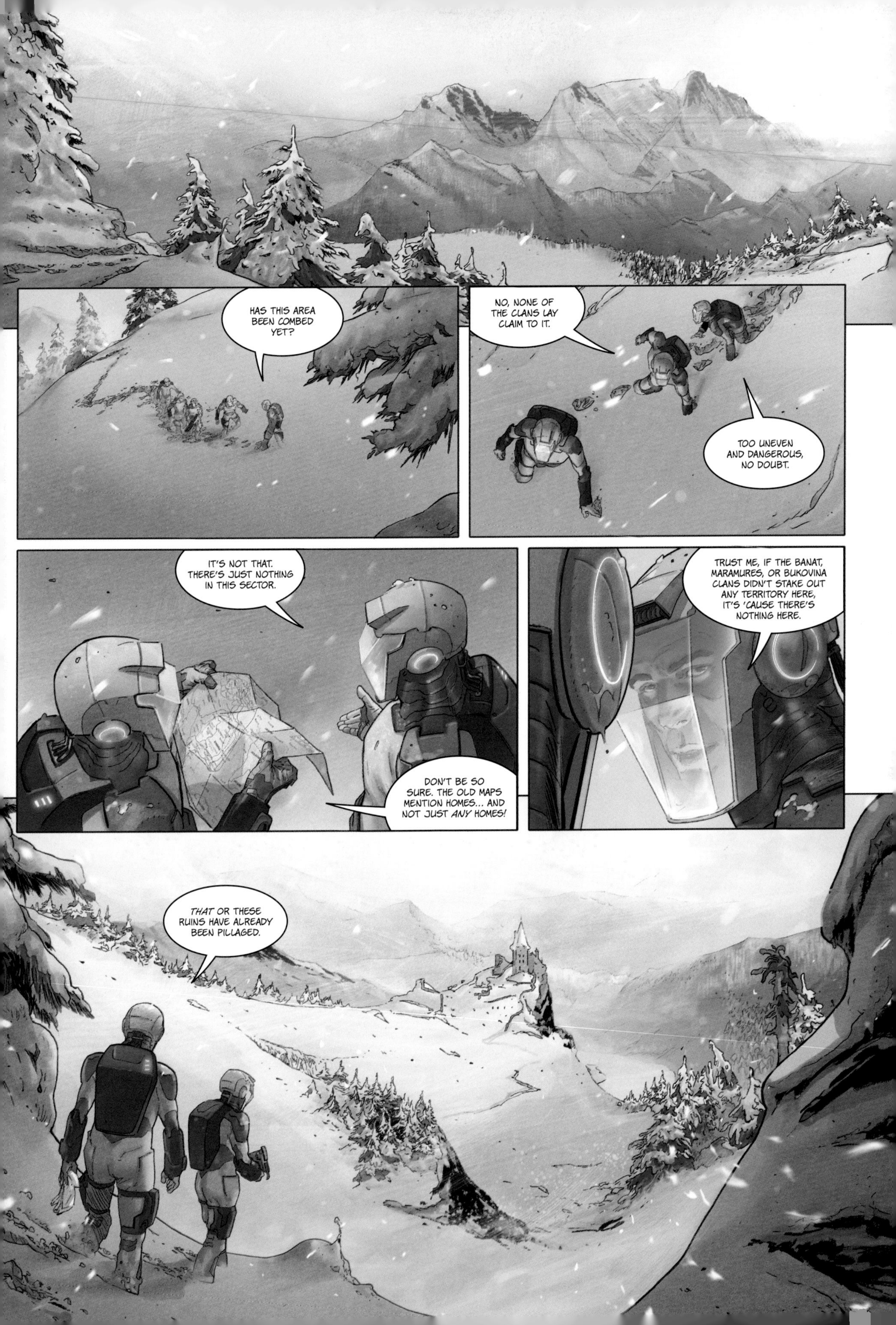
HAS THIS AREA BEEN COMBED YET?
NO, NONE OF THE CLANS LAY CLAIM TO IT.
TOO UNEVEN AND DANGEROUS, NO DOUBT.
IT'S NOT THAT. THERE'S JUST NOTHING IN THIS SECTOR.
DON'T BE SO SURE. THE OLD MAPS MENTION HOMES... AND NOT JUST *ANY* HOMES!
TRUST ME, IF THE BANAT, MARAMURES, OR BUKOVINA CLANS DIDN'T STAKE OUT ANY TERRITORY HERE, IT'S 'CAUSE THERE'S NOTHING HERE.
THAT OR THESE RUINS HAVE ALREADY BEEN PILLAGED.

PRIBILOF ISLANDS, BERING SEA, ALASKA – 2014.

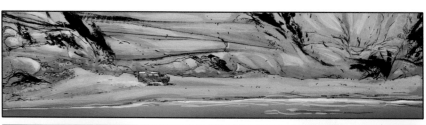

THANKS FOR LETTING ME KNOW ABOUT THIS.

WE'VE HEARD ABOUT YOUR BIOLOGY SEMINARS AT SAINT PAUL.

WE FIGURED THIS WAS YOUR FIELD OF EXPERTISE.

THIS ISN'T THE FIRST TIME WE'VE COME ACROSS DEAD MARINE CREATURES...

...BUT WE'VE NEVER SEEN ANYTHING LIKE THIS BEFORE.

DO YOU KNOW WHAT IT IS?

I NEED TO GET A CLOSER LOOK. AT FIRST GLANCE, I'D SAY IT'S A BEAKED WHALE.

HMM. NO, I'M NOT SO SURE, ACTUALLY.

I'M GOING TO CALL A RETIRED MARINE BIOLOGIST I KNOW. HE'S FOLLOWED MY CAREER FROM DAY ONE. THIS WILL INTEREST HIM.

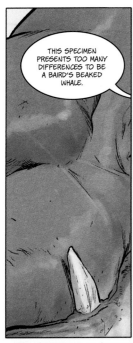

THIS SPECIMEN PRESENTS TOO MANY DIFFERENCES TO BE A BAIRD'S BEAKED WHALE.

THE SKIN AND THE FLESH ARE TOO DARK, THE DORSAL FIN TOO BIG AND TOO SOFT...

AND THE TEETH ON THE LOWER JAW... NO, NOT A MATCH.

YEP, THAT'S WHAT I THOUGHT TOO.

I'M GLAD YOU CALLED ME.

WE NEED TO TAKE SOME SAMPLES AND SEND THEM TO THE NATIONAL OCEANIC AND ATMOSPHERIC ADMINISTRATION TO FIND OUT WHERE IT CAME FROM. BUT I'M FAIRLY CERTAIN...

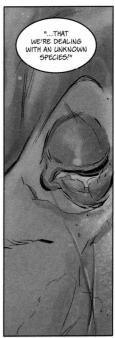

"...THAT WE'RE DEALING WITH AN UNKNOWN SPECIES!"

KAMCHATKA TRENCH – 2010 – DEPTH: 4,700 METERS.

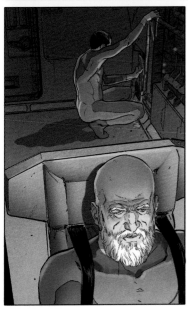

IF THEY CRANK UP THE FLOODLIGHTS ON THE D.S.R.V. TO THE MAX TO TRY TO BLIND THE MEG AND MAKE IT LET GO, IT'LL USE UP A LOT OF BATTERY JUICE AND JEOPARDIZE THE RESCUE.

PROBABLY WHY THEY HAVEN'T DONE IT YET.

TOMMY, YOU KNOW MEGALODONS PRETTY WELL. YOU GOT CLOSE TO THEM ON THE MEGSEARCH PLATFORM. ANY IDEAS?

I CAN'T EVEN TRY TO SUIT UP AND GET OUT THERE TO DRAW HIM AWAY. IT'S WAY TOO MUCH PRESSURE AT THIS DEPTH.

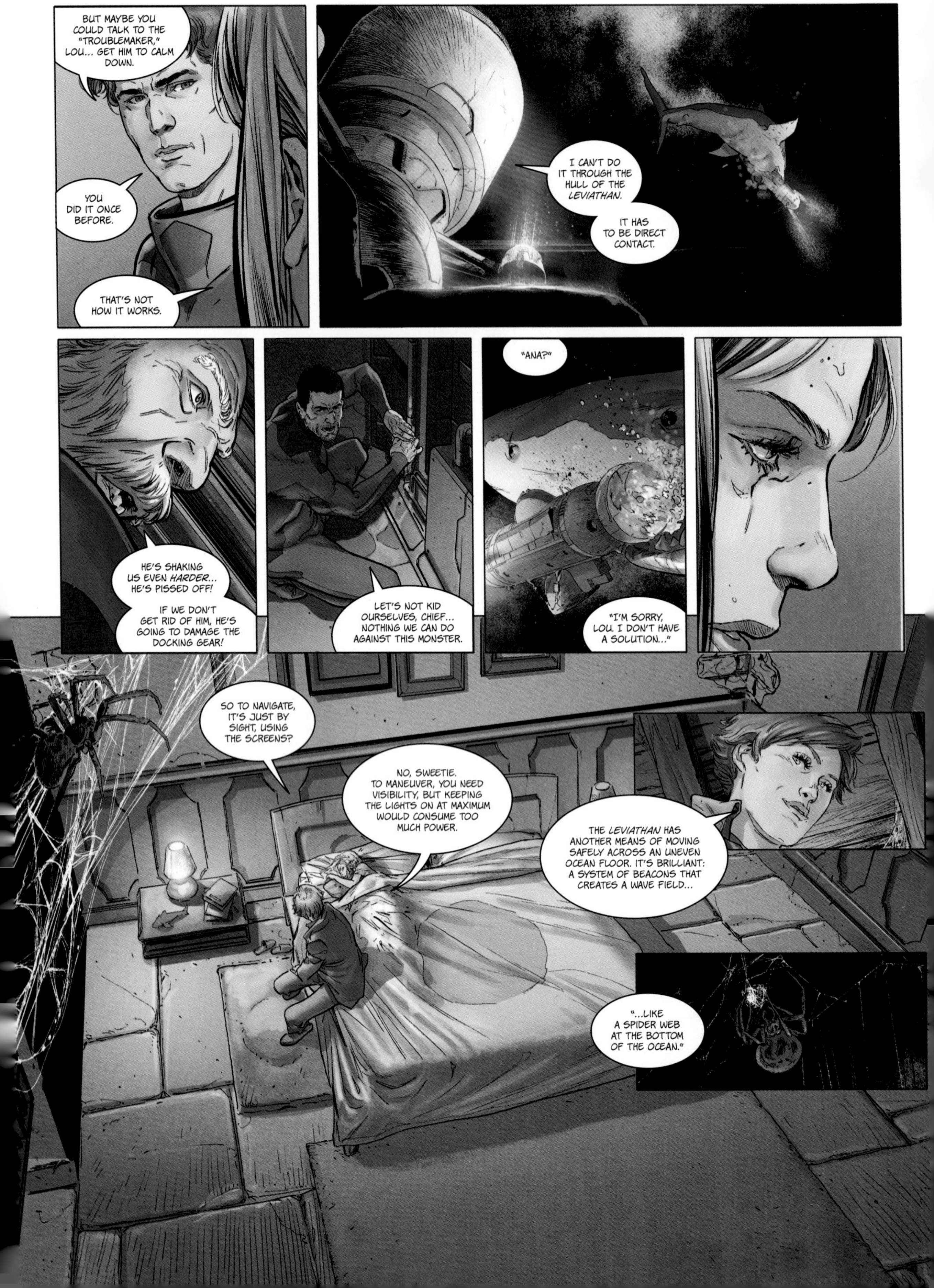
BUT MAYBE YOU COULD TALK TO THE "TROUBLEMAKER," LOU... GET HIM TO CALM DOWN.
YOU DID IT ONCE BEFORE.
THAT'S NOT HOW IT WORKS.
I CAN'T DO IT THROUGH THE HULL OF THE *LEVIATHAN.*
IT HAS TO BE DIRECT CONTACT.
HE'S SHAKING US EVEN *HARDER*... HE'S PISSED OFF!
IF WE DON'T GET RID OF HIM, HE'S GOING TO DAMAGE THE DOCKING GEAR!
LET'S NOT KID OURSELVES, CHIEF... NOTHING WE CAN DO AGAINST THIS MONSTER.
"ANA?"
"I'M SORRY, LOU. I DON'T HAVE A SOLUTION..."
SO TO NAVIGATE, IT'S JUST BY SIGHT, USING THE SCREENS?
NO, SWEETIE. TO MANEUVER, YOU NEED VISIBILITY, BUT KEEPING THE LIGHTS ON AT MAXIMUM WOULD CONSUME TOO MUCH POWER.
THE *LEVIATHAN* HAS ANOTHER MEANS OF MOVING SAFELY ACROSS AN UNEVEN OCEAN FLOOR. IT'S BRILLIANT: A SYSTEM OF BEACONS THAT CREATES A WAVE FIELD...
"...LIKE A SPIDER WEB AT THE BOTTOM OF THE OCEAN."

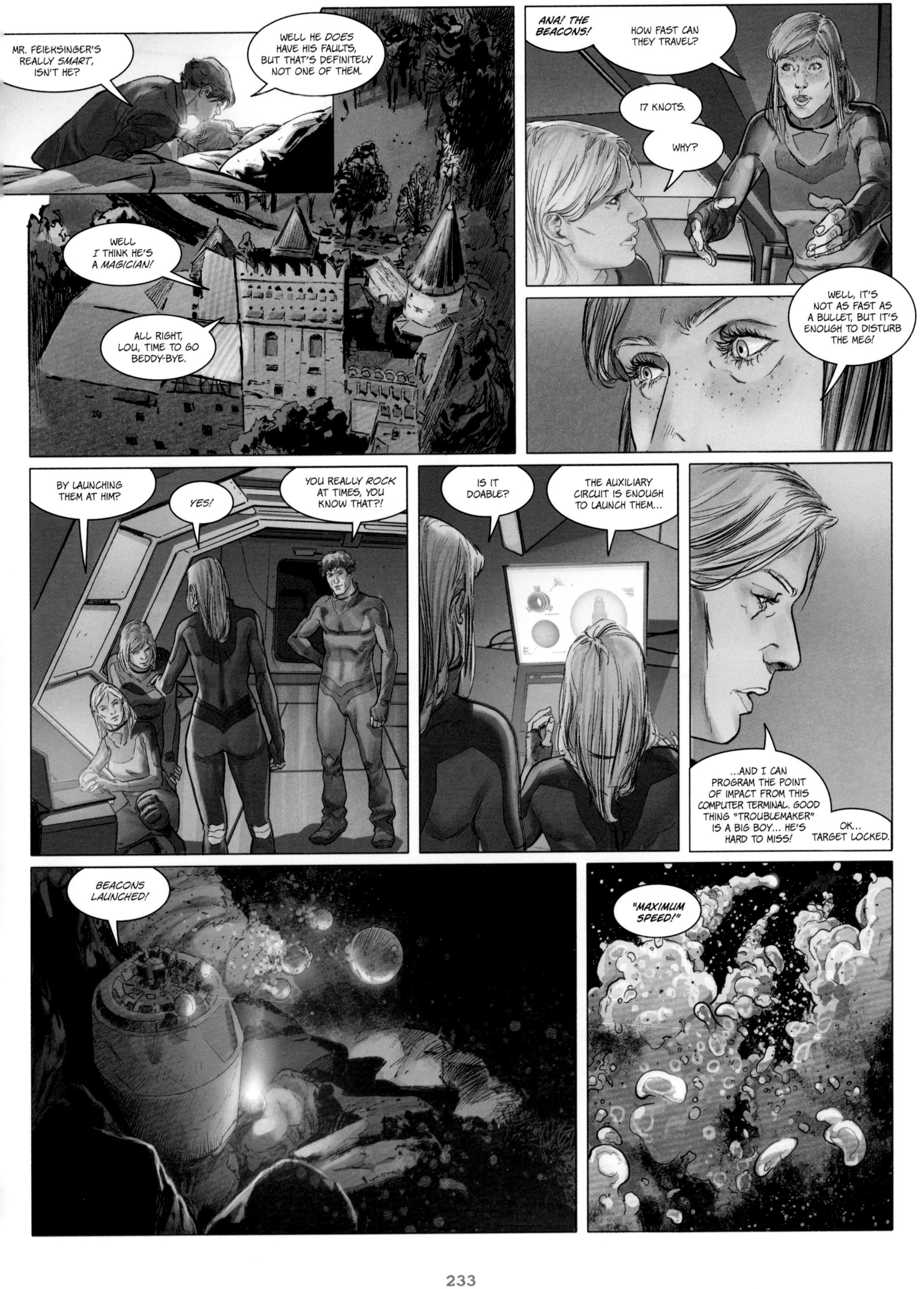

MR. FEIERSINGER'S REALLY SMART, ISN'T HE?
WELL HE DOES HAVE HIS FAULTS, BUT THAT'S DEFINITELY NOT ONE OF THEM.
WELL I THINK HE'S A MAGICIAN!
ALL RIGHT, LOU, TIME TO GO BEDDY-BYE.
ANA! THE BEACONS!
HOW FAST CAN THEY TRAVEL?
17 KNOTS.
WHY?
WELL, IT'S NOT AS FAST AS A BULLET, BUT IT'S ENOUGH TO DISTURB THE MEG!
BY LAUNCHING THEM AT HIM?
YES!
YOU REALLY ROCK AT TIMES, YOU KNOW THAT?!
IS IT DOABLE?
THE AUXILIARY CIRCUIT IS ENOUGH TO LAUNCH THEM...
...AND I CAN PROGRAM THE POINT OF IMPACT FROM THIS COMPUTER TERMINAL. GOOD THING "TROUBLEMAKER" IS A BIG BOY... HE'S HARD TO MISS!
OK... TARGET LOCKED.
BEACONS LAUNCHED!
"MAXIMUM SPEED!"

THIS GUY'S A STUBBORN ASS! HE'S GOT *YOUR* ROTTEN PERSONALITY, DONOVAN!

YEP! HE'S NOT LETTING GO!

HA HA!

WELL, CHIEF... AT LEAST THIS IS ONE *HELL* OF A WAY TO CHECK OUT!

HA HA!

TOO BAD, 'CAUSE I'M STARVING.

IF I HAVE TO DIE, I'D RATHER NOT DO IT ON AN EMPTY STOMACH!

YOU SHOULD'VE SAID SOMETHING.

WE COULD'VE ASKED THE GUYS THAT FIXED UP THIS WRECK TO INSTALL A BARBECUE!

TAKE THIS, BIG GUY. RIGHT IN THE GUT!

IMPACT IN 6 SECONDS.

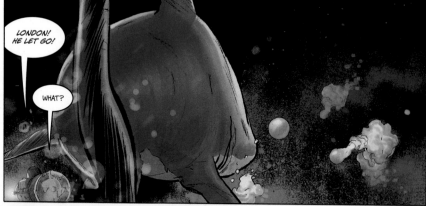

LONDON! HE LET GO!

WHAT?

HE DID! IT'S A MIRACLE!

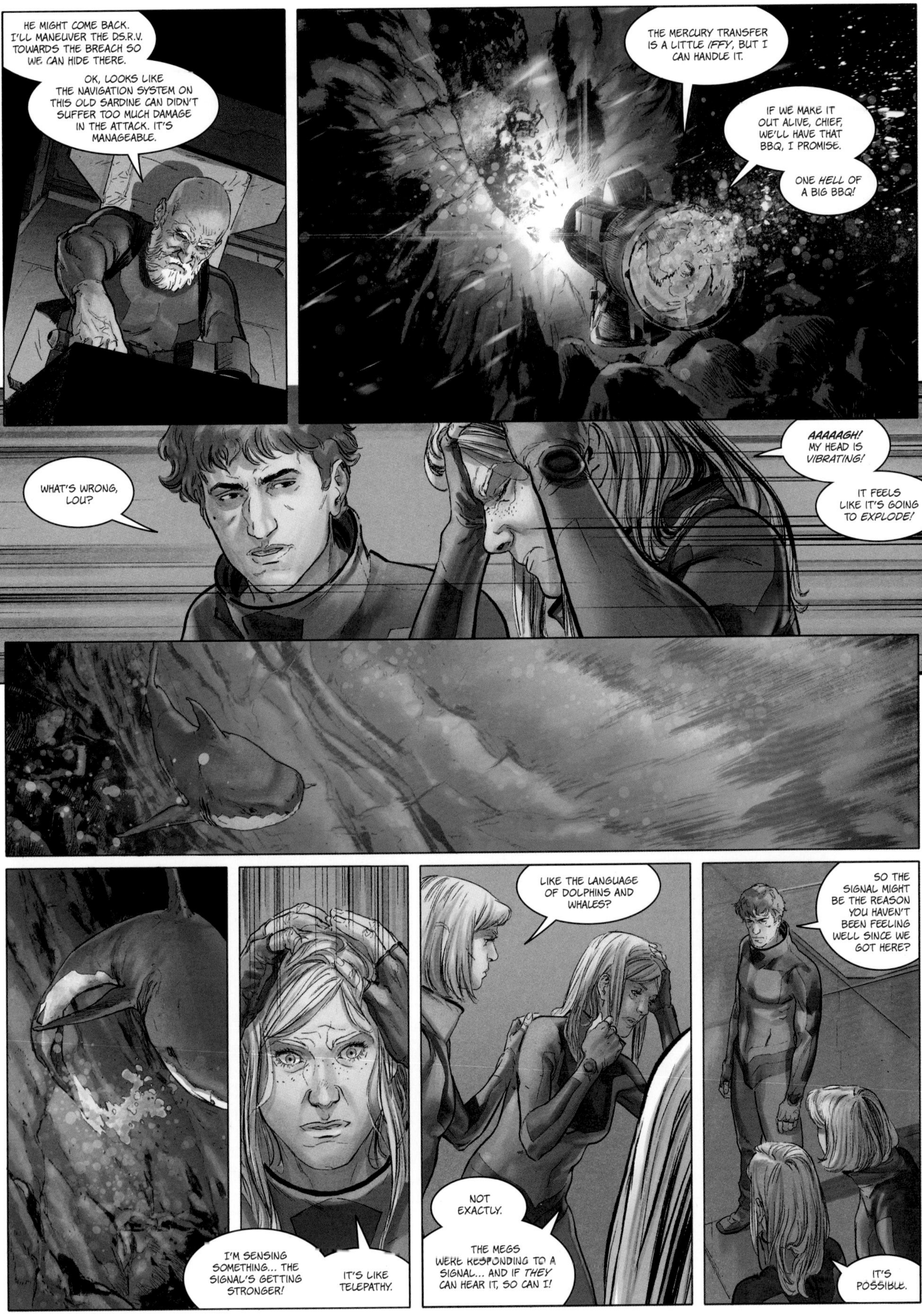
HE MIGHT COME BACK. I'LL MANEUVER THE DS.R.V. TOWARDS THE BREACH SO WE CAN HIDE THERE.
OK, LOOKS LIKE THE NAVIGATION SYSTEM ON THIS OLD SARDINE CAN DIDN'T SUFFER TOO MUCH DAMAGE IN THE ATTACK. IT'S MANAGEABLE.
THE MERCURY TRANSFER IS A LITTLE IFFY, BUT I CAN HANDLE IT.
IF WE MAKE IT OUT ALIVE, CHIEF, WE'LL HAVE THAT BBQ, I PROMISE.
ONE HELL OF A BIG BBQ!
AAAAAGH! MY HEAD IS VIBRATING!
WHAT'S WRONG, LOU?
IT FEELS LIKE IT'S GOING TO EXPLODE!
I'M SENSING SOMETHING... THE SIGNAL'S GETTING STRONGER!
IT'S LIKE TELEPATHY.
LIKE THE LANGUAGE OF DOLPHINS AND WHALES?
NOT EXACTLY.
THE MEGS WERE RESPONDING TO A SIGNAL... AND IF THEY CAN HEAR IT, SO CAN I!
SO THE SIGNAL MIGHT BE THE REASON YOU HAVEN'T BEEN FEELING WELL SINCE WE GOT HERE?
IT'S POSSIBLE.

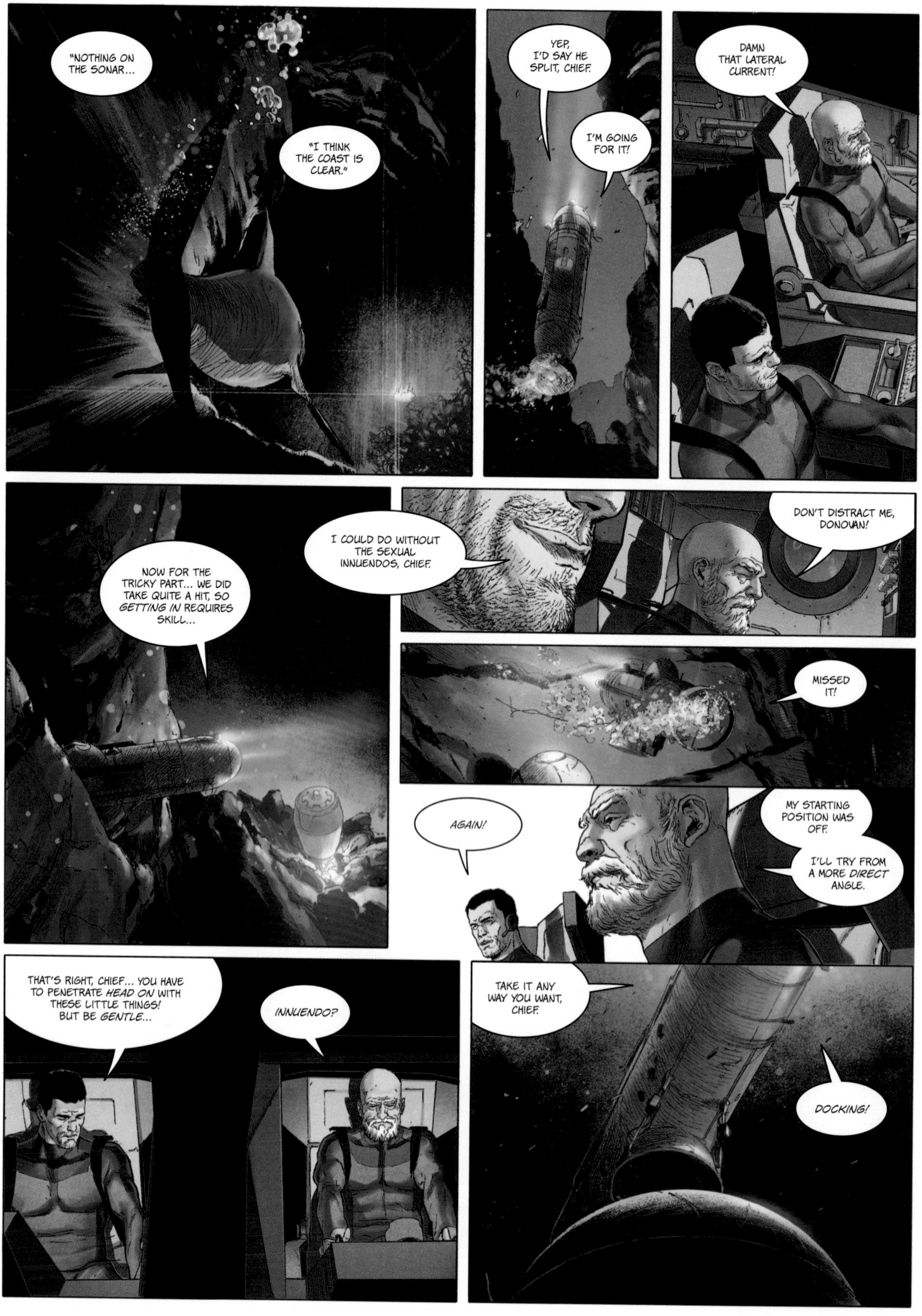
"NOTHING ON THE SONAR...
"I THINK THE COAST IS CLEAR."
YEP, I'D SAY HE SPLIT, CHIEF.
I'M GOING FOR IT!
DAMN THAT LATERAL CURRENT!
NOW FOR THE TRICKY PART... WE DID TAKE QUITE A HIT, SO *GETTING IN* REQUIRES SKILL...
I COULD DO WITHOUT THE SEXUAL INNUENDOS, CHIEF.
DON'T DISTRACT ME, DONOVAN!
MISSED IT!
AGAIN!
MY STARTING POSITION WAS OFF.
I'LL TRY FROM A MORE *DIRECT* ANGLE.
THAT'S RIGHT, CHIEF... YOU HAVE TO PENETRATE *HEAD ON* WITH THESE LITTLE THINGS! BUT BE *GENTLE*...
INNUENDO?
TAKE IT ANY WAY YOU WANT, CHIEF.
DOCKING!

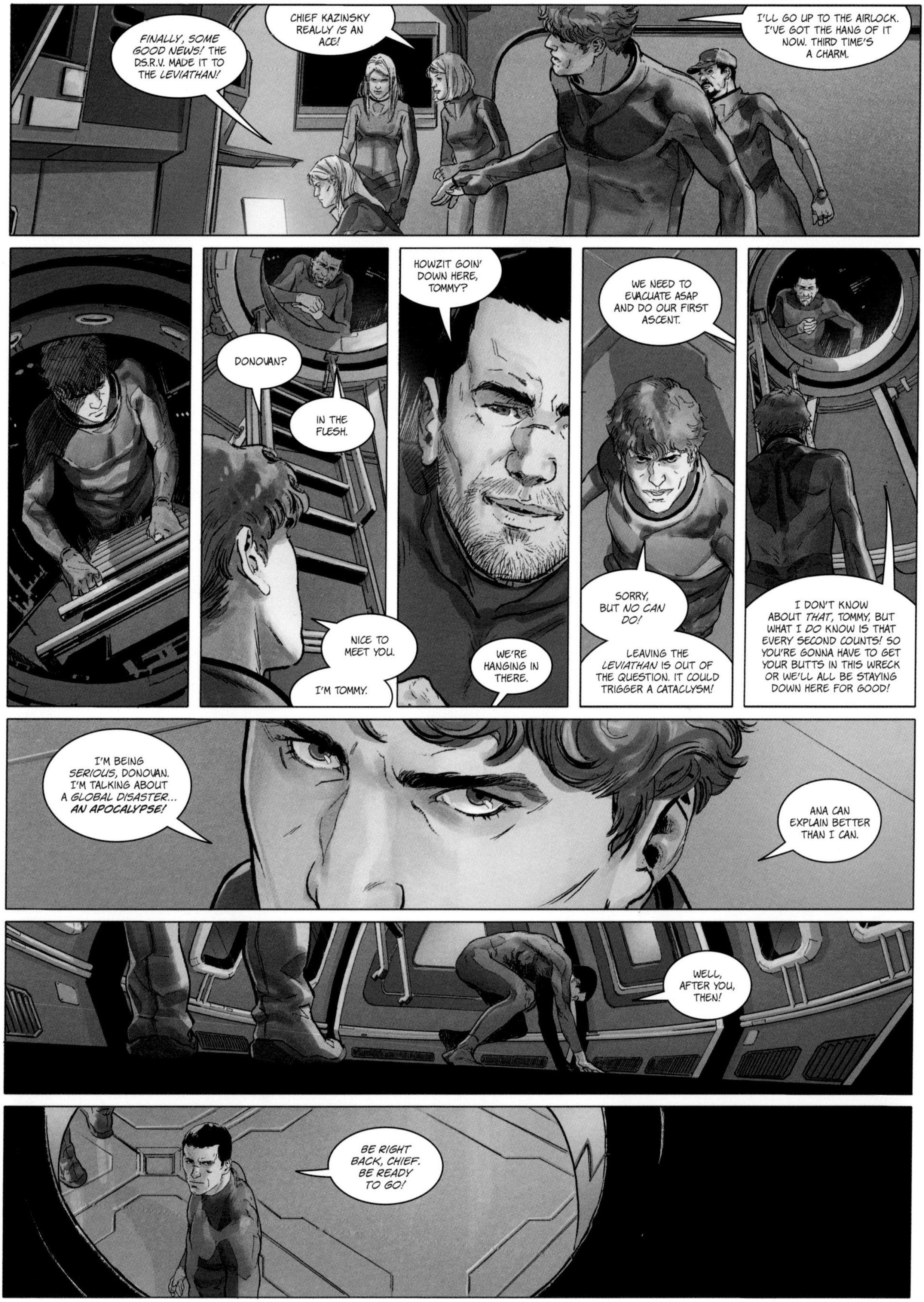
FINALLY, SOME GOOD NEWS! THE D.S.R.V. MADE IT TO THE LEVIATHAN!
CHIEF KAZINSKY REALLY IS AN ACE!
I'LL GO UP TO THE AIRLOCK. I'VE GOT THE HANG OF IT NOW. THIRD TIME'S A CHARM.
DONOVAN?
IN THE FLESH.
NICE TO MEET YOU.
I'M TOMMY.
HOWZIT GOIN' DOWN HERE, TOMMY?
WE'RE HANGING IN THERE.
WE NEED TO EVACUATE ASAP AND DO OUR FIRST ASCENT.
SORRY, BUT NO CAN DO!
LEAVING THE LEVIATHAN IS OUT OF THE QUESTION. IT COULD TRIGGER A CATACLYSM!
I DON'T KNOW ABOUT THAT, TOMMY, BUT WHAT I DO KNOW IS THAT EVERY SECOND COUNTS! SO YOU'RE GONNA HAVE TO GET YOUR BUTTS IN THIS WRECK OR WE'LL ALL BE STAYING DOWN HERE FOR GOOD!
I'M BEING SERIOUS, DONOVAN. I'M TALKING ABOUT A GLOBAL DISASTER... AN APOCALYPSE!
ANA CAN EXPLAIN BETTER THAN I CAN.
WELL, AFTER YOU, THEN!
BE RIGHT BACK, CHIEF. BE READY TO GO!

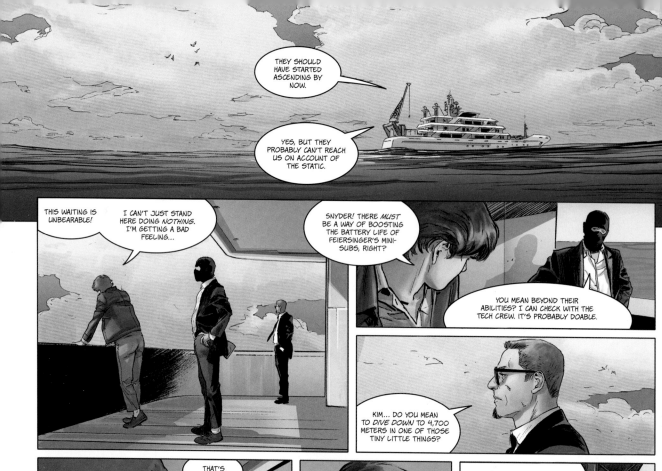

THEY SHOULD HAVE STARTED ASCENDING BY NOW.

YES, BUT THEY PROBABLY CAN'T REACH US ON ACCOUNT OF THE STATIC.

THIS WAITING IS UNBEARABLE!

I CAN'T JUST STAND HERE DOING *NOTHING*. I'M GETTING A BAD FEELING...

SNYDER! THERE *MUST* BE A WAY OF BOOSTING THE BATTERY LIFE OF FEIERSINGER'S MINI-SUBS, RIGHT?

YOU MEAN BEYOND THEIR ABILITIES? I CAN CHECK WITH THE TECH CREW. IT'S PROBABLY DOABLE.

KIM... DO YOU MEAN TO *DIVE* DOWN TO 4,700 METERS IN ONE OF THOSE TINY LITTLE THINGS?

THAT'S *SUICIDE!*

YOU JUST STAND THERE AND DO NOTHING, HARRY... AS ALWAYS!

COMPLETE *INACTION*... JUST LIKE ON MOUNT KAILASH!

THE *BABY* OF THE FAMILY... SPOILED, OVERPROTECTED AND INCAPABLE OF ACTION!

I'M *NOT THE BABY*, MISS MELVILLE. THERE'S A LOT YOU DON'T KNOW ABOUT OUR *FASCINATING* FAMILY TREE.

LONDON'S THE ONE DOWN THERE, YOU SAID. I DOUBT HE WOULD WANT YOU TO TAKE THIS RISK.

YOU MIGHT BE RIGHT, HARRY.

BUT I'M GOING ANYWAY!

238

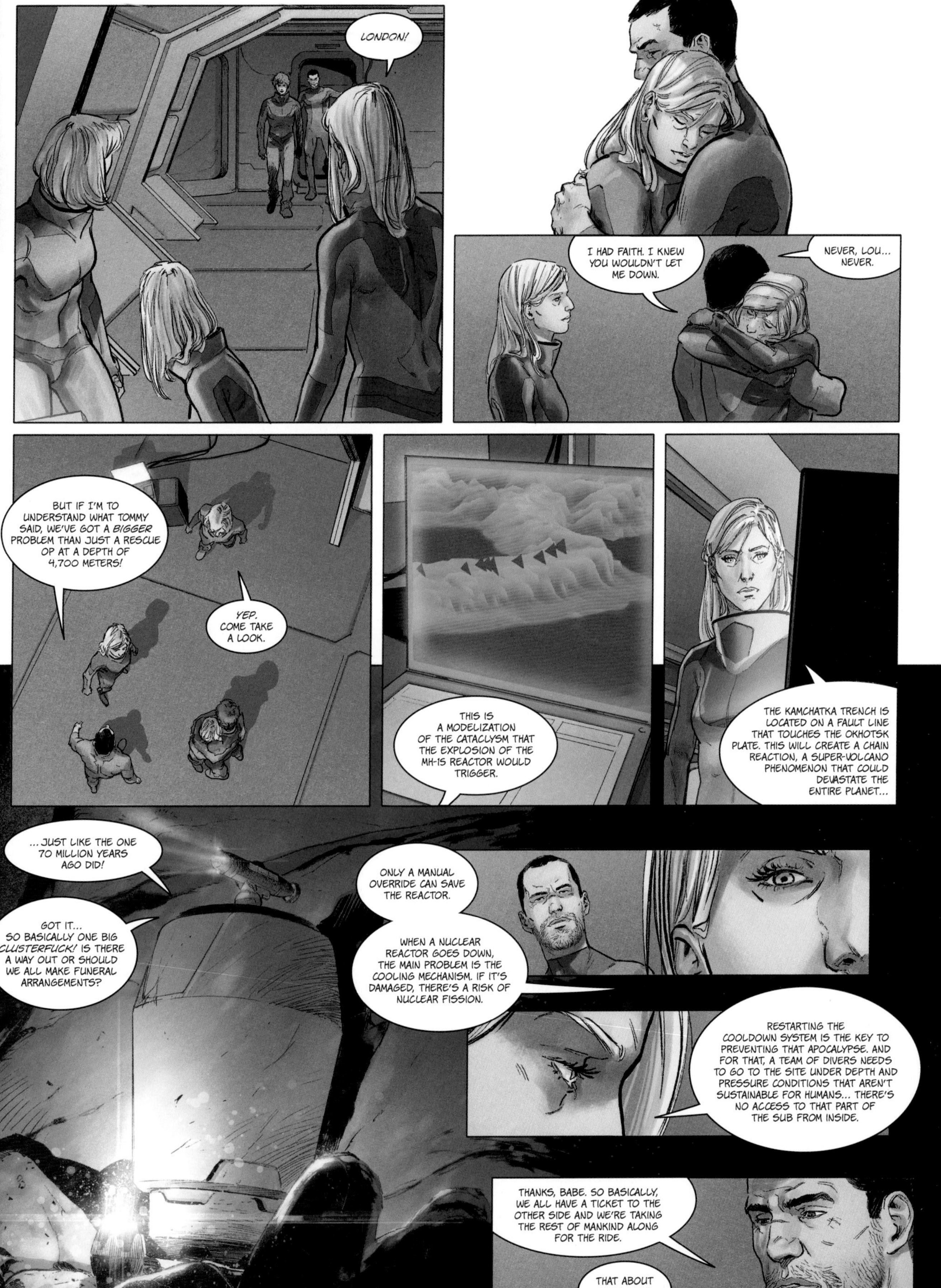
LONDON!
I HAD FAITH. I KNEW YOU WOULDN'T LET ME DOWN.
NEVER, LOU... NEVER.
BUT IF I'M TO UNDERSTAND WHAT TOMMY SAID, WE'VE GOT A *BIGGER* PROBLEM THAN JUST A RESCUE OP AT A DEPTH OF 4,700 METERS!
YEP. COME TAKE A LOOK.
THIS IS A MODELIZATION OF THE CATACLYSM THAT THE EXPLOSION OF THE MH-15 REACTOR WOULD TRIGGER.
THE KAMCHATKA TRENCH IS LOCATED ON A FAULT LINE THAT TOUCHES THE OKHOTSK PLATE. THIS WILL CREATE A CHAIN REACTION, A SUPER-VOLCANO PHENOMENON THAT COULD DEVASTATE THE ENTIRE PLANET...
... JUST LIKE THE ONE 70 MILLION YEARS AGO DID!
GOT IT... SO BASICALLY ONE BIG *CLUSTERFUCK!* IS THERE A WAY OUT OR SHOULD WE ALL MAKE FUNERAL ARRANGEMENTS?
ONLY A MANUAL OVERRIDE CAN SAVE THE REACTOR.
WHEN A NUCLEAR REACTOR GOES DOWN, THE MAIN PROBLEM IS THE COOLING MECHANISM. IF IT'S DAMAGED, THERE'S A RISK OF NUCLEAR FISSION.
RESTARTING THE COOLDOWN SYSTEM IS THE KEY TO PREVENTING THAT APOCALYPSE. AND FOR THAT, A TEAM OF DIVERS NEEDS TO GO TO THE SITE UNDER DEPTH AND PRESSURE CONDITIONS THAT AREN'T SUSTAINABLE FOR HUMANS... THERE'S NO ACCESS TO THAT PART OF THE SUB FROM INSIDE.
THANKS, BABE. SO BASICALLY, WE ALL HAVE A TICKET TO THE OTHER SIDE AND WE'RE TAKING THE REST OF MANKIND ALONG FOR THE RIDE.
THAT ABOUT SUMS IT UP.

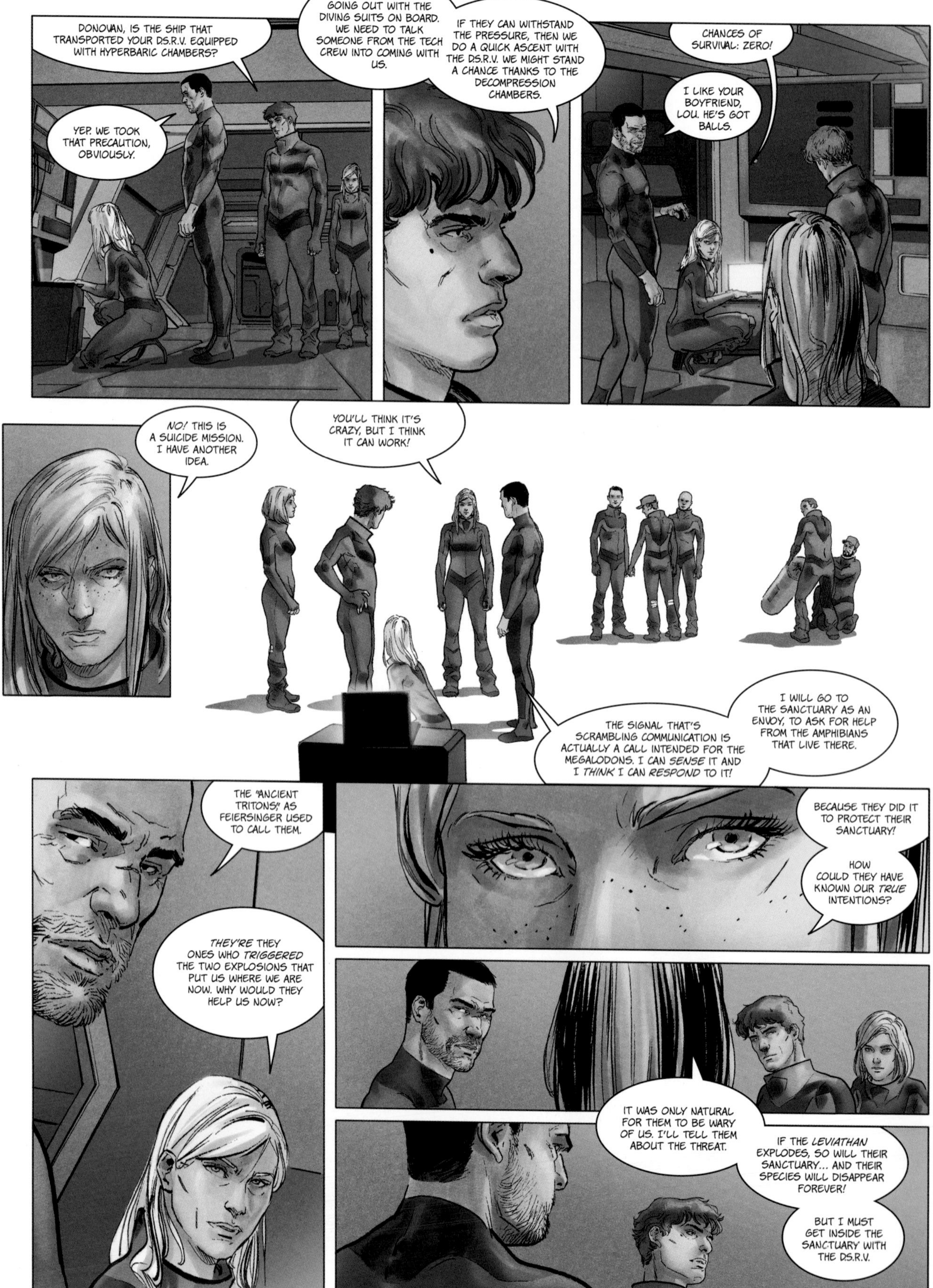
DONOVAN, IS THE SHIP THAT TRANSPORTED YOUR D.S.R.V. EQUIPPED WITH HYPERBARIC CHAMBERS?
YEP. WE TOOK THAT PRECAUTION, OBVIOUSLY.
WE CAN TRY GOING OUT WITH THE DIVING SUITS ON BOARD. WE NEED TO TALK SOMEONE FROM THE TECH CREW INTO COMING WITH US.
IF THEY CAN WITHSTAND THE PRESSURE, THEN WE DO A QUICK ASCENT WITH THE D.S.R.V. WE MIGHT STAND A CHANCE THANKS TO THE DECOMPRESSION CHAMBERS.
CHANCES OF SURVIVAL: ZERO!
I LIKE YOUR BOYFRIEND, LOU. HE'S GOT BALLS.
NO! THIS IS A SUICIDE MISSION. I HAVE ANOTHER IDEA.
YOU'LL THINK IT'S CRAZY, BUT I THINK IT CAN WORK!
THE SIGNAL THAT'S SCRAMBLING COMMUNICATION IS ACTUALLY A CALL INTENDED FOR THE MEGALODONS. I CAN SENSE IT AND I THINK I CAN RESPOND TO IT!
I WILL GO TO THE SANCTUARY AS AN ENVOY, TO ASK FOR HELP FROM THE AMPHIBIANS THAT LIVE THERE.
THE "ANCIENT TRITONS," AS FEIERSINGER USED TO CALL THEM.
THEY'RE THEY ONES WHO TRIGGERED THE TWO EXPLOSIONS THAT PUT US WHERE WE ARE NOW. WHY WOULD THEY HELP US NOW?
BECAUSE THEY DID IT TO PROTECT THEIR SANCTUARY!
HOW COULD THEY HAVE KNOWN OUR TRUE INTENTIONS?
IT WAS ONLY NATURAL FOR THEM TO BE WARY OF US. I'LL TELL THEM ABOUT THE THREAT.
IF THE LEVIATHAN EXPLODES, SO WILL THEIR SANCTUARY... AND THEIR SPECIES WILL DISAPPEAR FOREVER!
BUT I MUST GET INSIDE THE SANCTUARY WITH THE D.S.R.V.

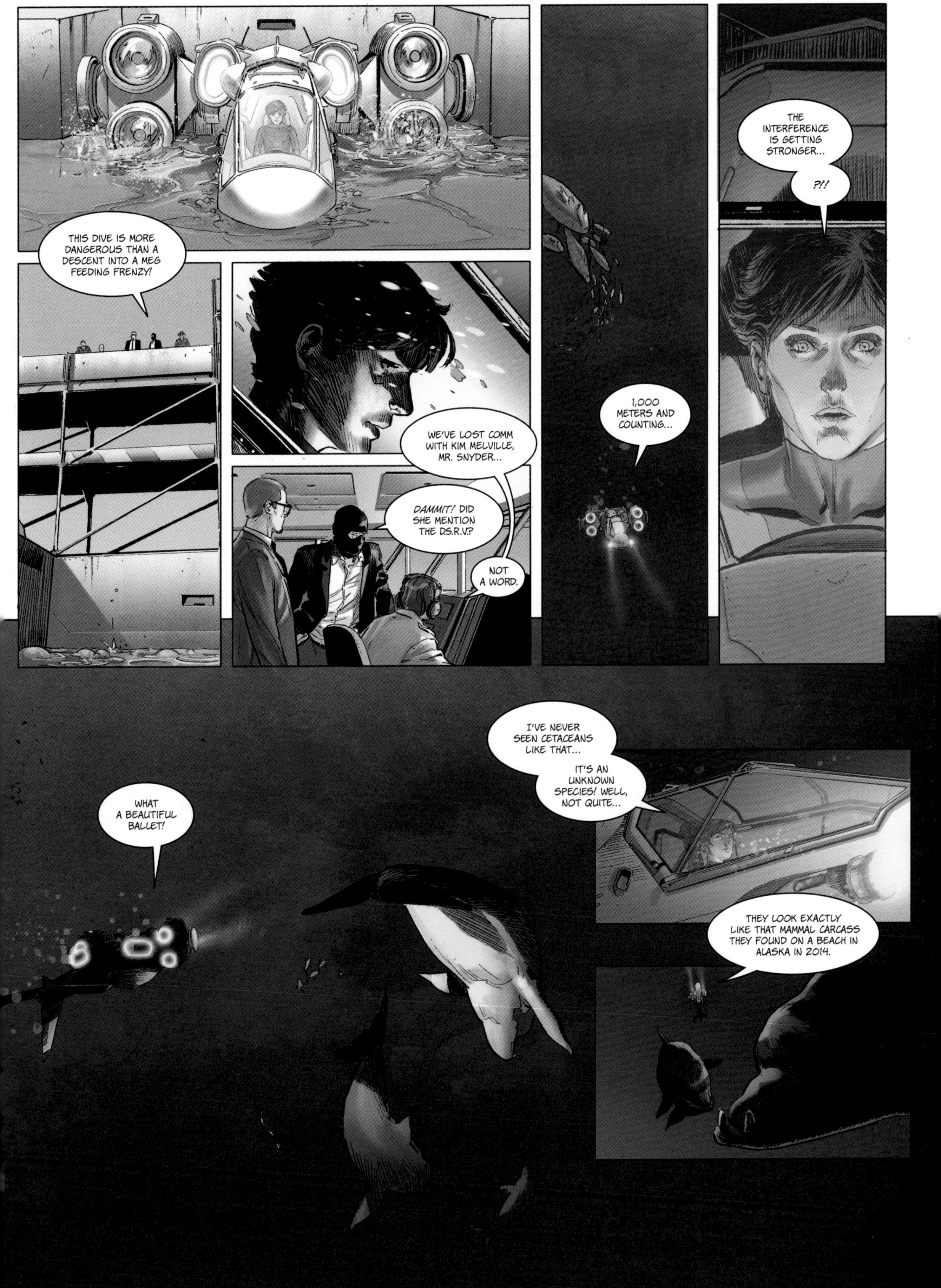
THIS DIVE IS MORE DANGEROUS THAN A DESCENT INTO A MEG FEEDING FRENZY!
WE'VE LOST COMM WITH KIM MELVILLE, MR. SNYDER...
DAMMIT! DID SHE MENTION THE D.S.R.V.?
NOT A WORD.
1,000 METERS AND COUNTING...
THE INTERFERENCE IS GETTING STRONGER...
?!!
WHAT A BEAUTIFUL BALLET!
I'VE NEVER SEEN CETACEANS LIKE THAT...
IT'S AN UNKNOWN SPECIES! WELL, NOT QUITE...
THEY LOOK EXACTLY LIKE THAT MAMMAL CARCASS THEY FOUND ON A BEACH IN ALASKA IN 2014.

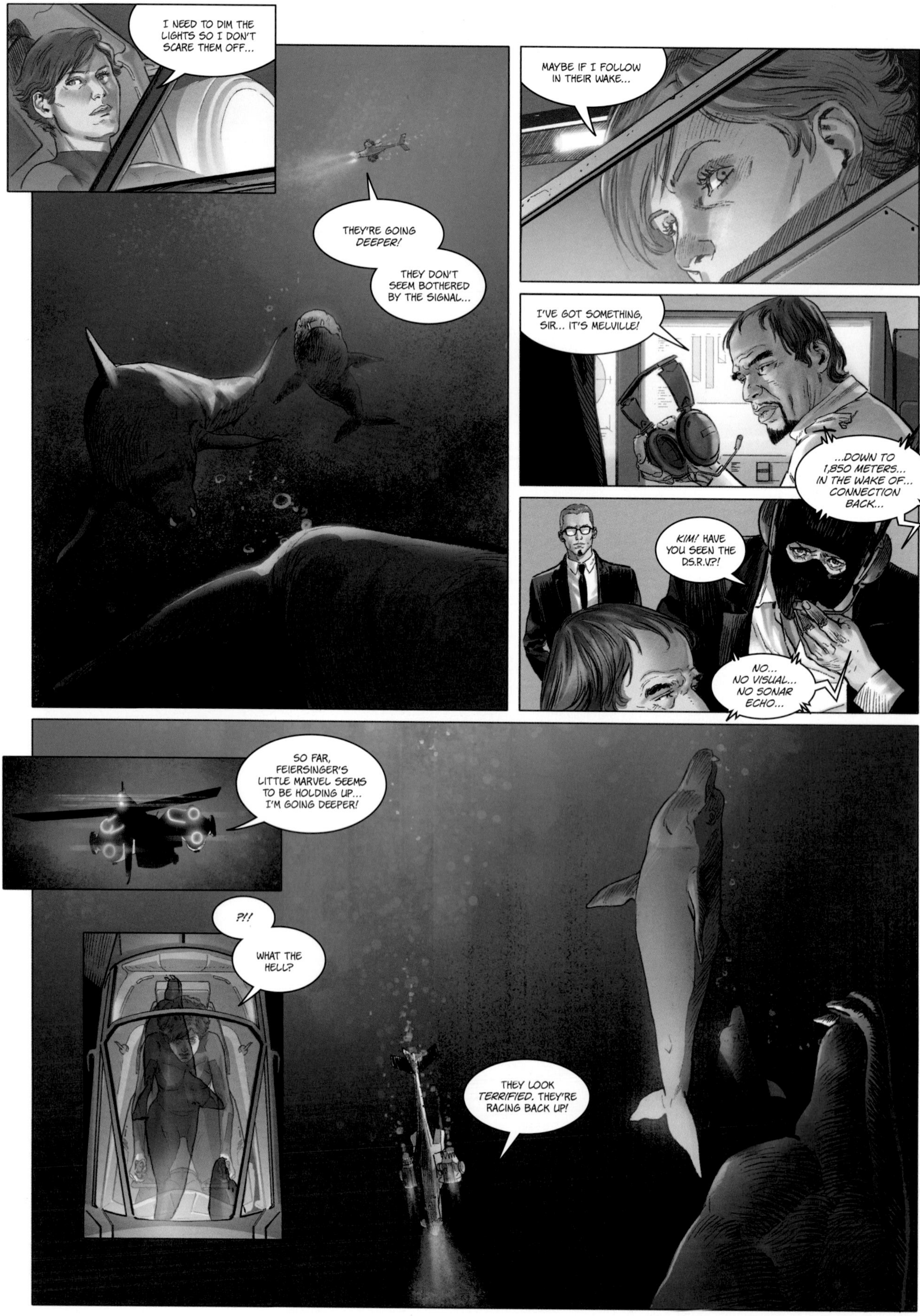
I NEED TO DIM THE LIGHTS SO I DON'T SCARE THEM OFF...
THEY'RE GOING DEEPER!
THEY DON'T SEEM BOTHERED BY THE SIGNAL...
MAYBE IF I FOLLOW IN THEIR WAKE...
I'VE GOT SOMETHING, SIR... IT'S MELVILLE!
...DOWN TO 1,850 METERS... IN THE WAKE OF... CONNECTION BACK...
KIM! HAVE YOU SEEN THE D.S.R.V.?!
NO... NO VISUAL... NO SONAR ECHO...
SO FAR, FEIERSINGER'S LITTLE MARVEL SEEMS TO BE HOLDING UP... I'M GOING DEEPER!
?!!
WHAT THE HELL?
THEY LOOK TERRIFIED. THEY'RE RACING BACK UP!

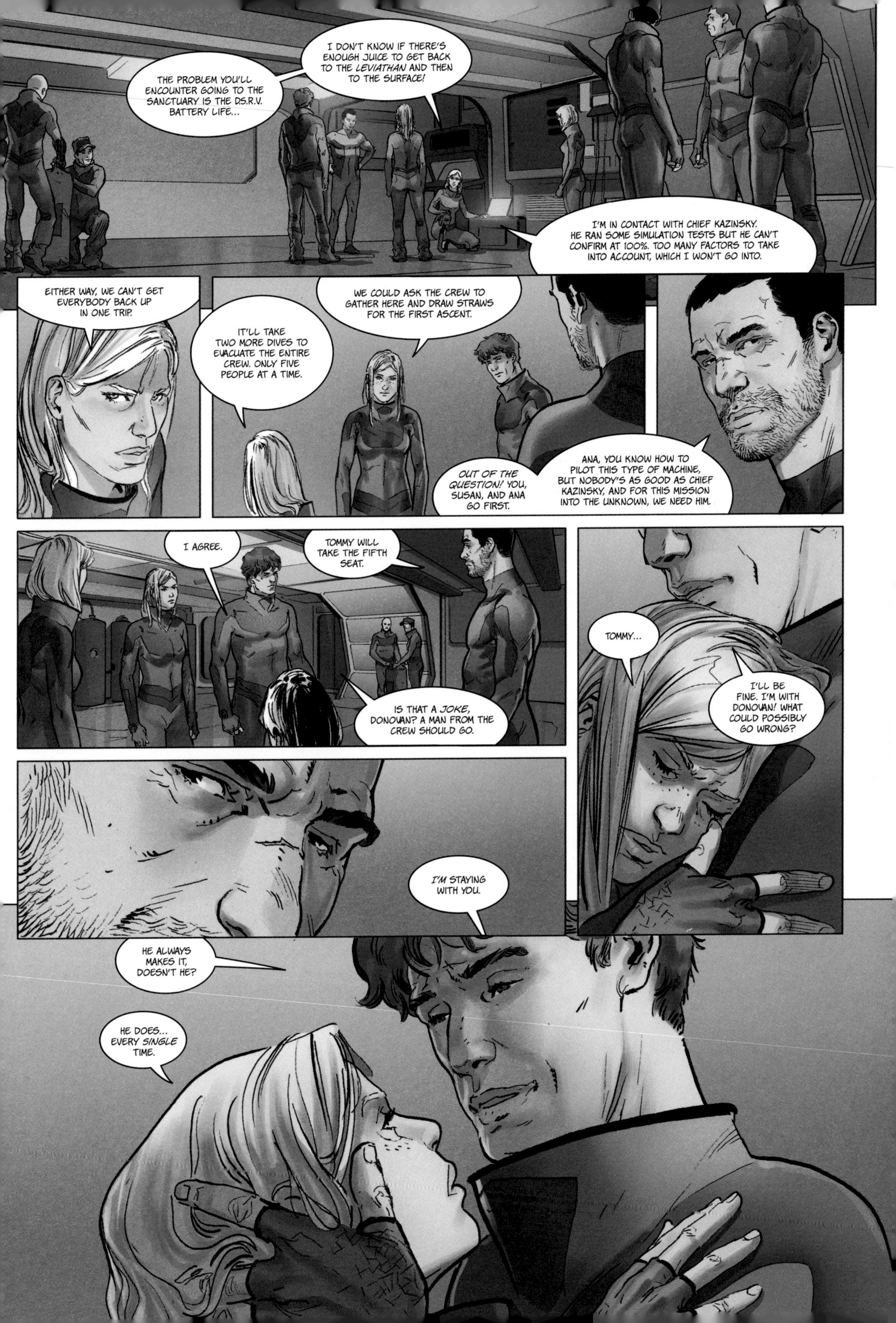
THE PROBLEM YOU'LL ENCOUNTER GOING TO THE SANCTUARY IS THE D.S.R.V. BATTERY LIFE...
I DON'T KNOW IF THERE'S ENOUGH JUICE TO GET BACK TO THE *LEVIATHAN* AND THEN TO THE SURFACE!
I'M IN CONTACT WITH CHIEF KAZINSKY. HE RAN SOME SIMULATION TESTS BUT HE CAN'T CONFIRM AT 100%. TOO MANY FACTORS TO TAKE INTO ACCOUNT, WHICH I WON'T GO INTO.
EITHER WAY, WE CAN'T GET EVERYBODY BACK UP IN ONE TRIP.
IT'LL TAKE TWO MORE DIVES TO EVACUATE THE ENTIRE CREW. ONLY FIVE PEOPLE AT A TIME.
WE COULD ASK THE CREW TO GATHER HERE AND DRAW STRAWS FOR THE FIRST ASCENT.
OUT OF THE QUESTION! YOU, SUSAN, AND ANA GO FIRST.
ANA, YOU KNOW HOW TO PILOT THIS TYPE OF MACHINE, BUT NOBODY'S AS GOOD AS CHIEF KAZINSKY, AND FOR THIS MISSION INTO THE UNKNOWN, WE NEED HIM.
I AGREE.
TOMMY WILL TAKE THE FIFTH SEAT.
IS THAT A *JOKE*, DONOVAN? A MAN FROM THE CREW SHOULD GO.
TOMMY...
I'LL BE FINE. I'M WITH DONOVAN! WHAT COULD POSSIBLY GO WRONG?
I'M STAYING WITH YOU.
HE ALWAYS MAKES IT, DOESN'T HE?
HE DOES... EVERY *SINGLE* TIME.

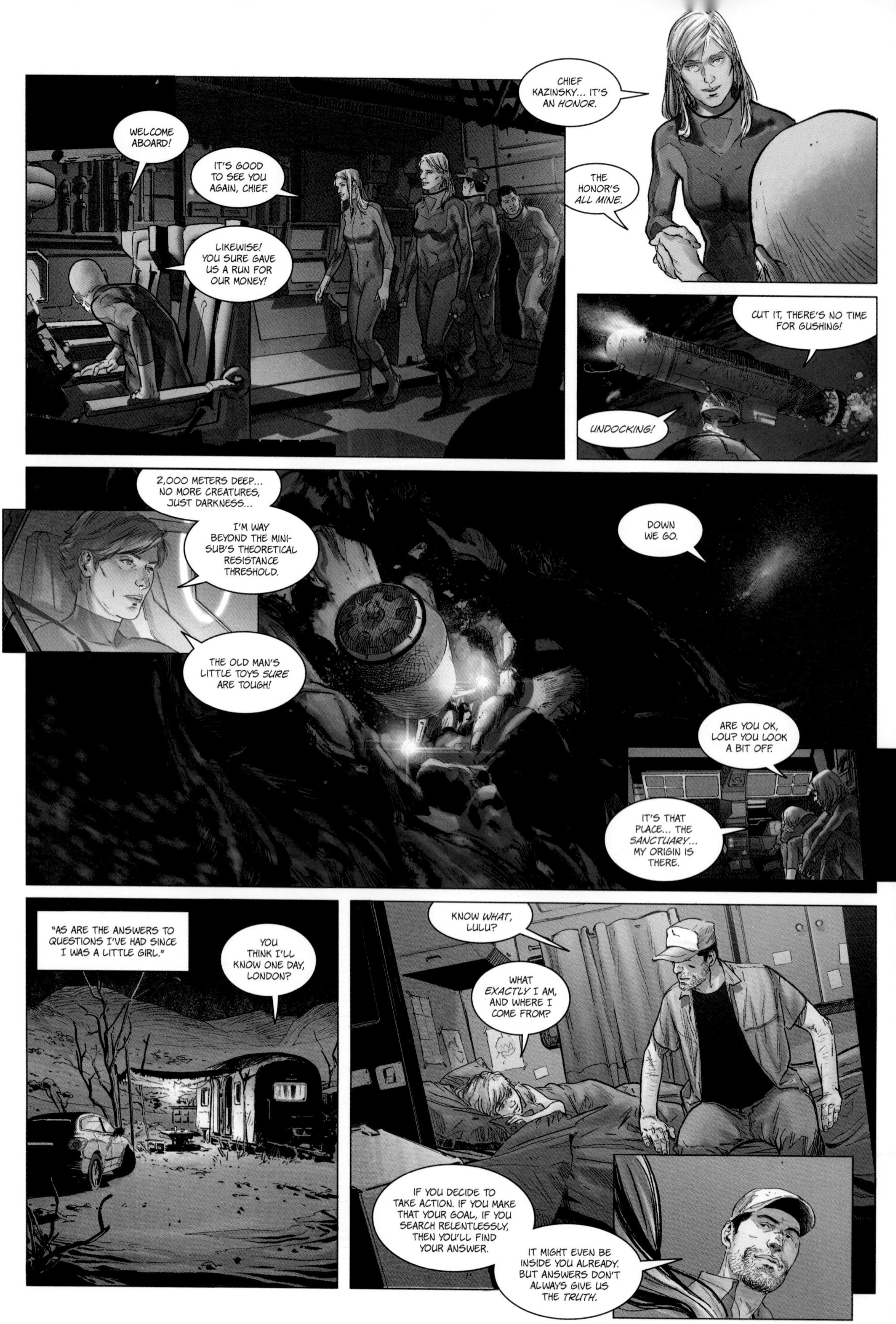
WELCOME ABOARD!
IT'S GOOD TO SEE YOU AGAIN, CHIEF.
LIKEWISE! YOU SURE GAVE US A RUN FOR OUR MONEY!
CHIEF KAZINSKY... IT'S AN *HONOR.*
THE HONOR'S *ALL MINE.*
CUT IT, THERE'S NO TIME FOR GUSHING!
UNDOCKING!
2,000 METERS DEEP... NO MORE CREATURES, JUST DARKNESS...
I'M WAY BEYOND THE MINI-SUB'S THEORETICAL RESISTANCE THRESHOLD.
THE OLD MAN'S LITTLE TOYS *SURE* ARE TOUGH!
DOWN WE GO.
ARE YOU OK, LOU? YOU LOOK A BIT OFF.
IT'S THAT PLACE... THE *SANCTUARY*... MY ORIGIN IS THERE.
"AS ARE THE ANSWERS TO QUESTIONS I'VE HAD SINCE I WAS A LITTLE GIRL."
YOU THINK I'LL KNOW ONE DAY, LONDON?
KNOW *WHAT,* LULU?
WHAT *EXACTLY* I AM, AND WHERE I COME FROM?
IF YOU DECIDE TO TAKE ACTION. IF YOU MAKE THAT YOUR GOAL, IF YOU SEARCH RELENTLESSLY, THEN YOU'LL FIND YOUR ANSWER.
IT MIGHT EVEN BE INSIDE YOU ALREADY. BUT ANSWERS DON'T ALWAYS GIVE US THE *TRUTH.*

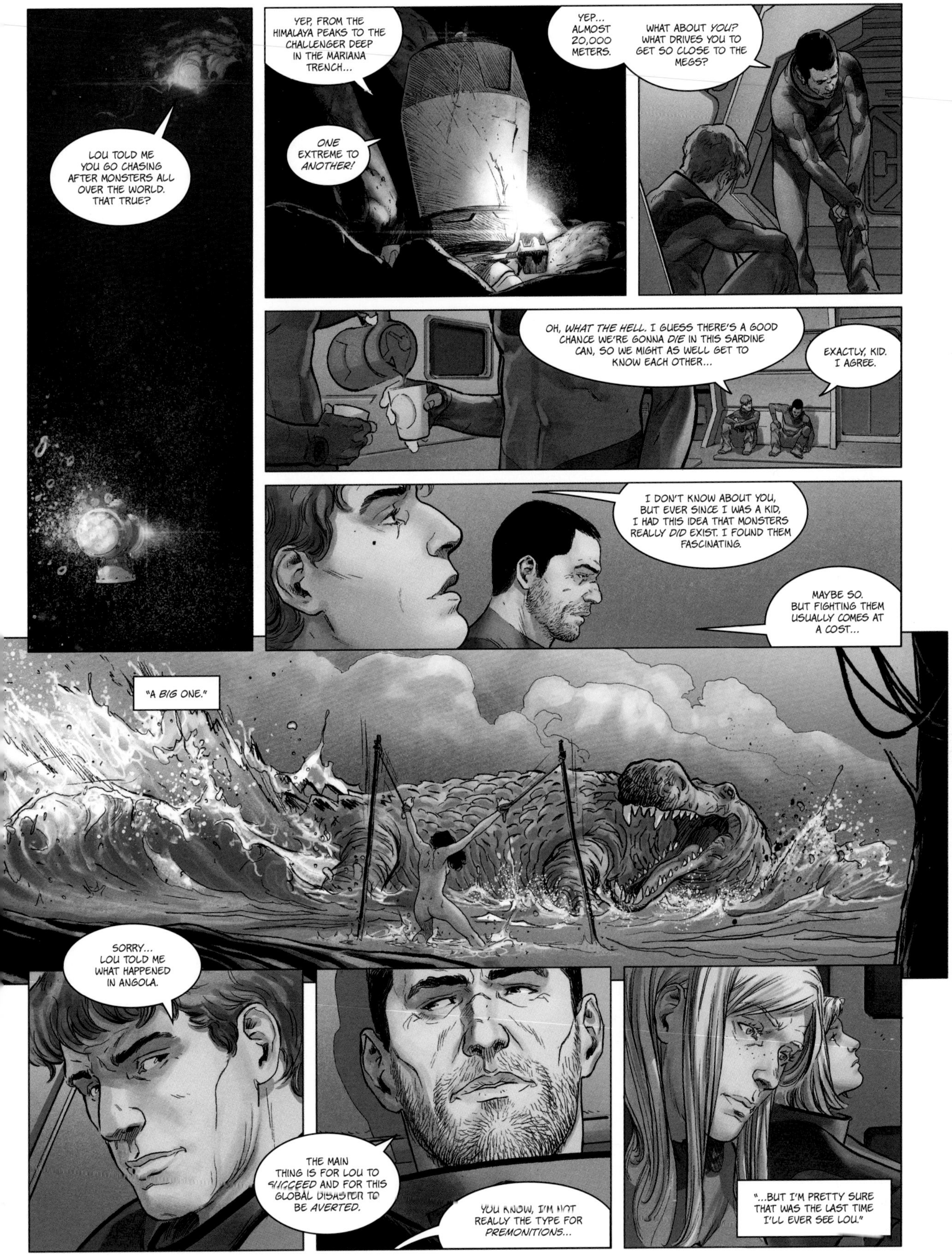
LOU TOLD ME YOU GO CHASING AFTER MONSTERS ALL OVER THE WORLD. THAT TRUE?
YEP, FROM THE HIMALAYA PEAKS TO THE CHALLENGER DEEP IN THE MARIANA TRENCH...
ONE EXTREME TO *ANOTHER!*
YEP... ALMOST 20,000 METERS.
WHAT ABOUT *YOU?* WHAT DRIVES YOU TO GET SO CLOSE TO THE MEGS?
OH, *WHAT THE HELL.* I GUESS THERE'S A GOOD CHANCE WE'RE GONNA *DIE* IN THIS SARDINE CAN, SO WE MIGHT AS WELL GET TO KNOW EACH OTHER...
EXACTLY, KID. I AGREE.
I DON'T KNOW ABOUT YOU, BUT EVER SINCE I WAS A KID, I HAD THIS IDEA THAT MONSTERS REALLY *DID* EXIST. I FOUND THEM FASCINATING.
MAYBE SO. BUT FIGHTING THEM USUALLY COMES AT A COST...
"A *BIG* ONE."
SORRY... LOU TOLD ME WHAT HAPPENED IN ANGOLA.
THE MAIN THING IS FOR LOU TO *SUCCEED* AND FOR THIS GLOBAL DISASTER TO BE *AVERTED.*
YOU KNOW, I'M NOT REALLY THE TYPE FOR *PREMONITIONS*...
"...BUT I'M PRETTY SURE THAT WAS THE LAST TIME I'LL EVER SEE LOU."

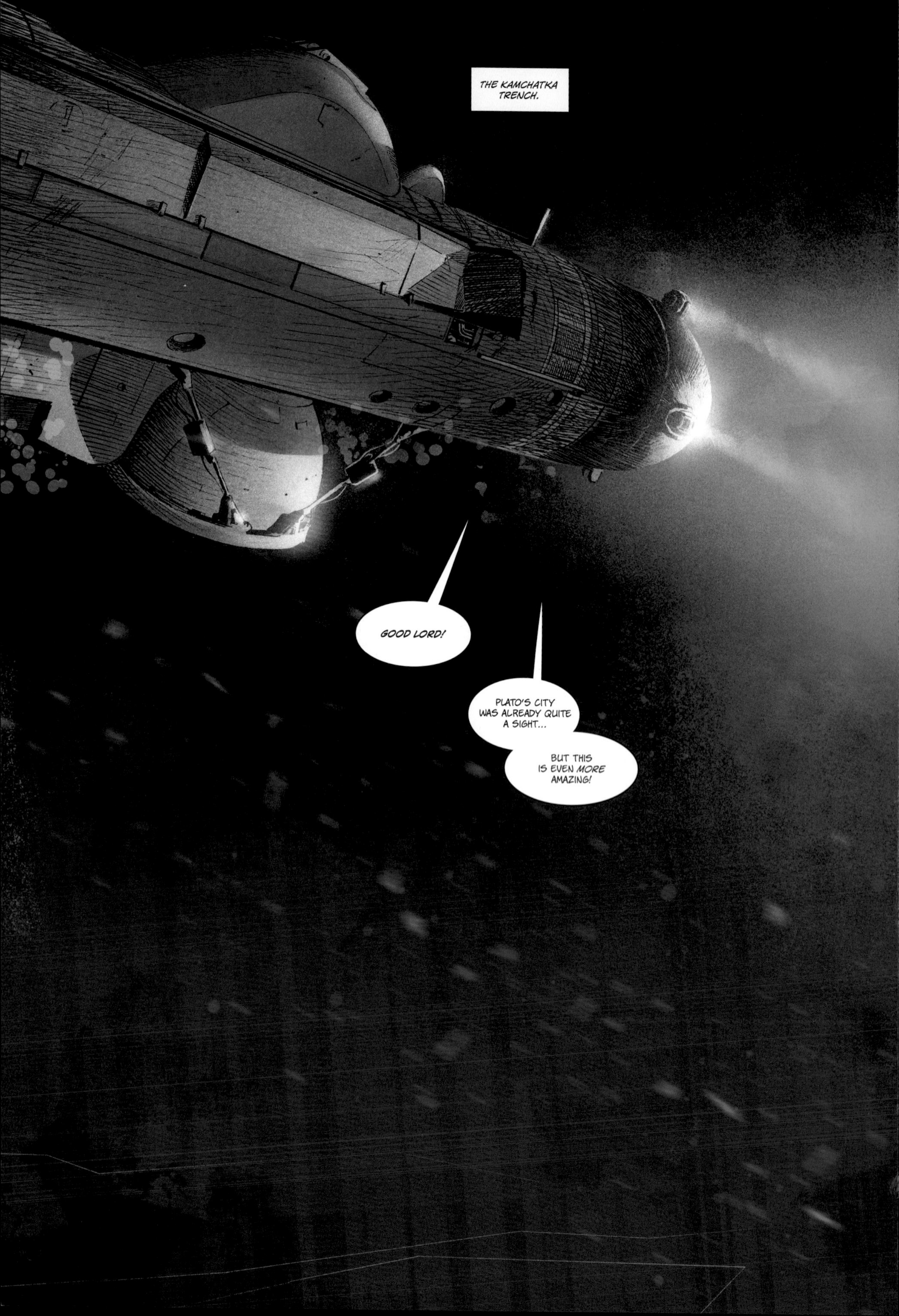
THE KAMCHATKA TRENCH.
GOOD LORD!
PLATO'S CITY WAS ALREADY QUITE A SIGHT...
BUT THIS IS EVEN *MORE* AMAZING!

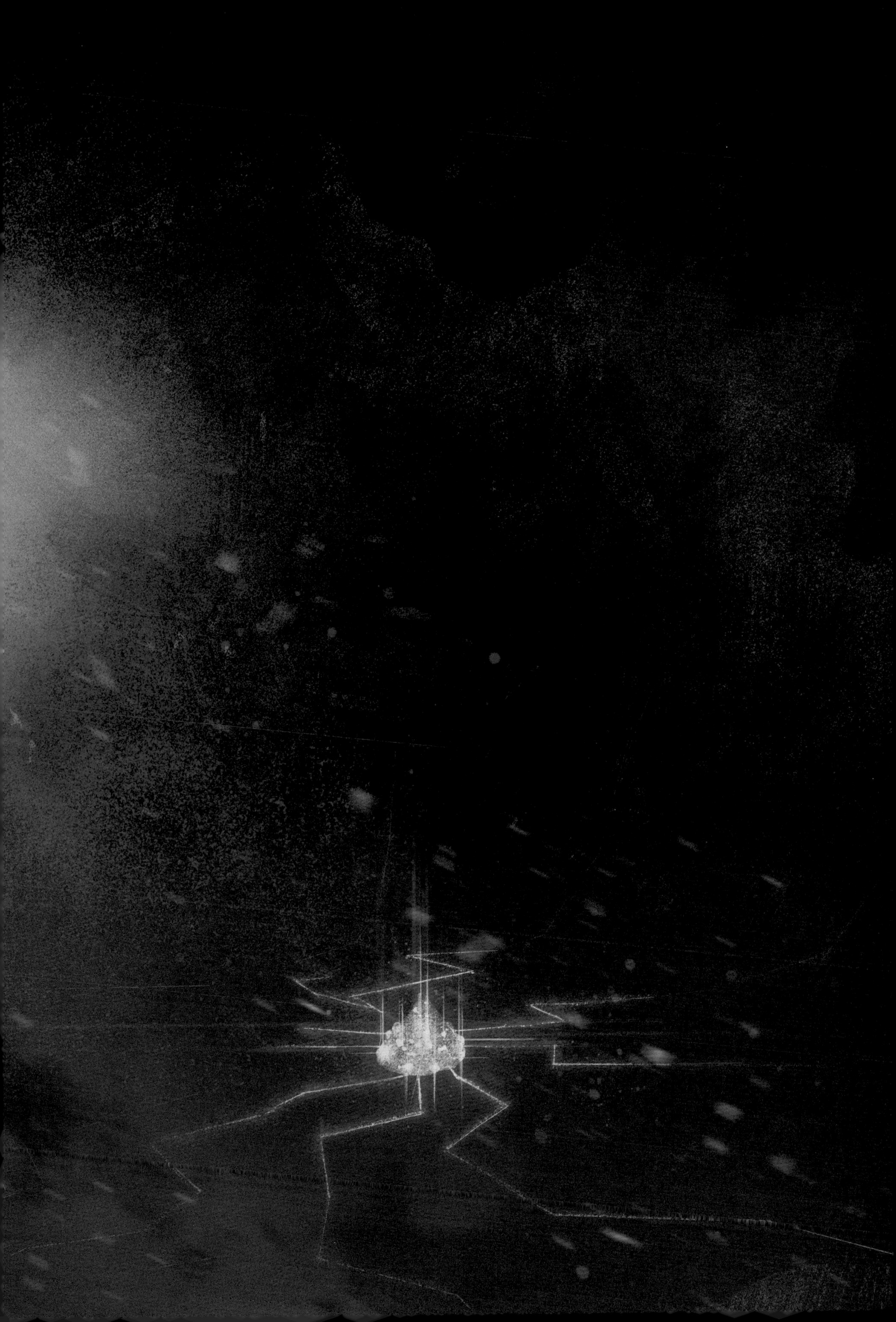

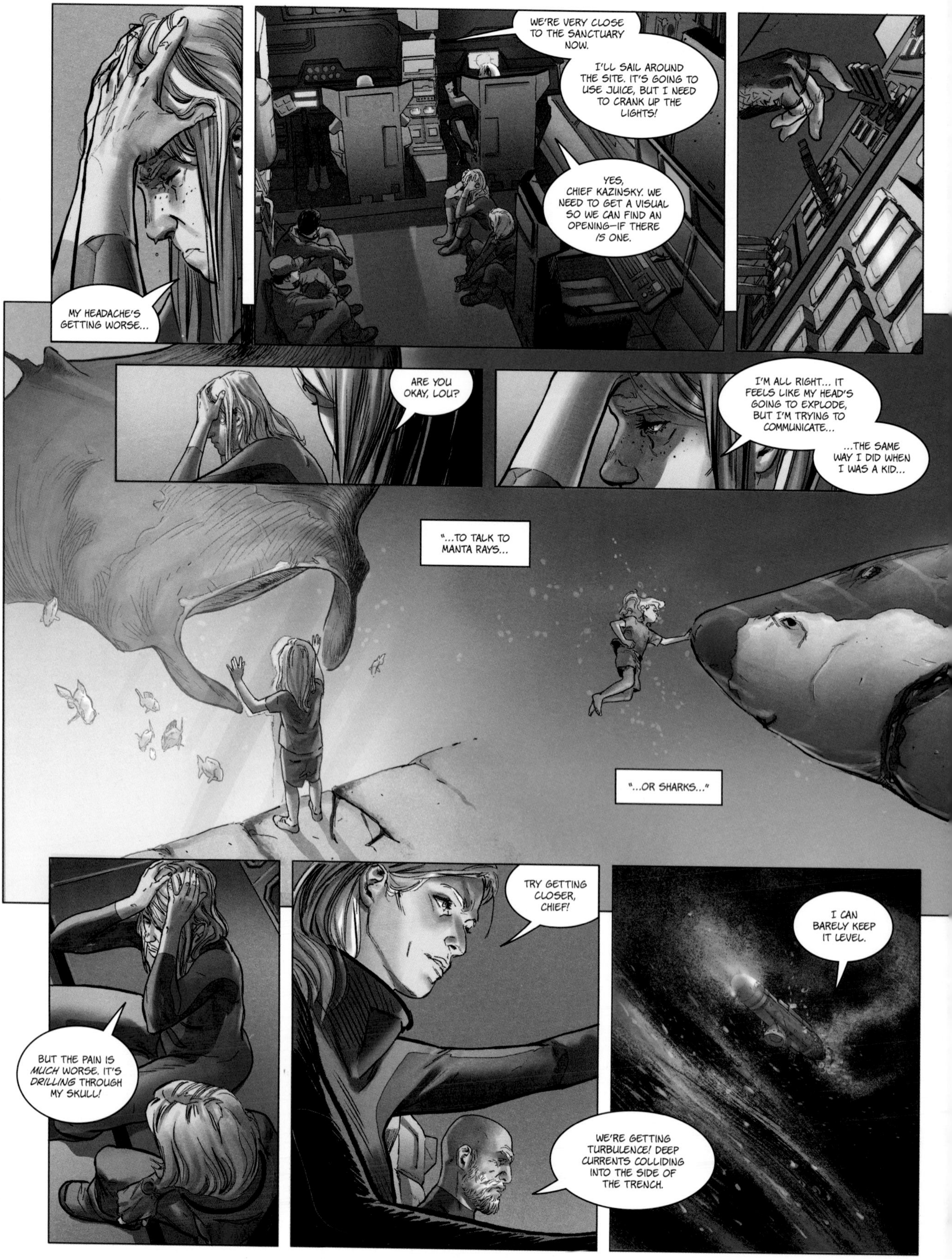

WE'RE VERY CLOSE TO THE SANCTUARY NOW.
I'LL SAIL AROUND THE SITE. IT'S GOING TO USE JUICE, BUT I NEED TO CRANK UP THE LIGHTS!
YES, CHIEF KAZINSKY. WE NEED TO GET A VISUAL SO WE CAN FIND AN OPENING—IF THERE IS ONE.
MY HEADACHE'S GETTING WORSE...
ARE YOU OKAY, LOU?
I'M ALL RIGHT... IT FEELS LIKE MY HEAD'S GOING TO EXPLODE, BUT I'M TRYING TO COMMUNICATE...
...THE SAME WAY I DID WHEN I WAS A KID...
"...TO TALK TO MANTA RAYS...
"...OR SHARKS..."
BUT THE PAIN IS MUCH WORSE. IT'S DRILLING THROUGH MY SKULL!
TRY GETTING CLOSER, CHIEF!
WE'RE GETTING TURBULENCE! DEEP CURRENTS COLLIDING INTO THE SIDE OF THE TRENCH.
I CAN BARELY KEEP IT LEVEL.

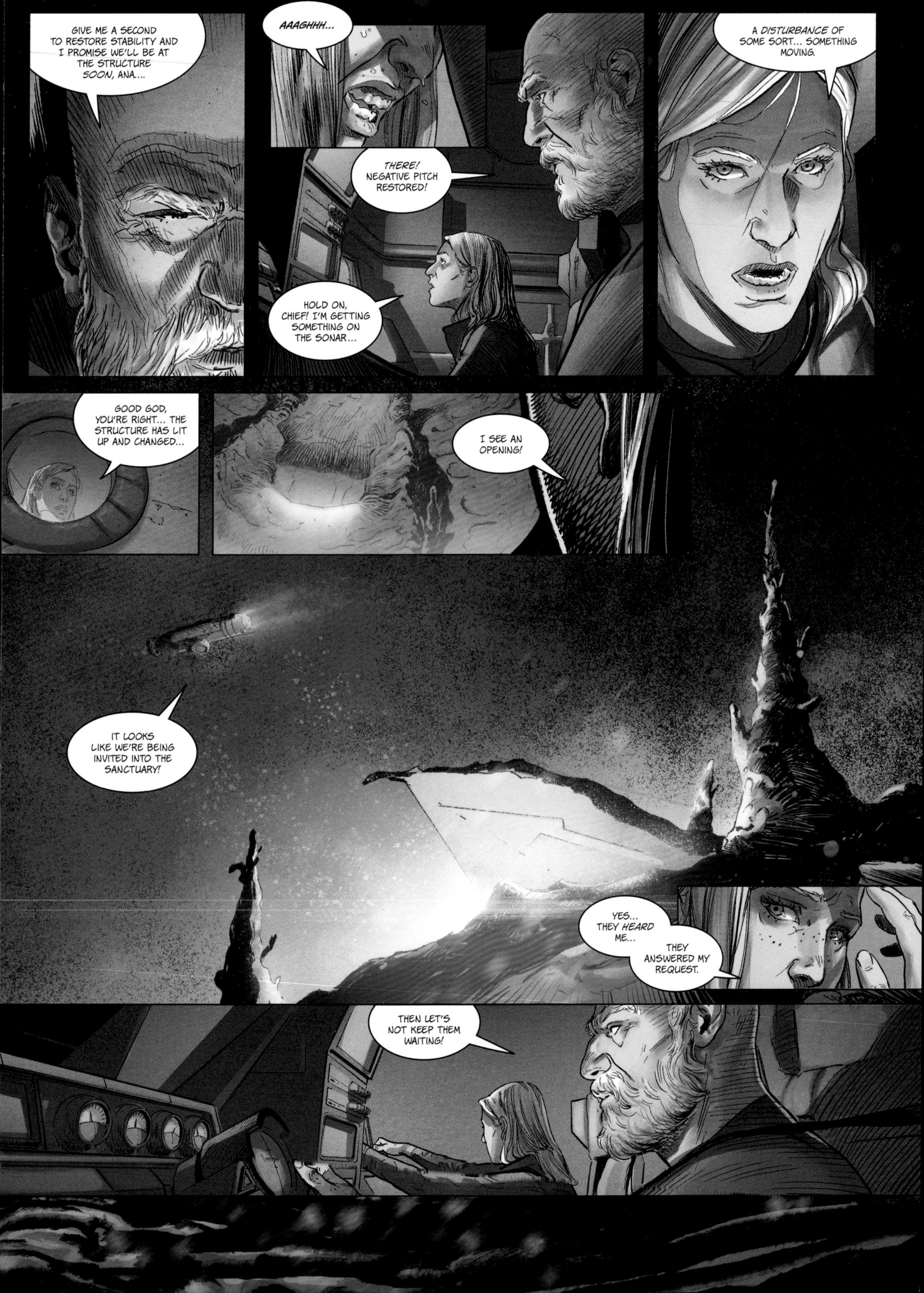
GIVE ME A SECOND TO RESTORE STABILITY AND I PROMISE WE'LL BE AT THE STRUCTURE SOON, ANA...
AAAGHHH...
THERE! NEGATIVE PITCH RESTORED!
HOLD ON, CHIEF! I'M GETTING SOMETHING ON THE SONAR...
A DISTURBANCE OF SOME SORT... SOMETHING MOVING.
GOOD GOD, YOU'RE RIGHT... THE STRUCTURE HAS LIT UP AND CHANGED...
I SEE AN OPENING!
IT LOOKS LIKE WE'RE BEING INVITED INTO THE SANCTUARY!
YES... THEY HEARD ME...
THEY ANSWERED MY REQUEST.
THEN LET'S NOT KEEP THEM WAITING!

INITIATING DESCENT TOWARDS THE OPENING...

WE'RE IN!

ANOTHER ECHO ON THE SONAR!

MAKE A 180, CHIEF! SOMETHING CHANGED AFTER WE ENTERED...

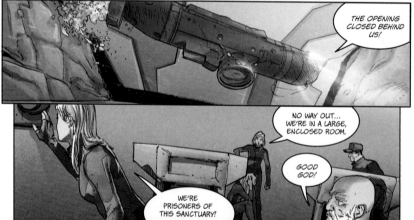

THE OPENING CLOSED BEHIND US!

NO WAY OUT... WE'RE IN A LARGE, ENCLOSED ROOM.

GOOD GOD!

WE'RE PRISONERS OF THIS SANCTUARY!

I'M GOING OUT THERE!

WHAT? BUT THERE ARE NO DIVE SUITS ABOARD THE D.S.R.V.!

NO BIGGIE... ALL I NEED IS A SWISS POCKETKNIFE.

CHIEF?

HERE YOU GO.

THANKS, CHIEF!

250

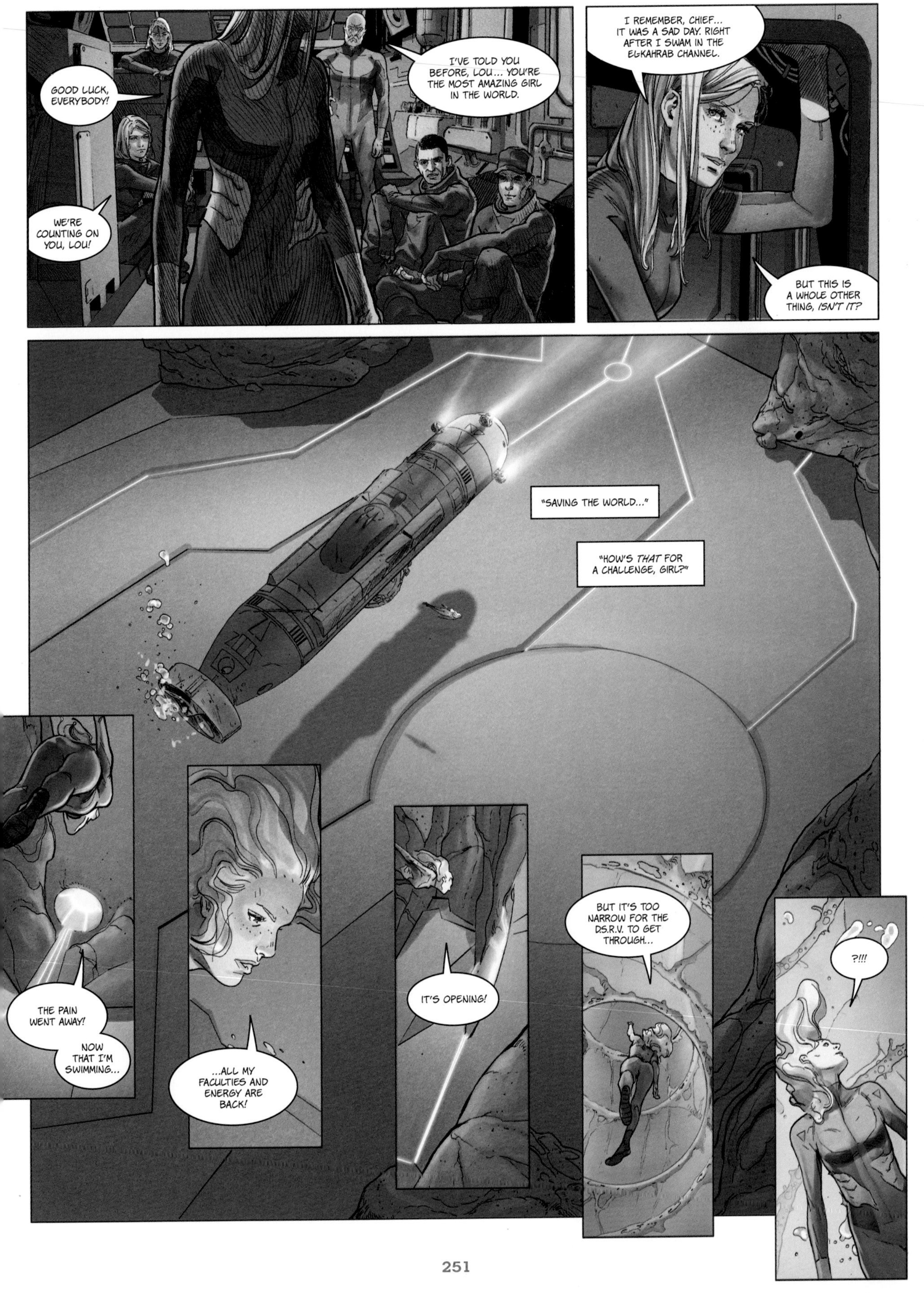
GOOD LUCK, EVERYBODY!
WE'RE COUNTING ON YOU, LOU!
I'VE TOLD YOU BEFORE, LOU... YOU'RE THE MOST AMAZING GIRL IN THE WORLD.
I REMEMBER, CHIEF... IT WAS A SAD DAY. RIGHT AFTER I SWAM IN THE EL-KAHRAB CHANNEL.
BUT THIS IS A WHOLE OTHER THING, *ISN'T IT?*
"SAVING THE WORLD..."
"HOW'S *THAT* FOR A CHALLENGE, GIRL?"
THE PAIN WENT AWAY!
NOW THAT I'M SWIMMING...
...ALL MY FACULTIES AND ENERGY ARE BACK!
IT'S OPENING!
BUT IT'S TOO NARROW FOR THE D.S.R.V. TO GET THROUGH...
?!!!

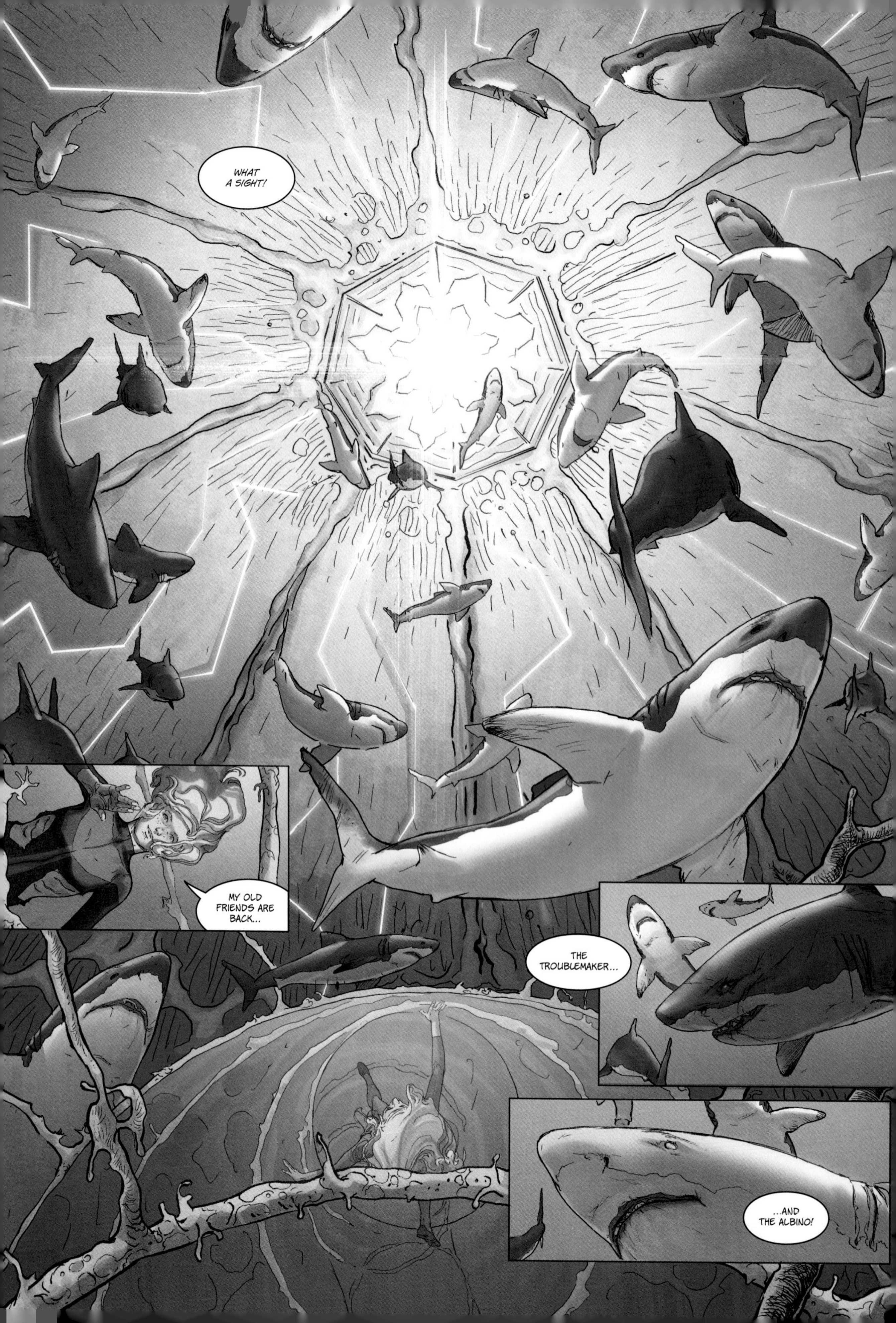
WHAT A SIGHT!
MY OLD FRIENDS ARE BACK...
THE TROUBLEMAKER...
...AND THE ALBINO!

LOU'S NOT BACK. SHE MUST HAVE FOUND A PASSAGEWAY.

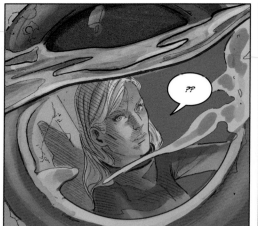

??

IT LOOKS LIKE... THE WATER IN THE ROOM IS DRAINING!

YEP! WE'RE FLOATING DOWNWARDS!

NOW WE'RE ON SOLID GROUND.

!!!

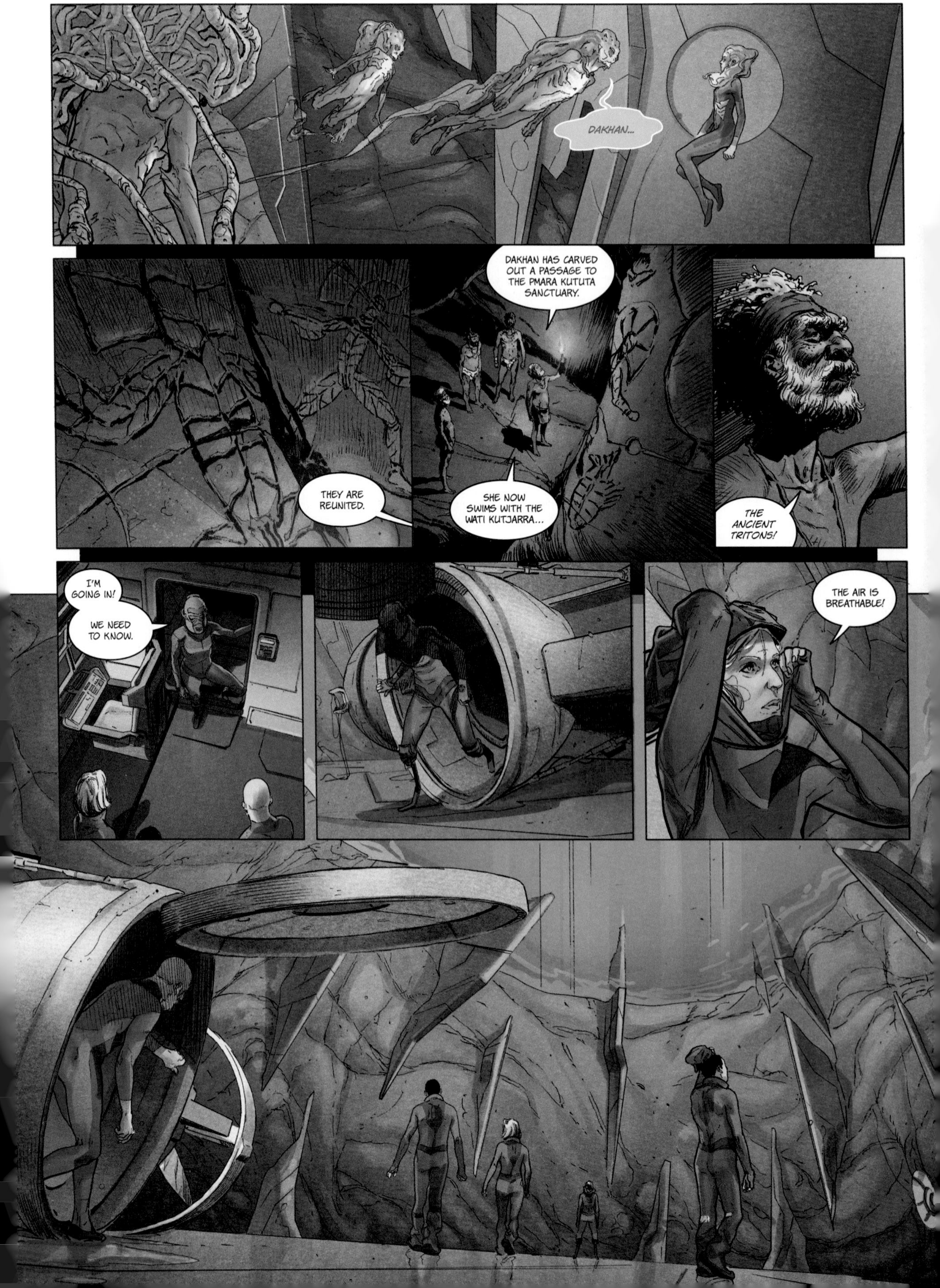
DAKHAN...
THEY ARE REUNITED.
DAKHAN HAS CARVED OUT A PASSAGE TO THE PMARA KUTUTA SANCTUARY.
SHE NOW SWIMS WITH THE WATI KUTJARRA...
THE ANCIENT TRITONS!
I'M GOING IN!
WE NEED TO KNOW.
THE AIR IS BREATHABLE!

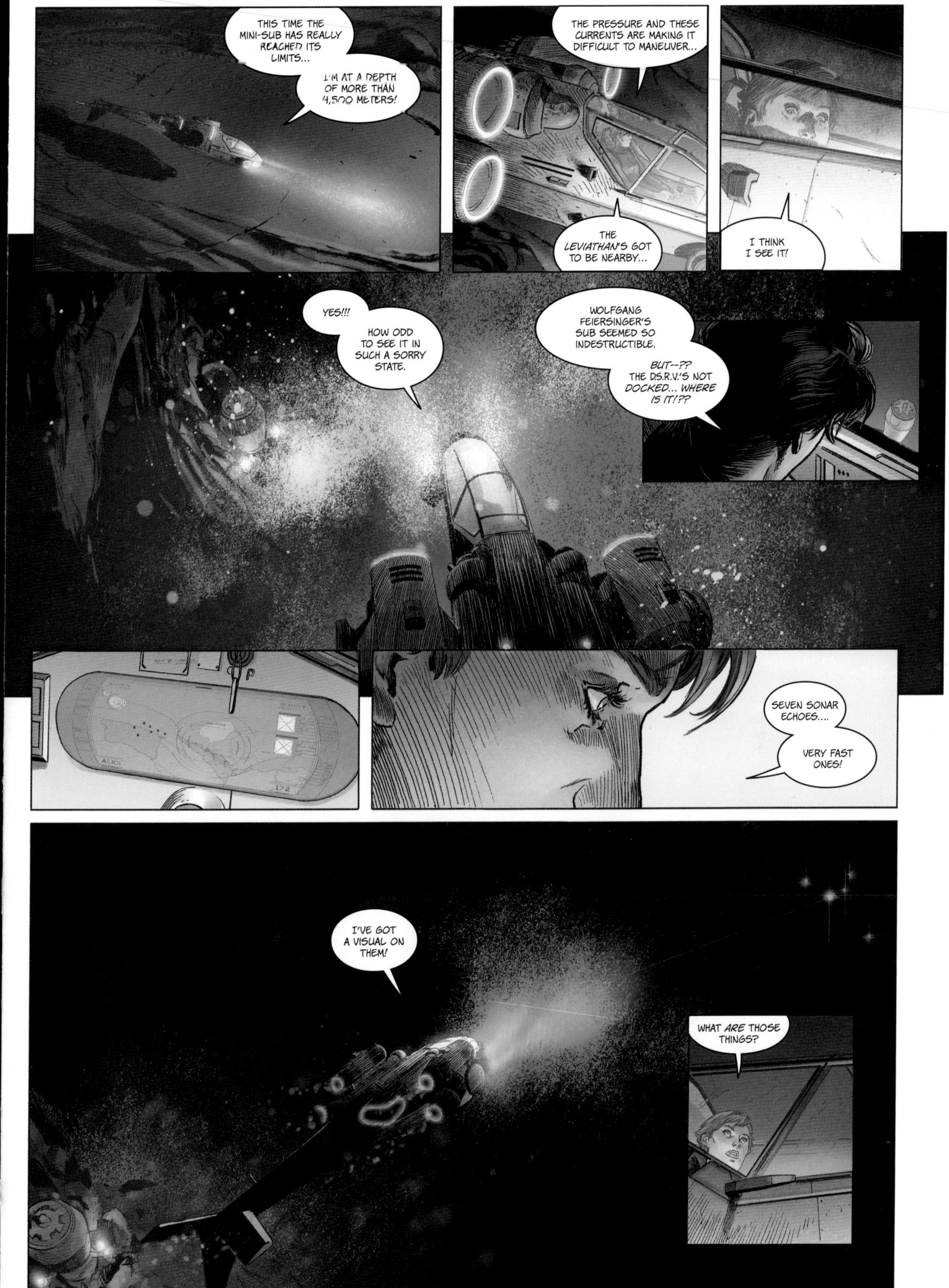
THIS TIME THE MINI-SUB HAS REALLY REACHED ITS LIMITS...
I'M AT A DEPTH OF MORE THAN 4,500 METERS!
THE PRESSURE AND THESE CURRENTS ARE MAKING IT DIFFICULT TO MANEUVER...
THE LEVIATHAN'S GOT TO BE NEARBY...
I THINK I SEE IT!
YES!!!
HOW ODD TO SEE IT IN SUCH A SORRY STATE.
WOLFGANG FEIERSINGER'S SUB SEEMED SO INDESTRUCTIBLE.
BUT--?? THE D.S.R.V.'S NOT DOCKED... WHERE IS IT!??
SEVEN SONAR ECHOES....
VERY FAST ONES!
I'VE GOT A VISUAL ON THEM!
WHAT ARE THOSE THINGS?

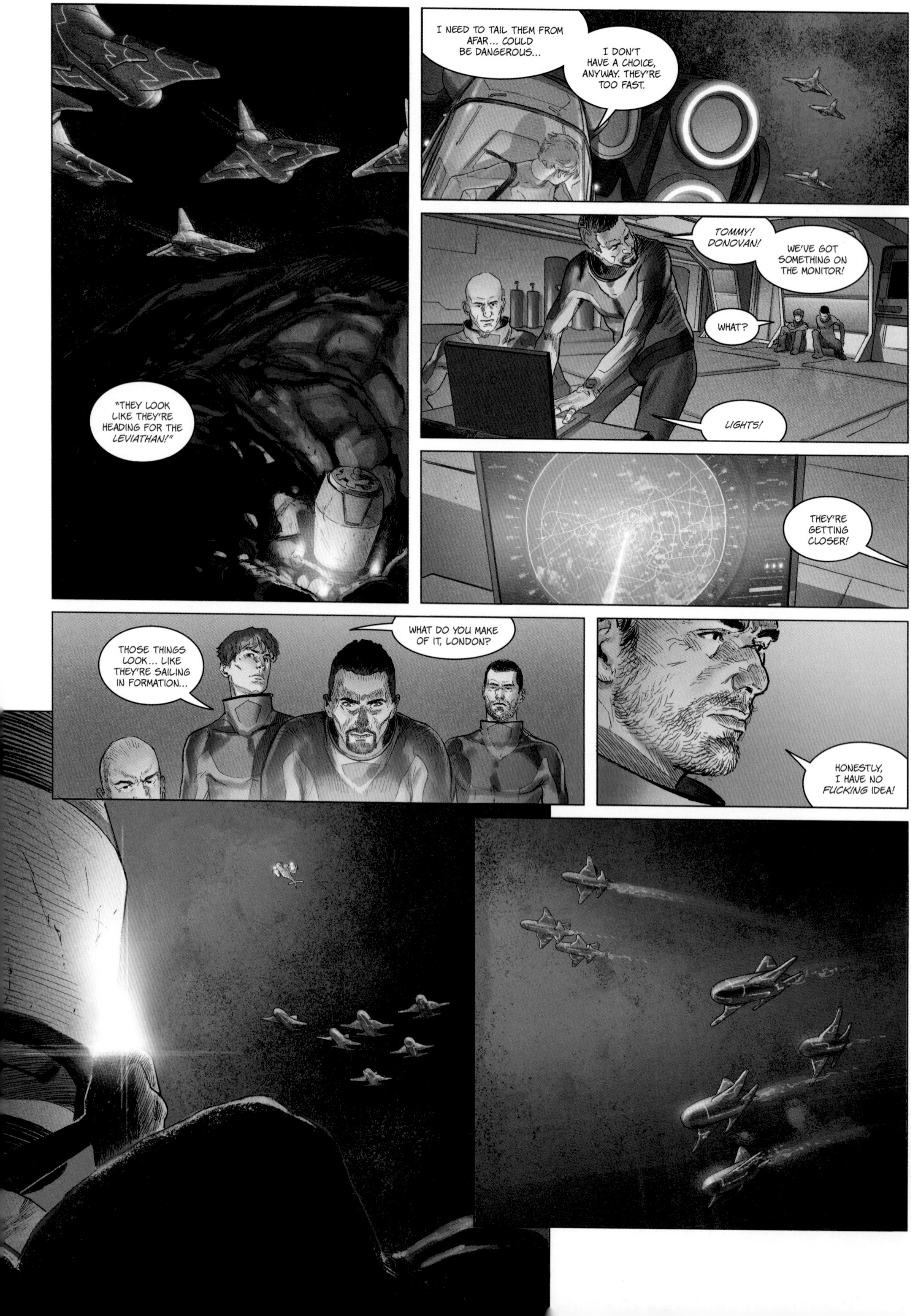
"THEY LOOK LIKE THEY'RE HEADING FOR THE *LEVIATHAN!*"
I NEED TO TAIL THEM FROM AFAR... COULD BE DANGEROUS...
I DON'T HAVE A CHOICE, ANYWAY. THEY'RE TOO FAST.
TOMMY! DONOVAN!
WE'VE GOT SOMETHING ON THE MONITOR!
WHAT?
LIGHTS!
THEY'RE GETTING CLOSER!
THOSE THINGS LOOK... LIKE THEY'RE SAILING IN FORMATION...
WHAT DO YOU MAKE OF IT, LONDON?
HONESTLY, I HAVE NO *FUCKING* IDEA!

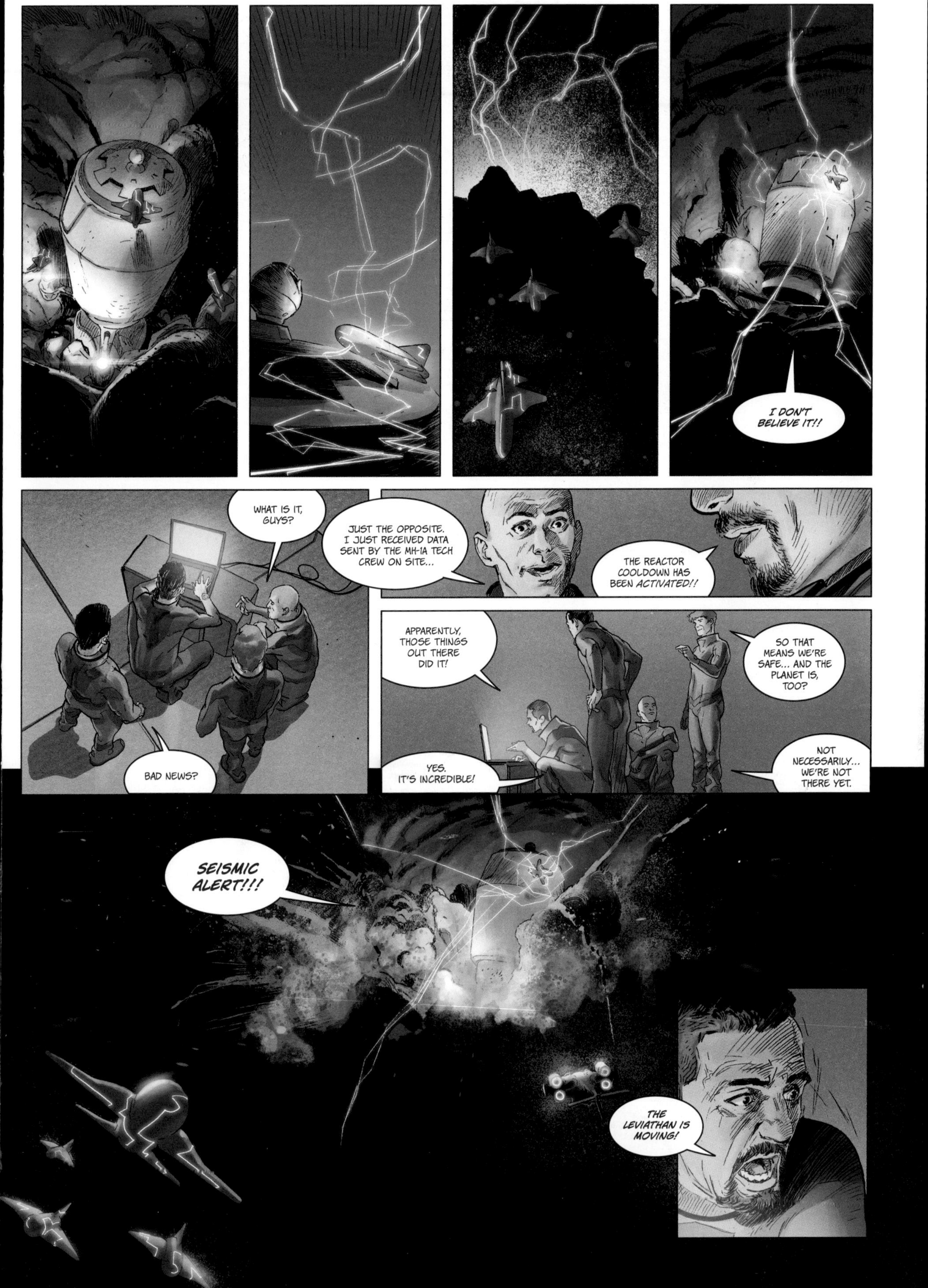
I DON'T BELIEVE IT!!
WHAT IS IT, GUYS?
BAD NEWS?
JUST THE OPPOSITE. I JUST RECEIVED DATA SENT BY THE MH-1A TECH CREW ON SITE...
THE REACTOR COOLDOWN HAS BEEN ACTIVATED!!
APPARENTLY, THOSE THINGS OUT THERE DID IT!
YES. IT'S INCREDIBLE!
SO THAT MEANS WE'RE SAFE... AND THE PLANET IS, TOO?
NOT NECESSARILY... WE'RE NOT THERE YET.
SEISMIC ALERT!!!
THE LEVIATHAN IS MOVING!

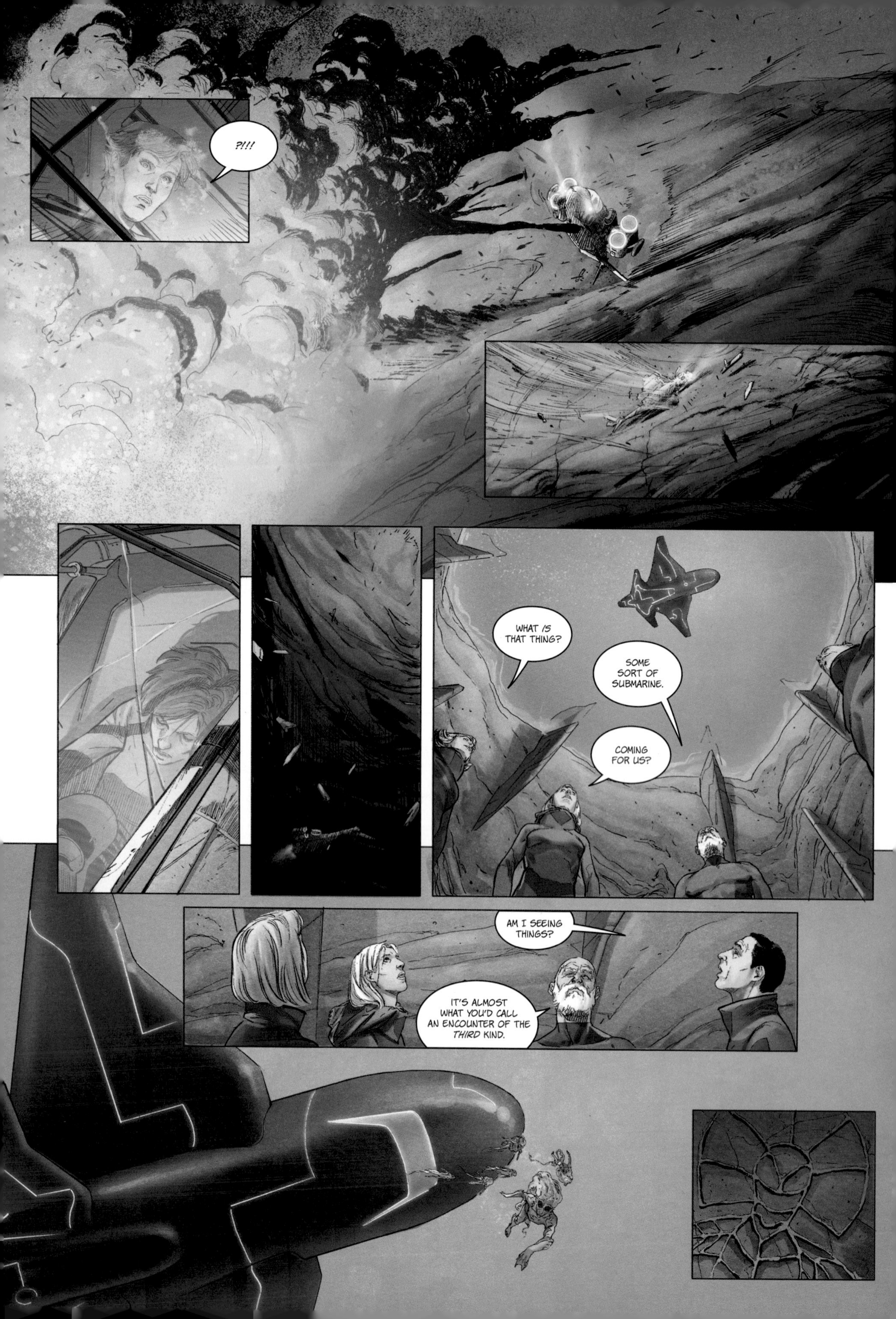
?!!!
WHAT *IS* THAT THING?
SOME SORT OF SUBMARINE.
COMING FOR US?
AM I SEEING THINGS?
IT'S ALMOST WHAT YOU'D CALL AN ENCOUNTER OF THE *THIRD* KIND.

WE'RE MOVING!

YEAH! WE'RE ASCENDING!

THE FEED FROM THE OUTSIDE CAMERAS SHOWS THAT TWO MACHINES ARE DOCKED ON THE *LEVIATHAN*...

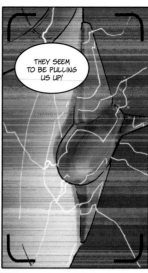

THEY SEEM TO BE PULLING US UP!

CAN WE RESTART THE REACTOR TO TEAR OURSELVES AWAY?

WHERE ARE THEY TAKING US?

NO, IT'S WAY TOO EARLY!

THE COOLDOWN WAS ONLY JUST ACTIVATED.

LOOKS LIKE WE'RE HEADING FOR THAT CAVITY IN THE WALL OF THE TRENCH, THERE...

A DOCKING SIGNAL!

SOMETHING'S LOCKED ONTO OUR AIRLOCK!

I THINK I GET IT... THEY'RE ASKING US TO COME OUT.

GIVEN THE SITUATION, I SUPPOSE WE HAVE NO OTHER CHOICE BUT TO TRUST THEM.

TELL THE OTHER CREW MEMBERS TO LEAVE THEIR POSTS. EVERYBODY UP TO THE DOCKING HATCH!

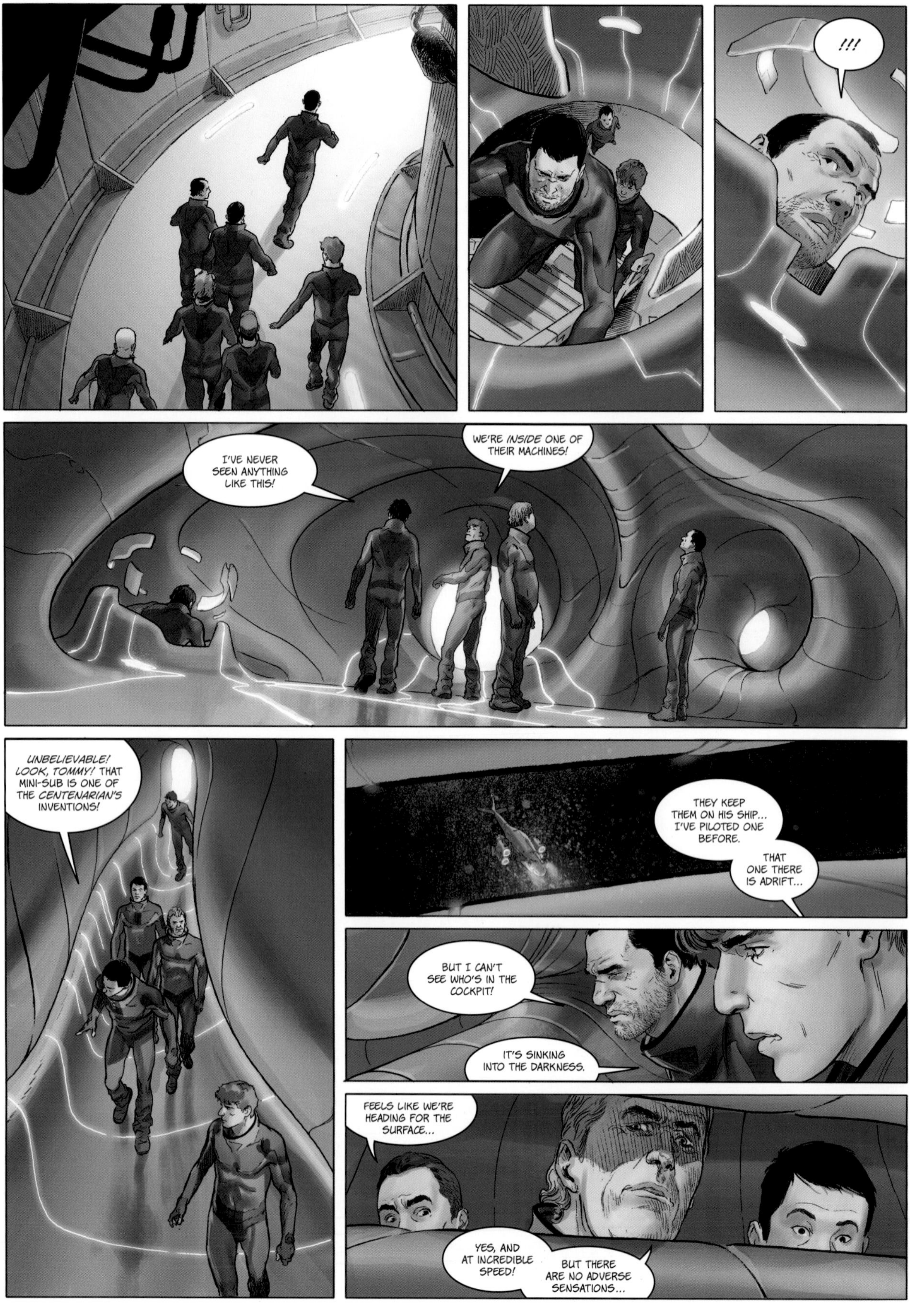
!!!
I'VE NEVER SEEN ANYTHING LIKE THIS!
WE'RE *INSIDE* ONE OF THEIR MACHINES!
UNBELIEVABLE! LOOK, TOMMY! THAT MINI-SUB IS ONE OF THE *CENTENARIAN'S* INVENTIONS!
THEY KEEP THEM ON HIS SHIP... I'VE PILOTED ONE BEFORE.
THAT ONE THERE IS ADRIFT...
BUT I CAN'T SEE WHO'S IN THE COCKPIT!
IT'S SINKING INTO THE DARKNESS.
FEELS LIKE WE'RE HEADING FOR THE SURFACE...
YES, AND AT INCREDIBLE SPEED!
BUT THERE ARE NO ADVERSE SENSATIONS...

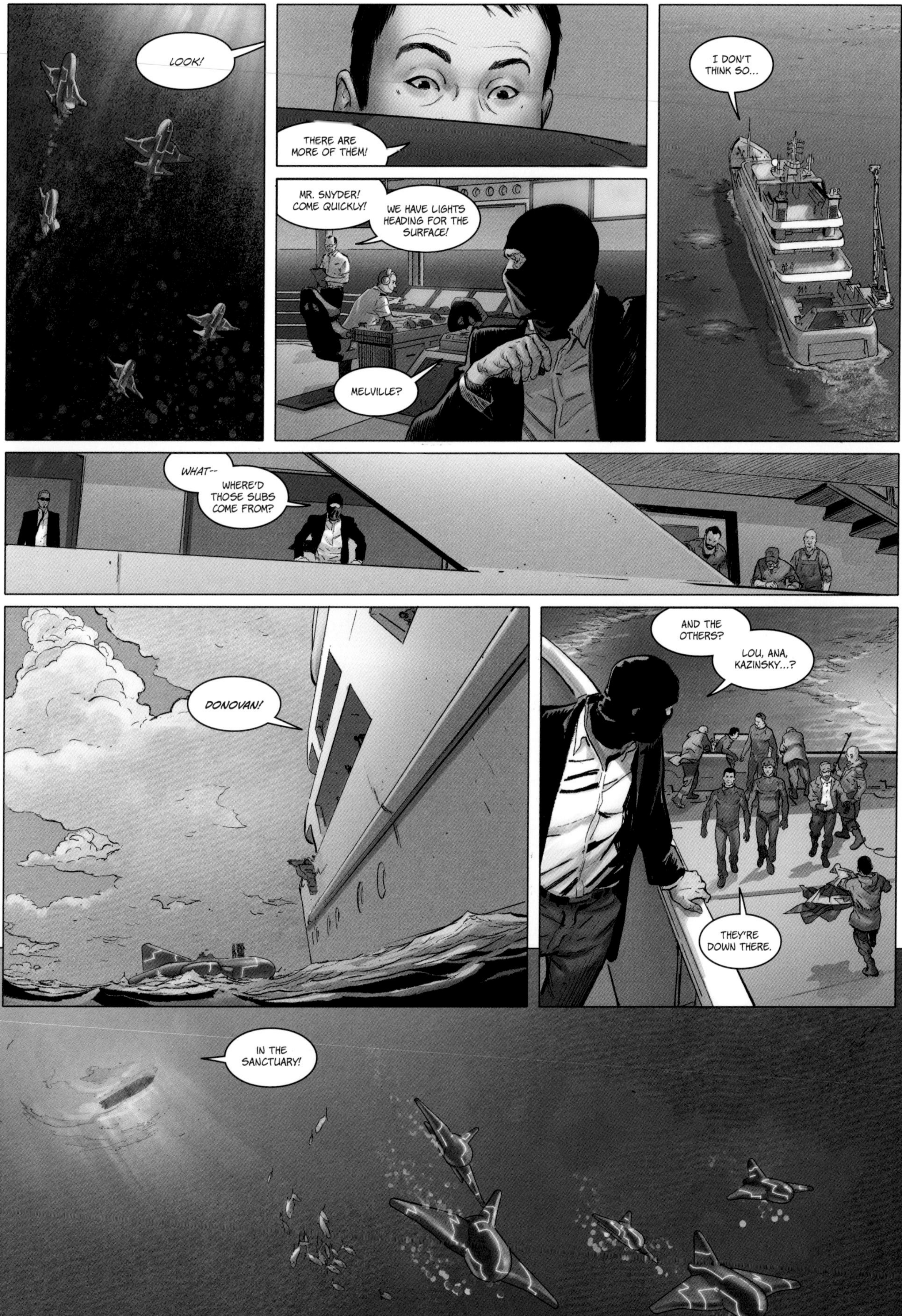
LOOK!
THERE ARE MORE OF THEM!
I DON'T THINK SO...
MR. SNYDER! COME QUICKLY!
WE HAVE LIGHTS HEADING FOR THE SURFACE!
MELVILLE?
WHAT--
WHERE'D THOSE SUBS COME FROM?
DONOVAN!
AND THE OTHERS?
LOU, ANA, KAZINSKY...?
THEY'RE DOWN THERE.
IN THE SANCTUARY!

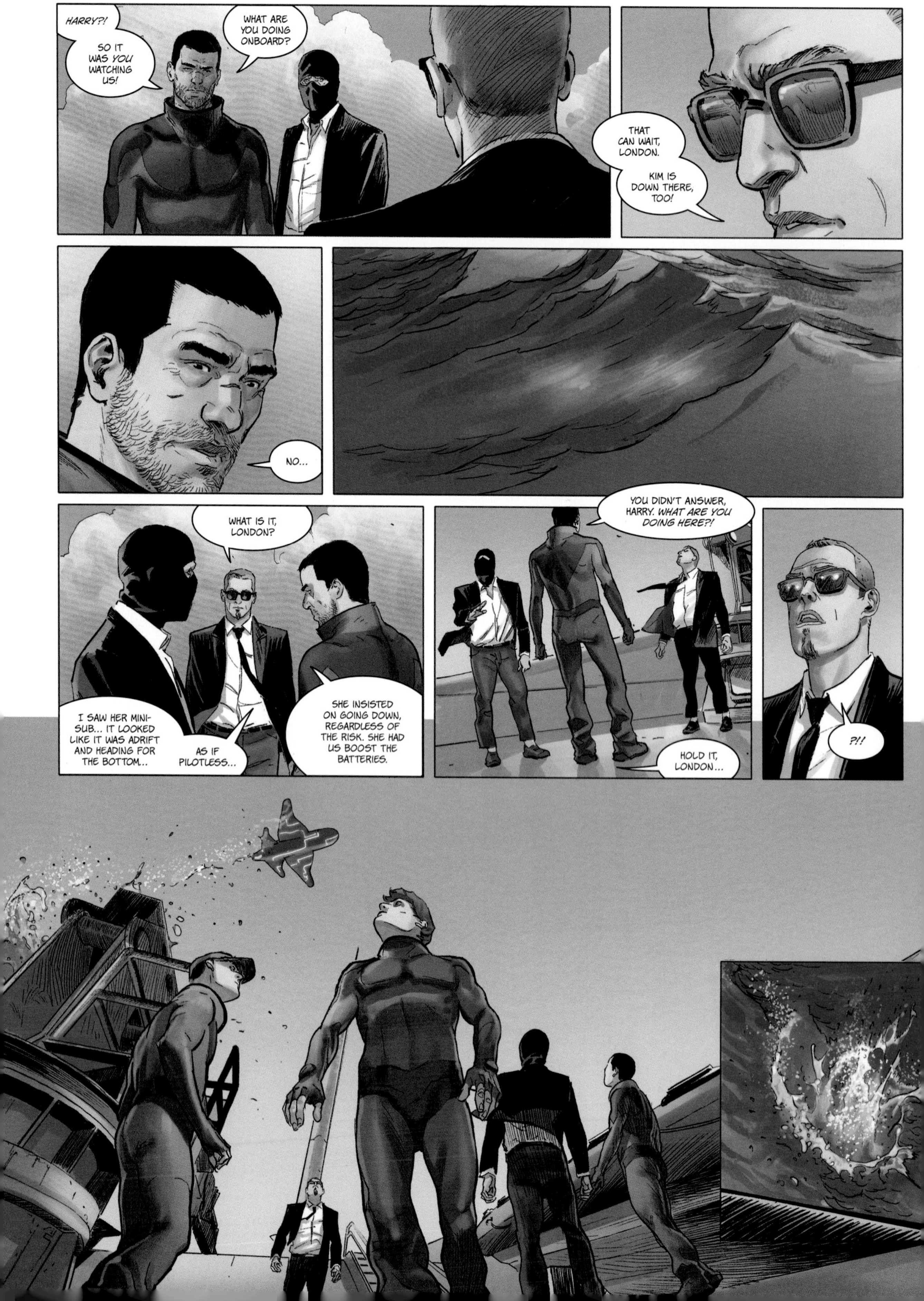
HARRY?!
SO IT WAS YOU WATCHING US!
WHAT ARE YOU DOING ONBOARD?
THAT CAN WAIT, LONDON.
KIM IS DOWN THERE, TOO!
NO...
WHAT IS IT, LONDON?
I SAW HER MINI-SUB... IT LOOKED LIKE IT WAS ADRIFT AND HEADING FOR THE BOTTOM...
AS IF PILOTLESS...
SHE INSISTED ON GOING DOWN, REGARDLESS OF THE RISK. SHE HAD US BOOST THE BATTERIES.
YOU DIDN'T ANSWER, HARRY. WHAT ARE YOU DOING HERE?!
HOLD IT, LONDON...
?!!

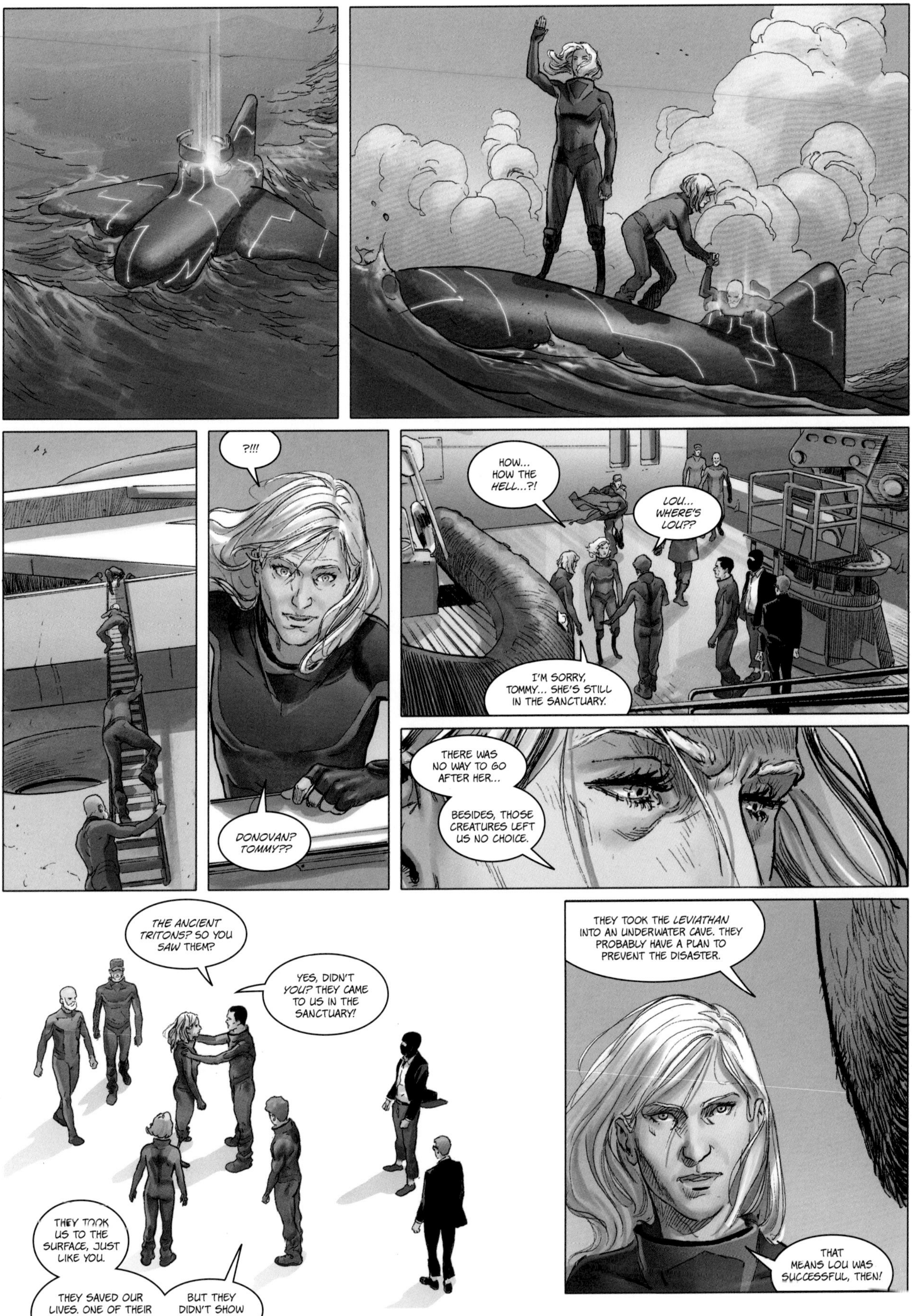
?!!!
DONOVAN? TOMMY??
HOW... HOW THE HELL...?!
LOU... WHERE'S LOU??
I'M SORRY, TOMMY... SHE'S STILL IN THE SANCTUARY.
THERE WAS NO WAY TO GO AFTER HER...
BESIDES, THOSE CREATURES LEFT US NO CHOICE.
THE ANCIENT TRITONS? SO YOU SAW THEM?
YES, DIDN'T YOU? THEY CAME TO US IN THE SANCTUARY!
THEY TOOK US TO THE SURFACE, JUST LIKE YOU.
THEY SAVED OUR LIVES. ONE OF THEIR VESSELS DOCKED ON THE LEVIATHAN.
BUT THEY DIDN'T SHOW THEMSELVES.
THEY TOOK THE LEVIATHAN INTO AN UNDERWATER CAVE. THEY PROBABLY HAVE A PLAN TO PREVENT THE DISASTER.
THAT MEANS LOU WAS SUCCESSFUL, THEN!

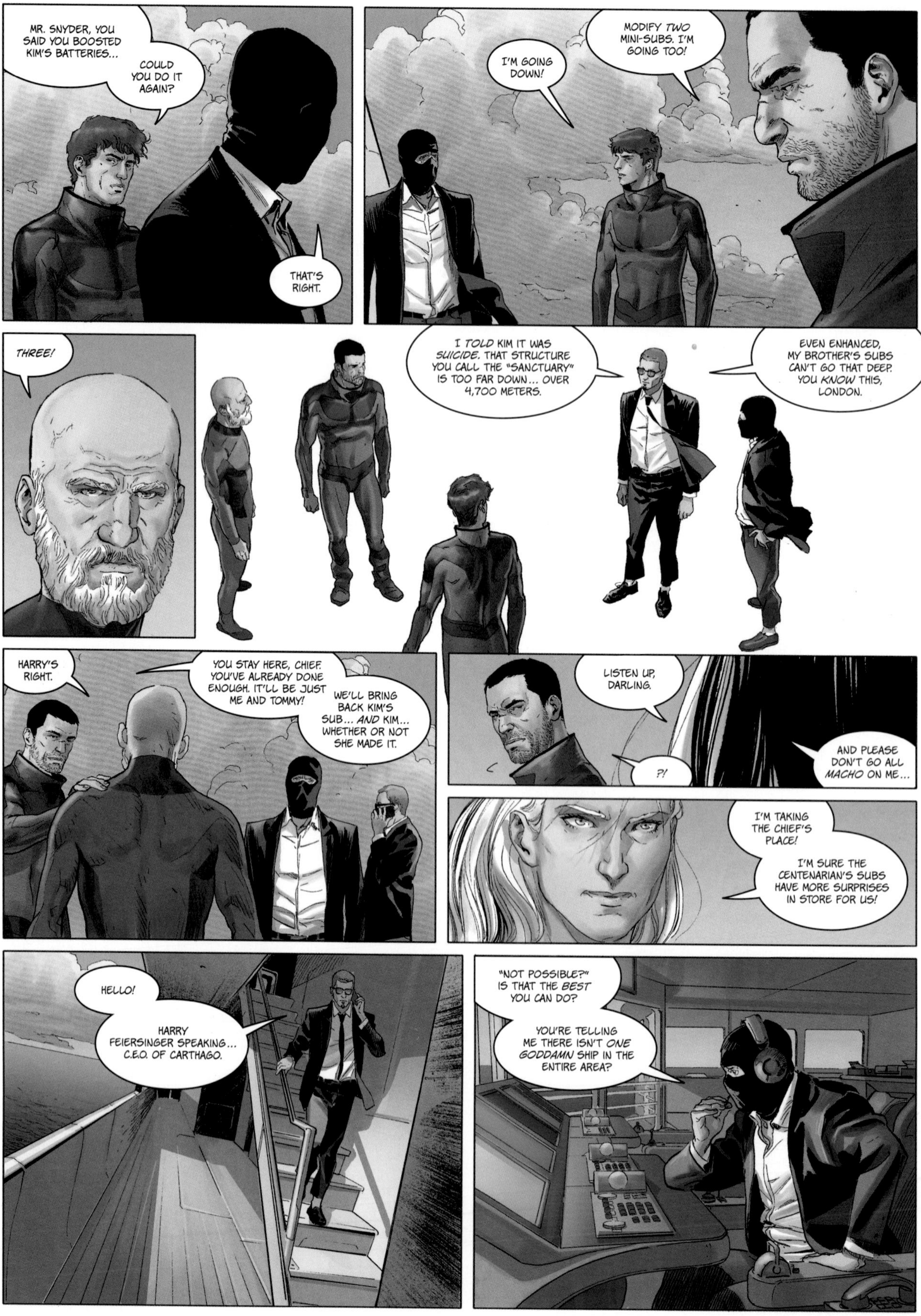
MR. SNYDER, YOU SAID YOU BOOSTED KIM'S BATTERIES...
COULD YOU DO IT AGAIN?
THAT'S RIGHT.
I'M GOING DOWN!
MODIFY *TWO* MINI-SUBS. I'M GOING TOO!
THREE!
I *TOLD* KIM IT WAS *SUICIDE*. THAT STRUCTURE YOU CALL THE "SANCTUARY" IS TOO FAR DOWN... OVER 4,700 METERS.
EVEN ENHANCED, MY BROTHER'S SUBS CAN'T GO THAT DEEP. YOU *KNOW* THIS, LONDON.
HARRY'S RIGHT.
YOU STAY HERE, CHIEF. YOU'VE ALREADY DONE ENOUGH. IT'LL BE JUST ME AND TOMMY!
WE'LL BRING BACK KIM'S SUB... *AND* KIM... WHETHER OR NOT SHE MADE IT.
LISTEN UP, DARLING.
?!
AND PLEASE DON'T GO ALL *MACHO* ON ME...
I'M TAKING THE CHIEF'S PLACE!
I'M SURE THE CENTENARIAN'S SUBS HAVE MORE SURPRISES IN STORE FOR US!
HELLO!
HARRY FEIERSINGER SPEAKING... C.E.O. OF CARTHAGO.
"NOT POSSIBLE?" IS THAT THE *BEST* YOU CAN DO?
YOU'RE TELLING ME THERE ISN'T *ONE GODDAMN* SHIP IN THE ENTIRE AREA?

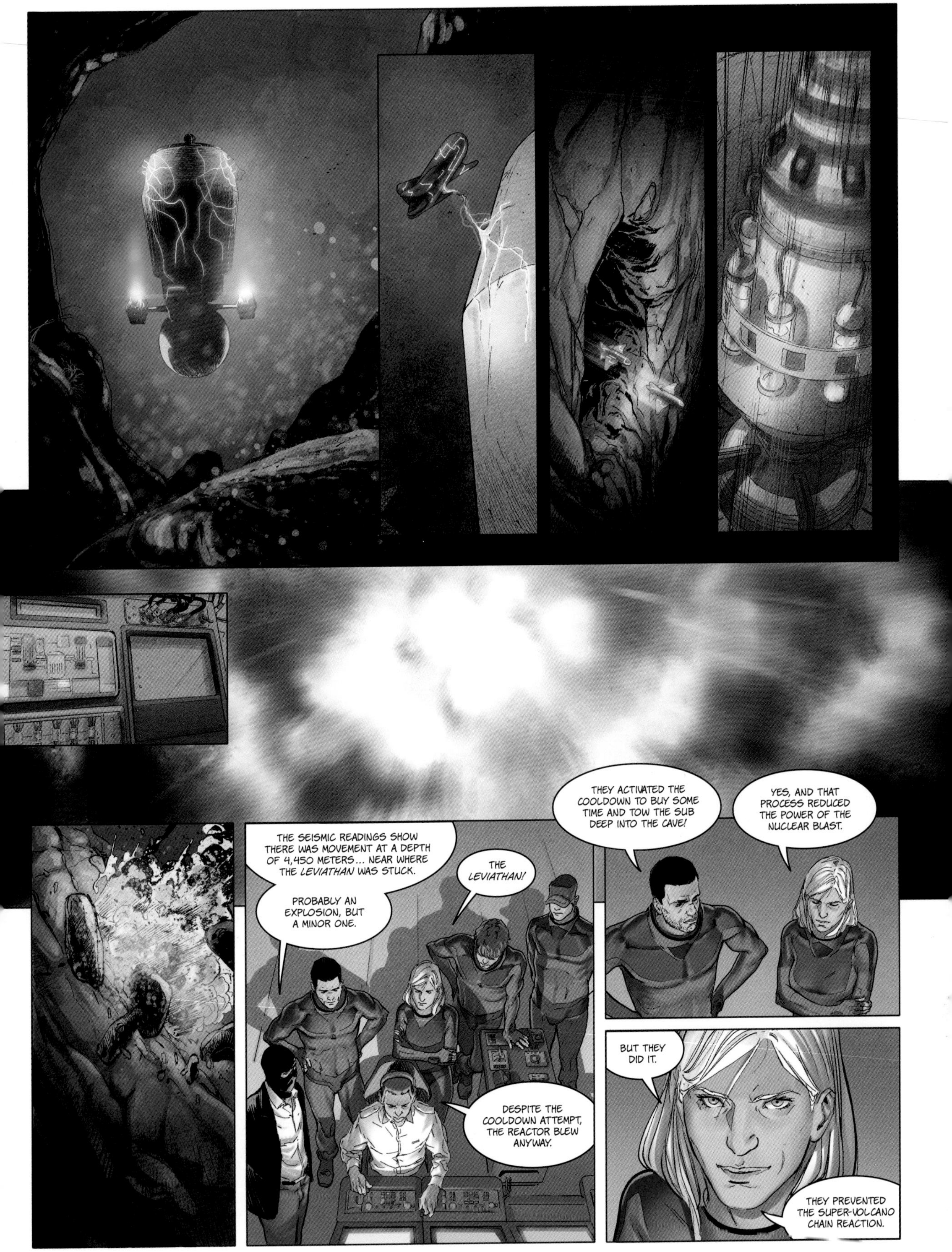
THE SEISMIC READINGS SHOW THERE WAS MOVEMENT AT A DEPTH OF 4,450 METERS... NEAR WHERE THE *LEVIATHAN* WAS STUCK.
PROBABLY AN EXPLOSION, BUT A MINOR ONE.
THE *LEVIATHAN!*
DESPITE THE COOLDOWN ATTEMPT, THE REACTOR BLEW ANYWAY.
THEY ACTIVATED THE COOLDOWN TO BUY SOME TIME AND TOW THE SUB DEEP INTO THE CAVE!
YES, AND THAT PROCESS REDUCED THE POWER OF THE NUCLEAR BLAST.
BUT THEY DID IT.
THEY PREVENTED THE SUPER-VOLCANO CHAIN REACTION.

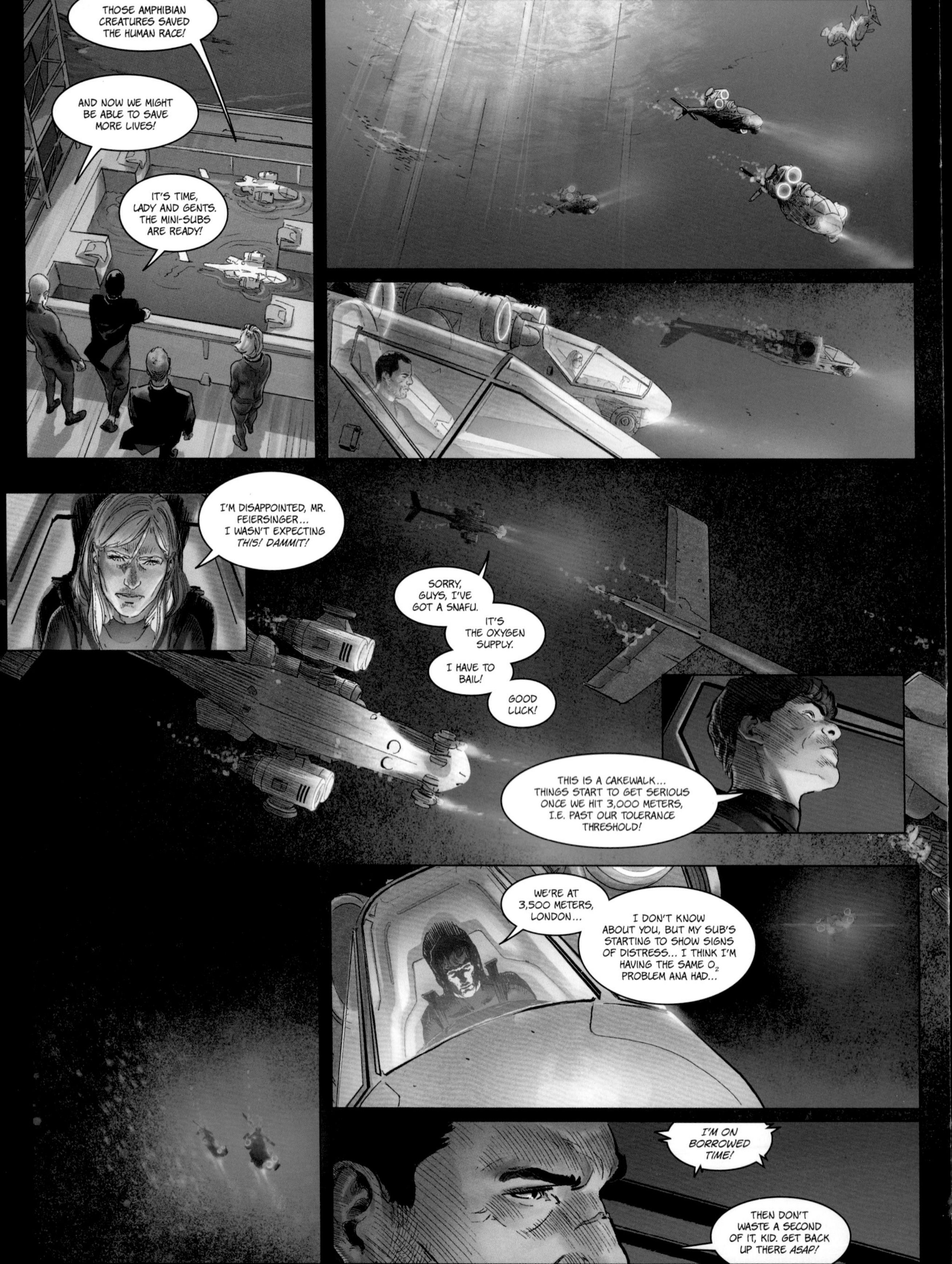
THOSE AMPHIBIAN CREATURES SAVED THE HUMAN RACE!
AND NOW WE MIGHT BE ABLE TO SAVE MORE LIVES!
IT'S TIME, LADY AND GENTS. THE MINI-SUBS ARE READY!
I'M DISAPPOINTED, MR. FEIERSINGER... I WASN'T EXPECTING *THIS! DAMMIT!*
SORRY, GUYS, I'VE GOT A SNAFU.
IT'S THE OXYGEN SUPPLY.
I HAVE TO BAIL!
GOOD LUCK!
THIS IS A CAKEWALK... THINGS START TO GET SERIOUS ONCE WE HIT 3,000 METERS, I.E. PAST OUR TOLERANCE THRESHOLD!
WE'RE AT 3,500 METERS, LONDON...
I DON'T KNOW ABOUT YOU, BUT MY SUB'S STARTING TO SHOW SIGNS OF DISTRESS... I THINK I'M HAVING THE SAME O_2 PROBLEM ANA HAD...
I'M ON BORROWED TIME!
THEN DON'T WASTE A SECOND OF IT, KID. GET BACK UP THERE *ASAP!*

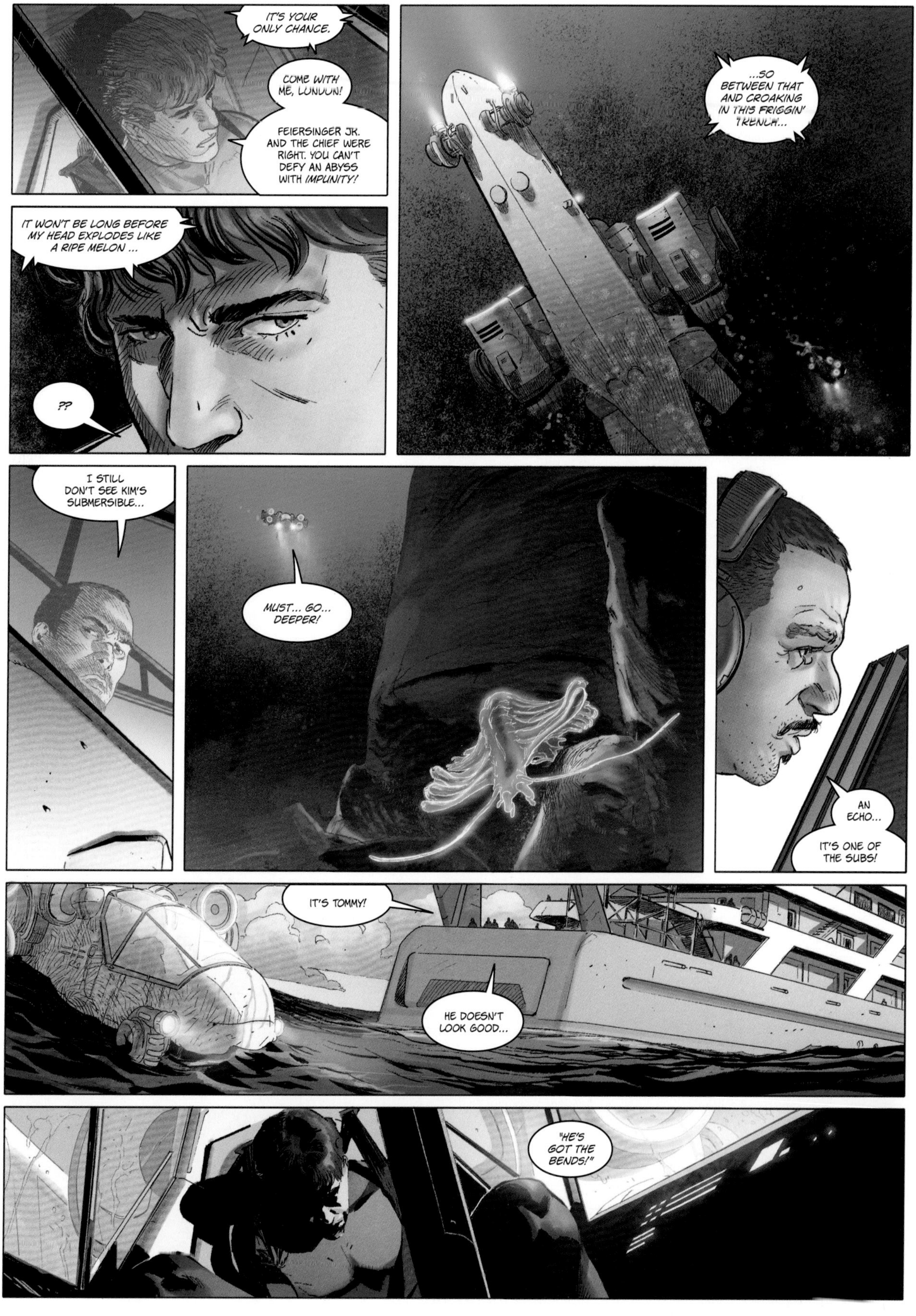
IT'S YOUR ONLY CHANCE.
COME WITH ME, LONDON!
FEIERSINGER JR. AND THE CHIEF WERE RIGHT. YOU CAN'T DEFY AN ABYSS WITH IMPUNITY!
...SO BETWEEN THAT AND CROAKING IN THIS FRIGGIN' TRENCH...
IT WON'T BE LONG BEFORE MY HEAD EXPLODES LIKE A RIPE MELON ...
??
I STILL DON'T SEE KIM'S SUBMERSIBLE...
MUST... GO... DEEPER!
AN ECHO...
IT'S ONE OF THE SUBS!
IT'S TOMMY!
HE DOESN'T LOOK GOOD...
"HE'S GOT THE BENDS!"

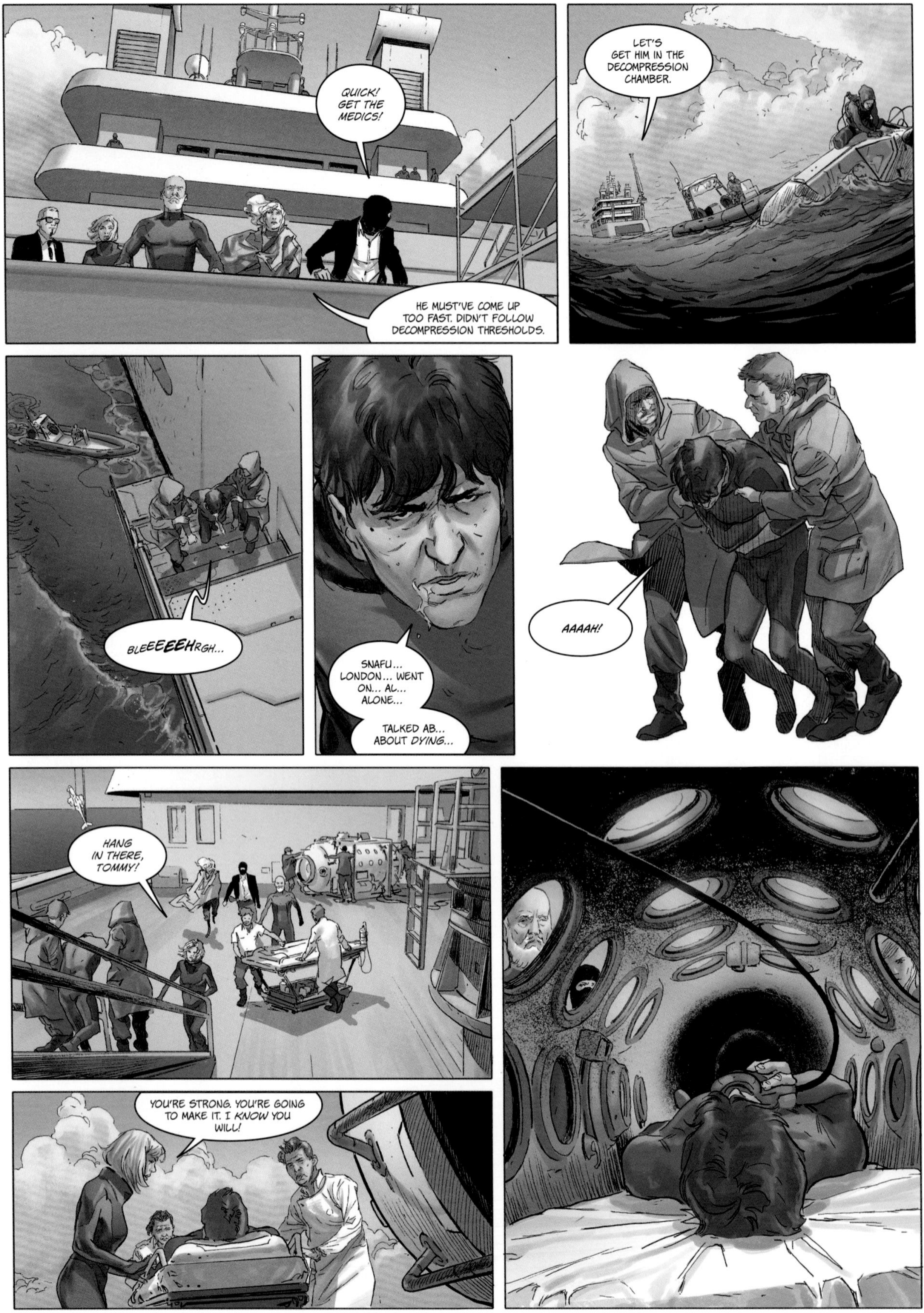
QUICK! GET THE MEDICS!
HE MUST'VE COME UP TOO FAST. DIDN'T FOLLOW DECOMPRESSION THRESHOLDS.
LET'S GET HIM IN THE DECOMPRESSION CHAMBER.
BLEEEEEHRGH...
SNAFU... LONDON... WENT ON... AL... ALONE...
TALKED AB... ABOUT DYING...
AAAAH!
HANG IN THERE, TOMMY!
YOU'RE STRONG. YOU'RE GOING TO MAKE IT. I KNOW YOU WILL!

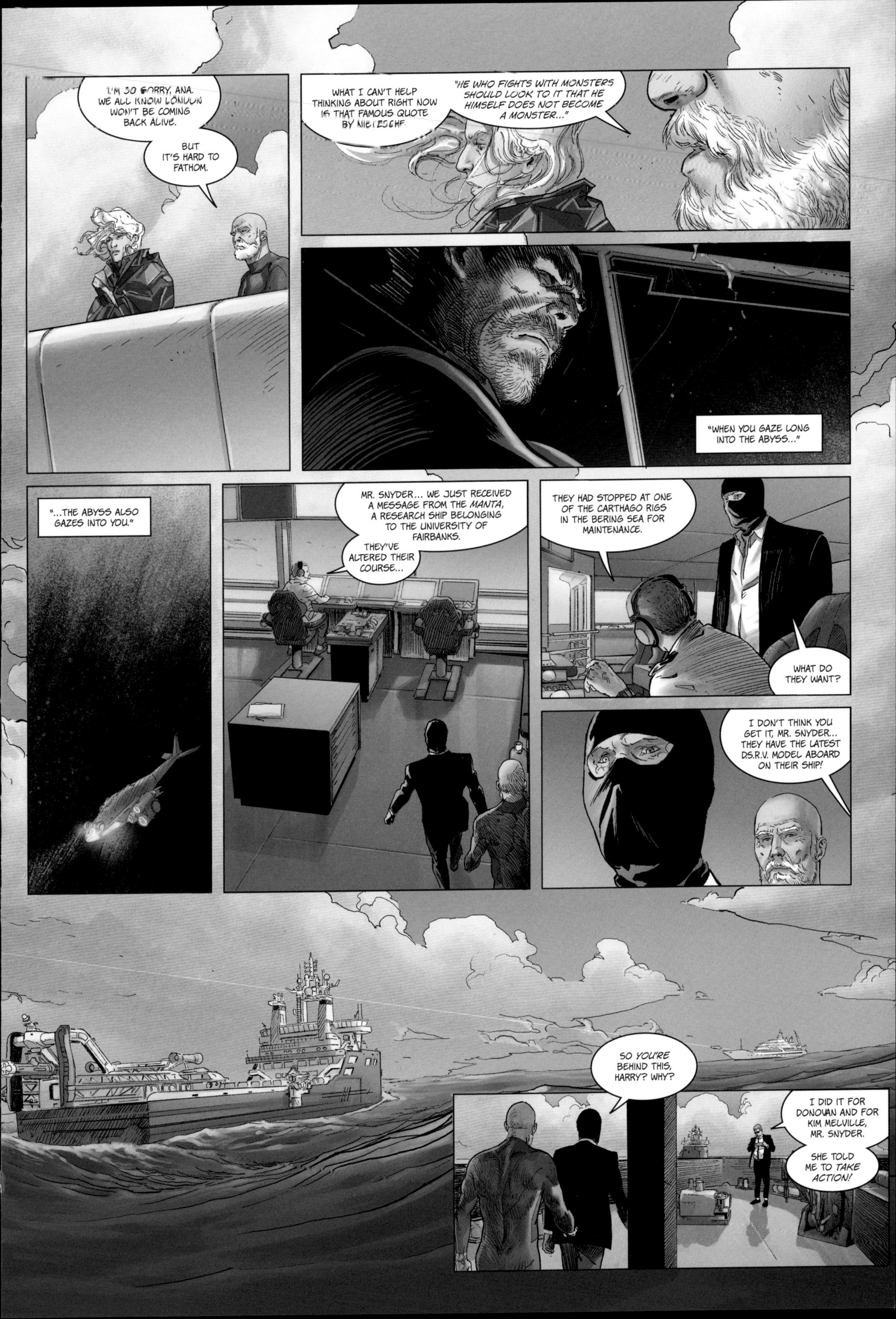
I'M SO SORRY, ANA. WE ALL KNOW LONDON WON'T BE COMING BACK ALIVE.
BUT IT'S HARD TO FATHOM.
WHAT I CAN'T HELP THINKING ABOUT RIGHT NOW IS THAT FAMOUS QUOTE BY NIETZSCHE:
"HE WHO FIGHTS WITH MONSTERS SHOULD LOOK TO IT THAT HE HIMSELF DOES NOT BECOME A MONSTER..."
"WHEN YOU GAZE LONG INTO THE ABYSS..."
"...THE ABYSS ALSO GAZES INTO YOU."
MR. SNYDER... WE JUST RECEIVED A MESSAGE FROM THE MANTA, A RESEARCH SHIP BELONGING TO THE UNIVERSITY OF FAIRBANKS.
THEY'VE ALTERED THEIR COURSE...
THEY HAD STOPPED AT ONE OF THE CARTHAGO RIGS IN THE BERING SEA FOR MAINTENANCE.
WHAT DO THEY WANT?
I DON'T THINK YOU GET IT, MR. SNYDER... THEY HAVE THE LATEST DS.R.V. MODEL ABOARD ON THEIR SHIP!
SO YOU'RE BEHIND THIS, HARRY? WHY?
I DID IT FOR DONOVAN AND FOR KIM MELVILLE, MR. SNYDER.
SHE TOLD ME TO TAKE ACTION!

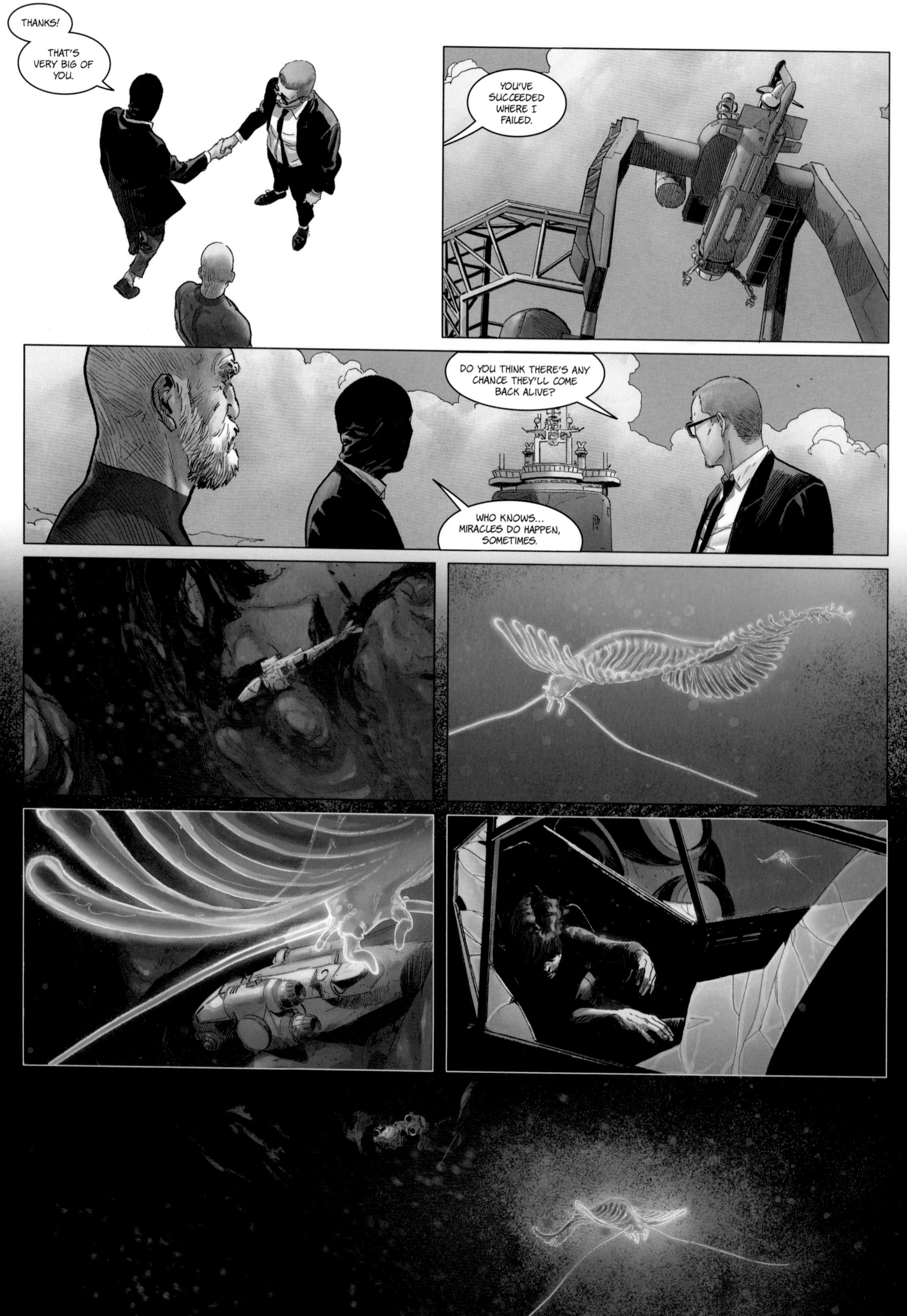
THANKS!
THAT'S VERY BIG OF YOU.
YOU'VE SUCCEEDED WHERE I FAILED.
DO YOU THINK THERE'S ANY CHANCE THEY'LL COME BACK ALIVE?
WHO KNOWS... MIRACLES DO HAPPEN, SOMETIMES.

SO THAT'S DEFINITELY DONOVAN'S MINI-SUB?

YES, MR. SNYDER. HE ACTIVATED HIS DISTRESS BEACON...

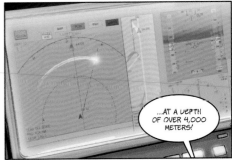

...AT A DEPTH OF OVER 4,000 METERS!

DIVING DOWN TO 5,000 METERS IS A PIECE OF CAKE FOR THIS D.S.R.V.

IT WAS DESIGNED TO GO TO 11,000... THE MARIANA TRENCH.

THAT WAS ONE OF THE MANTA'S PROJECTS: STUDY THE DEEPEST PART OF THE EARTH'S CRUST.

I WOULD HAVE LOVED TO SEE THAT!

KIM MELVILLE AND LONDON DONOVAN DID.

THEY WENT DOWN INTO THE CHALLENGER ABYSS WITH THE LEVIATHAN!

IT MUST BE AN AMAZING EXPERIENCE... THE EVEREST OF THE OCEAN FLOOR!

THE PRE-DIVE INSPECTION IS COMPLETE... THE D.S.R.V. IS READY TO GO!

WE'VE TRANSFERRED THE COORDINATES OF THE DISTRESS BEACON TO THE D.S.R.V.

YEP, DONOVAN'S IN TROUBLE DOWN THERE.

LET'S GO! NO TIME TO WASTE!

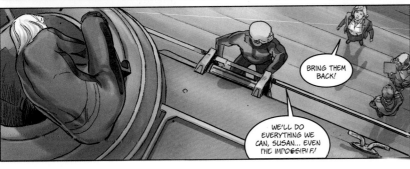

BRING THEM BACK!

WE'LL DO EVERYTHING WE CAN, SUSAN... EVEN THE IMPOSSIBLE!

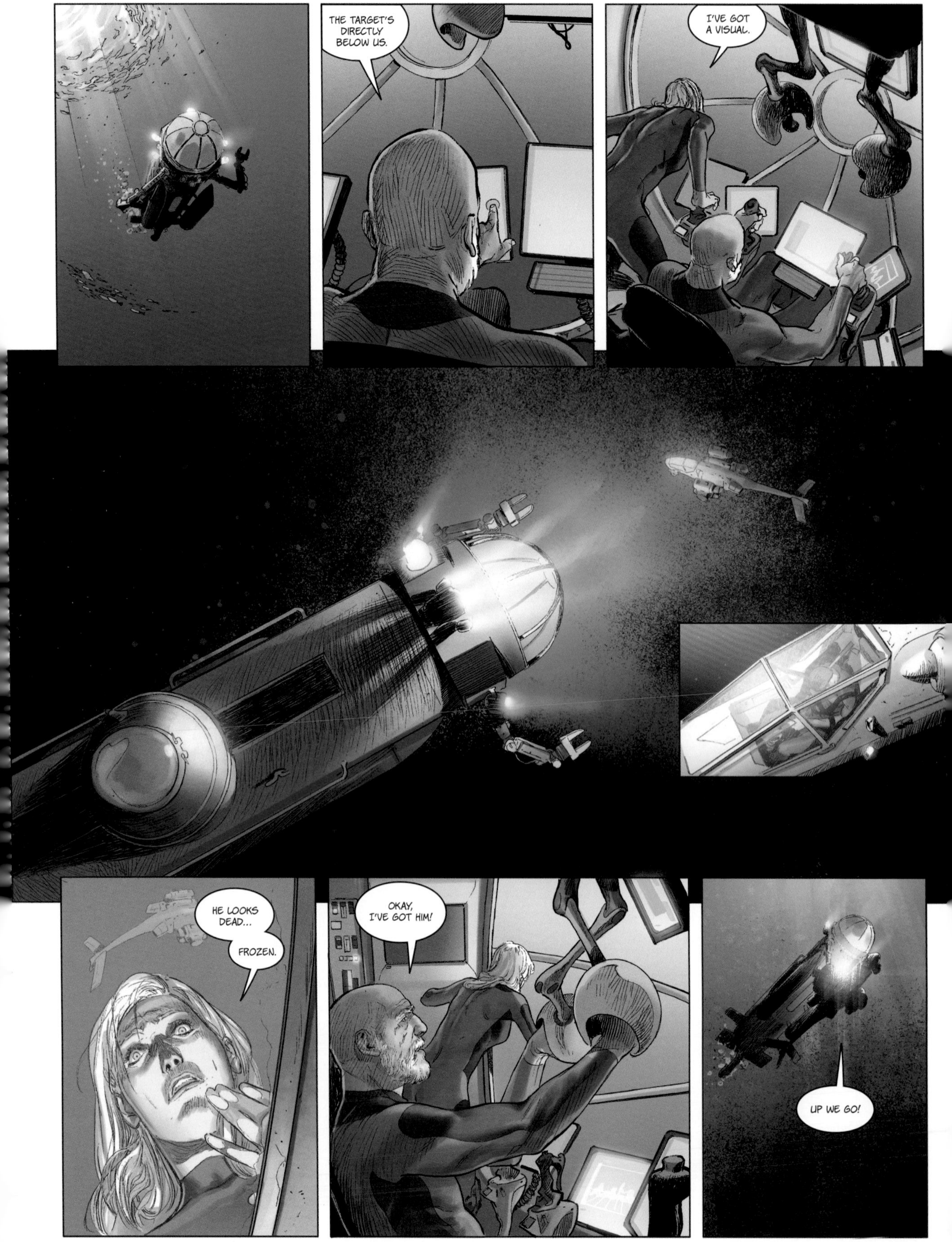
THE TARGET'S DIRECTLY BELOW US.
I'VE GOT A VISUAL.
HE LOOKS DEAD...
FROZEN.
OKAY, I'VE GOT HIM!
UP WE GO!

DONOVAN!!!

MOVE OVER! WE'RE GOING STRAIGHT TO MEDICAL.

THEY SAID HE'S BREATHING, TOMMY... JUST BARELY, BUT BREATHING!

HE'S GOING TO MAKE IT, RIGHT, ANA?

I DON'T KNOW... IT'S A MIRACLE WE DIDN'T BRING HIM BACK AS STIFF AS A BOARD...

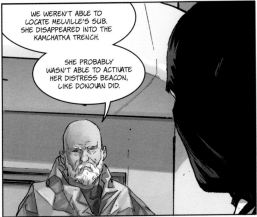

WE WEREN'T ABLE TO LOCATE MELVILLE'S SUB. SHE DISAPPEARED INTO THE KAMCHATKA TRENCH.

SHE PROBABLY WASN'T ABLE TO ACTIVATE HER DISTRESS BEACON, LIKE DONOVAN DID.

HER WORK WAS HER PASSION. AND SHE KNEW THE RISKS...

"ENDING UP ENGULFED BY THE DEEP BLUE!"

WHAT ABOUT LOU...?

WELCOME BACK TO THE REALM OF THE *LIVING*, MR. DONOVAN!

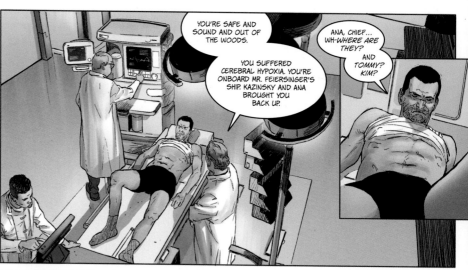

YOU'RE SAFE AND SOUND AND OUT OF THE WOODS.

YOU SUFFERED CEREBRAL HYPOXIA. YOU'RE ONBOARD MR. FEIERSINGER'S SHIP. KAZINSKY AND ANA BROUGHT YOU BACK UP.

ANA, CHIEF... WH-WHERE ARE THEY?
AND TOMMY? KIM?

THEY'RE FINE. BUT THEY DIDN'T FIND MISS MELVILLE'S SUBMERSIBLE. I'M SORRY.

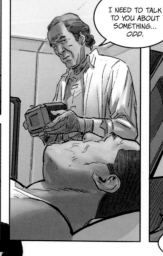

I NEED TO TALK TO YOU ABOUT SOMETHING... ODD.

DURING SURGERY, WE REMOVED SOME KIND OF IMPLANT FROM A SUBCLAVIAN VEIN.

ANY IDEA WHAT THAT WAS?

AND IT DIDN'T EXPLODE?

KIM...

SORRY?!

WOLFGANG FEIERSINGER... YOU *RASCAL!* WHEN DID YOU DISMANTLE IT??

"MAYBE AS EARLY AS TIBET, WHO KNOWS..."

DONOVAN??

YOU PASSED OUT.

PROBABLY ELEVATION SICKNESS.

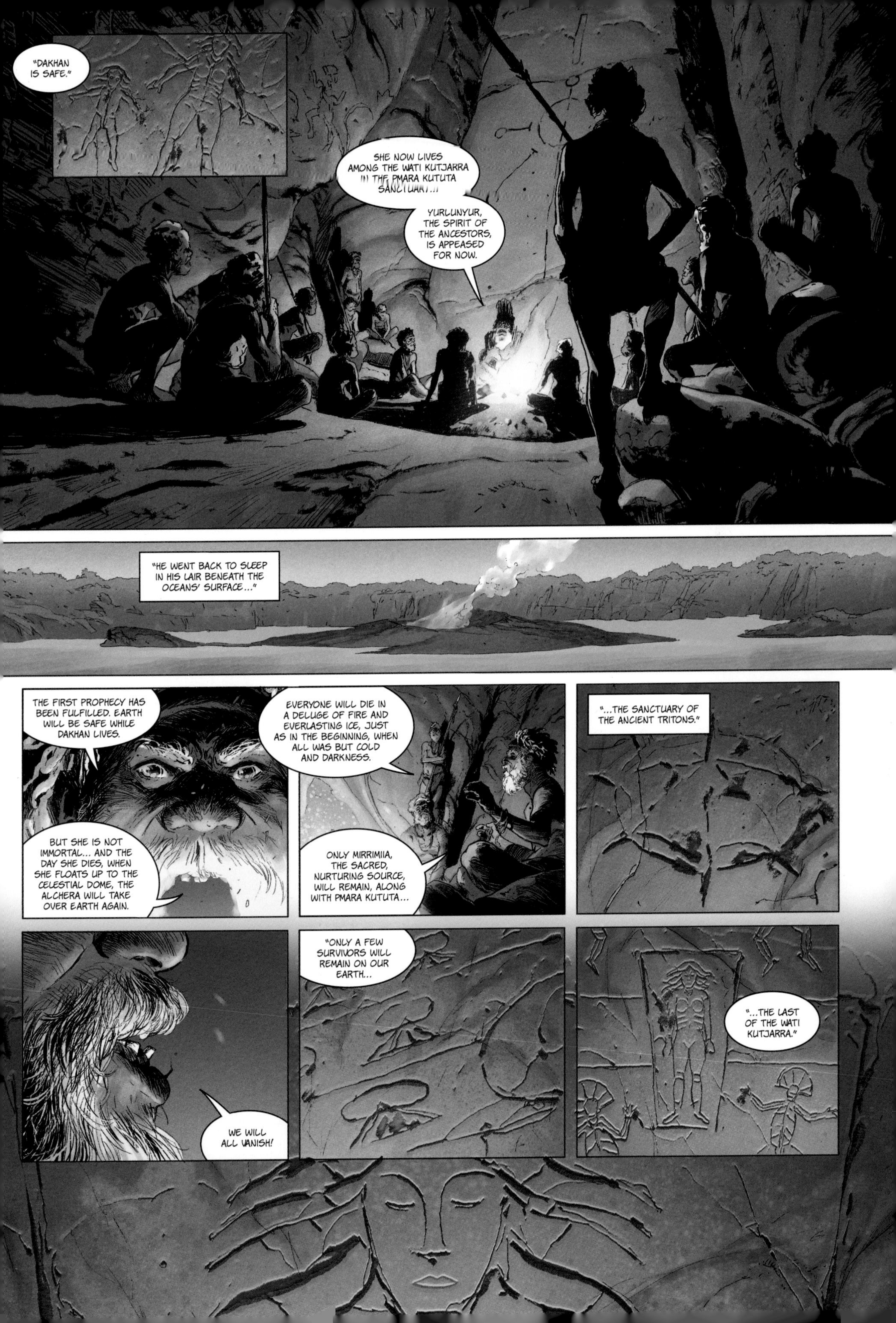

"DAKHAN IS SAFE."
SHE NOW LIVES AMONG THE WATI KUTJARRA IN THE PMARA KUTUTA SANCTUARY...
YURLUNYUR, THE SPIRIT OF THE ANCESTORS, IS APPEASED FOR NOW.
"HE WENT BACK TO SLEEP IN HIS LAIR BENEATH THE OCEANS' SURFACE..."
THE FIRST PROPHECY HAS BEEN FULFILLED. EARTH WILL BE SAFE WHILE DAKHAN LIVES.
BUT SHE IS NOT IMMORTAL... AND THE DAY SHE DIES, WHEN SHE FLOATS UP TO THE CELESTIAL DOME, THE ALCHERA WILL TAKE OVER EARTH AGAIN.
EVERYONE WILL DIE IN A DELUGE OF FIRE AND EVERLASTING ICE, JUST AS IN THE BEGINNING, WHEN ALL WAS BUT COLD AND DARKNESS.
ONLY MIRRIMIIA, THE SACRED, NURTURING SOURCE, WILL REMAIN, ALONG WITH PMARA KUTUTA...
"...THE SANCTUARY OF THE ANCIENT TRITONS."
WE WILL ALL VANISH!
"ONLY A FEW SURVIVORS WILL REMAIN ON OUR EARTH...
"...THE LAST OF THE WATI KUTJARRA."

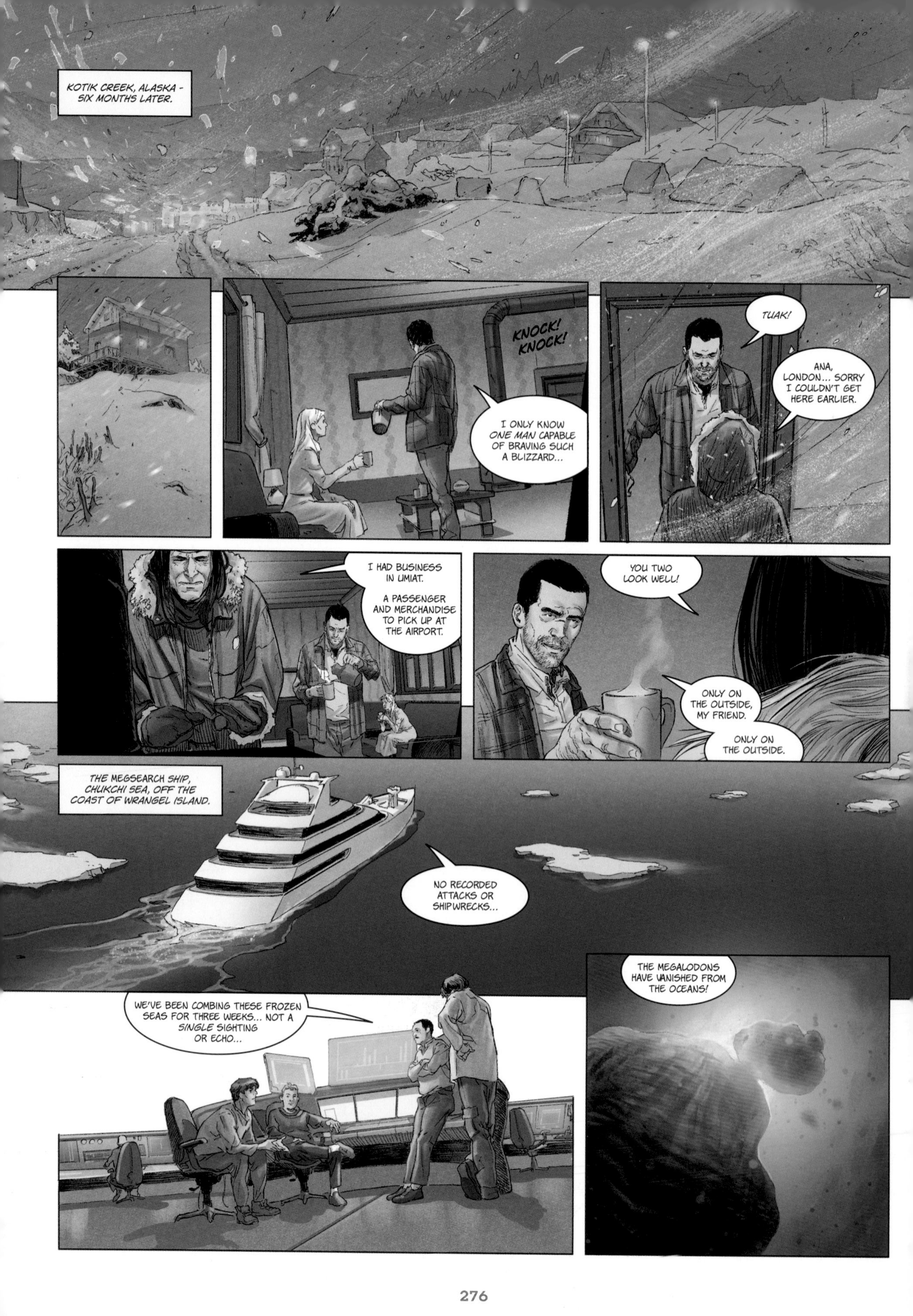

KOTIK CREEK, ALASKA - SIX MONTHS LATER.
KNOCK! KNOCK!
I ONLY KNOW ONE MAN CAPABLE OF BRAVING SUCH A BLIZZARD...
TUAK!
ANA, LONDON... SORRY I COULDN'T GET HERE EARLIER.
I HAD BUSINESS IN UMIAT.
A PASSENGER AND MERCHANDISE TO PICK UP AT THE AIRPORT.
YOU TWO LOOK WELL!
ONLY ON THE OUTSIDE, MY FRIEND.
ONLY ON THE OUTSIDE.
THE MEGSEARCH SHIP, CHUKCHI SEA, OFF THE COAST OF WRANGEL ISLAND.
NO RECORDED ATTACKS OR SHIPWRECKS...
WE'VE BEEN COMBING THESE FROZEN SEAS FOR THREE WEEKS... NOT A SINGLE SIGHTING OR ECHO...
THE MEGALODONS HAVE VANISHED FROM THE OCEANS!

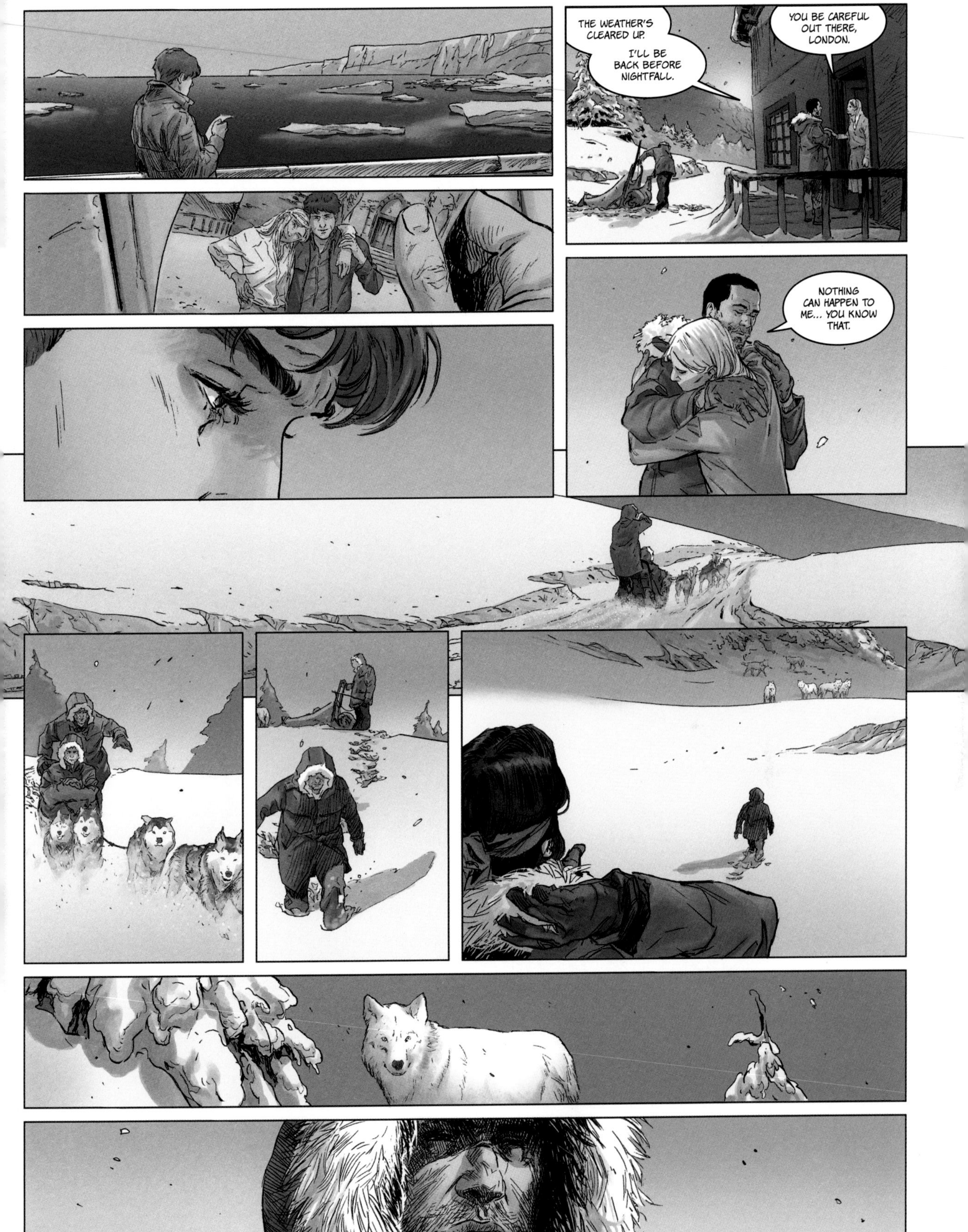
THE WEATHER'S CLEARED UP.
I'LL BE BACK BEFORE NIGHTFALL.
YOU BE CAREFUL OUT THERE, LONDON.
NOTHING CAN HAPPEN TO ME... YOU KNOW THAT.

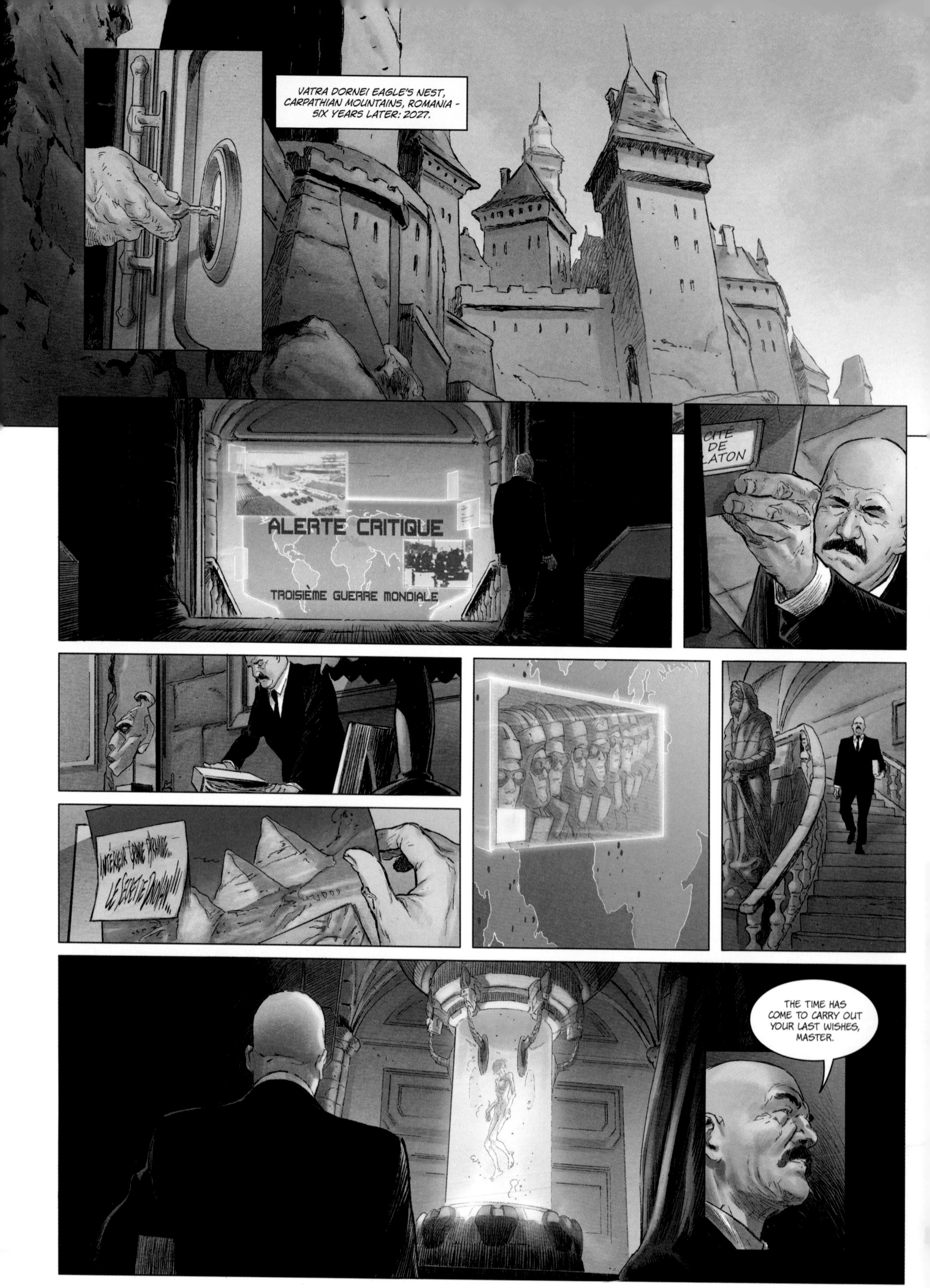
VATRA DORNEI EAGLE'S NEST, CARPATHIAN MOUNTAINS, ROMANIA - SIX YEARS LATER: 2027.
ALERTE CRITIQUE
TROISIÈME GUERRE MONDIALE
CITÉ DE
LATON
INTÉRIEUR GRANDE PYRAMIDE...
THE TIME HAS COME TO CARRY OUT YOUR LAST WISHES, MASTER.

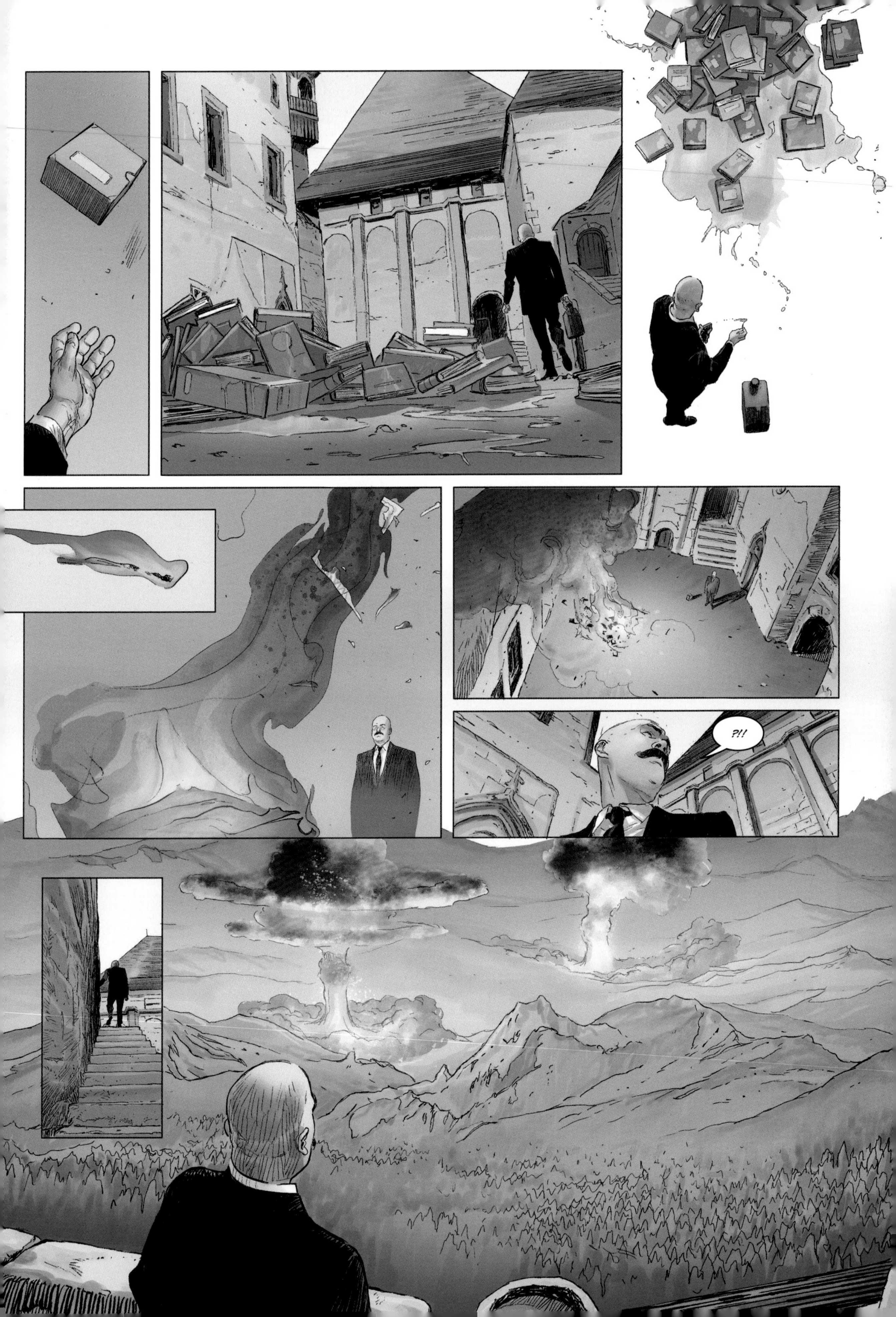
?!!

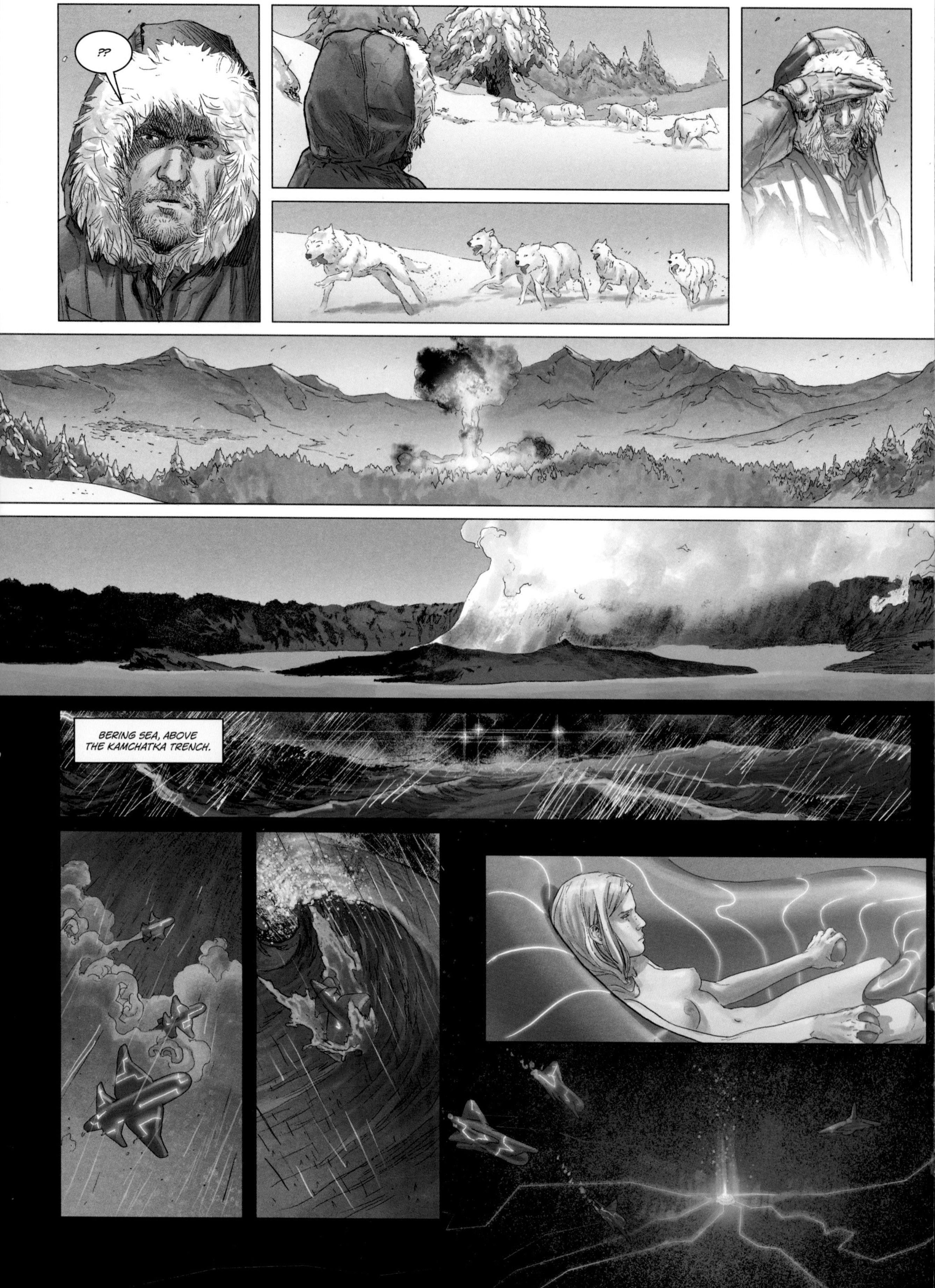
??
BERING SEA, ABOVE THE KAMCHATKA TRENCH.

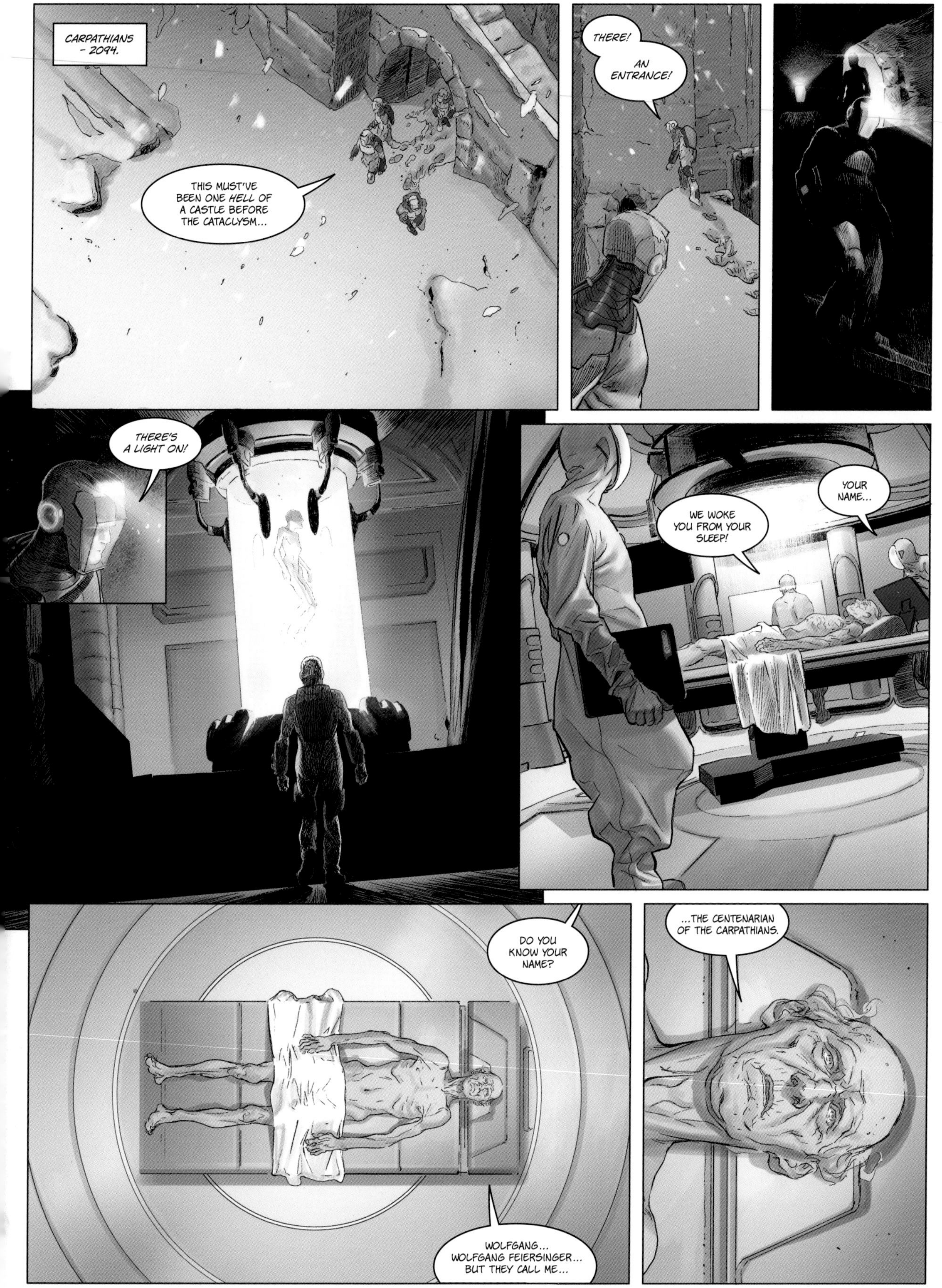
CARPATHIANS – 2094.
THIS MUST'VE BEEN ONE HELL OF A CASTLE BEFORE THE CATACLYSM...
THERE!
AN ENTRANCE!
THERE'S A LIGHT ON!
WE WOKE YOU FROM YOUR SLEEP!
YOUR NAME...
DO YOU KNOW YOUR NAME?
WOLFGANG... WOLFGANG FEIERSINGER... BUT THEY CALL ME...
...THE CENTENARIAN OF THE CARPATHIANS.

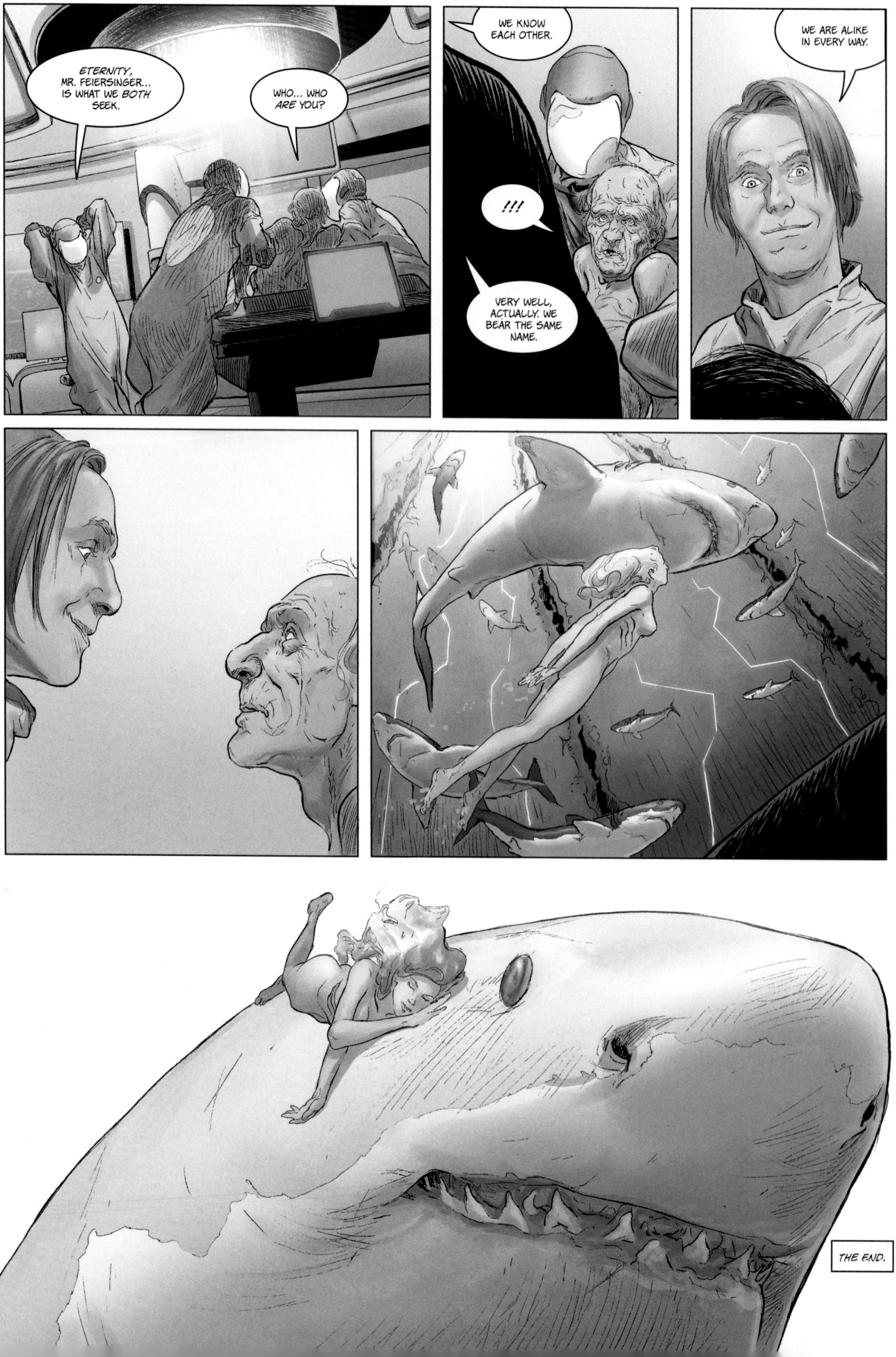

ETERNITY, MR. FEIERSINGER... IS WHAT WE *BOTH* SEEK.
WHO... WHO *ARE YOU*?
WE KNOW EACH OTHER.
!!!
VERY WELL, ACTUALLY. WE BEAR THE SAME NAME.
WE ARE ALIKE IN EVERY WAY.
THE END.

DEEP DIVING: BEYOND CARTHAGO

Bonus Section featuring the art of Ennio Buffi

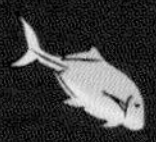

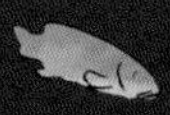

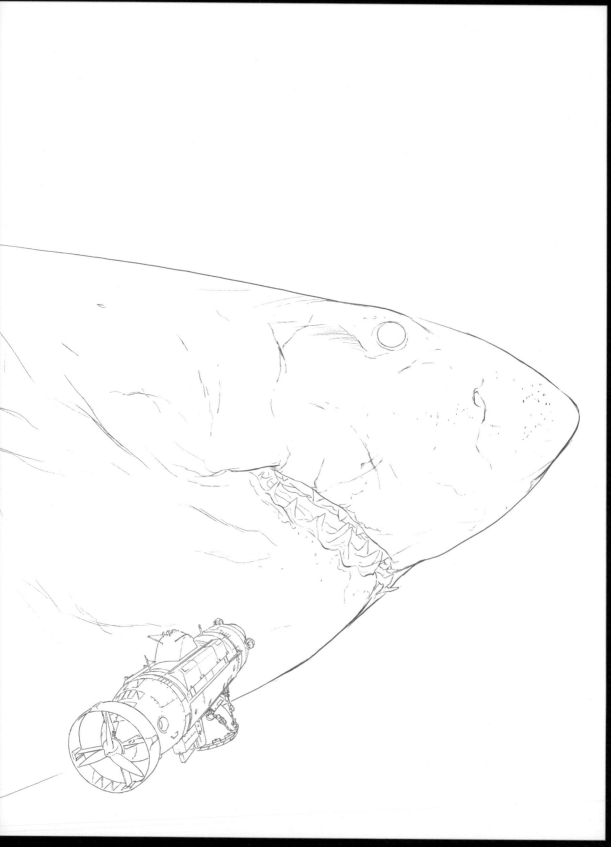

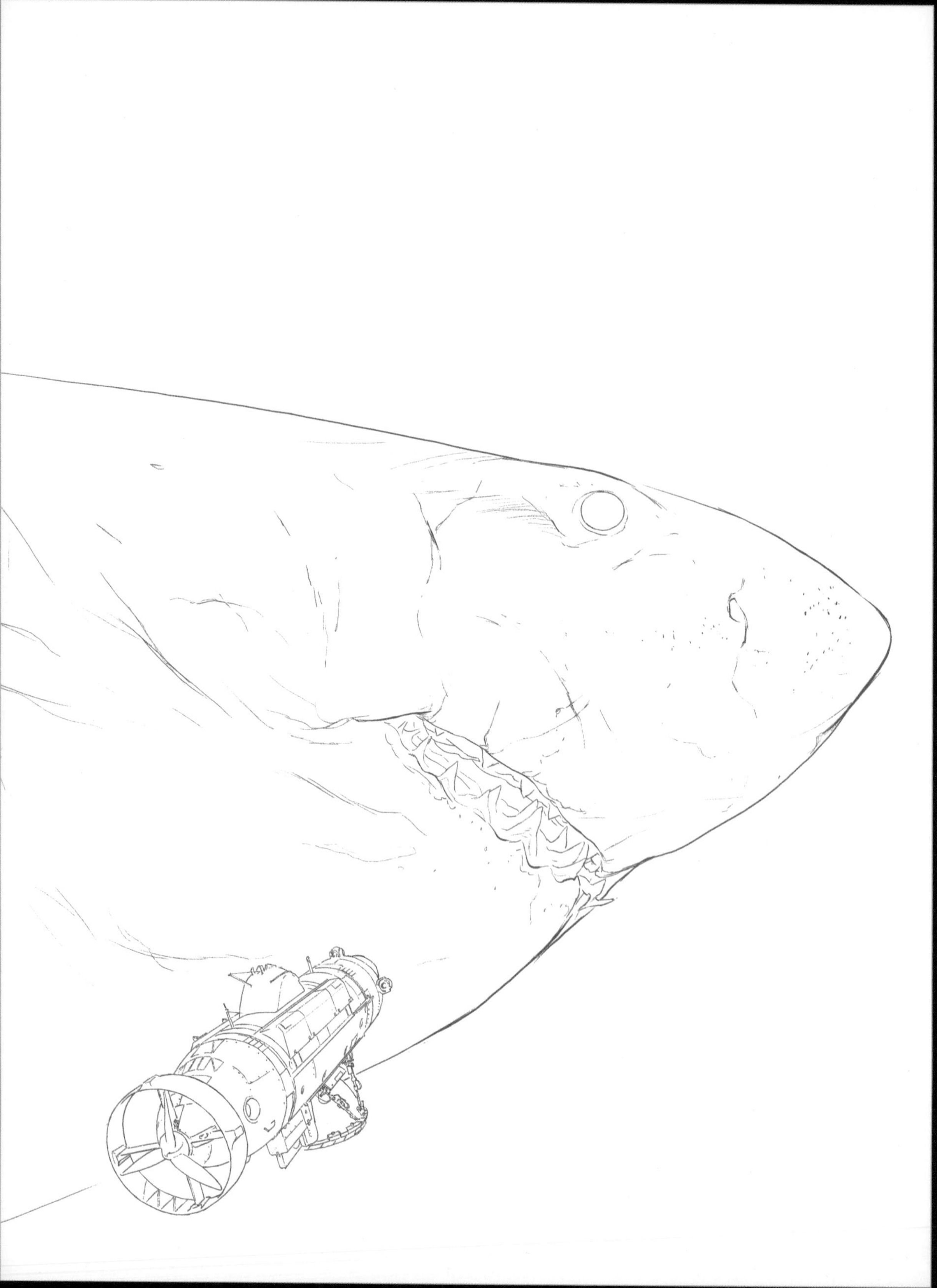

Cover illustration (inks) for the French Book 8.

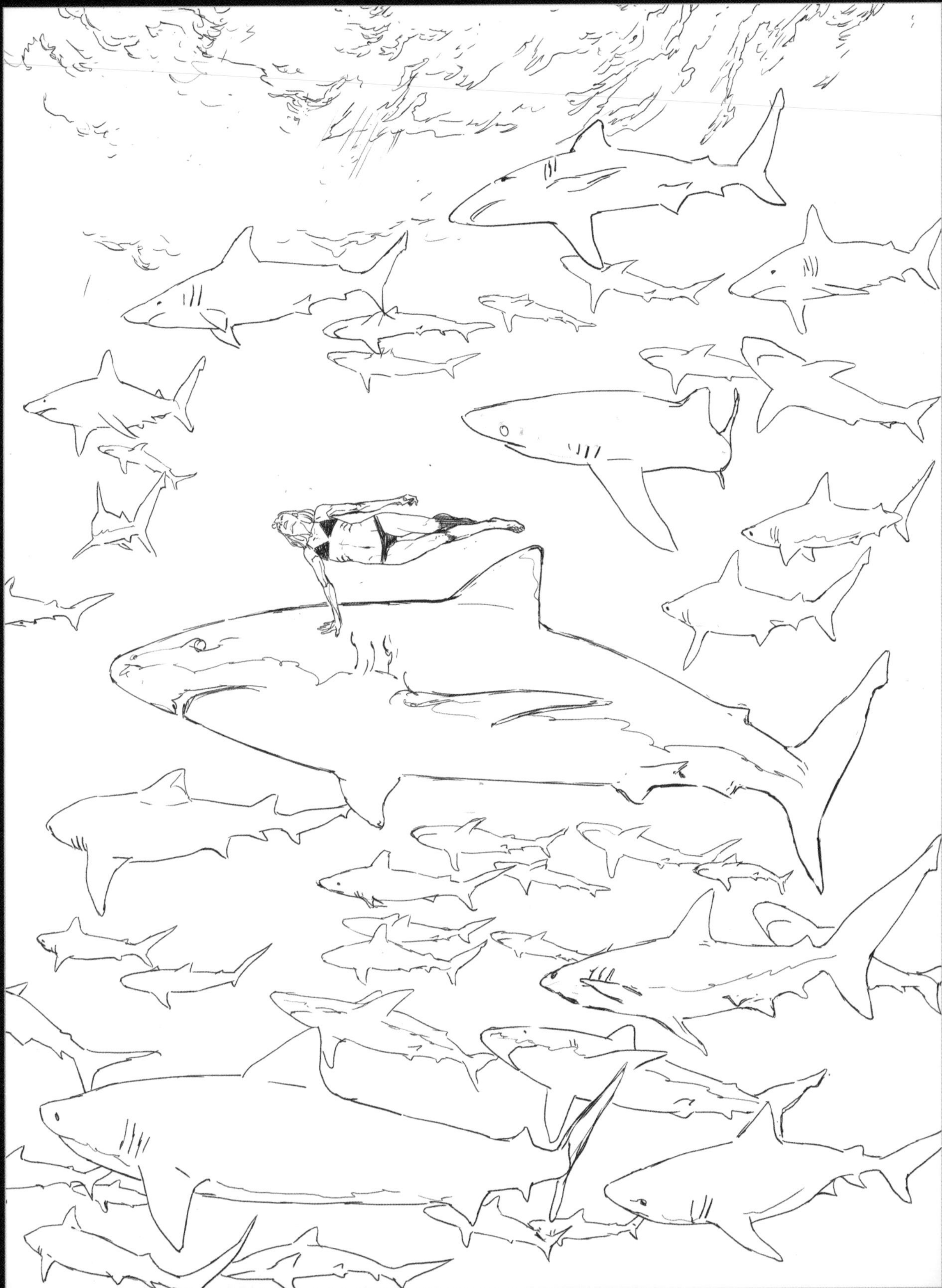

Cover illustration (pencils) for the first French Collection (Books 1–5).

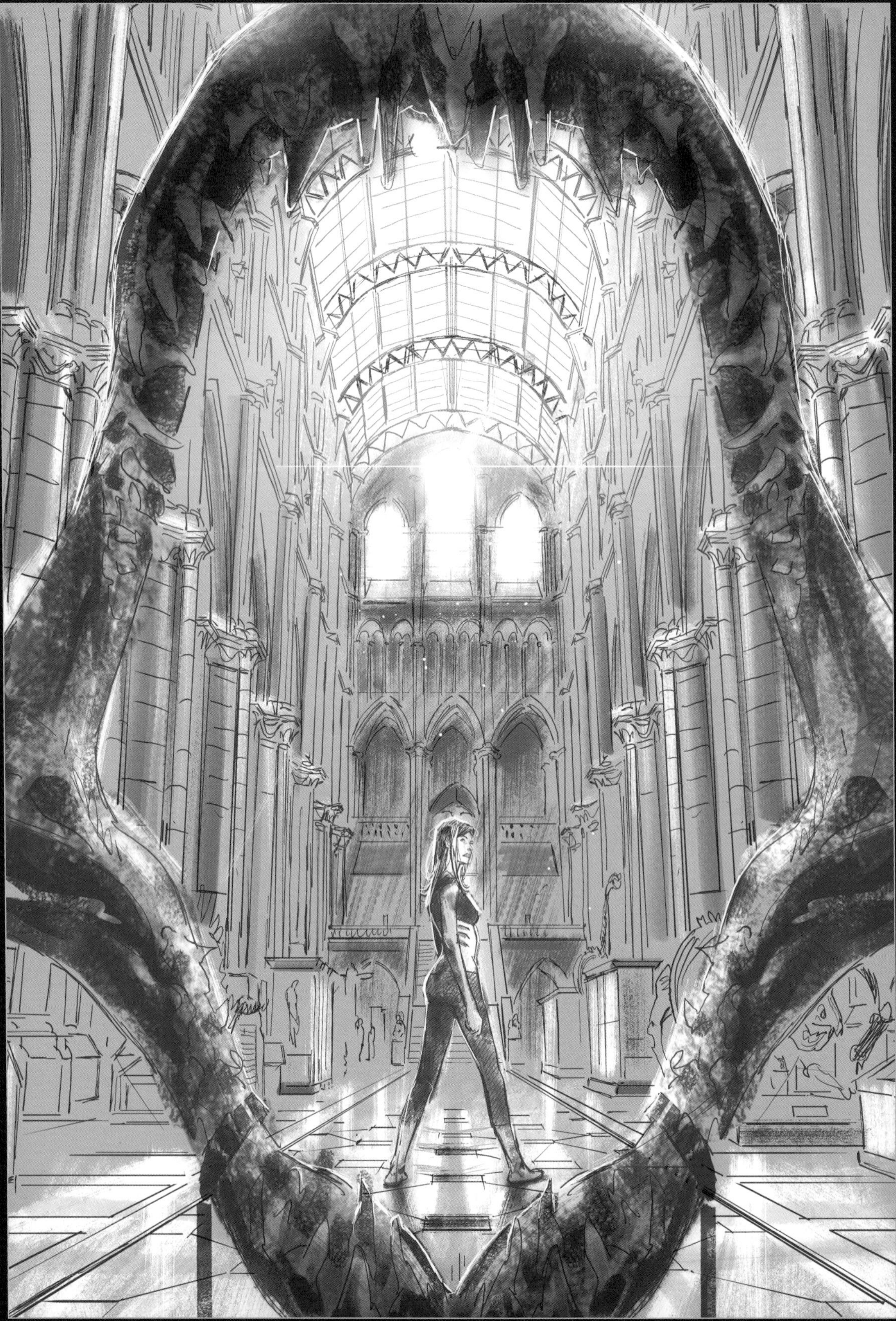

Cover illustration (pencils) for the French Book 6.

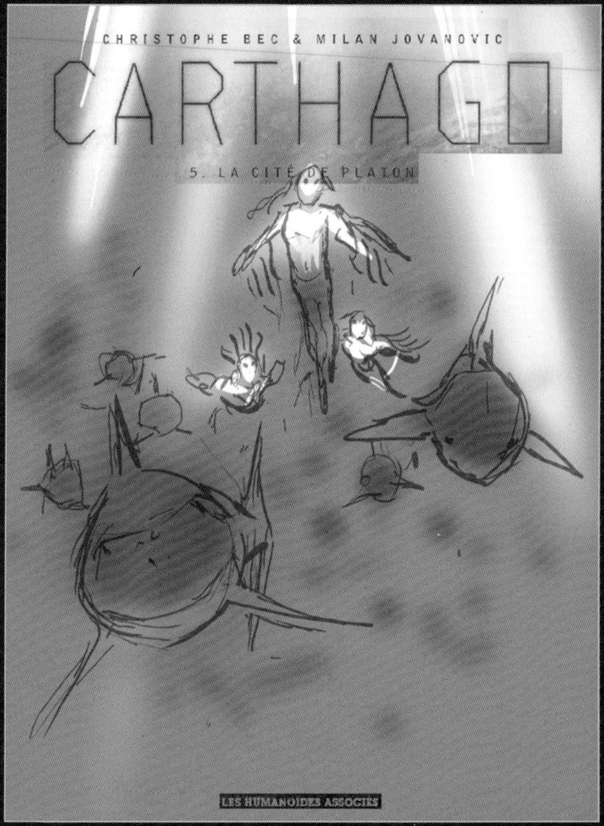
CHRISTOPHE BEC & MILAN JOVANOVIC
CARTHAGO
5. LA CITÉ DE PLATON
LES HUMANOIDES ASSOCIES

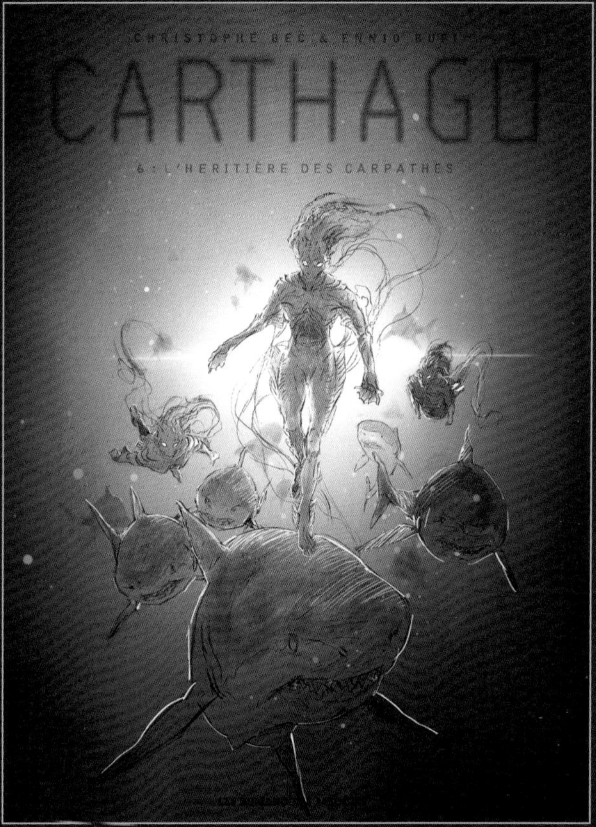
CHRISTOPHE BEC & ENNIO BUFI
CARTHAGO
6 : L'HERITIÈRE DES CARPATHES

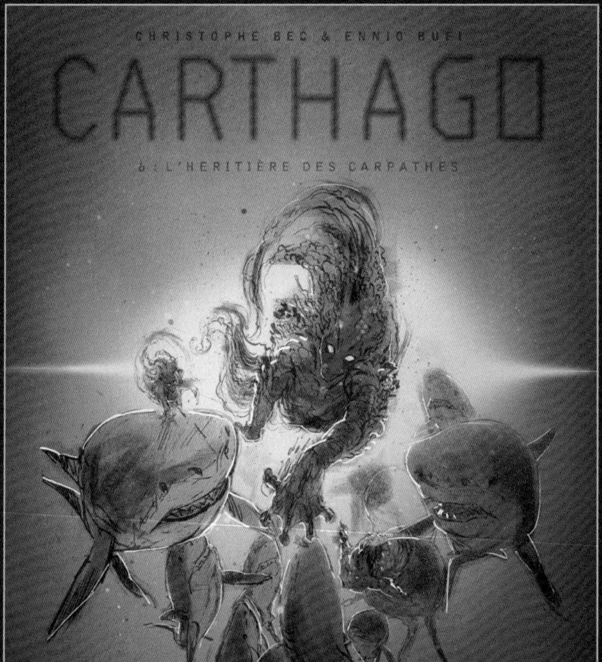
CHRISTOPHE BEC & ENNIO BUFI
CARTHAGO
6 : L'HERITIÈRE DES CARPATHES
LES HUMANOIDES ASSOCIES

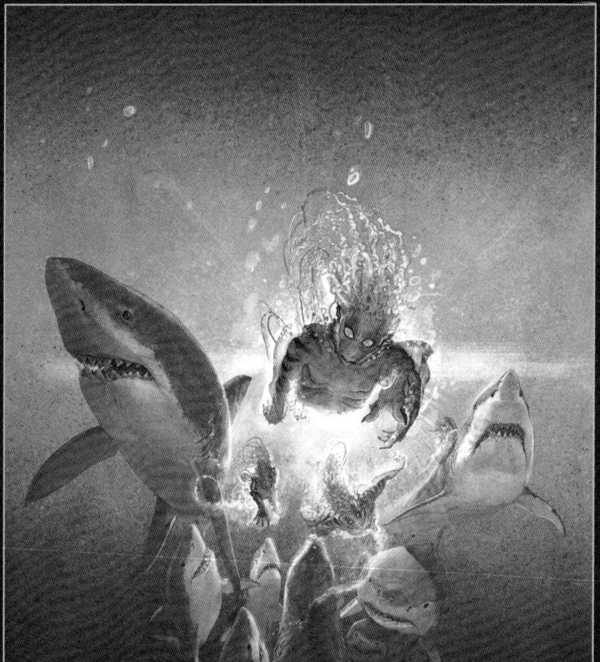

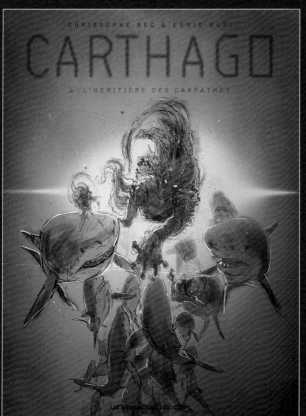

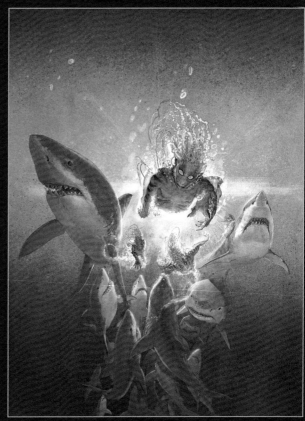

Cover sketches for the French Book 7.

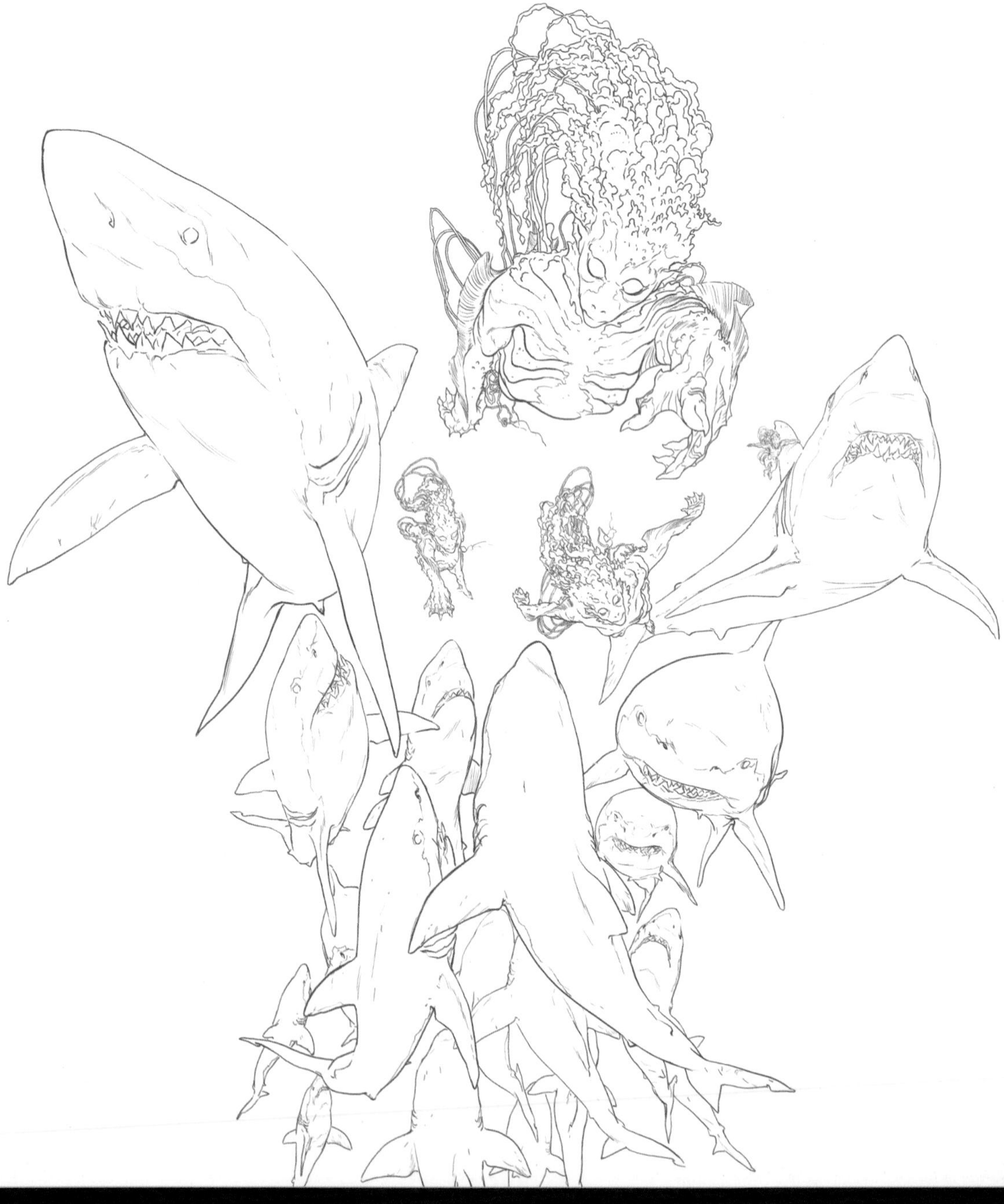

Cover illustration (inks) for the French Book 7.

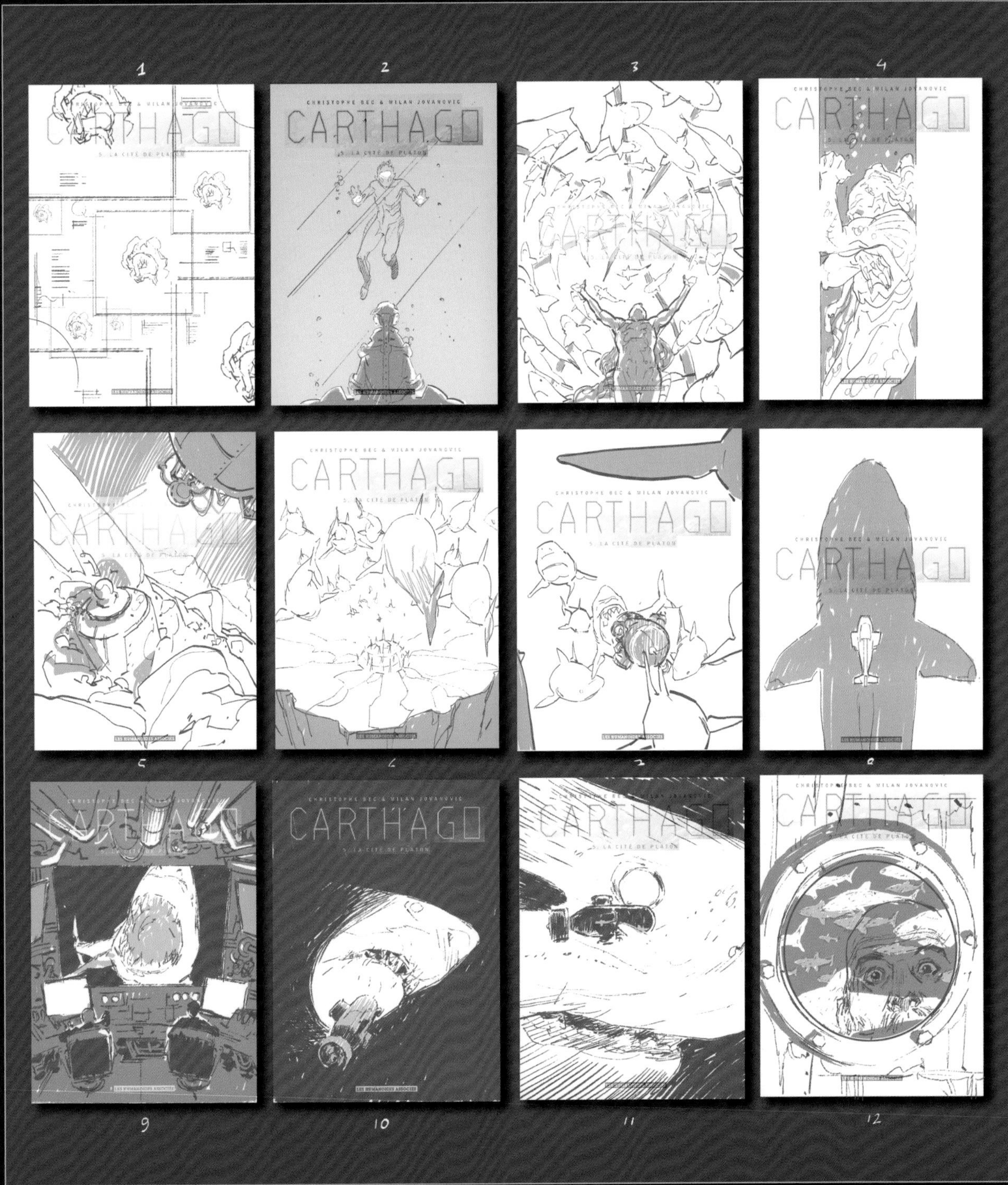
1
2
3
4
CHRISTOPHE BEC & MILAN JOVANOVIC
CARTHAGO
5. LA CITÉ DE PLATON
LES HUMANOÏDES ASSOCIÉS
5
6
7
8
9
10
11
12

Cover illustration (inks) for the French Book 9.

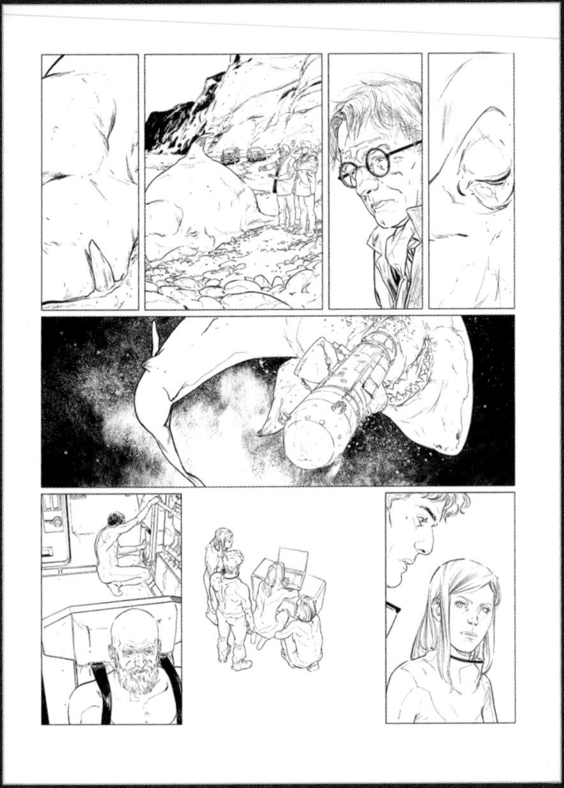

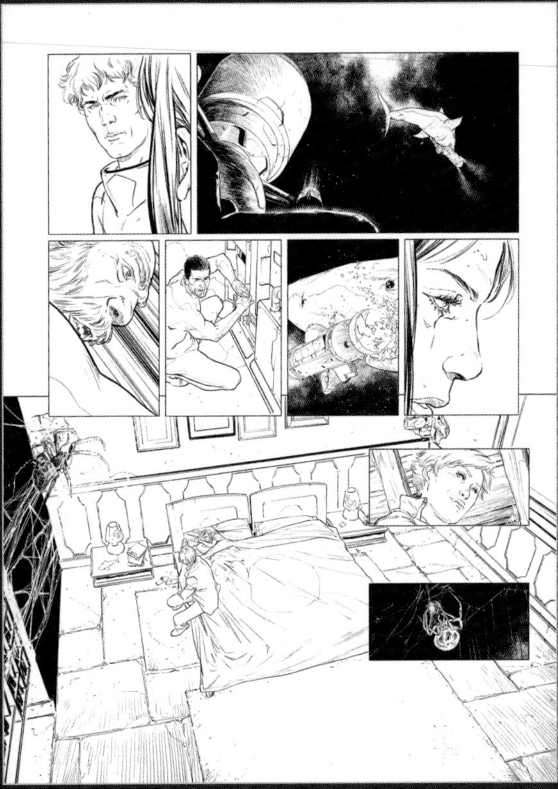

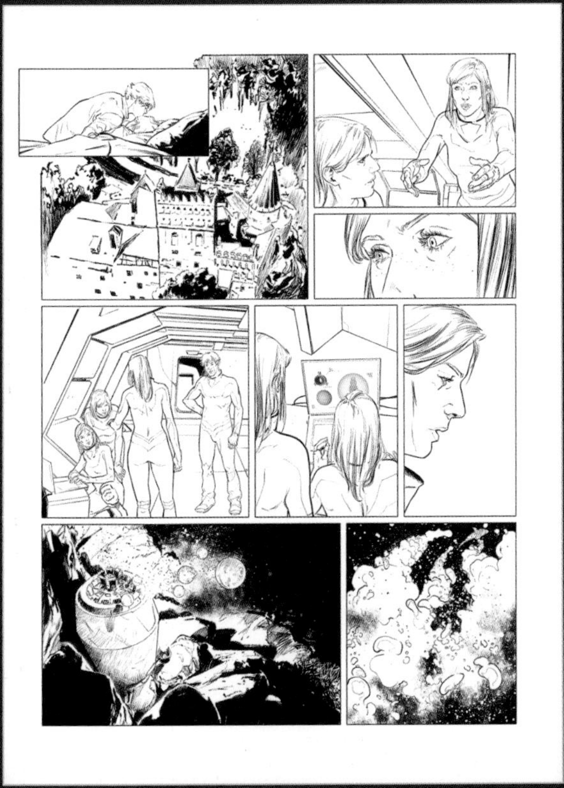

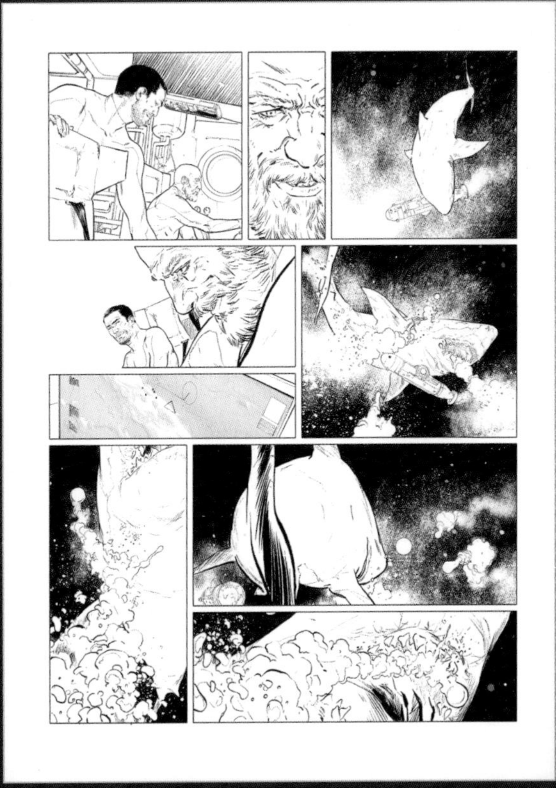

Original inks of pages 231 (top left), 232 (top right), 233 (bottom left), and 234 (bottom right).

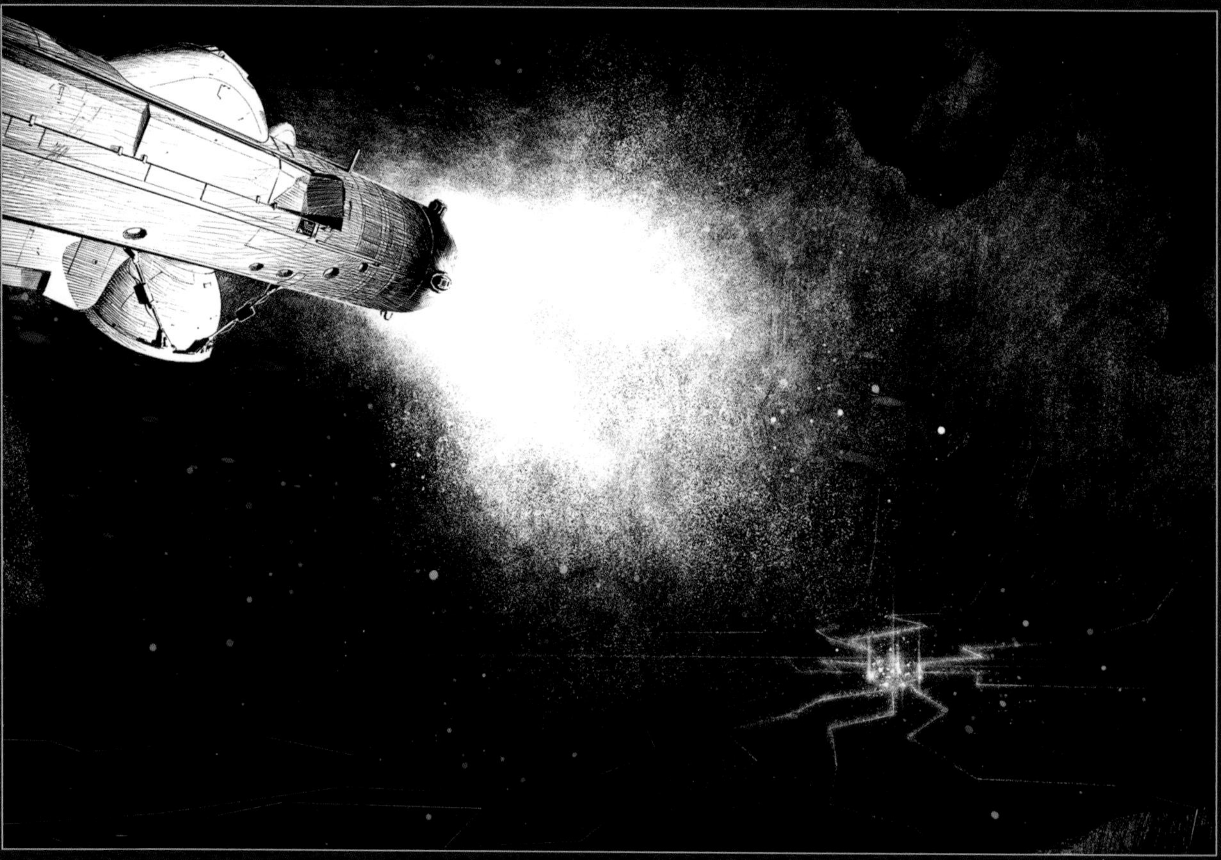

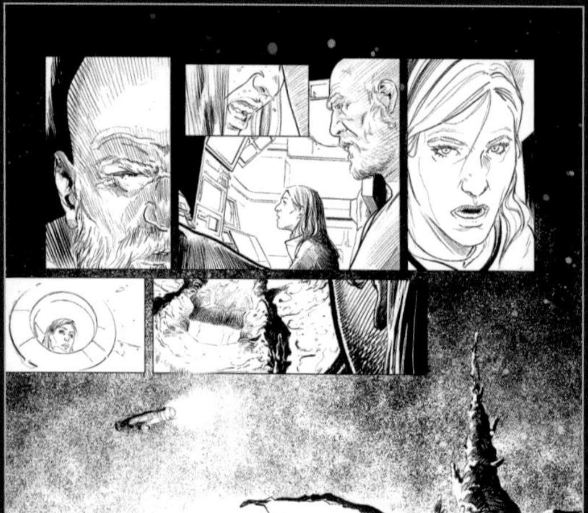

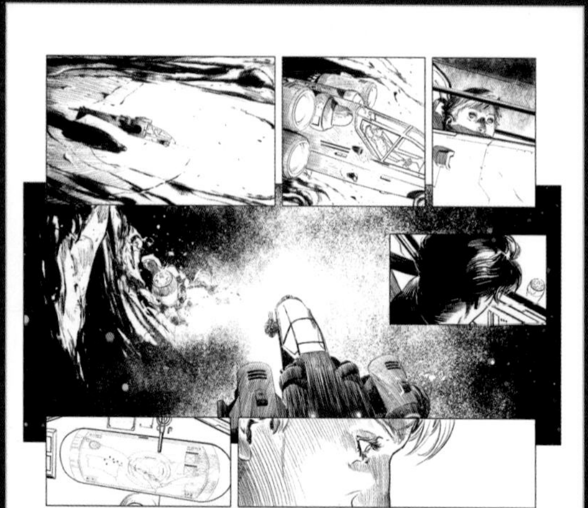

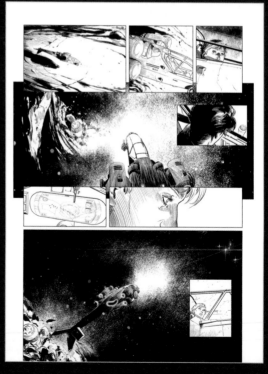

Original inks of pages 246–247 (top), 249 (bottom left), and 255 (bottom right).